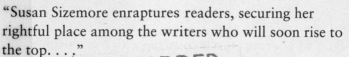

No one sets fire to
Susan Sizem

"Susan Sizemore enraptures readers, securing her
rightful place among the writers who will soon rise to
the top. . . ."

—*Romantic Times*

Praise for *I Burn for You*

"With her new twist on ancient vampire lore, Sizemore
creates an excellent and utterly engaging new world.
I Burn for You is sexy, exciting, and just plain thrilling.
It's the perfect start for a hot, new series."

—*Romantic Times*

"I adored *I Burn for You* and really hope it's the beginning of another wonderful vampire series from Ms.
Sizemore."

—*Old Book Barn Gazette*

"Sizemore has long worn two writing hats, that of
romance author and sf-fantasy scribe, and . . . the bonding of [her] two literary worlds is as powerful as what
Alex and Domini feel for each other in this sexy read
laced with laughter, the first in a burning new series."

—*Booklist*

"Sizemore's hunky vamps can visit me anytime! I was so
sorry to see this book end. This one is a must buy."

—*All About Romance*

I Thirst for You

"[W]ill appeal to fans who like their vampire heroes hot, sexy, and Prime (read: alpha male)."

—*Library Journal*

"Edge-of-your-seat thrills combine with hot romance and great vampire lore!"

—*Romantic Times*

"An action-packed, suspenseful roller-coaster ride that never slows. [Readers] will root for this passionate couple. Don't miss it!"

—*Romance Reviews Today*

I Hunger for You

"Sizemore's sizzling series gets more intriguing as it reveals more about this unique world. Hot romance and intense passions fuel this book and make it a memorable read."

—*Romantic Times*

"Sizemore will make readers believe that colonies of vampires thrive amongst us with this delightful supernatural romance. . . . Readers will hunger for more works like this one from Ms. Sizemore."

—Harriet Klausner, bn.com

"I couldn't put it down. . . . I highly recommend it to anyone who delights in a great love story with lots of action."

—RomanceJunkies.com

Books by Susan Sizemore

I Hunger for You

I Thirst for You

I Burn for You

The Shadows of Christmas Past
(with Christine Feehan)

Crave the Night

SUSAN SIZEMORE

POCKET BOOKS
New York London Toronto Sydney

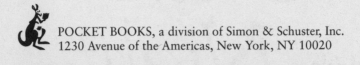
POCKET BOOKS, a division of Simon & Schuster, Inc.
1230 Avenue of the Americas, New York, NY 10020

I Burn for You, I Thirst for You, and *I Hunger for You*
were previously published individually by Pocket Books.

ISBN-13: 978-1-4165-1083-3
ISBN-10:   1-4165-1083-4

First Pocket Books trade paperback edition September 2005

10   9   8   7   6   5   4

POCKET and colophon are registered trademarks of
Simon & Schuster, Inc.

Manufactured in the United States of America

For information regarding special discounts for bulk purchases,
please contact Simon & Schuster Special Sales at 1-800-456-6798 or
business@simonandschuster.com.

CONTENTS

I Burn
for You

Constance Howard Brockway,
this is all your fault!
Thank you.

Very special thanks to Winifred Halsey
for staying awake all night to provide
me technical help.

Chapter One

$\mathcal{H}$e was growing hungry for the night.

Despite modern advances that made dwelling in daylight both possible and enjoyable, Alexander Reynard felt the longing to return to darkness stalking him. Especially right now, when driving through the heavy morning traffic in bright sunlight gave him a blistering headache, despite his tinted windshield and dark sunglasses. He used to enjoy the gift of being able to greet the dawn and all the bright hours after, but lately, light hurt. And he feared he was reverting.

Alec had forced himself to sleep last night through stubborn tenacity, to prove that he could still do it. He would not let nature conquer will. He *had* slept, and that may have been a mistake. For in his dreams, a woman came into his bed.

She had floated into his senses on a fragrant mist. Her skin had been warm and wet, her flesh firm and slick as satin. He'd woken up hot and hard in a tangle of sweat-soaked sheets. There'd been blood on his lips and molten hunger in his veins.

Head back, he'd howled his need into the dark. Though it had been a dream, the woman was real; he was certain of that. All he had to do was find her. Claim her. It had taken all his will not to run out into the embracing night and start the search then and there.

He didn't want this now. This was not a good time or place for the beginning of a quest.

Head pounding from the sun, Alec found a place to park on Hill Street near the huge Central Market. It was at least a three-block walk through bright sunlight to his destination; if he cut through the market, he could get out of the sun for a while.

Domini Lancer woke from disorienting dreams of angels, peaches, and making love. Once awake, a powerful craving for peaches remained. She even smelled peaches while she took a long, hot shower to try to wipe the dream from her mind. But she couldn't forget it, or the strong urge to buy some peaches on the way to work. She'd tried to ignore the ridiculous urge, yet here she was at the Center Market, right where her premonition had demanded she be. This absolute *need* to follow a dream had never happened to her before, and she was a little scared. Scared that maybe she was going crazy. More scared of whatever was about to happen. And even worse, scared that nothing was going to happen. She'd never had such a powerful premonition before, so if this turned out to be the usual petty crap her visions pulled on her, instead of something momentous, she was really going to be pissed off.

As was her boss, whom she'd called to say she'd be late.

Old Man Lancer didn't make any allowances for Domini being his granddaughter. His deep, whiskey-growly voice had been annoyed when he said, "Fine," and hung up the phone. Though he'd always comforted her when she had dreams that came true as a kid, as an adult he didn't cut her any slack, and she didn't bring up the subject of being psychic anymore. Maybe because both of them wished she wasn't.

Domini heard music, and turned around. Melissa Etheridge's "Angels Would Fall" was coming from a radio at a fruit vendor's stand—where a pyramid of peaches was piled high at the front of the stand, gold as the morning sun, almost shining with their own light in the dim market. She couldn't help but take a step closer. The music swelled around her, bright, lively, and full of aching secret passion.

Swaying to the sound, Domini picked up the peach at the very top of the pile. Its velvet fuzz brushed sensuously across her palm, more tempting than Eve's apple. She felt as if one bite of it might send her into a Sleeping Beauty trance—or make her fall in love.

She raised it to her lips.

"You want to pay for that first?" the vendor asked.

The music faded into the background; reality came rushing back in.

Domini blinked. She smiled apologetically and quickly dropped the fruit into the vendor's outstretched hand. "I'll have a dozen," she said, and handed eleven more peaches to the woman.

After she'd paid and taken the plastic bag of fruit from the vendor, Domini headed toward the nearest exit, boiling with frustration at the universe that had cursed her with such pointless foresight. For God's sake—was that *it*?

Why had it been so desperately important to race to Central Market, when all she'd been *meant* to do was listen to a song on the radio?

"I could have stayed home and done that," she grumbled.

"Do you always talk to yourself?" a male voice asked, his voice soft yet self-confident—caressing?

Domini turned to look for the man who'd spoken. When she moved her head, something soft as a breeze, intimate as a kiss, brushed against the back of her neck. It sent a cold shiver of fear down her spine and heat racing through her blood. The combination was as dizzying as peach brandy.

Though the market was crowded, suddenly she felt as alone as if she were standing on the moon.

And someone was watching her.

Domini turned slowly around, alert to any threat, to anything out of the ordinary. The routine of running a visual sweep of her location helped calm her.

The market was a huge open space, full of noise, bustling with people shopping at aisle upon aisle of stands, and breakfasting at the snack bars. Despite the overhead lights, neon signs, and sunlight flooding in from entrances on all four sides, there was a shadowed quality about the warehouselike building.

Nothing seemed out of place. It was a normal morning, with people going about their business and enjoying the sights and sounds of the place. There was no threat within.

Domini turned her attention to the entrance and instantly saw him standing in the doorway, just across the street from the Angels' Flight sign. He wore sunglasses, yet she knew the eyes behind the dark lenses were fixed on her. She stared boldly back.

His tall, broad-shouldered silhouette was haloed by the California sunshine. His features were shadowed by the brim of the sort of hat that reminded her of Indiana Jones. All she could make out was a square jaw and cleft chin, covered by dark beard stubble.

But how could he be the one who had spoken to her, when he was halfway across the market? Unless . . .

Unnerved, Domini turned and hurried for the opposite entrance. She didn't know what to make of all this; all she knew was that she had to get out of here *right now*. It was all she could do not to run, or look back over her shoulder to make sure he wasn't following her.

Alec watched the tall beauty go. He was left with a memory of long dark hair, a wide, full mouth, long legs, and lithe movement. As she fled, he fought down the urge to follow her with all the will he could muster. Her confusion and fear clawed at him. He forced himself to remain still as pain surged through him, wanting her with all his soul, bleeding inside at knowing she rejected anything to do with him. He told himself she had every right to run, and didn't let his primal response to flight rule him. He stayed on the leash, though breathing came hard and every muscle in his body tensed solid as stone.

Let her run. It will be all right.

Even as he told himself this, the shrouded part of him hated her for running—that creature believed in soul-bonding passion at first sight. But Alexander Reynard was more civilized than that. Or so he must believe, for the woman's sake, even more than his own.

What was happening to her was beyond her ken. And very nearly beyond his, at this moment. If they touched now, it would be raw and rough.

He hadn't expected to find her so soon, and losing her instantly dealt a blow to his soul. He wanted to throw back his head and howl, the way he had last night. But he would live with the loss for now, would fight down the arousal their brief touching of minds brought him. Or at least he'd live with it until he could offer her a man, not a monster.

He could have followed her easily. Her scent perfumed the air; her aura cut a bright swath easily discernible even in the tangled mix of life signs within the crowd. But he deliberately turned his back on that path. In a few minutes, he had a meeting at a nearby hole-in-the-wall joint, a meeting that was his purpose in coming into downtown Los Angeles. He would stick to that purpose, and endure what needed to be endured.

Alec made his tightly fisted hands relax, then he made himself walk through the market and out the other side, just as he'd originally planned.

Chapter Two

Many towns and all the big cities had a meeting place for the fringe peoples of the world. In Chicago, it was a boutique hotel. In New York, it was a bookstore. In New Orleans, it was an outdoor café famous for its coffee and doughnuts. Here in Los Angeles, the meeting place was a bar on the seedy side of downtown. It had a sleazy, dilapidated look that intentionally put off unwanted customers, which included most of the population. The bar's clientele paid very well for their privacy, and learned not to complain about the dirt and aromas to the bar's touchy proprietor.

While the establishment never closed, Alec was the only customer at the moment. He sat at a small scarred table in the center of the room and nursed a drink that looked like, but was not, a beer.

He hated to be kept waiting, and every now and then glanced toward the door with a look that grew more laser sharp with annoyance.

Finally, Alec made himself stop watching the door and reached for his glass again. The brew looked like a dark, rich stout, but was an herbal concoction that tasted something like—no, he didn't want to think about what it tasted like. Later, if he was lucky, he'd be able to enjoy a beer again, but for the immediate future he'd been told to abstain for medical reasons.

If things didn't work out—if the worst happened, and he went feral—it wasn't alcohol he'd be craving.

He rolled back the cuff of his white shirt and looked at the small tattoo of a stylized fox on the inside of his left wrist. It was fading, which wasn't a good sign.

Then the door opened, slammed shut, and Shaggy Harker bounded up to the table and swung into the other chair.

"Hey, buddy!" Shaggy's deep voice boomed through the room, the sound filling all the shadowy spaces. "Long time, man."

Alec was so startled he very nearly snarled at Harker, and that could have turned a meeting of old friends into a bloody mess, with both of them reacting on primitive instinct rather than thought. Alec's mouth and fingers ached as he controlled the reaction.

He managed something like a smile. "Long time," Alec agreed. "You look—hairy."

Shaggy threw back his head and let out a bark of laughter. "You look like shit."

"I feel like it, too," Alec acknowledged.

With a swift move, Shaggy wrapped his big hand around Alec's left arm. His grasp was surprisingly gentle. Alec went very still as Shaggy studied the fox tattoo.

"Ink's fading," Shaggy finally judged. "Bummer."

"Yes."

Shaggy loosed his hold and sat back with his arms crossed over his wide chest. Most werewolves were not bikers, despite the stereotype. Shaggy Harker just happened to be a werewolf biker. He was big and bearded, his long, silver-streaked hair tied back with a red bandanna. He was dressed in leather and denim and an old black T-shirt. A faint musky aroma washed across the table to tickle Alec's sensitive sense of smell.

Shaggy was smart, perceptive, and very much had his nose into everything in his territory. If someone supernatural blew into Los Angeles needing something, Shaggy was the one who could fix them up. If it was legal.

"You in town for the cure, man?" Shaggy asked, after the

bartender brought him a beer that was really a beer. "The docs at the clinic do good work," he added after taking a gulp of the cold brew. "You'll be fine."

Alec had little patience for sympathetic reassurance, but he let it go with only a cold look. His nerves were strung tight, which was his only excuse for acting so prickly. Or like a prick, to be more precise.

He signaled the bartender to bring Shaggy another drink, then made himself finish the glass he'd been nursing.

"I have an appointment at the clinic later this morning. There are stipulations about receiving treatment."

"Yeah, yeah," Shaggy said. "I know the drill for your folk. Part of your twelve-step is that you have to have a job, one that serves humanity."

Alec bristled at the casual comment. "I am a Prime of Clan Reynard," he sternly reminded the werewolf, whom he'd met on a mission to rescue embassy hostages several decades before. "The Clans serve. We are guardians, protectors," he said proudly.

"And touchy," Shaggy added. "I've never known anyone who could get bent out of shape faster than a vampire. Thanks," he said as the bartender deposited another beer on the table. He gulped down the brew, then wiped his mouth with the back of his hand. "Good thing you're buying, Alec—"

"You used to call me Colonel."

"Yeah, but that was before you went into Delta and got all casual."

It was true that the members of the army's elite covert fighting force acted like civilians much of the time, and rank was generally a nonissue. Yet . . . "I didn't know you knew about my transfer."

"Guessed when you disappeared so sudden-like." Shaggy shrugged. "We're both civilians now. You *are* out, right?"

"Unfortunately." Alec had reluctantly resigned his commission when the symptoms started. Delta Force was no place for a vampire when the drugs that let him function in the daylight world were losing their potency.

"You need a job?"

Alec rubbed the back of his neck, then rolled his head from side to side. "I need a job," he answered, when he'd worked some of the tension out of his muscles. The memory of seeing his woman in the market rose before him for a moment, but he pushed it away. "I very badly need a job."

"Think I might have something for you," Shaggy told him. "Heard old man Lancer's looking to add to his team. Your résumé hold up to a background check?"

"Of course," Alec answered. "What sort of team are we talking about?"

"Personal protection."

"Bodyguard."

"You got it. To the rich and famous. Protecting a movie star is an honorable enough job for a Clan boy, right?"

Alec wanted to snarl that a Prime was not a *boy*, but that was only his medication needing adjustment. "Depends on the movie star," he managed to joke.

"I'll get a friend of a friend to set up an appointment with Lancer for you," Shaggy said. "Maybe even today. That okay with you?"

"I appreciate it." He briefly looked the werewolf in the eye, a sign of respect, rather than challenge from an alpha male of one species to the alpha of another.

Shaggy nodded. "I'll call when I know anything."

Alec felt relieved at having set one item of his agenda in motion. He was almost looking forward to his first appointment at the very private medical facility that was his next stop. His senses, physical and psychic, were growing painfully sensitive. For example, he was uncomfortably aware of the werewolf's rising pheromone level.

Shaggy looked around restlessly and glanced at his watch. "Can't hang around and talk over old times." He grinned as he stood. "Got to get home. My old lady's in season, and we aren't getting any younger."

That explained the pheromones, but also told Alec far more than he wanted to know about werewolves' private lives. He got to his feet as well. "I have to be going myself. Good seeing you again."

"I'll be in touch." Shaggy waved a casual farewell, and was out the door faster than he'd come in.

Alec donned his jacket, driving gloves, sunglasses, and hat before walking out into the daylight. Not that long ago, he hadn't needed all this paraphernalia to face the sun. He felt like an invalid, needing it now, and hoped that the doctors at the clinic could bring him back to his normal life.

Then he could find *her*.

"Why, if it isn't Domini the Dominatrix finally sauntering in."

"I have never sauntered in my life," Domini informed Andy Maxwell, who lounged against Nancy's reception desk in the front hall.

As usual when off duty, Andy looked at her with feigned salaciousness. He wasn't really a sexist pig, but a good friend with a twisted sense of humor.

She pointed sternly to the white marble floor. "On your knees when you speak to me, slave."

Andy promptly obeyed, then looked up at her with anticipation.

Domini laughed; the silliness made her feel normal.

Nancy peered over the top of her glasses. "You two stop that."

They both knew who the real dominatrix was in the company. "Yes, ma'am," they answered together. Andy bounced to his feet and leaned against the desk again.

"Your grandfather wants to see you," Nancy told Domini.

"Right now?"

"I buzzed him as soon as I saw you get off the elevator."

The wide glass wall and door of Lancer Services' office suite gave Nancy a very good view of the long hallway that led to the gleaming copper doors of the elevators. "And you go back to your cube," Nancy told Andy, "before I tell him you asked me for a date again."

"I just came out for staples," Andy protested as Domini left the reception area. "And to flirt a little bit—"

Domini shook her head with amusement as she drew out of earshot. Andy *was* a flirt, all right, but he liked his job too much to break the old man's rule about no fraternizing among the staff. Concentrate on business or get out, that was Grandpa's philosophy.

Concentrating usually wasn't a problem for Domini, but she was having a hard time getting the image of the man she'd seen watching her out of her mind.

Domini knocked and then walked into her grandfather's office. The Old Man was on the phone, so she grabbed a bottled water out of the small fridge, took a seat in the deep brown leather chair in front of his desk, and blatantly listened to Benjamin Lancer's side of the phone conversation.

"D-Boy is just out, eh? How civilized is he? Any PPA training? Good. We can polish him up quick enough. Can he wear a suit? Okay. Send him over."

"Found someone to replace Hancock?" Domini asked after her grandfather put down the phone.

The desk was a wide, modernistic glass-topped affair; a present from a grateful corporate client a few years back. It didn't suit the Old Man's taste, but it, and the rest of the office's decor, set a low-key but expensively professional tone that reassured the company's clientele. A sleek new flat-screen computer and the telephone took up one side of the desk. The Old Man generally propped his feet up on the other side when there weren't any clients around. Nancy made it part of her job to see that the desk was clean and gleaming before any client meetings.

He put his feet up on the desk. "Looks like," was the gruff answer.

"That's a relief. A team leader type?"

"Won't know till I see him, will I?"

Domini shrugged agreement.

People came and went a lot in this business. Lancer only hired the best, and the best eventually tended to go freelance or start their own agencies. Tommy Hancock had recently taken an offer from the Secret Service, so there was a certain amount of pride, and no hard feelings, about his leaving. But replacing someone of his caliber was proving harder than usual. The Old Man had been starting to be frustrated about it. He didn't look frustrated now, which pleased Domini on several levels. Though he thrived on stress, she wished he'd take life a little easier. God forbid she should suggest it, however.

Though he didn't look a day over a very fit sixty, Old Man Lancer was pushing eighty. There was more silver than brown in his hair and beard. His skin was tanned, and the only wrinkles that showed were deep crow's-feet around surprisingly blue eyes. She'd heard someone describe Ben Lancer's eyes as neon blue, and they were the one physical feature she'd inherited from him. There was maturity in his voice rather than age. The tone was deep, dark, and had a rough timbre to it, like the taste of good whiskey. Whiskey was also a drink he tended to overindulge in once a year, on the anniversary of losing Domini's grandmother.

With that date looming over the horizon, Domini was glad the Old Man had one concern off his mind. Especially as she might be presenting him with another one.

Since he'd sent for her, she first asked, "What's up?"

"Holly Ashe called," he answered.

Domini smiled. "Called the house? She knows I have my own place now, and my cell number even if we haven't seen each other in over a year."

She and Holly had been best friends from preschool all the way through high school. Domini went on to college; Holly went on the road. They kept in touch, though since Holly's singing career went white-hot, contact had been less frequent. There had been a lot of phone calls and e-mails when Holly broke up with her longtime lover, but that had been a year ago, when Holly was touring Europe.

"So why did Holly call you?"

"Her management's looking to beef up her security. She remembered her old friend's family business, and she wants you to be her bodyguard."

Domini slugged down half the bottle of water. "I'm sure you told her that isn't exactly how it works."

He nodded. "Took the assignment for the company. You'll go through her people to set up the details."

Domini almost dropped the bottle. "You want me to run a detail for a friend?"

Those sharp blue eyes narrowed. "I want you to do the workup and briefing for the team. That all right with you?"

When Benjamin Lancer asked a question like that, he expected only one answer. "Yes, sir. How large a detail? Duration of contract? Who's your point person?"

A slight smile creased his weathered face. "I noticed you didn't ask if you were going to be on the team."

She smiled back. "I assumed that Holly insisted that I would be."

He nodded. "Good girl."

A compliment from him was rare, so Domini basked in it for a moment. She was also relieved. Doing groundwork meant several days spent mostly in the office. That would give her more than enough time to recover from the weirdness of the last few hours. She needed to be sharp, focused, and above all, behaving like a normal human being while in the field. People's safety depended on her out there.

For a moment she hesitated on telling her grandfather

about the incident, since it now looked to be a nonissue. But this profession demanded honesty, and her grandfather expected her to be honest. He'd raised her that way.

She cleared her throat. "I need to tell you something."

"I noticed your butt's still in the chair when you've got work to do."

Domini grinned mischievously. "Don't you want to see my pretty face first thing in the mornin', Grandpa?"

He glanced at his watch. "Not exactly first thing, is it? What'd you want to tell me, girl?"

"I had a dream last night. It wasn't a normal dream. It was a premonition—"

"Thought you didn't get those anymore."

"I don't talk about them, it's not the same thing."

Ben Lancer gave her a glower that should have had a trademark symbol on it, it was so definitive. "Hmmph. Go on."

"This dream was way different than anything I'd had before. It was . . ." She didn't want to say *erotic*, because she wasn't sure the word was big enough to fit the sensations that had overcome her. "Disturbing. I woke up with this need . . . a craving—"

Her grandfather's boots hit the floor with a shocking thud as he sat up straight. Those bright blue eyes held hers with laser intensity. "Compulsion?" he asked. "Somewhere you had to be at a certain time?"

If she didn't know him so well, Domini would have sworn that was fear she heard in his voice. His tone made her nervous. "Yes. How did you know?"

"How do you feel now?"

Domini shrugged. "Better. Steadier. But I was really disoriented until I got out of the market. I normally get very low-level premonitions. It's not like I *see* important events before they happen—"

"You did once, when you were three. You woke everybody up screaming, 'Shake! Shake!' We barely got out of the house before the quake knocked it down."

Domini was startled. "I don't remember that."

"It happened, whether you remember it or not. You said market?"

Domini took a deep breath, and went on. "The Central Market. That was where I was—okay, compelled—to go. I needed to buy fresh peaches."

"You were late for work because you needed fruit?" His disgust was palpable. He sat back in his chair. "I thought you were forced to go there to meet someone."

Again, she was surprised. "There *was* a man." Even speaking about him sent a shiver through her. "How did you know?"

He was leaning forward again, his hands flat on the thick glass desktop, studying her intently. "Tell me about him. What did he look like? Did he approach you? Speak to you?"

Domini felt thoroughly shaken now. "Forget it. I don't want to talk about it." She stood and turned toward the door.

"Wait—"

Domini bolted out the door.

"Just what I don't need," she muttered as she hurried to her own desk. "One psycho psychic in this family is more than enough."

Chapter Three

"Yeah?" Domini answered the ring of the internal phone line, later that day.

"Get in here," the Old Man answered.

"Be right there." She promptly hung up and headed back to the boss's office.

He wasn't alone.

A man standing beside the desk turned when she opened the door. Though the room was brightly lit, all she made out at first was a silhouette of a man, tall and broad-shouldered, standing unnaturally still but exuding grace and strength and power all the same. Domini blinked and he came into focus, but the impression of danger did not go away.

He was not the handsomest man she'd ever seen, but he was the most—something. The word that came to mind was *strong*, not just in the physical sense. His features were so strongly defined, his square jaw and high cheekbones could have been chiseled. There was a deep cleft in his chin and he had green eyes, which she couldn't quite make herself look into directly. It would seem too much like an alpha challenge to do so.

"Domini, you're staring," her grandfather said.

"Well, who wouldn't?" she heard herself mutter. The alpha smiled slightly, which brought her back to herself with a jolt. She was so not acting normal today.

Define normal?

She ignored the thought. "You wanted to see me, sir?"

"Would I have told you to come in if I didn't?"

Her grandfather's gruff rudeness told Domini that the

stranger was not a client. She'd realized that anyway. He would never be the one in need of protecting. Standing perfectly still, with a totally neutral expression on his face, he was the most dangerous person in the room—which said a lot, considering that neither she nor her grandfather were mild-mannered kittens.

So, this was the D-Boy.

"Alexander Reynard," he introduced himself. "Interesting name, Domini."

He spoke softly, and his voice had a velvety rumble. It was the caressing kind of voice that tempted one to lean closer.

"It's an old Scottish name," she answered. "It's a term for a schoolteacher."

"Oh?" he asked. "I thought it was a variation of Domanae, which means 'mistress.'"

Domini blushed, remembering her teasing with Andy Maxwell. Had this new guy been talking to the staff already?

"Never mind what her father decided to call her," the Old Man broke in. "Domini, show Mr. Reynard around. You'll be supervising his orientation for the next week, starting tomorrow morning."

Alec watched as Domini curbed both surprise and irritation. She was busy. He disturbed her. It took great effort for him to reach through the dull fog surrounding him, to read her. It would be better to save his energy, so after a few more moments he broke off the contact.

Her gaze flicked Alec's way and darted away again. "Yes, sir," she answered her grandfather.

Mistress indeed, Alec thought. A prize. Mine.

For an instant he held an image in his mind, a vision of how in ancient days, his kind were rewarded for mighty deeds with the bodies of the most beautiful women in the world. Long before his time, of course, but he knew the legends of the good old days. No one was going to bring this woman to his bed but him, which suited him. He only wished she wasn't here right now.

But it didn't surprise him to find her here; fate loved cruel jokes. To be so close and yet utterly distant . . . He dared not touch her, or taste her, or make any claim. Not in his condition.

He was all right for now, with a cocktail of drugs pouring through his system. The doctors had dosed him with a temporary fix to get him through the interview and the rest of the day, but because of the drugs, he could barely touch the senses of the woman meant to be his. He was grateful, in a way; it was only the drugs that kept the fury of *having* to be drugged in check. Catch-22, vampire style.

While she talked to her grandfather, Alec stared at Domini as blatantly as she had at him. The old man noticed without even looking Alec's way. Alec refrained from smiling at Lancer's protectiveness, for if he did, the smile would be predatory.

When he'd seen Domini in the market, it had been her spirit more than her physical appearance that he'd noticed. Then he'd seen that she was tall and dark-haired. This close to her, he could appreciate her long-legged athlete's body, but too much perusal of all the curves and lines of her figure was not wise right now, not even when he was numbed by the drugs. Later, when he had time to slowly strip her naked and look, he would caress and taste to his utter satisfaction. For now, Alec concentrated on Domini's face.

She was not classically beautiful and certainly not Hollywood beautiful, for which he was thankful. Not blond, not a size zero; nothing had been surgically altered or injected to try to make artificial perfection out of the perfectly lean and lithe form given her by nature. She was a hardbody, which took hard work, sweat, and dedication. He appreciated that, admired it, wanted—

Face. Concentrate on her face, before you get hot and bothered and do something stupid.

Domini's eyes were amazing, bright blue surrounded by thick, dark lashes. Her chin was sharp and stubborn. Her skin, pale and flawless but for one mole to the right of her lower lip. The beauty spot added a saucy air of wantonness to a mouth that was already more than amazing. Those full, ripe lips were made to be kissed for at least several hours a day. A man could make a full-time job of worshiping that soft, sensuous mouth.

"Come on, I'll find you a desk and show you around," Domini said, jarring him back to the present.

"Thank you." Alec exchanged a long glance with Ben Lancer. Lancer's look held a warning that no fraternization was allowed, especially with his granddaughter. Alec nodded, but it was in acceptance of the risk of breaking the rule, rather than agreement to abide by it.

For Domini, the walk down the corridor that led to the warren of office cubicles had never seemed so long. She felt like she was being tailed, almost stalked. Maybe he disturbed her because she couldn't hear him behind her. The corridor was not carpeted, and he was not wearing soft-soled shoes, so why were there no footsteps? And why couldn't she hear his breathing? She was damned good; was a Delta Force veteran that much better?

Stupid question—of course he was, or she would know he was there.

When his hand touched her shoulder, Domini was shocked, literally. Sensation burned through her like a bolt of electricity. A gasp caught in her throat as she spun to face him, hands held up defensively. Only to find herself facing a mildly surprised, very good-looking man, who said, "Sorry."

She should have been the one to apologize, but she felt stupid and—scared. Something else as well, something that sent her heart pounding in her ears and the blood sizzling through her veins. She didn't know what it was, but she knew Mr. Alexander Reynard caused it.

"Cat got your tongue?" he asked after silence stretched taut between them.

Domini quivered inside at the sound of his cool, lilting voice. Looking at him made her knees go weak. And—she wanted him to touch her again.

She turned around. "Come on." It was a victory that her voice didn't shake.

A few more steps, and they reached the large room partitioned into a dozen low-walled cubicles. Here she felt on firmer ground. Here she actually could find something reasonable to say to the man.

A few people turned from their telephones and computer screens as they passed, and Domini paused each time to introduce Reynard. Most of the office area was empty, so the journey to Reynard's future workspace didn't take very long.

The cubicle contained a pair of workstations with computers, phones, and file drawers. Two very comfortable desk chairs took up most of the floor space.

Domini gestured for Alec to have a seat. She leaned against the doorway, arms crossed, and explained, "Agents share the cubes. We're not in the office much, so it's not likely you'll have company crowding you when you're doing office work."

She pointed toward the workstation on the left. "This'll be yours. Nancy will set you up with supplies and passwords and a keycard for the secure areas. We'll go through the fun stuff tomorrow, if that's okay with you." She checked her watch. "I have an appointment in an hour."

He nodded. "Fine. Fun stuff?"

"Hardware, surveillance equipment. Nothing as fancy as you're used to, I'm sure."

He gave her a genuine smile. He had dimples. "I can't talk about what I'm used to."

Ex–special-ops people always said cryptic stuff like that, if they even talked about what they'd done at all. Naturally this whetted curiosity, but Domini refused to wheedle for information that wouldn't be given. It only encouraged the spooks' sense of superiority. And this man exuded so much confidence that she definitely didn't want to stroke his ego.

So, what would you like to stroke?

Where had that thought come from?

Domini returned to business. "We have two floors of this building. Offices here, fun stuff down a flight. We have a good exercise room downstairs, but most of our people also do classes at various martial arts schools. Though we don't carry guns on our protection details, we can get you a discount at the Pherson shooting range, and we have an arrangement with Delano Defensive Driving School. You'll be put through the driving course during your orientation. Let's see, what else?

"We're a dress-down, dress-up organization with very high-end clients, so your wardrobe has to reflect their lifestyles. You'll have a generous annual clothing allowance. Nancy has a list of recommended clothing stores and tailors."

She checked out Reynard's suit while trying not to eye *him*, not entirely succeeding. "Doubt you'll need Nancy's advice. Armani?"

He fingered the well-made, dark suit jacket. "Found this on Rodeo Drive. Wanted to impress my prospective employer."

Which brought up another question that she should have considered before now. "How *did* you impress the Old Man? He usually takes a couple of weeks to vet a new hire."

Alec gestured at the cube's other chair, and watched Domini take a seat. He had managed some mental influence on the Old Man, but only enough to smooth his way into the job. He hadn't lied about his skills. Lancer could trust Alec to do the job he hired him for, even if he'd been telepathically influenced not to run the normal background check.

"Your grandfather trusts the mutual friend who recommended me for the position," he told the clearly suspicious Domini. "And I know that you're about to say he doesn't trust many people."

She narrowed her extraordinary blue eyes. "Reading my mind?"

"Lucky guess."

Alex stood, and Domini rose to face him. He offered her a hand, which she pretended not to notice. Too bad; he very much wanted to touch her again. *Needed* to, and intended to. For now, he allowed himself the merest thought of how her skin would be warm and satin-smooth against his stroking hands.

Domini's eyes widened, letting him know that on some unconscious level she responded to his desire. She blinked and stepped carefully past him, while he resisted the temptation to reach for her. He didn't know if this was a victory of the drugs or his own self-control.

"Thank you for your help," Alec told her. "So, we'll resume the orientation tomorrow morning?"

She nodded. "You'll need to fill out forms and get an ID photo before you go. I'll leave you with Nancy to take care of that. Be nice to her," she added. "Nancy's the real boss around here."

He put a hand to his heart. "I will be the epitome of charm."

"That won't work on Nancy." Domini led the way back through the offices, saying over her shoulder, "Try bribery. She makes out like a bandit during Secretary's Week."

"Roses and chocolates it is, then." Alec hung back a few steps, so he could fully appreciate the view as Domini walked away.

Chapter Four

"Does this hurt?"

"If you ask me that again, I will rip out your throat." Alec was strapped down naked on a lab table built for vampires, but that didn't make the threat any less meaningful.

The drugs had worn off, and Alec was feeling very testy indeed. His fangs brushed against his lower lip and his claws scraped against the metal table. Anger pumped through him, and his control was very, very thin.

"I'll take that as a yes," Dr. Casmerek responded calmly. "These tests are necessary," he went on. "The consequences will be far more uncomfortable if we don't find out exactly what types of adjustments we need to make."

The doctor went on about proteins and allergic reactions, while assistants continued to poke needles into Alec's sensitized flesh and attached monitors to every section of his head and body. Alec closed his eyes and tried not to struggle. He hated being restrained. No matter how much he knew this was for his own good, he still felt like a prisoner. Worse, he was helpless and defenseless, something no Prime could take for long. Instinct fought with reason, and the effort left him panting and covered with sweat.

The doctor, who was a very specialized specialist, was totally trusted by the Clans. He was completely devoted to helping his patients, but right now Alec hated Casmerek with all his might. Alec was powerless, and Casmerek in control. Never mind that Alec had surrendered the control by his own free will; he *needed* the mortal's help. That was not the way it was supposed to be.

Maybe it would be better to return to the old ways. There were many, even among the Clans, who thought this modern solution wrong and unnatural. Many argued that the drugs that helped them live in daylight, that protected them against silver and garlic and the other allergens that limited their powers, were an abomination. For thousands of years the Primes, the venerable Elders, the House Ladies, the Matri, and the sheltered young had lived in the darkness and controlled the thirst with strength of mind and willpower and devotion to duty. With the coming of modern science much had changed, but the will still existed; mental disciplines could still be applied to curb the fire in the blood and mind.

Alec realized he must have been speaking aloud, possibly even raving, when Casmerek said, "You will need to draw upon every mental discipline the Primes know until your biochemistry is back in balance. It's that mental discipline and probably sheer stubbornness that have kept you going the last few weeks. I wish you'd gotten here sooner."

"Well, I couldn't," Alec snarled. "I was in Uzbekistan."

"Which is a fact I'm sure I'm not supposed to know." He dared to pat Alec's bare shoulder, and ignored Alec baring his fangs threateningly at this gesture of comfort. "We're used to keeping secrets here, so don't worry about it, Colonel."

"Don't call me that."

He didn't deserve the title. Not when he'd had to abandon his men, his assignment, all for the selfish need to—

"You've only done what was necessary for you to do. Leaving the service when you did saved lives. You'll realize that when you're feeling better. How are we doing?" the doctor asked the techs.

"Ready to go," one of them answered.

"Good." Casmerek turned his attention back to Alec and patted his shoulder again. "We're going to turn off the lights and leave you now. All you have to do is go to sleep. Close your eyes. Rest. Dream. The machines will do the rest."

Alec heard the technicians leave the room, and Casmerek's voice faded as the doctor moved farther and farther away. "In the morning we'll have run all the baseline tests, and then we'll take it from there. Go to sleep, now," he urged in his gentle voice.

Alec closed his eyes as the lights went out, and he was suddenly alone in the dark—a monster who should be lurking in closets, or hiding in nightmares. Wherever it was he should be, he was here, and he was very afraid of the monster who was himself.

The night was punctuated by smoky torches at each corner of the temple courtyard, hung high upon the rough stone columns. The scent of pitch and burning straw carried to her through the cool air of the desert night. The deep portico beyond the pillars was far darker than the night itself. The courtyard held the light of the moon, the stars, and the torches, though they sent out gray smoke that swirled like river fog through the enclosure. This was a place of dark mystery, a place set apart, a place where a god would walk—and do whatever he pleased.

Though she saw no one, she knew she was not alone. A shiver ran through her, compounded of deep fear and a thrill of excitement. She had been chosen. Though it meant her doom—for how could one not be consumed when touched by a god?—she faced her fate with the pride of a king's daughter.

She circled the courtyard slowly, drawing nearer to the altar set in the center of the sacred place. Then she realized that the place of sacrifice was in fact a bed, more ornately carved and gilded than any bed frame in the king's palace. The bedcoverings were richly embroidered, the mattress thick and piled high with pillows.

She sensed movement as she reached out to touch a carving

on the bedpost. She heard and saw nothing, yet knew which way to turn to face the Lord of Darkness.

She confronted a tall, broad figure clothed in an all-enveloping cloak and hood. She knelt but did not bow her head, showing respect but not subservience.

The cloaked figure moved silently toward her, as graceful as a hunting cat. "Did you come here of your own choice?" His voice was soft, rich, commanding attention and response.

"I came," she answered. "That is as much as you need to know."

The Lord of Darkness had rid the city of evil ones that killed in the night. He had asked for a woman as reward. It was fitting that the king give his city's savior a daughter to honor such great service.

They had drawn lots in the women's quarters. Each of the king's six unmarried daughters had taken a turn to draw a stone from a jar, one white stone among the five black ones. She had drawn third, and the white stone. So she had donned her jewels and her best gown and combed out her long, black hair as if preparing for her wedding. She had refused to weep, had kissed no one good-bye, but had gone silently with the priests who led her here, then left her to the god's will.

And here was the god.

She should remain humble and silent. She asked instead, "What do you want with me?"

He answered with a gesture toward the bed. Then he dropped his cloak. By both moon and torchlight, she saw that he was naked.

He was pale as milk, and perfect.

His face was beautiful, though the sharp lines of it might have been carved from stone. His expression was solemn, harsh, and very sad. She could not look at his face for long, yet she could no more look away from him than willingly stop breathing. He was taller than a mortal man, as a god should be. Taller and more—everything.

He was like a statue come to life. Everything about him was sharply defined, from the rippling muscles of chest and thighs and arms to the rampant phallus that inexorably drew her gaze.

She had never known arousal before, but surely this heavy, hot, aching growing inside her must be it.

She licked her lips, hardly aware of the gesture until the Lord of Darkness's soft chuckle caressed her ears.

"Can a god laugh?"

"A god can do anything that pleases him." He was before her suddenly, moving with cat grace and god speed. He took her by the shoulders with a touch that surprised her by its gentleness, and drew her to her feet, brushing her body against his as she rose. His flesh was warm, and not made of stone at all.

His fingers were skilled and quick. Her finest dress pooled around her feet within moments. It was but another moment before he picked her up and placed her on the bed. She did not realize she'd put her arms around his neck until he gently loosed her hold. He held her hands in his and kissed one palm, and then the other. The light touch sent a flame of desire through her.

Then he tilted her head up and covered her mouth with his. She had not realized what deep, fiery pleasure the touching of lips, the delving of tongues, could bring. The kiss was headier than unwatered wine, a rich feast of sensation.

It was said the Lords of Darkness had fangs and claws, so she was not surprised, and only a little afraid, when she felt sharp teeth press against her lips. The excitement of his touch overwhelmed her fear. Perhaps fear enhanced her excitement. All she knew was that she moaned with loss when his mouth left hers.

"No—!"

"Peace," he whispered. He held her face in his hands, so that she must look into his eyes. They glowed faintly in the moonlight, as any night beast's would. "This night you are mine, to do with as I please."

The look in those eyes demanded an answer, an assent. Her body was crying out for his touch. She was a spoiled daughter of the king; she wanted to demand he make love to her. She swallowed hard and gathered her wits to remember why she was here. "I am yours," she told him. "A gift for the god."

"Do you want me? Do you want my body to cover yours? Do you want me inside you? I will have your consent."

He had gone out of his way to arouse her, and now he was asking her? "Don't be ridiculous." She grabbed his thick black hair in her fists and pulled his mouth back to hers.

This second kiss was as intense, but he did not let it last as long. "The night grows late," he whispered against her mouth.

His hands skimmed over her then, and he kissed her throat and between her breasts and suckled at the tips, and moved on to her belly and thighs. Wherever he touched he left traces of fire behind. The heat pooled deep down in her belly, making her grind her hips and arch up against him, insistent, begging for more.

Every now and then there would be a slight sting as his sharp teeth penetrated her skin, pain that was more pleasure than pain. If he took a drop or two of her blood with each kiss, she welcomed the small sacrifice for the bright bursts of joy it brought. His fingers delved between her legs, caressed and teased her until she thought she would die from the tension building inside her.

He made her wild with longing. Finally she opened to him, and lifted her hips. He knelt between her legs and looked down. She held her arms out beseechingly, and looked up a long, long way to meet his gaze.

Only she couldn't see his eyes, because he was wearing sunglasses. His features shifted as he smiled, and a glint of moonlight sparkled off his fangs.

"Reynard," she demanded angrily. "What the hell are you doing in my dream?"

"Your dream?" he answered. "I thought it was mine."

*   *   *

Domini sat up in bed, shaking and covered in sweat. "What the hell?" she muttered, and swiped hair out of her face. She was checking herself for bite marks when she realized it had just been a dream, and that she still wasn't quite awake yet.

Good Lord, two nights in a row of weirdness. What was the matter with her?

Domini got out of bed, and discovered that she was shaking so hard she could barely stand. Her knees were like jelly, her breasts felt heavy and tender, and her insides ached. She sat on the edge of the rumpled bed, staring into the darkness, the image of the smoky temple courtyard overlaying her shadowed bedroom.

"So that's what an erotic dream feels like."

She was edgy, weary, drained. Arousal was fading to dull ash, leaving her with a growing sense of frustration.

"It was just a dream." It had been a wild, crazy ride, but—it was only a dream. One where she'd made love with a man she'd barely met who turned into a vampire. It was still so vivid that she could almost feel the sweet sting of the vampire's kisses.

Why a vampire? She hadn't dreamed of vampires since she was a little girl and her mom insisted Grandpa stop telling her horror stories before bedtime. Maybe she'd seen a movie billboard or television ad about a vampire movie. Maybe it was something she'd eaten. Maybe Reynard was just a spooky guy.

"I wonder if he does look that good naked. . . ." She shook her head sharply. "*Stop* that."

It was weird, it certainly wasn't the sort of dream she usually had, but it wasn't like last night's disturbing premonition. This time all that had really happened was that a lot of exotic props bubbled up from the warehouse in the back of her mind, and her subconscious went on a randy rampage.

But how was she supposed to face Reynard in the office tomorrow morning?

Calm down, girl. It was only a dream. After all, it wasn't as if Reynard was going to know what went on in her mind in the middle of the night.

*   *   *

Alec woke up in chains.

He snarled and howled in desperate fury, and fought against the restraints. He had to get to her. How dare they keep him from her!

People surrounded him while he struggled. Hands held him down. Needles pierced his skin, bringing white-hot pain, bringing calm, bringing peace, bringing him back to himself.

"I had a dream," he said, recognizing who these people were, where he was, and why he was restrained. "I'm all right," he told the anxious faces. They were here to help him, but he hated them—because they would keep him from getting to her. "It was just a dream."

Someone patted his bare shoulder. It was meant as comfort, but Alec would have bitten the hand off if he could have gotten to it. These people did not know what it was like to be Prime, and in the bonding state.

Gradually, the drugs sent him back into a drifting half-sleep. The monitors and alarms died down and stopped flashing and buzzing. The medical personnel left, one by one.

Alec smiled. He had not dreamed alone. He knew where the dream came from. He had thought of the ancient customs when he was with Domini Lancer, and his drugged subconscious had built on that sexual fantasy. In his sleep he took Domini as the old ones took mortal women; tasted her and pleasured her and was very near to completing the act, when Domini became aware that she was dreaming.

She woke up—and left him hanging out to dry with a raging hard-on, nearly out of his mind.

But the fact that she'd shared his dream meant she was aware of their connection, even if only on the deepest subconscious level of her being.

"Cool." He drifted back into deep sleep even as he murmured the word.

Chapter Five

"Good morning," a voice said.

"Go away," Alec growled.

"I realize vampires are not morning people, but you need to wake up now, Alec."

He opened his eyes. Dr. Casmerek was standing over the bed with a chart in his hands. Looking past Casmerek's broad frame, Alec was glad to see two technicians unfastening all the probes and monitors and restraints. He flexed his arms and legs. The metal table was still cold against his bare skin, even after hours lying on it. At least the lighting was dim and didn't bother his eyes.

"Am I free to go now?"

"Hardly." Casmerek looked at his watch. "It's five-thirty in the morning. Sorry to rouse you so early, but I wanted time to talk before you leave. You can get up now," Casmerek added as the technicians left the room.

Alec sat up, and looked at the inside of his arms. The marks from the intravenous needles faded as he watched, and he noticed unhappily that the Clan mark on his left wrist had faded a bit further. He held his wrist up for the doctor. "When can I have this redone?"

"In a couple of weeks, perhaps. We have photographs of it on file that we can check against to see if it fades further." Casmerek handed Alec a small paper cup containing a half dozen pills of various shapes, colors, and sizes. While Alec gulped down the drugs, Casmerek pointed toward a doorway on the other side of the room. "Take a shower and get dressed. Then we'll talk in my office."

Shortly after, Alec took a seat across a desk in a room decorated in soothing shades of pale green and blue. There were no windows in Casmerek's office, but beautiful landscape paintings on the walls made up for the lack of sunlit scenery.

"Will I live?" Alec asked.

"For several centuries yet," Casmerek answered, "even without the medication. But to live in daylight during that time"—he passed a metal case across the desk to Alec—"follow the instructions on using these religiously."

Alec snapped open the case to check out the carefully packed contents. "Pills, capsules, syringes, eye drops, skin cream."

"A supply of medicated animal protein—"

"We call it blood where I come from," Alec said dryly.

"—will be delivered to your home twice a week."

"When will I be able to stop taking the medication?"

"We have to start with the preliminary test results and go from there. Vampire physiology does its best to reassert itself every chance it gets. We're working on tracing mitochondrial DNA and gene mapping, which hold out a great deal of hope for the future, but for now, we're limited to tailoring a treatment for each individual case.

"I can't give you any firm date on when you'll be fully recovered. All we can do is take it one step at a time. Now, about last night." He looked over steepled fingers at Alec.

"We were monitoring your sleep cycle. The REM readouts went so wild for a few minutes that it was like we were recording the brainwaves of more than one person." Casmerek gave him a curious look.

"Interesting," Alec answered.

"It was a strongly erotic dream," Casmerek went on. "Perfectly normal for a Prime, of course."

"Nothing hornier than a Prime," Alec agreed.

"Was the dream about anyone specific? Someone you know?"

Primes might be highly sexed, but they protected even the most casual of lovers. They defended their bondmates to the death.

"None of your business," Alec informed the doctor.

"It is if it affects your treatment."

The bonding was an essential part of being a Prime. It was at the heart of what made one a vampire. The bond was sacred; it was as fundamental as the night.

After he'd seen Domini in the market, Alec had made a promise to himself to protect his mate from the dark part of his nature, to wait until he was totally in control of himself before he pursued her.

But he hadn't expected to meet her face-to-face so quickly. He hadn't expected to stand beside her, talk to her, breathe in her scent, and touch her skin. He hadn't expected to dream with her. Maybe he wouldn't be able to control the mating urge.

All he could do was try. He was Prime. The woman was his. He would do whatever was necessary to protect her.

Dr. Casmerek had worked with Primes long enough to know when to let a subject go. He nodded and went on. "Practicing the meditation skills you learned as a child is also vital for your treatment."

"I haven't stopped practicing them."

"I'm sure, but we've still set up a refresher course with an elder."

Casmerek was watching him closely, so Alec did not let the wariness show. "What clan?" he asked calmly.

"An Honored Father of Clan Shagal."

Alec relaxed. "The Jackals are friend to all."

"The Matri who will act as your therapist is also of Shagal. Don't look at me like you're about to bite my head off, Reynard. A mortal isn't going to be of any help if you need to talk things out. You can sit in a chair and glower at her for all I care, but you will see her."

"I have more respect for the Matri than to glower at one."

"You might think all these measures are overkill, but believe me, you are far closer to the edge than you think you are. We know what is necessary to help you."

"Fine." Alec stood, grasping the plastic handle of the case so hard he could feel it begin to crack. He'd had enough of being treated for one day. "I have to go to work now."

Domini held a white paper bag up before her as she entered the kitchen, following the smell of brewing coffee. She rattled the bag to get his attention. "Yo, Grandpa, I brought doughnuts."

Ben Lancer was wearing a white terry bathrobe. He was barefoot, and his silver hair was still damp from a shower. He'd been staring at the ocean out the kitchen window when Domini came in.

"Don't you know how to knock?" he asked, turning to face her.

He asked her that every time she dropped by, which was almost every day of the week. They generally had breakfast or supper together, if they weren't on a detail. He always pretended to be surprised to see her, though she knew the gruff old codger looked forward to her visits. They had a long-running chess competition going, and sometimes they'd drop into the game without bothering to say a word. Grandpa had also gotten her into Everquest, so they played the online role-playing game together on their laptops when either of them was out of town.

"Why knock when I have a key?" Domini answered, as she always did. And knew the codes for the other layers of security surrounding the Malibu property.

"What if I'd had a woman with me?"

"Then both you and I would be very much surprised."

"Point taken." He poured her a cup of coffee, then sat opposite her at the kitchen island. "What kind of doughnuts?" He opened up the bag and pulled out an old-fashioned chocolate doughnut. His favorite, as Domini well knew. "You ever going to learn to cook?" he asked after he'd taken a few bites.

"I wasn't built for comfort, I was built for speed."

"Is that a way of telling me I have no one to blame for your lack of domestic skills but myself?"

"Yep."

"Well, at least you know how to shoot."

Domini and her grandfather settled into a comfortable silence, concentrating on doughnuts and coffee. Grandpa made great coffee. She enjoyed the sound of the surf pounding on the beach in the distance, and the calls of the gulls. She enjoyed the salty fresh scent of the breeze that came in the windows and the doors that opened to the deck. She loved this house. It wasn't all that large, compared to some of the mini-palaces that lined this very prime stretch of oceanfront real estate. She'd spent much of her life here, and still thought of it more as home than she did her own small house.

She always felt safe here, yet she didn't feel safe right now. She felt—like she was walking on the edge of a knife and suffering from vertigo. She was bound to fall one way or the other, and she had no idea what waited for her at the bottom. She wished she could pinpoint why she felt this way; then she could do something about it.

The old man put down his cup, looked her over, and glanced at the clock. "Not exactly dressed for work."

"I'll change when I get there. I need to work out."

She was wearing shorts, a T-shirt, and athletic shoes. She suspected he would always prefer to see her in something feminine, even while she was kicking butt. He was kind of sweet that way.

She dusted powdered sugar off her fingers and sat back in her chair. "Speaking of work, I have a question about Reynard."

"What's wrong with him?" he asked, never one to let anyone else take the offensive.

"I haven't seen enough of him to think there's anything wrong." Seeing Reynard naked in a dream didn't count—though there certainly wasn't anything wrong with Alexander Reynard in the altogether. Not that anyone could actually look that good naked, and that wasn't what her grandfather meant, anyway.

"You're blushing."

"Sugar rush," she countered. "Is there any way I can get Andy or Castlereigh to take on the new guy's orientation? I'm busy setting up the Ashe detail."

He gave her his sternest look. "This guy make you uncomfortable?"

Dream images danced through her head, and her pulse rate picked up. Uncomfortable? Oh, yes. Very yes.

"Training him gets in the way of setting up protection for Holly. I have at least three venues I need to check out today."

"Then take him with you."

She sighed. "I should have known you'd say that."

"You should have thought of it yourself."

"I did."

"Then you *are* uncomfortable around him."

Domini held up her hands in surrender. "All right. Fine. I'm uncomfortable around him."

"Glad to hear it."

She eyed the Old Man suspiciously. "What do you mean?"

"I mean that I'm uncomfortable around him, too. That boy ain't what he seems, and what he seems to be is one dangerous, in-control dude. Got the feeling he's much more than simply dangerous. Want you to keep an eye on him."

Domini was flabbergasted. "Me? If you thought he was lying, why did you hire him?"

"I wonder why I hired him so fast, myself. I acted on impulse, and I'm too old for that."

"You should have waited for a full background check. He may not be who he says at all."

"Or more than he says. Don't think he was lying; he just didn't tell the complete truth. That's not necessarily a bad thing, but I want to find out why a good friend recommended him to me on such short notice. I'm not going to completely trust Reynard until all his references check out."

"Glad to hear it." It bothered her that her sharp-as-a-laser-scalpel grandfather was questioning his own judgment. She was also relieved that he was quickly doing something about the lapse.

"Until then, I want you to keep an eye on him out in the field. You, I trust completely." He poked at the doughnut bag. "Any more chocolate ones in there?"

"I brought you three, and I think you've only snarfed down two. If you're going to have another doughnut, so am I."

What were a few hundred more calories, if it meant putting off being thrown together with the sexy and unnerving Mr. Reynard for a while longer?

Chapter Six

The testosterone was so thick in the workout room that Domini could practically chew it. A group of her coworkers were having a high time flinging each other around on the floor mats. Practicing martial arts wasn't uncommon, but at the moment the place looked like a Jackie Chan movie. There was one man in the center of the fray, with at least six men coming at him from every direction, using at least six different martial arts styles. The man in the center was tossing them around as if the skilled protection agents were mere straw dummies. From the whoops and catcalls and laughter, it was obvious that the men getting beat up were having a ball.

Guys were funny that way.

Domini was impressed, and couldn't help but grin at the sight of a bunch of macho puppies taking on an alpha wolf. Her smile faltered when she saw it was Alexander Reynard making mincemeat out of Grandpa's finest.

She waited in the doorway, crossed her arms, and watched. There was nothing else she could do. The mats were in front of the door to the women's locker room, where she kept spare clothes. To get to the locker room she'd have to pass the gauntlet of male bodies, and they'd just ask her to join in. She enjoyed practicing with the male agents, but she wasn't prepared for sparring with Reynard.

Domini couldn't take her eyes off him. It was as if there was no one else in the room. He wore only an old pair of gray sweatpants and his body was almost exactly as she'd dreamed it—but not as pale, and even better muscled. The dream lover had been beautiful, but the fighter was magnificent!

He moved with tiger grace, every movement deadly poetry. His dark hair was pulled back off his chiseled face. Reynard's features were as still and concentrated as a statue's. His eyes gave nothing away, not showing by a flicker what move he intended next. He had long, narrow feet and long-fingered hands, and they moved with deadly, lightning speed as he kicked, spun, tossed, hit, jabbed, and ducked, putting down all comers. He was the most dangerous thing she'd ever seen, and the most compelling. She didn't recognize his fighting style, but he was obviously a deadly artist.

And she'd never seen anyone move that fast.

"It's unnatural."

She didn't think she'd spoken loud enough to be heard, but Reynard suddenly spun around, looked at her, and said, "It's Krav Maga."

His gaze bored into hers, green as moss, with sudden fire in their depths. His Zen-like fighting aloofness was a mask, and that fire drew her. She was across the room to the edge of the thick blue mats before she knew she'd moved.

"Krav Maga," she heard herself say in awe. "Wow."

"Yeah," Andy Maxwell agreed, coming to stand beside her. He was sweating hard, and she noticed bruises forming on his neck and right wrist. He looked about as awed as she felt. "I've been wanting to see this stuff in action." He rubbed his neck and nodded toward Reynard. "This dude is hot."

Masculine grunts of agreement issued from all around the room.

Reynard's gaze stayed on her. "Care to give it a try?"

She shook her head. "I don't—"

"You backing down, Dominatrix?" Andy questioned. "That's not like you."

"Come on, Domini," Joe Minke urged. "Give it a try." He was holding his hand over his ribs.

"Alec could use a new victim," Connor Marsh said. "He's used us up already."

None of them sounded the least bit resentful at having taken on the newest member of the firm and lost. It wasn't easy to win the respect of the professionals that worked at Lancer's, but Alec seemed to be more than holding his own, and this was only his first real day on the job.

Reynard caught her gaze again, which kept her from staring at his naked chest and washboard belly. This close to him, she caught the warm scent of his body, and the dream images rolled up out of her subconscious. For a moment she saw a glint of amusement in his eyes, and she had the horrible sensation that he knew exactly what she was thinking about.

Part of her wanted to run. Another part said, *Oh, don't be ridiculous!* and wanted to drag him down onto the thick mat. But that was the dream talking, and the discussion going on in the training room was about fighting, not fu—

"Krav Maga?" she repeated, trying to keep her mind on reality. "Where'd you learn that?"

"Army."

The unarmed fighting style had been developed in Israel, down and dirty and deadly. Krav Maga training was part of the bag of tricks favored by special forces and black-ops operators all over the world. And they didn't get much more elite than Delta Force.

Just one more reminder that Alexander Reynard was a very dangerous man, more dangerous than anyone she'd ever encountered. The knowledge sent an emotional rush through her that was part primal terror, and part primal "I want to have your babies."

Alec had been spoiling for a fight when he arrived at the Lancer offices. He'd come down to the exercise room to work off some tension, and found the group of agents there waiting to check him out. He'd have done the same with a new man transferred into his Delta unit, or with another Prime looking for Clan acceptance. He'd smiled at the other men, accepting their challenge. He fought them without arrogance and with humor, hadn't hurt any of them too badly, and the challenge gradually grew into a teaching session.

He realized now that he'd been waiting the whole time for this moment, for Domini Lancer to walk in and see him doing what he did so very well. He was preening for his mate. In a way it made him feel like a raw young Prime, strutting his stuff in the hopes a female would choose him as one of her consorts. But it was also a demonstration that told his woman that he could protect her. Or have her.

He wondered if she noticed.

To make sure, Alec gestured for Domini to take a turn on the mat.

A rush of heat that made her toes curl went through Domini as Reynard took a wide stance, knees flexed, and beckoned her toward him. His smile could have cut diamonds as his gaze swept through the group. All the other men backed away.

He looked back at her. "Come at me."

She shook her head. "I don't think so."

"Chicken," Andy called.

"Silence, slave," she retorted automatically, her attention on Reynard. What would she do if he touched her?

Fall down, she told herself sternly, and stepped onto the mat. This was a fighting exercise, and her style was aikido.

Aikido was a defensive art; the object was to use an attacker's own energy to deflect the assault. She had a second *dan* black belt in aikido.

"I'm going to die!" she squeaked as Reynard lunged toward her.

After all the years of training and practice, her response was instinctual. She countered his extended arm with a wrist block and fell away.

Or should have.

The next thing Domini knew, Reynard held her right arm up against her back, with her thumb locked in an unbreakable grip. Her chest was pressed to his, and he was looking down at her, smiling. He wasn't hurting her, but the threat was there. He could do with her as he pleased, and they both knew it.

She countered by hooking her ankle around his, which only made things worse, because he went down on his back, and she came down on top of him. His hold on her hadn't loosed a bit. His smile had turned into a savage grin. And his teeth were very sharp. They stared into each other's eyes. Applause erupted all around them, and someone whistled.

He let her go then. Domini was blushing hotter than she ever had in her life when she got to her feet. For the few seconds Reynard held her, she'd forgotten anyone else existed but the two of them.

She tossed her hair out of her face and said with strained dignity, "I'm going to change for work now." She glanced around the room at the grinning male faces. "Don't you gentlemen have places to be and things to do?"

"Took you long enough."

The humor in Reynard's voice was the only thing that kept Domini from jumping out of her skin. She didn't normally surprise easily. She glared across the room at him from the locker-room doorway. "What are you doing here?"

He gave a casual, one-shoulder shrug. Very economical of movement, was Mr. Reynard. "Waiting for you."

The contrast between the bare-chested street fighter and the conservatively dressed man leaning against the Bowflex machine was striking.

But he's bare-chested under his clothes. She could have sworn this inane thought earned her a low, dirty laugh from Reynard, except that he didn't make a sound.

He did give Domini a slow, intense, foot-to-head once-over

that left her toes curling in her sandals and made her wish she'd wore more clothes.

Or less.

She'd taken her time in the locker room, getting cleaned up, putting on makeup, then swearing because the business suit she normally kept in her locker was at the dry cleaner. She ended up wearing a short, sleeveless pink-and-white-print sheath dress. It had been appropriate for accompanying a client on a shopping trip, but she'd rather wear something a bit less girly for today's assignment, which was doing walk-through evaluations of several places on Holly's schedule for the next few days.

Something less girly for facing Reynard would also be nice, although she couldn't tell from the look on his face if he liked what he saw of her bare arms, legs, and neckline. Which was possibly more irritating than an outright lewd eyeing of her assets.

And why was she standing here letting him do it, anyway?

He held up a hand. There was nothing threatening in the gesture, yet Domini felt held in place by it. "About what happened . . . We need to talk."

Domini wasn't quite sure exactly what Reynard wanted to discuss. She gave a wary shrug. "About what?"

"What happened when we fought."

"You won. Nothing to discuss."

"I have a problem with that."

Oh, lord, what did he want from her? To acknowledge how great he was? "Why? I don't mind that you beat me. No, I mind," she added after a raised eyebrow from him. "But I'm not—"

"You were scared." He took a step forward. "You went into a fight scared, already thinking you were going to lose."

"I *knew* I was going to lose. And it was an exercise," she reminded him. "Not a real fight."

He came closer, the look in those compelling green eyes more concentrated. She got the impression he was trying to see into her mind, her soul. Domini resisted the urge to step back.

"You have no reason to fear me. You will never have a reason to fear me."

She considered this, and him. Reynard was tall, dark, and dangerous to the core. She didn't know him, had no reason yet to trust him. Worst of all, he disturbed her in a way no man had ever done before.

She said, "It isn't up to you to tell me how I should feel. Now, I need to get to work."

His eyes sparked and his jaw tightened, but he gave her a curt nod. "Let's go."

"Fine." He followed her silently from the exercise room and down the hall. "You're spooky," she told him when they stepped into the elevator. "How can you move so quietly?"

He chuckled. "Maybe I'll teach you someday."

He stood too close to her for comfort, and he pressed the button for the garage level before she had a chance to. The overhead lights seemed too bright to her, the space far too small. She was used to take-charge guys; it didn't usually bother her. But with Reynard it was somehow—personal.

Was he trying to intimidate her? Impress her? Did he even notice he was doing it? Was it all her imagination? That had certainly been working overtime since meeting him.

They remained silent while the elevator moved down. She didn't look at him, but her awareness of Reynard was tactile. He might as well have been running his hands over her, with all the heat growing in her from merely being near him. Part of her wanted his touch. She couldn't help but remember what being held by him felt like, even though they'd been in a fight. Sparring with him was anything but an academic exercise.

He evoked strange, new sensations, and she couldn't afford any distractions. Why shouldn't she fear him, when he brought this—awareness—bubbling up from some deep well in her sub-conscious?

Protecting their clients required teamwork and respect, if not absolute trust.

She turned to Reynard and forced an affable smile. It was up to her to make this work, since she was in charge. "So, Alexander, can I ask where you're from?" She hoped he wouldn't give her any special-ops secretive bullshit.

"My branch of the clan came from France originally, but we settled in Idaho."

"Idaho? Like potatoes?"

He shook his head. "That's the southern part of the state. We're from farther north, up near the Canadian border."

"I've been all over the country, and on foreign travel details as well, but never to Idaho. But even when I travel, the clients do the sightseeing; I keep my attention on them."

"I know how you feel," Reynard said. "You know the bit: join the army, travel to exotic places, meet interesting new people—and shoot them. I've never had much chance to play tourist."

Alec hoped Domini was appreciating his effort to hold a civilized, superficial conversation. There was much that needed to be discussed, but it was too soon to talk of who they really were and what they meant to each other. Too soon to speak of souls and hearts and bodies bound by passion for eternity. That was kind of heavy for a first date.

Besides, he couldn't offer her anything yet. Not when he was at risk of going feral. There was an animal caged inside him, banging hard against his discipline and the drugs, hunting for a way to the surface. If the animal broke free, it could be years before Alec saw the light of reason again. It wasn't that a feral couldn't bond with a mortal, but the results weren't pretty. He wouldn't force himself on Domini like—

"Yo, Reynard, you in there?"

Alec blinked as a hand passed before his face. "More than

you know." He gently grasped Domini's wrist, but only for a moment, as she easily circled her hand away from his. Aikido was such a graceful art.

He dug into his pocket and brought out sunglasses and his car keys. He gestured toward the burgundy Jaguar with darkly tinted windows. "I'll drive."

She frowned. "We should take a company car."

His only reply was to jingle the keys again.

Irritation radiated from her. She didn't like giving him control over any part of the situation, didn't like his taking the initiative. But it was easier to protect her if he was doing the driving. He wasn't going to budge, and luckily she decided not to push such a small matter any further. Alec could practically hear her grinding her teeth in frustration, and he civilly didn't show even the faintest flicker of smugness. He pressed the button on the key chain that unlocked the doors.

"Well," she said, looking at the dark windshield, "this'll help, since I forgot sunblock."

Alec glanced at the pale skin of her arms, legs, and throat. "You burn easily?"

She made a face. "Born and raised a child of the desert, but I turn into a french fry if I step outside in less than SPF 45."

Alec snorted. "Tell me about it." He reached into his inner jacket pocket and brought out a capped metal tube. He tossed it to her. "Try this sunscreen. My own special brand."

He hid a very sharp smile by sliding into the driver's seat, more than a little amused that they had serious sunburn issues in common.

Chapter Seven

"No, don't stop here," Domini told Reynard when he started to pull into a parking space in front of a Japanese restaurant. "They're out of wasabi. Can't have sushi without wasabi."

"Fair enough," he said, and drove on in the bumper-to-bumper midday traffic.

Domini spotted another sushi bar a couple blocks down the street. She pointed. "Let's try there."

"No parking spaces."

"Right. You want to try a drive-through?"

"What you want, I'm happy to give you."

Domini glanced sideways at Reynard's odd turn of phrase. She saw a profile of sharp cheekbones and jawline, his sculpted face made enigmatic by his dark wraparound sunglasses. "I can grab takeout on the way home. Right now we need to get a solid meal and get back on the road. We still need to stop by Kodak Center, then get the detail briefing in so we can start the assignment tonight. What do you want to eat?"

You. What Alec wanted was blood, a few warm, sweet drops drawn from skin soft beneath his tongue. The thirst hadn't hit him so hard in years. He wanted his hands on her, her body beneath his, her moans of pleasure in his ears, and her salt, copper, honey taste in his mouth.

"A burger sounds good," he answered, his hands clamped on the steering wheel.

The woman who sat beside him was a ticking time bomb and didn't know it. But he'd had decades of practice at being a very good actor. Wild men did not get sent on dangerous covert missions, and they certainly didn't lead them.

There was a very childish, churlish part of him that said she should *know* he hungered. She was his bondmate, wasn't she?

Domini is not on the menu, Alec firmly informed the beast inside him. If he tried making love to her the way he was now, the experience would terrify her and taint their relationship from the beginning. As strongly psychic as she was, she might be able to throw up mental shields around her heart and mind that he could never break through. Not that he wouldn't keep trying, and that would destroy them both.

So keep it together, he told himself. Keep your eyes on the road. Keep an eye on the rearview mirror and the blue RAV-4 that's following us. *Do not* reach over and run your fingers along her bare arm. Don't touch the hint of thigh showing below her provocatively short skirt. Don't brush your hand through her hair, or across those amazing lips.

"I need a really cold drink." *To dump in my lap.*

"Thirsty?" she asked.

"You have no idea."

Domini kept part of her attention on spotting a drive-through, and part on the realization that Reynard hadn't questioned her comment about the sushi place, which sounded strange even to her, and she *knew* she was psychic. Maybe he was simply indulging the whims of the boss's granddaughter, but he hadn't seemed to notice that what she'd said was a little odd. Was he as crazy as she was?

For all that Reynard's idiosyncrasies were fascinating, she decided to dwell on them later, for increasingly her gaze kept returning to the passenger's-side rearview mirror. Every now and then she caught sight of traffic as Reynard changed lanes and turned corners. She was beginning to see a pattern, and she didn't think it was her imagination.

"There's a Toyota RAV-4 behind us. About three cars back . . ."

"Has been for a while," he replied.

She slanted the enigmatic Mr. Reynard a curious look. "Someone from your shady past catching up to you?"

"Why would you think that?"

"It's your car."

"Ah, but they picked us up as we left the club in Westwood where Holly Ashe is doing the benefit. I spotted them again when we left the show venue in Venice. Quite a coincidence to see the same vehicle in both locations. Ms. Ashe's concert schedule is public information. I checked it out on her website myself."

Domini seethed as she listened to his calm recitation. "You might have mentioned the tail sooner," she pointed out.

"Figured you'd notice eventually."

"If I was any good, you mean."

"I didn't say that."

"I'm here to test you, Reynard. Not the other way around."

Alec was so very tempted to get into a fight with her. Her blue eyes sparked with anger, her emotions seethed, barely under control. Her voice was cold as ice, with fire beneath it. He wanted to stoke that fire, take it higher, to its inevitable conclusion.

Instead, he calmly said, "You're a competent professional protection agent, Ms. Lancer. I come from a specialized, far more dangerous, even more paranoid world than you do. You look after people but don't expect anyone to come after you. I always expect people to come after me."

"Why would anyone come after—" She cut off her angry words and held up a hand. "Wait."

Alec enjoyed watching the thoughts flicker quickly across her face and the swift shift of emotions as she analyzed what he'd said.

"I've read through the hate mail that made Holly decide to hire better security. There's one nutcase under a restraining order, but he claims he has lots of friends that hate her as much as he does. I don't think he made that up. I'd say those letters came from several different people, and there's a pattern that makes me think they're working together. Another pattern is the theme of getting her alone. There's a song on her first CD called 'I Want to Get You Alone,' and it's referred to quite a few times in the letters. So—these people aren't interested in approaching Holly during public appearances—"

"Unless they can't get any other opportunity," he cut in.

She nodded. "Right. They want to find out where she's staying. They want to hunt her down to the place where she thinks she's safe."

"So they set up surveillance at places she'll be, places—"

"—her security people were bound to check out. And when our car was spotted at more than one of these places—"

"—they made us."

She nodded. The way they'd been finishing each other's sentences was an indication either that they shared a mind, or that they made a good team. She wasn't sure which was more frightening. "I think we'd better lose the tail," she suggested.

He smiled. "Couldn't we waste them?"

The eagerness in his tone was contagious, but Domini squashed her perverse interest in finding out how a Delta Force operator really worked.

"I think we should let them follow us long enough to get their license plate numbers, and then get the hell out of Dodge. We don't want them trailing us back to the office." She added a note on her PDA about not allowing a vehicle as conspicuous as the dark red Jaguar anywhere near Holly Ashe. "You do know how to lose a tail, right?" she asked.

Reynard gave her a very dubious glance from over the top of his sunglasses. "Let me know when you make the plates," he said, and pushed the sunglasses back up on his nose.

Alec adjusted the driver's-side mirror to give her a better view behind them. Domini held her PDA at the ready, concentrating on her assignment. The RAV-4 was three cars back, so

Alec braked, shifting down into first gear. This resulted in getting the two cars in front of the blue Toyota to change lanes to get away from his slow driving. The Toyota slowed to stay with them; the person following them wasn't experienced enough at it to move inconspicuously within the flow of the traffic.

"Got it," Domini said.

The moment she spoke, Alec stepped on the gas, upshifted, and switched lanes. Then, moving smooth as silk, he switched lanes again and took a left-hand turn against a light, accompanied by squealing brakes and honking horns and cars swerving to keep from crashing. The RAV-4 tried to follow, but it wasn't a Jaguar, and the driver was nowhere near as skilled as he was.

"How very—Starsky and Hutch—of you," Domini commented as they sped away.

Alec grinned as he took the next right. The few moments of action had helped calm him. "That was fun."

"We definitely lost them." Her tone was amused when she said, "I don't think you'll need that evasive driving course as part of your orientation."

"Happy to hear it. Now, about lunch," Alec said as he brought the car to a gentle halt at a red light. "Do you think you can find us a sushi place where they do have wasabi?"

Chapter Eight

"How do you like the view?" Domini asked.

"There's a view?" Holly replied.

Alec watched as Domini pointed to the west side of the living room of the small but luxuriously appointed house. "Holly, you see those cloth things hanging on the wall? They're called curtains. If you pull them back, you can see a whole lot of lights twinkling in the valley below."

"No kidding?" Holly Ashe stood in the center of the room, her bare feet sunk almost to the ankles in the slate-gray carpet, and chewed on a fingernail. "Don't I pay people to open curtains and stuff for me?"

"Don't expect me to do it," Domini answered. "You still owe me lunch money from high school."

Ashe put her hands on her bare hips. "You were always cheap."

Ashe wore almost microscopic frayed denim shorts and a sequined red lace bra, along with a lot of jewelry and tattoos. Domini, to Alec's disappointment, was wearing loose linen slacks and a short-sleeved embroidered peasant blouse.

"Look who's talking," Domini told her friend. "I suppose you paid a fortune to look like a tramp, too."

"Tramp?" the singer laughed.

"If I called you a pop tart, you'd hit me."

"I'd try. Do I look like Britney Spears?"

"In that getup, yes."

"You're fired."

"Your manager hired us. Not cheaply, I might add."

"Cheap is as cheap does, as your grandpa would say. Besides, that wasn't lunch money I owed you, it was drug money."

Domini thoughtfully put her hand on her cheek, then pointed at the singer. "Oh, yeah, right."

Then the two of them broke up laughing at some old private joke.

Alec smiled internally at this nonsense, as he stood impassively and inconspicuously with his back to a wall in a spot with a good view of the whole room.

The two women had been bickering like giggly teenagers, apparently enjoying themselves immensely, ever since Holly Ashe was whisked out the guarded back entrance of her hotel and into the back of the limo where Domini was waiting.

While Domini and Holly seemed very different on the surface, they clearly had the sort of friendship where they could go for years without communicating, then pick up as comfortably and easily as they'd left off. Alec found it kind of cute, especially seeing Domini's lighter side. Had she been officially on duty, she would be behaving differently, of course.

It was Domini who set the tone for this part of the assignment at the detail briefing. Old Man Lancer presided over the meeting and made all the final decisions, but they were based on Domini's assessments. The threat level against their client was deemed high enough that she'd been talked into staying at a safe house equipped with state-of-the-art surveillance technology. Ms. Ashe was to have a minimum of two agents as well as a driver on duty at all times. There would also be an agent monitoring the security equipment in a room set aside as a command post. Andrew Maxwell was named team leader.

Andy was currently outside, making a sweep of the grounds. Castlereigh was in the command post, monitoring camera, audio, and infrared equipment. Alec had been assigned as Ashe's driver, but he was handling the inside-man job until midnight. He'd been surprised to end up on an assignment his second day on the job, but no one argued with Ben Lancer—though Domini had looked for a moment as though she was going to. Alec understood quicker than she did: Lancer wanted her to keep an eye on his newest employee. Domini was working the Ashe detail, so it made sense to assign Reynard to where Domini was going to be.

Domini had come along to "hang with my friend and make her as comfortable as possible, until she gets used to having you jokers around."

The approach was working so far.

"So, you want to look at the view?" Domini asked Holly.

"Nope," Ashe answered.

"Want something from the kitchen?"

"Nope."

"Have you suddenly decided to pout, after you agreed coming here was the best way to keep you safe?"

"Yep." Ashe was looking more stubborn by the moment.

"Why?"

"'Cause I hate not being in control of my life."

Domini moved to stand in front of her friend. "Are you scared of these people?"

"No! My management's being stupid."

Domini put her hands on Holly's shoulders. "If you're not scared, you should be."

"I don't want to talk about it."

Ashe shot a quick look toward Alec.

Domini exchanged a glance with Reynard, and they reached silent agreement about the situation without even so much as an exchange of a nod. She put an arm around Holly's shoulder and turned her toward the hallway that led off to the right of the living room. "Let's check out your bedroom."

Holly laughed. "Hey, I've been waiting for you to say that for—"

"Cut that out!" Domini dragged her friend down the hall into the spacious master bedroom and closed the door behind them. Two suitcases and a guitar case were laid on the bed. "Want help unpacking?"

Holly looked around and gave a mock shudder. "Everything's beige."

"The decorator used terms like *ecru* and *champagne*. It's supposed to be soothing." The room was the largest in the house, brightly lit, the decor intended to help keep a client calm and disguise the fact that there were no windows in the bedroom. Domini gestured to a doorway on her left. "Walk-in closet, with a huge bathroom on the other side. Bathroom's done in blue."

"I'm impressed at your knowledge of the real estate."

"The company owns the house. The best part's the state-of-the-art command center."

"Can I have a tour of that?"

"No. Can I help you unpack?"

"I'm used to living out of a bag, hon. Besides, I'm not staying."

Holly picked up the guitar case and started toward the door. Domini stepped in front of her, took the case from Holly, and set it on the floor. "You're staying for the next three nights."

Holly was smart enough not to argue with that tone, so she batted her eyelashes at Domini. "All by myself?"

"I'll be in the bedroom on the other side of the hall tonight."

Holly went back to the bed and took the bags off it, every movement stiff with tension. "I hate living like this," she muttered.

Then she settled down cross-legged in the center of the king-sized mattress, folded herself into a yoga lotus position, and closed her eyes. Domini watched as Holly's muscles relaxed and her expression became more peaceful.

Maybe I should try yoga sometime, she thought, aware that her own nerves were strung as tight as a bowstring tonight. Nothing has happened, she reminded herself. Nothing is going to happen. You aren't going to let it. Holly looked so small and vulnerable in the center of the big bed.

Domini had always thought of Holly as the brave one, because of her honesty, because of the way she went out into the world on her own, because of how she passionately embraced everything in life. Where Domini needed shields, Holly was almost skinless, recklessly open to every joy, hurt, and sorrow life had to offer. That was brave. Stupid beyond anything Domini could imagine, but brave.

Domini smiled affectionately and lay down on her side at the foot of the bed. She leaned on an elbow and propped her head on her hand. Though she seemed relaxed, she was positioned between her client and the door. Domini wasn't on duty and didn't think anything was about to happen, but why take any chances when another person's safety was involved?

Holly finally opened her eyes and leaned forward, a wicked look on her face. "Is he going to be with you?"

"What?"

"In the other bedroom. He going to be with you?"

Domini was completely confused. "Who? What?"

Holly laughed. "Don't tell me you're still oblivious? You know who I mean: the stud out front."

"Stud?"

"The guy holding up the living room wall."

"Reynard?" Domini cleared her throat. Reynard was meant to be unobtrusive, but Domini had been aware of him even though she'd tried hard to concentrate on Holly. She sighed.

"I heard that."

"Holly—"

"What's with the guy? He's so—male. Has he got like three testicles or something?"

Domini nearly squirmed with discomfort at that image. "Come on, Holly," she said. "You know I don't look at men any more than you do."

"You don't look at women, either. You've never looked at anyone." Holly pointed at her. "But this man, you're looking at."

"I'm working with him. We have to look at each other occasionally."

"You're looking at him with your body. I don't blame you," Holly went on as Domini shot to her feet. "And it wasn't me that had his attention, even though he was pretending not to look at anything. He has the hots for you."

Domini glared down at her grinning friend, then she took a deep breath and sat again with great dignity. "This is a ploy to get your mind off your own problems."

"The yoga didn't work, but no, it isn't." Holly plumped and stacked the huge pile of decorative pillows at the head of the bed until she had them just the way she wanted them, then leaned back on them. She spread her arms out across the pillows and said, "Let's talk about me."

"Always an interesting subject," Domini agreed, and settled back down on the wide expanse of satin.

"You'd look good naked on that," Holly observed.

Domini ran a hand across the champagne satin. It was marvelous to touch. "No, I'm too pale. I should be naked on stronger colors. Now, what about you?"

"I'd look good naked on this."

"I *meant,* what do you want to talk about?"

"You're in the business of protecting people from stalkers. Why are these people after me? I've never had any trouble before."

"It's your turn. Celebrities draw nutcases, and you've been lucky up until now. You managed to keep your private life quiet for a long time, but the breakup with Jo made screaming headlines in every tabloid for months. Remember when the unauthorized biography came out?"

"I didn't read it."

"I did. More pictures than words in it, going all the way back to you in diapers. There's one of you standing next to me at *my* sixteenth birthday party. There are even pictures from our high-school yearbook in it. And you remember what happened at the prom?"

"My real life's in that bio?"

"In a twisted, lying way, yes. More importantly, it didn't help that you talked about Jo doing you wrong to every media person that stuck a camera in your face."

"Against your advice," Holly added. "I was crazy then, I admit it. Passion will do that to you."

"If passion makes you crazy, then it's better not to feel it. Passion got you slapped with a restraining order to keep you from performing the songs you wrote about the breakup."

"My lawyers got that overturned. The controversy helped album sales," Holly offered. "But I guess it also got the attention of the bastards who're stalking me." She looked thoughtful for a moment, then asked, "Think Jo has something to do with this?"

"No. Jo's been checked out," Domini answered. "Are you behind it—to get Jo's attention?"

"No! How could you think that?"

Holly's outrage hit Domini like a slap in the face. She hated that her friend looked so betrayed, but she answered calmly, "I don't think it, but Lancer's is thorough. We consider all the possibilities when we take on a client. We're here to protect you—even from yourself, if we have to."

"Gee, thanks. I'm impressed." Holly shook her head. "But I'm not likely to go around raving about how I'm an impure abomination, and my kind must be stamped off the face of the earth. Not that I mind being impure, of course," she added. "You should try it sometime."

"I have. It's boring."

"Try being impure with Mr. Triple Testicles."

"Lancer's has a no-fraternization policy."

"I won't tell your grandpa."

"You know Grandpa: he'd know anyway." Domini looked at her watch, then got to her feet. It was just after midnight. The shift had changed, and she wanted to talk to the new men on the detail. "Time for me to get to sleep. You, too," she advised.

Domini left the bedroom, very glad after Holly's speculation that Reynard wouldn't be waiting in the living room. By tomorrow, she'd be able to get the question out of her mind. Mr. Reynard's reproductive equipment was no one's business but his own.

Chapter Nine

"*It* wouldn't hurt you to get laid."

Alec nearly spit out the water he'd just taken to wash down his pills. He wasn't sure if he was more shocked at the elder's suggestion, or at hearing an Honored Father of the clans using such language.

"Don't look so startled," said the Matri seated beside the elder in Alec's living room. "We both sense your need. Sex would be good for you."

"It's the best way for a Prime to release tension," the elder reminded him. "Still works for me," he added with an affectionate look at the woman seated beside him. The couple were holding hands. "Of course, if you would rather kill something, that can be arranged." Elder Barak looked as though he hoped Alec would rise above the need to kill.

"Sex is easier," Matri Serisa said.

They had arrived at his front door a few minutes after Alec got home. The regally calm woman's presence had helped ease the tension of two males meeting for the first time. Alec hadn't been able to stop a quick snarl and baring of fangs, but the Matri touched his cheek soothingly and sent cool, calming thoughts into his mind. He'd caught a hint of her age and wisdom that left him stunned—stunned enough to step back and bid them welcome when they stepped into his dwelling.

They were an elegant couple, dressed in black, both with large dark eyes and curling dark hair, the man's with far more gray in it than the woman's. She wore a gold pendant in the shape of the Egyptian god Anubis, and a carnelian ring carved with the same design on her left hand. They introduced them-selves as Barak and Serisa of Shagal, and said they thought it best not to wait for the mortals at the clinic to arrange the meeting. They couldn't seem to get it through those well-meaning humans' heads that there were certain nuances and courtesies that needed to be observed. . . .

"For us to be comfortable with each other," Serisa diplo-matically put it.

"To keep us from going for each other's throats," the blunter Barak added.

Though Alec gave them permission to enter his sanctuary, he resented their appearance in his life, even if they had brought him a case of fresh blood from the clinic as a wel-come present. He'd hoped they'd simply introduce themselves and then leave, giving him a chance to get used to the idea of talking to them in the diplomatic way of Clan Shagal.

But no, half an hour later, they were still here. In some ways their presence soothed his aching senses. He had not spent time around his own kind in years. He'd forgotten how the habits and rituals of vampire society were another way of imposing civilized behavior on instincts that hungered for possession and dominance.

Matri Serisa had insisted on serving them bloodwine and water. And she'd brought cookies. While bread and fruit to go with the wine and water were more traditional ceremonial foods for the ritual of getting to know new vampires in your territory, the Matri told them she had a taste for almond bis-cotti. Who argued with a Matri's desires?

"I thought I was supposed to practice meditation and have some sort of therapy sessions with the two of you," he told them.

Serisa's large dark eyes danced with laughter. "We're vam-pires, Alexander. Action *is* therapy for us. Sex is a necessity."

"We hunger," Barak said. "We need to feed."

"I'm not sure I could feed without killing right now," Alec

admitted. "As for making love . . ." He shook his head. "I don't think I could keep it under control."

"Perhaps not with a mortal woman," Serisa told him. "But with one of us—" She gave a delicate shrug and the brush of a hand across her skirt that somehow conveyed a world of eroticism. "There can be a great deal of mutual pleasure when a female bends to the will of a Prime."

An image of such a wild encounter went through Alec's head and straight to his groin, but the woman he pictured struggling beneath each hard, dominating thrust was no vampire female. He rubbed his hands across his face. "I really wish you hadn't said that."

Serisa chuckled, low and enticing. She rose gracefully and came to Alec. Her thigh brushed his as she leaned close, and placed a pack of matches in his hand. A telephone number had been written on the inside of the matchbook cover. Alec stared at the neatly printed numbers as Serisa stepped back. "What's this?"

"It's the cell-phone number of a young woman of the Family Caeg. She finds herself in town and at loose ends," Serisa told him. "She's spending the evening at the local hangout."

There were three nations of vampires: the Clans, who lived among men as protectors; the Tribes, who scorned all things mortal except what they could use and cause pain to; and the Families, who chose a gray, shadowy, opportunistic way. While the Clans took the high road and the Tribes traveled gladly in darkness, the Families moved uneasily in between, friends to neither, allies to both.

Alec gave Serisa a hard look. Forgetting the respect that was a Matri's due, he asked harshly, "Why would you have me mate with a woman from Caeg?"

"Why do you think?" Barak answered. "You are needy. Family Caeg is in danger of inbreeding. You might get lucky." Barak held up a hand to stop Alec's protest before it could be voiced. "It's not unheard of to sire a child outside the Clans."

"With a mortal woman perhaps, but—"

"Do you have a mortal in mind?" Serisa quickly cut Alec off. She sensed his reactions and shook a finger at him. "Dr. Casmerek suspected as much. I forbid it. I stand in your Matri's place, and in her name I forbid your touching a mortal woman at such a dangerous time."

"You don't have to forbid it," Alec snapped. "I know I can't have her."

Yet a war was beginning to rage within him, between what he wanted and what was best for Domini. Through the battle, the siren song of the promise of an eternal bond would call and call . . .

Perhaps he should follow the sage advice of these clan elders. The Caeg woman was willing, and the conception of a child was a rare and wondrous thing. He could at least meet the woman. The night was young enough.

"All right," he told the pair from Clan Shagal as he ushered them toward the door. "I'll give her a call."

Domini's heart was hammering with terror, her palms were sweaty, her head ached fiercely, and her mind was a complete blank. *Okay. Where the hell am I?* More important, why was she here? And how did she get here?

The *how* was obvious, sort of. She was sitting behind the wheel of one of the company cars. The car was in park, the engine was off, and she was parked on a side street near the center of downtown Los Angeles. She knew her approximate location because the tall, elegant towers of Financial District offices and hotels loomed up in the near distance. The dashboard clock told her it was the middle of the night.

This was worse, much, much worse, than the compulsion that had pulled her out of sleep and to the market two nights ago, and the erotic dream from the night before.

I can't remember a thing. She dug into the smooth leather upholstery with her nails and pounded on the dashboard with her fists until she got the fear and frustration under some control. *Why can't I remember?*

Okay. Take it a step at a time. What's the last thing I do recall?

She remembered going into the bathroom to brush her teeth. She'd looked into the mirror and—

Seen Reynard kissing a woman reflected in the glass.

She whirled around to face the couple, and—

Here she was.

Okay. Rewind. Where was the bathroom?

At the safe house. She'd left Holly's room and gone into the bedroom she was staying in. She remembered looking at her watch before taking it off and placing it on the nightstand. The time had been 1:44 A.M. Domini looked at her wrist now. She wasn't wearing her watch. She remembered taking off her shoes, and the luxurious feel of soft carpet under her feet. Domini glanced at her feet and wiggled her bare toes. Okay, no watch, and she was barefoot. Current reality corresponded with memory. She remembered the walk to the bathroom, turning on the light, and taking toothpaste out of the medicine cabinet. She'd closed the cabinet door and looked into the mirror.

And anger had rushed over her, as red and hot as lava.

If this was passion, she didn't like it. She tried to forget about the vision, but she felt her lips draw back in a snarl and the earlier rage heated her blood.

Domini leaned back against the headrest and took long, deep breaths, making herself relax, willing the world to make sense. The exercise helped calm her, but the world refused to cooperate as far as being sensible went. The fact remained that she'd blanked out and ended up in a part of town where keeping streetlights repaired was not a high priority.

The thought of a cold beer suddenly made her mouth water, and she got out of the car and followed the craving.

Barefoot was not the safest thing to be on this particular dark side street. For a few steps the cool, gritty hardness felt good on the soles of her feet, then she stepped on a piece of broken glass.

The pain sent Domini staggering against the nearest wall, swearing under her breath at herself for not being more careful—and for being out here in the first place. She leaned against the wall and lifted her foot. She was lucky: her big toe was bleeding a little, but no glass was imbedded in the cut. She waited for a few moments until she was sure the bleeding had stopped, then moved forward again, much more carefully. She didn't know where she was going, but she knew she'd know the place when she got there.

She was looking for a bar, she supposed, since she had a taste for beer. She was glad to discover that along with the car keys, she had a few dollars folded in her pocket. No ID, though—not that anyplace open at this hour in this part of town was likely to card anyone.

Domini crossed a deserted street and limped along until she reached the center of the next block and knew she was at the right place. The low brick building was thoroughly unremarkable, and there was no sign to identify it. Seedy didn't begin to describe it. A heavy curtain blocked any light from escaping the one wide window. The door was scarred and needed painting, but the brass door handle was worn smooth and shiny with use. She could hear noise inside, muffled and faint. She almost expected someone to appear at a peephole and ask for a password. She glanced at her bare feet. Would a dive like this have a "no shoes, no shirt, no service" policy? She opened the door and stepped inside.

She'd expected the place to be dim and smoky, but she hadn't expected almost total darkness, and to choke on the first breath she took as the door closed behind her. Not all the smoke she took into her lungs was tobacco. The miasma that drifted all the way up to the low ceiling consisted of some weeds she could recognize, some she couldn't, and there were hints of candle smoke and incense beneath the more pungent herbal odors. The floor beneath Domini's feet was sticky, she didn't want to know with what. Her palms grew sticky with nervous sweat as the noise level slowly died down and every eye in the house turned her way. Danger swirled around her, more substantial than the smoke. Some of those staring eyes shone with a hungry animal glow. She caught hints of fangs glittering in the shadows. A sound like a collective gasp washed across the length and breadth of the room, and Domini knew instinctively that the hunters within had caught the scent of fresh blood.

If she turned and fled now, they'd come after her.

You're making this up, she told herself, even as her heart hammered in her ears and the primitive part of her brain screamed at her to run for her life. Domini kept her back to the door as she peered through the shifting haze. There had to be a reasonable explanation. Maybe she'd walked into a Goth hangout, or a party of makeup artists.

Or a vampire bar.

Which was a logical explanation, in a way, but not a sane one. Of course, waking up parked outside this place was neither sane nor logical, now, was it? And driving away once she came to her senses would have been the sensible thing to do, now, wouldn't it? But no, she had to follow some stupid compulsion that she knew deep in the depths of her soul was all Reynard's fault, and—

She knew Reynard was here. And that he was with a woman. Anger flared through her.

And this was her business *how?*

Domini decided to ignore her unreasonable jealousy, and what she thought she saw. The sane thing was to just get the hell out of Dodge.

But when she turned around, someone was standing behind her. He was tall, dark-haired, handsome. He held an empty cocktail glass in one hand and looked her over like she was the dish of the day. He was wearing a lot of leather.

"Hello, Blackbird," he said. "It's been a long time."

"Excuse me," Domini said, and tried to step around him. Though her back was to the room, she knew she was still being watched. The energy from all that attention felt like static electricity on her skin.

He moved with her, keeping her from the exit. He held his free hand toward her, just short of touching her. "You don't remember me? Anthony? San Francisco? 1969?"

Domini shook her head. "Never been there. Wasn't born then." She looked him over. "Neither were you, Tony."

Anthony tossed his empty glass onto the nearest table, then held both hands out toward her. "Am I drunk, Blackbird?"

"Will you get out of my way?"

Instead he leaned closer, his hands not quite touching her shoulders as he peered at her intently, drew back his lips, and sniffed. Domini saw his canine teeth extend into fangs. She backed up, deeper into the smoke.

The crowd parted and he followed, his fanged smile turning from puzzled to predatory. "A cuckoo in the nest." He chuckled.

The sound of his laughter jarred against Domini's senses. And his change *hadn't* been a special-effects trick. When she took one more step, she backed up against the bar. The vampire moved in, put his hands on her waist, and pulled her to him. His body was hard, his hands were strong, and she had very little room to maneuver.

As she leaned sideways to break the hold, she barely caught sight of the shadow as it rushed out of the swirling smoke. She was flung backward, and Anthony went down.

Domini hit the bar hard enough to knock the breath out of her. For a moment, all she saw was the smoke swirling around the ceiling. She heard shouting in a language she didn't know, animal snarls, the crash of breaking furniture, and a howl of pain. When she tried to sit up, hands grabbed her arms from behind, lifted her onto the bar, and held her. Her captor held her with bruising force, but at least she could see the fight.

Two vampires circled each other in the tight space that had

been quickly cleared in front of the bar. Behind the antagonists loomed the solid mass of the avidly watching crowd, like the hungry eyes of a wolf pack glowing out of the night.

Between her and the crowd, the fighters circled and slashed with deadly grace—two intensely masculine figures of muscle, fang, and claw, one in a white shirt, the other in black leather.

There was a quick flurry of movement, a blur of black and white—and red—too quick for Domini to make out details. The dim room and swirling smoke didn't help. Then the smoke cleared away, like a curtain pushed aside. The fighters grew still, crouching statues facing each other. Domini counted a dozen racing heartbeats before the one in black—Anthony—slowly straightened. The thin slash of a cut marred his cheek. He didn't seem to be in pain as he smiled; a smile full of irony, without a hint of fangs showing.

Anthony bowed, ever so slightly, to the vampire in white. "Felicitations." Then he disappeared into the crowd and the dark.

The instant Anthony was gone, the winner sprang out of his crouch and straight at her. In the blur of speed, Domini made out fragmented details. A spot of blood like a small red rose dotting the front of the pure white shirt. A swirl of hair darker than a raven wing, a hard-set jaw, green eyes blazing like emeralds under spotlights. Shoulders wide as a mountain, hands as deadly as sharpened steel. Then the kaleidoscope of images came together into a recognizable form.

"Reynard."

Domini wasn't even surprised.

The grip behind her let go, and as Reynard lifted her into his arms, Domini swirled down into a dizzying vortex. Her head fell forward onto his chest, and everything went dark.

Chapter Ten

"*Mine.*"

The word came out a rough rasp, full of as much pain as pleasure.

With his body pressed against hers, Alec held Domini upright against the brick wall just inside the dark alley. Full of the debris and stench of derelict lives, the alley was nowhere to make love, but it would do for the hard, quick sex he needed.

"*Mine.*" He wanted her to acknowledge it. "Wake up," Alec commanded, using all the force of his mind. This brought only a faint moan and flicker of eyelids.

His. Won with blood; to be claimed with blood.

Alec held his prize tightly, her arms above her head, her slender wrists grasped in one hand.

With his other hand, he pushed her clothing aside to reveal belly and breasts as soft as white velvet. Her lithe body was warm, pliable, waiting to be covered, filled, possessed. His hand roamed freely; his lips brushed her throat where the pulse beat strong and steady. His mouth lingered at this spot, breathing in the scent of her, savoring her spirit while his hand caressed her breasts, then strayed down until his fingers pushed her thighs open and slipped between her legs.

Domini woke with a shocked gasp when he began to stroke and tease her soft, sensitive flesh. She bucked, but he held her mound pinned against his palm, his fingers working inside her, coaxing the beginning of pleasure from her.

Pleasure is mine to give. Mine to take.

When Alec felt her respond, he lifted his head to look into her eyes, deep into her soul, into her thoughts.

Mine. Only mine. Forever.

Domini's world was made of heat curling through her, of eyes of green fire branding her, steel grip binding her, a voice dominating, demanding acknowledgment, submission. A heavy, hot weight covered her, pressing into her breasts and stomach. And—

Inside her.

A mouth covered hers, hard, overwhelming. A prick of pain touched her lips. A taste of copper slid across her tongue and was gone.

Blood for blood, a voice whispered in her mind. *Always.*

Not her blood, she realized. His. The pain his, but he'd shared that with her as well. He'd bit his lip before he kissed her.

Confusion warred with the fire licking through her insides. She was helpless, totally without control; fear sang through her heightened senses. But her tongue danced with his and her hips swayed to the tune his fingers played inside her. She could not help herself. She'd never known that being out of control could be so—

Exciting?

The confident voice in her mind was like velvet over steel. A sheathed knife, beautiful but holding the potential for violence.

Exciting?

There was no mistaking the edge, no denying the demand for truth.

Yes!

I excite you. As no other has, or ever will. Truth.

He had her soul under a microscope. There was no escaping his overwhelming will. Nothing to give but truth.

Yes.

Good.

His silky, smug pleasure infuriated her. Anger helped counter the spell, helped bring her back to awareness. He was not the world.

I am your world.

Bullshit.

Alec was so shocked, he stopped kissing Domini. "What?"

It was a mistake. It brought him out of their shared mind, closer to awareness. Their gazes locked, and Alec no longer saw only himself reflected in her eyes.

"What are you doing?" she demanded.

"Fucking you."

"Oh, no you're not!"

"Despite evidence to the contrary . . . ?"

His voice held dark humor, darker determination. There was magic in his eyes. Domini fought off the urge to look into their swirling green depths. That way lay the molding of her will into anything he wanted of her.

She squeezed her eyes closed and said, "Get off me. Get away from me." She fiercely imagined herself free of him; willed it. If magic was real and he had it, then so must she.

"*This* is real."

Domini heard him as if from a great distance as he continued touching her. She tried to block out the sensations, but ripples of pleasure kept rolling through her, building . . .

"Stop it. Stop it. Stop it!"

He didn't. It just got worse. Better.

Alec loved the mastery of forcing pleasure on her, but his own need clawed at him. Enough of games; it was time to claim his own pleasure.

His hands left her for a moment as he reached for his fly. She was still trapped with her back pinned tightly against the wall, but her hands came down fast. Her fists would have slammed into his temples if his reflexes weren't faster than any mortal's.

Alec grabbed Domini's shoulders. "Don't try to attack me."

"Don't try to rape me," she snapped back.

Rape? This wasn't—he'd won her—she was his—

"What would your mother say?"

Where fists had failed, her words hit hard enough to box his ears. How did she know exactly the right question to ask?

"Damn you!" he snarled—and stopped being a Prime in heat—barely.

What *was* he doing? What was he thinking? His Matri would exile him, or worse, for taking a mortal woman like this. Yes, she was his, but he'd already vowed not to force himself on her. How soon he'd forgotten that vow.

Though not without provocation.

He took her by the shoulders and shook her. "What the hell were you doing with Tony Crowe?"

"What were you doing with that woman?" she shouted back. "What was I doing in that bar?"

"What woman?"

"The one—the one—" Domini blinked and shook her head. "The one I saw you with."

"You didn't see me with any woman."

Maia Caeg had been long gone before Domini showed up. One kiss had told them both that nothing would come of the meeting, and the incident had only added to his building frustration. Frustration that wasn't getting any better.

"In the mirror," Domini answered. "I saw you in the mirror." She knew her words made no sense. Nothing made sense. Her mind and body were alive and singing and singed by an inner fire, and she didn't know where she was, but she was nearly naked, and the reason was ridiculous. "Why the hell should I care who you kiss?" she added, puzzled.

Alec was shocked that the connection was already so strong on her side. They were nowhere near to being bonded, yet she knew when he was with another woman and reacted accordingly. He might have been smugly pleased if this weren't so dangerous for Domini's sanity. Considering his condition, it was no doubt his fault—some kind of psychic leakage, messing with her head as well as his. Not good for him; certainly not good for her.

But she wasn't ready for an explanation yet. He wasn't ready to tell her she was hopelessly entangled with a vampire trying to fight off madness and feral impulses. He was dancing on a knife edge and had her dancing with him. He couldn't let these incidents go on.

The need to protect her was even more basic than breathing or the call of blood. So he'd handle it. Somehow, in their day-to-day life, he'd keep his distance, keep his cool.

But first they had to get out of this alley and into what she needed to think of as the *real* world, until he could properly bring her into his.

Keeping his hands on her shoulders, he leaned far enough to let her adjust her clothing. He needed the contact; he needed to touch her—but also needed to keep her from running. When she was done, Alec picked Domini up and carried her out of the alley. He turned left when he reached the street.

"Where are we going?" she asked.

"Your car."

Domini was weary beyond belief; so weary that she was beyond fear. Her limbs and eyelids were growing heavier by the moment. It might be from the fading adrenaline rush. She suspected it was from Reynard.

"You're messing with my head."

"Not at the moment."

"Then why am I so sleepy?"

"You've had a long day." Or maybe it was because he was practicing a mental exercise for calm, and she was reacting to it.

Or—and he smiled hopefully at this thought—maybe the smoke was getting to her, now that he no longer was hooked into her mind. She'd been in the bar for some time, and she'd breathed in a lot of the drugged air. The place was kept pumped full of drugs that affected mortals for a reason: to make any humans believe they'd imagined any strange things they saw, should they be foolish enough to stumble into the very private establishment.

"You're stoned," he told Domini. "This is very good for both of us."

"I wasn't stoned a minute ago." Her voice was slurred, but her indignation came through loud and clear. "I do not do drugs . . . okay, maybe Ecstasy once in high school, but we were at a rave and I didn't know what Holly handed me when I told her I wanted something for cramps . . . and I've just told you more than you want to know . . . haven't I?"

"Not necessarily. Here we are." He'd followed her scent back to her parked car. "Keys."

When she didn't respond, he gently set her down, to lean on the side of the car while he dug into her pockets for the keys. Once he found them, he opened the door and tucked her into the driver's seat. He got in on the passenger side and found Domini slumped over, her forehead resting on the steering wheel.

"Can't go to sleep yet," Alec told her, and propped her up. There were thoughts and memories he had to make sure were planted in her mind before he could let her rest. He took her chin and turned her head toward him. "Open your eyes. Look at me."

Domini blinked a few times, then her gaze held steady on his.

Alec smiled at her, careful that not a hint of fang showed. It wasn't going to be easy to invade her thoughts, even with the drugs, but it had to be done. He kept up a steady, gentle pressure on her natural mental barriers, waited until her pupils were fully dilated, her breathing slow, deep, and steady. Then he said, "You were at the safe house. What did you tell them when you left?"

The answer came slowly, with no expression in her voice. "Nothing."

"You're sure? No one questioned you?"

"I left. Didn't talk to anyone."

Good. A clean palette to start with. There were bound to be questions from the protection team when Domini returned.

"You're going to go home to set your VCR. Tell them you forgot that you wanted to tape something."

"What?"

He had expected her to simply comply with the command, but why would Domini make it easy on him?

"A basketball game," he told her. "Tell the team leader that you remembered you'd miss the Sparks games this week while on the detail, and wanted to set your VCR for all of them."

"I don't follow the Sparks. I'm a Clippers fan."

"You follow the Sparks now. You love the WNBA."

"I love women's basketball."

"Then set the tape for it."

"I don't have a VCR."

"Everyone has a VCR."

"I have TiVo."

"Fine, then set that."

Alec fought down impatience, drawing on the same meditation techniques used to keep the hunting instinct at bay. He needed to be patient, gentle, persistent, convincing. He should be proud of her level of resistance, not irritated at her literal attention to detail. God was in the details, right? So was a successful brainwashing. They'd get through this, no matter how long it took.

"After you set the TiVo," he went on, "this is what you are going to do . . ."

Chapter Eleven

"Are you supposed to be here?" Ben Lancer asked.

Though it was a joke with them, this morning Domini wasn't in the mood for her grandfather's gruff ways. "Just once, you could show you're happy to see me."

He turned from the kitchen counter and gave her a narrow-eyed look. "What'd you bring for breakfast?"

She held up two white paper bags. "Bagels, cream cheese, and lox."

He gave a cursory nod. "Then I'm happy to see you. You look like shit—and you're supposed to be at the safe house this morning."

Domini set down the bags and got out plates and knives. "Holly won't be up until noon or later. I'll be there when she needs me." She took a seat at the kitchen island and began slicing bagels.

She wanted to rush into his comforting arms and ask him to make the dreams go away. She didn't know what was the matter, but maybe Grandpa could make it all better. Or maybe, since she was a grown-up now, she needed to figure things out on her own. Either way, she wanted the comfort of being with him this morning. He was the only family she had, the only sure thing in a shaky world, and her world was getting shakier all the time.

It wasn't just the odd visions and weird dreams. Something was in the air, something that told her her world was about to change forever. A feeling that she was about to fall off a cliff, and she'd either crash and burn or figure out how to soar like the condors she loved. Her parents had crashed and burned—and she'd never know why she hadn't seen that coming. She couldn't see what was before her, but she could sense . . . *something*.

Or maybe it was just her overactive imagination. Whatever it was, she liked her calm, ordered, controlled way of living. Ever since her parents' death, her grandfather had made her world stable, structured if not safe. He'd never let her think the world was safe. She wouldn't even have moved out of the house if he hadn't made her. She'd learned to appreciate a certain amount of independence, but she feared drastic change. Okay, maybe she feared growing up, and that was stupid. It didn't change the fact that she needed her grandpa.

The Old Man wouldn't mind being needed, he just wouldn't want her to go all mushy on him. The Lancers hung tough, even when they thought they were going crazy.

Actually, she *was* feeling better about the going-crazy part this morning. Maybe the world was unstable, maybe she was confused and melancholy, but a voice whispered deep in her head that she wasn't insane. It was as if a weight had been lifted from her last night, even as she had another long, complicated erotic dream. With vampires. Again.

The vividness of it—not even counting the sexual aspects—had stirred up old images, old memories. Snatches of stories? Overheard conversations?

"Grandpa?" she asked as he set a coffee mug in front of her. She sounded like a plaintive kid, and he raised an eyebrow as he took a seat opposite her.

"What?" He took a sip of coffee and a bite of bagel.

"I had another dream last night. Not a compulsion or a premonition, just a dream." She *had* felt the need to run home to record some basketball games, but that was only because she'd forgotten to earlier. Domini wished she hadn't dropped off to sleep on her couch afterward, when she should have returned to Holly. But Holly had been perfectly safe then and now;

Domini had called to check before coming over to the Malibu house. She felt vaguely irresponsible, but maybe not as guilty about it as she should. Which in itself was bothersome.

"If it was just a dream, why are you staring off into space with that worried look on your face? And why do you want to talk to me about it?" he asked.

Domini drank down her grandfather's excellent coffee, not sure why she was stalling. She wasn't quite sure what she wanted to know, or why she needed to ask him. She was afraid to hurt him. He was a tough old bird, but he was also a fragile old man, about some things.

Domini finished her coffee, then put the mug on the counter. "Does Blackbird mean anything to you?" It was an odd question, a snatch of conversation pulled up out of a dream, but so oddly familiar and—

"Course it means something to me." The old man's voice was steady, but his vivid blue eyes held painful shadows. "You know that."

She did. It came back to her now, though she hadn't heard the word in years. Domini closed her eyes for a moment, damning herself. She'd hurt him, damn it all. She had no right to—

"What's this about?" he demanded.

Domini held up a hand, and shook her head. "Nothing. I told you I had a dream."

"Premonition."

"No. It's—stuff coming up from my childhood, I guess. Mixed up with grown-up stuff." An explanation hit her suddenly, and she laughed. "You know, I bet it's from seeing Holly. Being around her makes me feel like a kid again. Makes me remember—stuff."

Domini didn't mention the part Alexander Reynard played in last night's dream, or the dream the night before that. There were some things one did not share with one's only living male relative. Or with anyone else, come to think of it. She couldn't imagine even telling a shrink about watching Reynard in a fight where the combatants had fangs and claws. Or the rough sex after.

It had only been a dream. One so vivid, her body still felt used, still felt unfulfilled. The tang of hard, coppery, hot kisses was still in her mouth. Her lips were tender, and—

She looked at the bruises on her wrists.

"What you staring at?" her grandfather asked.

She held up her wrists to show him. "I'm always getting bruised at the aikido dojo, but I can't remember when I got these." Someone had obviously grabbed her hard and held on for a while. The finger marks felt almost like a brand. But she was a fast healer. "I've got a pair of cuff bracelets I can wear if they haven't faded by tonight."

"Tonight's the ceremony?"

She nodded. "The venue's got tight inside security, but we'll still have three people on the red carpet. Andy Maxwell's running the team. Reynard's on point."

His usual frown deepened. "Who made that assignment? Reynard hasn't been on board a week yet."

"Andy's decision. He trusts Reynard."

Those bright eyes hit her like lasers. "Do you?"

Domini's reactions to Reynard were in total chaos. She took a deep breath, as though California air held enough oxygen to actually clear her head, and said, "I trust his professional expertise."

She remembered how almost eerily still and watchful Reynard was on the job. She remembered him standing unobtrusively in the living room of the safe house, his stance seemingly relaxed. Yet there had been such concentrated protectiveness emanating from him that even Holly had picked up on it. Holly described his intense vigilance as a macho thing, but Domini read it as understated confidence that nobody and nothing got past him. Ever.

Her own reaction to Reynard in all his glorious Delta Force grandeur was complex, and no part of a professional discussion with her boss. "He's competent to do the job."

"Point it is, then," Ben confirmed the team leader's assignment. "Where will you be tonight?"

"I'm on flank."

The Old Man snorted. "Which means you get to wear a pretty dress and walk the red carpet with our principal."

"Well, no one would think Reynard was Holly's date, would they?"

"Point taken. You don't mind?"

"Why would I? Remember, we went to the prom together."

"But not as a date," he reminded sharply.

Domini hid a smile. Ben Lancer wasn't narrow-minded, but sometimes his generational biases showed.

"Not as a date," she agreed. "But neither of us were interested in any of the boys in high school."

"At least Holly had an interest in someone," he said. "While you—"

"Grandpa."

"I wouldn't mind having great-grandchildren."

"I can still provide those." An image of Reynard flashed unbidden into her head. She shook it and said, "There are several ways to have babies without too much personal involvement from the sperm donor."

"I don't want to raise another baby," he answered. "You'll need a man around to help you with that."

Domini did not want to have this conversation. She finished the last bite of her bagel and got to her feet. "I'd better head back to the safe house. There's always the chance Holly might wake up before noon and need me."

Domini felt a tad guilty at leaving. For disturbing her grandfather, for his disturbing her, and because she'd been less than truthful with her excuse for leaving.

She would head over to the safe house in a while, but right

now she planned to head directly to her aikido dojo. Maybe an hour spent practicing her martial art form would help center her disturbed spirit and work off the restless thrumming of her body.

It didn't help her mood when the first car she noticed as she pulled into the road was a blue Toyota RAV-4. It was sheer paranoia to think it was the same car that had followed Reynard's Jaguar, but that didn't stop her from keeping an eye on the little SUV in her rearview mirror. Traffic was heavy, so she couldn't make out the license plate. The RAV-4 soon disappeared from sight, but she didn't relax until she was sure she wasn't being followed.

"I hear you had a date last night."

Alec held onto his temper and gave Dr. Casmerek a steady, direct look. He was sitting on a table in one of the clinic's examining rooms, his shirt off, and the doctor had just administered the second of three painful shots. Vampire skin was tough.

It was six-thirty in the morning, and he hadn't slept. He did *not* like the mortal prying into his business. But Alec also knew Casmerek wouldn't have brought up the subject casually.

"The Caeg woman and I didn't get it on, if that's what you want to know."

"Hmm," the doctor responded, and picked up the third needle. "I suspected Barak and Serisa would try to fix you up. That wasn't the liaison I was referring to."

Alec did not ask what the physician was referring to. The complicated drug regimen had him feeling almost like his old self, but even his old self didn't take lightly to inquiries into his private life.

He held his arm out for the last injection, a serum formulated after the clinic staff studied the results of his tests. Alec hoped this witch's brew worked, otherwise, like vampires in the past, he'd be a victim of the daylight.

Not a victim, Alec corrected himself harshly. It was not a

weakness to be a vampire. Daylight was merely inconvenient. They'd lived without it for thousands upon thousands of years.

I could live without the light; I don't have to put myself through this. But then I wouldn't be the man I want to be. Couldn't fulfill my Clan vow with the totality I want to give.

"Tony tells me it was quite a party." Casmerek interrupted Alec's thoughts, punching in the needle.

Alec glared, the sort of glowing, red-eyed supernatural glare designed to bring a mere mortal to his knees.

Casmerek didn't even look up. His gaze remained steadily on what he was doing as he slowly guided the plunger down on the injection.

Alec supposed he was grateful for the doctor's meticulous care. "Tony a patient of yours?"

"No." Casmerek finished the injection and put the used needle into a sharps disposal container. "But he knows you are." He held up a hand before a question could explode from Alec. "Anthony Crowe was a police detective—"

"Was?"

"He currently runs his own private investigation business, and oversees our security here. He still thinks and acts like a cop. Tony makes it his business to know when Primes are in town, and why. He didn't expect you to challenge him for a mate. A mortal one," Casmerek added, with a significant look.

"It's not what you think." At least it hadn't turned into the sort of orgy Casmerek thought it had. "I saw Tony hitting on a mortal woman who'd wandered into the wrong place. He didn't pay attention when she wasn't interested. We foxes are more chivalrous than the crows. I got her out of there, hypnotized her into thinking it was all a dream, and took her home."

"No sex?" Casmerek sounded deeply suspicious.

Alec shook his head. He loathed having to explain himself like a horny half-grown boy to his Matri, but he needed Casmerek's help. "I followed doctor's orders." Though he had come far too close to the edge.

"Then why did you tell Tony—"

"Macho Prime stuff."

"Hmmm." Casmerek stepped back. "You can get dressed now."

Alec got up from the table. "How am I doing?"

"I'll let you know."

"What does that mean?"

"It means that you continue to follow the regimen you're on, and we'll do tests in a couple of days to see if that cocktail I just gave you has any effect."

Alec wanted Casmerek to tell him that he was fine now, that all the allergies—or whatever they were that made a vampire vulnerable—were under control.

Before putting on his shirt, Alec checked the tattoo on his wrist. "I don't think the ink's faded any more."

"Doesn't look like it," Casmerek agreed. "Don't be so impatient, Alexander," he cautioned. "The process might be slow, but it does work."

How could he help but be impatient? The mate he'd been waiting for all his long adult life was within his hands' reach, and he couldn't touch her. Shouldn't touch her.

Would touch her.

His fists tingled and clenched tightly at the memory of touching her warm, yielding—

"Forget about it," he muttered. When the doctor gave him a curious look, Alec said, "I'm going now."

After Alec left the building, he made himself look toward the sun cresting the barren hills to the east, without the benefit of sunglasses. He couldn't do it for more than a few seconds, but he counted it a victory of pure stubbornness that he accomplished it at all. Then he put his sunglasses on and went to his car.

As he stood by the door of his Jaguar, the sensation of being watched struck him. Alec stood frozen in place, letting all his physical and mental senses roam. They weren't as sensitive as usual, due to all the drugs in his system, but his perceptions were still far more acute than any mortal's. Even in the daylight his sight was excellent, though nothing compared to his night vision. His hearing matched any owl's, and he was brother to the wolves when it came to smell. His reflexes were as incomparable as Deja Thoris. On top of that, he came equipped with strong telepathy, a modicum of mind control, and the occasional dose of second sight.

And the clinic has its own security, he reminded himself. The best in the world, since it was run by vampires. All of whose senses were more acute than his were at the moment.

This knowledge didn't keep Alec from standing perfectly still, his palms flat on the roof of the Jag, while he breathed and listened. After a minute or so, he concluded that the prickle of warning was probably a side effect of the new drugs in his system.

Someone dancing on my grave. He got in his car and drove home, since he wasn't due at work until late afternoon. *Plenty of time to gulp down a pint of O-positive and get some sleep.*

Chapter Twelve

"My feet are killing me," Domini complained as she and Holly stepped aside for a waiter carrying a tray of hors d'oeuvres. The food looked great, but little of it was being eaten. Ah, the Hollywood obsession with staying a size zero.

"Well, look at what you're wearing," Holly whispered back. Their heads were close together so they could hear each other over the loud buzz of conversation. The media room in the recording executive's mansion was huge, yet crowded. The decor was black marble, gray granite, and stainless steel, all sharp angles and calculated coldness.

Domini followed Holly's glance down to her shoes. She was wearing ankle-strap high heels to go with her short black lace dress and matching bolero jacket. Holly was dressed with the studied casualness her image consultant had put together, but neither of them stuck out in this crowd of media and recording people.

"*You* get to dress like a rock-and-roll slut in jeweled Keds," Domini pointed out. "I'm wearing Prada. But it's not the shoes' fault my feet hurt; I've got a cut on my big toe."

"Want me to call over Mr. Testicles to kiss it and make it all better?"

Domini successfully fought the urge to glance across the crowded room to where Reynard lingered by the open patio doors. She kept her attention on the succession of people who approached Holly, while Reynard concentrated on an overview of the room. No attack was expected; they just wanted to get Holly used to having a team around her during social situations. It would help her feel more relaxed and secure when she faced the gauntlet of the crowds of media and fans later in the evening.

"He's on duty right now; he can't kiss anything," she answered Holly.

"He's staring at us."

"He's protecting your ass."

"He'd rather have yours. When he isn't looking at me, he's looking at you," Holly went on. "And he looks at you a lot different than he does at me."

Domini couldn't help but glance Reynard's way this time.

Holly laughed. "Made you look."

Alexander Reynard didn't appear to know that either she or Holly existed, which was exactly how it was supposed to appear. He wore a tux and held a champagne glass full of ginger ale in one hand. He stood at an easy slouch, seemingly listening to a perky, petite young blonde in a backless red dress.

Frankly, the man looked like a movie star. It wasn't only his sharply defined good looks that set him apart. There were plenty of handsome men here, but Reynard had that indefinable charisma. He wasn't *doing* anything, but he wasn't being unobtrusive, either. There was utter confidence and cool in the way he carried himself. It was attracting attention, mostly of the female kind. Domini supposed Reynard's polish came from knowing just how silly this sort of affair really was, compared to a black-ops military operation.

She took a sip of her own ginger ale and brought her attention back to Holly as a couple in matching tattoos and body piercings approached.

It turned out the pair were record producers, and Holly was delighted to see them. Domini stood back while the trio engaged in a technical discussion that would have left her reeling in boredom, had she actually paid attention to it.

After a few minutes the producers wandered away, and

Holly turned back to Domini. "So, you finally have the hots for someone, don't you?"

Domini sighed. "You have no mercy."

Holly laughed. "Hell, no. Not when I have a captive audience."

It was Domini's turn to laugh. "Captive? Do you know how much you're paying me by the hour?" A television celebrity passing by paused and gave Domini an interested look. She glared, and he kept moving.

Holly cackled. "Look what you've done to my reputation."

"Serves you right for picking on me."

"I'm not picking, I'm . . . concerned."

"You're meddling. You always meddle with my love life when you're between girlfriends."

Holly put a hand on Domini's shoulder. "I want you to be happy."

Domini leaned over and said quietly, "Sex is not necessary for happiness."

"We've had this discussion before." A slow, wicked smile lit Holly's face. There was steel in that smile, and a hint of the burning charisma the tiny woman could use to mesmerize a crowd of thousands. "This time," she went on with utter confidence, "this time, my friend, you are only going through the motions of being indifferent to lust." She gestured toward the other side of the room. "You want him." Holly brushed her fingertips down Domini's arm. "You're heating up just thinking about him."

Domini jerked away from Holly's touch. "Stop it."

Don't stop, Alec thought, growing warm himself. Not when you're at a really good part.

He was completely unashamed of using his psychic ability and sharp senses to eavesdrop on Domini and Holly's conversation. Ashe's safety was his duty, and Domini was his lady.

Each life was his to cherish, one for this moment and one for eternity, and he put all he was, body, mind, and soul, between them and any danger. He had no trouble focusing on their conversation while keeping watch.

When he'd begun listening in, he was fascinated and a bit flattered—Mr. Testicles?—at the way the conversation was going. How could he help being interested in finding out what Domini thought of him?

He wondered if Holly had any inkling about how psychic her combination of charisma and empathy was. He guessed that Domini and Holly's friendship was based in part on the talents that set them apart from the normal world. They'd grown up as the strange and out-of-sync ones, but they were also the ugly ducklings who'd turned into swans. In Domini's case, anyway; Ashe was more of a bird of paradise.

He understood about being different, but perhaps not as completely as the two young women did. Vampire young, precious and rare and cherished, were sheltered from any contact with the mortal world. He'd gone out into the world as a young adult, and decided he liked associating with the mortals his people protected. A vampire didn't *need* the medicines that brought the daylight life, but for those like him who wanted to do more, experience more, the drugs were essential. He desperately craved the full life that only the drugs could offer. To see his beloved by sun and candlelight, if nothing else.

He continued to watch the room and to flirt with the young woman hitting on him, while he listened for Domini's response to Holly Ashe.

"You want him, don't you?" Holly whispered to her friend.

Ambivalence swirled through Domini's mind. "I don't know what I think—"

"Feel."

"Feel about Reynard. I don't know *the man. He's good at what he does, but I have absolutely no clue about his background or what he likes."*

"You don't have to know someone to want to screw them. Lust does not require an exchange of résumés."

"I'll admit to having erotic dreams about the man. That's a first for me."

Alec was gratified that Domini had to fight very hard not to look at him.

"Not a bad start," Holly said. *"You gonna jump him?"*

"Of course not."

"Why the hell not?"

Holly's disgust tickled across Alec's senses, and he couldn't help but smile.

"Because I have no intention of losing my job," was Domini's answer. *"I've got too much time, training, and loyalty invested in Lancer Services. Grandpa'd bounce me out of the company as fast as he would Reynard if I got caught fooling around with him."*

"You could always find another job."

"But I can't find another grandfather. No way will I betray Ben Lancer's trust. Besides, Reynard hasn't shown any interest in me."

"But you want him to. Even I can tell that Mr. Testicles is a prime example of the breed."

Alex smiled. *How right you are, my little friend.*

The conversation between Domini and Holly was interrupted as their hosts, Emmett and Joni Brakie, approached Ashe and asked to speak to her in private. Ashe nodded. The power couple frowned when Domini stayed in step as they hustled Ashe off, but all they dared to do was frown when Domini gave them a hard, no-nonsense look.

That's my woman, Alex thought, and swiftly followed the group through the thick crowd.

Domini caught a flicker of movement out of the corner of her eye when Emmett opened the door to a private room. A quick sweeping glance showed her that nothing was there, but warning prickled along her skin. She waited to be the last person in the room, and made sure the door was securely shut before crossing a wide expanse of plush blue Chinese-patterned carpet to stand near Holly. In direct contrast to the spare, modern decor of the media center, this room was full of old-fashioned luxury. Blue velvet curtains hung from tall windows, and tall crystal vases of white calla lilies lent a subtle scent to the air.

Holly headed straight for a shiny baby-blue grand piano and immediately began playing something by Chopin. She stopped after a few seconds and turned an accusing look on her host. "Brakie, when's the last time you had this thing tuned?"

Emmett Brakie shrugged. "I don't come in here very often." He waved her toward a pair of blue brocade couches that faced each other across a low white marble table. "Come have a drink."

Joni Brakie was standing behind a bar in a distant corner of the room. "Wine?" she called.

"Mineral water." Holly glanced at Domini and murmured, "Got to keep my head in the shark pool."

Domini gave a faint nod and followed Holly across the room.

"We've been thinking," Joni Brakie began as she took a seat next to Holly on the long couch.

"About your tour schedule," Emmett said. He sat down on the other couch, but leaned forward across the wide expanse of tabletop. "We think you should add a few dates."

"To support the new single."

Emmett picked up the ball from his wife. "Airplay's not as strong as we'd like."

"Maybe add some more in-store appearances," Joni went on. "We have some charity events lined up."

"Here in Los Angeles," Emmett said.

"This week."

"We know your schedule's already tight, but—"

"Hold on," Holly finally interrupted, much to Domini's relief.

Domini was prepared to protest the security problems the Brakies' plans entailed, but she needed to know her client's opinion before she could voice her own.

"I'm not interested." Holly held up her hands in front of her. "I'm not even the person you should be talking to about this."

"You are the one who needs to make these decisions," Joni insisted. She put her hand earnestly over Holly's. "You don't want your career to lose momentum, do you?"

"We want to support you. Push you into the spotlight."

"Cutting back on your schedule right now is the last thing you need," Joni said. "It's against the bold, brave image you've been building."

"Your coming-out was bold, and—"

"I was never in." Holly cut Emmett off once more. "People are threatening to kill me," she reminded the owners of her recording company.

"People threaten to kill me all the time." Emmett waved her protest away. "Dealing with crazies is the price of fame. Consider it a compliment."

Domini spoke up. "We prefer to think of it as a threat."

"We'll add extra security for you," Joni said to Holly.

Domini knew that was a promise the Brakies had made for other artists, and had followed through in the most desultory fashion. Which was one of the reasons Holly's management had called in Lancer Services.

"We've always treated you right, haven't we?" Emmett asked, a touch of hurt in his voice.

Holly flinched slightly at his tone. "Yeah. I know."

"We'll take care of you," Joni promised.

"Ms. Ashe, it's time to go."

Reynard's calm, commanding voice sent a shock through Domini's entire body, and she whirled to face him. Where the hell had he come from? She hadn't heard him come in.

A chill crawled up her spine, and she watched silently as Reynard approached Emmett Brakie, who'd risen from his seat.

"We aren't finished—" Brakie started.

But Reynard looked deeply into the music mogul's eyes, and Brakie grew silent. Joni Brakie stepped up to touch her husband's arm, but she was caught by Reynard's glacial green gaze as well.

"You are finished with Ms. Ashe."

They stared at Reynard. Joni smiled faintly, as though appreciating Reynard's angular good looks. Emmett's expression was rapt, as though he was about to learn the secret of obtaining ultimate power.

"Any interference with Holly's current schedule might jeopardize her safety. You don't want that."

"We don't want that," Joni repeated.

"We don't want that," Emmett echoed.

Reynard gave a slight nod. "Good." Then he turned to Holly and gestured. "Come."

Holly looked almost hypnotized, but relieved. "Happily," she said.

Joni and Emmett Brakie sat back down on their big blue couch. They were holding hands.

"What the hell?" Domini muttered. "What did you do?"

As Reynard shepherded Holly out the door, he threw her a brief glance over his shoulder. The power in that look was scalding. She had to fight to turn away from the fire in those eyes, and to fight against the sensation of that power probing against her mind.

"It is time to go." His voice was soft, persuasive, tinted with immense assurance.

She wanted to slap him.

"Where did you come from?" she demanded as she followed closely behind him and Holly through the crowded mansion. "Nobody came into that room after I entered. I was watching."

"I did."

Her senses rebelled. She would have known. She would have seen. All she'd felt out of the ordinary was a breeze. That couldn't have been him, moving too fast for anyone to see, even though that's what she half believed.

"What'd you do to those people?"

"I'll tell you sometime."

The party continued around them as they headed for the front door. He didn't push anyone out of the way, but Reynard was as efficient as Moses parting the Red Sea at getting people to move aside for Holly. Domini would have admired it if she weren't so freaked about what had happened in the music room.

"Nothing untoward happened," he said as they stood outside and waited for Holly's limo to be brought up. He wasn't looking at her, but he spoke in the same tone he had with the Brakies—as if all he had to do was tell her something to make it so. "Something needed to be done. You didn't seem to be in any hurry to stop those fools."

She bristled at the implication that she hadn't been doing her job, but she didn't let it distract her. "Don't try to tell me that you learned hypnotism in the Delta Force."

"Of course not. I was merely firm with them. People like the Brakies aren't used to taking orders. It makes for a nice change."

"You should have knocked before you walked in." The protest sounded lame even to Domini, but she was disturbed, maybe even frightened. There was something very *wrong* with Reynard's behavior. Maybe it could be explained away, but . . .

He turned his head just enough from scanning the cars moving in the wide brick drive to show Domini a faint smile. "We're on duty," Reynard reminded her. "This is no time to argue."

That, she couldn't argue with. Damn it.

Their two cars pulled up as she tried to think of something scathing but nonargumentative to say, and Reynard handed Holly into the back of her limo.

"Later," Domini snarled at Reynard before following Holly into the limo.

"I'm sure." He closed the door and went to join Andy Maxwell in the lead car.

Chapter Thirteen

He'd been showing off, which was *not* the sort of thing a vampire was supposed to do. Alec admitted that part of it was trying to impress his girlfriend, but not all of it. He'd hated standing by and seeing Holly Ashe being put in jeopardy from within as well as from without. Her so-called friends were no more interested in her welfare than the strangers who threatened her life. He'd watched Domini become more and more concerned, and waited for her to say something. When she didn't, he acted on impulse and instinct. He felt good about that.

He doubted Dr. Casmerek would approve.

The key to survival was subtlety, as any Prime in control of his powers knew. Walk in the Light, Work in the Darkness, as the saying went.

But what fun was there in being a vampire if you couldn't show it off sometimes?

"What're you smiling about?" Andy Maxwell's voice came through the receiver in Alec's ear.

"Enjoying my work," he answered through the headset mike.

They stood on opposite sides of the walkway, just inside the black velvet rope that marked off the magic territory where the stars treaded a red carpet. The noisy crowd of fans was at their backs. A swath of media announcers, camera crews, paparazzi, and publicists made a human barrier between the security men and the famous folk slowly making their way toward the auditorium entrance. Alec and Maxwell were watching opposite sides of the area outside the ropes, but caught the occasional glimpse of each other.

"Not just looking at the beautiful people?"

"Can barely see them from here. Our girls are up," Alec said as he spotted Domini and Holly.

Holly was being interviewed while Domini stood back and watched. Domini was wearing an earpiece, artfully concealed in her large jet bead earrings, so they could contact her if there was any trouble. A herd of gorgeous women occupied the densely packed length of the carpet, but none of them were as beautiful to Alec as Domini Lancer. Where many had style, she had substance, purpose instead of ambition. Then there was the matter of those long, sexy legs, meant to be wrapped around him, that swan neck, and the mouth made for ravishing.

"Does she have any idea what she does to a man?"

"None whatsoever," Maxwell answered.

Alec had no doubt Andy Maxwell knew he was talking about Domini. "Good." He had no doubt Maxwell took the warning.

"Don't fall," Maxwell warned back. "It'll hurt when you land."

Too late, Alec thought. "I'll keep that in mind."

He turned his full attention back to the mass of bodies piled tightly together on the other side of the velvet ropes. He had continued his visual scan while he talked to Maxwell; now he opened his mind, as well. He didn't try for thoughts, but dove into the roar of emotions like a swimmer jumping into pounding surf. The world went white for a moment, then Alec came through the blinding cacophony and swam above the flow.

It was amazing how much anger, hate, envy, and greed swirled like veins of lava through the superheated longing, lust, and admiration. The fans loved their celebrities, and were equally eager to eat them alive. The urge to both adore and sacrifice the object of adoration was nothing new to the human psyche, and Alec recognized the lack of personal animosity that fueled most of it. He was looking for genuine threats, trying to focus on anyone whose hatred was targeted specifically.

It took several passes through the shifting levels of passion before he brushed against a blaze of loathing so raw and angry, it sent a wave of nausea through him.

Alec drew his mind back and put up mental shields instinctively. Once he was wholly back inside himself, he lowered the shields just a little, enough to inch back toward the hatred. This time he used his eyes as well as his mind to search for the source. When he found it, it wasn't at all what he expected.

The old woman was so bent and withered, she could be a hundred in human years. She looked as ancient as some of the most senior Matri, and had much of the stubborn strength and force of will as the Mothers of the Clans, as well. She was vitally alive, and it was clear to anyone with psychic eyes that it was the hate that kept her going. There was no magic in the ancient one, but there was a whole lot of mean.

She was surrounded by three men, all much younger. They clearly existed to do her bidding, and reminded Alec of ferocious leashed dogs. None of them matched the photos he'd seen of the man who'd threatened Ashe. The hounds' gazes scanned the crowd, as protective of the old woman as the Lancer security team was of Ashe.

The ancient one's glare was as hot and as straight as a laser beam. Alec followed her intent gaze, and it was no surprise that the look was directed at—

Not Ashe.

But Domini.

"What the—" Alec muttered the words even as he moved.

"Trouble?" Maxwell's voice asked in his ear.

"Having a closer look at someone," he answered, calm and cool. Though Alec followed instinct, by long habit he made mortals think he was following by-the-book procedure. Mortals and civilians liked to think there was logic to the world.

"Not a deal," he added as he moved stealthily closer, weaving unnoticed into the clog of publicists, reporters, and camera crews that filled the area between the carpet and the velvet rope.

It was very hot among the lights that had been set up at close intervals for interviewing the celebrities. The heat hit him hard, the stab of the lights even harder. Artificial light shouldn't have sent the stab of pain through his skull, but the pain was there, disorienting and nearly blinding.

Somewhere along the line, he must have forgotten to take a pill or a potion. He swore, pulled out a pair of sunglasses, and pushed on.

Something nasty tickled the back of Domini's neck, scratched at her nerves. There was the sensation of being tapped on the shoulder by a wicked claw. The feeling spun her away from Holly's side, looking for the danger at her back.

As she turned, the first thing she saw was Reynard, pale as sculpted marble under the lights, and cool as the distilled essence of the Rat Pack in Armani and designer shades. One instant he was on the edge of the interview area; the next, he was a few feet away. She filed the incongruity for later and kept turning. Whatever he was to her, Reynard was no threat to Holly.

Domini faced the noisy crowd. It was difficult to see beyond the brilliant lights. She made out packed bodies, reaching hands, blobs of faces. Auditorium security patrolled the perimeter, watchful but showing no signs of concern. There was no evident physical threat; just a feeling.

She squinted and followed that ugly, dangerous feeling, narrowing her focus to a spot where she saw a little old lady, wizened down to the size of a cricket and tough as old leather. Domini couldn't see the woman clearly, but that was her impression.

"Hate in her heart and venom in her blood," Domini muttered.

"What?" Holly asked, turning away from an interviewer.

"Nothing. We should head inside now," Domini answered calmly, trying to block off the psychic input.

ABOMINATION!

The word exploded in her head with the force of a bullet, black and boiling and sickening. Domini staggered back, blind with pain, and came up hard against a rock-solid wall of flesh covered in silk.

Strong arms came around her. A voice whispered, "I'm with you. You're safe."

The darkness cleared from her vision, the pain evaporated like fog in sunlight. She was aware of Reynard's scent. His arm circled her from behind, his presence alert, protective, with leashed fury held just under the surface. She realized he had mental barriers up that put a guard between her and the attacking voice.

These impressions were insane. So was her impulse to turn in to his embrace and rest her head against his heart.

Domini took a breath and opened her eyes. All the insanity was over in less time than it took anyone to notice. It probably looked like she'd stumbled and he'd caught her, which was exactly what had happened. Holly was the star, and all eyes were directed at Holly, not at her companion or the man who'd come up behind her.

Domini moved away from Reynard, and they both took a step back while Holly laughed and answered one more question.

"I thought I saw something," he said to Domini's inquiring look. "It was nothing," he added after sweeping a look across the crowd.

It was true. There was nothing obviously threatening in the area. Nothing physical, she thought. But something real.

It was only an old lady with a bad attitude, no matter how ugly it felt.

But Reynard had known. He'd felt the invisible threat.

He'd moved like the wind; he'd spoken inside her head. It was as real to him as it was to her.

Or maybe he'd seen her flinch or change expression, and he'd reacted—but Domini didn't believe it for a moment. Giving him a hard look, she whispered, "What are you?"

His body was still, his expression bland, his eyes unread-able behind the dark glasses. Maybe he counted on her telling herself it was all her imagination.

"Time to take Ms. Ashe inside." He stepped back. "The car will be waiting as per procedure after the show."

She nodded stiffly, annoyed but grateful he'd reminded her that there was a routine to follow, a schedule to stick to, a client to protect. She needed to hang on to that until she could be alone.

Domini took Holly by the elbow. "Show time," she said, steering her friend past the last interviewer. "Let's go."

Chapter Fourteen

It was two in the morning and Domini was finally off duty, in her own home, in pajamas, with a glass of wine in her hand.

ABOMINATION.

The word still echoed in Domini's mind, worsening her splitting headache and a horrible sense of disorientation. She'd tried aspirin, she'd tried meditation; now she was curled up on the patio swing, sipping a glass of merlot and looking up into the light pollution that hid the southern California stars. She had twelve hours off, and she wanted to enjoy them.

ABOMINATION.

The word rolled over and over, wanting her to worry over it like a sore spot in her brain. She didn't know why it should be such a puzzle. Most of the time her psychic gift manifested itself by showing her little sound bites of the future. The last several days, her oddly wired mental faculties had been acting up. So, she'd picked up a particularly strong emotion from an old lady who didn't approve of Holly Ashe's lifestyle. It was a simple, straightforward enough explanation, even if it did require a belief in telepathy and other psychic phenomena.

But it hadn't felt like it was aimed at Holly.

It had felt more like a stab in her own heart. Like she'd been branded. Marked.

Domini shivered, but made herself give a cynical laugh. "Right."

A coyote howled, and she heard it slinking through the dry bushes. She took a sip of wine, closed her eyes, and tried to savor

the cool night air. It was quiet up here in her fairly secluded little canyon.

It would be lovely to go to sleep, but when she closed her
eyes, images from tonight's detail began to replay in her head.
With Reynard smack in the center of every move she made,
every place she looked, every decision and thought. And that
damn word still buzzed viciously underneath.

Technically, tonight's detail had gone perfectly. Holly had
breezed through the party and the awards show without any
incident. Now she was at the most trendy club in town, with a
fresh protection detail discreetly keeping her company. She'd
wanted Domini to come along clubbing as a friend, but Domini had opted for home. Tomorrow morning she could write
up her report of almost perfect procedural actions. But should
she also talk to her grandfather about Reynard?

"By the way, Grandpa, the guy's not only a spook, he's
spooky." It sounded not only flippant but stupid—and were
black-ops commando types the same thing as spy spooks?

She finished the wine and noted that her headache was finally fading.

Abomination.

"Not me, lady," she muttered. "I'm just a working girl trying to get by."

And at least the shout had eased off to an insidious whisper.
A silly word for the twenty-first century, anyway. It reeked of
fire and brimstone, with satanic overtones. Very apocalyptic.
Very melodramatic.

Come to think of it, the word appeared in several of the
hate letters sent to Holly.

But the old lady never actually spoke the word, Domini recalled. No overt threat was made.

It wasn't your imagination.

Damn it, Reynard, get out of my—

She cut off the thought and sat up straight. She'd only had
one glass of wine, right? She took deep, calming breaths and

listened to the night all around her. The coyote whimpered once in the bushes, then silence came down to gently enfold the yard. Domini tensed, mistrusting the silence. Then she got up and went into the house.

Alec stayed very still, refusing to pet the scruffy critter that was licking his hand. *Children of the night, get lost,* he thought at the coyote, but it paid him no mind. The thing was half domesticated already, and found having a Prime in its territory more interesting than terrifying.

Alec waited on one knee in the deep shadow of a bush to see what Domini would do next. No lights came on in the house. After a couple of minutes he began to hope that she'd gone to bed. If she had, it would make his patrol easier.

He rose to his feet, and a second later the back door opened. Domini came outside, carrying an object in each hand. When she lifted one of the objects to her eyes, he realized they were night-vision binoculars.

She scanned the yard before he had a chance to hide.

"Busted," he said to the coyote, and stepped to the center of the yard so Domini could get a good look at him. The animal followed him and sat down at his feet, leaning its weight against his leg.

"Good evening," Alec said to Domini. "Nice place you've got here. Nice Glock," he added, seeing the 9mm pistol at her side.

"Why are you here?"

He took a step forward. "I'm here on business. We need to talk."

"In the middle of the night? In my backyard?"

"They want you, not your friend." Alec spoke the words calmly, but her shocked response rocked through him. Shock, yes, but not surprise, at least no more than on a superficial level. "How did you guess I was in the yard?"

"Realized the coyote was upset. They have a den—" She peered hard at him, at the form at Alec's side. "What are you doing with my—with that animal? Get away from it, it's wild."

"Barely. You've been feeding it, haven't you?"

"They have cubs. What am I supposed to do, let them eat Mrs. Gregory's cats? Those cats mean the world to Mrs. Gregory. But babies have to eat, so—"

"You take the predators' side." Alec found her attitude sweet. But then, a predator would.

"If they were feral dogs instead of coyotes and went after domestic critters, I'd shoot 'em. Feral animals are confused and crazy. They don't know what the hell's going on."

He could sympathize. "Making them more dangerous than a truly wild thing."

"Yes. And how did you distract me into this conversation?"

"I'm not sure," he admitted. "But I like getting to know something about you." He gestured the animal away and took a step closer to the patio. "People who work together should be friends." He continued to inch forward as he spoke.

"Only on Sitcom World," she answered. "This is Planet Earth."

"This is Los Angeles," he countered. "Not quite the same thing. Of course, after spending twelve- to twenty-four-hour days with your coworkers, I can see why you'd want some distance from most of them."

"Most? How about all?"

He smiled. "You don't want to keep your distance from me."

His voice was soft, persuasive, and exuded complete confidence.

"You drive me crazy, Reynard."

"Lancer, I haven't even started."

Domini figured maybe it was the wine. She must have had more than one glass; otherwise why would she be standing here, carrying on an inane conversation?

Maybe it wasn't the wine. Maybe it was Reynard. He did things to her.

"What sort of things?" he asked in a velvet whisper, suddenly standing in front of her. It took him no effort to take the Glock from her. "Like this?"

Alec knew he wasn't playing fair with the one person in the world he ought to face on level ground, but the game had gone on long enough. Besides, her shiver of fear when he took the gun was arousing.

He put a hand on her shoulder, not allowing her to step back. Her skin was smooth satin stretched over supple muscle. His thumb found and caressed the point where the pulse beat quickly in her throat. Her gaze shot to his, panic warring with anger in her bright eyes. Excitement coiled like smoke through all her other reactions. Her vulnerability was ruthlessly tamped down within the space of a breath, but the predator in Alec took dark pleasure in it.

He let her spin away from his touch and held the gun out to her when she turned to face him again, several feet away. "Haven't I already told you that you have nothing to fear from me?"

Domini hadn't believed him the first time he said it. She certainly didn't want to believe him now. Except . . .

She snatched back the gun. Then she made sure the safety was on and set it down beside the binoculars on the swing. Her skin still tingled warmly where he'd touched her. Looking at Reynard, standing there gorgeous and half smiling, Domini was aware that she wanted him to touch her again. She'd never wanted anyone's hands on her before. She clasped her hands behind her back to deny the other thing she wanted: to touch him.

He gestured toward her back door. "Let's go inside."

What the hell. It was obvious that she couldn't make Reynard go away until he wanted to. It was also obvious to her that she didn't want him to go, even though she should. That was probably obvious to him, too.

"Come on in." She turned and scooped up her stuff before opening the back door. "You want a glass of wine?" she offered over her shoulder.

"I don't drink . . . wine," he answered, following too close behind her. "But I could use a beer."

Chapter Fifteen

Two references to *Dracula* in less than an hour, Alec chastised himself as he took the beer Domini handed him. *That definitely puts me over my weekly vampire cliché limit.*

"What are you smiling about?" Domini asked.

"Telling myself bad jokes." He glanced at the label on the beer bottle and saw that he was holding a microbrew apricot ale. "Chick beer," he complained.

"If you want a Bud, you'll have to go back to that bar where—"

Alec watched as Domini's eyes filled with confusion. He watched while the memory almost surfaced. "What?"

She shook her head, her dark hair swinging around her pale face. "Nothing."

"You sure?"

He half wanted her to remember, to know that she hadn't been dreaming, that the world was crazy but she wasn't. And that he'd had his hands on her, had very nearly taken her. Damn, but it would have felt good.

Wrong, but good.

He noticed a bruise on her wrist, and remembered that she'd worn a silver bracelet with that sexy black lace dress earlier tonight. It had covered the mark he'd left on her, which brought a twinge of guilt. Alec wondered if she'd subconsciously known he wouldn't have been able to touch the bracelet. In his current condition, his people's allergy to silver was in full force.

"Living room's this way," Domini said after a drawn-out silence.

She sat in the room's one chair and left the couch for him. Alec took a quick look around as he sat.

The furniture was light brown leather, the coffee and end tables carved pine. A flat-panel television screen and other electronic equipment on steel shelving took up one wall. A desk with a computer and other office equipment took up another. There was a bookcase near the desk, with framed photos and a couple of blown-glass paperweights on the top. He recognized pictures of her grandfather and of Holly Ashe, and assumed the photos of a couple were Domini's parents. The walls were neutral beige, decorated with vibrant Navajo wall hangings and a painting of condors soaring over a desert canyon. Another bright rug covered the middle of the Spanish tile floor. She switched on a halogen floor lamp that was too bright for his taste. His eyes really were giving him a lot of trouble tonight.

"You okay?"

"Fine." He made himself stop squinting and focused his attention on Domini.

Domini thought he looked tired. He'd been up as long as she had, and there was weariness in his eyes, and edginess as well. A dark fuzz of beard shadowed his square jaw and highlighted the cleft in his chin. A form-fitting black T-shirt stretched over hard muscles, and dark jeans molded his thighs. It took an effort to tear her gaze away from Reynard's powerful body, but when she did, she saw that he was giving her the same sort of once-over. And she remembered what she was wearing.

Alec liked her cotton knit shorty pajamas, which were red with white polka dots. The top was low-necked, held up by thin ribbon straps, and the bottoms were very short indeed. He watched with growing pleasure as a slow blush crept across her pale cheeks and long throat. The blood just beneath the surface of her soft skin called a sweet invitation to him. It took a great deal of effort not to lick his lips, and it took more not to pounce.

"I never thought of you as the polka-dot type," he said, stretching an arm out on the back of the couch.

She sat up straight, which made the pajama top dip lower on her breasts. "There's a great deal you don't know about me." She eyed him with renewed hostility. "I don't know anything about you."

"I'll tell you anything you want to know," Alec answered, and meant it.

There was much he shouldn't tell her yet, but if she wanted the truth from him, he would give it to her. He wouldn't volunteer a thing, of course, and she'd have to ask some very specific questions—questions no one was likely to think of in this modern age. But if she asked them, he'd answer. Whether she'd believe the answers . . . Well, his part was to offer truth. Hers would be to find belief. She was going to have to believe, eventually. But it would be better for them to come at it together, slowly, when he was in complete control of himself once more.

Tonight Alec felt like an animal was trying to claw its way out inside him. He'd forgotten to take his scheduled medication earlier in the day, and taking a double dose before coming to patrol Domini's house might not have been such a good idea. If he'd been at top form, Domini wouldn't have noticed his presence.

And he wouldn't be sitting here having a beer and enjoying the rush and thrum of lust he got from simply looking at her.

"What do you want to know?" he asked her.

"Why are you here?"

"I wanted to make sure you were safe."

She looked at him with complete and utter consternation. She also looked—touched. Something went soft in her eyes, in the tautness of her shoulders, and the tilt of her head. She didn't realize it, but Alec did, and it pleased him more than he could have believed possible.

Of course, the softness was quickly replaced by the annoyance of a modern woman well aware that she could take care of herself, thank you very much. Girls who grew up with Lara Croft, Captain Janeway, and Xena, Warrior Princess, for role models didn't take well to the idea of being rescued by brave, brawny men. The attitude could be hard on a man's ego, especially on a man who'd been born around the turn of the twentieth century.

"Chivalry is dead, have you noticed?" He took a sip of beer.

She instantly picked up on what he meant. "I don't mind men opening doors for me."

"Just stay out of your way when you come through carrying riot gear."

"Exactly."

Alec stood. "I obviously shouldn't have come."

She reacted just as he hoped, by jumping to her feet, disappointment in her eyes. She managed to sound firm when she said, "No, you shouldn't have. But since you're here, you're not going until we've talked."

He smiled. "You don't want me to go." The anger that shot from her energized all his senses. "Okay, I played you," he told her, and didn't apologize for it. He smiled instead, which served to fuel Domini's annoyance. Which fueled him. The woman made him hot. "There you are, a tower of indignation in polkadot pajamas. Maybe not a tower," he amended, coming closer. "Towers don't have such nice bumps . . . and curves."

Domini saw something wild in Reynard's eyes, so wild they almost glowed. The way he looked at her sent heat lightning blazing through her. His smile was sharp, predatory. She felt as if he were about to eat her up.

He was Reynard the fox, cunning, clever, beautiful, and dangerous. The danger drew her as nothing ever had before.

Domini felt her senses spinning as the wildness in Reynard lured her toward him. At this moment, she couldn't avoid him if her life depended on it.

While her eyes stared into his, she held out a hand and discovered she was close enough to touch his face, to draw her fingertips down his throat. Beard stubble teased against her palm, sending shocks of heat through her. The texture and scent of his skin skirled around her. His gaze held her. She could see herself reflected in green depths. And deeper down, there were flames.

Reynard's eyes closed when she touched him, and he let out a low moan. The sound broke the eye contact and the spell long enough for her to drop her hand, to take one long step backward.

She was trembling so hard she nearly fell back into the deep embrace of the chair, but she tried to make it look voluntary. Why wasn't she just throwing him down on the couch to have her way with him? Her heart hammered in her chest and her insides boiled, while she fought not to let the turbulence show.

"Sit down. Talk," she managed.

Reynard gave an elegant shrug, suddenly looking cool and unconcerned, as though he'd never made any suggestive remarks or touched—

Okay, he hadn't touched her; she'd touched him. And she'd been tempted to touch him a lot. She'd come damn close to breaking company policy.

Alec tucked his hands out of sight when he sat down. He'd managed to keep his fangs drawn back, despite the pain the effort caused him. But his claws had inexorably dug into his fisted palms while he fought the need to take her then and there. One touch from her was all it had taken to nearly send the madness over the edge. His control was thin, his body and soul demanding the taste and total possession of her. But he couldn't let it show, couldn't act on it.

Why not? the demon inside him wondered, silky and seductive. *She belongs to me. She wants me.* He sighed. *She'd be terrified of the real me. Here I sit with my own blood on my hands, and my fangs trying to pop out to sink into her flesh.*

All I want right now is hard sex and hot blood. A vampire's supposed to seduce his lovers, earn their trust, calm their fear; share passion, give pleasure. I want to mark, to possess—

"Reynard? You okay?"

Alec swung his gaze toward Domini, forced his attention to focus. "No."

He shouldn't have had the beer. Dr. Casmerek had told him not to drink, right? He couldn't remember any of the doctor's myriad instructions right now. He didn't think the treatment was working. Alec turned over his left wrist and stared at the fox tattoo. Was it still fading?

"I'm tired," he said before looking back at Domini.

"Been a long day," she agreed. Then she blinked, and a gasp caught in her throat.

"What?" Alec asked.

"Nothing," Domini managed to answer.

A premonition had just streaked through her. In the vision she'd watched Reynard answer his cell phone, heard a voice on the other end say, "Your appointment at the clinic needs to be rescheduled. The serum formula has to be adjusted."

What clinic? she wondered. What serum?

Somehow she knew it would be dangerous to ask.

"How long have you known you were psychic?" he asked after the silence drew out between them for a while.

Domini went stiff. Her fingers dug into the arms of the chair. "How did you know I—"

"The sushi incident was the first clue."

For a moment she struggled to remember what he was talking about. "Oh, right," she finally said. "The place that was out of wasabi." Thank God he hadn't picked up on her vision about him and his medical problems. She waved a hand, trying to be casually dismissive, but the movement was stiff and jerky with nerves. "Probably just my imagination. I have a very active imagination."

"So do I," Alec answered. He managed to smile without

showing any extra-sharp teeth. "Someday we'll try our imaginations out on each other."

He enjoyed the faint outrage that swept through her as she puzzled that out. "Was that a come-on?"

"A statement of intent," he told her. "But let's concentrate on the conversation we're supposed to be having, or neither of us will get any rest before we have to go back to work."

Domini pressed her fingers to her temples for a moment and said, "You've finally said something I agree with. How long have I known I'm psychic?" she went on. "All my life. It's no big deal, no woo-woo talent. Nobody's going to offer me a syndicated television show where I talk to the dead for money, or anything like that."

"I'm rather partial to the pet psychic lady on *Animal Planet*."

"Me, too," she admitted. "Apparently I could do that as a kid."

"Bet you still do," Alec said, recalling her relationship with the coyotes. "But not consciously."

"Right."

"Your skepticism is charmingly postmodern, but it gets in the way of your psychic development."

She made a gagging sound. "Don't make me throw up on you, Reynard."

"You should be happy that I appreciate your gifts, instead of making such a vile suggestion."

She couldn't help but smile. "Vile? What an old-fashioned word."

He smirked. "Didn't know that Delta Force operators have large vocabularies?"

"To go along with your large egos?"

"All sorts of things are large on us D-Boys."

Domini recalled Holly's speculations about Reynard's testicles, and firmly kept her gaze away from his groin. "What's my being psychic got to do with anything?" she asked.

"What's it got to do with Holly Ashe's stalkers, you mean? Does Ashe know you're psychic?"

"We grew up together."

"So maybe they used her to find you."

"They? Who?"

"I don't know yet," Alec said. "But there was something familiar about the old woman."

Domini leaned forward, a rush of excitement going through her. "You saw her? You—heard—her?"

"I saw her. You're the one who heard her. It was directed at you, and you flinched like she'd slapped you hard. There was telepathic communication between you."

She shook her head. "Not between. It was only her. She—hated."

"That was obvious. What did you hear?"

Domini collapsed against the chair back. "Abomination." The word still left a bad taste in her mind. "She called me *abomination*."

"Ugly word. Why abomination?"

"Obviously she thought I was Holly's girlfriend."

He shook his head. "No. It was *you* she hated, not a lifestyle." He leaned forward, gaze boring into hers. "Why?"

"Damned if I know," was all she could answer, even though part of her wanted to proclaim that his opinion was nonsense. Nonsense she half believed, maybe because Reynard wasn't freaked by her being psychic—which was freaky enough in itself. She swiped a hand across her forehead. "I am so confused."

Reynard rose to his feet.

Domini was almost too weary to appreciate the smooth play of tight, toned muscles as he moved. But she was only sleepy, not dead, and looking at him was a pleasure, albeit a muted one at the moment.

"You're getting sleepy," he told her.

She yawned, then shook a finger at him. "You trying to hypnotize me? Won't work."

His smile had a secret, knowing quality to it. "You might be surprised."

"Don't want to be surprised." She yawned again. "Wanna sleep now."

"I didn't see anyone when I did the sweep of the area. You're safe enough tonight," he said.

She didn't bother to argue. "Good night, Reynard."

"Not going to see me out?"

"No."

"Or kiss me good night?" She didn't answer, and he walked to the door. There he paused. "About the coyotes—I know someone who takes an interest in wild canines. He'll relocate them to a safer habitat. He's called Shaggy. I'll have him get in touch with you."

Touched by Reynard's concern for the animals, Domini smiled as he left. "Fine."

Chapter Sixteen

"*H*e was *petting* the coyote. How weird is that, Holly?"

Domini took a sip of orange juice and gazed out over the terrace, the pool, and a hedge of waxy green hibiscus with vivid orange blooms to the city below. Only a faint morning heat haze obscured the vista.

Holly swallowed a bite of toast, then said, "Maybe the coyote recognized an alpha male."

"Maybe." She couldn't deny Reynard's aura of masculinity. "But what's even weirder is that I didn't notice it at the time. It didn't seem strange until I woke up this morning and remembered everything that happened."

"I think it's *interesting* that he showed up to see if you were all right."

"You want to say that you think it was *romantic,* but you're afraid I'll hit you."

Holly tossed her hair out of her face, the movement setting several dangling earrings tinkling together. "You can't hit me. I'm surrounded by bodyguards."

Domini glanced at her friend's long scarlet nails as Holly sipped her coffee. "I wouldn't attack anyone with claws like those. I could get hurt."

Holly held them out in front of her. "Too bad these have to come off before the show tonight. Can't play guitar in these fakes." She picked up her cup and returned her attention to Domini's quandary. "You sure it was a coyote? Not a stray dog or something?"

"I'm sure. I'm also sure that wild animals do not approach

humans. The critters that hang out in my neighborhood will take the food I set out, but only when I'm not around. They're cautious. What's Reynard got that drew a wild animal to him?"

Holly snorted. "I think we've been over that ground already."

Domini sat back in the green metal patio chair. A pair of doves settled on the blue-and-yellow Moroccan tiles that edged the pool. As she watched them bob around searching for food, she wondered why she was here, having this conversation with Holly. She knew why, of course, but she didn't like facing her own cowardice.

What would Grandpa say if he knew about last night? Technically, nothing sexual had gone on between her and Reynard. But she'd wanted it to. Was thinking about it against company policy? It certainly made her feel guilty and confused.

"But does lust count?" she murmured.

Holly overheard her and said, "Normally I'd say yes, but I have no idea what you're talking about. Except Mr. Triple T., that is."

Domini let out a disgruntled laugh. "I wouldn't be surprised if he does have three testicles. The guy is so weird."

"How weird?"

"So weird that I automatically accept that he accepts my psychic abilities."

"I accept it."

"You've known me since day care. Reynard's a stranger. A weird one."

"What can you possibly find weird about a handsome, competently dangerous male who accepts your gifts and worries about you? So he pets wild animals—isn't that just the testosterone attracting them?"

"I think you mean pheromones."

"Which is why you did our chemistry homework for both of us. And speaking of chemistry . . ."

Holly didn't look as teasing as she sounded. "What?" Domini asked, then answered the question herself. "You're getting back together with Jo."

"I ran into a mutual friend last night. Not mutual anymore, really—she took Jo's side," Holly said. "So I wasn't expecting anything nice when she came up to me in the club, but what the hell, I had a bodyguard. So when she started talking, I let her. Only she was friendly. And finally we got around to talking about Jo, and I let slip how I miss her sometimes, and—and she said that Jo misses me, too. And that Jo's worried about me because of all these threats. And this friend gave me a phone number. And I gave her a phone number. And maybe I'll call."

She shrugged, pretending it didn't matter, though her eyes were glowing with hope. "Or maybe Jo'll call. Maybe we were stupid and let all this fame crap get in the way. She's a big-time artist and I'm a big-time artist, only we come from different worlds. I'm from Malibu, and she grew up in the Hamptons, but East Coast–rich and surfer-girl–rich sensibilities aren't exactly the same. But maybe we've matured and—"

"You are getting back together with Jo." Domini spoke the words slowly and clearly. She took Holly's wrists, made sure her friend was looking at her, and repeated clearly, "You are getting back together with Jo."

"How do you—" Holly's eyes went wide. "Oh!" She grinned. "You *saw* it?"

Domini nodded. "Just now." She sighed with relief. "Which means that now you'll stop nagging me about my lack of love life."

"You don't lack one anymore."

"I—" The protest died on Domini's lips as the thought of Reynard caused warmth to flood through her synapses. While Holly eyed her with amusement, Domini said, "Okay, I'll admit to being in lust with him. I don't like it, but I will find a way to cope."

"Sex works."

Domini shook her head. "The guy's weird."

Holly said seriously, "He cared enough to come by your house to see if you were safe. That's nice."

Domini chose not to argue. Reynard was one of the people responsible for protecting Holly, and he had exhibited nothing but professional behavior.

Okay, to her eyes he moved too fast, saw too much. It was like the guy had super powers—and calling it Delta Force training didn't wash with her. But she shouldn't be discussing a fellow Lancer employee with their client. She wasn't going to undermine Holly's trust in Reynard's effectiveness just because she suspected the guy was—

That was the problem. She didn't know *what* he was. Never mind the *who,* it was the *what* that preyed on her mind.

"I need to get to the dojo. Nothing like an aikido class to clear the mind," Domini said, and looked at the fading bruises on her right wrist.

The marks on her left wrist were gone, but the prints of fingers and thumb were still quite clear on this arm, though pale yellow now. At least the faint rash silver sometimes gave her had cleared up as soon as she'd taken the cuff bracelet off last night. Odd that the allergy had acted up, since it hadn't bothered her for a while.

Domini stood to go. "I need to do some research. And office paperwork," she added with a sigh.

Domini's first stop was by Nancy's desk in the reception area.

"Hi." She leaned her arms on the high countertop. "Quite the star-studded night, last night."

Nancy looked up with a grin, happy for a bit of celebrity gossip. "Who'd you see? What did they wear?"

Domini chatted about the rich and famous for a few minutes before asking, "The Old Man in?"

Nancy shook her head. "Lots of meetings outside the office today."

Domini looked disappointed. "Too bad. I wanted to see him. Could you let me know when he comes in?"

"Sure."

"But call me on my cell when you spot him. I'm going to be all over the office today."

"No problem."

With her back now covered, Domini walked away from the reception area and straight to Benjamin Lancer's office, where the computer she wanted to use was located. Fortunately her grandfather's office door wasn't locked, so Domini didn't have to do anything more nefarious than slip inside. Hopefully this wouldn't take long.

She supposed she should feel guilty about snooping on Reynard, but she didn't. She needed to know more about him. Maybe she could have gotten a look at his paperwork from Nancy, under the pretense that she was handling Reynard's orientation, but Nancy would have made sure the Old Man was briefed on Domini's request. And she wasn't ready to discuss Reynard with him yet, even if Grandpa had asked her to keep an eye on him.

Mostly because she was afraid she'd spill her guts about being attracted to the man. She wasn't sure where such a conversation would go with Ben Lancer. He might come down hard, angry and hurt, on the "no fraternization between my employees" side. Or he might go all soft and sentimental and remind her he wanted great-grandchildren. Either way, somebody was likely to get fired. She didn't want it to be her. And she didn't have any proof that it deserved to be Reynard.

"Yet," she muttered, and proceeded to break into the password-protected personnel files. It took her only three tries to figure out that her grandfather used *Domini* as his password, which made her squirm with guilt but didn't stop her.

There was basic information on Alexander Reynard in his

file. Very basic. His full name had no middle initial; his last employer, U.S. Army; rank, colonel, retired. No mention of Special Services or Delta Force, of course. Date of birth given as July 14, 1968, Coeur D'Alene, Idaho. His address, home and cellular phone numbers. No references were listed. No one to contact in case of emergency. Health records were blank, including the company's routine drug-testing results.

Since he'd only been with the company a few days, she *could* assume that the results from his medical exam and tests weren't in yet. But she didn't. He shouldn't be out in the field without those results being logged.

It wasn't like Nancy not to enter data immediately. It wasn't like her grandfather, Andy Maxwell, or herself to vet someone without proper background documentation. Why had he left the army? Who were his references?

What the hell was the matter with all of them?

Some kind of voodoo? Mass hypnotism? What *was* it with Reynard?

Totally dissatisfied, Domini shut down the computer and went to her own workstation. She checked her e-mail and phone messages, then wrote and posted the log of her last shift on the Ashe detail. She read Andy Maxwell's log, and was annoyed that Reynard had only sent a short e-mail from his home computer rather than fill out the proper form.

"Not company policy, D-Boy," she muttered with a certain malicious glee. But Andy was team leader on this assignment; it was up to him to deal with personnel problems.

It was also disappointing to realize that when she objectively wrote down the actions taken to protect Holly, she couldn't find any way to see Reynard's behavior as sinister.

And why do I *want* to get him in trouble? she asked herself. Because he terrifies me, she admitted.

There was something—unnatural—about him. And he wanted her to know it, she was sure of it. If he went away, she wouldn't have to follow her curiosity and the lure of her fascination about what was hidden in the shadowy heart of Alexander Reynard.

Now, there was a melodramatic thought—but she couldn't laugh. Reynard was disturbing. Distracting. Damn sexy.

Maybe that was the dark heart of her fear. He'd walked into her comfortable, contented life and just—shattered it.

And they hadn't even done anything yet. She rubbed her bruised wrist as she wondered what would happen if they ever got around to kissing.

Domini shook her head and forced herself to concentrate on her job. She got out Holly's file and reread the threatening letters, the police reports, and psychological profiler threat assessments, concentrating on finding any evidence or pattern that might jibe with Reynard's theory that Holly wasn't the intended victim. It was ridiculous, of course, to think that someone was using Holly as a cat's-paw to get to her. But—

That ugly voice still throbbed in her head. The old woman's vicious stare cut into her soul. Domini shuddered, then jumped as the phone rang.

"Lancer. What?"

"You okay, Dominatrix?" Andy Maxwell asked. She must have sounded shaken when she answered the phone.

Domini took a deep breath, then said calmly, "I was reading all the icky letters sent to Holly. Put me in a bad mood."

"With good reason. My bad mood comes from still waiting for the police to share the DMV information on the car that followed you and Reynard."

Followed me? The thought sent a chill through her. Or followed Reynard?

"We provided them with the plate numbers and were promised full disclosure on anything to do with Holly Ashe's stalkers," Andy continued. "I'll give them another day, then I'll ask the Old Man to make a call to LAPD."

"We having an afternoon briefing for tonight's detail?"

"On-site briefing at seven—that's what I called to tell you," he answered. "Alec can't make it into the office today."

"Can't?" The word dripped sarcasm. "Who's in charge of this detail, Andy? Listen, Reynard's—"

Reynard's mouth came down hard on hers. Fangs sharp as ivory daggers grazed her lips. His tongue invaded her mouth as his words invaded her mind.

Mine! Mine! Mine!

No! Her protests were growing fainter, will draining out of her like blood from a wound. Please!

Her begging only drove him on. The kiss forced on her was harsh and demanding, tasting of coppery blood. Tasting of defeat. The vampire's lust pounded through her, emotion as real and hard as the cock pounding ruthlessly inside her. There was no escape, only a storm overwhelming her. Driving total possession into her flesh, her blood, and being. She was spread out beneath him like a sacrifice. Her skin was smeared red with her blood, and his.

"The guy's got a toothache, Dominatrix." Andy's words, sounding thoroughly disgusted, brought Domini back to herself.

She shook so hard, she could barely hold the phone to her ear. She blinked, trying to bring her vision back into focus. What the hell was *that?* Her insides ached as if she'd—

"Domini? You okay, Domini? You having some kind of attack?"

"How did you know? There's a vamp—"

"You having an asthma attack or something?" Andy's concerned voice cut across her words.

"I'm—all right." Domini wiped a hand across her forehead, and was surprised to find sweat instead of blood.

Blood. The memory of it was so strong she could almost smell it. Almost taste it. Blood and sex—why did she keep dreaming about Reynard as a vampire? Only this hadn't been a dream. Yet it hadn't felt like one of her premonitions, either. What the hell *was* it, then?

A dose of paranoia? A really sick, perverted one. Something that had slithered up from some dark well of her own imagination. No matter how much Reynard freaked her, she couldn't blame him for this.

She forced her mind back to things she *could* blame Reynard for. "Why the hell isn't he coming in today?" she demanded of Andy.

"I told you, a toothache. He needed a quick trip to a dentist. Cut him some slack; he'll be on duty tonight."

"How do you know that?"

"'Cause he said he'd be there."

Domini took a moment to calm down, to relax her tight muscles. To remind herself that she hadn't been violated in any way. *Think about taking care of Holly. Concentrate on the job and nothing else. Forget about Reynard. Let him go.*

She didn't know how she was going to do that.

"I'll see you at seven. Good-bye." She hung up.

Chapter Seventeen

"Perhaps screaming would help." When both Alec and Barak gave Serisa a dark look, she added, "Not you, of course. Perhaps if you made someone else scream—"

Alec heard the Matri's voice filtered through the layers of pain and violent, feral urges that made up his existence now. He could not lose control. Not for one instant.

"It hurts." He could admit that much.

Alec knew he was in his own house, but he couldn't remember when the elders had arrived. He couldn't remember why. He forgot about them as a picture of Domini flashed through his mind, like a glimpse of a photograph being tossed on a fire.

She was in danger. From some unknown source. More immediately, from him.

He had to get to her.

He had to stay away.

Don't think about her now. Can't think about her now. Must have her. NOW!

Barak stooped next to where Alec knelt on the floor.

"Look me in the eye, Prime." Barak spoke evenly, calmly. Alec hated him for his control.

His eyes were closed again. He didn't want to open them, but he did, for every word between two male vampires could be considered a challenge. There was too much light, and it burned like fire, but Alec met the challenge and looked Barak in the eye.

There was no pity in Barak's gaze, nor was there any mockery. So it would not be necessary to attack him. Damn—it would be good to attack something and hear it scream.

What a hell of a day this had been. It started with a phone call; he recalled that intermittently. He'd arrived home from Domini's, slept a little, then woken and paced, his headache growing worse with every second closer to dawn. None of the pills or injections helped. Maybe he'd taken too many. Maybe not enough. He remembered the taste of medicated blood, and how it had made him sick.

Just after dawn, someone from the clinic called to calmly tell him that his appointment was canceled. There was no explanation, but there was the bad news that the serum wasn't working. He was told that he might experience feral hallucinations.

Maybe that was why the elders came . . .

He recalled that he'd behaved almost normally for a time after the call, even though pain leaked deeper into his body with the rising of the sun. He'd drawn every curtain, blocked off every source of light, but the pain still grew. He'd meditated. He worked through it. He thought he'd even remembered to call the office and make some excuse for staying away. He thought—

"Your eyes are open, but you're not looking outside your own troubles."

Concentrate, Barak's voice whispered in Alec's mind. The whisper had steel in it. *You haven't lost control, but the* fear *of losing it is what's driving you toward the edge. What is the worst that will happen if you lose control?*

The image came immediately into Alec's mind. Into Barak's view.

His mouth came down hard on Domini's as his words invaded her mind. Mine! Mine! Mine! The kiss was harsh and demanding, tasting of coppery blood and sweet domination. Desire pounded through him as he pounded ruthlessly into Domini. Driving into soft heat. Driving total possession into flesh, blood, and being. She was spread out beneath him like a sacrifice. Her skin was smeared red with her blood, and his.

Mine. You are mine. Know it. Love it.

Mine. Want me. Forever. Love it.

She cried out, pain and torment mingled with the desire he forced on her. She writhed beneath him, struggled, submitted. Her mind was conquered, her body rose to meet his brutal thrusts. He roared out his pleasure, reveled in mastery, took her. And took her again.

Mine. Forever mine!

It was beyond Alec's power to shield his dark, feral desires from Barak's knowledge.

Ah. I see.

The thought was a soft sigh in Alec's mind, almost like a blessing. It banished the ugly images for now. Alec sensed no disgust from the elder, no judgment. He only sensed Barak's sympathy.

You understand?

I have known this fire.

It is evil—to want what I want—the way I am now. I cannot—

You fight nature—but I understand why. The timing is shit for a mortal bonding, but fate frequently screws with us.

Alec almost laughed, but any trace of humor fled when he felt Barak withdrawing from his mind. He hadn't wanted the intrusion, but he hated being alone within a mind that felt ready to shatter like glass.

"You'll hold it together," he heard Barak say. "For her sake."

Serisa sighed. "He's obsessing about the mortal I forbade him to see, isn't he?" She did not sound pleased. "Still, he needs a woman right now." After a thoughtful pause, she went on. "He needs to share blood, and passion; needs the fight, the conquest, and domination. He needs the strength that comes with the night, and he needs to be a Prime. Perhaps even a mortal woman would be able to bring him through this. One who understands the risks—"

"Not just any mortal woman will do."

There was a long and pregnant silence from Serisa before she said, "Damn. His timing is shit."

"So I have informed him, my love."

"Then we should bring her to him."

"No!" Alec cut into the conversation. His mouth throbbed. He had to talk around the aching fangs that had drawn down to graze his lower lip. "She's too gifted. Too fragile. I will protect her from myself." He glared at Serisa, though his eyes felt like burning coals. "I will protect her from you."

Serisa knelt on the floor in front of him and touched his shoulders lightly with her strong, long-fingered hands. Even though she was not of his Clan, even though she'd angered him, she was still a Matri. A Matri's touch brought reassurance. Her words were to be listened to.

"I admire your attitude, child." She brushed her fingers through his sweat-soaked hair. "I truly do. But you must understand what is happening to you. You've had a bad reaction to the first serum Dr. Casmerek formulated for you. The reaction is causing your body to go through an experience you've been through once before. One you don't consciously remember."

Her hand moved from his shoulder down to his groin. Agony speared through him from the spot where she touched. He was hard as a rock, and hadn't even realized it.

"Puberty is not fun for our kind," she said. "The transition from adolescent to Prime or to mature female is excruciating. It is the feral time. We forget it, can blank out the anguish when we're young. Unfortunately right now you are a Prime, fully aware of what you are going through."

"Fortunately," Barak added, "you can fight the need."

Serisa gave Barak an annoyed look. "I don't see why he should have to."

"Because he wants to," the elder answered his bondmate. "My duty is to help him control his feral urges."

"My duty is to keep him from suffering. I will not see him

scarred because he is at war with himself. The drugs that let him function in the light are his enemy today. A defender of the children of the sisters deserves all the help we can give him."

"Then take me to the clinic," Alec broke in. "Get me to Casmerek."

The older couple exchanged a look.

"What is it?" Alec asked. "What's wrong?"

"The clinic is closed for the day," Serisa answered. "All outpatient appointments are canceled. All vampires on staff who aren't part of the security team have to stay away."

"There might be a security problem," Barak explained.

"Nothing is known for sure yet," Serisa said. "But the clinic's staff is very cautious."

Alec leapt on this information. Security was something he understood, something he could focus on. Besides, he knew. "The place is being watched. I felt it the last time I was there."

Through the haze of pain caused by the room's dim light, Alec saw the older vampires exchange a worried, skeptical glance. They thought he was hallucinating, didn't they? Anger spiked through him.

It made the claws spring from his fingertips, and he let out a furious hiss as he scraped deep gouges in the floor on either side of where he knelt. Glancing down, Alec saw that these were not the first marks he'd left in the brightly polished hardwood floor. The incongruous thought that his landlord was going to have his hide for this damage flashed through Alec's aching head, and he almost smiled.

Alec forced his attention back to the clinic. He needed something he could concentrate on besides the pain. Besides Domini.

"Hunters," he said. "The clinic's being watched by hunters."

"We have a truce with the hunters here in California," Barak said.

"Unofficial, of course," Serisa added. "We haven't bothered them, and they haven't bothered us, for several years. It could be a bloodbath for their people and ours if they stepped over the line after so much time."

"Who else is a threat to us?" Alec asked. "The Families are neutral. The Tribes don't approve of the medical research done for the Clans, but they're too pragmatic to risk endangering a resource they might need. Only hunters hate us."

"It's not as bad as the old days," Barak said. "They understand now that not all vampires are the enemies of mortal kind."

"Not all of them," Serisa said bitterly. "Are you forgetting we lost a son to their worst fanatics? The ones that call themselves Purists?"

"I will never forget losing Joshua," Barak told his bondmate. "I can still hear him screaming as he burned, and the later screams of the Purists when I tracked them down. They paid. I won't hate all vampire hunters because of them. I will avoid them if I can, fight them if I have to. But not kill them, even the Purists. You know that."

Serisa nodded. Then she spoke to Alec again. "We keep track of the local hunters, as they try to keep track of us. If they're watching the clinic for some reason, we'll find out about it. And take care of it." She took Alec's face between her hands. "Right now, let's concentrate on taking care of you. Barak, bring Alexander's medicine case and the dosage instructions. It's not the medicines that have messed him up, but the serum. I still think he needs several nights of tempestuous sex, but if he won't, he won't."

"You don't have to talk like I'm not here."

She patted Alec's cheek and smiled. "Petulant. Good. That's better than vicious. And you're alert enough to worry about the clinic and not just your own needs. Between meditation and the drugs, we're bound to make it better."

Alec made himself believe her. He had no choice.

"Let's get started," he said. "I have to be at work at seven."

Chapter Eighteen

"Well, don't you look like death warmed over, Mr. Reynard?" Domini said when Reynard sauntered across the crowded parking lot behind the club.

The lights mounted on tall poles at each corner of the lot were bright and white, causing Reynard's long, lean shadow to spear out behind him. Had he lost weight overnight? He certainly looked lean and mean in the tight jeans and body-hugging black T-shirt, but there was a hollowness to his already austere features. She thought he looked tired under the swagger. Seeing him put her on edge. Worse, it made her worry about him. The dichotomy was so disturbing, she couldn't help her tart comment.

His reply was equally snide as he reached the black SUV parked next to the rear entrance. "Thank you for your concern, Ms. Lancer."

On closer inspection, she added, "You're looking extremely pale and pasty as well."

"The lights do nothing for my complexion," Reynard said as he joined her in leaning against the hood.

Large men in shirts with SECURITY stenciled front and back patrolled a perimeter between the fans and the Lincoln Navigator parked next to the rear entrance. The Lancer team was spaced around the SUV. Domini and Reynard faced the growing crowd while they talked to each other.

"And you're wearing sunglasses at night again. Why is that?"

"Trying to fit in with the milieu."

"I don't see anyone else in sunglasses."

"It's the best I can do to appear cool, as I have no interest in body piercings or full-body tattoos. This place look like the set of *The Fast and the Furious* to you?"

She swept a look around the lot. "No rice rockets. More girls."

"I suppose."

Alec wondered if his effort to sound laconic was working. Domini had sniped at him the moment she saw him. He sniped back. Vampire courtship. Snapping and snarling could come next. And after that . . .

This exchange could prove dangerous.

Duty. Discipline. Responsibility. He lived by these standards, but right now, his insistence on fulfilling his obligations as Prime and Lancer operative was maybe not the best idea he'd ever had. Help from the elders and pure stubbornness had gotten him here. But now that he was here, he was having trouble looking Domini in the face. His feral imagination had gone into overload today, and the harsh fantasy images he'd conjured not only haunted him, they embarrassed him.

But he couldn't bear not to be with her. It was ridiculous, since his head told him she'd be safer with him elsewhere, but he kept returning to her side.

Did she really need protecting from anyone but him? Was he imagining a threat to her to legitimize being near her?

Domini had hoped Reynard wouldn't show. Was her belief that he was hiding his true nature and intentions her way of denying . . . what? Desire? Fear of losing control? Fear of losing herself in the throes of passion?

She scoffed at such an old-fashioned notion. Who said passion required loss of control, of self?

Holly. And not just in her songs; Holly lived with total commitment to her emotions. Domini had watched her fall in and out of love with complete abandon and frequent heartbreak ever since they'd hit puberty. Domini had helped pick up the pieces plenty of times, and it was never pretty. Crazy thing was, Holly never gave up on falling in love.

Lust, passion, and desire were not safe, and they didn't make for sane behavior. Domini had enough trouble with staying sane on a normal day-to-day basis. Add passion to the mix, and—

"Our principal's still in the car," Reynard said, jolting Domini out of her reverie. He checked his watch. "Why?"

"On the phone," Domini answered. "She wanted privacy for the call."

Holly was talking with Jo. Domini shook her head. Talk about not giving up on love. If the media got hold of this—

"Isn't Ashe supposed to be onstage in a few minutes?"

Domini noticed the members of Holly's entourage pacing restlessly on the other side of the SUV. Her road manager looked very unhappy.

Domini shrugged. "We go into the club when Holly wants to."

She wasn't going to complain about a client's screwing up a schedule. That was Andy's job, if he thought the delay posed a security threat. She did notice a pair of the club's bouncers glaring at them from their post by the rear entrance. She offered another shrug to the beefy bouncers, then her attention returned to Reynard.

"Can I ask you a question?"

He crossed his arms. They were long and sinewy, and the stance emphasized the width of his shoulders. She was used to hard-bodied, hard-edged men, but none so impressive as this one.

"You can ask."

Domini took a quick breath and blurted out, "Do you believe in vampires?" She didn't think it was a stupid question to ask. She thought it was a dangerous one.

It got her a sardonic look over the top of his sunglasses. His eyes were very bloodshot. "You mean, like do I believe in things like tooth fairies and Bigfoot?"

"Do you?"

"I absolutely do not believe in Bigfoot."

She noted that he hadn't answered the question. He moved closer to her, with uncanny speed that no longer surprised her. He was no more than an inch away from her when he spoke. "How about you? What do you believe in?"

"I absolutely do not believe in tooth fairies."

"Vampires do," he said. "They go through two sets of baby teeth, so they really clean up on the money-under-the-pillow thing. In fact, many vampire college funds are started with tooth-fairy money."

His facetiousness amused her against her will. Added to his looks and the sizzle of strong sex appeal, the combination was frighteningly potent.

"Do you believe in vampires?" he asked her.

"I used to dream about vampires when I was a kid," she admitted. "I've been dreaming about them again the last couple of days. Ever since I met you."

Domini couldn't tell how Reynard took what she said, not with his green eyes hidden by sunglasses and the angular structure of his face bleached out and oddly shadowed by the bright white light overhead. He *looked* like a vampire, damn it! Not that he could be; the dream images were only her subconscious's way of warning her of—

He brushed his fingers along her cheek and throat, not quite touching, yet still sending hot and cold shivers through her. "You're afraid I'm going to possess you, is that it? That I'm going to suck the life out of you?" His voice was low, and very angry.

Domini took a step sideways. He turned, watching her, but giving her distance. She crossed her arms. "Something like that."

He stepped back. His voice was angry ice. "I am so flattered."

Domini turned her back to Reynard and made a survey of the area. The crowd of fans surrounded the building and spilled up the block in both directions, but this early in the evening they were pretty well behaved. The tricky part would be getting Holly out of the club later, not taking her inside.

She felt Reynard's gaze on her, and looked over her shoulder. "What are you looking at, Mr. Reynard?"

He quirked an eyebrow and looked down over the top of his sunglasses. "Ms. Lancer, I can't help but notice that you have a buzzard on your butt."

Domini was wearing a short skirt that rode low on her hips, and no doubt a bit of the tattoo at the base of her spine was showing. She brushed a hand across the small of her back. "It's a condor."

"Interesting," Reynard murmured. "Do you have something similar on the front?"

"You'll never know, Mr. Reynard."

He moved up behind her so close that she could feel the heat of his skin. "Really?" he murmured, lips close to her ear. "I don't think you want to bet on that."

Domini shivered. No. She didn't.

Andy Maxwell came around the front of the SUV, and he was not looking happy.

"What?" Domini asked.

"You recommended the club hire extra security from Tanner for the evening, right?" She nodded. "Those people walking the security line and the extra bouncers aren't from Tanner. The club management contracted with Dennis Weader instead."

"Damn."

"Problem?" Reynard asked.

"Could be extra work for us," Andy told Reynard. "Weader the Weasel doesn't run the most professional security firm in town."

Domini snorted. "He hires itinerant steroid-abusing bodybuilders and the occasional ex-con," she elucidated. "He's not particular about checking references." She gave Reynard a hard look, but he didn't react to her implication.

Holly emerged from the back of the SUV just then, and Domini was relieved to get the show on the road.

"You going to ask me how my romantic life's going?" Holly asked as Domini fell in beside her.

"You're grinning like an idiot. I don't need to ask."

Domini linked arms with Holly, making sure her friend was between her and the back wall of the building. Andy was in front, with Reynard taking the rear. They set a brisk pace. Holly's posse was already filing through the rear door.

Holly swiveled her head to give Reynard a look. "How's things going with Mr. T.?"

"It's only a few feet to the door. We'll talk later."

"You're no fun."

Blatantly listening, Alec said, "That's what I've been telling her."

He appreciated Holly's chuckle and Domini's dirty look, but his attention was drawn to the bouncers on either side of the door. He slipped the dark glasses off to get a better look. Ashe's people obscured his view, but he got a better look as Domini and Holly reached the entrance. The bouncers turned toward them to shield the women further. The one nearest Domini looked at her intently. There was something familiar about the man's profile . . .

The guards who'd flanked the old woman in last night's crowd! He would have seen it sooner if he'd been on top of his game.

Domini caught a glitter from the corner of her eye, and she saw the knife in the door guard's hand when she glanced sideways. She immediately gave Holly a quick, hard shove into the building.

The man lunged at Domini before she could step inside. At her—not Holly. The realization shocked her, but training made her instinctively block the blow and spin out of the line of attack. But there were too many people around them, pressing in on all sides. Caught in the bottleneck around the entrance, she stumbled into someone.

The impact bounced her back toward her attacker, who slashed again. There was nowhere for her to go, and this time the knife grazed her arm. Blood arced out on her hiss of pain.

Someone shouted. Someone else screamed. Bodies bunched

up and milled around Domini. She lost sight of her attacker, then he pushed the person between them aside and was on her again. As she blocked another blow, she saw his eyes blazing with fanatical hatred.

"Abomination!"

Alec heard the attacker snarl the ugly word through the cries and shouts as he tossed a dozen people aside to get to Domini. He smelled the scent of her blood—if she had more than a scratch on her, the bastard was dead. No. The bastard *was* dead, period.

The blade was flashing down a third time as Alec finally reached Domini. He pushed her aside and grabbed the attacker's wrist. The man screamed as the bones were crushed, and the knife dropped from his lifeless fingers. Alec considered using it, but rejected it in favor of using his bare hands.

He pushed the man to the ground and dropped down beside him. Alec pressed a thumb into the man's broken wrist, and took great satisfaction at hearing the bastard howl.

"What's going on? Where's Domini?" a voice said.

Alec swore under his breath and looked up to find Maxwell looming over him.

Where *was* she?

He made sure the attacker was unconscious before he sprang up and looked around. Shadows and light played havoc against his aching eyes. People were getting to their feet, pressing forward. The one person he needed was nowhere in sight. Noise and waves of too many strangers' emotions pressed against Alec's strung-out senses.

He turned around in a blur. "Domini!"

And saw her, a crumpled heap in the shadows against the wall. Where he'd pushed her.

He was there instantly. "Domini?"

Maxwell followed. He reached them as Alec gently turned her over. "Is she okay?"

Alec sighed with relief as he felt the life rushing warm

through her veins. He ran his hands over her, through her hair. "A bump on her head," he told Maxwell. "No broken bones." The cut had already stopped bleeding, and Alec gathered her close in his arms.

Maxwell knelt beside them. "Ashe is safe inside. What happened here? How many were there?" He glanced back toward the parking lot. "We've got a lot of bruised people calling 911 on their cell phones."

Alec frowned, knowing that the police and EMTs would be arriving any minute. That was not the way he wanted this played. He looked at Andy Maxwell, eye to eye. After a few moments Maxwell's pupils dilated, his expression went lax. "Go inside," Alec ordered. "Look after Ashe. I'll take care of the situation out here. Go," he ordered.

Maxwell rose to his feet. "Take good care of Domini," he said, and did as Alec said.

"I will."

But first, he set her gently down and returned to the attacker. He extended a claw and slashed it down the man's forearm. As blood flowed, Alec bent forward and took a long, deep breath. The man stirred, then opened his eyes. Alec looked into them, saw the dawning recognition, and the fear.

"I have your scent now," he told the man. "And you the mark of prey. We'll play later."

He heard police sirens approaching, so he backed away, scooped Domini's limp body into his arms, and disappeared through the crowd.

Chapter Nineteen

Far in the distance, Domini heard a telephone ringing. It rang and it rang, and she really wished it would stop, because it made the aching in her head worse.

Miraculously, her wish was granted. But then the ringing was replaced with the sound of a voice. She didn't recognize the voice, but it was familiar, and curiosity made her want to listen. Wanting to listen made her want to wake up, but she figured that would only make her head hurt more. Besides, being awake meant thinking. Nameless fears and dark memories floated in the back of her mind, and she preferred they stay there. If she woke up she'd have to face them.

Though reality phased in and out, the voice went on, and she couldn't help but strain to hear.

"Yes?" Alec's voice was rough, and he was feeling rougher when he grabbed the telephone receiver. He'd been scrambling through the medicine case open on the kitchen table when he couldn't take the annoyance of the ringing phone any longer. "Who and what?"

"Anthony Crowe," came the answer. "We have Purists in town."

"Tell me about it."

"They tried to break into the clinic. I don't want anyone anywhere near the place until I personally give the all-clear."

Alec recalled that Tony Crowe provided security for the clinic. Crowe also had taken his sarcastic comment literally. "I know about the Purists. We had a run-in with one a couple of hours ago."

"We?"

"He attacked my woman. Not *me,* but my woman. I didn't nail him, but I can track him," he told the local Prime. "You have a problem with that, Tony?"

"I'm not territorial, and no other Prime or the Matri's Consort will object to your protecting your woman. I'll spread the word for you."

"Good. Thanks."

"Wait," Crowe said, and paused a moment. "You're with a mortal, right? I remember her."

Alec fought down a growl at the interest in the other Prime's voice. "We've had that discussion."

Crowe laughed. "Nothing like the jealousy of a bonding Prime. As to your lady, why would the Purists—?"

"I have no idea." After a thoughtful pause, Alec said, "Maybe you can help. You're the private dick."

"I've been known to be public about it. But I was young and blood-drunk at the time. Have you asked her why she was their target?"

"Not yet; she's unconscious. She knows nothing about us. Or them. I'm sure of that. But they have something against her. Can you look into it? Just in case I don't get a chance to ask when I track down the one who bled her."

Vampires took a fatally dim view of anyone causing their loved ones blood loss. Blood was sacred, the blood of a lover a sacrament. And blood paid with blood. The mortal vampire hunters were well aware of vampire beliefs and taboos. They desecrated these beliefs with hatred and contempt whenever they got the chance.

"I'll see what I can do," Crowe answered. "In fact—"

"What?"

"Never mind. I just recalled something. It's probably not anything, so I'm not saying until I check it out. But why don't you ask your lady if the word *blackbird* has any meaning for her? I'll be in touch."

Though she lay on the couch in the living room, Alec became aware of a slight change in Domini's breathing, of her consciousness focusing. She'd been drifting in and out of wakefulness for a while, he realized, but awareness of her state had only grown gradually in him.

"Fine," he answered impatiently. "Thanks, Tony."

Alec put down the handset, gulped down a quick selection of pills, and hurried toward the living room.

"Well, don't you look like death warmed over, Ms. Lancer?"

Domini sat up slowly, then gingerly lifted her aching head to discover Reynard leaning against a doorframe, arms crossed over his chest. The room was lit only by a few pillar candles on several tables. Reynard was wearing a white Oxford shirt tucked into dark slacks, with the sleeves rolled up over his forearms. The expression on his face was concerned.

"Why am I at your place?"

"You weren't injured badly enough to take to the emergency room." His nonchalance was grating. He sauntered into the room and took a seat beside her. Very close beside her.

Domini slowly turned her head enough to look at him. He brushed his thumb across her forehead. She was caught between the urges to lean forward and back away. She wasn't sure whether accepting or rejecting the comforting warmth of his touch would be cowardly. Getting up would probably make her dizzy, if being so near Reynard didn't do it to her first. She felt grungy and rumpled, and resented that he'd been able to shower and change while she'd been out. Well, at least they both didn't smell like the grimy residue of a back alley.

Alley? No, not quite. They'd been in back of—

"How's your head?"

"Aching." She automatically touched the small bump just above her left temple. "What hit me?"

"A wall."

"A whole wall for one little lump?"

"I put ice on the lump," he told her.

She didn't even have the strength to stiffen in alarm when he put his arm around her. She didn't go so far as to rest her weary head on Reynard's shoulder, but she did lean it on the long, strong arm across the back of the couch. She closed her eyes, breathed in clean masculine scent, and tried to piece together the events that had brought them to this spot. She supposed that she must have been struck, but—

"Do you have any memory at all of what happened?"

She kept her eyes closed and murmured, "I'm thinking about it."

"Want me to fill you in?"

"I hope it doesn't come to that."

"You're not feebleminded."

"But feeling pretty feeble at the moment."

She felt the soft chuckle ripple through him all along her side. It was pleasant to be so close to him. She didn't know how she could be so suspicious of this man, yet so comfortable with him sometimes. Why did being so close to Reynard come so easily; why did wanting him bubble just under the surface? Probably because she'd been knocked on the head. People with head injuries were not responsible for—

"How's your arm?"

"My arm?"

"You were scratched."

"Oh. That explains why it stings. Didn't notice until you mentioned it. It's not important."

"Really?"

She didn't mistake the dangerous edge to his tone, but she was distracted by another thought. There was something important she was missing. Some responsibility. What responsibility was she forgetting?

"Holly!" She sat up straight as alarm bolted through her. "Good God, where's Holly?"

He glanced at a wall clock. "Probably offstage by now. Though I believe her sets can go on for several hours if the mood takes her."

"You mean—she's at the club? But she was—" Memory flooded back. She jumped to her feet, ignoring the momentary dizziness. "Attacked. There was a man with a knife. I didn't—"

"Holly wasn't attacked. You were."

"—protect her," Domini finished over his words.

She rubbed her hands nervously across her face while her stomach tied itself up in aching knots. She was an idiot. A fool. A complete fuckup.

His hands landed and locked on her shoulders, and he pulled her to him. She looked up to meet furious green eyes.

"Shit happens!" Reynard exploded. "If there's one thing I learned in the army, it's that no matter how hard you plan and prepare, sometimes the op gets blown to hell. You were set up, Domini, ambushed. People you thought you could trust turned on you. You couldn't see it coming. None of us saw it coming. You did nothing wrong. When you saw the knife, you got Ashe out of danger. You put her inside the building, well out of harm's way. It was *you* the bastard went after. You. Do you even know why?"

Domini was acutely aware of being held in a steel grip, of the fact that they were standing so very close together. She was even more aware of the strong emotion that sang through him, into her. The air thrummed around them, grew heated.

She blinked and found her voice through the crackle of tension. "I really wish you'd stop moving at the speed of light," she told him. "It's disconcerting."

He drew her even closer. She could swear she saw fire dancing in those hypnotic green eyes. "You want disconcerting?" He kissed her.

It was a big mistake. A terrible mistake. And Alec reveled in it.

Bad idea, Domini thought. Very bad idea. Her arms came around him. Her mouth opened beneath his. *Very good kiss.*

His hands moved over her. Hard warrior's hands, but his touch was almost tentative, in exciting contrast to his harsh, hungry kiss. Reynard touched her as though she were fragile, some precious creature made of glass. It only made her want more.

Tentative or not, those hands were quick and clever. Her short little skirt was pooled around her feet within moments. She laughed against his mouth, and felt it send a shiver through him.

His hands skimmed up her hips, up her back, and under the thin knit top she was wearing. *The man has practice in unhooking bras.*

He cupped her breasts, then his head moved down to cover a nipple.

Practice in touching. Practice in tasting.

Her back arched as she let out a sharp gasp, and she barely noticed when he drew them both down to their knees. The wood floor was smooth and cool. She was melting. It was like nothing she'd ever expected.

He caught her surprise and wonder, caught the thought that she'd never expected to be so aroused. He was not her first lover, but the first who sparked passion. It was a sweet thing to his pride, and it also hurt him to learn that she'd been so disappointed before.

"Never again." He whispered the words against her breast, too low for her to hear. It was hard for him to keep from taking everything he wanted, to keep the possessive animal at bay.

He loved the way her body felt, velvet skin curving over firm muscle. He stroked her—oh, so carefully—holding back. Holding on.

"This isn't safe," he told her when his mouth came back to hers.

"No," she whispered. "But it's helping the headache."

"I won't hurt you." The words were intense, like a vow.

He tried to pull back, but she held on tight. She saw concern cross his face, so fierce it looked like pain, but she wasn't about to let him get away. She wasn't going to let this stop.

She grabbed Reynard's shirtfront and pulled. Buttons popped. Once his chest was bare, she moved to kiss his throat, then farther down. While his hands fisted at his sides, her fingers kneaded his shoulders and long lean back, smoothed down to his narrow waist. His scent was pure erotic perfume, sharp and clean and—

And she was suddenly aware of her own sweat, and the grit of dirt on her skin and in her hair. "I'm filthy. How can you stand me?"

His eyes were half closed, and gleamed like a cat's. Candlelight suited him, the shadows softening the stark lines of his face. But nothing softened the coiled tension in him; the shadows only seemed to bring that out more.

While he knelt there watching her with those burning cat's eyes, Domini rose to her feet and pulled her shirt and bra over her head. She'd never known such power, knowing that he couldn't take his eyes off her, that she was making him sweat, making him hard. She couldn't take her eyes off him, either. She could barely breathe for wanting him. Lust sang through her, heat rose in her, and she couldn't help but run her hands down her body, reveling in her own desire.

She remembered the dark dreams she'd had recently, how all the images of monsters had tangled up her thinking about the real man, in her fears about bad sex. She threw back her head and laughed at such foolishness.

Domini stepped back and held out her hands. "Come on, I won't hurt you," she said. "Where's your shower?"

It wasn't just a shower, it was a perfect-for-sex shower, a double-sized cubicle with a seat and mirror tiles and lots of water nozzles set to spray in all directions. He hadn't let her turn on the lights, but there were candles in the bathroom, too. The reflection of their lights glowed on the tiles like stars through mist. By the time he was naked, steam was rising from the water jets and he followed her inside. The shower gel she cupped in her hands was scented with juniper. It glided smoothly over both their skins.

Skin slick with water and fragrant soap, Domini wrapped herself around him, immediately guided him inside her, and exploded with her first orgasm, too consumed with need to want anything but more.

She could eat him alive and still not have enough.

Alec moaned as she closed in around him, a hot, tight, sweet, engulfing pressure. The force of sensation when he entered Domini set him reeling. Her orgasm slammed into his senses, lightning-swift and hot. He collapsed, falling back onto the shower bench, bringing her with him. Streams of hot water pulsed against his skin, flowed over them. The pleasure was almost painful, the desire almost too consuming. She rode him in a white-hot frenzy.

Alec held on to her and let it happen. He couldn't take control. He couldn't lose control. He buried his face between her breasts and rolled with the thundering rhythm of her heartbeat. The blood surged powerfully beneath her skin, hot wine spiced with sex. Alec craved and craved and fought the craving.

No teeth! No teeth! No teeth!

The mantra was accompanied by a pulsing ache where fangs tried to extend into his mouth. He tasted blood on his tongue, but it was his own. He wanted to howl like a maddened wolf, but only panting moans of pleasure escaped him. The woman pounded against him, driving him deeper and deeper into her, wild, relentless. Her orgasms shot through him like bullets, only making matters worse, better, totally beyond bearing.

After an endless glorious time, Alec couldn't take it anymore. He grabbed Domini around the waist and tumbled them out of the shower. They fell, soaking wet, onto the cool tiles of the bathroom floor. He rose above her and moved into her in swift, hard strokes that quickly brought them up, up, and explosively over the edge.

For a long moment, Alec went white blind with the blended

sensations. Then the world went dark, and after a moment's panic he realized his eyes were closed.

"It's all right," he rasped, stroking the drowsy Domini's wet hair. "Everything's all right."

She stirred a little, caressed his cheek, and gave a long, satisfied sigh. "Everything's fine," she agreed drowsily.

Alec reached into the shower to turn off the water. Then he helped her to sit up and grabbed towels. When they were reasonably dry, he hauled her over his shoulder and carried her into the bedroom. She made no protest when he laid her on the bed and fell in beside her. She might have been asleep before she hit the mattress. Just as he was, a second later.

Chapter Twenty

Alec felt much better, even though he hadn't slept for long. So good that he wanted to howl in triumph at the moon, to mark a notch in the bedpost with a claw, to laugh, and to cry out—and to sleep. Deep, dreamless, restful sleep called to him. He hadn't felt so good in weeks. Some of the tension was drained from him, some of the pain. Even some of the fear of madness had eased, from having kept the animal side of his nature at bay for now.

Maybe Serisa had been right. He desperately needed physical release. He desperately needed Domini, and he had managed, at least this once, to make love in the mortal way. He still wanted, craved, the sharing of blood, the mating of mind, soul, and flesh—but if he let himself go now, the dream images would turn to ugly reality. He sighed.

When he did, Domini shifted position. Her hair brushed across his chest, tracing a line of pleasure across his sensitized skin. He reacted with a gasp, and a deep chuckle.

She was nearly asleep, but she stirred at the sound. "Did I tickle you?"

It was something like a tickle, he supposed, though he wasn't sure exactly what being tickled felt like. He longed to explain how his kind experienced sensation differently than their mortal cousins, more intensely. But he couldn't explain with words; he could only explain by taking her there. A normal mortal could not share the intensity, but a bondmate was no normal mortal.

"You could call it ticklish," he told her.

"So now I know one of your secrets," she murmured, and settled back to dozing.

And I know none of yours. For it occurred to him that Domini did indeed have secrets, at least one, and it was deathly dangerous.

It was a secret he needed to know if he was going to protect her. Going into her mind to find out what he needed would be the easy way, especially in her relaxed state. Easy, but not ethical. He'd invaded her mind once already, out of desperation and the need to protect her, and he knew damn well that doing so had been wrong, even though it had seemed like a good idea at the time.

What did he know about Domini Lancer? He held her close. He knew that she could see the future in fits and starts, but she thought that was all she could do. She worked hard, lived alone, had a soft spot for wild animals like condors and coyotes that many others thought of as scavengers and pests. She loved her grandfather and had at least one good friend. She had magnificent breasts, he added as she shifted against him again. And she smelled great.

Alec determinedly turned away from thinking about Domini's physical attributes. "You awake?" he asked.

"No," she answered.

"Talk to me," he urged. "Tell me about yourself."

He felt her float a little closer to full consciousness. He liked the way she felt, drifting like that, her thoughts as well as her body at rest. It soothed his own tense spirit.

"Tell me about your family," he suggested. "Brothers? Sisters? Parents?"

"No. No. Dead."

She didn't feel so relaxed now. Pain welled up from under the satiated contentment, like a little rift of lava finding the surface of the earth.

"How did your parents die?"

Domini stiffened beside him. She took a tight breath and said, "Five-car pile-up on the freeway. They weren't the only ones who didn't walk away."

"Were you with them when—"

"No." Definitive. Angry. "I didn't see it coming, either. I was surfing when my parents died. Having a good time when I should have—"

"Psychics frequently never see anything really important about their own futures," he said. "It's a defense mechanism; it helps to keep you sane. If you know the hard stuff that's coming, you're more likely to freeze than try to avoid it."

"Bullshit." She freed herself from his arms, sat up, and turned to look at him.

"It's a gift, Domini."

"Curse. It's getting worse all the time. And what the hell do you know about being psychic?"

He sat up and propped his hands behind his head as he leaned against the headboard, to keep from grabbing her. She had no idea how arousing she was, naked and burning with anger. "I'm psychic," he said. "In a different way than you are, but I'm the last one who'd call you crazy."

"That's not reassuring, Reynard."

Her reaction sparked answering anger in him. He grabbed Domini, using the swiftness she found so disconcerting, and pulled her close. "Suddenly we aren't friends anymore?" His voice was a low whisper brushing across her lips.

She grew hot with fury, and he grew hard against her.

"We aren't—"

He had her beneath him in an instant. Within seconds, he proved to her that they were more than friends. He made love to her swift and hard, and it burned off the anger in both of them, turning it into quick, satisfying lust. She writhed eagerly beneath him, rose to meet him, and they came together in the same explosive instant.

Alec lay, stunned, on top of Domini for a long time. Slowly he became aware of her fingers brushing tenderly up and down his back, and through his hair. He didn't think she was mad at him anymore.

He didn't blame her for the anger, not when he'd stirred up an old, deep pain.

Alec finally rolled off Domini and off the bed. He put on the clothes he'd stripped off earlier, then pulled a long shirt out of a drawer and draped it over Domini's naked belly.

"I see that you only have the one tattoo."

"Uh-huh." She lifted her head a little from where she lay delightfully spread-eagled on the mattress. She touched the shirt. "What's this for?"

Alec looked down at her hungrily. "While I appreciate the view, it's far too tempting to see you like that. Get dressed; we need to talk."

"Don't want to talk." She held a hand up, languid as a cat. "I want to—" She sighed. "Sleep, if nothing else. Too tired to—"

He took her wrist and pulled her to her feet. He drew her close for one hard, possessive kiss. When he stopped kissing her, Domini collapsed against him, her head on his shoulder.

"That was supposed to stimulate you."

"You've stimulated me enough for one night."

He rubbed a hand up and down her back and cupped her behind. Then he moved away from her before an erection could take his mind off of anything but having her again.

"If you won't let me go to sleep, can I at least sit down?"

"Fine." Alec eased her down on the edge of the bed, then made himself take a seat in the chair. Touching her would not help him stay clear-headed.

"How's your head feel?"

Domini was confused. Muscles in areas she hadn't used for a while were strained and aching, but not in a bad way. The man was hung like the proverbial horse. It occurred to her that she hadn't checked the number of testicles he sported when she had the chance. Holly would be disappointed in her lack of observational skills.

"Holly," she muttered, putting a hand to her forehead. "Now I remember why I had a headache."

"Had," Reynard repeated. "Good. It's gone."

"I'm a fast healer." She glanced toward a clock on the bedside table. "Is that A.M. or P.M.?"

"A.M."

"Damn." She gave him an annoyed look. "Reynard, do you always stay up all night?"

"Frequently. Why did someone try to kill you?" He stabbed a finger at her. "Don't try to pretend he was after Holly; Holly was the decoy used to find you. How? Why?"

"I figured that out."

Alec sat back in the chair, crossed his arms, and stretched out his long legs. Domini noted that some of the candles that lit the room had burned out. She was rather glad of the semi-darkness; the candlelight lent an intimacy to the scene that made it easier for her to confide in him.

"I went through all the letters the stalkers sent her again," she told him. "This time I focused on the number of times the word *abomination* was used. It only appeared twice, both times in reference to Holly's childhood. *Abomination from birth* was one term. *Abomination's child* was also used. The first time I read the letters, everything seemed like the ramblings of a vicious, deranged mind. Coming at it from a fresh angle, it occurred to me that maybe, just maybe, they weren't talking about Holly, but about someone she's known all her life." Domini twisted her hands tightly together. "Me."

"But you didn't really believe it until someone came at you with a knife."

"I didn't really believe it even then," she admitted. "That's why I didn't react fast enough. It shocked the hell out of me, and I froze."

"Because you can't think of any reason why anyone would attack you?"

She nodded. "Or why anyone would set up an elaborate smokescreen to get at me. If someone wants to harm me—"

"Kill you."

She acknowledged the brutal truth with a nod, even as a cold shiver went through her. "I'm easy enough to find," she finished. "Why go to all this trouble? How'd they connect me to Holly? No, wait." She lifted a finger. "I think I know that one."

He tilted his head sideways. "Really?"

"An unauthorized biography of Holly was published recently. I'm mentioned in it."

"Any photos?"

Domini thought this a strange question, but nodded. "I'm in a couple of photos a high-school classmate sold to the sleaze who wrote the book. But why would anyone come after me because of pictures from when we were teenagers?"

He shrugged. "I don't know. Just throwing out questions. There are people in this world who take great pains to stay in the shadows. This sort of cloak-and-dagger plot is their style."

She gave him a hard look. "So speaks the black-ops operative?"

He nodded. "Does the word *blackbird* have meaning for you?"

"It was my grandmother's nickname." A knot fisted in her stomach. "Why?"

"I have no idea. But a private investigator I asked to look into this asked me to ask you."

"Why would he—?"

"I don't know. I'll be sure to ask him when he checks in."

Domini rose and began to pace the room. Fear raced through her. "Maybe this has something to do with my grandfather. Maybe they're trying to hurt him through me."

Alec felt her worry, and wished he'd never brought the subject up. He should have spent the night hunting down the one who'd attacked Domini, instead of making love to her.

Tomorrow, he thought. I'll find the bastard tomorrow night. Dawn wasn't far off and his eyes were beginning to ache, even though the sun hadn't yet inched over the horizon.

He rose from his seat and stepped in front of Domini, cutting off her restless pacing. He took her in his arms and looked into her eyes. "Don't worry. There's nothing we can do right now. Everyone's safe for now."

Domini nodded. Alec didn't like using the hypnotic tone on her, but she needed rest as much as he did. He turned her toward the bedroom, eased her down onto the bed, and slipped in beside her. He aroused her, then made love to her as the candles burned out one by one. By the time he could feel sunlight pressing against the thickly insulated bedroom curtains, Domini was sleeping peacefully in his arms.

With her beside him, despite the pain, Alec found peace enough to quiet the beast inside and to sleep himself.

Chapter Twenty-one

Domini woke up remembering that she'd had a dream where someone called her Blackbird, but she couldn't quite remember when. Not last night, she thought. Last night? What time was it now?

She opened her eyes and looked at the bedside clock. "Is that A.M. or P.M.?"

"P.M.," Reynard answered.

"Oh, my God!"

An arm like a steel bar came over her when she tried to sit up. The body beside her was firm, warm, and scented with sleep. The room was dark but not unfamiliar. The bed was comfortable, and she felt like she'd shared it with this man all her life.

It didn't surprise her that she'd slept through the day and into the night. With everything that had happened, she'd been totally wasted.

"How's your head?"

Domini thought about it for a minute. "Spinning."

"You're dizzy? Are you in pain?"

She smiled at the concern in Reynard's voice; it sent a pang of joy through her to know that he cared. Oh, dear.

"Confused," she answered. "Chagrined. No physical pain." She tried sitting up again, but his arm was immovable. "I ought to make some calls."

"Already made."

He smiled, which sent a flutter through her. She had to clear her throat before she said, "You talked to my grandfather? You told him what happened?"

His gaze darted away from hers. Was he blushing? "Not exactly," he replied. "I called the office, and got us both a sick day."

"Bought us some time," she said. "Before we get fired."

"You needed the rest."

"I needed the job." Wanted the job. Loved the job. Had believed she'd never break any of the company rules.

She needed to talk to her grandfather. What surprised her was that lust had so easily overridden her ethics. She'd never thought passion could catch her off guard like that. Now she had to face her grandfather's disappointment. Damn, she hated hurting the Old Man.

Had it been worth it? With a man she didn't know—but every couple started out strangers to each other, didn't they? A formal introduction wasn't needed before the primal mating urge took over and screwed up your life.

Well, she certainly knew Reynard in the biblical sense now. And the urge to continue knowing him wasn't nearly satisfied; the primal craving still burned in her. If she let it loose, they wouldn't get out of bed for a long time yet.

Domini sighed. The longer she put off facing Benjamin Lancer the worse it would be for both of them.

"Can I get out of bed now?"

Reynard sat up and leaned over her. There were dark circles under his eyes and his cheeks seemed a bit more hollow than usual, but he still looked gorgeous to her. He dipped his head to brush his lips over hers.

Domini fought the thrill that went through her. Losing the fight, she ran her hands through his hair and pulled him into a deeper kiss.

Domini closed her eyes and soared, but the niggling of her conscience kept her from completely losing herself. It made her turn her head away and relax the fists she'd pressed against his naked back. Even though she wasn't directly looking at Reynard, she was acutely aware of his disappointment. After a moment, he rolled to his side of the bed. She wanted to follow him, to reach out to him. To—

"Passion sucks," Domini muttered, and sat up.

She was on her back again in an instant. Reynard loomed over her out of the darkness, holding her down. The combination of anger and hurt in his eyes stunned her.

"It's all right to fall in love, Domini." The intensity in his soft whisper was more painful than a shout. "Most people want to fall in love."

Spoken by Reynard, the word sounded big, deep, complicated. It had never occurred to her that anyone would fall in love with her. She was barely coming to terms with the concept of lust, and here was Reynard using the big L word. Guys weren't supposed to be the first one to bring that up, were they? Was Reynard telling her she was in love with him? Was he in love with her?

People didn't fall in love in less than a week.

People fall in love in less than an instant. Some people fall in love before they even meet.

"I've been looking for you all my life," he said. "You've no idea how long that's been."

His words hit Domini with a double punch that sent her reeling. *He loves me. He's a telepath. He loves me. He's talking inside my head. He loves me. He can read my mind. Can you read my mind?*

Yes.

And he had for days; she realized that now. She'd heard him—talking inside her head. And she'd been answering. It had seemed so, so—natural.

He had told her he was psychic. It wasn't his fault she hadn't paid attention, hadn't asked the right questions. Any questions.

Yet his being in love with her was almost more frightening

than his being a telepath. No, not almost. She could get her mind around the concept of his having psychic talent. She didn't want him to be in love with her. Did she? Not that he'd actually told her he was in love with—

I'm in love with you.

She glared. "You're not going to make this easy, are you?"

"Love isn't easy." He gave a short, bitter laugh. "Even lust isn't easy, not when it's a consuming passion."

"Passion." She sighed. "Reynard, I'm not even used to the *idea* of passion. It's never happened to me before." With anyone else she would have been embarrassed to admit this, but she owed him the truth. Wanted to give him the truth. "I don't trust you," she pointed out. "I don't even know if I like you."

There was a menacing glitter in his green eyes when he said, "You don't have to like me. But do you love me?"

She was speechless, and afraid. His angular face was the only thing she could see in the dim room. His scent was on her skin, his taste in her mouth. The heat of his body covered hers, and his hands held her down. And her awareness went deeper than fear; it went into the core of her; it pounded through her heart, quickened her pulse, and heated her blood. Her body and her soul whispered that she *wanted, wanted, wanted* him and no other, and her mind was not involved in the equation.

He was a part of her. She couldn't imagine herself separate from this need. Was that love?

"I want to fuck your brains out," she finally answered. "Repeatedly. Is that a good enough answer for now?"

His expression turned bitter, but he said, "If that's all you can give me, I'll take it. For now."

Domini realized that they'd both used the word *now.* Which implied that they both assumed a future for them, a time together that stretched beyond last night, this bedroom, this moment.

"What am I getting myself into?"

"Life," he answered. "You haven't been living until now."

"Which implies I didn't exist before you came along and got into my pants?"

"Yes."

He didn't sound smug, or arrogant. He sounded sure.

Domini's heart gave a quick, hard lurch, then it melted. She should have been furious or insulted, but instead she—

"Damn it, Reynard, don't do that to me!"

"What?" He touched her cheek. He drew a finger down her throat and chest and came to rest over her heart, where he pressed gently. "Make you feel loved?"

She gulped in air. "Yeah—that."

He shook his head, and dark hair swirled around his sharp and shadowed face. "I can't help it."

Pleasure swept through her, as strong as the passion that drew her to him. The man made her feel, more than anyone ever had. "It's not the emotions that scare me," she confessed. "It's—there was this pattern to my life. Comfortable. Secure. Now I feel like there's this kaleidoscope under my feet—no set pattern, no—" She shook her head. "Can we stop talking about this now? I need to get up. Go to the bathroom, get dressed, check my voice mail. You know there's—"

"Life outside the bedroom," he finished for her. "Yes. And I could really use a shower."

She sniffed delicately. "You and me both."

He rose to his feet and held out a hand. "Care to join me?"

She laughed and shook her head. "We both know where that would lead." She waved toward the bathroom. "Go ahead." She switched on a bedside lamp and waited until Reynard went into the bathroom before she got up. This gave her the opportunity to study his truly fine backside, and to get out of bed without having him around to look at her. She didn't know why she was suddenly shy about being naked, but she was. She needed clothes on, so she could think about something besides sex. The same way Reynard had done last night, come to think of it.

Maybe they had some things in common, after all.

She pulled on the long T-shirt from the night before, then padded into the living room, flipping on light switches and lamps as she went. Candlelight might be very romantic, but it wasn't what she wanted right now.

In the living room, she gathered up her abandoned clothes and sat down on the couch. She extracted her cellular phone from the pocket of the miniskirt, flipped it open, and discovered the battery was dead. Domini swore. So much for checking her voice mail. Though she could probably find a phone in the kitchen. She vaguely recalled hearing Reynard talking to someone in there while she was lying in here, recovering from the incident outside the club. Or maybe she'd dreamed it.

"Incident?" She gave a faint, ironic laugh. Someone had come at her with a knife.

And Reynard had saved her, brought her to his home to recover. He had been looking out for her all along. He'd suspected someone was after her, had watched her house, and hired a detective.

She was touched by his concern. Annoyed by his intrusion and his assumption of command over her actions, but maybe that was a D-Boy's idea of a romantic gesture. He was used to being a protector, to being in control and taking independent action.

Maybe she should cut the guy some slack. He told her he loved her, and showed it by protecting her. How could she resent that? She had trouble trusting him—but wasn't that based on dreams, imagination, and a couple of weird visions? Were dreams and visions proof of anything? Other than that she'd been half-crazed with fear of having sex?

It was all *her,* wasn't it? Not him. He hadn't done anything that wasn't kind, caring—loving.

The realization brought a dreamy smile to her lips.

"He attacked my woman. Not me, but my woman. I didn't nail him, but I can track him. You have a problem with that, Tony?"

Domini sat up straight, the smile wiped off her face as the words bubbled up out of her memory. She'd been lying here, half in and half out of consciousness. Reynard was in the kitchen, and she'd overheard him talking to someone on the phone. The detective he'd hired?

"He called me his woman." She sighed, and for a moment the gooey pleasure of being claimed by him almost overwhelmed the memory of the other things he'd said.

He'd called the man Tony. Tony was the detective. Tony had told him to ask her about Blackbird.

She'd had a dream where a man named Tony called her Blackbird. A very vivid dream with vampires in it.

Domini got up and headed into the kitchen. She hoped Reynard kept Pop Tarts or at least frozen bagels around, because if he expected "his woman" to go all domesticated on him, he had disappointment in his future.

When she turned on the overhead lights, the first thing she saw was the metal briefcase lying open on the kitchen table. The case was full of pill bottles.

"Drugs," she said, moving to the table to take a closer look. Was Reynard on drugs? Was he dealing drugs? Why *had* Colonel Reynard left the army? She picked up a round bottle that contained large, clear capsules. Turning it in her hand, Domini saw the prescription label. She didn't recognize the name of the drug, but Alexander Reynard's name was on the label, and a doctor's name was also listed, along with the dosage.

Her heart rose and sank almost at the same time. She was relieved that whatever Reynard was taking was legally prescribed by a physician, but she was concerned that he needed to take medicine. Almost panicked that he needed so many different medicines.

What kind of illness required this much treatment?

There was only one she could think of. She wanted to reject it, but the word AIDS rose in her mind. It left her shaking, with fear, with anger, and compassion. Was Reynard HIV-positive? Was the virus in his blood? Was that the true symbolism of her blood-drenched visions?

Had he had unprotected sex with her and not told her?

Domini shook her head fiercely. No. She couldn't believe that of him. Something else had to be wrong with him. He *couldn't* have some fatal disease; she couldn't bear it. Not when she'd just found him.

What could be wrong with him? She remembered that he was sensitive to light. What caused that? Porphyry? Some horrible chemical or biological weapon he'd encountered while defending his country?

Why hadn't he told her? Was there anything she could do to help?

Still worrying, she opened the refrigerator door.

Stacked plastic bags full of neatly labeled, bright red blood took up all the available space on every shelf.

Domini's skin went cold. She didn't believe it at first. This was some sort of nightmare; another hallucination. She could not—*could not!*—be seeing what she saw.

Blood.

Why would Reynard keep blood in his refrigerator? There had to be a logical reason; something to do with his medical condition.

I know why he keeps blood. I know why he moves so fast. I know why he needs such strong sunblock. I know why he pets wild animals. I know why he reads minds.

"I know." Her heart hammered wildly in her chest; she felt hollow with the fear that raced through her. "I know," Domini repeated, and stumbled backward and to her knees. She needed to get up. She needed to run.

"I see you found my stash."

Reynard's voice was soft, pleasantly conversational, and it utterly terrified her.

All she could do was look up, and it was a very long way from where she crouched on her hands and knees, but she made herself meet Alec's gaze.

Only to discover that he was wearing sunglasses in the glare of the kitchen lights. She couldn't look him in the eye, even though she tried. Bastard.

"You're a vampire," she said, even if saying it got her killed. "You really are a vampire."

"Yes," he answered, completely conversationally. "I probably should have told you sooner."

Chapter Twenty-two

The bright kitchen lights increased Alec's blazing headache, but he left them on. The light would make Domini feel safer. He moved closer to her, slowly and carefully, hands held out empty before him. He didn't think she took any notice of how nonaggressive he was being. She stared at him, but he wasn't sure she was seeing.

Her emotions, on the other hand, beat at him. She was screaming inside her head, and he could hear it.

But it wasn't with fear.

He reached a hand toward her. "Domini . . ."

She rose to her feet slowly, gracefully, quivering with fury. "I'm not crazy."

"You're not crazy."

"You're a vampire."

"Yes," Alec affirmed again. This did nothing to calm her. Anger flared like neon fire in her bright blue eyes.

"I'm not dreaming this, am I?"

He inched closer and cupped her cheek. "Sweetheart, you haven't dreamed any of it."

She took a sharp breath. "None of it?"

"None."

"You let me think I was *insane?*" Her fist connected with his jaw.

"I can expl—"

"You sent me visions of vampires, didn't you? *Made* me see things."

"Not on purpose! We share—"

"You damn near raped me in a back alley, and made me think it was a dream?!"

Alec's guts twisted with guilt. "I—"

She threw another punch at him, sending his sunglasses flying. Before Domini could try again, Alec had her wrists in a tight grip. "Stop it," he ordered, and twisted her around, holding her back to his chest with her arms crossed in front of her. The intimate embrace wasn't just defensive; he needed her close to him, needed her touch, even though it increased his awareness of her pain and anger. He needed to share those hard emotions, to love all of her even while she hated him. The hate would pass. Or so he prayed.

He closed his eyes against the light. He opened his mind to hers, though he faced a storm, and spoke directly to her, thought to thought.

Listen to me. Just listen. I never meant to impose my— delusions—on you. Never meant to hurt you.

It was real! she silently yelled back. *The bar. The fight. Your winning me. Your hands on me—in me!*

Real, he admitted. *My hands are on you now. Am I hurting you?*

You're holding me prisoner.

I'm keeping you safe.

From what?

Yourself. Me.

Keeping you safe from me.

That, too.

Domini could feel Reynard's smile. It was the oddest sensation. It was pleasant, soothing, like a balm on her burning thoughts. She had to fight the urge to calm down, and she fought it by trying to feel beyond Reynard's smile, to probe deeper into the mind touching hers. There was an instant, less than a heartbeat, when she stepped through a door, into fire. Saw the twisted face in the flames.

The door slammed on her faster than she'd found it.

No! You can't—see me—know me like I am now.

There was anguish in his thoughts, real fear and shame. Fear for her. Shame at what she'd seen.

Why not? Domini demanded.

Remember the bad dreams you've had? Those were my bad dreams, too.

Domini didn't understand what she'd seen deep inside his mind; it had been too brief, too intense, to take in. But she remembered the dreams.

We'll share so much, Domini. All the good things. You have my promise. Later, when I'm more myself.

How much more yourself could a vampire be? she asked. *Showing fangs? Turning into a bat or a wolf, sucking blood? Ripping out throats and—*

"Spare me the gory details, please."

He sounded so exhausted, Domini almost wanted to hug him. "Spare *you*? You're the scary one."

"I never set out to frighten you."

How could he say that? And sound so very sincere? There was a fire inside this creature. Chained violence, she realized, horrible dark urges trying to get out. He had a grip on her that was unbreakable, arms like steel binding her close to him.

"I'm at your mercy," she reminded him. The fact that she had to remind him seemed almost ludicrous.

He kissed the side of her throat. Domini stiffened, waiting for the sharp prick of fangs, the spurt of blood. What she felt were soft, warm lips, the brush of his breath against her skin. It felt good, and it set her shivering, partly with anticipation of pain, partly with longing.

Damn it! How could she still desire him, knowing what he was? *I've been screwing the living dead, for God's sake!*

Reynard pressed his hips closer to her, and she could feel that one part of him certainly wasn't dead.

Neither is the rest of me. "I was born a vampire. I've never been a mortal. It doesn't work that way. Not with Primes. I should have told you about myself sooner," he went on. "Or not at all. We shouldn't have become lovers yet, even though it was meant to be."

"Meant?"

"We were born to be mated," Alec said. "Bonded. To be together for as long as we both shall live. I understand that you can't feel it yet, not with the way I am now. And I don't blame you for fearing the monster inside me; I shouldn't have approached you so soon. But fate led me to you, and you to me. Remember the market?"

Fear fisted Domini's heart. "The dream—compulsions? It was you? You called me there?"

"I was drawn to you. You to me. That's how a bond begins. We happened to be in the same area at the same time, close enough for our dreams to touch."

"Right."

"No, that's how it really works. I wasn't looking for you. I came to L.A. to take the cure—"

"Cure? You guys have a vampire Betty Ford Clinic? You're trying to stop being a vampire?"

"I can't stop being a vampire. I don't want to. My body is rejecting the medicines that let me live in the daylight world. I don't *need* to live in daylight, but I want to."

"All that stuff in the case—that's antivampire medicine?"

"You aren't listening to me, are you?"

Domini tested his hold on her, but though his grip wasn't painful, there was no breaking away from him. They were locked together until Reynard decided to let her go. "I'm paying attention," she said. "How can I not be?"

"Because you won't let me get past your preconceived ideas of what a vampire should be."

"There's a monster inside you," she reminded him. "Isn't that what a vampire is?"

They were so close that she felt his shrug all through her. "Let's talk about us."

She knocked her head back against his shoulder. Maybe she couldn't hurt him, but she could still express her anger. "Us?"

He remained infuriatingly calm and patient. "You already know I love you, even if you won't believe it. As for that beast inside me—yes, I fear what I could do to you, and I fight it. I'll never hurt you. And soon you'll realize that you can have no other lover."

She didn't *want* any other lover. She hadn't wanted him, to begin with. Even before she knew he was a vampire, she knew he brought too much complication to her life.

No—he brought color to what had been a black-and-white life. Once you saw in color, how did you live without it?

"No other lover sounds terribly romantic," she said.

"Doesn't it?" His cheek brushed across hers. It was freshly shaved and smelled of soap, all normal and nice. "I am a romantic. All Primes are."

Her skin tingled where he'd touched her. It would be easier if there was at least a whiff of rotting corpse or evil about him.

"Prime. What's that?"

"Prime male of my Clan. Prime of the Fox Clan," he answered, and there was pride in his tone, arrogance. "Alpha male, you'd say, only much more so. We're a testosterone-intensive species, we vampires. Our men more male, our women the ultimate in female."

She couldn't believe it, but a bolt of jealousy went through her. "Vamp girls are the ultimate in female, huh? Then why'd you pick me?"

"It was meant to be."

That seemed to be his answer to a lot of things. "I don't believe in fate."

"You can see the future."

"Yeah, but . . ." Okay, he had her there. "Only sometimes."

"The ability will improve and stabilize after we've been together for a while. I'll help you free all your mental abilities. And—" He kissed her throat again, and the back of her neck.

It set her quivering. "There are many ways I'll teach you to feel, to excel."

Good lord, but she was dancing with the devil here. He made such sweet promises: of love forever, of carnal delights, of knowledge and power. "Tempting," she admitted. But that was the devil's job, wasn't it? "Will you let go of me now? Please?"

"Will you run?"

"Would I have a chance if I did?"

"No."

"Then I won't try to run." *Not yet.*

Alec heard her thought, but he loosed his hold and stepped back. He didn't expect trust and belief to come instantly. Not with a beginning like this. He almost wished he hadn't walked into Lancer Services a few days ago. But if he hadn't, he wouldn't have been there to protect Domini from the Purists.

And he still didn't know why the most fanatical group of the vampire hunters were after her. The fact that the Purist used a knife meant that the grudge was very personal. Why?

Her safety and the reasons why he needed to keep her safe were really the most important matters for them to deal with right now.

She'd backed away from him, all the way across the kitchen. She wasn't checking the room for exits, but she was deliberately not looking at him, either. She was trying to physically and mentally distance herself from him.

He had a terrible headache again, some of it from the angry energy she'd poured into him. Her fear hurt him; it also enraged that part of him she called monster. The monster wanted to throw her across the kitchen table and take her, to force blood as well as sex on her. Once she tasted him, she wouldn't be so superior, so disparaging. She'd crawl on her knees to beg the monster for one drop more of what only a vampire could give.

The monster, of course, was the damned pubescent part of him that he had to keep in line. He absolutely could not risk sharing blood with Domini while the beast was so close to breaking free. The pills were only so much help. If a new serum wasn't developed soon, he was going to have to be locked away from civilization until his body made the adjustment back to the nightside of life on its own. But how could he abandon Domini when she was in danger?

"Where's Dr. Casmerek when I need him?" he muttered.

Domini jumped, and pivoted to face him. "What?"

He didn't answer but moved slowly, every movement as nonthreatening as he could make it. He picked up his sunglasses and turned off the kitchen lights. "That's better."

"I can't see in the dark," she protested.

"It's after dawn." As she glanced toward the lowered shades over the kitchen's window, he added, "I don't have to look outside to know when the sun rises. It's a vampire thing," he replied to her skeptical look.

"I don't want to know about vampire things."

"You must know something about vampires," he told her. "Otherwise vampire hunters wouldn't be after you. That's who tried to murder you. They're called Purists."

She shook her head. "I've never heard of them. Until a few minutes ago I truly believed vampires were fictional, the stuff of horror movies and bedtime stories."

Alec glanced at her over the top of his sunglasses. "Bedtime stories? You must have had an interesting childhood."

"My grandfather likes horror stories." She twisted her hands together nervously.

He walked toward her. "I think you're keeping family secrets."

She backed up as he approached. "I don't know any family secrets. I mean, I don't have family secrets. The Lancers—"

"Blackbird."

"You keep my grandmother out of this!"

"I think I'd better ask your grandfather about this woman."

Domini stopped retreating and stood facing him squarely, her hands on her hips. "Oh, no, you don't! It's too close to the anniversary of when he lost her. He doesn't—he's never dealt with the loss. I won't have you upsetting him."

She looked like a tigress, and Alec smiled fondly at her defense of the old man she loved. But his judgment was that the man didn't need or want protecting.

"You're the one who needs protecting, Domini," Alec reminded her. "It would hurt your grandfather as much to lose you as it did to lose his wife. You don't want to see him devastated by loss again, do you?"

Domini's lips compressed, and her nostrils flared with an angry breath. She shook her head. "Oh, you're good, Reynard."

He held his hands out in front of him. "I know." He looked her over and said, "While I think you look delightful wearing nothing but my shirt, I think your grandfather would prefer it if you were showered and dressed. Even in what little you were wearing last night."

He was sure she'd accept any excuse to put off his confronting the Old Man. And Alec wanted her out of sight long enough so that he could take this morning's prescription cocktail without having her there. While he intended to share his life with her, he was still a Prime, unwilling to show any weakness. Even the weakness of downing a few pills.

"Go on," he urged when she hesitated. He offered her a smile, and further incentive. "Then when you're ready, I'll let you drive the Jaguar."

Chapter Twenty-three

The drive to Malibu through heavy morning traffic was a grim, silent affair, with Domini growing more nervous by the second. Once at the house, she dragged out every step toward the door.

There, she turned on Reynard and demanded, "Don't you have to ask permission to enter a dwelling or something?"

He answered by twisting the doorknob until the lock broke and pushing her into the house ahead of him. Breaking in so casually set off a very sophisticated alarm system, one that he found and almost instantly shut down. The skill had nothing to do with being a vampire, Domini supposed. More than likely, breaking, entering, and securing a residence was training he'd gotten from the United States government. At the moment, she didn't particularly approve of this use of her tax money.

Once the alarms were neutralized, Reynard sighed, and some of the tension went out of him. Domini realized that the morning light must be bothering him badly, despite his sunglasses and sunblock.

She tried to curb any feelings of sympathy and headed straight for the kitchen. She hoped to somehow warn her grandfather . . . but he wasn't in the kitchen for her to warn.

The room was empty, and for some reason this frightened her. Maybe she'd really been counting on him to rescue her. Grandpa'd always been there for her before.

"There's no one here," Reynard said, after he drew the blinds to shield the room from the bright light coming through the deck doors facing the ocean. "We're alone."

There was an empty stillness inside the house, easy enough for Domini to detect once she filtered out the outside sounds of the ocean, the wind, and the gulls. Where was the Old Man?

Her first thought was that something had happened to him, but there was no sign of any struggle. All looked normal: there were dishes in the sink, the dregs of coffee in a mug, and breadcrumbs on a cutting board. A glance at the clock on the microwave showed her that it was later in the morning than she'd thought.

"He's at the office," Reynard concluded. He put a hand on her arm. "Let's go."

Domini shook him off. "Give me a minute."

She expected the vampire to drag her off, or at least protest, but Reynard stepped back and stood very still, his hands balled into fists at his sides, while she picked up the telephone handset. Domini felt a desperate need to catch up with the real world after several days of visiting the Twilight Zone. One way to reconnect seemed to be to call home to check her voice mail. Of the dozen messages in the inbox, only two were of any importance. One was from Holly.

"Andy said you saved my butt, then went off to have mad, passionate sex with Mr. Testicles. Actually, he said that you got hurt and Mr. T. was taking care of you. You aren't hurt bad, are you? You and Mr. T. are finally screwing like bunnies, right? You must be, or I would have heard from you. I *will* hear from you soon, Lancer. Thanks for taking care of me during the L.A. visit. The Venice show went off fine last night. I'm at the airport right now, off to Vancouver in a few minutes. Andy and a team are coming with to keep me safe on the road. Jo's meeting me there, so wish me luck and love. Wish you the same. Call."

"Wish you both," Domini said, and saved the message.

The other message was from her grandfather. He'd left it an hour earlier. "If you happen to decide to put in an appearance, I'll be at the office. Come in. We need to talk. Maxwell assures me that you're all right. I'm assuming you're catting around with Reynard. If so, consider your ass fired. Both your asses. Come talk to me anyway."

"Thanks, Grandpa." She saved that message, too. She put the phone back on the wall base.

"Let's go," Reynard said, taking her arm. "He wants to see us."

It occurred to her that he probably had extra good hearing, along with the other superpowers. "He didn't say he wanted to talk to you."

"But I want to talk to him." Reynard gave her a thin, tight smile, as though that was all he had the energy to offer. "Besides, maybe I want to be old-fashioned and ask for your hand."

"You can have the hand, if you promise to leave the old man alone."

Anger flashed over his already stern expression. "Come on." He tugged her back toward the front of the house. "Let's go."

Despite the growing heat of the morning, the dimness inside the office parking garage was blessedly cool against Alec's burning skin. It was much easier to see in here than out on the street. After he closed the car door, he leaned against it and took deep breaths, no longer feeling like he was drowning in light.

Even with the sunscreen, glasses, and dark polarized windows, riding in the car left him so sunsick, he was blind and wracked with pain when he finally stepped out into the parking garage. He knew it was a bad idea to leave Domini alone behind the wheel of the Jaguar, but he had to regain control before walking into the Lancer offices.

He was relieved that she made no effort to start the car and drive away. Oh, he could catch her if he had to, but the temper fit that would follow would not be good for their relationship. He hoped she sensed he was on the edge and was reacting with appropriate discretion.

Alec hooked his sunglasses onto the neck of his T-shirt and pressed his palms against his aching eyes. Even a week ago, sunlight had felt good against his skin; his vision had been sharp and clear both day and night. He could barely remember now how he'd noticed that his body was beginning to betray him. He'd been concerned but confident that Casmerek's renowned clinic would soon put everything to rights. He'd come in for a tune-up; he hadn't meant to go through hell. The treatment was complicated by the physical and psychic changes brought on by bonding. Maybe he should have mentioned it to Casmerek, but Prime pride and possessive paranoia got in the way.

He had the Purists to blame for this torture, as well. They threatened not only Domini but the clinic. The first serum hadn't worked, but the clinic was still his best hope. If he could get back there—

There was another way, of course. He could accept the night, give up sunlight and the discipline it took to live side by side with humans. It would only take blood and sex to ease the pain of the transition. Alec smiled, and felt the throb of fangs just beneath skin. He was so weary. It would be easy to give up, give in.

And betray everything the Clans stand for.

He wasn't a selfish Tribe boy, to do what he wanted when he wanted, or a pragmatic male of the Families, who did what was convenient in the name of survival. He was Clan. He'd taken vows. Honor meant something, even though it was driving him mad.

Alec sighed. Soon he wasn't going to have a choice. Clan, Family, or Tribe, he was still a vampire. Nature would have its way eventually.

But not yet. For Domini's sake, he'd abide by the rules as long as he could.

He forced his eyes to focus, his senses to be alert. The sooner he talked with Ben Lancer, the sooner he could get on with hunting the Purist who'd attacked Domini.

Besides his red Jaguar, three dark Mercedeses, a black

Hummer, and a dark blue Lincoln Navigator were parked in the Lancer office slots. There was a white Grand Cherokee parked near the building entrance, but no other cars occupied the spaces on this level.

Alec went around to the driver's-side door and opened it. "You have no idea how noble I'm being," he informed the woman he loved.

He took her hand and helped her out of the low-slung sports car. She didn't need the help, but his touch was a warning not to run. The feel of her soft skin on his was a comfort as well, and kept his mind off the pain.

"You all right?" she asked him.

He noted that Domini was annoyed with herself for caring, but she did care.

"Maybe you should go home, lie down, and have a rest—"

"Come on." He twined his fingers firmly with hers and led her toward the building entrance.

He was taken by surprise when the door of the white Jeep opened as they neared it. Alec let out an angry snarl, thrust Domini behind him, and spun to face the Jeep. Instinct told him to make the leap with all claws and fangs extended, and he was barely able to hold instinct at bay. Instinct should also have let him know the other Prime was nearby before he actually saw him.

Anthony Crowe stepped cautiously to the concrete and held a hand out toward Alec. He held a white envelope in his other hand. "Peace, Brother Fox." He spoke quietly, and moved slowly to close the SUV door gently behind him.

Alec took the time the other Prime gave him to calm down. "Peace, Brother Crow," he answered when his vision had flashed back from red to something closer to normal.

From behind him, Domini said, "Hi, Tony."

Alec was aware that she was both relieved and annoyed at this evidence that she *really* hadn't imagined the encounter in the vampire bar. And that she was still *really* angry at him for having made her think it was her imagination. Okay, he'd been wrong to manipulate her like that. He wasn't going to apologize for it again.

You didn't apologize to begin with.

Alec heard her thought and ignored it. "What are you doing here?" he asked Crowe.

"Several reasons," Crowe answered. "I spent the last few hours waiting around to see if the Purists have any interest in Lancer Services. Haven't noticed anyone but me watching the place. Second, I wanted to let you know that Casmerek's team have packed up everything and headed out of town. Don't worry, he'll be in touch with you soon." Crowe took a cell phone from an inside jacket pocket and handed it to Alec. "You'll hear from the doc only on this number."

"Thanks." Alec put the phone in his pocket. Then he glanced at the small FedEx package. "What's that?"

"The main reason I'm here." Crowe passed the envelope to Alec. "I made those calls about your lady, and this came with instructions to deliver it to you."

Domini supposed this might be a good time to attempt an escape, but instead she peered curiously over Reynard's shoulder. For one thing, she didn't figure she could outrun two vampires. And for another, she was completely flabbergasted at the idea of vampires getting FedEx packages. It didn't seem right, somehow, that supernatural creatures used cell phones and overnight delivery services. They should use mysterious white-haired messengers in swirling black capes who arrived at the stroke of midnight, holding out red velvet cases in their pale, long-fingered hands. She did notice that the address was written out in thick, dark ink, in rather ornate handwriting.

When Reynard hesitated to open the package, she grew impatient. "Who's it from?" she asked, practically bouncing on her toes with curiosity.

"His mother," Tony answered.

Domini stared at the other vampire. "What?"

"My Matri," Reynard said.

"Your who?"

"Which in this case happens to be his mother." Tony noticed her confusion and said, "Brother Fox, haven't you explained anything about your Clan to this girl? If you're getting married, she should know about her in-laws."

"We're not getting married," Domini announced.

"That's not what I heard," Tony answered.

Domini chose to ignore him and watched as Alec tore open the envelope with shaking fingers. What spilled into his palm was a small red velvet bag and a small folded square of heavy writing paper. Now, this had more of a vampire look to it.

The mysterious effect was spoiled somewhat by their standing in a concrete parking garage, and Tony Crowe's sharp whistle when he saw the bag.

"What is it?" Domini asked.

"Is that what I think it is?" Crowe asked.

They both peered closer.

Alec's stomach twisted with nerves. He very much did not want this to be what Crowe thought it was. The velvet pouch weighed heavily in his palm. It was almost warm, as though with the memory of the hand that had worn it, as though with the thoughts of the woman who had sent it only hours before.

He tugged open the braided silken strings that held the bag closed, and spilled the ring into his hand. The ruby-and-gold signet ring of the Matri of Clan Reynard. The same fox symbol he wore as a tattoo on his wrist was incised deeply into the rounded ruby bezel. It was a beautiful thing, ancient, symbolic.

The ring must be returned to the Matri. Whatever command came with the ring must be obeyed instantly, without question. To fail to obey was a sentence of expulsion from the Clan, and of death as well. The clanless one would be hunted down and killed by all those he'd once called brother, sister, kinfolk, and parent. The ring of the Matri was far heavier than the pure gold and priceless gem that made up its physical form.

Crowe was solemn and silent, taking a step back. Domini's attention was sharply focused on Alec, curiosity mixed with sudden wariness. She sensed this was important, too important for any flippant questions or comments.

Alec unfolded the paper and recognized his Matri's handwriting.

Bring me Domini Lancer.

Fists of ice closed around Alec's heart and pounded into his gut. A small explosion of rebellion tried to evaporate his already shaky thinking processes. He didn't know what the Matri wanted, and for a second he didn't care. The world around him went blood red and boiling hot with his fury. He threw back his head and howled with rage.

Domini was *his.*

Lady Anjelica had no right to ask him to give up—

No right? Anjelica was Matri of the Clan.

His heart cracked open, but the fury subsided. The world went from red to dark. He was hollow, empty, an automaton.

He was Prime. He was Clan.

Duty. Honor. Obedience.

He sensed Domini's fear and confusion, even concern for him, but he could not bear to look at her. She belonged to the Matri now.

Alec tucked the ring back into the pouch, then turned to the cautiously watching Anthony Crowe. "We need to get to Idaho," he told the Prime of the allied Clan. "Can you help with the arrangements?"

Chapter Twenty-four

They were heading toward an isolated airport. The human captive was the designated driver.

Domini was following a map displayed on a small GPS screen in the center of the Jag's high-tech dashboard. Outside, the afternoon sun burned down on rolling desert hills spotted with the huge whirring fans of tall wind turbine towers. Traffic was light now that they'd left Route 10, and for someone used to driving in constant gridlock, this was weird.

She found the barren landscape eerie, but nowhere near as disconcerting as being on a road trip with Reynard. His head hurt. She knew, because her head hurt. She couldn't deny that they had a psychic connection; the more she was around him, the more attuned to him she was becoming. She suspected he was concealing a great deal of pain, and hiding something worse than physical pain. He was irritable, which set her nerves on edge. He was angry, but wouldn't say why. And there was the caged fiery beast prowling inside him, as well. The cage was weakening, and she didn't know what would happen if the monster escaped.

All she knew was that he and Tony Crowe had had a brief discussion involving routes, secrecy, and abandoned airfields. They'd sounded like a couple of drug smugglers coordinating an important shipment. Neither of them had asked her opinion about anything.

During their conversation she took the opportunity to make a break, running toward the building entrance, hoping to get to human help before the vampires noticed. Reynard proved to her that while he might not be feeling well, he could still move

fast. He'd been waiting for her, leaning in front of the door before she got there, his arms casually crossed.

She'd let out a small squeak of rage, then swore vividly at him.
He smiled. Actually, it was more of a snarl, and it showed her
for the first time that he did have fangs: sharp, predatory, and
thoroughly frightening. When she backed up in terror, she ran
into Tony Crowe. He nudged her back toward Reynard, who
grabbed her by the arm. She was then stuffed into the driver's
seat of the Jaguar once more. Reynard called up directions to the
Salton Sea Recreation Area on his GPS, and told her to drive.

Hours later Domini was still driving, and she was tired.
There'd been one break for a gas and potty stop, but he'd
given her no chance to escape.

The air-conditioning and dark windows didn't keep the
heat at bay. Sweat sheened both their skins, but there was a
lot more of her exposed than there was of Reynard in his dark
shirt and jeans. Her micro-length skirt and midriff-baring top
gave her no protection at all. She hesitated to ask for a hit of
his super sunblock, because she was certain Reynard needed it
more. She'd come to believe that the vampire definition of
sunburn was spontaneous combustion. Maybe this was a
good thing in the overall us-versus-the-monsters scheme of
things, but she couldn't imagine it happening to Reynard.

Why she worried about him, she didn't know, but she did.
More with every passing mile.

"You know, Mr. T., you make a terrible traveling companion."

Reynard lifted his head a bit and took a long gulp from a
bottle of water. His throat still sounded parched when he
asked, "Where are we?"

Domini checked the map on the screen. "We just passed
Thermal. Heading toward Mecca. Nearly there," she added as
the blue smudge of the inland sea grew larger on the map.

She'd never been to this part of California; she'd never been
farther south than Palm Springs. She vaguely remembered from
a geography class in junior high that the Salton Sea had been

created by a Colorado River flood a long time ago. The Sea was actually a salty lake, only fed by polluted farm drainage. It had been quite a tourist spot once, but now it was mostly used by migrating birds.

"Pretty forlorn place you're taking me to," she said.

"That's the idea."

"Not my idea of a fun date."

Reynard put his head back against the soft leather headrest, seeming to have lost interest in the conversation. Then his hand reached across the gear shift to stroke the inside of her exposed thigh.

Heat rushed through Domini, and she let out a sharp gasp. The car veered across the sun-baked road.

"I could make it your idea of a date," he said.

Domini got the car under control. "I concede that." His fingers moved higher and continued to stroke. Domini's breath quickened.

She made herself concentrate on anything but what Reynard was doing. She saw a grove of date palms in the distance, and realized they were at the outskirts of a small town. A sign said to reduce speed to forty-five. She had to move Reynard's hand away so she could downshift.

"Mecca," Reynard said as the Jaguar moved through the outskirts of the small town. "Nine miles to go."

"Nine miles to what?"

"Nine miles to the Salt Shore Motel." He crossed his arms over his chest. "Wake me up then."

"I live to serve," she grumbled.

"Don't we all?" was his enigmatic answer.

She couldn't get a word out of him the rest of the way.

"What a lovely abandoned motel in the middle of nowhere you've brought me to, Reynard. I am *so* impressed."

"It's not abandoned," he answered after he closed the door. "The clerk told me that there are guests in two other rooms."

Domini had to admit that though the furnishings were seedy, the place was clean. An ancient air conditioner wheezed loudly away in the room's one window, drowning out any other noise and thinning down the late afternoon heat. The concrete walls were thick, but painted a cheery coral. The pale green indoor/outdoor carpet was thin but recently vacuumed. The spread on the queen-sized bed was beige chenille. The rest of the furnishings consisted of a chair and a table by the bed. There was a lamp on the table that boasted a bulb of such low wattage, it didn't even seem to bother Reynard's sensitive vision. There were also a chest of drawers and a television resting on an old coffee table. Hardly the Hotel Bel-Air, but at least there was a bathroom.

"Mind if I take a shower?"

Reynard was already pacing the room, like a restless prisoner measuring out the dimensions of his cell. He gestured jerkily toward the bathroom. "Fine."

Domini hesitated for a moment, studying him. She didn't like the look of him at all. He was more like a caged animal than a prisoner.

She curbed the impulse to go to him and take him in her arms. She was frightened of what would happen if she did. "You're getting worse, aren't you?"

He managed to curb his pacing long enough to give her a sardonic look. "You think?"

"Why?" she asked.

He went back to pacing. "Lots of reasons. I'm horny. Hungry. I'm hurting. I want to *bite* something."

"You left your medicine at your house."

"Yes." He gave her a sharp look. "I wish one of us had noticed that before now."

She could have pointed out that she wasn't the one who arranged this little road trip, but nagging an antsy vampire probably wasn't the safest course of action.

"You want to lie down?" she asked. "Can I get you a glass of water or anything?"

"Anything?" He took in a sharp breath. His muscles looked as tense as steel. "Domini, you have no idea—" Reynard rubbed his hands over his face. The lean lines were sharper than ever, pared down by pain. It gave him the beauty of a suffering saint, or the fierceness of a hungry predator. "It'll be dark soon. Maybe that will help."

He didn't sound at all confident. Reynard went back to pacing, and she went into the bathroom. There was no window in here. She stripped off the clothes she'd been wearing for far too long and stepped into the tiny shower cubicle. The shower head was positioned too low for comfort, and she couldn't get the over-enthusiastic spray of water warmer or cooler than tepid. The pipes rattled like thunder, and the water roared enough to wake the dead. But at least there was a tiny square of soap and thin towels, so she managed to get clean and sort of dry.

Domini felt a bit more civilized when she was finished, but she hated having to put on her dirty clothes yet again. This was definitely not her idea of a glamorous resort getaway.

As kidnappings went, though, it could have been worse.

"There's a vampire out there," she said to her reflection in the bathroom mirror. "How do you define *worse?*"

A hungry vampire, she added, and a shiver of terror raced up her spine. Reality hit her hard, and she had to grab hold of the sink to keep from falling to her knees. She stayed where she was for a long time, shaking, her empty stomach twisting with nausea that left her panting with the effort not to throw up.

She was alone with a vampire.

Even worse, she wasn't alone with a vampire. There was the manager who'd rented them the room, and other people staying here.

Reynard had admitted to being hungry. To wanting to bite something. Someone, he meant. She didn't think he *wanted* to— feed, or attack anyone. But she feared that soon he might not have any choice.

Domini opened the door and stepped into the bedroom.

The chair and chest were smashed to kindling. The television had been shoved to the floor. Not only was Reynard still pacing, he'd left deep claw marks in the wall, baring pale lines of concrete beneath the cheerful coral paint. He whirled to face her. There was madness in the eyes that stared out of the tortured face, madness that struck her like a blow. His nails had grown sharp and pointed. She had to take a deep breath and remind herself that it wasn't blood under his nails, but dark pink paint. She tried to tell herself she imagined the feral gleam in his eyes. He was breathing hard, and pain radiated off of him like desert heat. He'd been keeping himself on a very tight leash, and now the leash was slipping badly.

Domini pushed the rising fear aside. "Are you going to hunt humans?" she asked him. "Do you need to drink blood?"

"I need blood."

He was on her in an instant, his hands tight on her shoulders, his body pressing hers hard against the wall. She was aware of his weight, his strength, his heat, his arousal. There was no mistaking the fire in his eyes, a reflection of the burning inside him.

An answering fire stirred in her, quickening her breath, her body, her blood.

Reynard's face dipped close to hers; his lips brushed across hers without touching, yet she was aware of the slight bulge of needle fangs hidden beneath his lips. He breathed in her scent. She felt her heart begin to race in time with the frantic beat of his. His thoughts burned into her.

What do I want? What do I need?

The words mocked her, and himself.

"Me?" she asked.

"You!" The word was a snarl, of desire, of denial.

He spun away from her abruptly, before she could answer. Before either of them could move closer.

"I can't take what I want. You aren't mine to take."

Domini was left shaken, with only the battered wall to hold her up. Reynard was on the other side of the room, standing beneath the cold blast of the air conditioner, face turned upward and eyes closed. The wrecked room, the shredded walls, were evidence of his pent-up violence. Only the bed was left untouched, like an altar waiting for a sacrifice.

The monster wanted her. The monster needed her.

She glanced toward the door, only a few steps away. She took one step, her knees weak. She didn't think she had the strength to run, but she managed to walk out the door without Reynard noticing.

Domini had no idea what she intended to do when she stood outside. There were three cars in the small motel lot, each parked outside one of the occupied rooms. Domini fingered the Jaguar keys in the tiny pocket of her tiny skirt. She could leave if she wanted, run away from the whole mess. It wouldn't be hard to get in the car and drive away; she doubted Reynard could catch up to her. She doubted he'd even notice.

Then what?

Wash her hands of the whole affair? Write it off as a nightmare, or a hallucination brought on by her psychic gifts?

What would happen to Reynard? He was hurting. He needed help. She couldn't just leave him, and it wasn't like she could call the paramedics.

He did need help, and soon. She could feel the barriers shredding, the wildness building in him as though the emotions were her own.

She didn't believe that he wanted to hurt anyone. He hadn't hurt her; he'd protected her. He'd protected Holly.

He'd made love to her. They'd made love. He'd made her feel like . . .

He tilted her head up and covered her mouth with his. She had not realized what deep, fiery pleasure the touching of lips, the delving of tongues, could bring. The kiss was a rich feast of sensation.

She felt sharp teeth press against her lips. Excitement overwhelmed fear. Perhaps fear enhanced her excitement. All she knew was that she moaned with loss when his mouth left hers.

"No—!"

"Peace," he whispered. He held her face in his hands, so that she must look into his eyes. They glowed faintly in the moonlight, as any night beast's would. "This night you are mine, to do with as I please."

The look in those eyes demanded an answer, an assent.

"I am yours."

"Do you want me? Do you want my body to cover yours? Do you want me inside you? I will have your consent."

She grabbed his thick black hair in her fists and pulled his mouth back to hers.

This kiss was as intense, but he did not let it last as long. "The night grows late," he whispered against her mouth.

His hands skimmed over her then, and he kissed her throat and between her breasts and suckled at the tips, and moved on to her belly and thighs. Wherever he touched he left traces of fire behind. The heat pooled deep down in her belly, making her grind her hips and arch up against him, insistent, begging for more.

Every now and then there would be a slight sting as his sharp teeth penetrated her skin in ever more tender places. If he took a drop or two of her blood with each kiss, she welcomed the small sacrifice for the bright bursts of joy it brought. His fingers delved between her legs, caressed and teased until she thought she was about to die.

She opened to him and lifted her hips. She held her arms out, and looked up to meet his gaze.

Only she couldn't see his eyes, because he was wearing sunglasses. A glint of moonlight sparkled off his fangs.

"Reynard, what the hell are you doing in my dream?"

"Your dream? I thought it was mine."

Domini blinked, and found that she was standing in the motel parking lot, looking up at the sky. Stars were coming out as the last glow of sunset faded. For a moment she didn't realize what had happened.

Then she remembered that it *had* been a dream. A dream she'd shared with Reynard. Or was it a memory of a shared past, where he'd saved a city, and she'd been his reward?

He was the one who needed saving now.

Had they done this before? Been lovers through time? Soul mates?

Domini gave her head a hard shake. This was no time to go off on metaphysical theorizing. Not when a supernatural creature was tearing up the room behind her, and could be tearing up the rest of the building and the people in it any minute. He hadn't attacked anyone so far, but he was close to it.

She remembered the nightmare dream—vision—whatever it was.

The vampire's lust pounded through her, emotion as real and hard as the cock pounding ruthlessly inside her. There was no escape, only a storm overwhelming her. Driving total possession into her flesh, her blood, and being. She was spread out beneath him like a sacrifice. Her skin was smeared red with her blood, and his.

Which was real: the pleasure of the first dream, or the degradation of the second?

You don't live in dreams, she reminded herself harshly. Reality is what's back in that room.

Alexander Reynard needed her.

Domini turned on her heel and walked back to the door. Newfound determination didn't stop her from shaking like a leaf, but she went of her own free will. She knew what she had to do.

Domini opened the door and stepped inside. "You need me," she told the vampire who whirled to face her. She held out her arms. "You need me, and I'm here."

Chapter Twenty-five

"No!" He held his hands out before him, shaking his head with denial. "I can't!"

"The hell you can't," Domini answered. "I didn't just go through that whole crisis of conscience thing to come back in here and have you say no. If anybody's going to be self-sacrificing here, it's me."

She moved slowly closer to him. He backed up with each step she took, but she had the advantage; the wall was to his back. Eventually Reynard had nowhere else to go.

"Alexander," she said, putting her hands on him, cupping his face when he tried to turn away. His skin burned against her palms. "You've proved to be nothing but a good man. You're suffering. Let me help. I may not be the woman you deserve, but I'm here now, and you need me."

He took a deep breath and managed to say, "You don't belong to me."

"I belong to me." She smiled gently, stated very firmly, "I give myself to you. Whatever you vampires have going on about me doesn't mean shit. I don't care about magic rings. I don't care about secret societies. That's all bullshit, nothing to do with me. Nothing to do with us."

"It has—to do with—me."

"*You* have to do with me. Right here, right now. Nothing and no one else exists."

"Only us?"

It hurt to hear the way his voice rasped with pain. "Yes, Alexander."

"No. Too dángerous. You—go."

She shook her head, then stepped back and pulled off her clothes.

Alec could not help but look at Domini. He saw her with all his senses. It was the warmth of her flesh that called to him, the softness. The scent of her was sweet and sharp, all female. He meant to deny himself, but she smiled and held her arms wide, let all the barriers of her mind drop. She offered herself completely. Freely. Not unafraid, but with determination and her own rising hunger.

He could do nothing but reach out and touch.

He meant to be gentle, but intentions meant nothing. Claiming her meant everything. He drew her close, then lifted her into his arms. It was but a step to the bed.

Domini was aware of the unyielding firmness of the mattress, of the way the springs creaked beneath her weight, even of the faint bumps of the chenille bedspread. The moment Alexander touched her, she became supersensitized. Everything became *more*.

"Stay still," came his rough whisper. "Let it happen. Don't try to run. Don't fight. I don't want to hurt you."

His warning was not reassuring, but she stopped thinking a moment later when he kissed her. The kiss tasted of hot copper and electricity.

His hands moved over her, bringing pain, followed by pleasure. The combination was more than heady: at this moment, in this place, with him, it was perfect. Fear had no place here, only arousal.

He touched her everywhere, harsh, gentle, stimulating. His nails made the faintest of pinpricks, on her breasts, between them. Tiny spots of blood welled. His mouth found each mark, licked and suckled the beads of blood, took nourishment and gave back pleasure. Where fangs sank into flesh, she did not know.

Domini closed her eyes and let herself completely go. No

barriers, nothing but sensation. Her orgasm sent flame through her blood and melted her bones. And that was only the beginning.

Fire filled her, consumed her, raised her up to explosive heights, brought her down into wells of swirling darkness where their twin heartbeats hammered together, then cycled her upward again. It took her higher and further each time, then dropped her deeper. She soared toward the sun, then dove into the depths of heavy darkness. She drowned, and each time she felt the spark go out of her, she was kindled back into fiery life.

She gradually became aware that their hearts were no longer in rhythm. His was stronger, so much stronger. His heart thundered, roared with life and power, while hers was drawing down to a faint echo, straining to keep time.

Straining to keep alive.

Domini understood what was happening. A trace of fear coiled through her, like smoke through flame. The fire would soon take her. Or the darkness. Either way, she would be consumed. She was dying.

She could not speak or move. Her spirit floated in a lava flow; slowly boiling away to nothing, but she'd lost all awareness of her body. She could barely find the will to call out a silent whisper. She hadn't enough strength to even call for help. All she could manage was his name.

Alexander.

An image of sparks turning to ash and falling around him like rain entered Alec's mind, interposing itself over the frenzied pleasure of feeding. The ash turned thick as snow, a blizzard blanketing the feverish greed, dulling it down to something manageable. He cried out angrily, not ready to lose the searing pleasure, the utter, satiating satisfaction. He had forgotten the power only the taste of blood could bring. Red lightning. There was nothing else like it in the universe.

Alexander.

The voice that called to him was faint, fading, unfamiliar in its weakness.

Alexander.

He barely recognized his own name. Didn't want to recognize it, because then he would have to *be* Alexander. Alexander was not the beast who fed and fed and wanted ever more.

Alexander was—

The man who loved Domini.

Domini?

The world came back in on him with a hard, heavy rush that brought him to orgasm and left him sprawled on top of a soft, limp form. His vision shifted from seeing the world as degrees of heat, to something closer to human sight. He didn't remember when he'd entered her, taken her body as well as her blood, but they were twinned together, his seed inside her, her taste on his tongue.

And she was dying.

Alec let out a cry of pain. He'd taken too much, too quickly. He'd given nothing, shared nothing. She'd offered, but he should have refused. He'd lost control, lost himself. Now he was losing her before they'd even had time to—

Alexander.

Her voice was fainter than before.

His name sounded so beautiful in her mind. To hear it as her dying thought was soul-shattering.

"Selfish, stupid idiot!" Alec lifted his head, the fog clearing from his brain.

He sat on the edge of the bed, drew Domini into his lap, cradled her head against his shoulder, and brushed a wing of dark hair away from her face. He could detect no breath, and her normal paleness was changed to moonstone translucence.

He didn't have much time, and the only sharp objects available were his own claws and fangs. A quick, hard bite into the vein in his left wrist, then he opened her mouth and held his wrist to it.

Drink, he urged as blood began to flow into her. *Drink.* Alec sent the command into her fading thoughts. *Drink, and live. Please live.*

He waited, holding his breath, full of terror and guilt. And waited.

Domini!

Alexander?

She sounded miles away, fading fast.

I am with you, he sent his thoughts after her. *Do as I say!*

Bossy . . .

Alec laughed, though fear still rushed through him. *No time to argue. Suck, sweetheart. Swallow. Do it.*

No answer drifted back from the place where Domini sank into darkness. Alec could do no more—only wait, and pray, and bleed.

He caressed her throat, hoping that would make her swallow. He tried to find her pulse, but it was only the faintest flutter.

What the hell have I done—

Domini jerked, her mouth clamped around Alec's wrist, and she began to drink, fiercely reclaiming her life.

Alec let out a long gasp, and lost himself in the intimate pleasure of giving the same fire he'd taken.

There was the light, and there was the voice. Both in the distance from where she hung in the dark. Both called to her. The flames had gone from the dark, hunger remained. She called out, and the voice answered. The light did not command, it did not call. The light offered peace, but the voice, the voice wanted her to live. The voice offered life. He wanted her.

She was Domini, he was her Alexander, her Alec, her Fox, and she wanted everything he was.

She was hungry for him. He offered, and she feasted.

Domini took from the fire, brought it inside her.

The tasting of sweet fire filled her senses for the longest time, but gradually, incrementally, Domini became aware of other things, things beyond the feeding. She had a body. She was aware of drying sweat and a cold breeze blowing over her. There was another body, hard and male, strong arms holding her, a heart beating like a drum. Underneath the drumbeat was another sound, an irritable, persistent ringing noise that hurt her ears. What was it?

A telephone?

A telephone. Yes.

After a while, it stopped.

Soon after that the darkness came back, but different now. She floated in it, mind and body and soul happy, exhausted, sated. She was herself again, too tired to move, almost awake, almost aware.

Aware enough to know Alexander was moving around the room when she wished he was beside her. She thought he might be getting dressed. That was too bad. She was not awake enough to protest that she wanted him to come to bed.

She heard the phone ring again. Then the knock came on the door. Then there were voices. Alexander barked out a question. There were answers. The air currents on her skin changed, and she knew he'd opened the door.

Alec had to open the door to the two men, but he blocked the doorway with his body. Dr. Casmerek, he recognized. The other must be the pilot.

Casmerek peered past Alec's shoulder. "What have you done?"

"She's mine," Alec answered.

"Let me in."

He was Prime. No one came near his mate. If Casmerek had been anything but a human physician, Alec's claws would have come out. As it was, he did show the faintest hint of fangs. The pilot had the sense to back off into the darkness.

Casmerek did not back off. He tried to take a step forward, but Alec put a hand on his shoulder. "Have you harmed her? Does she need a transfusion?"

Alec turned his wrist out so the doctor could see. "My blood. Only mine."

Casmerek's eyes widened. "Bonding? In your condition?" His features grew stern. "Step aside, Alec," he said calmly and with great authority. "For her sake. You know I won't harm her. She helped you; I can see that. Now let me help her."

Alec backed up, and the doctor followed. But he didn't let Casmerek near his woman. Instead, he wrapped the bedspread around Domini and lifted her in his arms.

"The plane's waiting?"

"Yes," Casmerek answered. "I brought the new serum. I was going to treat you during the flight."

"No need to change the plan." Alec marched out of the wrecked motel room. The darkness felt good. He hadn't felt so alive, so much himself, for a long time. He held Domini tight against his chest. He had her to thank for this night.

The doctor hurried into the parking lot after them. "You're going to feel like hell tomorrow," he said, as though he'd read Alec's thoughts.

"Maybe."

Alec glanced at the pilot waiting in the shadows, leaning against a pickup truck with "Salt View Airport" painted on the door. Both the motel and the private airport were owned by the Clans. Both the humans were not only well paid, but had ties of family, friendship, and loyalty to the Clans.

Alec climbed into the back of the truck, cradling Domini in his lap. "Let's go," he ordered, a high-handed Prime who expected to be, and was, obeyed.

Chapter Twenty-six

She knew her name was Domini; everything else was a blur.

The air smelled of pine; fresh and sweet, with just a hint of dampness to go along with the north woodsy tang. She remembered hearing raindrops on the windowpane sometime while she drifted in and out of sleep.

The bed was large, the mattress soft, the linens softer, and they smelled of lavender. This was not her bed.

She managed to open her eyes. It was a nice room, but totally unfamiliar. She made out botanical prints in dark wood frames hanging on a cream-colored wall. Sheer curtains fluttered in the breeze from a slightly open window. A pine-scented breeze was damp with recent rain. There was a pretty little pink glass lamp on the bedstand beside her. The lamp was turned on, but the bulb was about as dim as her thought processes at the moment. In the pinkish light she discovered she was wearing an old-fashioned long-sleeved cotton nightgown, elaborately embroidered white on white. How had she gotten into it?

When she tried to sit up, lights flared behind her eyes in fireworks that would have been pretty but for the pain. She fell back on the thick down pillows and lay very, very still. Maybe she wasn't ready to get up yet.

She let that thought percolate for a while, until it made her angry, and stubborn. She tried sitting up again, but this time she took it slowly. Her head still hurt when she moved, but she expected it, and she coped. There was a door on the other side of the room. She intended to go out that door.

Questions were beginning to form, and she wanted answers. She wasn't going to get them lying around in a soft bed in a pretty room somewhere very far from the smog, dust, and dry heat of Los Angeles.

She wanted to go home. And she wanted—

Loneliness stabbed at her, sharp and cutting, more painful than the ache in her head.

She wanted Alexander Reynard. Alec. Her Alexander.

"Where's Alexander?"

As if speaking the words activated a magic spell, the door opened—and a dark angel stepped in. The woman was beautiful; tall, lean, elegant, with supermodel cheekbones, green eyes, and long black satin hair; she was dressed all in black. She held her right hand out, and Domini recognized the ruby-and-gold ring the woman wore.

Domini wondered if she was supposed to curtsy, or kiss the ring.

"I am Lady Anjelica," the woman said, in a warm velvet voice. "Matri of Clan Reynard. Welcome to my Citadel."

"Uh-huh," Domini said, nodding slowly. She wondered if the woman was aware of how silly that all sounded. "And what century are we living in?"

The other woman only laughed.

"I'm living in the twenty-first. I suppose the title sounds a bit much to someone not used to our ways." She smiled, and her green eyes glinted with humor. "Would it help put you at ease if I told you that back in the sixties, I was known as the original Foxy Lady? Of course, that was long before you were born, though I swear you look exactly like your grandmother did then. We were quite the pair—"

"Whoa! Whoa! Whoa!" Domini waved her hands in front of her, which didn't help her headache, but the confusion was worse than the pain. "You didn't know my grandmother. You couldn't. You're a vampire; I can tell."

Lady Anjelica nodded. "Of course you can tell I'm a vampire. You and Alec have been busy." She shook a finger at Domini. "I wish you and my son hadn't begun the bond before I had a chance to talk to you both, but Dr. Casmerek tells me the feral incident couldn't be helped. I thank you for helping him. But what you don't yet understand is that his blood is beginning to change you."

Domini didn't understand a lot of what Lady Anjelica said. She couldn't remember—she couldn't remember past— "There was a ring. Your ring. Alexander—" His face flashed through her mind, pain-racked, tight with control, beautiful to her. She missed him desperately, needed to be with him. "Where's Alexander? Where's Reynard?"

A look of concern crossed Lady Anjelica's face. "He will be all right," she soothed Domini. "You can see him when he's better."

"I need to see him now."

"I understand."

Her expression was compassionate, but Lady Anjelica stood squarely between Domini and the door. Domini knew there was no getting past her. That didn't stop Domini from wanting to try; only the knowledge that she didn't know where to look stopped her. Maybe if she concentrated on *wanting* to find Alexander, the wanting would lead her to him. But she didn't think the headache was going to let her concentrate enough for that. Besides the pain in her head, her whole body felt weak and drained, and not quite right. And there was panic growing in her, gnawing at her control.

"What happened?" she asked. "Why do I feel like this? Where am I? What happened?"

"All very good questions," Lady Anjelica answered. "Most of the answers, you'll be able to work out for yourself after you've had a bit more rest. And lots of nourishment. You were down a couple of quarts. You'll need lots of feeding to get your strength back."

"Down a couple of—"

What exactly did the vampire woman mean by "feeding"?

Domini found herself sitting on the edge of the bed. She was very confused, and even more dizzy. The pulse in her temples pounded, and she squinted to keep the other woman in focus. Nausea clenched her gut. "A couple quarts of what?"

"I think you need a bit more sleep," Lady Anjelica answered. Domini knew from the soft, insistent tone that the vampire was ordering rather than suggesting.

She waved a hand weakly toward Anjelica. "Don't do that. I don't like it when you people do that." Her voice was a muffled slur.

"It's for your own good."

"You sound like Alexander."

"I am his mother."

"You look more like a sister."

"Thank you. I'll explain many things to you later. Sleep now," she ordered, and helped Domini lie back on the bed. Domini couldn't keep her eyes open any longer.

When she woke up again, Domini did feel better physically, but she wasn't happy about it. Not when she was haunted by dark dreams she couldn't recall, and woke with a lurking sense of dread. Something was coming, something she didn't want to face.

This time no one appeared in the room when she got up. She found clothes neatly folded on top of a chest at the foot of the bed. She found a bathroom as well, with vanilla-scented soap and thick, plush towels.

The clothes fit, from the underwear to the long black broomstick skirt, pine green silk sweater, and black slides she slipped on her feet. She felt much better with clothes on, armored to face the day, or the night, or the vampires that waited outside the door.

Well, she wasn't so sure about facing Alexander's mother. It wasn't just that the vampire queen, or whatever she was, was all magical and formidable, and far too glamorous for any other female's ego. It was that she was Alexander Reynard's *mother,* for God's sake!

She'd never been involved with a man long enough or seriously enough to meet his parents before. But she had a feeling that the only way she was going to get to Alexander was through his mom, so a meeting with Lady Anjelica was in the offing. Might as well get it over with.

Domini tried the door handle, and was surprised to find it wasn't locked. And *maybe* she was a touch disappointed that it wasn't. Being locked in would have been evidence of her being a prisoner. She had been brought here against her will, right? At Lady Anjelica's order. Domini's memory was still a little fuzzy, but she was pretty sure she hadn't volunteered to be a "guest" at the Citadel.

Domini walked out of the bedroom to find herself on a landing of polished hardwood that overlooked a huge room two stories below. Looking over the smooth wooden railing, she saw furniture, rugs, and a decor that was far more North Woods Lodge than Hollywood Vampire Castle. Of course, Reynard's house in Los Angeles had been perfectly normal, too. Maybe hearing the place called a citadel had given her notions. There wasn't a cobweb or coffin in sight in this airy house, and much of one wall of the great room that stretched up three stories was made of windows that looked out on a large lake.

"Pretty, isn't it?"

Domini jumped, and whirled to find Lady Anjelica standing beside her, leaning on the rail.

Anjelica was dressed in gray slacks and a gray-and-red patterned burn-out velvet tunic, her long hair framing her exquisite features. There was a wicked look on Anjelica's face.

"You enjoy giving people heart attacks, don't you?" Domini asked.

"Strokes," Anjelica answered. "Elevated blood pressure lends a certain carbonated effect to the victim's— I'm joking, I'm joking." She touched Domini's shoulder. "Don't look so horrified. Honestly, you young people have no macabre sense of humor these days."

"Not at the moment. Nice place," Domini added politely.

"Glad you like it."

"Can I leave now?"

"Come along," Anjelica said, ignoring Domini's request. "We need to talk." She walked down the landing and turned left at a long hallway. Domini followed. "My morning room," Anjelica said as she ushered Domini into a large windowless room at the end of the hall.

The decor here was more feminine, though strong colors dominated; the overhead lighting was subtle, and the furniture was leather, with a pair of chairs and a love seat grouped around a low table in the center of the room. There was a fire going in a white marble fireplace, and framed photographs on the wide mantel. A small desk was set against one wall, and a few other tables and straight-backed chairs were scattered around the room. The carpet was a deep plush, in a blue-and-white Chinese pattern.

"The great room downstairs is lovely in the morning, but I'm not much of a morning person," Anjelica told her.

Domini realized that Anjelica's conversation was meant to put her at ease, but what really drew her attention were the wonderful aromas coming from dishes on the table.

Domini's stomach rumbled as she walked past Anjelica and headed straight for the low table, where a small feast was set out on fancy china.

Domini pointed at a tall carafe. "Is that coffee?"

"I thought you might like some breakfast."

"Yes, please."

"Have a seat."

Domini had already settled into one of the leather wingback chairs. She poured two cups of coffee and passed one to Lady Anjelica before taking a long gulp. She sat back in the deep, butter-soft chair, savoring the coffee. "Wonderful."

"Try the orange juice," Anjelica directed. "It's good for you. There's eggs, bacon, and sausage. Never mind the cholesterol, you need protein right now. I'll talk while you eat, because there's a great deal you'll want to know, and much I can tell you before you need to ask any questions."

What Domini wanted was to know where Alexander was and if he was all right, but before she could ask, Lady Anjelica said, "I should tell you about Alec. About Primes in general, but Alec specifically, since he is your Prime. Eat your eggs while I explain."

Domini gave in to curiosity and hunger and let the woman talk.

"Primes are adult male vampires. They are proud, imperious, possessive, strong, territorial, intensely sexual, stubborn, haughty, protective, arrogant, handsome. Depending on the situation, they can be the most wonderful men in the world or complete pricks. There tend to be more male vampires than females, so Primes frequently have sexual liaisons with human women. Sometimes those liaisons become long-term romantic relationships. And sometimes the same sort of lifemate soul-bond forms between a Prime and a female human as does between a vampire male and female. This bonding is on a psychic and physical level, and permanent. The Prime and his human soul mate share blood and psychic energy, which increases the human's life span and psychic gifts to match the life span of her mate. Due to a rare genetic abnormality in humans, occasionally, very rarely, a mortal woman bondmate can make the transition to vampire. This change doesn't grant immortality, because vampires are not immortal, though we do live significantly longer than our human cousins. Very close cousins, but I'll explain more about physiology, biology, and history in a bit."

"Okay," Domini agreed, around a mouthful of food. "Go on about Alexander and me."

She remembered now that she'd offered him her blood, and he must have shared blood with her. Anjelica's comment about her being down a couple of quarts made sense now. The experience had led to her feeling like hell, but Domini was willing to bet that her reaction came from the fact that Alexander had been so—feral—at the time.

"Absolutely correct. He took more of your blood than he should have, but he couldn't help it. He loves you," Anjelica said, "which is why he stopped before it was too late."

"I'm getting used to having my mind read, but I still don't like it."

Lady Anjelica didn't apologize for the intrusion, but said, "You'll develop barriers eventually."

"Fine. Go on."

"In the normal course of events, what appears to have happened between you and Alec is the meeting of two people meant to be bondmates. But the circumstances are not normal at all."

Dread clutched at Domini again. She was barely managing to accept the bondmate stuff. If you accepted that there were people like her who could see glimpses of the future, and that vampires really existed, then it was possible to believe that soul-deep love-for-all-time was possible. Now Lady Anjelica was throwing a wrench into the works.

"You're saying that your son and I *aren't* meant for each other? You don't approve?" Domini was not unaware of the irony here. A couple days ago, *she* wasn't sure she and Reynard belonged together.

"It is not for me to approve or disapprove," Lady Anjelica told her. "You are bonding. There is no stopping it. The problem might arise when the Matri of Clan Corvus finds out her granddaughter has bonded with a Reynard Prime, without any prior agreement or contract between clans." Anjelica waved an elegant hand while Domini gaped at her. "But that is a matter of paperwork and ceremony. I'm sure Cassandra Crowe and I will work something out; the Blackbird is a reasonable woman."

Domini stared at the vampire matriarch, dizzy with dread and the effort to make sense of what she'd heard. All that she knew was that her grandmother's name was Cassandra, and that her nickname was Blackbird. Everybody seemed to know that her nickname was Blackbird—at least all the vampires she met knew it. "What the hell are you talking about?"

Anjelica put down her coffee cup. "Let me explain about the Clans a bit, first. There are different sorts of vampires, different cultures, really. The Clans have always been the most closely associated with humans. We like humans—and not just as menu items. Though we do need to drink blood, we don't have to kill to satisfy that hunger. We don't even have to drink human blood, though we prefer it. There's certainly a medical reason for the craving, and we have researchers working on the connection.

"The Clans do everything possible to work for the welfare of our human cousins. We always have and always will. There is an ancient, sacred bond between us and our human cousins. Once upon a time, we were treated as gods by humans. We brought justice, protected them. Times changed, and humans changed, and vampires became reviled and hunted. But the Clans stayed true to our vows to protect humans.

"We went underground, and each of the ancient Clans that had once been kings on Earth took the name of a creature that humans needed, but hated. We became the snakes, the wolves, the foxes, the crows, jackals, and so on. We took the names of creatures that humans called vermin, and wore them with honor and irony. Never let it be said that vampires don't have a sense of humor.

"Corvus," she went on, "is the Crow Clan, as Reynard is the Fox, Jackal is Shagal, and so on. Your grandmother is from Clan Corvus."

Domini wanted to protest, but arguing with Anjelica wouldn't get the story out sooner.

"Since there are significantly fewer vampire women than men, traditionally, vampire women rarely had the same sorts of sexual liaisons as the Primes. For the last century, though, some of our young women have ventured out into the world for a few decades before settling into their responsibilities as heads of the Clans. Once upon a time, Cassandra Crowe took herself a human lover."

"No."

Anjelica ignored Domini's faint protest. "They lived together for several decades. They had a son. Such offspring rarely exhibit any vampire traits. They might be a bit psychic, but for the most part they are completely human. Your father was human, Domini, but sometimes vampire traits skip a generation." She paused. "You are not completely human, Domini."

"That does it. I'm out of here."

Domini sprang to her feet and marched to the door. Nobody, nohow, no way, was telling her that she was a vampire.

Domini! Come back here.

Anjelica's order snapped around her like a whip. Domini fought the urge to obey and kept on going.

I will not be disobeyed in my own house.

Don't bet on that, Domini thought back.

It took all her will, fueled by stubborn anger, but she made it to the door. Reaching for the knob and turning it was the hardest thing she'd ever done. It seemed to take a long time, but the door finally opened.

And when it did, Alexander came rushing in like a charging linebacker. He grabbed her, and his momentum carried them halfway across the room.

"What's the matter?" he demanded frantically, holding Domini in a tight embrace. Domini put her arms around him and held on tight to his hard muscle and flesh.

"Mother," he said, pulling her closer, "what the hell have you done to my woman?"

Chapter Twenty-seven

"I've been telling her the truth," Anjelica said, coming to her feet. "Truth I need to tell you, as well. I'm glad you feel up to joining us."

Alec was aware of his mother's anger. He had dared to enter the Matri's presence without asking permission; he'd also spoken rudely to her.

He didn't care. Even a Clan Matri had no right to cause pain to someone in the fragile beginning of a bond. He'd felt Domini's agitation and pain from the other side of the estate. Her need had been strong enough for him to throw off the effects of the sedatives Casmerek had given him, and come to his lover's aid.

He had not expected to find that his mother had caused Domini's distress.

"Domini is overreacting," his mother said, tightly controlling her impatience. "I was explaining her heritage to her, and she took it amiss."

Alec ran his hands soothingly up and down Domini's tense back and turned a puzzled look on his mother. "Her heritage?"

"Apparently her grandfather has been keeping secrets from her. I think that's what's disturbing her the most. Isn't it, Domini?"

Domini whirled out of Alec's embrace to face Anjelica. "I am not a vampire!" she declared.

The venom in her tone struck pain through him, but Alec reminded himself that Domini really didn't know anything about vampires yet. It certainly didn't help that he'd nearly killed her a few nights ago. "Of course you're not a vampire," he soothed. "Bonding to one, yes, but you cannot become—"

"She can and she will be changed," his mother interrupted. She turned a stern gaze on Alec. "Dr. Casmerek has done the blood tests to prove it. Why do you think the Purists pursue her?"

With everything else that had happened, Alec had all but forgotten that the fanatics had attacked the woman he loved. He put his hands on Domini's shoulders and gently turned her to face him. "Is there something you haven't been telling me?"

Her gaze met his in a fiery glare. "Of course not!"

"She had no idea about her family history," Anjelica said.

If Domini truly was of vampire lineage, their possibilities together might, just might, change drastically. Alec didn't dare to let himself hope yet. Having a bondmate, vampire or human, was more than many Primes ever achieved. Having Domini as his bondmate was more than enough. But . . .

Alec looked back at his mother. "Are you sure about this? How?"

"I knew her history before Dr. Casmerek ran his tests. Why do you think I sent for her?"

"I have no idea why. You commanded. I obeyed." He snapped the words out, hating that anyone, even his Clan Matri, dared to interfere with his private affairs.

"Sit down, both of you," Anjelica said. "And I will explain."

Domini was quivering with fury in his embrace. He knew that if he dared to let her go she would only try to march out again. The Matri would tell him to stop her, he would, and he and Domini would argue.

To avoid that argument, he forced his own anger at Anjelica to cool, and brought Domini to sit beside him on the love seat. He put his arm around her, keeping her close to comfort them both, and to keep her from bolting again.

"Anthony Crowe knew that his second cousin and I have always been friends," Anjelica explained after she resumed her own seat. "When no one at the Crowe Citadel knew where their Matri had gone on vacation, he called here to ask if I knew. I did, but if a Matri doesn't want to be disturbed, another Matri isn't going to disturb her for less than a Clan-threatening emergency." She gave Alec a faint smile. "When I asked what his business was, Anthony told me that you were involved with a young woman named Lancer who looked amazingly like his cousin Blackbird, and that Purists were active again in Los Angeles. Not only were they threatening vampires, but the Purists had an interest in the Lancer woman. He suspected a Crowe connection because of the strong resemblance between the women. He doesn't know about Blackbird's life among mortals, but I do. I knew who Domini had to be, so I sent for her."

Alec was still annoyed at Anjelica's interference, but he was also curious. "If she's Corvus, why not send her to the Corvus Clan?"

"Because I have a use for her."

He frowned at the Matri. "Other than being my mate, I take it."

"Yes."

"I'm sitting right here, you know," Domini chimed in. "What do you want with me?" she demanded of the Matri.

Anjelica looked directly at Domini. "I want you to talk to the hunters about the Purists."

After a pause, Domini said, "Of course you do." She turned to Alec. "This makes sense, how?"

"It does makes sense, when you know who the players are," Alec assured her.

"Explain to her, Alexander," Anjelica told him.

Domini's anxiety and anger weren't getting any better, and she was projecting all she felt very strongly. Her emotions were open to him; he wondered if Domini sensed his possessiveness for her, and his leashed anger at the Matri.

He did not want to talk. He was back in his right mind and certain of his physical responses. He wanted to celebrate this rebirth by taking his mate, over and over, until they were both blind, deaf, and dumb from sated lust. Then he wanted to start all over again.

Instead, he curbed desire and said, "It's a staple of fiction, and a matter of fact. Where there are vampires, there are vampire hunters. Not all vampires are good. Not all hunters are as bad as the Purists. Over the millennia we've come to, if not exactly truces, at least unspoken understandings with the less fanatical of the hunters. They hunt the vampires that behave like monsters, and mostly leave the Clans alone. It's an uneasy understanding. Most hunters believe that the only good vampire is a 'staked through the heart, head cut off, mouth filled with garlic, burned to a cinder' dead vampire. Most vampires hate the hunters for all the persecutions of the past. Many resent the hunters taking out any vampire, no matter how evil, because there are so few left. There's bad blood on both sides, and no real trust. The situation is always tense, ready to spill over into bloodshed.

"The Purists are a supersecret fanatical cult that arose among the hunters a century ago. They hold to the original hunter doctrine that all vampires are the evil spawn of Satan and need to be destroyed."

"Hence the name Purist," Domini put in.

"Precisely, my love."

Are they right?

Alec caught Domini's thought, and told himself that no one could be damned for stray thoughts that crossed their minds. He exchanged a glance with his mother, and saw that she had also overheard Domini's flash of uncertainty.

"May I interject some facts and figures about what vampires really are?" Anjelica asked. Because she was the Clan Matri in her own citadel, the question was, of course, rhetorical. "We are not supernatural beings. We were not created by a pact with the devil, or any other such mythological nonsense. As long as there have been humans—no, as long as there have been hominids—there have been vampires. We are simply descended from a slightly different branch of the evolutionary tree."

This anthropological explanation drew Domini's complete attention. "Really? How so? How do you know?"

Anjelica was equally enthusiastic about explaining. "There is a legend about two sisters. Vampires have kept this legend alive for thousands of years. Our belief is that at the beginning of time, a pair of twin sisters were born deep in the heart of the world, in Africa. One sister walked by day, but feared the night. She was physically weaker than her twin, but very fertile. She gave birth to the race of men. The other sister was gifted with very long life, but she was not so prolific. The night was hers, as were many other gifts. She not only feared daylight, but it had the power to kill her. She was the mother of vampires. In the last few decades, proof has begun to emerge that there is a great deal of fact to our origin legend. You've heard of Eve?"

"You're not talking about Adam and Eve, are you?" Domini guessed. "You're referring to the study that traces all the mitochondrial DNA of everyone on earth back thousands of generations to the one hominid female that was the mother of us all. Some scientists, and the media, call her Eve."

"You watch the Discovery Channel a lot, don't you?" Alec murmured.

"Yes," Domini answered. "And I have a minor in anthropology."

Anjelica smiled with pleasure at Domini's interest. "That is indeed the Eve I referred to. Human scientists traced human origins back to this one primitive hominid woman. And vampire scientists have done work on finding Eve's sister. They have traced our DNA back to the same source—to the same family, rather."

"This is all very interesting," Alec said. *To someone, I suppose.* "But Domini and I would like to spend some time together—alone."

Anjelica lifted her head proudly. "Domini needed to understand that there is scientific proof that neither we, nor she, have any connection to demons or monsters."

"Fine. I'm glad that's settled."

He was aware that Domini was still uncomfortable, but only time and experience would fully settle her doubts. He wasn't all that comfortable with the scientific explanation of vampires, but if it helped Domini, he wasn't going to point out that he preferred a more romantic version of vampire origins.

"Now that I've explained about the Purists, will you tell us why you want Domini to talk to the hunters?"

"Because the hunters will be far more comfortable meeting face-to-face with a human to discuss our mutual problem with the Purists. We desperately need a liaison, and Domini's background will help her talk to both sides. There's tension building among all branches of vampires over recent increases in Purist attacks. Many of our kind are being swayed back to the old belief that the only good hunter is a dead one. I'm trying to keep a war from starting, and Domini can help stop that war. Fate has brought her to us at the moment we need her."

"I need her," Alec stated his claim. "She is mine."

"Domini's aid is needed by all the Clans," Anjelica went on. "I have called a Convocation." She glanced at the gold watch on her wrist. "I've been planning it for weeks, to begin tonight. Guests have been arriving from all over the country for several days."

"Convocation?" Domini asked Alec.

"Sort of a cross between a party, a religious ritual, and a board-of-directors meeting," he explained. "They're usually a lot of fun." Though he wasn't interested in socializing right now; he wanted to be alone with Domini. "Fun for those of us who don't have to work," he added with a respectful nod to his mother.

Anjelica actually took that as the hint he intended. "I have guests to greet," she said. "Staff to brief." She glanced toward her desk. "A speech to finish writing."

Alec rose to his feet, bringing Domini with him. "Then we'll leave you to your work." He had his lady out in the hallway and the door closed behind them before Anjelica could answer.

Anjelica sent telepathic laughter into his thoughts. *Show Domini the gazebo,* his mother thought at him. *You'll be private there.*

It was an excellent suggestion. Alec sent a thought of thanks, then said to Domini, "I'll show you the gardens and the lakeshore. You'll like the grounds."

Domini welcomed the chance to check out the area. She'd been trained to find all entrances and exits to wherever she was staying; you never knew when escape routes might come in handy.

"You're feeling better," she said as they stepped outside into the daylight.

It was overcast, a bit cool, but the pine-scented air was very refreshing. Alexander held her hand in his. It made her feel warm and secure, and the touch of his flesh sent little thrills of desire through her.

"How can you tell?" he asked, and raised her hand to his lips to kiss her knuckles one at a time.

It took Domini a moment to concentrate on anything but how those kisses made her feel. "You're not wearing sunglasses," she finally managed. "And you look . . ." The best she could manage was, "Good." Which was not nearly an adequate description.

His face was no longer gaunt or deathly pale. The sparkle in his eyes was wicked, but it wasn't feral. There was no sign of pain or weakness about him; just the opposite. He exuded confidence, strength, command, and bone-deep allure. He made her heart race and her knees weak, and sent desire careening through her. The man had it, knew he had it, and was perfectly comfortable living with an overdose of raw sexual appeal.

"Prime," Domini muttered.

"Uh-huh."

She'd spent time around movie stars, rock stars, and other high-powered men who oozed charisma and sexual confidence. She'd always been told that power was sexy. She'd certainly seen how women were attracted to that scent of power, but now she understood.

And Alexander Reynard stood there smiling at her in the middle of a vibrant garden, while she ignored the beautiful landscape and took in the wonder that was him. He accepted her awe as his due.

"You're—impressive," she said.

He drew her closer. "And you like it."

She draped her arms around his neck, pressed her body against the hard length of his, and let her fingers roam through his thick, dark hair. "And you like that I like it."

He put his hands on her, stroking her hips, her waist, and up and down her back, drawing small noises out of her and making her very aware of his own arousal.

He finally took a deep breath and held her out at arm's length. "We can't stay here," he said.

"Why?" she wondered dreamily, trying to draw him back to her.

"Because we can be seen from every window in the back of the house." He turned her around.

Domini took in the huge three-story building. "That's a lot of windows," she agreed.

"Let's go down by the lake."

He put his arm around her shoulders and steered her to a red-brick path that took them in a zigzag pattern through the terraced grounds. Some of the property was beautifully landscaped, but much of it was wild woods. They crossed a meandering stream on log footbridges a couple of times.

Domini caught glimpses of other buildings through stands of trees and beyond low walls. "How big is this place?"

"We have a few acres, and a number of buildings. There's a small private school with dorms for the adolescents. Other things the Clan needs."

"How many people live here?"

"Most of us who call the Citadel home don't live here all the time. With the Convocation, there'll be a lot of guests."

"Where is this place?"

"On the shores of Lake Coeur d'Alene." He looked up at the mountains that rose in the distance. "Nice, isn't it?"

"Yes. How'd we get here?"

"We took a private plane from one private airport to another, then a helicopter to the helipad out by the garage. We have several copters, planes, and pilots always on standby. The Clans are fairly wealthy."

"Medieval treasure hordes?" she ventured.

"Investments in pharmaceutical firms, mostly. Biotech, genetic research, anything to do with medicine."

"How very—humanitarian of you."

"Partially."

They rounded a turn in the path and came upon a man sitting on a bench beneath a huge old pine tree. The man stood when he caught sight of them.

Alec winced, like a boy who'd been caught by the truant officer. "Dr. Casmerek," he said. "You've met the doctor," he told Domini, "but you don't remember him."

"Seems to be a lot of that going around," Domini muttered.

"I've been waiting for you, Alec. Nice to see you vertical, Ms. Lancer." The doctor came forward and held out his hand.

Domini was amused to realize after a moment that the doctor was more interested in taking her pulse than shaking her hand. Though she was aware that Alexander didn't approve of any male touching her but himself, she dutifully presented her wrist to the physician.

She wasn't amused a moment later when Casmerek's fingers settled on her skin; she found that *she* didn't like anyone's hands on her but Alexander's. But the doctor's exam was quick and impersonal.

He soon stepped back and said, "You're doing fine. You," he said, looking sternly at Alexander, "left the infirmary in the middle of your inoculations."

"Inoculations?" Domini gave Alec a quick, anxious look. "I thought you were all better."

"He is better," Casmerek said. "But he still needs—let's call them treatments for very serious allergies."

"Garlic, hawthorn wood, silver, that sort of thing," Alexander added.

Domini rubbed her wrists, remembering the bracelet that had irritated her skin a few days before. "I have trouble wearing silver sometimes," she said. "Wait a minute—I thought it was werewolves that were allergic to silver?"

"Not that I'm aware of," Alexander answered. "But silver's murder on vampires."

"And if you want to be one hundred percent in shape for tonight's gathering, Prime," Dr. Casmerek cut in, "you need to come with me right now."

Alec wanted to snarl with frustration. He was standing outside in the daylight and feeling just fine. He wanted to be with Domini. But Casmerek would never thwart a Prime without good reason. If he said Alec needed the rest of the shots, Alec needed them.

"All right, Doc. Give me a second." He took Domini's hands and kissed them one by one before letting her go. "I'll see you tonight. Do me a favor, sweetheart." He kissed her palm one last time. "Wear anything but black to the party."

Chapter Twenty-eight

"Don't wear black, he said," Domini told Maja as they came down the stairs. She paused to take in the view of the room below, and Maja came to a halt beside her. "Do you see anyone wearing anything *but* black down there?"

"No." Maja was wearing a long-sleeved column of black velvet, very elegant, very Morticia Addams.

Maja had appeared at Domini's side when Alexander left her in the garden and hadn't let Domini out of her sight since. She wasn't particularly talkative, other than to tell Domini that she'd been sent to keep her company by Lady Anjelica and to answer "No" to any question Domini asked her. Her demeanor was completely neutral, and totally watchful. If Domini hadn't been so frustrated at having Maja dogging her every movement, she'd have complimented a fellow professional on her competence.

For all her polite inconspicuousness, Maja's presence reinforced Domini's belief that she was more a prisoner than a guest in Lady Anjelica's house. It infuriated her more than it frightened her. Being frightened all the time was far too wearing on the nerves. Besides, right now, all she wanted was to find Alexander; no one and nothing else in the Citadel mattered.

Except, possibly, what she was wearing.

She was wearing scarlet, and a lot of bare skin.

Domini had found the short, strapless red satin sheath among a closet full of clothes in her guest bedroom. The clothes and shoes stored in the closet ran in a wide range of sizes, leaving Domini to conclude that unexpected company was common. There'd been several dresses suitable for evening wear in Domini's size, two of them black. She'd decided to wear the red dress and a pair of stiletto heels partly to look sexy for Alexander, and partly because being inconspicuous was what she did at work, and tonight was a party. She hadn't planned on standing out quite so much in a crowd of strangers, though.

She continued down to the main floor and stepped into a sea of beautiful women in black—silk, satin, beading, lace, embroidery—all of it expensive, much of it stylish, some old-fashioned, some of it Goth. The men—and what men they were!—were dressed as darkly as the ladies. Many of them favored leather.

Heads turned her way instantly. Conversations stopped. She told herself it was the dress, but she could feel the psychic energy levels shift. She was being looked at, studied, assessed, and not with eyes alone. It reinforced that she was human, and that these people were not.

She needed Alexander. To see him, touch him, talk to him. She missed talking to him when he wasn't around. She'd wanted him all afternoon, her body humming with desire and anticipation. It was surprising how she'd gone from being wary of him to caring for him. But she also wanted to be near him because he was the one thing she was sure of in this place.

Maybe the one thing she was sure of in her life.

If her grandfather had lied to her about . . . If what Lady Anjelica said was true . . .

Domini pushed her doubts aside. She captured a glass of champagne from a roving server and moved farther into the huge room. At least, she hoped it was champagne—for all she knew, vampires served carbonated plasma at their parties. She bravely took a sip, and discovered the flute did indeed hold champagne. Very good champagne.

Maja finally left Domini, walking past her, and was instantly surrounded by an admiring knot of vampire men.

Domini was glad to be rid of her watchdog, but it left her adrift in a room full of strangers. What was she supposed to do? Walk up to the nearest group and introduce herself? No one had filled her in on this culture's etiquette.

She supposed the best she could do was keep circulating until—

"Hello, beautiful."

Domini swung around to face the man who'd spoken. Even in heels, she had to look up quite a ways to meet his gaze. His eyes were dark, and his hair was blond. Broad shoulders filled out a high-necked, Russian-style tunic. His smile was confident to the point of being cocky. Even though she didn't have a clue about how vampires aged, her impression was that he was young.

"Hello, gorgeous," she answered without thinking, because he was.

He smirked. She'd figured he would.

"I'm Kiril."

Domini was very aware of all the eyes on them, but Kiril didn't seem to notice, or at least care. He stood in front of her, and—preened for her pleasure, was the only phrase that came to mind for his attitude.

She took a sip of champagne. "You're trying to impress me, right?"

"I don't have to try." He held up a hand, his wrist turned outward so that she could see a small, stylized tattoo. "Wolf Clan," he announced proudly. "House Ariadne." He took a step closer to her. "I'm looking for a mate." He made a small gesture that somehow took in every other male in the room. "As are we all."

Domini's brows rose in shock. "Direct, aren't you?"

"I am Prime."

"You're a putz," someone behind Kiril said.

As the blond Prime whirled around, snarling, Domini thought she caught sight of a hint of fangs. He lunged toward another big blond. Domini backed off hastily, while a laughing crowd formed around the fighting pair.

She remembered how Alexander and Tony had fought over her at the bar in Los Angeles. Apparently battles to claim mates were part of this alpha male culture. Looking around, she saw that there were far more men than women in the great room, and that each woman was surrounded by groups of men. No wonder Maja hadn't stuck with her when they joined the party. Why hang with a mortal female, when there were so many fine-looking studs to choose from?

Domini put more distance between herself and the altercation. She had no interest in being a party favor for the winner. Besides, if she couldn't find Alexander, she'd just find an unguarded exit. With everyone's attention focused on the brawl, maybe—

"Where are you going, pretty one?"

Oh, God, not another one!

When Domini turned around this time, the Prime who smiled at her was whipcord lean and sharp-featured, with thick, burgundy red hair that fell all the way down his back. He looked her over with a hot gaze that left her blushing, and far more intimidated than she'd been by Kiril's arrogance.

Domini fought the urge to take a step back. She faced the stranger and said, "You know I'm a human, right?"

"Yes." He came closer.

Domini did back up this time. "And involved with someone already?"

The vampire took a deep breath. "His blood's in you," he agreed with Domini. "But not so much that another couldn't claim you." Long fingers reached out and touched her cheek. "During Convocation, all is fair."

Domini took another step back. He followed, of course, and she finally noticed he was herding her toward a dark corner. Come to think of it, the room had a lot of dark nooks, crannies, and corners.

The red-haired vampire put his hand on her bare shoulder. "Warm, soft, and lovely," he murmured.

"Cold, hard bitch," she answered.

She threw her champagne into his face, glass and all, and spun away. He smiled and lunged forward over the wet floor and shards of broken crystal, and she used his momentum to toss him over her hip onto the hardwood floor.

He was on his feet before she could blink, and moving toward her again. "I like this game."

Domini stepped back and ran into a solid wall of muscle.

Strong hands came around Domini's shoulders. "I don't play games," Alexander said. "Go away, Colin, before I let my lady wipe the floor with you."

Domini didn't see Colin's exit, because Alexander turned her around, murmuring, "Kids," under his breath. Then he kissed her.

Pleasure swept through her, and the aching kindling of desire. His hands roved over her shoulders and back, and sifted through her hair. Her hands mirrored his movements while she drank in his scent and taste.

After a few minutes she came to herself enough to realize that he'd backed them into the dark corner she'd avoided earlier, and she was delighted at the privacy. Alec held her close as he nuzzled her throat, then kissed a line up her jaw and temple. His wide shoulders blocked her view of the room, but she heard music, laughter, the murmur of voices, and the occasional shout or snarl.

It pleased Alec that she wasn't wearing black. He reluctantly left off kissing her so that he could look at her. Her blue eyes were bright with desire, and her lush lips swollen from his kiss. She looked edible, but along with desire, he felt her curiosity, and a hint of annoyance.

"I'm sorry I'm late. Don't be offended by Colin or the other boys; they can't help but hit on anything in skirts."

She arched a brow. "Well, that's flattering."

He glanced briefly over his shoulder. "Flare's come back to the Citadel. That's one of the reasons for the Convocation; every unattached Prime who could make it is here."

"Including you?"

He was pleased at the jealousy that shot through his lover. "I'm not unattached. And Flare's my sister."

"Flare?"

"Francesca. We call her Flare for her quick temper and tongue. My bet is that the Matri had to send Flare her ring, too, or she wouldn't have come home."

This was all interesting, but it was hard to think when he kept gently brushing her shoulders and chest and throat. The contact sent pulsing shivers through her. She touched his face in turn, tracing the long line of his jaw, his sensual lips, and the indentation in his chin. She wanted him, had never wanted anyone else, knew that she would never want anyone else. And she knew it was more than lust.

"I like you," she told him. "Even if you are wearing black." He wore a draping black jacket that set off his wide shoulders to perfection, with a black, tab-collared shirt beneath. She fought an impulse to rip off the shiny black buttons of his shirt to get to the skin beneath. "Then there's the lust thing."

Was it the bond they kept talking about that made her feel this way? Was it love? Were the two one and the same?

He put his hands around her waist and pulled her away from their cozy, dark corner. "Let's go somewhere."

"California?" she suggested, coming back to herself through the pleasurable burn of desire. "I need to go home. I need to talk to my grandfather."

He gave her a slightly annoyed look. "Did you ask to use a telephone?"

"Yes," she replied. "I was told the Matri didn't think I should make any calls. Polite or not, I'm a prisoner."

"Cherished guest," he corrected.

"Bullshit."

"I see," Alec said.

He swept Domini into one of the small alcoves off the great room and pulled the heavy drape across the doorway for privacy. The windowless little room had lounges piled high with thick pillows, low romantic lighting, and plush rugs; it was meant for nights like this.

"You see what?" Domini asked, after she'd taken in the romantic little boudoir.

Alec made sure that he was between Domini and the doorway when he answered. "I see that the Matri wishes you to stay here, incommunicado. Her word is law, Domini. There is nothing I can do about it."

Domini was outraged at such blind obedience. "What do you mean, there's nothing you can do about it?"

He ignored her anger. "Not blind," he answered her thoughts. "I stand by the choice I made to live as a son of the Clan on the day I came of age."

"But—"

He held up a hand to get her attention, then spoke very formally. "Lady Anjelica wants to keep you safe. And I would do anything to keep you safe. I *will* keep you safe. You saved my sanity," he added. "Even if I did not owe you that, I love you. And even if I did not love you, or owe you, you are a human in danger. A Prime's true and sacred duty is to protect humans from harm."

Domini glared at Alexander, her lips pressed tightly together. It wouldn't be right to make a man choose between what he saw as his duty and the woman he said he loved. Not and still respect herself. Not if she respected him.

But her grandfather needed her. He had to be frantic about her disappearance, and she desperately needed to talk to him. He was an old man, and she was all he had. If he had secrets, she needed to hear them from him.

"Then I suppose I'll have to escape on my own," she told Alexander.

He crossed his arms, looking dangerous and implacable. "I suppose you can try." He sighed and dropped his aggressive pose. "Or you could accept the Matri's hospitality and my protection. At least until she presents you to the Clan Council."

He came to her and took her in his arms. She stood stiffly in his embrace, fighting the temptation to be comforted, to give in. "I love you," he whispered. *I love you.*

And that did melt her heart, if not the stubborn shell that surrounded it.

She clung to him, accepting his comfort, even if she could not accept her imprisonment. She knew that he drew comfort from her as well, even though he thought she was a stubborn, prickly pain in the butt.

True, she acceded. *I don't know why you think you love me. Not that* you *aren't as stubborn and prickly.*

More puncturing than prickly, he corrected.

"Oh, yeah, fangs and claws."

"Standard equipment," he answered. "All the better to— Domini?"

You were down a couple of quarts. The memory of Anjelica's words ran with a tingling shock through Domini's mind, followed by Colin's, *His blood's in you, but not so much—*

"What the hell did they mean?"

Even as she asked, the memory came up out of the dark and hit her. The motel, the wrecked room, the suffering only she could aid. The choice. The fear and the burning ecstasy that mixed together into hunger. Deep, dying hunger. Sated by the sweetest taste in the world. Giving, taking, giving back and taking again.

They'd shared—

"More than blood," Alec told her. "More than sex. Both, but more." He held her face between his hands, looked into her eyes, and faced her shocked confusion. "That is how the bond begins. Our minds and souls recognize each other, our bodies crave no other touch, but it is the sharing of blood that makes a lover into a bondmate. I'm glad you remember, so I can thank you. But I wish it could have started now, when I could be gentle, careful." He stroked her cheek. "The way I will be in the future."

He glanced at the bed. Now would be a perfect time to strengthen what had started in that motel room. It would bind her closer to him, and help ease her doubts.

He moved his hands over her, soothing and arousing her. "You're strong, Domini, brave and giving. And you wonder why I love you? We were lucky. I might have driven you mad. But you gave yourself freely, and I think that saved us both. I might have killed you. I almost did. This time," he promised, leading her toward the bed, "it will be better."

As he talked, desire sang through Domini. She knew he played her like some fine instrument, and he was an expert musician, but she loved the tune. She covered his mouth with a hard, demanding kiss. She reached for his shirt buttons, to rip them off and—

The blue RAV-4 came to a halt beside a trio of palm trees. Sunset turned the water beyond the white crescent of beach molten bronze. The houses perched above the shore were dark silhouettes in the fading light of dusk. But the driver and three passengers weren't interested in the beauty of the place.

Another car pulled up behind them. Then a van rolled to a stop behind the second vehicle.

With the full team assembled, everyone got out of the vehicles. Everyone was carrying a weapon.

"Grandpa!"

Domini staggered away from Alexander. She couldn't see; her head was too fogged by passion, and the fading images of the vision. She stumbled to her hands and knees on the thick rug, and stayed there while her mind cleared.

"Domini?"

She was on her feet before Alexander could reach her. She waved him away when he would have taken her back into a comforting embrace.

"I have to get out of here," she said. "I have to." She turned, and ran in blind desperation out of the curtained alcove.

Chapter Twenty-nine

Alec moved faster than Domini. He caught her by the shoulders and drew her close as she stepped into the great room.

"Calm down," he whispered in her ear. He held her tight so that she couldn't move. She quivered beneath his hands. He projected calm at her while he looked around and stared down gazes that turned their way. "Don't *ever* run. Don't show fear. Don't panic. No one here wants to harm you, but there are kids here barely out of adolescence. Don't tempt them."

"I am not afraid of vampires," Domini whispered back angrily, her words precise and clipped. "I am afraid of vampire hunters. Your Purists are going to go after my grandfather, and I am going home to help him."

"What did you see?" Alec asked. "If you had a vision, I didn't share it."

"Why should you? It was my vision."

"We're bonding. We share—"

"Maybe your mind was occupied with thoughts of fucking," she snarled.

"So was yours," he countered.

"Until I saw my grandfather in trouble."

Alec tried to remain reasonable, calming. "You are worried about the Old Man. It's likely your subconscious—"

"Is minding its own business. When I see the future, Reynard, I see the future. I know a vision when I have one. And I saw—"

"There you are," Anjelica declared, emerging from the crowd and coming toward them. "Come along," she said, and everyone dutifully followed her into the central area of the great room. Domini and Alec were swept forward in the center of the crowd.

Domini was too intelligent to continue fighting with him in this situation, Alec knew. And far too intelligent to try to flee. So he twined his fingers with hers rather than hold her so tightly. *Relax,* he told her. *Enjoy the party.*

Domini visibly got hold of her temper. Anger remained hot in her eyes, but she put on a smile and squeezed his hand, as though to reassure him.

What was it Anjelica said about Primes? Domini thought as she was led across the room. How they could be the most wonderful men in the world, or complete pricks? Lady Anjelica obviously knew what she was talking about, as her darling son was certainly on the prick side of Prime behavior at the moment. How dare he try to convince her that she hadn't seen what she'd seen, just because it didn't suit his or his beloved Clan's agendas?

Domini managed to train her attention on the present as they approached the freestanding fieldstone fireplace in the center of the room. A fire burned high in the hearth, and lit candles of all shapes and sizes were set out on the mantel and the deep stone bench that circled the fireplace. Five grave, dignified women stood before all this light. They were beautiful and ageless, and exuded confidence and power. Matris, Domini guessed; Clan leaders. No one had exactly explained the rules to her, but it wasn't hard to figure out that Clan society was matriarchal.

A group of men stood to one side of the Matris—strong, vital men, with hints of gray in their hair, lines of experience on their handsome faces. They were all past their youth, in the prime of life. Senior Primes? Silver foxes, definitely—and Wolves, Crows, and whatever the other Clans were called, she supposed.

Another group stood on the other side of the Matris; mostly younger Primes, but Maja was there. So was another young woman. She wore a burn-out velvet dress with nothing but pale skin beneath the semi-sheer black material. Her dark hair was cut buzz short and she was wearing far too much dark eye makeup, which didn't disguise the fact that she was probably the most beautiful woman in a room full of beautiful women. This had to be Flare, and she didn't look any happier to be there than Domini was.

Alec led Domini over to the younger group, and they took places in the front row. Domini found herself standing next to Flare, who threw her a hostile look before she turned a dagger stare on her mother.

Lady Anjelica took her place in the center of the Matris. Everyone at the party was gathered around the fireplace now.

Anjelica said a few words in a language Domini didn't know, and whatever she said got her a round of applause—except from Flare, who sneered. Something of a drama queen, Domini decided.

"Welcome," Anjelica said after she finished her speech in Vampirese. "Especially welcome home to my daughter Francesca."

More applause. More sneering from Flare, with a head-toss and a dirty look for everyone thrown in for good measure. Annoyed as she was with him, Domini couldn't keep from sharing an amused look with Alexander.

"And welcome to all the Primes who have come to Convocation for no other reason than to impress Francesca."

More laughter, and quite a few Primes exchanged challenging looks.

"It is time that Francesca founded her own House. I look forward to being a grandmother many times over in the next few decades."

There was another spattering of applause, especially from the Matris, who nodded their approval.

Domini found all this interplay interesting, until Lady Anjelica turned her attention on her and Alexander.

"My son Alexander brings the Clans good fortune, as well." Anjelica raked her gaze over the crowd before looking back at Domini. "All of us seek our bondmate," she said. "Some of us find this mate among vampire kind; many find their fulfillment with one of our human cousins. My son has found his mate."

More applause and enthusiastic cries of congratulations filled the room. Alexander looked pleased and proud, and Domini couldn't help but feel a flutter of pleasure herself. When he put his arm around her shoulders, she leaned against him, happy to be with him, happy for him. She still planned on getting to her grandfather as soon as possible, though.

Anjelica held up a hand for silence. "Alec has brought us more than a bride. He has also brought back a daughter of the Clans. Welcome, Domini, bound to Prime Alexander, Reynard of House Reynard.

"Domini is human born, but bears a Founder's spark," Anjelica continued. "She is one of those rare women born of the day, but meant for the night."

Domini looked at Alexander. "This highfalutin stuff make sense to you?"

He was grinning. "Every word."

When she looked back at the crowd, Domini noticed that many of the women did not look particularly pleased at Anjelica's news. Vampire politics, she supposed.

"What am I being thrown into, here?" she whispered to Alec.

"Founders can start new clans," he whispered back. "Become Matris."

"Aren't all vampire women Matris?"

"Matris are heads of Clans. Most women are heads of Houses within their Clans."

Anjelica finished her speech by throwing up her arms and declaring, "Tomorrow I will present Domini to the Matri, with whom we have much to discuss. Tonight, the Convocation of the Clans celebrates!"

The crowd cheered. Alec kept his arm around Domini and steered her into the party.

"That was very—"

"In a minute," Alec cut Domini off as Primes stepped up to them to offer their congratulations.

She kept quiet, but he felt her bursting with questions, and was aware of temper and impatience simmering under the polite veneer she put on. She really didn't pay attention to anything until Kiril stepped up to them.

"Congratulate me, cousin," the big blond announced. He held up his arm, proudly showing off a wolf's-head tattoo. "I am going to be a fireman."

Alec gave the young Prime a pleased pat on the shoulder. "Congratulations. Welcome to the Force."

"Force?" Domini asked.

Kiril ducked his head in pleased embarrassment. When he looked back at Alec, his eyes were full of hero worship. "Will you be returning to the army?"

Alec shrugged. "Perhaps someday. For now, my lady and I will continue as bodyguards."

"We will?"

"Good," Kiril said. His attention was diverted as a woman walked by. "Excuse me," he said. "Maja!" he called, and headed after her.

"Isn't he cute?" Domini asked as the young Prime moved away.

"You've met?"

"He showed me his tattoo."

"Did it impress you?"

"Should it have?"

Alec disengaged himself from Domini to push up his left

sleeve. He showed her the newly freshened fox on his own wrist. "Those of us who follow the old tradition of protecting humans wear our Clan mark like this. Not all of us choose to use the daylight drugs, but those who do, go into the military, police forces, that sort of thing. Becoming a fireman is a good beginning for a boy like Kiril."

"Boy? Idiot, you mean. You protectors are all idiots," said a female voice behind them.

Domini stood back as Alexander turned to face his sister. "How can you say that, Flare?"

"You know it's true." Flare gave a bitter laugh. "Humans don't need you, even if it does give you Primes a chance to play out in the real world."

"I thought you liked humans," Alec answered.

"I like them better than I do our kind. I like the real world, too."

"It's time you left their world."

"Because the Matri says so?"

Domini winced at the female vampire's toxic tone. She didn't like anyone speaking that way to Alexander, and she stepped between the siblings.

"Excuse me," she said to Flare. "I think—"

Flare's angry laugh cut Domini off. "What you think doesn't matter. What a woman wants doesn't matter. Are you going to defend your right to be a breeding sow because you're *bonded?* The bond's a prison. It makes you want whatever my brother wants. He's Prime. Primes want sons." Flare gestured at the room full of men. "All those Primes want is to get us pregnant and keep us that way. Whatever you were told, you were brought here as breeding stock, and nothing more. You're just a womb, and don't let anyone tell you differently."

With that angry pronouncement, Flare turned on her high spiked heels and marched away. Several men followed her.

Domini turned back to Alexander.

He looked embarrassed and wary. "My sister's always been melodramatic."

Domini noticed that he didn't rush to deny what Flare had said. "Uh-huh."

His gaze followed his sister's haughty march through the room. "She's really not happy about being home, and she likes to give speeches even more than Mom. And her hormones are—"

"Was she telling the truth?"

He took instant umbrage, with a haughty, "Reynards do not lie."

"Uh-huh." She didn't know how much longer her frayed temper was going to hold.

"What do you mean, *uh-huh*?" he demanded.

"It means there are a hell of a lot of things you aren't telling me. You've got all these vampire rules and regs and expectations, which I'm supposed to obey without question. You expect me to trust you and to believe you, just because you're great in bed," she snapped. "But that's not how relationships work, and it's not how I work. And I didn't sign on to be anybody's baby factory! Do you understand me, Reynard?"

Alec grabbed Domini's shoulders and pulled her to him until their faces were an inch apart. "Not anyone's children but mine. No one's babies but mine. Understand me, Lancer? You are *my* bondmate, and you will give *me* sons!"

Wait a minute—that wasn't what he'd meant to say!

The woman he loved looked at him with cold fury, and not a little fear. Emotionally, she was holding herself as distant from him as she had before they'd shared blood. It hurt him more now, because of what had happened between them.

Silence reigned around them, and everyone at the party stared. Never mind that struggles for dominance went on throughout every Convocation. This was no place for him and Domini to have a fight. From clear across the huge room, he saw his mother making her way toward them. Her interference was the last thing they needed.

"Damn!" Alec turned around and dragged Domini through the open doors, across the deck, and down into the dark garden. He didn't stop until they were assured of some privacy.

Then he let Domini go, held his hands out in front of him, and said, "That was the testosterone talking. Pure Prime possessiveness. I didn't mean it the way it sounded."

She wasn't ready to be placated. "How did you mean it?"

"I mean that I love you, and want us to have children together. If we can found a Clan—"

"I'm not a vampire."

"You are from Clan Corvus."

"So your *mother* says."

He felt his temper trying to get out of control again. "My mother doesn't lie."

Domini whirled back. "Don't you understand that I can't believe this vampire stuff coming from her?" She grabbed him by the shoulders and shook him. "It's my grandfather's story to confirm or deny. This is between him and me. Even if Anjelica is telling the truth, this is something I have to hear from *my* family. I have to talk to him. More importantly," she added, hands squeezing Alec's shoulders tightly, "I have to help him. I can't talk to him until I know he's safe."

Domini caught hold of her temper, and her desperation. A deep disappointment replaced her fury. She let Alec go, and stepped back. "Love is about trust."

Alec hated that he could not comfort this pain. "We're trying to keep you safe." It was all he had to offer.

"I know," she said, surprising him. "And I want to keep *him* safe."

"You don't know that you saw trouble." He held up a hand. "Remember that people with precognition rarely see any important visions of their own future." He hated to do it, but he added, "You told me that you did not foresee your parents' deaths."

She was exhausted, full of grief, but hope still burned deep inside her. "Maybe this time I got lucky. What I saw hasn't happened yet. You can change the future if you try. *I need to try.*"

She sounded so sure, so desperate, that it tore Alec's heart. Love is about trust, she'd said. Trust your instincts. Trust the one you love.

At his back was the Citadel, full of light and friendship, his family, Clan, and all he believed in. Before him was his woman. Bondmate. Soul mate. She wasn't asking for her freedom, but she was asking him to believe in her. She told him what she must do.

"God damn it!" Alec snarled.

He turned his back on Domini and walked deeper into the shadows of the garden, where he took out his cell phone.

Domini watched his hunch-shouldered form anxiously, hearing only a faint murmur of what he was saying. When he turned around and approached her, she didn't know what to think. He held something in his hand, and tossed it to her when he was close enough.

She caught the car keys automatically.

"Spare set to the Jag," he said. He took her arm and led her across the lawn at a brisk pace.

"Where are we going?"

"The helipad's down by the garage. I told you we always keep flight crews on duty."

"Flight crews? Where are we going?"

"You're going home." He stopped to take her into a fierce hug. "Go talk to your grandfather. Do what you have to do." *Come back to me.*

Elation made her light as a balloon. "I love you!"

He kissed her fiercely. *You bet your ass you do, Lancer!*

She laughed, and the sound and sensation filled both their minds.

He hurried her down the path, and helped her into the small helicopter that would take her to the private airfield. She hugged him tight and kissed him again, but they'd said all that was needed. For now.

When she was in the air, Alec turned back to the house to face the wrath of his Matri. All he could tell her was the truth: that the needs of a bondmate overrode everything else in the world.

Chapter Thirty

"It took you long enough to get here."

"The traffic on I-10 was pretty heavy," Domini answered from the doorway where she stood between the kitchen and living room.

She'd arrived only a few moments before, squealing the dusty Jaguar to a halt in the driveway. She'd run to the front door and knocked frantically until he opened the door, because she'd forgotten her key. He hadn't said a word when he saw her, but he had turned around, and she followed him.

Ben Lancer turned away from the kitchen sink, holding a carafe full of water. It was late afternoon, but he was in his bathrobe, and making coffee. Must be Sunday, he always slept in on Sundays. "You've been gone five days."

"I told you, the traffic was heavy."

He looked her over from head to foot. She was still wearing the short, strapless red dress. She knew she looked like hell from lack of sleep and nerves.

"Been to a party?"

"Yes."

"With Reynard?"

"Yes. And possibly with some old friends of yours."

"Possibly?" The word came out as a deep, dark, suspicious rumble.

She'd anticipated this moment all the way back from Idaho. Now that it had come, she didn't know how to start. "Blackbird," she said at last. "Cassandra Crowe. Corvus Clan."

He carefully put the coffeepot down on the black marble counter. "So, Reynard's exactly who I thought he was."

"*Excuse* me?" She had not expected this response at all. She was annoyed to find her world spinning out of orbit again; you'd think by now, she'd be used to it. "You knew he's a vampire?"

"I thought so. It's getting harder to tell these days. The drugs the daylight ones take are getting better all the time. Knew you were destined to meet a vampire the minute you told me about your compulsion dream. That's how bonding starts with Primes and humans: fate kicking into high gear. Then Reynard showed up. The way he looked at you—I thought, yeah, he's got the hunger the way only they can get it."

"Hunger?"

"Lust, honey. I can recognize it, even at my age."

Reeling, Domini said, "I need to sit down."

"Why don't you go get cleaned up?" he suggested instead. "You'll feel better when you're not dressed like a tart." He poured the water into the coffeemaker.

Domini didn't know which one of them was buying time with this diversion, but she went along with it. She took a few minutes to clean up and change into shorts and a shirt she kept in her old bedroom. It was odd how she kept bits of her belongings all over town, she reflected as she got dressed. Clothes here, at the office, at her dojo, at her place. Had she left any at Alexander's? Probably. Maybe it was because she didn't know where she belonged, or who she really was.

"Oh, please," she snorted at her reflection in the bathroom mirror as she brushed out her hair. "Well, at least I have a reflection. Quit stalling, Lancer."

She went back to face her grandfather, who'd also gotten dressed. He handed her a cup of steaming coffee, and they both took seats at the kitchen counter. He handed her a bagel, and she ripped into it like she was starving. Come to think of it, she couldn't remember the last time she'd eaten. Breakfast with Lady Anjelica?

"Where've you been?" he asked after he put down his empty cup.

"Idaho," she said around the bagel. Then she swallowed, and added, "at a sort of party."

"Convocation? A Clan gathering?"

Domini nodded.

"What was it like?"

"Weird. Noisy. Sort of like I was part of the cast of *My Big Fat Vampire Wedding.* There was business going on, too. The Matris were gathered to talk . . . I don't know. Anjelica wants me to do something—diplomatic, I guess, but I have the impression the others have to approve. They—the vampires—were nice enough."

"Clans are all right, mostly. At least they make an effort to be civilized. Never can tell which way the Family ones will jump. And the Tribes are pure bloodsucking bastards. Glad you fell in with one of the Clan males, or I would have had to kill him. You look confused, girl. Didn't they tell you all about vampires?"

Domini shook her head. "I— Maybe there wasn't time."

"Can see why they'd want to show you everything in a good light. The Clans are real snobs about how superior they are to other kinds of vampires."

"There was mention that not all vampires are good guys."

"Damn right, they're not." A considerable silence followed. Finally, the Old Man asked, "Was she there? At the Convocation?"

Domini knew that lost and lonely tone far too well. He always sounded like that when he talked about her grandmother. Especially around this time of year, around the anniversary of when—

"You always said you lost her." Domini swallowed a painful knot in her throat. "I thought you meant she was dead. She left you, didn't she? Abandoned you."

He turned a sharp, angry look on her. "Don't you ever think

that! She did what she had to do. She did her duty." He looked down at the black counter. "It nearly killed me."

Domini knew how he felt, after only a few hours away from Alexander. There was a tugging ache in her being. She put her hand on her grandfather's shoulder. It was still hard muscled; there was no frailty about Benjamin Lancer. She thought she knew why now. "You shared blood with her, didn't you? It makes you live longer, doesn't it? But if you were bonded, why would she leave—?"

"We never bonded, exactly. The connection went deep between us, though. Once you love a vampire, you don't ever stop. The psychic and physical connection works differently with vampire females and mortal males than it does with human women and Primes. Species survival. Vampire women need a connection with their own kind if they're going to have vampire children."

"You had a child with her."

He gave her a slight smile. "Your dad wasn't a vampire, now, was he?"

Domini smiled back. "Not at all." Dad had been normal, prosaic; a kind, loving, practical man. "Not a bit of dangerous alpha male in him. Not like you still are."

"His mother and I were a tough pair. Reckless, too. We were glad when Junior turned out so sensible. Guess the wild streak skipped a generation to you. He didn't even know about her being a vampire. I raised him, and kept my secrets. Shouldn't have kept them from you. I knew I'd have to tell you one day, from that time you predicted the earthquake when you were still in diapers. I tried to prepare you."

"The bedtime stories you used to tell."

He ducked his head. "Got me in hot water with your mom."

"I remember."

Domini went to rummage in the refrigerator for more food. As she absorbed the conversation she realized that she hadn't really believed he'd refute any of it. It was only the confirmation that she needed. Loving Alexander made it real; made her real. Grandpa's saying it was so made it really real.

When she came back to him with a cold slice of pizza in her hand, she finally answered his earlier question. "Cassandra wasn't at the Convocation. She's a Matri, did you know that?"

He nodded. "That was why she had to leave me. She was heir to her Clan's leadership."

"Oh. You know a lot more about vampires than I do."

"Had a few decades to learn their real ways, and unlearn what I thought I knew."

Domini finished the pizza. "There's so much that doesn't make sense to me. Why would Lady Anjelica want me to be a liaison between the Clans and the hunters? Do you know about the humans that hunt vampires? About the Purists?"

He got up and went to the deck doorway. He stared out at the rolling green Pacific, and the tenseness in his body language frightened her.

"Grandpa?"

"Let's go into the living room and get comfortable," he said.

She'd never known her grandfather to be interested in comfort. "Must be a long story," she said as he moved across the kitchen. A horrible certainty sent a chill through her, and she stood and touched his arm as he reached her. "You know about the Purists."

He said nothing, but took her hand and led her into the living room. It was darker in here, away from the sunlit kitchen. There was a view of the sea as well as the front lawn, with its hibiscus bushes and palm trees, but the curtains on both sides of the room were closed. He didn't turn on any lights before they sat down on the couch.

"Some stories need darkness, I guess," she said.

"Some do," he agreed.

Domini shivered with dread. But she'd never feared the truth. What kinds of ghosts was he about to conjure?

"This story is all about the dark," Ben told her. "You know about your grandmother." He let out a deep, aching sigh. "Now you need to know where I come from."

"Oh, shit." The words hissed out with a jolt of dread.

"Don't swear in my house." He rubbed the back of his neck, looked her in the eye, and went on. "Hunters and vampires have been at war since the Middle Ages. We killed them. They killed us."

"We?"

"Hush, and listen. Eventually folks on both sides got tired of the bloodshed. After a while the hunters started only going after the really bad ones, the ones even the other vampires disowned. But some among the hunters thought we were soft on the demons. That all vampires were demons, and demons need to burn. My grandparents and my parents, uncles, aunts, my brothers and sisters—and me—we were evangelists for returning to the old ways. That's why the Lancers founded the Purists."

Domini jumped to her feet. "What?"

He grabbed her hand and tugged her back down. "We had our reasons," he told her. "Good ones."

"But what could—"

"I told you, the Tribes were bastards. One of the things the Tribes like to do is keep humans, like cattle. They feed on their prisoners, use them as sex slaves. When I was about eleven, my mother was taken by a Prime of the Phoenix Tribe. He must have liked her, or maybe what he did to her was just to show his contempt for the hunters. He took her blood, used her body, and made her drink his blood."

"They bonded?"

"It was nothing like a bond. It was rape, repeated rape. Body, mind, and soul. It took us two years to track her down. My grandfather wanted to kill her, stake her through the heart, and burn her corpse—like any vampire. But my father wouldn't hear of it. He loved her, even if she was defiled and he never touched her again. My mother hated vampires. Hated them more than any other Purist. Eventually she became the leader of the movement."

Domini had a sudden memory of the old woman in the crowd outside the awards ceremony. Ancient but tough, and so very full of hate. Domini had a strong suspicion of who the ancient one was. It sent a cold shiver through her to think that her own great-grandmother had tried to have her killed. She needed to tell her grandfather this, but first she wanted to know more about her grandparents. So she kept it to herself as he went on with his story.

"I hunted vampires, hated vampires, until I was sixteen. That's when I got caught by one myself. Blackbird caught me, but she had a fight on her hands to do it. I was hurt pretty bad, but instead of killing me, she took me to her Clan's citadel. I thought they were going to treat me like my mother had been treated. Instead, they civilized me. I was as wild as an adolescent vampire boy. Long and short of it is, I found out that not all vampires deserve killing; Blackbird and I fell in love; and we ran off together, away from her people and mine. We lived happily together for nearly thirty years. That's longer than most marriages last," he added regretfully. "Better than most marriages, too." He took Domini's hands and asked, "You love Reynard?"

"Yes," she answered, without hesitation.

She hadn't realized until this moment that she had no doubts, no questions, about what he was, what they had, and what they could build. Even if he wanted her to have lots of babies. There was nothing wrong with their having babies, when they were ready for them. Besides, Grandpa had been nagging her for great-grandchildren.

"Stick with him, or you'll regret it."

"I will." She slipped her hands from his and got up to cross the room and throw open the front curtains. She didn't want any more conversations in the dark. Even if daylight was starting to fade into evening shadow, the windows still let in a little light. "Then again, when he finds out my ancestry, he might not want me."

"He'd better want you."

"I don't know. Those people called me an abomination, and— Oh, my God! I completely forgot."

She turned to look outside. Were some of the shadows moving?

She crossed to the couch. "They know about me. About you. The Purists tracked us down somehow. They trapped me, setting up Holly's stalker as a smokescreen to attack me. Alexander saved me, and took me to his citadel. Last night, I saw them coming after you," she went on. "I've never had such a strong vision of the future. I ran home to help—then I forgot it when we started to talk about vampires."

He rose to his feet. "What did you see in this vision?"

"That they're going to attack the house."

He reached under a coaster on the coffee table and picked up the key to his gun case. "When?"

"Uh . . ." Domini glanced out the window again. "Now."

Chapter Thirty-one

"Thanks for the call, Alec."

"No problem, Tony," Alec answered as he slid into the passenger seat of Crowe's white Grand Cherokee. Crowe was parked two blocks down from the Lancer house. It had been a long trip, one he would have made even if his Matri hadn't agreed that the plan was a good one.

"Your tip was what we needed to put these Purist assholes out of business."

"Not my tip. My lady's."

"Whatever. You called it in; gave us a target for the op."

Alec chafed at having been told to report to the Los Angeles Prime, instead of heading directly to Ben Lancer's house. He was used to commanding operations, and had no intention of being relegated to observer status. Not with Domini's life on the line.

"What's your team setup?"

Crowe gave him an aggravated look. "I've been a cop in this town for fifty years, D-Boy. I think I know what I'm doing. Besides," he added with a grin, "this is Shagal territory, and Old Barak's really running the show. He's a good strategist. The plan's to let all the Purists show up, then surround them and take them out when they attack the house."

Alec turned a furious glare on the other Prime. "You're putting human lives at stake."

Crowe held up a hand for silence, then cocked his head to one side to listen to the telepathic voice speaking in his head. Alec concentrated and picked up Barak's words as well.

We've got three vehicles parked under the palms. Fourteen humans have exited the vehicles. They've broken up into four teams and a couple stragglers. Each team is approaching the house from a different direction. Move up behind them. Take them before they reach the house. Alive.

"Alive?" Crowe sneered. "What fun is that?"

No blood on the beaches of Malibu, the elder thought back. *Take them prisoner now. We'll deal with them later.*

"No blood," Alec repeated. He opened the car door and stepped out into the night air. He took a few deep sniffs, and found the scent he wanted. No one attacked his mate and got away with it. "No blood? I don't think so."

Crowe called out to him, but Alec quickly set off on the trail without looking back.

"I don't suppose you had the chance to get the alarm system repaired?" Domini asked her grandfather. He shook his head. "Want to call the police?"

"No." He gave her a stern look. "Some things need to be kept in the family."

Like vampires, and vampire wars. The Purists had gone out of their way to hide the attack on her behind a facade of threats to Holly. "Why are they attacking openly now?"

"Desperation," came the terse answer. "Local vampires are onto them by now. They're too fanatical to just leave town, so they'll try to take us out before they run. They'll make it look like a robbery-homicide."

"Charming." They were in the kitchen, and she was holding a 9mm Glock. "I don't think I want to let them make it as far as the house."

"Me, either."

Grandpa held a shotgun, and they both had plenty of ammunition. Lancers didn't take kindly to being attacked.

"Wish I had the AK-47 back from the shop," he complained. "And that this damn house didn't have so many windows."

It was full dark now. Domini took a quick glance out the window with a pair of nightscope glasses. "There's a lot of movement out there; at least two waves of attackers." She turned her head to look down at her grandfather, who was crouching by the center island. His attention was directed toward the glass deck door. "How many Purists are there?"

As she spoke, glass shattered. A bullet from a silenced weapon whizzed past, inches from her head.

Domini turned and fired before ducking to the floor. A scream of pain erupted from the yard.

"However many they started with, there's one less now," Ben said.

I said no blood! Barak's angry thought shot into Alec's head.

Tell the Lancers that! Crowe's thought shouted back.

Alec smiled, feeling Domini's surge of adrenaline through their bond. *That's my girl.* He went back to concentrating on his prey. The man was crouched behind a dense hibiscus bush at the back of the house, near the deck staircase. Holding back from the main attack because of his broken wrist, Alec surmised.

Move in! Faster! Barak ordered. *Clean this up now!*

Vampires moved across the Lancer property toward their chosen targets. They moved silently, seeing in the dark, with superior hearing and scent, and able to sense thoughts and emotions. They were stronger and swifter than their human enemies as well, and the surrounded Purists didn't have a chance. Especially since the Purists were outnumbered, and the vampires had surprise on their side.

Alec sensed the Primes' elation as one by one they took out their targets. He kept his gaze on the Purist crouching in the bush, a gun clutched tight in the human's good hand. When the Purist thought it was safe to move, Alec followed him up the back stairway, a shadow one step behind his enemy. His hand, claws fully extended, was less than an inch from the man's shoulder.

Time for the punishment to begin.

A flicker at the edge of her vision and a faint whisper of warning in the back of her mind made Domini glance toward the deck. She saw a shadow silhouetted against the last dregs of sunset light. And a shadow behind the shadow, reaching out.

"Grandpa!"

"I see him."

The blast of the shotgun shattered the wall of glass. The Purist outside was hurled back and sideways onto the deck.

He hadn't been hit by the shotgun, Domini realized. Something else had pulled him down.

There was a struggle going on on the deck. Bodies rolled around, sliding and crunching on broken glass. Domini moved forward cautiously, trying to get a better view. She kept low, her Glock at the ready.

Inches away from the deck, she finally got a clear look at what was going on. Then she laughed, an unholy, triumphant sound. It made her bondmate turn around and grin at her. His fangs flashed in the faint light.

Sitting on the chest of one of the Purists, Alec stopped pummeling the other man's face and said, "Hi, hon. Be with you in a minute."

"Take your time." She'd never been so delighted to see anyone in her life. She had no sympathy for the man at all. "You came to rescue me, didn't you?"

Alec gave up punishing the Purist and hauled the man to his feet. He kept a firm hold on the cowering human as he spoke to Domini. "Yeah." He gave her a diffident look from under his eyelashes. "Do you mind?"

She shook her head and chuckled. Her emotions bubbled with pleasure. "Not a bit."

Benjamin Lancer came to stand behind his granddaughter. He leveled his shotgun at the Purist. "What have you got there?"

Barak came storming up onto the deck before Alec could answer. "Give me that," he demanded. He snatched the Purist from Alec's grip, knocked him out, and hauled him over his shoulder. "Sorry for the disturbance, Mr. Lancer," he said, and disappeared with his burden into the night.

Domini pointed after Barak. "What's he going to do with them?"

"Hypnotize them," Alec said. "The local vampires have rounded up all the Purists. They're going to make them forget all about vampires' existence. And the Lancers' existence," he added as he noticed the old man's frown. "The Clans don't kill if we don't have to," he pointed out.

"I know that," Lancer answered. He stepped back into the house through the shattered doorway, and pushed Domini forward onto the deck.

Alec scooped Domini into a tight embrace, and kissed her like he'd never kissed her before. *I couldn't let you face the Purists alone,* he whispered to her mind.

I know. I thought you'd come. I hoped . . .

You did?

Not until after they attacked, actually. But it did cross my mind that you might show up. She devoured him with the kiss, grinding her body against his. *I love you. Do you know how much I love you, Reynard? When you're with me, when you're not.*

I'll always be with you.

Forever?

Forever, Lancer.

Alec stopped kissing her and held her out at arm's length. She was grinning widely, the fire of battle as well as desire in her eyes. "You look like you enjoy a firefight way too much."

She pressed a finger into the cleft in his chin. "Hey, I'm bonded to a D-Boy, aren't I?"

They were so alike. Soul-deep alike. And just enough un-alike to add plenty of spice. He burned to take her to bed as soon as possible.

He pulled her close. "Woman, I think we're going to have an interesting life together."

"A long one." He nodded. She added, "With lots of kids. Eventually."

"Eventually," Alec agreed. He patted her on the bottom, then rested his hands over the tattoo riding low on her back. "And we'll call ourselves the Buzzard Clan."

"Condor," she corrected, and kissed him. *Someday we'll be the Founders of the Condor Clan.*

I Thirst for You

For Micki Nuding. Great editors inspire,
and Micki, that book you sent me
was truly inspirational!

Chapter One

Two things pain can do for you: sharpen you up or dull you down. It never does anything for your mood. He'd been in pain for over a week, and the crystal clarity he'd run on was dulling down to shards of scoured glass. He'd been running on adrenaline, when he needed blood. That had to change—soon—if he was going to survive. Blood was survival.

If he survived long enough out here, once he was free he could start thinking about revenge. He *yearned* to think about what he'd do to those who'd imprisoned him—but letting those thoughts surface could easily lead to hallucinations, a sure way to get himself caught again.

"Not going to happen," he growled, the sound a rumble of thunder in the desert night. The name of the game was survival, and survival meant paring himself down to pure animal instinct.

Blood.

That was the only order of business.

He crouched on the ground, where scorpions scurried to get out of his way, rested his hands on the thick base of a saguaro cactus, and concentrated on finding blood. Animal blood wouldn't do; it had to be human. Preferably female.

He could hear the soft breathing of doves nesting in the cactus. Bats fluttered and flitted overhead, and he could hear their sonar squeaks piercing the air. Hearts beat all around him, so many small living things going about their nocturnal business. He was surrounded by life, but had never been so alone.

He blocked out everything else and searched for the one heartbeat that had to be out there. *Had* to be waiting for him.

When the need was the greatest, that was when you found The One. Wasn't that how the old myth went?

Eventually his head came up, then turned, nostrils flaring. "Son of a bitch," he muttered.

A slow smile creased his pain-ravaged features. He rose, gave a quick look up at the full moon, and whispered an ancient word of thanks.

Then he turned south and ran, spending all his remaining energy in a burst of desperate speed.

The stars were huge overhead, and the moon rode high in the sky. Stevie Nicks's voice was in her ears, singing about sorcerers and sapphires. Maybe she should have been enjoying the deep silence of the desert night, but she preferred the music coming through the headphones of her Discman as she lay on a sleeping bag outside her tent and drank in the vast emptiness.

She'd always liked being alone, but since the plane crash she craved privacy more than ever. She'd been called brave and heroic, and she hated that. She'd been the pilot, and she survived—which seemed so *wrong* to her. The admiration made her cringe; so did the sympathy. She hoped the solitude would be healing.

She'd always absorbed other people's emotions too easily, and it was worse now, since her head injury when the plane hit the ground. The physical wound had closed, but her mind was still open. Things poured into it, thoughts and emotions, things that had nothing to do with her. She used to be able to control it most of the time. "Empath," a witchy friend had called her once, a Sensitive.

Once it had been kind of fun to have this psychic ability; now it made her a fugitive. Now the need to be alone was the reason she'd camped out in the national forest south of Tucson. Here, she had some peace from the joys and pains and hungers that didn't belong to her.

Right now she concentrated on the music to get away from

the pain that *did* belong to her. Four people had died in the plane crash. Four others had lived besides her, but lives saved didn't make up for the guilt of lives lost. No one called it pilot error; it had been a freak storm. Wind shear. Lightning. An act of God. But she should have . . .

Something. There must have been something she could have done.

Try not to think about it. Try to move on. She'd heard those words so many times. But where did you move on to when by all rights you should be dead?

Maybe she *was* dead, and hell was having to hide away from the rest of the human race to keep from—

Hell? You don't know anything about hell.

The thought raced out of the night, straight into her heart, like an avalanche with a New York accent.

Then hunger shot through her, hunger that was a burning pain that set her writhing on the ground and clawing feverishly at the earth. It absorbed her, nauseated her, leaving her twisted up in a sweating, cringing ball when the pain withdrew. Gradually she realized that the pain was not hers . . . but that it was coming for her.

And she realized she did *not* want to die. In that way, the rising fear was a gift.

Terror pumped adrenaline through her, bringing her to her feet, and she turned to run from the unknown danger.

And found that she had turned toward the very thing she feared, as he came rushing at her like a runaway freight train out of the night.

She caught a quick glimpse in the bright moonlight of a big man, densely muscled. At least, he was shaped like a man. But his eyes belonged to a hungry, hunting beast. Fire burned in those eyes, the deep red of glowing coals, and the anguish in them was terrifying.

*   *   *

The woman's fear speared him, but he kept on coming. He had no choice: he was hunter, she was prey. He felt her pain when she pivoted and twisted her ankle trying to escape him. She ran despite the sprain; instinct made him follow.

After being pursued so long, being the pursuer brought him pinpricks of pride, and pleasure. He almost remembered what it felt like to be Prime.

It was a short chase. He followed the pounding of her heart and quick, sobbing breaths a few yards, then grasped her around the waist and brought her to the ground. They landed in the spiky shoots of a yucca, but he pulled her out before any cactus spines penetrated her skin. Her blood belonged to him—every drop—and how he took it was under *his* control.

Another time he might enjoy subduing her struggles, but he didn't have time to waste with love play. He was growing weaker.

He carried her back and sank to his knees onto a sleeping bag in front of her tent.

He ripped off her loose-fitting shirt while she fought and scratched at him. He was aware of her surprise when he didn't go for her bra or try to rip off her pants. He stroked a thumb down her long, lean throat, feeling her blood like blue heat beneath the satin skin, loving the strong, fast pulse. His fangs were already out, had been hard in his mouth for days.

He pushed her down and fell on top of her. Her scream punctured what remained of the shielding that protected his mind, and her fear drove through him like a stake. Shock sent him into her mind. He found psychic injury, a torn-open place that left her nearly helpless all the time.

He pulled out quickly, unwilling to take more from her mind than he must. And at least he could ease this for her—so there would be a give as well as take.

He drilled a thought into her head and made sure she understood.

Then he forgot about everything but need. He kissed the side of her throat once, because he could not bear to make this intimate act completely impersonal. Then he sank his fangs into her. His need was so desperate, he couldn't make the bleeding a slow, sensual sipping. What he did brought her to powerful orgasm within a moment.

It brought him life, and he drank and drank and drank.

Chapter Two

Jo Elliot woke up not sure what had happened but, even semiconscious, knowing it was *not* a bad dream. It was real, as real as the crash, and just as life-changing. Though her hazy mind couldn't focus, her body was deeply aware of that.

She gradually recognized the cooing of doves, a sound she'd always loved. Then the buzz of an airplane engine in the distance. She recognized the make of the motor.

Very nearby she heard the sound of breathing—not just her own, but someone else's, whose breaths were unnaturally slow and deep.

And there was weight on her, hot and heavy against her thighs and hips and across her chest. She didn't want to open her eyes; she didn't really want to see what held her down. Skin pressed to hers, sweat to sweat. His face was next to hers, it was his breath that sounded in her ear.

He had come out of the night, and he had . . .

She didn't know what he had done. Whatever it was, she felt weak. Used. Her bones were melted, and her brain was fried. She felt hungover and hard-ridden, but—

She had no memory of rape; no memory of pain. Yet *something* had happened. And she knew he wanted more.

She didn't want the new day to begin, because a totally new reality waited for her. Because he wasn't going to let her go.

"That's right," Marcus Cage said. He lifted his mind from her surface thoughts and his head from her shoulder. He looked at her, knowing she deliberately kept her eyes closed, not wanting to see what the monster looked like. Thanks to last night's feasting, his fangs were under control and safely sheathed once more. He looked like a man, but he felt like hell.

It was a few minutes after dawn. He wanted to get out of the growing light, but he took a few moments to study his captive. She had short blond hair and fine-boned features, with a short, sharp nose, high cheekbones, and a stubborn, square chin. She was on the skinny side, with breasts smaller than he liked, but he admired her long, slender neck. Marc was definitely a neck man.

But he didn't need sentimentality to memorize his beloved's features. Now that he had her blood in him, he could find her at the bottom of a pitch-black mine shaft during a total eclipse. And he didn't have time to waste on anything, not even on letting her get used to the idea of his being there.

He took her by the shoulders and gently shook her. "Look at me," he ordered. "Get used to me. I'm not going away."

Her captor's deep, rumbling voice penetrated Jo's mind, and his touch sent a bolt of electricity through her. Suddenly she was almost as angry as she was afraid, and her eyes flew open.

"Get off me!"

"Fine."

He got up and pulled her to her feet after him. Standing, Jo had to keep looking up to look him in the eyes. He was very big, with a hard-muscled body. He'd obviously spent a lot of time pumping iron. In a prison exercise yard, was her guess. His body was magnificent, but a heavy jaw and large nose spoiled any chance of his ever being called handsome. He looked like a thug, but there was something about his full-lipped, sensual mouth and the expression in his dark brown eyes that belied the initial impression of his being a monster.

A beast that thinks, she thought; a beast that feels.

"That still makes me a beast," he said.

A beast that reads minds?

His huge hand was across her mouth before her involuntary scream came out. His other arm was around her, holding her to his chest. She was aware of the sharp male tang of his sweat and the heat coming off of him in almost visible waves. It was barely past dawn, yet his slightly olive skin was already starting to burn.

She could almost, not quite, feel his pain. It wasn't anything like last night. He had himself under control now, but it was like a wild animal straining on a leash. It could get loose again. She became very still, afraid of provoking that animal.

"I'm going to let you go," he said. "And you're not going to run."

He wasn't asking, he wasn't threatening, it was a statement of fact. Jo didn't even bother with nodding agreement. When he stepped back she stayed put, oddly aware of his absence.

She was trying not to think about his reading her mind. Marc almost chuckled, but knew that a normal person running into the paranormal coped with the weirdness any way they could. He'd be sympathetic if he had the time, and if this woman was a normal mortal. She was probably one of those psychics who pretended they weren't different. That kind of virgin was fun to court under normal circumstances, but right now there was no time for anything cute or coy.

"You belong to me," he gave her the flat-out truth. "What's your name?"

He looked around to see if anything among her camping gear would be useful. The light hurt him—and he needed to feed again as soon as she could tolerate it, so they had to get to somewhere sheltered quickly.

"Do you have a gun?" he asked. "A knife? Do you know what could happen to a woman alone out here?"

"Jo. Yes. No. You," she answered his questions in the order he'd asked.

"Where's the gun?"

She pointed toward the bright blue Jeep Cherokee Sport parked beyond the small tent.

"Pack up," he said as he headed toward the Jeep.

"What do you mean, 'pack up'?" she called after him.

He turned to face her outrage. "It's your stuff," he told her. "I don't know what to do with it." He couldn't help but smile at her. "Or do you expect me to be a gentleman and do all the heavy lifting?"

"I expect you to steal my car and go," she said. "Just—leave. Okay?"

She looked really pretty when she was angry as hell, with the sun shining in her golden hair. He also liked that she was standing up to him. It was too bad he couldn't do what she wanted.

He came back to her and held out his hand. "Forgot the keys."

She fished them out of her pants pocket and slapped them in his palm. "Go."

"Pack up," he repeated.

He found a 9mm Beretta in the storage compartment between the front seats. He came back to where she was folding up the tent, the weapon in his belt. "You probably think that if you'd had this with you last night, it would have done you some good," he told her. "It wouldn't have."

Jo pretended to ignore him as she finished with her gear, but she was all too aware of him. She could feel the intensity of his dark eyes on her as she moved and knew she wasn't imagining it.

When she bent to roll up the sleeping bag, she saw a couple of white buttons lying on it, and she realized that her shirt was hanging open. A vague memory stirred. There were a few brownish specks on the bag as well, where her head had been not so long ago. Drops of dried blood? Jo put a hand to her throat. Her neck was aching—because she'd slept on it funny, right?

Even as she made this logical excuse, she turned on her captor. "You bit me!"

He answered with the faintest of gestures with a hand that moved far too gracefully for someone of his size. "Hurry up," was all he said. "Forget the tent."

"What?"

"Do it."

Jo knelt beside her clothing duffel and quickly shrugged off the ruined shirt, then pulled a Hysteria tour T-shirt over her head. The screaming face on the black background certainly suited the situation. There was no way she was going to change anything more than her shirt in front of this man, even though she was grungy and sweaty and—

"You're not the only one who needs a shower. Come on."

"Stop that!" she snapped. *He's not really reading my mind. He's just reading body language, making obvious guesses.* "And give me a hand if you're in such a hurry," she added.

He sauntered away from the Jeep and took the sleeping bag in one hand.

Jo kept the duffel. When he moved to the back of the Jeep, she fished the spare keys out of the duffel's side pocket and sprinted for the driver's-side door.

"Cute," was his comment when he appeared in front of her and snatched the keys from her hand.

Her momentum caused her to run hard into his big, broad body. It was like hitting a wall. She bounced back and landed flat on her butt on the rocky ground. She could read no expression on his face as he loomed above her for long, menacing seconds; but her own terror brought up images of his brutalizing her for daring to attempt escape. The unnatural speed with which he'd intercepted her added to her fear.

When he reached down, she flinched and tried to scramble away. He picked her up and hauled her over his shoulder as if she were light as meringue. The ease with which he handled her was as shocking as his speed. Okay, he was a big guy and she'd lost weight after the crash, but she wasn't a feather.

He carried her to the Jeep and put her in the passenger seat. "Fasten your seat belt," he told her as he closed the door.

"It's going to be a bumpy night." He heard her mutter the line from an old movie as he went around to the driver's side.

Marc might have laughed, but he was too strung out to allow any emotion through. Even with the blood he'd taken from her last night, he was still on the edge of being feral. Flight triggered pursuit. Although the ancient instinct was the first thing a young male was taught to control, the instinct never went away. If she ran again, he might bleed her dry this time. He was still fighting hard against the need to drag her beneath him and take her, blood or no blood. Catching her meant he'd won, and winning was an aphrodisiac.

He gave his head a hard shake. He had no time for this! He got in the Jeep and slammed the door, grateful for the small shade the interior provided. He hoped the Cherokee came equipped with air-conditioning.

Now, where to go? Having the SUV and the woman gave him a chance, but only a small one. They weren't going to stop coming for him—Gavin wasn't the kind who ever stopped.

He'd heard a plane in the sky around dawn, but they hadn't spotted him then. Luck couldn't be counted on to last. He badly needed a place to sleep, to eat, and to get the drugs out of his system; a place to lie low and recoup. But where?

He couldn't head home; that would put his Family stronghold in jeopardy.

Maybe there was a map in the duffel on her lap. Marcus reached across the seat and had to tug it away from her, because she was holding it in a death grip. Her nerves were as tightly strung as his, and he knew she was too afraid to be aware of what sang between them. He wished *he* could stuff the awareness down a hole in his consciousness.

He undid all the many zippered compartments of the bag and combed through it. Since she'd had a spare set of car keys, there might be a spare weapon in the bag as well. He found only a few items of clothing, some cash, a Discman, a · CD case, and her driver's license.

"Josephine Elliot," he read. She lived in Phoenix. She was twenty-seven and was five feet five inches tall. She certainly didn't match the weight listed on the license.

He flipped through the CD case and was disgusted with the music selection. Chick stuff like Alicia Keys and Norah Jones.

He looked at her chest. "I'd thought you'd have better taste, Josephine."

Jo realized he was talking about the rock band logo on her shirt. "This was a present. Leave my stuff alone."

"I like road music. You have any rap? Hip-hop? And what are you doing with a cop gun like a Beretta?"

"It was a present," she said again.

"Your dad a cop?"

"Mother." She didn't know why she was telling him these personal things. "And my sister."

Her dad was a pilot, as was her brother. She'd always wanted to fly.

She'd flown, and then she'd fallen, and now here she was with a monster. No one expected her home for at least a week, and no one knew exactly where she'd gone. She didn't even have her cell phone with her. *Stupid, stupid, stupid*. What had she been thinking?

She hadn't been. She'd been hurting. She'd let the hurt take over her life, and look where it had gotten her.

Captured by a dangerous stranger, whom she was attuned to in a way she'd never experienced before. She supposed the hyperawareness was some sort of survival instinct.

Marc found a pair of wire-rimmed sunglasses on the visor. They didn't fit him very well, but they blocked the blistering desert light.

He also found a bottle of fancy "sports" water in Josephine's bag. Though he'd drunk deeply from the woman the night before, he was still dehydrated, along with all his other problems.

He drank half the water, then tossed the bottle to Josephine. "You need liquids," he told her. "And plenty of sleep."

She unscrewed the lid and gulped down the other half of the bottle. Then she eyed him nervously. "Now what?"

"Sleep, Josephine." He used his dwindling reserves of energy to make the command a telepathic one that she couldn't help but obey.

Then Marc started the Jeep and drove back along the track she'd made to her campsite. Eventually he'd find a road. He'd decide which way to go when he got there.

Chapter Three

Jo lifted her head from the pillow and sniffed. "What's that?"

She knew what the aroma wafting through the small motel room was, but normally her stomach wouldn't have rumbled or her mouth begun to water as she caught a whiff of cooked meat.

Her captor closed the door and crossed the few steps to the bed, where he'd left her tied to the metal frame.

She had vague memories of the day, very vague. She'd dozed a lot, and he'd run the air-conditioning too high. There must have been a stop for gas. She'd heard his deep voice asking questions, though she had no recollection of anyone answering, no memory of any stranger's emotions intruding on her.

She'd lifted her head while they were stopped, intending to call for help. But he'd been beside her instantly. He held a bottle of cold water to her lips, and she drank greedily. And there'd been candy bars. She remembered salty peanuts and chocolate that she'd devoured with greedy lust at his urging. His voice was like chocolate, dark bittersweet whispering in her ear, or maybe inside her head, urging her to take care of herself while somehow making it sound like sin.

Now the aroma of greasy meat brought her fully back to consciousness. She looked around and found that she had some memory of being guided into this room by a hand on her arm.

It was a small, square cell of a place. The walls were a dull gray, the furniture sparse and shabby, and the double bed sagged in the middle. An air conditioner covered the room's only window. There was a door that led to a bathroom and the door to the outside. She had a feeling he was always going to be between her and the door to freedom.

"That's right," he said, and put two brown paper bags on the bedside table. He switched on the lamp, which gave more of a fitful glow than any real illumination, then squatted beside the bed and untied her.

He'd used strips from her shirt to restrain her. "I don't have that many clothes with me," she complained.

"This one was already ruined," he reminded her.

"I could have replaced the buttons."

It was silly to complain about something so unimportant as a piece of clothing, but it was easier than thinking about why the shirt had been destroyed.

A shudder of fear went through her. She wanted to ask how long he was going to hold her prisoner, why he was keeping her, what he was going to do.

She asked, "What's in the bags?"

"Hamburgers." He pulled the only chair over by the small table. It creaked when he sat on it. He took one of the burgers out of the bag and handed it to her.

The wrapped bundle was warm and heavy in her hand. The fragrance made her mouth water. The look she turned on him was accusatory. "I'm a vegetarian."

"Not anymore."

She wanted to refuse to eat, but why be a hypocrite? She wanted it. She wolfed it down in three large bites, then licked mustard and ketchup off her lips. She held out her hand, and he put a second burger into it. She didn't make such a quick job of this one, but settled back against the headboard with the thin pillows at her back and her legs folded beneath her, and savored. He handed her a small carton of orange juice, and that was delicious, too.

Marc settled his big frame as comfortably as he could on the

wooden chair and watched Josephine. The food he'd brought
her wasn't anything fancy, yet she took absolute, sensual pleasure out of it. She took these moments to forget he was there,
to forget her fear and simply enjoy what she had.

She was living in the moment, and that was a good thing.
She hadn't been doing that when he'd found her. She'd been
living in the past, and in pain.

He ate two of the burgers he'd brought, but they only satisfied a small part of his need. He was hungry for her, but it
wouldn't be safe for her if he indulged that hunger so soon.
The mark he'd left on her throat hadn't healed yet, a sure sign
he'd taken too much too quickly.

It still amazed him that she'd been there for him. All her psychic
senses had been wide-open, waiting—calling. Though this mortal
woman didn't know the psychic connection her soul craved, he recognized his future mate, even maddened by thirst.

He'd never believed in fate and legends, or even the ancient
moon goddess the Families revered, but old Selene had come
through for him in his darkest hour. Now it was up to him to
make the most of the miracle and protect what the goddess
had given him. As much as he could. His own freedom had to
come first.

"How are you feeling?" he asked, gently probing the edges
of her mind.

"Where are we?" she asked.

He sensed that she was still hungry and passed her a third
hamburger. "There's milk." She held out a hand, and he
twisted off the cap of the plastic bottle before handing it to her.

"You haven't answered me," Josephine said after she drained
the milk.

"Eat," he suggested.

"We're in a motel." She looked around, with more attention than when he'd come in. "How? Where?"

"There's no phone. No one knows you're here."

He'd paid cash for two nights, and had been as hypnotically persuasive with the run-down motel's owner as the drugs in him and his weakness allowed, telling the old man to forget about him, to ignore the man in room two. He'd been equally persuasive with the counterman at the greasy spoon across the dusty road that ran through this tiny excuse for a town.

She brought an annoyed gaze back to him. "What's your name?"

"Cage," he answered.

He got a skeptically raised eyebrow at this. He knew it sounded dramatic, but vampire culture was like that.

"Really. Marc Cage."

Marcus Cage of Family Caeg, to be formal about it. Someday the knowledge might mean something to her, but this was no time to consider possible futures. Always live in the moment when in trouble, concentrate on getting out.

She wished she hadn't asked, didn't know why she had. Putting a name to the brute humanized him somewhat. Which might not be a smart move. She didn't want to think of Cage as a person. He was her kidnapper. She had to keep emotional distance. She didn't want to worry about what he was feeling and thinking, other than as it applied to her survival.

There were some basic things she needed to know: *Are you going to kill me? Are you going to rape me?*

"What now?" she asked.

"You want more to eat?" When she shook her head, he got up, and said, "Come on."

He took her arm again once she was on her feet. She hoped they were going outside; maybe she'd get a chance to shout for help. Instead, he took her to the bathroom.

"Ladies first," he said, and pushed her before him into the room.

Jo looked at the toilet, then back to where he stood blocking the doorway. "I don't use that with anyone watching."

"I won't watch." He turned his back to her. "I'll even close my eyes."

"You could wait outside."

He didn't answer, just stood there filling the narrow doorway like a statue carved out of dark marble. After a few moments she gave in to the call of nature. While she did, he stripped off his clothes. She tried not to look, but by the time she was done, her view was of his naked backside.

Every muscle was so beautifully sculpted, Michelangelo could have signed the work. His skin was as smooth as marble, perfectly proportioned from wide shoulders to narrow waist and down to the curve of his ass and hard-muscled thighs and calves. He had no scars, she noted. There was not a mole or freckle on him.

"Done?" he asked.

"Yes." She stood and backed into the farthest corner of the small bathroom.

"I'm turning around now," he told her.

She gasped.

He chuckled. "Don't stare. It's rude."

When he moved, she closed her eyes. That was no protection, of course. Pretending this juggernaut of a man wasn't there was stupid. He was standing next to her in only a couple of steps. She was aware of his presence like a shadow passing across the sun. Only instead of being cooler, she grew warm.

His hands touched her hips, then skimmed up her waist. She pressed herself back against the wall, wedged between the sink and toilet. There was nowhere for her to go, and his hands were on her. Her head spun, and her body went heavy and hot in a way that was totally unexpected and unwanted. It took her a moment to realize that he'd taken off her shirt, and that she'd lifted her arms to help him do it. What was the matter with her?

Marc wasn't surprised when Josephine's eyes flew open, and

the dreamy expression that briefly crossed her face disappeared in a burst of panic. Her reaction shook him enough to make him remember the reason they were in the room. He stepped back and turned to the shower. "You want to go first?" he asked, and turned on the water.

Jo abandoned modesty as soon as water began spraying out of the showerhead. She took off the rest of her clothes and squeezed past the naked man into the stall. He passed her a sliver of soap and closed the thin plastic curtain. She made the most of the sudden privacy to quickly wash off days' worth of grime. She worked the soap into a pitiful lather and scrubbed at her hair and skin. It was surprising how quickly basic things like food and cleanliness came to feel like the ultimate in luxury.

"Save some for me," she heard Cage say.

"No," she called back over the sound of the water.

"Then we'll have to share."

She knew it was a mistake even to try to tease this man when the shower curtain was shoved aside a moment later.

Marc slid his big body into the small space. Cramped as it was, he almost felt like he'd died and gone to heaven as water washed over him, and the scent of Josephine's skin, warm from the water, sleek and slippery with soap, was crushed against his chest and thighs. He grew hard instantly. His erection pressed against her. He put his arms around her, having to move slowly and carefully in the confined space. He stood for a long time, holding her, letting the water work on tired muscles, waiting, hoping she would relax.

After a while he began to touch her. He had to move very slowly in the tight space, but the gentleness helped her. He needed her to get used to his touch. He wanted her craving it, and perhaps that would come in time. If they were to bond, it was necessary for desire to grow between them.

He glided his hands up and down her back, over her lovely,

rounded buttocks, over her hips and up to her waist. He sleeked his hands down her thighs, then came up to rub his fingers through her hair, massaging her scalp.

Her head moved against his hands, and the small sound she made was one of pleasure at last. The fear was still inside her, quivering in her belly, beating in her heart, roaring in her head, but her skin enjoyed his touch.

Her head fell back, her face full in the stream of water. He kissed her then, his mouth covering hers as the water beat against his back. He was all too aware of her breasts pressed against his chest, of her taste, of the clean scent of her skin. She opened her lips for him.

Though she stayed still in his embrace, a fear-driven spike of adrenaline shot through her. She wasn't ready for this.

Besides, more than her body, he still needed her blood, and couldn't spare giving her his. She wasn't ready for that yet, either.

This was no time for him to think about a bonding courtship.

He lifted his head and turned off the water. "Time for bed," he told her. He snatched thin white towels from the shelf over the toilet and handed her a couple.

Jo shook as she dried herself off. She was so weak she could barely stand, so confused she couldn't think, so aroused she could hardly bear the shame. Her head was spinning, and she couldn't feel what he was feeling. Maybe because she was feeling too much herself? Maybe because he could shut himself off from her? She should be glad of that, yet it made her feel lonely. She was used to reading emotions. Now she had to do it the hard way, and she looked at him.

What she saw was a man weary to the point of collapse. Her heart went out to him, though sympathy for the devil was stupid.

It made her even more confused when the devil picked her up and carried her to the bed cradled in his arms like a baby. She couldn't manage to protest, not even when he turned off the dim light and lay down beside her. The sagging mattress made sure that they rolled together.

For a long time she was acutely aware of her back pressed to his front, the animal warmth they shared, his arm across her body, holding her prisoner yet somehow comforting. She was aware when his breathing shifted from wakefulness to sleep. She counted those slow breaths like another person might count sheep. Eventually she drifted off, too.

Chapter Four

*D*oors. Where had all the doors come from? Endless corridor of doors. Each one locked, with little barred windows. People could look in, but no one could get out. Everything was white. Cold, frozen white. No fire outside, only on the inside. He burned—pain, fever. Fear? Nofearnofearnofear. Don't give them fear.

Fear. There was nothing but *fear, and the ground and the sky changing places over and over. Screaming metal, screaming wind. Screaming inside, silent outside. It would be so easy to scream, impossible to stop. No time to scream. Her hands working, eyes working, voice calm. Training. All training. A puppet going through the motions. Trying to live, waiting for death.

Death was part of the plan. Had to be. Cold, calculated, step-by-step torture leading down to the door marked Death. Endless nights and days of torture. Needles filled with fire. Needles filled with ice. Fading in and out—pain that came with sleep, pain that came with waking. And hunger. Always the growing hunger leading to weakness, madness, murderous need.

As the needle slid into her arm she looked into the stranger's face. It was cold, hard; the only expression in the eyes was one of faint curiosity. A merciless man in a merciless place. She was a lab animal laid out on a cold metal slab. Restraints held her down. Her skin was freezing cold. Everything was white,

walls, ceiling, floor. Gleaming metal monitoring machines re-
flected the whiteness. There was a door in the distance, behind
the torturer's head. She had to get to that door, to all the doors
beyond that door. She had to get out.

"You're going to kill me."

Her voice was not her own, but deep and male. Her skin
was not her own, but her mind filled the muscular body, and
her mind wanted answers.

There was no answer. They never talked to her.

Then the reaction to the injection kicked in, and the world
turned to fire.

He couldn't make his hands work. They didn't look like his
hands, they were soft and small, and shaking. There were con-
trols in front of him he didn't know how to use, even if he
could stop the shaking. His gaze riveted on lights flashing
ominously red, and data he had no idea how to read. Fear
clawed at him, and the guilt was beyond bearing.

He was going to die. Worse, others were going to die be-
cause of him.

Through the cockpit window he saw the mountain rushing
toward him. Rushing, but in slow motion. Everything hap-
pened far too fast, and far too slowly at the same time. It
made him dizzy. His head began to spin, and the plane began
to spin, augering in toward the ground.

No one to blame but himself.

Falling. Falling.

Marc flinched hard as his soul crashed back into his body.
It brought him half-out of the bed, and off the woman
tucked half-beneath him. He wiped a sweaty hand across his
face—fear sweat, he hated to admit. His heart rate had
kicked up, pounding close to human normal as the dream
still half filled his head. He sat up, placing his bare feet on
the rough, worn carpet.

He looked at his hands, flexing fingers that were large and competent. In the dream they had been numb and useless. *He'd* been useless.

At least he hadn't hit the ground. He'd heard somewhere that if you dreamed of falling and hit, you died in your sleep. Of course if that were true, how would anyone who'd actually finished the fall convey the information back to Urban Legend Central?

The thoughts made him smile, almost made him feel normal. It reminded him that there had been a time when he'd been more than a creature pared down to fixation on his continued existence. There'd been a time when Marc Cage wasn't an abusive jerk.

New nightmare images rushed in, dizzying, devastating, and he realized suddenly that the nightmare was not his. He turned to Josephine, who was caught in a nightmare of her own. He touched her shoulder and discovered muscles stiff as stone. Through the physical contact, he felt what was going through her subconscious.

The white room. Cold. Fire. The watcher.

She was curled in a frozen ball of pain and fear that didn't belong to her, any more than his nightmare had belonged to him.

"Josephine." He spoke her name out loud, then in her mind. *Josephine.*

The sound was like an alarm far away, beyond the doors, beyond the impassive observer's face, beyond . . .

Come back to me, Josephine.

Not a sound. It was a name.

Josephine.

Hers.

She blinked, and the restraints faded. The face faded. The room faded.

The pain—

Jo woke with a soundless scream. Her eyes flew open to—

"It was a dream."

The rich, deep voice wasn't hers—but she had sounded like that. In the—

"It *wasn't* a dream." She turned a glare on Cage. "Those were memories. What the hell happened to you?"

"You had a dream. A bad dream. That's all."

He put his big hands on her shoulders, and she felt engulfed by them. His presence was overwhelming, more than just physically. He caught her gaze and held it. There was a lot of power in the depths of his deep, dark eyes.

"It was a nightmare."

He *wanted* her to believe it.

The memories of the white room and torture were clear and crisp and horrible, but she went along with his wishes and nodded. She couldn't bear to do anything else at the moment.

"You had a dream about a plane crash," he said.

That wasn't what she'd dreamed at all. Had *he* dreamed about the crash? Was that possible? It seemed like he could read her mind and bring her comfort if she'd let him. Maybe it was possible—no. She shook her head.

"You're a pilot, aren't you? And the crash happened. That's what left your psychic senses open and screaming when I found you."

"I wasn't screaming until *after* we met."

"I heard you."

She found herself looking at his chest rather than his face. She would not look into those eyes. She would not let him pull her life out of her. He had no right.

But—what had *he* been through?

It didn't matter, she told herself. And it *must* have been a dream, as he said—psychic senses—what the hell was he talking about? The head injury had just messed up her head.

"Being around people hurt." She hated that she admitted that much, but he was the only one who seemed to understand.

"Survivor's guilt," he said. "That's what made you so vulnerable. It's not safe to be alone out in that desert. People disappear out there every year and are never heard from again. You weren't consciously looking for trouble when you found it, but you were waiting. You didn't have your gun nearby—"

"You said it wouldn't have done any good."

"With anyone but me, it would have." He shook her gently, like reprimanding a child. "There are easier ways of committing suicide, Josephine."

"I don't want to kill myself!"

"But you're guilty about being alive."

His words stung like ice water in her face. "This is none of your business, Cage."

She was fully awake now, all the dreams and memories shoved in the back of the mind where they belonged. She was also aware that they were two naked people on a bed, bodies touching, emotions running high.

"Wrong."

That was all he said, one simple, adamant word. A word that unequivocally stated that everything about her was his. Absolutely everything.

"Oh, good lord." Tears sprang to her eyes, and she wasn't quite sure why. She wasn't exactly afraid. Something inside her sizzled, but it wasn't exactly anger.

His arms slipped off her shoulders and came around her. He pulled her close and just held her. Her head rested on his shoulders, and the tears came. She tasted salt on her lips and felt the moisture on his skin, where her cheek rested against him.

"You shouldn't cry," his bass voice rumbled in her ear. "You're already dehydrated."

She sniffled and lifted her head off his shoulder. "Bite me."

He didn't take this as the insult it was intended to be. "Later," he told her.

She wondered what time it was, how long they'd been sleeping, how long they'd been awake. The room was dim and cool, like a cave they'd run to to hide from the world, a place to lick their wounds and recover strength. There was danger all around. She sensed it from Cage.

She'd never been *so* aware of anyone in her life—mentally, psychically, physically.

He was being hunted, and she, as a hostage, was his ticket to freedom. She had to remember that she meant nothing to him besides his own selfish ends.

Her emotions danced like static electricity through all Marc's senses. His Josephine was a confused whirlwind of feelings. He shouldn't have comforted her or confronted her. But she needed both, even if she didn't want it; even if giving it and drawing her closer to him endangered them both.

Even worse, he'd made claims and staked territory, and she knew it. Stupid Prime instinct. It wasn't good for a species when the mating drive kept trying to override the need for survival. Or maybe it was the need to bond that overwhelmed every sensible instinct in a psychic species.

He was an idiot. Worse, he was thirsty, and his control was slipping. He wasn't all that noble, or much of a gentleman. Her naked body was pressed close to his, and the feel of her was exciting him more by the moment. It wasn't only blood he craved. It had been a long time since he'd had a woman. It had been a long time since he'd had any contact that didn't bring pain and humiliation. There were a lot of bad memories he needed to wipe away. Like any Prime, he needed to establish dominance and control in every possible way.

And it would be so good to share pleasure once more.

He ran a hand down the length of her relaxed spine, appreciating her soft, supple skin. Her head came up off his shoulder again and she was suddenly stiff, faintly trembling with a surge of fear.

All right. He knew how to make love. He could make her want him, if he started slowly and gently and used everything he knew from decades as a sexually active Prime to get her so keyed up, she'd beg him to take what he wanted. It would only be a matter of slow, deliberate, delicious coercion, arousing her flesh so thoroughly that it would override any objections her mind could bring up.

Or he could bite her. When a Prime drew blood from a partner, he gave pleasure in exchange. It was a fair price for life-giving sustenance, but she'd already been roughly overwhelmed by that kind of pleasure once; it had nearly been too much for her bruised mind. So much so that she probably didn't remember exactly what had happened out in the desert night. If he drank from her now, he was in control enough to give her the time of her life. He could sate her body, satisfy his blood thirst, then have her in as many ways and as many times as he wanted. That kind of sex would make up for a lot of privation.

She was a helpless prisoner, and he was totally in control. She couldn't stop him.

Marc let her go and scrambled to his feet. He turned his back on the woman and rubbed his hands across his face. He knew too well what it felt like to be helpless and at his captors' mercy. Not that they'd had any.

He was shaking when he turned back to her. She was kneeling on the bed, back arched, hands fisted at her sides, her face turned up to look at him. He couldn't keep from devouring her with his eyes, and those eyes saw beneath sweet female flesh to the tracery of vital life beneath the skin. He could sense her body heat, smell the mingled scents that made the unique perfume that was her. Combined with all that was the vibrant swirl of her emotions.

He was hard and shaking with need.

"You have no idea how you look to me, do you?" His deep voice was rough with his need.

She met his gaze, blinked. "Your eyes are glowing."

"Yeah. That happens."

Her gaze slid down the length of his body. "Are you going to rape me?"

Her frank stare almost made him want to cover his erection. He concentrated very hard on calming down and managed the faintest of gestures. "I'm not," he answered.

"Right now?"

He shook his head. "Not ever."

She slid cautiously toward the end of the bed and brought up the worn bedspread to cover herself. "Never?" she persisted. "Can I trust you not to touch me?"

"No," he admitted. He was no saint, or a chivalrous Clan boy who'd die before dishonoring their chosen lady. "But I'm not going to touch you right now. That's all you can count on. We don't need the complication."

He didn't give her much to go on, but Jo found Cage's honesty reassuring. She watched, wrapped in the bedding, while he turned away and put on his ragged trousers. Muscular as he was, he still moved with compact grace that was hard not to appreciate.

Had his eyes really been glowing? There was so much about him that was strange. "Didn't you have a sunburn yesterday?" she asked as he walked toward the bathroom.

"I'm a fast healer. Come on," he added. He gestured for her to follow. "I need your help."

She didn't want to be confined with him in there again, but didn't suppose there was any getting out of it. She rose to her feet and wrapped the bedspread around her like a sarong. It wound around her slender body a surprising number of times, which somehow made her feel safer, though it weighed her down when she moved.

He waited at the doorway to gesture her in before him. "Help you do what?" she asked as she moved past him.

"Shave," he answered. "Maybe you'll even get lucky and cut me."

Chapter Five

"Why do you want to shave your head?" Jo asked.

His hair was already quite short. It was curly and black, and currently covered with a lather he'd managed to work up from the thin bar of soap. The blue plastic razor in her hand was from the few toiletries in her bag.

She turned the razor over and over in her fingers. It would make a pitiful weapon, which was probably why he was letting her hold it. And when had she started thinking about everyday objects as weapons?

Was acquaintance with Cage turning her into a survivor, or a barbarian?

"Change is good," he said.

For a moment she thought he was answering her thought, then she remembered that she'd asked him about why he wanted to get rid of his hair.

"Is this really a fashion statement?" she asked suspiciously. "Or are you trying to look different than the face on the wanted posters?"

"Clever girl." Seated on the toilet, he reached over her to turn on the tap, then leaned over the sink. "Do this before the soap dries."

Well, how hard could it be? Jo made a careful pass with the razor across Cage's head.

"Ow."

"Sorry." She didn't know why she apologized—automatic politeness? Then again, why antagonize her captor?

"Am I bleeding?"

Then again, why not? "Do you want to be?"

He chuckled, and the deep, rich sound filled the tiny room. He turned his head to look at her. "Do you want a taste?"

The question sent a shiver through her, and the oddest momentary sensation—like a craving—through her.

"You're sick, Cage."

He didn't answer, but turned his head so she could get back to work.

To really see what she was doing, she had to lean over Cage's big body, putting a hand on his shoulder to steady herself. Disconcerting as the closeness was, there was something almost comforting in the pattern of drawing the razor across his skin, rinsing it in the running water, then moving on. Her work progressed slowly, but Cage was patient. She rather liked the sound the razor made scraping off his short, thick hair. Every now and then her breasts brushed his back or her thigh touched his side, and the contact sent little shock waves through her.

She was relieved to take a step back, and announce, "Done."

Cage splashed water over his head to get off the remaining soap. Then he stood to look into the mirror over the sink. "Not bad. Reminds me of my days in the Marines."

He took the razor from her and made a quick job of shaving his face.

She barely recognized him when he finished. She preferred men with hair, which gave her another reason for disliking him. Yet the lack of hair somehow emphasized his strong cheekbones and throat, made his dark eyes seem larger, and made his large, sensual mouth the focus of his face.

All she could say was, "You were a Marine?"

"Back in the day." He smoothed a hand over his freshly shaved head. "You do good work." He rubbed the dark sprinkling of hair on his chest. "You do body waxing?"

She gestured around the dingy little bathroom. "We offer a full line of treatments at the Grubby Acres Resort. Aromatherapy, massage, and facials available. Would you care to see a price list, sir?"

"I'd rather have something to eat."

The mention of food made her stomach rumble. She was so hungry all of a sudden that it made her wonder how long it had been since their last meal. How long had they been asleep? Was it day or night? There were no windows in the bathroom, and the small bedroom window was filled by the noisy air conditioner. The low-wattage lightbulb in the bedroom's only lamp gave a feeling of perpetual twilight. How long was he going to keep her here, hidden from daylight?

Claustrophobia gripped her worse than physical hunger, but a few deep breaths calmed her. By the time she had herself under control, he'd moved into the bedroom. Jo followed, with the bottom of the bedspread held in her hand to make it easier to walk.

Cage's back was to her, and she saw that he was counting out bills from the cash he'd taken from her. With his attention diverted, she swiftly unwrapped the cloth from her body and tossed it over his head.

She managed to make it to the door while he threw off the cloth; she grabbed the knob and had it open . . . then he tackled her.

She heard the door slam as she hit the floor hard. The impact knocked the breath out of her, keeping her from howling in angry frustration. Though fighting the big man was impossible, she hit him on the shoulder.

"Let me *go*," she said when she got her breath back. "Just let me go!"

"No."

Marc probably understood her need for freedom better than Josephine did. He admired that she'd managed to surprise him, even as he was annoyed that he'd relaxed enough to let that happen. He needed her for cover to keep himself alive.

He also needed Josephine the way a Prime needed the woman meant to share the mating bond with him. He was already attached to her, body and soul. His prayer had been answered, which was a miracle, and a mistake. His side of the bond was only going to get deeper as he fed, and as their minds and personalities meshed.

She was rightly frightened of him, rightly furious, and she hadn't tasted him yet. Those would all help her fight her attraction to him, and lack of bonding on her part would come in handy if he had to abandon her.

He had to protect his Family; he had to protect the secrets of his world. He couldn't let caring for Josephine put him in danger. He wouldn't willingly walk away from her if he could help it; but if he had to abandon her to survive, he would.

Right now, he didn't want to walk away. He had a naked woman beneath him, and he was fiercely aware of every inch of her, of every curve, every muscle. Her scent fueled his thirst for her.

But this was no time for him to get a hard-on again—not so soon after he'd promised not to touch her right now.

He gave his head a hard shake. Then he got up, scooped her off the floor, and carried her back to the bed. He found the rags of her shirt he'd used before and tied her hands to the bedframe. This time he added a gag. The look of hatred she gave him shot straight through him. He tossed the bedspread across her before he left. The last thing he wanted to see was a naked woman waiting on the bed when he walked back into the room.

Why tempt himself if he didn't have to?

"You don't have to sulk; I know you're hungry."

"I am not sulking," Jo informed Cage. He was sitting on the chair, she was perched on the edge of the bed, and the nightstand, piled with food, was between them. The aroma of the fried chicken was making her mouth water.

"Try it, you'll like it."

His deep voice was almost as persuasive as the smell. She put her hand up as he tried to pass the paper plate with a piece of fried chicken on it to her. "I told you before that I'm a vegetarian."

She rubbed her wrists, which were bruised from trying to work off the strips of cloth that had bound her. No luck there. The first thing he'd done when he returned was untie her and let her get dressed. He'd changed, too, out of his torn and dirty sleeveless T-shirt into a clean white cotton one. He'd taken the shirt out of a package that he'd brought back with the food. The shirt was a little tight on him and outlined the ripped muscles of his arms and chest.

"This is all I could find to wear," he said, when he noticed her looking at his shirt. "The gas station has a few supplies, not much." He gestured toward a plastic bag he'd left near the door. "I got you some shampoo."

She refused to show the gratitude that she felt. After all, if he hadn't driven off before she could pack up her tent, she'd have all of her toiletries with her.

He handed her a cola, and she gulped it down. "Thanks. The gag made my mouth dry."

She didn't expect him to look guilty, and he didn't. "Eat," he urged. "You need protein."

He'd brought a bag of fried chicken, corn on the cob, fried potatoes, rolls and butter, along with milk and sodas. She wanted it all, but she eyed him suspiciously. "Why do I think you're trying to fatten me up?"

He looked her up and down, assessing her in a critical way. "You need more exercise. A cardio routine, weights, yoga for flexibility."

"Don't tell me; in your real life you're a personal trainer?"

He gave a slight shrug. "Gym rat. Working out's good for you."

"I've just finished six weeks of physical therapy, thank you very much. I don't want—" She snapped her mouth shut.

Her life was none of his business. His life was none of hers.

She wished it didn't interest her. Since he was all she had to focus on, it was natural to latch on to any information she found out about him. Information might help her find a way to escape. So far, she knew he was an ex-Marine and into working out. That made him a fit, trained soldier—points in his favor, not hers.

There were other things about him that she couldn't comprehend, but they were also not in her favor.

"Eat the chicken," he urged. "You know you want to."

"It's cruel to eat animals."

"Not chicken. They deserve what happens to them."

"How can you say that?"

He laughed at her outrage. He ripped quickly through a drumstick, then said, "My great-grandmother has a farm in upstate New York. Most of my family are city mice, but I used to spend summers in the country when I was a kid. You know anything about the butter-and-egg business?"

"Yes," she answered, and watched his strongly arched eyebrows go up in surprise.

He bit into a chicken breast, then went on. "I got to know her chickens really well. Meanest bastards you ever met. They'll chase you and peck you. And they're really stupid, as well as bad-tempered. Trust me, chickens are not our friends. Chickens are food." He finished off the breast and picked up another chicken leg.

Jo'd been watching him the whole time he'd been eating, and talking, and eating. She couldn't take it anymore. "Give me that."

He let out a deep, rumbling laugh when she snatched the meat out of his hand.

He put another piece on her plate, along with corn and potatoes. "I told you you were hungry."

She hated that he was right—and that the meat was really, really good.

Chapter Six

Jo turned on the shower and thought back to what Cage had said. He'd used the words *my great-grandmother has.*

Has. Not past tense.

So, his great-grandmother must be a really old woman. And he'd mentioned the butter-and-egg business.

Her own great-grandfather had gotten out of that profession back in the mid-1940s and moved the family from New York to Arizona. He'd seen the end coming of what had been a flourishing nineteenth- and early-twentieth-century way of life. She'd heard stories about it when she'd visited him in a retirement home when she was little. The old-time industry, with individual companies brokering eggs and butter from small farms and re-selling them, had been driven out of existence by supermarket chains and factory farms by the 1950s.

And something in the way Cage spoke about the butter-and-egg business made it sound like he'd been a kid back when his great-grandmother sold her eggs to the butter-and-egg brokers.

That was impossible, of course, because Cage could be no more than in his early thirties.

He had to be messing with her head, taking psychological advantage of her. And feeding her up for something, she just knew it.

At least I'll be clean when the apocalypse comes.

And at least she wasn't sharing the small stall with the over-sized Cage.

Even when he wasn't coercing, the man was *influencing* her. She didn't know how he did it. She supposed it was because her world had been reduced to him and the hotel room, where there was only the lamp for light, and the drone of the air conditioner blocked off all other sound. The room didn't even have a clock, and she didn't know where her watch had gotten to. There had to be other people around, but oddly, she couldn't sense any but Cage's presence.

Jo turned off the shower with an angry twist and grabbed a towel. Hiding in the bathroom wasn't going to help. She got dressed and marched into the bedroom while her anger was strong enough to make her brave.

Cage looked up from reading a newspaper, and asked, "Were you really going to run out of here buck naked?"

"Of course."

"I'm shocked." He regarded her carefully in her shorts and black T-shirt with a large white X splashed across the front. "I really am." He shook his head. "Women these days."

She got the feeling he was quite serious. "Spend much time in a hospital, and you lose any self-consciousness." Which was none of his business. "I want out," she announced. "You have to let me go."

He tilted one arched eyebrow. "We aren't going to have the 'you haven't got any right to be doing this' conversation, are we?" He folded the paper and gave her his full, serious attention. "Of course I don't have any right to do this. I'm not a sociopath. Sociopaths believe they can do anything they want, simply because they can."

"But—"

"I'm not a nice man," he continued, "but I do know right from wrong."

"But if you know this is wrong—"

"I suffer guilt and anxiety, but I can live with it."

He was teasing her. He looked serious, he spoke with calm earnestness, but he was teasing her. She could feel it. She could feel him, read him, at least a little.

Of course, he didn't want her to be afraid of him. That was

what this was about—he was trying to keep her off-balance. He could control her easier if she—

Oh, for God's sake, the man was huge! And faster than any mortal had a right to be. He didn't have to play psychological games to control her. When she'd tried to escape an hour ago he'd stopped her, but had he tied her up or beaten her? No. He'd tossed her the shampoo and told her she needed something to occupy her.

So he *was* just teasing her. Though he was also telling her the truth. She didn't understand why, but—

"I know," he said. "Try not to think so hard. It'll give you a headache." He picked up the newspaper and handed her a couple of sections. "Try the comics," he suggested.

The paper was a copy of the *Republic*. The date could have been today's or a couple of days ago. She'd had two meals and a couple of showers, but that didn't give her any real indication of the amount of time Cage had been holding her.

"Where'd you get this?" she asked him.

"Stole it out of the back of a car."

"You get to have all the fun."

"Yep."

"Where is here?" she asked him.

"Don't know."

She hated his getting all terse on her. "I'm ready to start clawing at the walls, Cage."

He gave her another raised-eyebrow glance, and his expression made her blush. "If you want something to claw, sweetheart . . ."

His voice was deep, dark, and suggestive of sin.

She perched primly on the side of the sagging bed, her feet firmly on the floor, and made herself read the front page. There was a story about wildfires in several spots across the state; it was suspected that the fires were arson. She didn't understand why anyone would purposefully start a fire that could ravage a countryside and endanger people. She put down the paper.

"Are the fires near here?" she asked, unable not to worry about them. And to be reminded of her real life. She wondered if her brother was flying a plane for the Bureau of Land Management overhead right now.

"I don't know." He was reading the sports section.

Jo got up and paced the room. "You should find out. It could be important."

"I'll do that."

His laconic routine was infuriating her. Ordinarily she didn't have much of a temper. She had never raised her hand in anger. She didn't get into shouting matches or emotional scenes. But Cage brought out very strong emotions in her.

"I'd *love* to throw something at you right now," she told him.

"You could."

Marc wished she would. She had no idea what she was doing to him, how the craving was growing. The faint soap on her clean skin didn't disguise her female scent, which nearly drove him over the edge with desire. The way she moved like a hunted animal brought all his predatory instincts to the surface. And he was getting very, very thirsty.

What was the matter with him? The source of all he needed was only a few feet away; all he had to do was reach out and take her. Instead, he sat burning up, a newspaper covering the evidence of how hard he was.

Go ahead, he prayed. *Throw something. Give me an excuse to pounce.*

Normally, he'd simply seduce a partner and bring them mutual satisfaction, then say good-bye the next morning. But that wasn't an option. There was only one road for them to go down, but he didn't know how to start on it. Maybe a month from now—if he could get them out of this alive.

Cage's deep voice penetrated Jo down to her marrow, and

something in her soul responded to the call. The next thing she knew she was standing in front of him, shaking like a leaf, but not wanting to run away.

She found enough courage to look him in the eye, and ask, "Was that terror or telepathy, Cage?"

Marc had enough control left to smile. "That's Sergeant Cage."

He put his arm around her shoulder and pulled her to sit beside him on the bed. The old springs sagged inward, making them lean back. The bed was trying to make them lie down; why not go with it?

Her body heat sent aching need through him. Her heartbeat pounded inside his head. Her blood and her being called and called . . .

He couldn't resist rubbing his cheek against her soft blond hair, still damp, fragrant, seductive. Everything about her was seductive. Need curled tightly around him, in him, from her, for her. He fought to keep from stroking her skin, from caressing her breasts. He wanted to arouse her as much as he was aroused.

He didn't know why he resisted his impulses; maybe he was too used to ordinary dates. He wanted her body as much as he needed her blood. He could take it, and would if he must, but if he could have her heart and mind as well . . .

"Listen to me, Josephine. Listen to me."

"What do you want?"

"I'm thirsty. You have to understand what I need." His fangs were growing. The fight not to extend them was so hard, he could barely get out the words. His thoughts reached out when the words failed.

Fire.

She was suddenly burning up from the inside.

I'm on fire.

The fire was inside him, driving him mad, killing him.

He needed her help, was begging for it. How could she refuse anyone in that much pain? His pain blinded her, deafened her. All that was left was her sense of touch. She was aware of hard, tense muscles, of his arm around her, and the solid wall of his chest.

Help.

She didn't know what she could do, but her hand came up to touch his face. She stroked his cheek. His flesh was hot with fever.

His hand grasped her wrist and brought it to his mouth. Soft lips and warm breath brushed across her skin. Pain sharper than needles followed the kiss. Then she was filled with brightness, and bliss flooded her, consuming her until everything went dark.

Chapter Seven

He had given her pleasure, and he hadn't taken too much blood. Though she'd fainted, her life wasn't threatened. He'd been in control of his desire, and hadn't had sex with her even though he was still hard.

Chivalry hurt like hell. His balls were about to fall off, and here he was stretched out beside a sleeping woman, totally aroused and knowing he wasn't going to do a thing about it.

Well . . . "Never trust anyone completely, even yourself," he murmured, and slipped his hand under her shirt to cop a feel of her firm, round breasts. Nice breasts; small, but very nice. He touched a nipple with the tip of his forefinger and enjoyed the way it stirred and stiffened. When he touched her other nipple, she let out a soft moan that sent a shiver of lust through him. He reluctantly pulled his hand back. She wasn't conscious; it wasn't fair.

He could feel her blood coursing through him, healing him. He was regaining strength, regaining his powers. He should be sleeping, letting the fresh blood work its magic while he slept.

Maybe he was too horny to sleep. And, strangely, he enjoyed watching Josephine sleep. There was no fear in her face right now, no tenseness in her muscles. She looked boneless as a sleeping cat, with her head turned to the side on the thin pillow, one hand at her side, the other arm stretched out across the mattress.

Studying her, he became aware of her scars for the first time. Straight lines of scarring with little dots of stitch marks on her left knee and right leg, burn scars on her left arm. He suspected he'd find more scars under her clothing. She'd mentioned being in the hospital, and physical therapy. He remembered living through the nightmare of her plane crash. She'd had a rough time recently, and now he was happening to her.

Well, life wasn't fair. And her scars would start healing as soon as she tasted his blood. At least he could make her physically whole once more, another fair exchange.

Marc rolled onto his back and worked on relaxing. It didn't help that Josephine turned onto her side and fitted her body against him, her head on his shoulder. It pleased him, even as he wondered if he could use this unconscious trust.

Tender and treacherous, that's me. But he had to be alert to any opportunity that might help him stay alive and free.

After a while, though, the comfort of Josephine's presence lulled him into healing sleep.

"Take her."

The voice whispered in his ear like the buzz of a mosquito, and made him shake his head. "What?"

"You know you want to."

Of course he wanted her. "Yes." He opened his eyes and looked around. White. Everywhere white. Familiar, imprisoning white. "No!"

"It was all a dream. Welcome home. Take her."

He knew that voice. The devil's own voice. The voice of the torturer turned seducer.

"Make her yours. Body and soul. Take what you want. Give her what she needs. Make her need."

Josephine lay on the cot in his white cage, naked, spread out like a feast. Her eyes were open, on him, full of fear, and he found the fear delicious. Her heartbeat raced like a frightened rabbit's. The frantic rhythm filled his senses.

"Blood need sings inside you. Take what you need. Everything you need."

Everything was a hell of a lot. He was Prime, and no Prime claimed a mate in only one way. The merging had to be total:

fangs into flesh, thoughts blending, blood mingling, bodies thrusting and straining, completing—

"Inside her, in every way. Your blood in her, your cock in her. Do it."

Why not? It was what he wanted, all of him inside all of her. He ached as only a Prime could with wanting all of her.

He knelt between her outstretched legs, and slowly slid up the inside of her thighs. Her skin was soft velvet. His fingers moved against her, stroked warm, yielding flesh. He leaned forward, ready to guide himself into her, glanced up, and met her gaze.

She said, "I'm sharing this dream, you know."

Then someone knocked on the cell door.

The knock came again, harder and louder.

The sound brought Marc to his feet, waking as he hit the floor. His first thought was that she'd said "dream"—not "nightmare."

Then the knock sounded again, and he was instantly across the room. He put his ear to the door, and opened his senses. He didn't recognize the heartbeat or the scent of the man outside.

"Anyone in there?" a stranger's voice called. "Highway Patrol."

Marc swore silently, and opened the door to face a stout, uniformed man. At least it was dark outside, and he wasn't weak and drug-addled anymore. He was prepared to do whatever he had to do.

"Yes?" he asked.

"Sorry to wake you." The patrolman gestured toward the Jeep parked in front of the motel room door. "I thought the place was completely evacuated. Didn't the owner warn you about the fire before he left?"

Marc shook his head. "Fire? Sorry. I don't know what you're talking about."

"The wind shifted a couple of hours ago. The wildfire's

moved out of Grace Canyon and is spreading this way. Looks like it might join up with the fire burning across the Kennedy ranch. The whole county could go up in flames."

Marc read fear beneath the patrol officer's professional calm, and irritation that he'd found a fool sleeping in a place that should be empty. There was also a strong sense of duty about getting the fool to safety.

"No, we didn't hear anyone knock earlier," Marc said.

Since he'd told the owner to forget about him two days ago, the man had left without delivering any warning.

"Thanks for waking us." Marc yawned and ran a hand across his freshly shaved head, like a man still not quite awake. "We'll get out of here right away."

"Get to the crossroads at Kennedyville, over Jessup Pass," the patrolman said. "Then head west."

West was the last place Marc intended to head. "Right. Thanks." He turned, and, for the man's benefit, said, "Honey, wake up. We have to get going."

While he spoke, he mentally sent suggestions for the man to remember that it was a married couple he'd rousted out of the motel if he remembered anything at all. He closed the door and rested his palms on it, willing the man to go away. After a minute Marc heard the rough cough of a car starting, then engine noise receding quickly in the distance.

Once he was sure he was alone, he stepped outside and took a look around. He stopped in the center of the asphalt parking lot, with the low length of the motel building at his back. The lot was empty but for Josephine's Cherokee. The windows of the small diner and gas station across the street were dark, as were the few houses that made up the rest of the small town.

He looked up to where a crescent moon rode high in the sky and gave the old moon goddess a friendly nod. The crescent moon was part of Family heraldry, so he counted the sight as good luck.

He was going to need luck, he decided, when he looked at the sinister orange glow of fires on the horizon to the north and east. The desert night was cool, but he was aware of the heat from miles away.

He had no doubt why the fires were burning. He had to move quickly and put in as many miles as possible before daylight began to sap his strength. Though he could deal with daylight, life was easier at night.

He moved the Jeep across to the gas station and helped himself to a full tank. Then he packed their few belongings, and as much water as he could in the containers they'd used over the last couple of days. He consulted a map, aware of the minutes ticking away, but needing to be sure of routes.

After he'd made all the preparations, he picked up the still-sleeping Josephine and placed her gently in the passenger seat. Then he got in and drove, heading east, toward the ominous glow of the fire.

Chapter Eight

"This has got to stop," Jo muttered. The bed was bouncing, and there was a tang of smoke in the air. She wasn't really awake, but aware enough to be annoyed. "Cigarettes will kill you."

I'm not smoking.

Cage's voice in her head slowly rolled over her, like a velvet-covered boulder. It left her wanting more.

Say something else.

Prose or poetry?

She almost laughed. Almost laughing reminded her that she hadn't found much of anything humorous lately. That Cage could spark her sense of humor was—

Scary?

Let's not be that dramatic, she answered the thought.

Disturbing?

Oh, please! Merely disconcerting.

Don't let the bad guy make you laugh; he can use it against you?

Something like that.

And do what? Cause Death by Stand-Up? No one dies laughing, Josephine.

Keep talking, Cage. If I can't have chocolate, I'll take your voice.

Whoa. Where had that thought come from?

"You can have both," Cage said aloud.

He couldn't really read her thoughts, could he? He couldn't put himself in her head, her dreams?

She'd dreamed about the white room again, only this time Cage had been there with her. She hated that place. It was all very symbolic of being a prisoner, and the sterile setting she got trapped in during her dreams also reminded her of the hospital. Understanding what her subconscious had dragged up didn't make the place seem less real, though. This time the dream hadn't been about pain, but sex.

"Power games, either way."

Jo finally opened her eyes.

She realized that she was out of the motel room at last. The Jeep was bumping along a back road in the middle of the night. A high ridge reared up on the left, while flatter ground rolled off to the right. An ominous snake of light followed the line of the ridge. The smell of smoke came from that way.

Her mouth was dry from fear when she spoke. "That's one of the fires I read about."

"Yeah."

How could he sound so calm? "What the hell are you doing?" she demanded.

"Don't worry," he answered. "The hills are between it and us."

Oh, God, what was the wind like out there? Direction, speed? The brush and trees were dry, very, very dry. And the dry streambeds weren't wide enough to make good firebreaks this time of year.

"Fire can jump," she told him. "The wind can whip it into a storm. Stop the car, City Mouse, and let me drive. I'm getting us out of here."

Marc took umbrage at her thinking he didn't know what he was doing, even if he didn't, exactly. "We'll be okay."

"People do not run toward infernos, Cage." She spoke slowly and carefully, as though explaining to a child.

He was aware of how hard she was holding down the urge to panic and how annoyed she was at him for always keeping her on the edge of it.

"It can't be helped," he explained. "The fires have been set to flush me out, and that's not going to happen. So we go opposite the way any sane person would go."

"Into the wildfire?" Her voice rose with the words.

"Around the fire. Stay calm; we can do this."

"*We?* I didn't volunteer to be broiled." Josephine took several deep breaths, but her agitation didn't lessen. "And what do you mean, the fires were set to flush you out?" Was he crazy?

She looked ahead and noticed that the headlights weren't on though she could see the road by the glow of the death trap over the ridge. "Why aren't the headlights on?"

"So we won't be seen from above by circling planes. If they have nightscopes, it might not help, but the heat from the wildfire might make the scopes useless."

Jo stared at Cage in disbelief. "This *isn't* about you."

"Yeah. It is."

"You cannot really believe that the fires were set because of you."

He looked at her with his head tilted to the side. "Impressive, isn't it? They really want me back."

"The police don't set fires to help them with manhunts."

"We're not escaping the police. And I'm not a man." He looked at the road again, then at the ridge. "I think the fire's coming over the hill up ahead."

While she sat pressed back against her seat, trying to take in the enormity of her captor's insanity, he switched the Jeep into four-wheel drive and eased the SUV off the road to drive cross-country. The going was rough, but the vehicle was tough, and Cage drove very carefully.

Jo could make out very little of what lay in their path. "I hope you can see in the dark," she muttered, as the Jeep bumped and swayed over landscape and low bushes.

"No problem."

Of course not. He isn't a man.

She couldn't stop the crazed giggle that rose in her throat.

She put her hands over her mouth, breathed through her nose, and fought giving in to hysteria. She was going to have a good fit when the chance finally arose.

As Jo wondered exactly what Cage thought he was, she ran a thumb over her slightly aching right wrist. That brought back a vague memory.

Had he bitten her? She concentrated, trying to draw up memories that were oddly fuzzy. Had he been drugging her? She'd certainly been sleeping a lot. But she had a strong feeling that he'd bitten her, twice—and when he did, things went all erotic on her. Something left her shaken, out of control and—all right, admit it—fully satisfied. There was a deep sharing that took place. And the sharing of thoughts and dreams wasn't in her imagination.

Or was it? She hadn't been too stable before Cage happened to her. All she could be sure of was that, once again, she was out in the desert at the wrong place and time.

"There's more than one fire," she told the kidnapper driving her Jeep.

"I know."

"If they connect, we're going to be in more trouble than we already are."

Marc finally grew exasperated. Didn't she know he was doing the best he could? Maybe it was risky, but it was the only way he could elude his pursuers. "You're a city girl from Phoenix. How do you know so much about fires?"

"I've camped all over the Southwest all my life," she answered.

"Bet you were a Girl Scout. Got a badge in firefighting?"

"I certainly was a Scout," she responded proudly. "Besides, my family business is flying. I used to fly charter helicopters and transports for the BLM every summer."

"BLM?"

"Bureau of Land Management. I've taken firefighters and

supplies in and out of fire areas since I was a teenager. I've seen fires from the air and from the ground, and I'd rather not see this one at all."

Her anger hit him like a hot wind off one of those blazes, and he knew that she had good reason to fear for her life. While fire could kill him, it would take far more than third degree burn damage and far longer exposure to flame to kill him than it would to kill her. Josephine was fragile mortal skin and bone, and she knew exactly what fire could do to her.

He worried about her, but there was more at stake than saving their skins. He kept on driving, carefully avoiding cacti and boulders, and the many creatures out there that were afraid for their lives. Since Josephine was an empath, maybe part of her fear was a reaction to the mood of the desert animals. Even if it was hard on her in a dangerous situation, Marc admired his woman's gifts.

He also admired how she'd reacted when he questioned her competence. She was no cream puff. "You fly helicopters?" he asked, trying to distract them both from the fire behind them. "That's cool."

"Yeah," was her flat answer.

He could almost feel the temperature in the Jeep go down. She didn't want to talk about flying, but maybe she needed to. He persisted. "Been flying long? What kinds of craft are you rated for?"

"Planes, copters. It's a job. It was a job. I'm never getting in a plane again."

"It wasn't your fault your plane crashed."

"How do you know?"

"It's understandable that you're scared to get in the air again. But when you fall off a horse you get back on, right? It's the same with anything that scares you."

Anger, regret, fear, and pain seethed through her. "When

you fall off a horse, you don't kill other people," she finally answered. "When you take responsibility for other people's lives, and fail—" Her voice trailed off into a painful sigh.

Why did she have to bring up taking responsibility for somebody else?

"You might want to think about yourself," he suggested. "Do you want to fly again?"

"This isn't exactly a good time for me to think about my future, now, is it?"

Her annoyance flicked against his senses, and her words stung.

Marc figured it was time to shut up and drive, something that was increasingly difficult, even with his excellent night vision. It wasn't just the rough terrain; the night was alive with animals fleeing for their lives. He was aware not only of their movement, but of racing hearts, and the scent of fear mixed with smoke.

When one scent grew stronger than the others, Marc rolled down his window and took a deep breath of the acrid air. There was something out there—

Josephine coughed. "Smells like a fox."

"Yeah," Marc answered, as a large animal dashed in front of the Jeep.

"What was that?"

"A fox."

Jo peered through the windshield. "Too big to be a fox. It doesn't look like a coyote, though. It's circling back. Maybe it wants to hitch a ride."

"Maybe."

A quick glance at Cage told her that her captor wasn't joking. He was frowning furiously, his gaze swinging from side to side. When the large animal dashed in front of the Jeep again, Cage swore under his breath. Then he rolled up the window and stepped on the gas.

His reaction sent a shiver up her spine. "What's out there?" she asked.

"Nothing." He stared straight ahead, his jaw set so hard that his neck muscles strained.

A howl sounded behind them, mournful, afraid.

"Did you hear that?"

"No."

"If you didn't hear it—"

"Blast!" Cage slammed hard on the brakes. When the Jeep jolted to a halt, he growled, "Wait here."

The door opened and slammed shut, and Cage was gone into the night. Jo stared after him, her mouth open in surprise. After a few seconds she looked around, all too aware of the danger in which he'd left her.

"Great. *Now* he gives me an opportunity to escape."

Chapter Nine

Cage sprinted back to the Jeep before Jo could make up her mind to climb into the driver's seat. She was almost grateful he didn't give her time to work through whether or not she should leave him to take his chances with the fire.

He wasn't alone, but was carrying a small woman in his arms. A slender red-haired man trotted along beside him. The fact that the couple were naked was almost as surprising as their being out here in the first place.

Cage opened the back door and set the woman down, then he got behind the wheel. The man climbed in after her and took the moaning woman in his arms. Cage put the Jeep in gear and made a wide turn, heading back toward the road. He looked straight ahead, grim and angry. Jo was consumed with equal parts relief and curiosity, but didn't dare ask any questions when frustration was boiling off Cage in a psychic shock wave.

She turned to look at the couple in the backseat, and saw that the woman was heavily pregnant.

"Thank you," the naked red-haired man said. "We were trapped. If you hadn't come along—"

"How did you get out here?" Jo blurted out. "Why are you here? Why are you naked?" Maybe that wasn't any of her business, but it was a natural question. "Are you in labor?" she asked the woman. The woman nodded, then turned her head, burying her face against the man's bare shoulder.

"Know anything about birthin' babies, Girl Scout?" Cage asked her.

"No," she answered. He was driving faster back than he had into the desert. Jo was grateful that he was heading for the road, and for the seat belt that secured her. All this jostling around couldn't be good for the woman. "Do you know anything about birthing babies, Cage?"

"Do I look like a midwife?"

"More like an angel," the man in back said. "You saved our lives, Prime." The man then said something in a language Jo didn't understand.

Cage answered. "Not my dialect. I'm not Clan, furball." Jo saw a look of fear flash over the man's sharply triangular face. It changed to relief when Cage added, "I'm not Tribe, either."

"Yes, of course. I and my mate will find a way to repay your kindness."

"I know you will," Cage answered.

Jo felt like she could learn a lot from this conversation, if only she had the key to translate what they were actually talking about. The language was English, but she felt like she was eavesdropping on a pair from a foreign culture.

"You know each other?" she asked.

The Jeep reached the road, and Cage turned onto it, thankfully heading away from the fire. When he floored it, Jo sighed with relief. The woman let out another loud moan.

"We better get her to a hospital," Jo said.

"No need." The man gently massaged the woman's abdomen. "All we need is to be safely away from the firestorm. We left our car at a convenience store outside Kennedyville. Take us to our car, and we'll be fine."

"Okay," Cage agreed.

"She needs a doctor," Jo insisted, but was ignored.

"What the hell were you doing out here?" Cage asked.

"We wanted to have the baby the old-fashioned way. So we hiked out into the desert, made a den." He sighed, and rubbed his cheek against the woman's head. "It seemed like a good idea at the time."

Jo noticed that the pregnant woman also had red hair. And there was something odd about the couple, something fey and feral. She recalled the musky smell of fox, and the creature that had circled the Jeep before Cage stopped and jumped out of the SUV. There'd been a flash of movement ahead of him, hadn't there? Had he followed the fox? And what did the red-haired naked guy mean by making a den?

"Uh—"

"Don't ask," Cage cut her off before she could ask. "It's saner that way."

Instead of focusing on the utter weirdness of the couple, Jo took some comfort in the fact that Cage had saved them. Not only had he stopped for the pair, he was taking them to safety, even though he believed he was risking his own freedom. It was obvious he wasn't happy about this decision to act humanely, but he was doing it—so he couldn't be all bad, right? Which had to bode well for her own safety?

A warm glow spread through her, despite her fears and reservations, and she couldn't help but look at Cage with reluctant admiration. Which was stupid, considering they shouldn't have been out in the desert with the wildfire in the first place. But if they hadn't been, the pair in the backseat would likely have died. Maybe it was fate.

Fate? Oh, boy. Maybe the events of the last few days had driven her crazy, too. And why was she sitting here thinking too much, when she should be doing something to *save* herself? There were people in the backseat, for God's sake! She could find a way to ask them to help her, to let them know she was a prisoner. They could warn the authorities—

Cage's big hand landed on Jo's thigh. Its weight and warmth startled her. He squeezed gently, and that was all the warning she needed. *Not a word,* that touch said, *not a sign, not a look or movement out of place.* Cage would only go so far in this act of kindness; he already believed he was risking his own freedom. She dared not push him, and put the pregnant woman's safety at risk.

He gave her a warning glance, and she gave a sharp nod in return. He smiled a little. Bastard. When she tried to push his hand away, he slipped it higher up her thigh.

"Keep your hands on the wheel and your eyes on the road," Jo said.

The woman gave out a long, loud moan.

"Faster, Prime," the man said. "Please."

"Prime what?" Jo asked.

"He is Prime," the man answered. "Don't you know your own mate's bloodline, woman?"

"You take care of your mate, and I'll take care of mine," Cage told him. "We're coming up on a crossroads," he added. "It's not far beyond that."

They'd passed a scattering of dark and deserted buildings straddling the roadside a few minutes before, and Jo suddenly realized that it was the place where Cage had kept her prisoner. Where were they, anyway? She didn't recognize the name Kennedyville, though she'd probably flown over the place plenty of times.

There were maps in the glove compartment. If she could get a look at one, it would help her get her bearings. Knowing where she was and what day it was might help her regain a sense of reality.

Well, it was *her* Jeep. Was she supposed to ask permission? Or furtively sneak a look at one of her own possessions when Cage wasn't looking? Maybe she was a mess, but she wasn't a mouse, city or country. She'd been forced into a scary situation, but she'd been scared before and held it together, until she hit the ground. Then there'd been pain and suffering and guilt, which she'd been almost starting to work through when this jerk came along. What she had to do now was get it together, and get out.

Jo pushed Cage's hand away, then leaned forward and opened the glove compartment, taking out a map and small flashlight.

"What are you doing?"

"Navigating," she told him.

He said nothing, so she concentrated on the map while Cage drove over increasingly rough road that switchbacked along the side of a mountain. She really wished he'd turn the headlights on, even if he obviously wasn't having trouble seeing. The people in the back huddled together silently, except for occasional distressed sounds from the woman in labor. Jo winced in sympathy at every sound she made.

After a few minutes of studying the map by dim light in the bouncing vehicle, Jo announced, "Near as I can figure, we're heading into the Jessup Mountains." They hadn't traveled far from where she'd been captured and were heading back that way.

"I could have told you that," Cage said. They crested the mountain as he spoke and started down. Beyond the pass the road was straighter, if not much smoother, and he put on more speed.

Jo flicked off the flashlight and studied his hard-jawed profile. "But would you have?"

He gave a one-shoulder shrug. "Hard to say."

The man in back said, "There! Up there. On the left. Hurry!"

"I see it."

Jo peered through the windshield, but had no clue what the men saw. It was at least another half mile before she made out the dark outline of a large, flat-roofed building up ahead. She didn't see the car near the building until Cage pulled up beside it in the small parking lot.

"Stay here," he told her once again, and got out of the Jeep.

Marc reached for the handle, but the rear door opened before he could touch it. He stepped back and let the pair he knew were werefoxes out of the Jeep, then followed as the male rushed to get his mate settled in their own vehicle.

"Wait a minute," Marc called, as the male got behind the wheel.

The male put down the window and stuck his head out. "Hurry. I have to get her home."

"I know." Marc rubbed his jaw. He was loath to trust anyone outside his Family with information, but sometimes you had no choice. "Are you Affiliated?"

The fox nodded. "Reynard Clan, House Isabeau."

Okay. That wasn't so bad. The Reynards were known as the noblest of the clean-living, good-guy vampire clans. And it made sense that a werefox would be allied to the Reynards.

"How's your memory?" he asked.

"Perfect. If you want me to get a message to the Clan, tell me and let me go."

"Thanks." Marc spoke a few words in his own language, preferring to speak from vampire to vampire. Somebody in the Clan would be able to translate and pass the information on to his own people.

"Got that?" The werefox repeated the message back to him. "Good," Marc said, and stepped back from the car.

The werefox started the engine, just as the Jeep engine came to life a few yards behind him.

Marc spun around, and his deep-voiced shout filled the night. "Hey!"

Dust and pebbles flew up in the Jeep's wake as Josephine raced out of the parking lot.

Marc had the keys to the Jeep in his hand, and the second set in his pocket. She must have had a third set secreted in the SUV.

He lunged toward the werefox's car, but it was already moving, and he couldn't grab the door handle. Marc shook a fist as the foxes drove away. Seemed like no good deed went unpunished.

Left alone, he howled in frustration and pain at being stranded right back where he'd started nearly a week ago. Only now he was worse off than before.

"Josephine!" The word was a painful howl of betrayal, grief, and rage.

Then he took a deep breath, gathered all his energy, and began to run after the woman fleeing him into the fading night.

Chapter Ten

Jo didn't know why she was crying as she drove away. She'd started crying the moment Cage got out of the Jeep, because she knew what she had to do and almost didn't have the strength to leave him.

"Stupid!" She swiped a hand across her eyes. She could barely see as it was, and she was shaking so hard she could hardly grip the steering wheel. Her hands were sweaty, her heart was pounding as adrenaline and fear pumped through her.

There was a voice in her head screaming that if she left him, he'd die, and the voice wasn't his. And that was just crazy!

When his deep bellow of pain pierced the night behind her, she told herself it was her imagination. She had to get away. This was no time to think, no time to feel remorse. Even if she did, she'd get over it once she was out from under Cage's strange influence.

Oh, my God! What if he takes those people prisoner? The thought struck her like a blow to the stomach.

Was she trading their freedom for hers? Why hadn't she thought of that? She risked a quick look in the rearview mirror and sighed in relief when she saw that the other car was heading in the opposite direction. If Cage had forced his way into their vehicle he'd be chasing her, right? He'd try to stop her from reaching the authorities. Though she honestly didn't believe he'd harm the pregnant woman he'd rescued.

So, they were safe. She was safe.

But what was that shadow in the road ahead of her? A fallen boulder? Why was it so dark?

"Because you haven't turned the headlights on, fool."

It was like riding around in the dark had become normal for her because it was normal for Cage.

She flipped on the lights, squinting into the sudden brightness. The high beams illuminated a man standing in the center of the road ahead of her.

Jo screamed.

Cage's muscles glistened with sweat. His white T-shirt clung to his heaving chest, and the eyes glaring directly at her were glowing fiery red.

Jo could only stare unbelievingly at the apparition before her. He held his hands up and shouted something. Then she realized that the Jeep was heading straight toward him and that he wasn't going to get out of the way. She jerked the wheel hard right, heading off the road and out of control.

Cage jumped onto the hood as the Jeep plunged down a short embankment and rode the SUV like a wild bull as it plowed forward. *Brake!* he shouted inside her head. *Put your hands on the wheel and your foot on the brake!*

Jo realized that her hands were covering her open mouth and hysteria was quenched by the ingrained emergency calm she'd learned as a pilot. Her hands found and fought the wheel, her foot found the brake. Within moments she brought the Jeep to a halt and turned off the engine.

It was only then that she wondered why she'd gone out of her way not to run over the man who'd pursued her.

A vision of what might have happened hit her hard, and she flew out of the Jeep and was on Cage even as he jumped off the hood to confront her.

"Idiot!" She grabbed him by the shoulders. He was too big for her to shake, but that didn't stop her from trying. "You idiot!"

"Me?" he shouted back. "You—"

"You could have been killed!"

The heat of the energy he'd burned racing ahead of the Jeep came off him in waves. He was panting, and she knew instinctively that he'd hurt himself with so much exertion. The hard muscles under her hands quivered with fatigue and fury.

"I could have killed you!"

Josephine's genuine distress pierced the anger that had driven him to nearly kill himself to get to her.

"Woman, what is the matter with you?" he demanded. He was seeing the world in pulsing red, everything but her. She was a bright, constant flame. His head was throbbing, his control hanging by a thread.

"The matter with me? I was trying to escape!"

"I know. What are you so upset about?"

"You could have been hurt."

"Yeah—but—I'm the bad guy!"

He couldn't help but be furious at her running. He couldn't help but give chase. What he found hard to understand was that she was upset *because* he might have been hurt by her. It messed up his mind, made everything complicated. How could he feel betrayed when she was so worried about his safety?

"You drive me crazy," he told her.

"Me? This is all your fault!"

"I know." He pulled her close. Then closer still. He wanted her. He wanted her so badly, it hurt. "I'm sorry."

He'd been sane once, hadn't he? Before he met her. Before they took him away and tortured all the civilization out of him. He'd been brought down to basic needs, and wanting Josephine was as basic a need as he was ever going to experience.

His head was pounding from exertion as much as confusion. As the adrenaline rush of anger wore off, the thirst roared to life. The need for blood mixed with the thirst for sex, and lust, won out. All his senses focused into acute awareness of the woman he held. She was soft, fragile, so very alive. The strength of her emotions was intoxicating even as they pounded at him with a mix of anger, fear, and overwhelming concern.

In a confused, mad way she cared for him, and that added more fuel to his desire. "Josephine."

Jo lifted her head off his chest at Cage's rough whisper, both body and mind responding to the need in his voice. When he bent to kiss her she opened her mouth, and something wild tore loose inside her when their lips touched. He was male, hard, huge, dominant, and demanding. All the danger and power he exuded was intoxicating. Kissing him, she tasted dark, heady wine. She responded, female to male, and she *wanted*—every touch, every taste, every rough caress, every hard kiss. Her hands moved over his smooth, hard, hot muscles, as fiercely intent on sensation as he was.

They sank to their knees onto the hard earth. His hands roamed up under her shirt to stroke her breasts, across her back, then to push down her shorts and cup her bare bottom. Every touch took her deeper into her own need. She ground her hips against his, and he moaned and rose to his feet, bringing her up with him. Her head spun, and she clutched desperately to his straining arms as he picked her up and moved to the Jeep.

"What?" she asked, pulling away when he would have kissed her again. Fear shot through her.

He calmed it with a whisper. "Scorpions. Snakes." He settled her in the backseat and climbed in on top of her.

Night creatures, she thought, of course. Like him. Dangerous and deadly, but not if you treated them right.

"Cage." She spoke his name on a moan, a sound of anguished longing and desperate pleading.

"Josephine."

His need poured into her, hers boiled up from deep inside her. The blending sparked fire, and hunger.

She reached for him, and her fingers scraped across the rough stubble of his shaved head. Sparks shot through her, sizzled through her nerve endings. The salty tang of fresh sweat on his skin excited her. Basic, primal need battered her. He moved, half-sitting to pull off his shirt and unfasten his trousers.

When he leaned close again she ran her hands over his hard chest and belly, reveling in the feel of his naked skin. "Beautiful." His big, solid body filled the cramped back of the SUV, filled the darkness with overwhelming sensory impressions.

His mouth came down on hers, then he nuzzled her breasts, suckled her nipples. Her back arched, and the breath caught in her throat as desire built deep inside her.

He grasped her by the hips, fitting her beneath him. *"Josephine."*

Then with one hard push he was inside her, filling her. When his hips began to pump, she went wild. She arched up, meeting every swift, powerful stroke, her fingers pressing deep into his shoulders. All she could do was ride the building pleasure. He was a hurricane, and she needed the storm washing over her. She needed him.

She might have screamed when the first orgasm took her. Someone did, but she was too taken with pleasure to be sure who made the sound, or even who was Cage and who was Jo. All she knew when the wave of ecstasy passed was that her desire wasn't sated yet.

"More. Give me *more.*"

The answer was a deep, animal growl, a prick of pain on her breast. A wave of pleasure immediately washed through her, took her up over the edge again. There was no coming down this time. Another peak came immediately, then higher to another, and another.

Chapter Eleven

Jo opened her eyes, blinked, and discovered Cage's shaved head resting on her shoulder. Her naked shoulder. "Oh, boy."

She almost wished she hadn't woken up, and not just because of the confusion that came with conscious thought. She had a crick in her neck, and her back ached, and that was only the beginning of the places that felt used and abused. She was beginning to understand the old-fashioned term of "being taken," and thought that if she soaked in a very hot tub of water for a couple of days, the muscle aches might begin to go away.

She didn't feel violated; she was just sore. It was a long time since she'd had sex, and she'd never had it in such close quarters. Cage's size made it even more cramped. He weighed her down now, flattened her, and in so many more ways than physical.

He still slept, sated, satisfied. Full. He'd taken her—in more ways than physical.

Taken, yes.

She sighed, a deep, weary exhalation. She found that she was cradling his head on her shoulder, her fingers slowly stroking the back of his shaved head. She didn't know why she liked the way it felt. She'd never been with a man with a shaved head before; it was rather exotic, in a peach-fuzzy sort of way.

I have no reason to like this man, she reminded herself. *What's to like, other than the fact that he hasn't killed me yet?*

And he hasn't raped me.

She couldn't blame him for what they'd done. She didn't blame herself, either. Later she might be embarrassed, even appalled, but it was only an adrenaline-driven chemical reaction on both their parts. She didn't want to think about it. She certainly didn't want to dredge up details from her memory.

Right now she just wanted to get comfortable, to stretch out and go to sleep. It was just after dawn, and the coolness of the desert night was already slipping away. She wondered if *she* could slip away, if she had the strength to. It wasn't that she lacked the will, it was that she felt weak, drained.

The man somehow took the energy out of her. It made her so tired. Tired and hungry. She wanted to eat a steak and sleep for a good long time. The man somehow made her crave meat. If there was anything she should blame him for, it was her abandonment of over a decade of being a vegetarian.

"I'm hungry," she said aloud, and was surprised at how rough her voice was. Maybe she *had* been the one screaming with pleasure—but she didn't want to think about that.

Marc woke up feeling Josephine's hunger; he was also aware of the growing daylight on his skin. Time to get dressed and get going. But the urge to care for her needs first was almost overwhelming. The woman beneath him was gentle and vulnerable and his to protect. It was her gentleness that led to what had happened between them.

All right, that wasn't precisely true. He'd intended to have her when he hunted her down; it was his right.

But then she'd turned it all around with her concern for his safety, her fear of hurting him. That turned his anger-born passion into something far more dangerous—for him, if not for her. By the time he carried her to the backseat of the Jeep, he'd had to have her because he couldn't live another minute without making love to her. But he hadn't been gentle or kind about it.

He lifted his head and looked at her, and they looked at each other warily for long seconds. He wanted to kiss her. But he didn't know what to expect.

"Am I supposed to apologize?" he asked.

She considered this very seriously before she said, "Let's call it an act of temporary insanity."

"I can go with that." It was easier to keep emotions out of this.

He didn't know why he should apologize for sex, anyway. It was a Prime's right to take pleasure, and a Prime's duty to give pleasure. He knew how well he'd performed on both counts.

It was just that . . . he hadn't been very nice about it.

He rubbed his forehead against Josephine's shoulder. "Goddess, I'm turning into a wimp."

"You could get off me," she suggested. "You can't be any more comfortable than I am."

He certainly wasn't—not with the way he was positioned between her open legs, and growing hard, being so close, so aware . . .

He took a deep breath and pried himself off her and forced his body to calm down. Never mind what he wanted to do; they had to get out of here. He put his head in his hands and rubbed his temples. The growing light was giving him a hell of a headache. And here he was, back near where he'd found her. He didn't know how long or how far he'd run before that night, but he was worried that it hadn't been far enough. Though he'd tried to get away from danger, it felt like he was running back toward a trap. Stupid hippie werefoxes. He shouldn't have stopped for them.

"What's wrong, Cage?"

He turned his head to look at her. She'd sat up as well, and had found the T-shirt and bra he'd dropped on the floor. Her blond hair was tousled, and there were dark circles under her eyes, but she didn't look too much the worse for wear.

"It all seems futile this morning," he answered her. "Life. Everything."

"You should have a cup of coffee," she advised. "It generally helps my mood in the morning." She stretched.

"I'll consider it." He put his hand around her outstretched wrist and turned her toward him. "Just how many sets of car keys do you have?"

She smiled. "I don't think I'm going to answer that."

"Fine." He shook a large index finger under her nose. "Don't try that trick on me again. Stay here," he ordered, and got out of the Jeep.

"You're always saying that," she said, and followed him out. "You're not the only one who has to pee, you know," she added, as they went to opposite sides of the Jeep.

She didn't try to run again while he got dressed. When he got into the front and found the sunglasses he desperately needed, she climbed into the backseat, and told him, "I'm going to take a nap. Wake me up when you've found food."

"Your wish is my command."

"Liar."

Actually, it was. He just didn't dare let her know it.

She woke up inside the stripped-down fuselage of an airplane. She recognized the old metal bones arching overhead the instant she opened her eyes. As she lurched upright, her mouth opened in a scream of panic. But Cage's hand covered her mouth before any sound came out.

She was in a plane!

She couldn't be in a plane! Never again!

She fought to get out, but he held her down. Kept her inside. Spots danced in front of her eyes, and darkness wavered on the periphery of her vision, but she couldn't stop trying to scream.

Let me out! Let me out! Let me out!

Calm down, it's all right. What is the matter with you?
Get me off. I can't—I can't—
Can't what?
An airplane. I can't be on an airplane. We'll fall. We'll
crash. I can't—
You can't crash. We're not flying. It's just an old wreck in
an abandoned boneyard. You're a pilot—you know about
boneyards.

Of course she did. They dotted the desert landscape, if you knew where to look for them. She began to calm down. He eased his hand away, and she gasped in air, then found herself panting from the lack of it.

His hand hovered near her mouth. "Don't scream," Cage said. "Just take slow, even breaths—and don't scream."

"Why not?" she asked when she could speak. "If the place is abandoned?"

"It hurts my delicate ears." He sat back on his heels. "Feeling better?" She nodded. "I should have realized you might have a strong reaction to being in an airplane. Sorry." He gestured around the bare interior of the hulk. "Maybe you should consider this therapy."

She took a good look around as well. "I consider it a B-29."

He rose to his feet and turned around slowly. "Really? This is a World War II bomber? How do you know?"

She was amazed by his sudden enthusiasm. "Because I know airplanes."

He sat down cross-legged in front of her. "And I'm into history. Tell me about this plane."

She shrugged. "It's a bomber. From World War II. Tell me what we're doing here."

"Camping out. I brought in all your gear from the Jeep; we stopped for groceries while you slept. Want a ham sandwich?"

She finally noticed that she was sitting on her sleeping bag. Her stomach growled when he mentioned food. "Yes. And water." She rubbed her throat. With the heat, she was dying of thirst.

The metal body of the plane provided shade, but it magnified the heat. Glancing toward the gaping hole where the cockpit window used to be, she judged by the light that it was late afternoon. At least she could see clear blue sky and the hazy outline of mountains in the distance; this didn't have the claustrophobic quality of the motel room. She didn't even mind that she was in an airplane, now that she was fully awake.

While he moved to her cooler, she sighed in frustration. Why was she always asleep when they were around other people? Did he give her some kind of drug to keep her knocked out whenever he needed? Was it magic?

"Hypnotism," he said, turning back with his hands full. He looked at her over the rim of the sunglasses he always wore in the daytime. "Or something like it."

She took the sandwich and wolfed it down, then gulped the cold water from the liter bottle he gave her. He had another sandwich waiting when she finished drinking. She polished the second one off quickly as well.

"Cookies?" he asked, when she was finished. He held up a bag of Oreos.

She eagerly reached out both hands for them.

He gave a rumbling chuckle, then sat down by her and opened the cookie bag. "You have to share." He took one and popped it in his mouth before handing the bag to her.

"You're eating that wrong," she told him, and twisted the chocolate cookies apart so she could lick the white filling off first. "Oreos aren't just food, they're a culinary experience."

"Oysters are a culinary experience," he said. "That's a cookie."

"Oysters." She made a face. "Oh, God."

"Goddess," he said. "My people worship a goddess."

She recalled that he'd mentioned a goddess before, though she couldn't remember when or where. "You're a Wiccan?"

He looked puzzled by the word for a moment, then said, "No. My people avoid witches as much as we do everyone else, unless we marry them. We Primes like our women psychic."

There was that word again—Prime. And talk of his *people*, and psychic powers. "Who are you, Cage? Who are your people?"

He stared silently into the shadows for a minute, then took off the sunglasses and looked at her intently. His eyes were as dark as triple espresso.

"I'm a Prime of Family Caeg. C-a-e-g. It means door. Our kind are very into heraldry, tradition, respecting our past, and preserving our ways. The Family's symbol is a crescent moon behind a tree branch—very shadowy and mysterious. The Caeg Family crest is a heavy old ironbound castle door. It's important to me, being a member of my Family within the Families. That's who I am." He tilted his head and gave a faint shrug. "And not a word of that makes any sense to you."

"It made a sort of sense, if you're into genealogy and coats of arms and stuff like that. Which apparently you are."

"I know where I come from. That's important. Family is important. Especially for a small ethnic minority trying to get by among strangers."

"Now, doesn't that sound dramatic."

Another of his shrugs. "That's us. Tight-knit, insular, urban, living in the shadows and out of sight, on the fringes."

"What about your great-grandmother's farm? That doesn't sound urban or insular."

"She is an exception," he answered. "And her place is a refuge, a safe place for kids to come of age. It takes a while for our children to mature," he added.

Jo gathered from Cage's solemn attitude that he had just revealed a profound and closely guarded secret to her, but she had no clue as to why it was so important. She still didn't know anything about Cage, the man. For a moment she couldn't even recall his first name, though she knew he'd told her what it was. "Marc," she said when it finally swam into her consciousness. "Your name is Marcus."

"A good Roman name."

"Are you Italian?"

"My family lived in Italy for many generations," he replied. "The family came to America in the 1800s and settled in New York. Before I was born."

"My family left New York long before I was born."

He smiled. "We have New York in common."

"And butter-and-egg men." It was perturbing that she enjoyed finding that they had things in common, though he looked puzzled at what she'd said. "You asked if I knew what a butter-and-egg man was a few days ago. We were eating fried chicken at the time."

"Oh, right! How do we have that in common?"

"I gathered in context that your great-grandmother sold her farm produce to New York buyers. My great-grandfather was one of those buyers. That's part of my family history, passed down lo these many generations."

"Maybe they knew each other."

"Doubtful. He died in a nursing home out here in 1984. He was nearly ninety."

"Well, Gram's nearly three hundred, so it's possible."

Okay, so much for thinking they had anything in common. "You're crazy, Cage."

It was also disturbing that she was relaxed enough around her captor to comment on his sanity to his face. Having sex with someone did not automatically mean that you started trusting and liking him, she reminded herself firmly.

But she was still curious. She looked around the remains of the old plane. Through a hole in one side she made out a row of other scavenged and discarded aircraft. "How do you know about boneyards?" she asked him.

"I saw a show on them on the History Channel," he answered.

"Oh, lord," she moaned. "I'm being held prisoner by a geek."

"A tired one." He moved to the sleeping bag. "Scoot over," he said, and lay down.

He snagged her around the waist and pulled her to lie beside him, her back against his front, his arm held over her. The position was intimate, and comfortable. Even comforting—though that couldn't be right.

"You're getting sleepy," he said. "Very sleepy . . ."

"Cut that out."

He chuckled and kissed the back of her neck. It sent a pleasant shiver through her and a small ache of desire. *Oh, dear.*

Well, she *was* still tired, and had nothing better to do. So she closed her eyes, relaxed against the big man, and felt far too safe and contented as she drifted off to sleep.

Chapter Twelve

When she woke up hours later, Jo found that she was lying face-to-face with Cage, her head on his shoulder. His arm was still around her, and hers was now around him. For a moment it felt exquisitely pleasant, then shock at being so comfortably intimate with him brought her completely awake.

It was only when she was fully alert that she realized that it was night, and the temperature had dropped like a rock. They'd cuddled together in their sleep like a pair of animals to share body heat.

That was a *much* better explanation than thinking they'd cuddled together for mutual comfort—and because the way their bodies fit together felt nice.

She sensed that he was awake; but he did nothing to stop her when she slowly rolled away and sat up even more slowly. She moved like an old woman, stiff and aching from the cold and from the hard floor. One foot was asleep, and when she rose carefully to her feet, her hips and thighs were sore.

Cage sat up as she stood, stretched, and groaned. "You okay?"

"I may never walk again. And don't give me that smug look, Cage, this isn't all your doing."

"It's too dark for you to tell I'm looking smug."

"I can feel smugness waves from your direction."

"That is only because you are a natural-born empath."

She didn't feel particularly empathic lately, not since he had shown up. In a way, this lack of picking up other people's emotional leakage was a blessing. Then again, thanks to Cage she'd pretty much been isolated from people, so there was no one but him for her to focus on.

"And, I," he went on, "am a natural-born—"

"Killer?"

"Stud."

"Don't give yourself too much credit for my condition," she told him, rolling her stiff shoulders, then stretching her arms over her head. "I'm full of pins and plastic, and nothing works right anymore."

"It'll get better," he assured her. "That I can promise you."

The sincerity in his deep voice touched her, reassured her as no promise from any doctor had managed to do, and she didn't know why. And the doctors hadn't promised that she'd ever be completely free of pain. "Does this goddess of yours promise miracles?"

His dark voice was full of mesmerizing promise. "She gave me one when she led me to you."

For a moment Jo was caught up in his spell. "Are you *my* miracle?"

"Yes."

The conviction in his voice shook her, sending a hot rush of pleasure through her. Then she blinked and made herself break the spell. She turned her back on Cage and did some more stretches to work the kinks out.

When he came up silently behind her and put his hands on her shoulders, she went perfectly still. Warmth spread through her, though her nerves began to wind tighter and tighter. He was like a wall behind her, huge, unmovable, and completely commanding her attention. The hands on her shoulders were a warm, heavy weight. The touch was gentle, but she was conscious of the latent power that could snap her neck or squeeze the life out of her.

She realized that she was holding her breath and let it out sharply as his hands began to move. His thumbs rubbed circles against her shoulder blades while his fingers massaged her shoulders and neck. She went almost instantly from growing fear to nearly purring with pleasure.

"Better?" he asked after a few minutes.

She'd forgotten all about her sore muscles, and she was warm all over. "I think my bones are turning to jelly." He stopped and stepped away, and she rounded on him. "Hey!"

He chuckled at her complaint. "If your bones turn to jelly, I'll have to carry you everywhere."

She laughed. "Lazy."

"That's better," he said. He reached out and brushed the hair out of her face, then ran a thumb along her cheek. "You feel better when you laugh, when you're not concentrating on staying scared of me."

She found herself rubbing her face against his open palm and pulled back. "Well—you're a scary guy."

"Nobody can be scary all the time. It wastes energy, and I'm a lazy guy. You said so yourself."

What Marc felt right now was tempted, more than anything else. Tempted to make love to her, tempted to taste her again, and tempted to initiate her into the beginning of a true bond. She needed the healing and completion he could give her when she took his blood, and he wanted to offer it with all his heart—stupid and dangerous though that was. He owed her, and he cared for her.

But he *wasn't* stupid, and he was still very much in danger. They were still out there. He didn't just have to escape, he also had to make sure they were stopped so they couldn't harm his Family and his people. And he couldn't bring Josephine into his world until it was safe.

Besides, some of the drugs they'd given him might still be in his system. He wasn't going to risk tainting her with the chemicals that had nearly killed him. The pain and disorientation he had fought for so long were mostly gone, but he was still exhausted from thwarting Josephine's latest escape attempt. His physical condition had upgraded from near death to just being tired and sore. He was also horny, of course, but that was a Prime's natural condition.

"We have to go." He needed to get to a place where he could feel secure in using a telephone.

"Go? You want to abandon such luxury accommodations?"

"When I find you someplace with a bed and a bathroom, you'll thank me." He hefted the cooler and carried it out the large hole in the rear of the ancient airplane. When he came back, she'd rolled up the sleeping bag and was holding it and her duffel. He took them from her, and she followed him out to the Jeep.

To his surprise, she circled the dusty vehicle like she was giving it a thorough inspection. The moon overhead was bright enough for her to see fairly clearly.

When she circled back to the rear of the Jeep she said, "At least I didn't bang anything up when I drove off the road. However"—she gestured toward the license plate—"where did that come from?"

Her power of observation pleased him. "Stole it off a car from Nevada last time I stopped for gas."

"Why?"

He owed her the truth, even if she wasn't going to like it. "I don't want a cop to try to pull us over. You've been gone for over a week. I figured someone would have reported you missing by now, and there must be an APB out on your Jeep."

She went still for a moment, then turned a look of cold anger on him. "Of course my family's looking for me."

"You told me that your mom's a cop. There'll be extra energy put into the hunt for you."

"How clever of you to think of that. You have a fine criminal mind, Cage."

"Thank you. I learned most of my little tricks while working for the government." The desert night was cold, but they stood in tense silence for a moment. Finally, he asked, "You want to drive?"

"Of course I want to drive. It's my car."

"Okay."

After another long wait, she said, "Well?"

"Waiting to see if you have any more sets of car keys."

"No." She held out her hand.

He dropped keys into her palm, then they settled into the front seat. She started the engine and flipped on the headlights.

"I wish you wouldn't do that."

"I can't see in the dark."

"We're on a salt flat, with the moon shining on it. That's not dark." He reached over and turned the lights off. "You can do it, Josephine."

She didn't argue and put the engine in gear. "Which way?"

He pointed. "There's a break in the perimeter fence over there; it leads back to the road. Turn right at the road."

Jo drove silently for a while, enjoying being in control of the machine. Driving wasn't as satisfying as flying, but it had proved an adequate substitute since recovering from the crash.

Cage relaxed beside her, his head tilted back. He appeared to be napping.

After a while, though, he said, "You're beginning to miss flying."

"No," she answered through a throat tight with sudden pain.

"You're not the only empath in this car. I can feel you feeling wistful, Josephine."

"I miss my freedom," she answered. "That's all."

"If you say so."

He reached over and took her right hand, and twined his fingers with hers.

His touch brought her comfort, and it occurred to her that maybe her touch brought him comfort, as well. What the hell was he running from, anyway? She'd never asked him that, had she?

"Cage? Marcus?" she ventured.

"Hmmm?"

When he turned his head toward her, she thought she saw a faint glitter in his dark, dark eyes. She decided it was an effect of the moonlight bouncing off the dried salt crystals on the ground and turned her attention forward again.

"What are we doing out here?" she asked him. "Who are you running from? And why?"

Marc was acutely aware of the connection between them, even if she wasn't. He owed her his life and his sanity, and she deserved more than his simply having fixed the hole in her psychic shielding. The first night he'd found her, she'd been nearly as messed up as he'd been. When his mind had touched hers, he'd automatically found what he could use, but he had paid for what he took. He hadn't given her a choice, yet he had given her something she needed in return.

Sometimes, though, it was necessary to pay with the truth. Maybe he wanted to tell her, anyway.

"What are we doing out here? Trying to get away from the people I escaped from. Who am I running from? A group of renegade scientists trying to discover the secret of immortality. And why? Because I don't want to be a guinea pig. I don't want them to learn the secrets of immortality, because that would destroy my people, and probably yours, too."

Josephine angrily wrenched her hand away. "Dammit, Cage, why couldn't you just tell me you're a hit man on the run from the mob?"

"Because I'm not part of the mob."

"You said you were from a—a family."

"Not *that* kind of family." He was outraged that she would jump to such a conclusion, just because he was from the East Coast and had an Italian background. He was a vampire, not a mobster! "I thought you wanted the truth."

"Truth?" Her voice rose on the word. "Mad scientists?"

"I didn't say they were mad. Cold bastards, yes, but not crazy."

"Secret of eternal life?"

"There isn't any such thing, but they think so."

"Right. Immortality . . ."

Jo started laughing, and after a few seconds, she realized that she wasn't going to stop. She laughed so hard she started to cry. She barely managed to get the Jeep stopped before she totally collapsed.

Marc watched her reaction with annoyance and growing concern. Maybe he shouldn't have been so flippant, but the horror still haunted him and he'd found it hard to speak about it.

Still, her laughter stung.

"That does it. I'm driving."

Chapter Thirteen

Jo suddenly remembered the white room in the dream, and a painful gasp brought her laughter to such a sudden halt that she choked for a moment.

She remembered horrible experiments—being strapped down, and needles and machines and cold, impersonal voices. Mad scientist nightmares.

But that was all they'd been—just bad dreams, symbols of her own captivity. After all the time she'd spent in the hospital, with the surgeries and rehab, of course her subconscious would create images that she found scary.

But what did her dreams have to do with Cage's claims of mad scientists and the search for immortality? Claims that sounded like some sort of comic book or Lara Croft scenario.

"Because they're my dreams, too," he said.

She turned in the car seat to glare at him. "Stop that!"

"What?" He grinned, and for a moment his eyes flashed red. Just for a moment. "Don't do that, Josephine."

"Do what?"

"Look away and pretend you didn't see it." He reached across the seat, took her chin, and made her face him. "You've noticed that I'm not like normal humans, but you've refused to think about it. I think it's time you thought about it."

"You can read my mind," she said. Then added, "Or at least I imagine that you can."

He arched an eyebrow. "Be honest, Josephine. Or I really will not let you drive anymore."

She stuck her tongue out at him, aware of how absurd the childish gesture was, but she couldn't help it. She was relaxing around him, and that was even more dangerous than letting herself fall into his fantasy world of super powers and . . . and . . . letting him get away with calling her Josephine.

It was such an ugly name, even though it had been in the family for generations. But Cage seemed to like it, and it sounded dignified and right in its old-fashioned way when spoken in his deep voice. Hell, Rapunzel or Snickerdoodle would sound good spoken in that voice. Yet she couldn't help but feel unique and special when he called her Josephine, like it was some secret love word between them.

Jo shook her head, realizing that she'd gone off on an inane tangent. She also knew that her mind had deliberately wandered, rather than do what Cage demanded, which was to examine how strange he really was. His speed was—his vision was—his psychic gifts were—

"Inhuman."

She was shocked that she'd said it, but he only shook his head.

"Not human," he said. "Not the same as inhuman. Or maybe it's easier for you to think of us as enhanced humans." He smiled wickedly. "Close enough to breed."

She ignored this remark. "Us? Your people? This family you've told me about."

"I haven't told you about my people because I can't share details yet. Just believe that the world isn't what it seems. You can accept that I'm different because you also have mental gifts that most people don't have."

Jo considered this very seriously. She couldn't logically explain her ability to read emotions, but until the ability turned on her recently it had been one she'd accepted, even enjoyed.

"Okay. I'll concede that the world is not exactly as—normal—as most people would like it to be. But what's the secret of immortality have to do with—"

"I'm a lot older than I look," he said. "They found out about me. A friend betrayed me and he helped them trap me."

"Who are *they?* How old is older than you look?"

He ignored her first question. "When I was a Marine, it was in Vietnam. I'm somewhere around eighty in human years, Josephine. That's why they were experimenting on me."

"In some ways this all makes sense," she said tentatively.

"But you don't completely believe me." He sounded disappointed.

His disappointment bothered her. She was beginning to trust him, wasn't she? He hadn't hurt her; he'd helped those people. The man had his good points. Except for the crazy parts.

"What about the police?" she asked. "What's your reason for not going to the police?"

"If I can find a Clan Prime who's a cop, I'll tell him. But I can't trust human cops."

"Why not?"

"Someone's spent a lot of money to finance the research and keep it secret. A lot of money pays for a lot of corruption. Cops can be bribed."

As daughter and sister to a pair of clean cops, she was offended that he assumed the police were easily corrupted. She also conceded that he *might* have a point.

"I need to think about it, okay?"

"I've got time."

Silence settled between them as she drove on. When they reached the road, she turned right as he'd instructed. He settled his head against the seat and closed his eyes. This road was sparsely traveled, but not deserted. The lights of the vehicles they passed were a reminder that she and Cage weren't the only people in the world.

"Don't you miss being around people?" she asked him after many miles of silence.

He cracked his eyes open. "I enjoy your company."

"Why? All I do is complain."

"But you do it so well. You also have trust issues."

She couldn't help but snort with laughter. Damn the man for making her situation seem funny.

"And you have problems with self-confidence, but that's understandable so soon after such a serious accident. I think we've made some progress there, but we'll keep working on them."

"Thank you for listing my shortcomings," she said sweetly.

"You're welcome. You're about to ask if I'm your captor or your shrink, and the answer is yes."

"And how am I supposed to report that on the insurance forms?"

"Not my problem." He pulled a map out of the glove compartment and didn't bother with the overhead light or the flashlight to read it. "Not too long to daylight. Pull over," he said after he finished with the map. "I'll drive now."

"I'm not tired."

"We're coming up on some towns," he told her. "So you understand why I'd feel better driving. Besides, it's time for you to get some sleep."

Jo stopped the Jeep on the shoulder of the narrow highway and turned a furious look on Cage. "You're going to knock me out now, aren't you?"

"Yeah."

"You blatant bastard!"

"Such language."

He leaned closer and took her face between his hands. His mouth brushed hers briefly, his lips very soft and tender. A spark of pleasure zinged through her, but it didn't quell her anger. She was tired of being manipulated. "I'm not letting you do this, Cage."

"It's safer for both of us."

"Safer for *you*."

"Josephine," he said, making her look into his deep, dark brown eyes. "Go to sleep."

"No!"

But he kept looking at her, and his voice whispered in her head, and she *was* tired, even without his telling her to be. Eventually, she did exactly what he told her to.

"This is bad." His deep voice echoed down the long, empty hallway.

"This is very bad," she agreed. She looked around fearfully. It might be empty, but the sense of watching menace was chilling. The air was freezing, and they were naked.

There was white everywhere—floor, walls, ceiling. The white hall stretched forever, lined with heavy white doors. Bare, bright lights glared down from overhead.

"My head hurts," she said.

"I can barely see," he admitted. "Light hurts."

She rubbed her bare arms. "The cold makes my skin burn."

He pulled her close, and they wrapped their arms around each other, sharing comfort and as much warmth as possible. His hard muscles were rigid with tension; she'd never felt so vulnerable. She couldn't feel safe being held like this, but she did feel loved. His concern helped.

He kissed her temple, then whispered in her ear, "We have to get out of here. We have to try."

She was afraid to try. She rested her forehead against his shoulder. It felt so hopeless. It felt like a trap. But she lifted her head and nodded. She'd try—for him.

"What do we do?" she asked.

"Try the doors."

He took her by the hand, and they walked down the long, long hall, bare feet slapping on the glacial white tiles. As they passed each white door, they tried to open it. Locked, one after another; they were all locked. The futility of it was wearying. Her fear grew with each step.

"Why won't they let us go?"

"We're valuable property. They need our blood."

At the sound of the word, the world changed. The harsh white light took on the glow of molten lava. All the white around them was suddenly splattered with scarlet. Blood ran down the walls and formed freezing rivulets on the floor. Their feet slipped in it as they continued walking, and they left a trail of bloody footprints behind them.

"They can follow us," she said.

"They already are," he answered.

They stopped, and as he listened carefully for the sounds of pursuers, all she could hear was the rapid sound of her own heartbeat. She wrapped her arms around him and rested her head on his chest. His heartbeat sounded slow, steady, and hers gradually stopped racing, matching the strong rhythm of his.

Soon, over the twin beating of their hearts, even she could hear the guards coming for them.

She held him tighter, never wanting to let him go. "I'm sorry. I should have believed you sooner."

He stroked his fingers through her short hair. "It's all right. I love you."

"I love you."

He pushed her gently away, took her hand again. "When I tell you to run, run. Don't look back."

"All right."

The sound of many heavy footsteps filled the cold air. The floor vibrated. Screams and shouts sounded all around them. The lights and the walls began to pulse. The white doors began to fade, slowly replaced by thick iron bars. Behind the bars, other prisoners howled in pain and terror. Skeletal arms reached out toward them.

She looked around at all the horror, all the people. "We have to help them."

He squeezed her hand tightly. "Run!"

They ran, barely keeping their footing on the blood-slick floor. She didn't look back, but she knew the guards were there, gaining on them with every step. They weren't going to escape.

"There!" he shouted.

A black door appeared ahead of them. They were close to the end of the corridor at last. A pair of guards reached him, grabbed him. He shook them off. As more came at him, he pushed her forward. He got them to the door and wrenched it open. There was nothing but void and blackness outside—and a long, long fall.

"No!" she screamed. "NO!" She couldn't go out there!

"You'll be safe. You have to be safe." The guards were all over him, beating him, chaining him. He ignored them. "I love you," he told her, and pushed her out into empty space. He slammed the door before the guards could reach her.

She screamed, and fell, and was alone—

And Jo woke up screaming in a bed, in a room, with Marcus writhing and moaning beside her.

Chapter Fourteen

It was the white room. No, the walls were white, but this wasn't—

Jo's heart was racing so hard, she thought it was about to hammer out of her chest. She could barely catch her breath for the panting gasps. She was covered in cold sweat, and the fear was so strong that she couldn't think about anything but the dream for long, horrible moments.

Knowing it was a dream didn't help. The reality of the horrible, cold white place was consuming. Even when the waking world began to come into focus, it was overlaid with a ghost vision of the long hall and the echo of footsteps chasing her.

She rubbed her shaking hands over her face, wiping away salty tears. She blinked the stinging moisture away and forced herself to be in this moment, this place, to be awake.

Gradually the room took on more reality than the dream. She didn't recognize anything around her, but it wasn't surprising to wake up in a strange place with Cage. This one was slightly nicer than the last motel they'd stayed in. The bed didn't sag, and the walls were a freshly painted off-white. She was relieved that the color wasn't antiseptic, cold white.

Cage had left the bedside table lamp on, and its warm glow was reassuring. She swung her legs over the edge of the bed, and her feet touched soft carpet.

"Definitely better accommodations," she murmured.

Cage thrashed in his sleep, his arm waving wildly. It struck her, and Jo landed on her hands and knees on the carpet, stunned by the force of the blow. Above her Cage moaned, and the bedsprings creaked as he twisted and turned, fighting some invisible enemy.

Not invisible to him, she knew. He was still caught in the nightmare, fighting to escape. Fighting to defend her. He'd helped her escape and was trying to keep them—

"A dream," she told herself, firmly. "Just a dream." But she couldn't shake the reality of the white place, with its many doors and aura of fear and pain. Slowly, she made herself crawl away from the bed. When she was a few feet away she managed to rise to her knees, then get to her feet. Behind her, Cage continued to moan. The sounds nearly wrenched her heart out.

"Not real," she reminded herself, though the words came through gritted teeth.

She looked at the door. It was real. For a moment she was absolutely terrified to approach it, afraid it would lead to the white corridor.

But that was only in the dream. This door would lead to freedom. He couldn't stop her. He was helpless, captive—frightened and alone.

She passed a hand across her forehead, dragging sweat-damp hair away from her face. "Only a dream."

"Josephine!"

She spun around at Cage's guttural shout, her body going tense. But he had only cried out in his sleep. He wasn't trying to stop her; he was a prisoner on the bed. He was lost in the nightmare.

I have to help him.

Jo shook her head hard, trying to toss the thought away. She turned back to the door, made herself concentrate on it. It was a plain wooden door, brown, not white. She reached out toward the doorknob. All she had to do was open the door and walk away. Cage wasn't going to wake up.

He might never wake up. He'd been willing to die for me.

It was a strange thought, but she believed it. Cage was a psychic, and he'd been caught in a mental trap. She'd been caught in it with him, but he'd found the way out for her, pushed her back into the waking world. He'd stayed behind so she could make her escape.

Jo closed her eyes and pressed her fingers to her temples. What was she thinking? What was the matter with her?

"Josephine!"

"Damn!"

She was going to regret this, wasn't she? But she didn't regret turning around and going back to the bed. She didn't regret being needed, knowing that there was something she could do.

Cage was lying flat on his back, his muscles tense as marble. Kneeling on the edge of the mattress, she grabbed Cage by the shoulders and shook. Her efforts barely moved him. She pinched his upper arms, she prodded his chest. Nothing.

"Wake up!" she shouted as she shook him again. She leaned close to his ear. "Wake up—Marc. Marcus Cage, you wake up right this minute!"

He moaned at the sound of his name and his head turned toward her, so she shouted again.

"Marc!"

She patted his cheek, but the pat turned into a caress along his jawline. Then her fingers traced his lips. They were warm and soft. Touching them sent little shock waves along her fingertips and coiled heat deep inside her.

"Marc! Come on, wake up. It's Jo—Josephine."

"Josephine."

He whispered the word like a prayer. The sound made her shiver. And a feeling that was bright as fire, sharp as pain, stabbed her heart. The emotion the sound awoke in her was more complex than any she'd known before. It was—

"Josephine." Not a prayer this time, but a demand.

The sound sent fire racing through her. She stroked his cheeks, traced his lips again, ran her hands down his neck and across his wide shoulders. His body was so hard, the muscles perfectly molded, so very male. Just looking at him was an erotic experience; touching him was a joy.

"My Josephine," he said, and finally opened his eyes.

His deep voice set erotic vibrations all through her. Her head came up, and she was caught by his dark brown gaze for a long moment. Need and hunger blazed between them as they stared at each other. Her breath caught, and her heart lurched.

"You're awake," she managed to say, though her voice was thick with desire. Fierce hunger set her head reeling. She gazed at his face, at his beautiful eyes, and full, sensuous lips, and wanted as she'd never wanted before.

The back of his hand came up to brush across her cheek. "Don't cry."

She wasn't crying, or if she was, it didn't matter. It wasn't because he was lost and hurting and she was scared of losing him. It was because she'd found him, or because she was finding something in herself. If she was crying, it was because she'd never felt anything so, so—*this*—before. Whatever it was. The only place it was, was in this bed, with him.

"I'm here." He drew her to him, holding on to her like a lifeline.

Maybe she was crying, because she was blind all of a sudden. Everything went blurry, like a heat haze coming up off a wildfire. All she had were her other senses, and they were demanding touch and smell and taste.

She touched her lips to his, all fear of him was lost. Kissing him was more necessary than breathing. More necessary than sanity. More necessary than right or wrong, good or bad.

No names, no history, no future. Just them. This bed. Now.

There was nothing gentle or tentative in her kiss; it was passionate and insistent. *Mine!* she thought.

Yes. Yours, was his response.

While their mouths were still locked together, in one swift movement she was suddenly on her back. The swift shift made her dizzy, like a feather in a hurricane. Or maybe it was the kiss, which made her head spin, made her drunk with desire. She reveled in the sensation.

She moaned in protest when his head came up, then gasped in pleasure when he bent over her again and took one of her stiff nipples into his mouth, sending a sweet ache through her.

Her hand landed on the back of his shaved skull and pressed his head back down to her breast. The breath from his silent laughter tickled her flesh. He suckled and teased her nipple, and brought his hand up to fondle her other breast. He nuzzled her, and gently scraped the tips of fangs over her skin. His mouth throbbed, wanting to bite down, but he kept the impulse at bay. Instead he made love to her man to woman, taking pleasure in giving simple, uncomplicated human pleasure.

He took his time, moving from one spot on Josephine's slender body to the next, learning her scents, her curves and hollows, what merely pleased her, and what drove her arousal higher. He kissed his way down her belly and between her thighs. His tongue found her swollen clitoris and brought her to a quick, hard orgasm. Her taste was a salty-sweet triumph to him as he worked his way back up her body. She moaned and writhed against him, alive with need, her hunger growing rather than being sated.

The more he caressed her, the more sounds of pleasure she made, the more she responded to his touch, the further he was drawn out of the hellish dream. She brought him back to life, away from the dark edge of oblivion. She made him hard as hell, made his fangs throb and his cock throb. He wanted to be inside her, but he didn't allow himself that pleasure yet. He wanted to savor Josephine for as long as she wanted him to make love to her. All her need poured into him, filled his mind, fired his body. What she needed, he needed. The need brought them together, body and soul.

The bond was beginning.

The realization made him happy, and he smiled. She gazed back but her eyes were huge with desire, unfocused, her expression completely rapt. If a bit of fang pressed over his lips, she didn't notice.

She lifted a hand toward him. "What—don't—"

"Stop? All right." He began to caress her again.

Her breasts were firm and very sensitive. He wanted to spend a lifetime touching, tasting, and teasing them. When he moved down, he found the scars along her ribs and across her belly. He kissed them and stroked them, letting her know that every inch of her body was beautiful. He told her so, whispering against her skin.

"You survived," he told her. "You're a survivor. You're strong."

Jo marveled at his tenderness, marveled at how it aroused her far more than any other words ever had.

"Even when these are gone"—he kissed the scars one by one again, moving deliberately down her body—"I will honor them. Love them."

This moved her too much. "Hush," she said. Lust was enough for her right now.

She ran her hands over his back and shoulders, stroked down his chest and the hard, rippling muscles of his abdomen. "Damn, you're hot."

"Don't swear, it's not becoming in a lady."

She laughed. His ability to make her laugh was as much a turn-on as everything else about him.

Somehow he made her whole; this stranger in her bed had become her whole world. She wanted this man and intended to appreciate him to the utmost. She was glad the light was on so she could see what she touched, what she claimed.

She ran her hands down the length of his back, traced his narrow waist and cupped his buttocks, before moving around to stroke his hips and the fronts of his bulging thighs.

She leaned her face close to his throat and drank in his musky, masculine scent. "Cage, you're amazing."

"You have yet to—oh!"

She'd reached the thick length of penis that jutted up between them. She stroked him from base to tip and back down. It was hot and heavy in her hand, as beautifully formed as the rest of him. His hips jerked, then he deliberately stilled at her touch, moaned.

"There is so much of you, Cage."

"No more than you can handle." He scooped her up and laid her down beneath him.

Her legs came up and open, her hips rose to meet him even as he pulled her forward. He entered her slowly, filled her. She was tight and wet and more than ready for him.

"More," she whispered, pleaded.

But he took his time, took her higher with long, slow strokes that filled her, excited her, made her beg for—

"More!" she demanded, and wrapped her legs around his waist. She ground against him, pulled him to her, as deep into her as he could go.

He groaned finally, and gave in to their mutual need. She threw her head back and rode out the building storm. When they came, it was together. Not just joined bodies reaching a blinding climax in an explosive instant. They were completely intertwined, ecstasy multiplied, blending, spiraling out of control as one.

Jo was outside herself for a long time, soaring, flying with Cage in some glorious place where she was not alone and where she never wanted to come down. But gradually her spirit sank back into her body, a body that was weak from the pleasure, where small aftershock orgasms rippled through her, keeping her insides quivering and her body singing.

Cage had collapsed on top of her, slick with sweat. His weight anchored her back into the world, back on the bed, and reality slowly took hold of her again. It grew harder and harder to keep her eyes open. Would she dream if she fell asleep? She wondered if the nightmare would return or if their sleep would be deep and peaceful.

"Oh, screw it," she muttered.

"Language," Cage murmured and was asleep as soon as he spoke.

She barely had time to be surprised as he took her with him into deep, delicious oblivion.

"*G*ood morning, do we have any Oreos left?" Josephine asked as he rolled over to let her slip out of bed.

He'd been awake for a while but had enjoyed holding her as she slept utterly relaxed in his arms. He'd always thought he wasn't sentimental, but for a few minutes he imagined doing this every night for the rest of his long life.

When she finally stirred, he greeted her with a lengthy kiss that she returned with enthusiasm. But before he could take it any further, she grew distracted. He sensed hunger in her even before she was aware that she needed to eat, and he reluctantly let her go. Mortals just didn't have any stamina, at least at the beginning of a relationship.

"You don't need chocolate," Marc answered. He'd noticed that she said *we,* and wondered if she did. "You have me."

"Sex is not a substitute for chocolate," she answered. "Chocolate is not a substitute for sex. A woman needs a balance of both in her life."

He propped himself up against the pillows and put his hands behind his head. Her bare back was to him as she stood by the dresser where he'd piled their few possessions. "You look beautiful this evening," he said. "I like a naked woman, even when she's rummaging through a grocery bag for crumbs."

"You look eminently smug and satisfied this evening," she answered.

"I have good reason."

Jo turned and looked at Cage. He was stretched out in the

middle of the bed like a potentate waiting to be entertained by his harem. Or, an analogy more to her liking, he looked like dessert. No, the main course of a very rich banquet, as sculpted by Michelangelo. She'd found the cookie bag and made a production of taking an Oreo apart and licking up the sweet filling while she let her gaze drift over the naked Mr. Cage. He was a big, powerfully built man in the prime of life, and she enjoyed the way just looking at him sent flashes of heat through her. She hadn't felt so alive, so sensually female, for a very long time.

"Prime," she said, remembering hearing him call himself that. The man from the couple they'd rescued had used the word as well, used it like a title. "Prime," she repeated.

Cage looked curiously at her. "Yes?"

"What's a prime?"

"I am. A Prime is a fully sexually mature male in control of his powers, a male who accepts responsibility for his actions, and responsibility for the safety, comfort, and happiness of those he takes under his protection."

"I—see."

He shook his head. "No, you don't. But someday the explanation will make sense to you, I promise."

Jo's stomach rumbled, and she ate another cookie while trying to puzzle through what Cage meant. After she swallowed, she asked, "So, Primes—like you—are people who live by a code of honor?"

"More like a code of tradition." He shrugged. "Works for our cultures."

"Cultures?"

"You're lucky I'm Family, because the rules for being Prime are even more complicated for the Clan boys, and the Tribe Primes don't follow any rules."

She wished she hadn't brought the subject up, as his explanations were making her nervous. She'd gone for hours thinking he was sane—why? Because he was good in bed?—and now he was telling her about arcane and strange rules for some underground society he was part of.

He couldn't have made the whole thing up since he wasn't the only one who'd used the term. Of course, the naked guy and his pregnant wife had been pretty strange, too.

"Who were those people?" she asked. "Did you know them?"

"What people?"

"Oh, as if I've had so much contact with crowds since we ran into each other. The couple you rescued, of course."

Cage rubbed his jaw, then the back of his neck. "If I tell you, you won't believe me."

She put her hands on her hips, and he suddenly grinned. His expression made her realize how much he was enjoying her nakedness, and all of a sudden her nipples stiffened, and moist heat flared between her legs.

She refused to give in to this sudden arousal, and continued to glare at him. "Try me." He started to get up off the bed to come to her, but she held up a hand and insisted, "Tell me about those people."

He sat on the edge of the bed. "I didn't know them personally, but I recognized what they are. They aren't the same as my people; but they are psychics, with different types of gifts." He rubbed the back of his neck again. "You're psychic," he reminded her. "I found you because I sensed your presence. Like calls to like. That's the most logical explanation I can give you."

"What's the illogical one?"

"You mean the truth?" He gave her a long, hard stare. "They're werefoxes."

"They were foxes?"

"Oh, no, you heard me right. Don't try to pretend you didn't."

She wished she hadn't insisted on an answer. Why couldn't she leave well enough alone and pretend that the man who'd kidnapped her wasn't crazy? And, by the way, she reminded herself, he *had* kidnapped her. She shouldn't forget that just because she'd made love to him. And wanted to make love to him again.

He was psychic, she had to give him that.

She suddenly felt tired and depressed. She wanted some privacy. "Can I take a shower? By myself?"

He looked disappointed. "Sure," he answered gruffly. "There's no window in the bathroom."

Cage certainly wasn't forgetting about their captor/captive relationship, even if she'd crossed the line when she had sex with him. "If I were going to escape, I could have done it last night," she snapped.

Stung by her bitterness, Marc came to his feet and stalked across the room to her. He hated the way Josephine flinched slightly at his approach, but she stood her ground. He tried very hard not to loom over her and kept his voice gentle. "What do you mean you could have escaped? Why didn't you? When was this?"

She blushed and looked away.

"Josephine," he insisted. Then he caught a flash of memory as it leapt through her mind. A memory that belonged to him, as well.

They ran, barely keeping their footing on the blood-slick floor. Without looking back they knew the guards were there, gaining on them with every step. They weren't going to escape.

He'd almost forgotten the dream; making love to her had flushed that horror out of his mind. It rushed back now with enough force to twist his stomach with fear. He went cold, as cold as he'd been running down that long, white hallway with Josephine at his side. That was wrong. She shouldn't have been there. Had it been a dream or a premonition?

He was confused for a moment, forgetting what they'd been talking about as the world around him spun out of what little control he thought he'd won back. Then he said firmly, trying to make himself believe it, "It was only a dream."

"It—was worse than a dream."

"You were in the lab. With me. They caught you, too." He pulled her into a tight embrace, wanting to put himself between her and any harm.

"I couldn't leave you." She spoke with her lips against his shoulder. The words were garbled, but he understood her meaning. "I couldn't leave you trapped there."

He remembered that they ran and ran, then they'd reached an open door. He'd pushed her through it, then turned to face their captors. She must have woken up. He must have stayed inside the nightmare.

"It was only a dream," he said. He ran his fingers through her short hair. She'd begun to quietly sob. "Only a dream," he promised. "Don't let it upset you anymore."

She lifted her head, and her eyes shone with tears and anger. "You were trapped! I couldn't leave you. I thought you were going to die in there. I went back for you." She blinked, and moisture glittered like crystals on her lashes. "Was that stupid, or what?" she asked.

"It was a nightmare," he said. "A bad one, but it was a dream." He was grateful for her concern, for her caring. He wanted to lie to her and tell her that she'd saved his life, but he couldn't. "I would have woken up eventually."

"So I should have just left you to sleep it off?" He nodded. "Damn."

She tried to pull away from him, but he held her gently in his grasp. "Josephine, what have I told you about that kind of language?"

She wasn't amused. "Let me go," she demanded.

He knew she was embarrassed now, and feeling like a fool. He hated having her feel like that. "Listen," he said, "your instincts are good, and your reaction's understandable. You were shaken by a very, very bad dream, a dream that you did share with me. There was telepathy involved, and your own special kind of empathy, and your own bad memories and what I've put you through kicked into the mix. That's a pretty weird combination. The weirdness didn't disappear immediately when you came to consciousness. You were still partly caught in the dream. You believed in the reality of it."

"Damn right I did. I was *there*."

"So instead of walking out the door like the smart woman you are, you did what you could to help me."

"But you said it was only a dream."

"Yeah, but neither of us believed it at the time. I was lost in the weirdness, too. So . . ." He kissed her forehead, then tilted her chin up so he could gently brush his lips across hers. "Thank you, Josephine."

She still needed some space and time to deal with her feelings on her own, so Marc reluctantly took a step back. "Go take your shower."

She grabbed some things out of her bag and fled into the other room. Marc stood very still, watching the closed bathroom door until he heard the shower start. Then he got dressed and began to pace the room restlessly.

Good goddess, what had he done? The dream was a warning, wasn't it? He hadn't been able to think clearly those first few nights, hadn't had the strength to make any decision not related to his survival.

But there came a time in every Prime's life when he could no longer just look out for number one. He'd taken Josephine under his protection; he was responsible for her. Had he told her that? He couldn't remember. It wasn't formal until the words were spoken.

He had told her she belonged to him, though, and that was enough. The Matri, his great-grandmother, matriarch of the Caeg Family, would certainly rule that he'd made a bondmate commitment to the mortal woman Josephine Elliot.

Rights and responsibilities aside, he'd gotten her into this; it was time he got her out.

He felt like he'd been running in circles when he needed to

be running as fast and far as he could away from danger. And didn't think he'd gotten very far from where he'd started. If it hadn't been for the wildfires, and the foxes, and Josephine's reasonable insistence on escape attempts that left him enervated, he could have made some progress by now.

He had to run fast and hard away from Arizona now to make up time. If not home, maybe he should go to one of the Clan citadels up north. If the foxes had gotten his message out, the Clans would all be up in arms by now. They'd be willing to mount a crusade, and he'd be happy to ally with them.

Those hunting him had all the resources, a cunning leader, and believed the prize was the secret of immortality. All he had was himself, and Josephine.

Soon he wouldn't have her. Not until he could come back and claim her safely.

He was already missing her when she came out of the bathroom. For a moment he sat on the bed and looked at her, memorizing her. Her hair was wet and slicked back off her face. She looked warily back at him, a slender woman in khaki shorts and a T-shirt with a Union Jack flag outlining her breasts. He was aware of how vulnerable she was, and it fueled the need to protect her.

"What?" she finally asked, breaking the silence.

Marc stood, tossed what was left of her cash on the bed, and walked to the door. He wasn't going to take her in his arms and kiss her good-bye. He'd find her when he could. Even without the beginning of a bond, he knew he could find her.

"Time to leave," he said. He held one of her sets of keys in his hand.

She looked from the money to him, totally confused. "Is that a major tip for the maid?"

"It's for you. Sit down," he added. He waited until she had before he went on. "Believe me when I tell you it's safer not to go to the authorities. To explain why you've been missing so long, tell them your car broke down and you had to hike around the fires. Tell them whatever you want." He gave her another long, hard look. He almost apologized for what he'd done to her. Instead, he said, "Stay safe, Josephine. Go home."

Then he did the hardest thing he'd ever done. He opened the door and walked away, leaving the woman he loved behind.

Chapter Sixteen

For a very brief moment, Jo almost acted on the insane impulse to run after him and beg him to take her with him. She was not crazy, though. She did not throw away the opportunity he'd given her to have her life back. But she didn't know what to do, either.

So she sat unmoving on the edge of the bed, her hands clasped tightly on her lap. For a long time she was numb, empty, full of dozens of conflicting emotions but no coherent thoughts.

She finally became aware of how empty the room was, how *alone* she was. Cage had an overwhelming, dominant presence. Without him there, the world was silent. She was alone in the room, alone inside her head. His emotions had bombarded her for days, keeping her constantly off-balance. She'd had to fight against his will, fight against sympathizing with him, fight against his crazy claims, fight caring for him, and fight and lose to a growing sexual attraction. She'd fought fear, and she'd fought uncertainty. What was she supposed to do with nothing to fight anymore?

She was free. The realization came slowly; but it came with no joy, no victory, no pleasure. There was relief at being alive, but she'd stopped believing he was going to kill her the night he rescued the—the foxlike people.

She shook her head, and realized her muscles were stiff. How long had she been sitting here? Where was he? Where had he gone?

Would he be all right?

Then her deep worry for him was replaced with the outraged thought, *He stole my Jeep!*

Her anger pumped enough adrenaline into her system to get her on her feet and make her finally, truly aware that she could go anywhere she wanted, do anything she wanted. Marc Cage wasn't lurking out in the hall ready to jump at her if she opened the door and tell her that her freedom was a practical joke.

No. There was a part of her that was aware of him moving away from her, a connection between them that tugged on her heart.

She shook her head again, trying to deny any psychic link. "Stop that. That's nonsense. Mumbo jumbo."

To keep from thinking about the mumbo jumbo that she more than half believed, Jo looked around. He'd managed to find them another motel room without a phone or television. The man had a gift for finding really out-of-the-way places in the middle of nowhere. "If you want a real secluded getaway, let Marcus Cage book the tour for you," she muttered.

Getting away had been the point, of course. She still didn't know who he'd been running from, or why.

But the point is, she told herself, *you aren't running from anyone. Get out of here and find a phone.*

Should she call the cops? Yeah. One cop. Her mom. Her family had to be frantic by now.

Jo stuffed the cash in her pocket, and went to the door. Turning the knob proved to be hard. Walking out into the hallway was harder. By the time she stood in the center of the narrow motel corridor, she was furious with Cage for breeding this trepidation in her. It didn't help that the hall reminded her of the dream.

At least Cage wasn't waiting for her. And this time no one chased her as she walked, then ran toward the door at the end of the corridor. When she reached the door she banged into it so hard she bruised her shoulder in her haste to get out. She forgot the pain the instant she stepped out under the open night sky; she looked around and saw lots of parked vehicles, a few people going about their business, and a scattering of buildings. She soaked in the sights and sounds as she turned around and around. The night air was cool on her skin. She heard a train in the far distance. A truck horn blasted the quiet evening air as a huge eighteen-wheeler sped past the motel. The stink of its exhaust filled her lungs.

"Ah, civilization."

Cage had left her in a small town, though she had no idea where. It didn't matter. He hadn't abandoned her to fend for herself in the middle of nowhere. She wasn't a prisoner; she could do what she wanted.

She spotted a restaurant across the street and decided to go have a salad. She was suddenly determined that the first thing she was going to reclaim about her life was being a vegetarian.

Actually, the very first thing she did when she walked into the restaurant was to use the pay phone by the cashier station to dial a collect call.

"Yes, Mom, it's Josephine," she said when she finally got through.

"Josephine?" her mom asked, sounding almost skeptical. "Josephine? Is that really you?"

What was wrong? Jo was hurt until she remembered that she hadn't let anyone call her by her full name since she was twelve. Her mother worked missing persons cases, and knew all the tricks the media, creeps, and crazies used to get at victims' families. No wonder she was suspicious.

"It's really Jo, Mom. Really. I'm fine."

"Oh, my God!" her mother shouted. "Oh, my God! You're alive! Sweetheart, we were so worried." Then Constance Elliot switched from mother mode to detective lieutenant mode. "Where are you? What happened? Can you talk?"

Jo looked at the woman behind the cash register and asked

the name of the town. The woman looked surprised, but told her. "Kennedyville, Mom. I—" She wasn't used to lying to anyone, especially to her parents. "I got lost. The Jeep broke down, and I had to hike around the fires."

"Really?" The skeptical tone had returned. "Kennedyville, you say?"

"Yes."

"Fine. You stay right there. I'll call the local sheriff—"

"No!" Jo interrupted. "No police, please."

"And why the devil not? You're a missing person. There's a very intense search going on for you."

"I'm sure there is, and I'm grateful. But I'm not lost, I'm found. I'm fine. Really. I don't want any attention."

"Jo, are you sure you're safe?"

"Yes." The cashier was staring at her, and Jo turned her back to the woman. She whispered, putting her hand up to muffle the conversation further as she gave an excuse that her very sharp mother would believe. "I can't stand any more media attention. Remember what it was like after the crash? I can't go through that again. They'll drag up my past."

"They already have. You obviously haven't caught any news broadcasts."

"No, and I don't want to. Mom, please, keep this quiet. Just come and get me, okay?"

She really didn't want to have to face the media again. The spotlight that had been turned on the pilot who'd survived had been agonizing. It had been hard enough being hailed a hero. She feared that a flimsy story of her getting lost wouldn't hold up if reporters decided to look into it.

"Just come get me," she pleaded. "Let the family know I'm okay, tell them I love them, and come get me." She didn't wait for an answer, but hung up the phone. She wiped a hand across her stinging eyes. Damn, she was crying again.

Language, Josephine.

I'll swear inside my head if I want to.

She had to be imagining Cage talking in her head. She was just tired and very stressed out. Maybe she'd have that salad, give herself time to get her thoughts together, then call home again.

Beyond the cash register, there was a row of booths and a lunch counter with a half dozen stools. The kitchen was visible beyond the counter, and the smell of coffee and deep-fried food wafted through the air. The food smelled good, and she stood and breathed in the scents for a moment.

The cashier was looking at her worriedly. "You all right, honey?" she asked. "You a refugee from the fire, too?"

Jo remembered how full the motel lot was, and she finally noticed that the restaurant was crowded. Refugees from the wildfire? Of course. Many of these people must have lost their homes, or been evacuated by firefighters. She knew that drill. She'd helicoptered people out of harm's way herself in years past. Other people had been caught up in their own emergencies while she was isolated in Cage's company.

She nodded to the cashier. "Yes. Can I get something to eat?"

The woman pointed to an empty stool at the counter. "Have a seat."

When Jo sat down and picked up a menu, she found herself missing Cage. And she found the quiet of the place disconcerting, as well. It wasn't that no one was talking; there were conversations going on all around her. A baby was crying in one of the booths. There was the clink and clatter of dishes and flatware, the hum of air-conditioning, and sounds of cooking from the kitchen. The type of quiet Jo was suddenly aware of was something she'd never experienced before as an empath. It was an emotional quiet, an absence of perception. One of her senses was suddenly missing. She couldn't feel them. She'd been empathic all her life. She'd learned to control it and done just fine. After the accident she'd felt too much, she'd been bombarded, overwhelmed. She had been drowning before meeting Cage, so soaked and saturated with others' emotions that running away from the world had been her only option. She'd yearned for the silence.

It was silent, and she had only her own thoughts and feelings to deal with. Was this what it was like to be normal? She wasn't sure if she liked the isolation or not.

Don't worry about it; it's probably a reaction from spending so much time with Cage. Maybe concentrating so intently on one person fried whatever brain circuit controls the empathy.

Her empathic gift would either come back, or it wouldn't. It wouldn't do any harm for her simply to be normal for a while. Normal was good. Normal didn't get people into trouble. She wasn't going to let herself worry about psychic stuff when she needed to concentrate on getting home and getting day-to-day life back on track.

"You ready?" the waitress asked.

Jo looked up. "Scrambled eggs," she said, suddenly not wanting a salad after all. "And toast with lots of butter and jelly, and hash browns, and maybe some pancakes."

"You want any sausage?"

"Yes." The answer surprised Jo, but she didn't retract it. "Just pile a lot of cholesterol on a plate, and I'll eat it." Cage would be proud.

The waitress laughed. "You sound like you've been lost out in the desert for a month."

"More like a couple of weeks," Jo said. "And I'd like coffee and orange juice, too, please."

It wasn't as if Cage had starved her, she thought, as the waitress turned away. Far from it, he'd been worried that she was skinny. That was rather sweet—except for the kidnapping part.

Don't romanticize him. Just don't. And don't sit here half in tears from missing him. That's too weird.

Her coffee and juice arrived, and she concentrated on them. When several large plates of food arrived, she was able to focus on the meal. There was a lot of food, and Jo took a long time eating it. She slowly worked her way through everything she'd ordered, happily accepting frequent refills of coffee.

For all she knew, hours had passed by the time a hand landed on her shoulder, and she looked up into a stranger's face. The man was in his late forties, with buzz-cut steel gray hair and bags under his eyes. He wore a police uniform.

"Jo Elliot?" he asked.

Not so long ago, the sight of a cop would have thrilled her, now all it did was annoy her. Hadn't she asked to be left alone? "Did my mother call you?"

A flicker of surprise crossed his features, but he calmly answered, "Our office was contacted by Lieutenant Elliot."

The restaurant was silent, with everyone watching. Jo hated the attention. "Thank you for your concern," she said quietly. "I'm fine, and I'm sorry for the inconvenience. I'm waiting for my family to come get me, so—"

"Your mother asked me to bring you to the office," he interrupted. The hand on her shoulder subtly urged her to stand. "You can wait for her there. That's where she'll be expecting to find you," he added, when Jo looked around the restaurant uncertainly.

It was true that she hadn't told her mother where to pick her up. The police station would offer more privacy than waiting here. Now that there'd been attention drawn to her, the last thing she wanted was more. She didn't want anything to do with the authorities. Marc had asked her not to go to them. Well, they'd come to her. Not because of him, they didn't know about her connection to him.

She overheard someone in the crowd say, "I think I saw her picture on the news channel. Isn't she the one lost in the fire zone?"

"I think so," someone else said.

This recognition from a stranger tipped the balance in favor of going with the officer even more than the fact that he had his hand on her arm and didn't look like he was going anywhere. "I'll wait at the police station," she told him. She paid for her meal and accompanied him to his car.

There was no conversation on the way to the small cinderblock building. Once inside, she was shown to a room with bare walls that held only a table and two chairs. She was told to have a seat, then left alone. For a while she was glad of the privacy, but as time passed she grew restless, and the silence and isolation began to wear on her nerves. When she got up and tried the door, she discovered that it was locked. She went to the window, but it was small and set high in the wall. There was no seeing out, and no getting out, as it was barred.

Nervousness turned to a sense of dread, which edged into fear. She tried shouting and banging on the door, but no one paid any attention. She paced around and around the table for a long time, but eventually sat back down.

She must have fallen asleep because her head was resting on the table when the door opened. She bolted to her feet as a man came into the room. She had to blink to bring him into focus. He was tall and handsome, with a cleft chin, blue eyes, and short blond hair. He was wearing a suit and carrying a leather case. There was a look about him that said "cop" to the cop's daughter, but not just any kind of cop. FBI, maybe. Something federal.

"Who are you?" she demanded. "Why am I being held here?"

"Sit down, Ms. Elliot," he said smoothly, with a smile and a gesture toward her chair. He closed the door behind him and crossed the room to take the chair opposite her. "I'm sorry to have left you waiting so long."

He folded his hands on the table and looked at her, very calm, very professional. He watched her for a few seconds, then he said, "I need you to tell me where to find Marcus Cage."

Chapter Seventeen

She'd already been expecting the question. She chose to ignore it.

She said, "I've had a rough few days. I'm very tired, and I want to go home to my family."

"I understand that," he replied. "I sympathize with your ordeal, and I don't want to add to the trauma any more than necessary. But I still need information from you." He took a leather wallet out of his jacket. "My name is Jonas Gavin," he said as he handed her the case. He sat back in his chair and waited while she flipped it open and studied the badge and identification card inside.

She'd been right about his being from a federal agency, but the FBI guess was incorrect. "Special Agent Gavin," she said, and passed the ID back to him. She didn't know what else to say.

"Call me Gavin," he said. "Most people do." He tucked the badge away and folded his hands again. His movements were deliberately calm and nonthreatening, and all she had was body language to tell what he was feeling, since her gift of empathy was gone. He turned a sympathetic expression on her. "Cage has put you through a lot, but it's safe for you to talk about him now."

The last thing Jo wanted to do was talk about Cage, and certainly not to this stranger. She didn't even want to think about Cage. She'd started her trip into the desert confused, despondent, and in physical as well as mental pain. Truth be told, she'd run off to feel sorry for herself in private.

All she wanted was to go home and take her life back. If

Marcus Cage had done nothing else for her, he'd shown her how precious home, family, and freedom were. He'd even given her some good advice and tried to make her face some of her fears. She owed him for shaking her out of her self-pitying depression.

"Marcus Cage," Gavin said.

Jo realized she'd been staring at the wall and had almost forgotten the man was there. She looked at him and wondered how she was going to get past him. She didn't know what to say. She didn't want to lie, and she wasn't very good at it, anyway. It would be annoying and ironic if Cage gave her freedom, but she didn't get a chance to use it because of him.

Then again, she didn't *have* to talk to Gavin, did she? The fact that she'd been locked in this room was ominous, but it had probably been mistaken zealousness on the part of local cops who'd been under orders to hold her until this federal type showed up.

She stood, and said, "I'm sorry your time has been wasted, but I'm not going to be any help to you."

Gavin let her get almost to the door before he said, "Your trying to buy him time won't help him. I think you want to help him." She heard him push back his chair and stand. "He's going to die if you don't help him."

Jo halted in front of the door as Gavin's words sent a chill up her spine. She stood frozen, shoulders hunched as though waiting for a blow. Guilt raced through her as she remembered the people who'd died in the crash. She hadn't been able to help them. She had a sudden image of Cage hurt and dying, and it terrified her.

But Cage was alive—free. Running. She didn't know what he was running from, she didn't know where he was going, but she wasn't going to let anyone try to stop him.

Why?

She forced the question away, took another step toward the door.

"If you walk away from this, he'll die."

She desperately wanted to run, but Gavin's calm certainty drew her back. She turned to face him.

"I want to help him, too," he said, when she looked at him. "I can't help him if I can't find him. You hold the key to that."

"I don't," she said, having at least that much truth to share with the agent. She shook her head. "I really don't."

"There are tears in your eyes," Gavin told her. "Don't tell me you don't know who I'm talking about."

"I'm not telling you anything," she snapped back. She forced herself to add, more calmly, "I've been out in the desert, lost near the fires. I don't know why you make assumptions about me. All I want is to go home." She turned around.

"The door's locked," Gavin said, before she reached it. "I know you're tired, but I can't let you go until you help me."

She spun back around. "Are you charging me with a crime? Do I need to call a lawyer?"

"A lawyer won't do you any good," he said. "Not with the kind of power my agency wields." He held his hands up before him. "But I'm not here to threaten you. I'm trying to make this easy on you."

He was so very calm, so neatly groomed, well dressed, polite, and totally in control. It looked like she'd traded one captor for another. And frankly, she preferred big, gruff, grubby Marcus Cage to the slick Mr. Gavin.

"You are threatening me," she told Gavin. "Locking me in this room is a threat."

He nodded. "You're correct, of course, but I need your cooperation. I need it quickly. Please believe that talking to me is for the best. I won't force anything on you. I won't hurt you. Terrorize you." After a long pause that left her enough time to go cold with dread knowing what was coming, he added, "Rape you."

The words still felt like a blow, no matter how neutral the

man's tone. "I haven't been raped," she answered, making herself look Gavin in the eye.

"You're sure?"

She didn't offer any more comment despite the look of concern in his eyes. She wished she hadn't even answered him; it was none of his business. What had happened was no one's business but hers and Cage's.

She was cold, goose bumps dotted her skin; it felt like the air-conditioning had been cranked up to stun. And the lights in this interrogation room were too bright. The walls were a dull beige, and it felt like they were closing in on her. She was deliberately being made to feel that cooperating with Gavin was the only way she was going to get out of here, wasn't she?

Or maybe she was being paranoid, and the man really was trying to be patient and as kind as possible under the circumstances.

And the circumstances were . . . ? Why was Cage running? Why were the feds chasing him? She'd been a pawn the whole time, kept in the dark, sometimes literally. What the hell was going on? She practically had to bite her tongue to keep from shouting the question at the special agent. If she gave in to curiosity now, it would be an admission that she knew Marcus Cage.

Gavin had put his briefcase next to his chair; now he picked it up and put it on the table. When he opened it he took out several items, among them her wallet and one of her Def Leppard T-shirts, as well as one of the white shirts Cage had worn.

"Our forensic team has been through the room where you and Cage stayed. There was evidence of sexual activity on the bed linens. We have a match for Cage's DNA, and I'm certain a sample of your DNA would show that you were his sexual partner." He'd been looking down as he spoke, now he raised his head to look at her sharply. "Are you sure it wasn't rape, Jo?"

"Of course, I—!" Jo clapped a hand over her mouth to keep from saying more.

She'd never been so mortified in her life, or felt so humiliated. It wasn't that she was ashamed of the sex, it was the clinical proof of its being presented to her by a stranger that was so awful. It made her feel as if she needed to justify her actions, as if she should apologize for making love to a man she'd wanted. Gavin was doing a good job of making her feel dirty, and that made her angry.

She'd made the choice to make love to Cage.

It might have been a reckless choice, but it had been the right one at that moment. What had happened between them was an act of fiery intensity and sweet fulfillment. She could almost still feel his body twined with hers, the perfect way they fit together, how they made each other whole. Just thinking about it made her ache to do it all over again.

"Mind your own business," she said to Gavin.

"Marcus is my business," he answered. He sat back in his chair. "I think you *think* you made love to him, Jo, but that isn't what really happened."

"I was there."

He shook his head. "Not really. Not exactly."

"You're about to bring up Stockholm Syndrome, aren't you?" she asked. "I know what it is; how hostages who spend long amounts of time in the company of their captors can come to identify with them. It's one of the things that helped me—"

She broke off again as she realized that she was telling Gavin things he wanted to know, that she had just admitted to being abducted and held prisoner.

"Being aware of a process doesn't mean that a person will be unaffected by it." Gavin leaned forward slightly, his gaze very intent on hers. "Shall I tell you what happened to you?"

"I know what happened to me."

"You were there when it happened, I know that. But you

are too involved with the situation to understand it objectively. I can explain it to you."

Of course she wasn't objective about it! She hadn't even had time to think about it yet. Could a person ever be objective about an experience like that? Could she ever be anything but emotionally attached to Marc Cage? She felt like he was a part of her, that she was a part of him somehow.

"Jo." Gavin tapped a fingertip on the table to get her attention. "Jo," he repeated.

"What?"

"You were detached from the present, just then. Your thoughts were on Cage, weren't they?"

"Yes," she admitted.

"He's done that to you."

"Done what?" Why shouldn't she think about Cage?

"He's conditioned you to center your whole existence around him," Gavin told her. "He probably didn't even do it on purpose. Marcus is not the sort of person who'd deliberately set out to brainwash someone, but he would do anything he had to in his current condition to survive. He completely isolated you from the rest of the world," he went on. "Everything you did was completely under his control. What you ate and when, where you slept, where you went, how long you stayed, all at his discretion. Everything you had, he gave to you, every little privilege was his gift to you. That's all true, isn't it, Jo? What did he call you?" he added. "Josephine, perhaps?"

"Yes. How did you know—?"

"He took away your name and gave you one of his choosing. He needed to make you his, to make you feel like you belonged to him."

She wanted to protest that people who cared for each other gave each other nicknames, pet names. But a nagging voice spoke up inside her, questioning that perhaps Cage had given her a pet name because he treated her like a pet. She *had* been dependent on him for everything, just like a puppy or a kitten. Or a prisoner.

He was a wanted man. He was on the run, with a government security agency hunting him. So he wasn't a garden variety criminal or prison escapee.

"Is he a terrorist?"

Gavin smiled. "No."

This answer came as a relief, though she didn't see why the agent found the question amusing. "What is Cage, then?" she demanded.

"Psychic," he said.

"You know about that?" she blurted out. "The government *believes* it?"

"Marcus Cage has a rare and dangerous gift."

"I thought he was a criminal!"

"He is, and an escapee. He is very dangerous in his current condition. Dangerous to others, and almost certainly fatally dangerous to himself if he isn't found soon. You have to help me find him. You have to help me for his sake, Jo. Never mind that he's a convicted criminal—"

"Convicted of what?" she interrupted. "Tell me he's not a murderer." *Please, not that. I can't bear it if he's a killer.* "He didn't hurt me," she added. "He let me go."

"He hasn't killed anyone, at least not yet. Despite his size and looks, he's not a violent offender. He was sentenced to three years in a minimum security facility for a white-collar crime."

Relief flooded her. He wasn't evil. She knew it in her gut, in her heart, but she was shaken enough by Gavin's descriptions of her captivity that she wasn't sure she could trust her instincts.

Then the incongruity struck her. "Wait a minute—if Cage isn't a dangerous criminal, and he escaped from a white-collar lockup, why the manhunt? Why are the feds involved?"

"There are things I can't tell you, Jo."

She laughed, and his evasiveness stiffened her resolve to have some control. She crossed her arms over her chest. "Then I guess there are a lot of things I can't tell you."

A flash of frustration cracked his calm veneer for the first time. "We don't have time for games."

"My life isn't a game. But you're playing games with me, setting boundaries for me. That's not acceptable. You drew me into this—"

"Cage dragged you into this."

"And I have a right to know what *this* is. What's going on? What's going to happen to him? Why is he—?" She took a deep breath before she added, "the way he is."

"Ah." Gavin nodded. "So you noticed."

"He's—not like other people," she said. "He—"

"Thinks he's a vampire."

"*What?*" She laughed. "Of course he doesn't—"

"Didn't he mention that to you? Didn't he tell you about his kind?"

"No. He talked about his family." A line of cold dread went up her spine, and she tried to shake the feeling off. "It sounded like they were from some secret ethnic minority."

"So he never said he was a vampire? In so many words?"

"No." She shook her head in disbelief.

"Didn't he bite you?"

Jo touched her throat, she looked at her wrist, she remembered a sting of pain and pleasure as Marc's mouth settled on her breast. "Yes, he bit me," she conceded. "But . . . he didn't mean anything by it. I suppose it's a fetish . . . a harmless turn-on and—"

"He drank your blood," Gavin cut off her rationalizing. "You don't want to remember it, or maybe he was able to use his telepathic gift to make you forget, or think it was something else. Believe it now, Jo. Cage drank your blood."

"Eeuwww!" She balked at this, totally disgusted. But she recalled how weak she'd been after that first night in the desert—how he'd come out of the dark like a nightmare come to life. He'd completely overwhelmed her, and— She touched her neck again. "He never said he's a vampire."

"What did he say?"

"That he wasn't mortal," she admitted. "That he was around eighty years old. That he'd escaped from people who were doing experiments on him. There were dreams," she added. "Horrible dreams."

Excitement burned in Gavin's eyes. "You shared his dreams?"

"Yes. I know that sounds crazy."

It didn't *feel* crazy, not with the way she still felt connected, mind to mind, with Cage. Or maybe it was soul to soul. She had a moment of absurd humor, thinking that maybe she'd truly met her soul mate in Marcus Cage, and it turned out he really was an insane criminal. Wouldn't that be just—typical?

"It doesn't sound crazy to me, Jo." Gavin sounded very, very reassuring.

And Jo very much needed to be reassured. "Why isn't it crazy? There's no such thing as a vampire, so why did he bite me?"

"It's all related." Gavin looked at her for a few seconds, then shuffled his papers and tapped his fingertip on the table. Finally, he came to a decision, and looked at her again. "You are owed an explanation. Nothing I say leaves this room. Agreed?"

"Of course." She knew very well that if she didn't agree, she wouldn't find out anything. And she very much wanted to know everything she could about Marcus Cage.

He hesitated a moment longer, then said, "Marc volunteered for an experimental government program. Volunteered: be very clear on that. He was nearing the end of his prison sentence when he found out about the experimental program. He didn't do it to shorten his time. He went into it with his eyes open. He knew he was physically strong, and he was aware of his mental abilities, and was curious to see if he could take them further. The purpose of the program was to enhance both."

"Enhance? How?"

"With new types of drugs, new surgical procedures, new microtechnology." He smiled. "Remember the opening of the old television show *The Six Million Dollar Man?*"

She did, and nodded.

"The price of the work has been a lot closer to six billion."

"But why do these *enhancements* to Marc?"

It was a stupid question. One she knew the answer to even as he said, "There have been science-fiction stories about building supersoldiers for a long time, but this program is the real deal—or will be, if the techniques are perfected. If not, if we can't correct the psychoses the experimental drugs have produced in the volunteers, then the program will be shut down. We set out to enhance Marcus Cage and succeeded to a certain degree. Are you following me?"

"You were trying to make Superman?"

Gavin nodded.

This explanation, bizarre as it seemed, made a lot more sense than Cage's being a vampire. "And you run these experiments out of Area 51, right?" Everybody knew about the supersecret government experimental base in the Nevada desert, but nobody knew what went on there.

"Are you taking me seriously, Jo? Because Marc's life is at stake."

She recalled how Cage had been able to read her mind, to hypnotize her almost at will. She supposed that drugs could have been developed to up the abilities of someone who was already psychic. She remembered how his eyes seemed to glow red sometimes. Was that some sort of night-vision device surgically implanted in his eyes? She remembered how he'd outrun the Jeep when she tried to escape. Enhanced muscles and cardiovascular system? She remembered how he was sensitive to light. Was that a drug reaction?

"Have the drugs you've given him made him delusional?" she asked Gavin.

"Exactly," he answered. "His mind has created a detailed

fantasy world where he believes himself to be a vampire. There are things we did to him that reinforce this belief. The drugs have given him a serious reaction to sunlight. He does crave blood. Again, the drugs did that to him. We are responsible for what's wrong with him, and we want to help him."

"He's an experiment gone wrong, enhanced with a lot of classified technology." Jo found it hard to believe that the people who created Cage were only looking out for his good. "That's why you want him back?"

"He's also an escaped prisoner, one with paranoid delusions that are only going to get worse," Gavin answered. "He's getting more dangerous all the time. You were the first person he took hostage, and he let you go. But he's going to reach a point where he can't let go, where he's going to drain an innocent victim's blood, and somebody is going to get killed. He won't be able to help himself. We really do want to help him," Gavin added. "I know you do, too."

He looked and sounded very sure, very earnest, and what he said shook her deeply. She sat and thought for a while. Gavin kept quiet and let her. She twisted her fingers together nervously in her lap, trying to decide whether to trust her heart or her head. Her heart said Marc had told her the truth. But the only element that Gavin's story didn't explain better were the things the werefox had said.

She looked up. "What's a Prime?"

"It's a term convicts use," Gavin answered. "It means an alpha male."

"Oh."

So, maybe the werefox wasn't a shapeshifting human after all. What was he, then? An ex-con who recognized Cage from prison? It made a hell of a lot more sense than tales of vampires and werecreatures. And Cage *was* sick. The drugs were driving him crazy. They might kill him.

She looked up again. "Can you save his life?"

"We want to try. We need your help. You can save him, Jo."

"How?"

"Lead us to him."

"How?" she asked again.

"You're connected, aren't you? Don't you feel it? The way you're protecting him convinces me that you're more than emotionally connected to him."

"I thought you said it was brainwashing?"

"Part of it was brainwashing, but not all. You spent days together, days full of intense emotional contact. He got inside your mind and under your skin psychically, along with messing with your head psychologically."

"Yes," she admitted. "We-we—" She couldn't explain it. Gavin did it for her. "Experiments have proven that prolonged telepathic contact, especially between sexual partners, creates bonds between the partners. If you think about it very hard, you'll find the link between you. That link can lead you to him."

He sounded completely certain. She wasn't at all sure.

"Search inside yourself," he urged.

"Use the Force," she muttered.

He chuckled. "Call it whatever you want to."

Jo thought about going inside herself and finding the place where Marc Cage had become a part of her. She didn't know if she could. She rubbed the back of her neck and rolled her tired shoulders. She was stiff, and as weary physically as she was emotionally.

She was worried for Cage and about him. She didn't want anyone hurt. And even after what he'd done to her, after what Gavin had told her, it had become utterly important to her to have him safe.

She looked at Gavin, who was leaning forward, anxiously watching her. He was waiting for her to make the decision.

"All right," she told him. "At least I can try."

Chapter Eighteen

"I should have had a snack before leaving," Marc muttered as he drove hunched over the wheel. Even though it was night on an empty road, his eyes were burning. His skin ached as it healed from the day's sunburn; his head ached as well. And he was thirsty. He hadn't expected to be thirsty so soon.

As flippant as the words were, Marc meant them on many levels. The first few hours hadn't been so bad, except for missing Josephine so much that the ache was almost physical. He'd grown increasingly aware of her agitation, of her worry. All he wanted to do was turn around and save her, even though logic told him she wasn't in trouble. She was safe, probably just having to deal with the mess he'd left her with. But the worry was slowing his escape. He kept going, but sometimes he found himself driving at only a few miles an hour. This was not hastening his escape.

And now his pain was physical as well as in his mind, and deep in his soul. He felt like hell, and all because he was bonding. That could soon be disastrous. It was also totally unexpected.

I shouldn't have let her go.

He'd always heard that the greatest thing that could happen to a Prime was finding a bondmate. Whether the bond was with a vampire female or with a mortal was of little concern to the Prime who found this permanent sexual and soul connection. It was the highest of highs, the greatest achievement of an adult male's life. Or so young males were led to believe.

But nobody ever talked about what it was like when you were separated from that mate. You learned about the glory, but what about the hell? He wasn't even fully bonded—the connection was new, tenuous at best, yet he missed Josephine as though a part of himself had been cut out and left behind. His soul bled more with every mile that stretched between them.

But he had to let her go, to keep her safe. It was the right thing to do. He'd find her again, explain everything to her, share everything with her, and complete the bond. But only after his world was secure for the vampire Families, the Clans, and even for the Tribes. The vampire world had to be safe before he could bring Josephine into it.

Chivalry is for idiots.

His fangs ached and throbbed, and his mouth had grown so sensitive that even sucking in a breath was agonizing. The burning was starting in his veins. It was only a faint trace of fire now, but it would grow into a maddening inferno if not dealt with soon. He needed blood.

He should have taken more than a few drops the last time they made love, but he hadn't been thirsty then. He'd only wanted to increase the pleasure for both of them. He should have drunk from Josephine before he left her, but he'd been so intent on doing the noble thing that it hadn't occurred to him.

Stupid.

Love made a male stupid. That was the only explanation for why he hadn't done something so necessary for his very survival.

If the bastards hadn't starved him, he wouldn't still be hungry. If they hadn't done things that nearly nullified the drugs that allowed him to dwell in the daylight world, he'd be able to control the blood craving better. Meditation might help if he had the time or energy for it.

Her blood would help more.

He tried not to think about what he needed and concentrated as hard as he could on driving. He was heading south toward Mexico on a rough mountain road. The track paralleled larger highways that would make the trip faster and easier. The gas tank was getting low, and, as much as he wanted to avoid people, he was going to have to turn toward a town at the next crossroads.

Or maybe not yet. The sunburn from driving in the daylight should have healed, but it was still bothering him. Even moonlight bothered him, though he was wearing sunglasses. Another day of driving in the light wasn't possible; he'd end up with third-degree burns. That agony would drive him to ground in the first dark place he came to, and he'd be helpless until he healed. They'd find him then, for sure.

He needed to find a place of his own choosing, while he was still in control, where he could hide from the blisteringly bright sunlight. Arizona was not vampire country. He didn't even understand how mortals could live in a place where the sky was cloudless, and the sun had no mercy.

Jo could explain it to him, he was sure, and with verve and enthusiasm. His Girl Scout was a native of a place called Phoenix, for the goddess's sake! She was from firebird country, and she probably loved the heat and the endless sky and the parched earth.

"We're moving to New York, hon," he told his absent lady. "As soon as I get things straightened out."

He wondered how long it would be before he could get back to her, then ruthlessly put the thought aside. The rule of survival was to concentrate only on survival. Since meeting Josephine, he kept forgetting that.

Up ahead, he spotted a crack in the cliff face. As he got closer he saw that it was actually an opening into a narrow canyon. It was wide enough to accommodate the Jeep, so he turned into it and cautiously drove a few hundred feet, carefully searching the canyon walls on either side for a place to hide from the sun. There was an overhang of rock above the point where the canyon ended, which would provide enough shelter. He'd hole up for the day. He backed the Jeep up to turn it around, then parked facing toward the road. After he draped Josephine's sleeping bag over the windshield to block out even more light, he got into the backseat, drank a couple liters of water, and tried to get into a comfortable position. It was cool and dark now, but he knew the interior of the Jeep was going to turn into an oven during the day. Still, that would be better than being exposed to the sunlight.

He'd long ago learned how to fall asleep anywhere, but when he closed his eyes he found it impossible to clear his mind. He was all too aware of his connection to Josephine. It was as if she were nearby, coming closer.

Marc told himself that was wishful thinking, and fought down his burning thirst to finally get to sleep.

"You're sure?" Gavin asked.

"Yes." Jo was growing irritated at the way he kept questioning her. They were seated together in the backseat of a Humvee. "I thought you said you believed I'm linked to Cage?"

"I do. It's just that we're on the clock here." He put his hand over hers. She didn't like him touching her.

There were two men in desert camouflage uniforms in the front seat. They wore helmets and headsets, body armor, and both were heavily armed. There was another Humvee full of soldiers in front of them, and a third behind. There were also a couple of large vans and a boxy vehicle she assumed to be an ambulance. None of the vehicles in the convoy had any official markings, and the hard-faced soldiers wore no insignia on their uniforms.

Jo had noticed these details when she was brought out of the Kennedyville police station and saw the waiting vehicles and personnel lined up along the narrow street. When she'd asked Gavin about it, his answer was to hustle her into the back of the Hummer as he said, "This is a classified operation."

Once everyone was in their vehicles, he'd asked her, "Which way?" and he'd been asking all the questions since.

Jo was getting more and more anxious as the convoy wound its way up a narrow mountain road. She knew these people were here to help Cage, but the show of force bothered her. Surely he could be persuaded to surrender without a fight. He'd seemed very dangerous when they first met, but as the days went by he'd shown kindness, and humor, and he'd seemed lucid most of the time.

She hated the thought of their hurting him, but she couldn't blame them for not taking any chances that he could hurt them.

"I don't want anyone to get hurt," she told Gavin.

"Do your job, sweetheart, and no one will."

His condescending attitude set her taut nerves even further on edge.

"Close your eyes," he said. "Think about Marc."

She pushed his hand off her arm, then she closed her eyes. They were near, very near.

"He's hurting," she said. She felt an echo of his distress. "Hurry."

She felt the surge of power as the driver obeyed. Messages were relayed over headsets, the men speaking in military acronym shorthand that she didn't understand. With her eyes closed, she was more aware of her other senses. Sunlight came through the back window, hot on her cheek despite the air conditioner. It was a blisteringly hot day, and she could smell the smoke of the wildfires. She was grateful that Marc had gone south of the fire zone.

"He's trying to get to Mexico," she said.

"Now?" Gavin asked.

"No."

"What's he doing now?"

She felt almost hypnotized, answering Gavin's softly spoken questions while she drew abstract images and directions out of her subconscious. "Sleeping," she answered. "Dreaming."

"Dreaming of what?"

That seemed like an odd question. What difference did it make to the operation?

She answered, "Me."

Outside the cave mouth, the world was gray and cold. The only warmth came from the woman he held in his arms.

"I don't like this," she said. "It doesn't feel right."

"Tell me about it." He looked around, peering through swirling fog and seeing nothing. He sensed monsters out in the mist, invisible, waiting. They were going to have to make a run for it, they both knew it. He looked back at her. "It's you I'm worried about."

"You can't protect me from everything."

"I can try."

"Let's do this together."

He drew her closer and kissed her, gently at first. But she was life to him, she was everything to him, so soon the kiss turned ruthless and demanding. His hands moved over her in the same way. He found her breasts, squeezed them and played with her nipples, then his hands moved down her body and between her legs. His caresses were not gentle, but she groaned into his mouth, ground her body against his. She was just as needy, totally in sync with his need. Soon he backed her against the cave wall, holding her up. One hard thrust brought him inside her, where she was hot and wet and so very tight. He loved the weight of her ass in his hands, loved the way she wrapped her legs and arms around him, loved the smell of her arousal and the taste of her mouth. He pounded into her with frantic intensity. He was aware of the lurking danger beyond the cave, and the danger added desperation to their mating. This might be the last time they ever came together. The last time . . .

Then an orgasm rippled through her, and the way her sheath tightened around his cock was the trigger that set off his own explosive release. The world went blinding, white-hot.

And while he turned to ash, the danger outside drew nearer.
"They're closing in," she said.

He heard her, but he couldn't see. His eyes were open, but the
fog had turned to white heat haze, with ominous shadows flit-
ting deep inside the shimmer. He'd lost control, he'd dropped
his guard. The enemy was taking advantage of his lapse, and
they were going to pay.

"I'm sorry," he said. "I'm sorry."

"Just run!" she shouted. "Wake up and run!"

The warning brought him awake, but even as he came up
out of the dream, he knew it was too late.

"Cage!" he heard Josephine call, somewhere in the far, far
distance. "Run!"

He felt her in pain then, sharp as a needle driven into his
mind. All he could do was roar in fury, and react.

The wave of absolute, blinding pleasure drove Jo to her
knees. She wasn't aware of the soldiers moving cautiously toward the Jeep, or of Gavin standing beside her. For a moment
her surroundings disappeared, and she was lost with Cage in
the dream, joined body and soul. Then they split apart, the
world flashed into focus, and she was acutely aware of who
she was, where she was, and the danger—

"Cage!" she shouted as she sprang back to her feet. "Run!"

Gavin swung around as she shouted, slapping her so hard
that she fell. She landed hard on the stony ground, her ears ringing and tears of pain obscuring her vision. But when Cage's roar
of outrage sounded through the midday heat, Jo was on her feet
again, running toward the sound.

Glass shattered as Cage erupted out of the Jeep. He rushed
out of the shadows, all muscle, speed, and fury. Orders were
shouted, someone threw a metal cylinder. It landed on the
ground and burst. Stinking smoke billowed into the air. Another cylinder landed, then another. Cage kept coming. Jo kept

running toward him through the acrid fog. The stuff burned her nostrils and mouth with a familiar stench and taste.

Gavin ran after her, but she eluded him. She only slowed when Cage lifted his hand, pointing it toward her.

She'd forgotten about her gun until the moment before Cage fired it. Gavin tackled her, throwing them both to the ground as the bullet whipped by overhead.

A coughing fit took Cage before he could fire again. Jo managed to twist out from under Gavin and caught sight of Cage as he stumbled to his knees, caught in a cloud of smoke. He fell forward onto his hands, then reared up again, his breath coming in harsh gasps. His skin had gone white, and he seemed to be choking to death.

Their gazes met for a moment. Though his eyes were glowing like dying red coals, the look of betrayal he turned on her tore her heart in two. Then the coughing took him even harder, and the gun dropped from his hand.

That was when the soldiers who had circled him began firing. Blood stained his arms, and a red stain spread across his white T-shirt at the left shoulder. The force of the bullet impacts threw him onto his back.

"No!" Jo shouted. She turned on Gavin in anguished fury. "You weren't going to hurt him!" When she fought to get away, he shoved her hard to the ground.

He got up and walked over to where Cage lay, his face turned toward the sun, and used his foot to turn Cage onto his stomach. One of the soldiers came up and fastened handcuffs around Cage's wrists.

Jo got to her feet and stood bent over, clutching her side, and finally recognized the smell that was so thick in the smoke. It was garlic.

Garlic? That couldn't be right. How could something as harmless as garlic be so toxic to Marcus that it weakened and choked him?

She didn't know whether he was alive or dead, but she had to get to him. She'd feel it if he were dead, wouldn't she?

She moved toward the circle of men surrounding Cage, but one of the soldiers grabbed her by the arm.

"Should I put her with the others, sir?" he called to Gavin. *Others? What others?*

Gavin backed away from Cage's prone form, and two men hurried forward with a stretcher.

"The woman, sir?" the soldier asked. "Should I take her to the van?"

Gavin turned her way. "No," he said to the soldier. He smiled. "I've got a better use for the bitch. Put her in with the creature. The vampire's going to be hungry when he wakes up."

Chapter Nineteen

"Please, God, don't let him be dead!"

They'd dumped the stretcher with Cage's limp body unceremoniously onto the floor, pushed her in after him, and locked them inside. The vehicle wasn't an ambulance; it was a mobile prison cell.

And it was her fault they were trapped in it. Her fault Cage was hurt—or worse.

A grid of bright lights shone down from overhead, reflecting with painful intensity off the highly polished silver walls and floor. Squinting, Jo knelt by Cage's side as the vehicle began to move slowly over the rough ground. The heat from overhead was as intense as the desert at midday.

She placed his head in her lap, then put her fingers on his neck, hoping to find a pulse. One hand hovered over his mouth, hoping to detect breathing. After a few intense minutes, she thought she felt both, but so faintly that what she sensed might only be hope and imagination. She finally decided that he was alive because she *felt* that he was.

"I'd know," she told him. She ran her hands across his heavily stubbled chin and the rough new growth of dark hair on his head. "I know."

"Hey!" she yelled. "This man needs a doctor!" She didn't think anybody heard her, but she had to try.

It was frightening that they'd gone to so much trouble to capture Cage, yet no one cared about his wounds. They wanted him alive, didn't they? Of course, Gavin had called him a vampire, and maybe vampires didn't need doctors.

Despite the hot lights, Jo shivered as she remembered what Gavin had said.

The vampire's going to be hungry when he wakes up.

Was Cage *really* a vampire?

Huge, heavily muscled Marcus Cage wasn't anybody's image of a vampire. Vampires were skinny and sepulchral-looking, like David Bowie in *The Hunger*. But—

Had the clues been staring at her all along, and she'd simply ignored them? Was she that stupid?

Gavin had certainly played her for a fool. And Cage—what had Cage played her for?

Whatever his game had been, she couldn't believe that he deserved to be Gavin's prisoner. And he would have escaped if it wasn't for her.

Jo wiped sweat off her brow with the back of her hand. Her clothes were damp and sticking to her hot skin. Why was it so bright in here?

Because vampires couldn't stand too much light?

She ran a hand along the smooth surface of the floor. It looked and felt like it was made of the finest silver; her great-grandmother's antique silver tea service had felt just like this. She tried to remember what she knew of vampire legends. Were they supposed to be allergic to silver? Silver crosses, maybe, but there weren't any crosses in sight, and . . .

"What the hell—?"

She'd noticed a slight rippling movement beneath the skin of Cage's wounded shoulder. She bent forward for a closer look, and jerked back with a gasp when the thing beneath his skin moved again. Then the bullet, flattened and covered in blood, slowly emerged from the entry wound. Rejected from Cage's body, it stuck for a moment in a bloody fold of T-shirt, then fell into Jo's outstretched hand.

She'd never been so surprised at anything in her life. It was enough to make her dizzy—or maybe that was just the heat from the lights. She held the small piece of metal up in front of her eyes. Despite the impossibility of what she'd just witnessed, she was holding the evidence in her palm. Cage's body had spat out the bullet!

She flung it away and looked at his wounds. Blood crusted his arms, but new skin had already grown over the bullet holes. And now that the bullet was out, the shoulder injury was already healing.

"Good God Almighty," she murmured. "What is going on here?"

"Blood," Cage said, as if in answer to her question. His nostrils flared, scenting the air, and he turned his head and snapped at her.

She saw the sharp fangs, and skittered backward before his teeth could close on her flesh.

She didn't recognize the monster that heaved up off his back and twisted onto his knees.

Marc could smell the scent of her blood, sense the warmth of her body, and the spike of fear that shot from her hit him like a blow. But he couldn't see her. His hands were bound in silver, there was silver all around him, and light poured into his eyes and over his skin—burning, blinding. He was helpless, hungry—and furious.

"Traitor!" he shouted at the woman he could sense but couldn't see.

"Fangs!" she shouted back, her voice shaking. "You've got fangs!"

All the better to kill you with.

"Stay out of my mind!"

He lunged toward the voice. Everywhere the silver touched hurt, reaching him through the many rips in his clothes. The bright sunlamps burned him, searing every bit of bare skin. Blood loss made him weak and even thirstier than he'd been before the ambush. And he could still feel the sharp tang of garlic gas in his nostrils and lungs. He bent over, choking and coughing in reaction to the stuff. He was almost thankful for the fit, because fighting for oxygen forced him to make a conscious effort to breathe, which forced him to think. And thinking kept him from following the instinct to fall on Josephine Elliot, rip her throat out, and drink every drop of her blood.

Oh, he'd take her blood, all right, and he'd take her. He'd make it hard and brutal, and make her love it. She deserved what she got—but he wasn't going to kill her. He fought that urge off; he was not a murderer.

He *was* a wreck. Gavin had counted on his having a multitude of bad reactions, and that planning had paid off. It took a lot to bring down a Prime, but Gavin knew the tricks to do it, which was no one's fault but his own. He'd gotten himself into this mess the day he trusted a mortal. He obviously hadn't learned his lesson the first time, since the second mortal he'd trusted had betrayed him as well.

This betrayal hurt so much that he threw back his head and howled with the pain, pain that was far worse than all the physical torture.

Jo crouched in the farthest corner of the silver box and covered her ears as Cage howled. He was an animal! How had she ever thought him to be anything else? He was the creature that ran out of the night, who assaulted her, hurt her, took her away from her life! Now look where she was—locked in a cage with him, left alone with him to be his prey.

"This is all your fault!" she shouted. It was a stupid thing to say to a monster.

"My fault?" Marc shouted back. "I'm not the one who turned me in."

Why was he bothering to argue with her? Where was he getting the strength to argue? He inched closer to her, sliding painfully across the hot metal surface.

She kicked at him. "Keep away from me."

"That's not going to happen." He ignored the impact of her foot against his thigh. His hands were fastened behind his back. That would slow his subduing her, but it wasn't going to stop him.

"You've got an erection."

Her disgust amused him. "Comes with the territory. The fangs and the penis are connected."

"Isn't that typically male?" She kicked at him again, then lunged forward, trying to get past him.

He let her move out of the corner, then turned and followed her scent to the other side of the mobile prison cell. Marc was thrown forward when the vehicle hit a bump. He landed on top of Josephine, who'd landed on her back. Finding her and pinning her down had almost been too easy.

Her fists found his shoulders and the sides of his head as he scrunched forward. The lights kept him blind, and his hands were useless, but his weight and strength were enough to control her.

He found a soft, bare spot of skin, and bit down. She arched with pleasure as he drank from her, so he gave as well as took. The nourishment didn't stop his suffering, surrounded by light and silver, but it helped the weakness, helped hold madness at bay.

But he couldn't take everything he wanted; it wasn't possible without the use of his hands. Yet even if he'd managed to get his cock out of his pants, he couldn't bring himself to rape her. His conscience would only let him go so far.

He ended up only taking a few sips of blood; enough to sustain him, but not enough to weaken her. *Saving a valuable resource,* he told himself. When he got a chance to run again, he was going to need his hostage healthy and strong.

"Move," Jo demanded. "Get off of me."

"No," he answered, his voice muffled against her skin.

She kept her eyes closed against the glare of the hot lights. If it was this bad for her, it must be unbearably painful for Cage.

His head was buried between her breasts. She doubted they were giving him a lot of shelter, as they weren't all that big.

She wondered how far they'd gone, and where, while she'd gone in and out of a semiconscious blissful fog. At least they'd finally turned onto a relatively smooth, straight road. Her back ached, a foot was asleep, and his weight was hot and heavy on her. It was too intimate, as well as uncomfortable.

"I don't want you touching me."

"I don't want to touch the floor. All I've got to rest on is you."

"I'm not a piece of furniture."

"You'll do."

He sounded so very angry and contemptuous, and she didn't know why it bothered her.

"You *bit* me, Cage." She remembered how it felt, the sharp intrusion of fangs sinking into her arm, the swift, hot pleasure that followed. Her body was still alive with the electric aftershocks of that pleasure.

"Biting's what I do."

He sounded totally unapologetic, which infuriated her. "It's wrong. You should have asked."

His head came up. Though his eyes were screwed tightly shut, she could feel him glaring at her. "Wrong?" His deep bass voice rang like a bell in her head. "You turned me in! You got me into this—"

"*Us* into this," she corrected angrily. "You're not the only one locked in this box. With a vampire. Who bites without permission."

He really is a vampire. How stupid was she not to have figured that out on her own? And why had the revulsion already worn off? Because the actual process of his taking her blood gave her orgasms? She hadn't asked for the pleasure, and experiencing it was no reason to forgive him for doing it.

"You shouldn't take people's blood."

"How else am I supposed to live?"

"I've seen you eat food."

"It's not the same thing. Food provides some energy, but I need human nourishment to really live." He sneered, which looked oddly menacing with his eyes closed. "You're skinny and kind of anemic, but you were all I could get. Traitor," he added.

His words stung her. No, the pain went deeper than a sting. That he could hurt her by insulting her quality as a food source showed how insane this situation was.

"I'm not sane," he said, picking up her thought. "I'm barely in control. Don't push me to do what Gavin wants."

"What does Gavin want?"

"For me to kill you. That's what you deserve for what you did to me."

"I didn't do anything to you!"

"What did Gavin promise you? Though it doesn't matter, now, does it?"

"You don't have to sound so pleased about my being a prisoner, too."

"I need any pleasure I can get. After all, I'm the one they're going to dissect, slowly."

Her stomach knotted at his words. Wild dream images of torture and humiliation rose in her mind, only they hadn't been dreams at all. Cage was being taken back to the white laboratory. And so was she.

She said, "If they went to so much trouble to capture you alive—"

"If you hadn't *helped* them capture me alive, I—"

Jo didn't notice that the vehicle had stopped until the door was flung open. A blast of cool night air flooded the silver cube as armed men swarmed in, and she and Cage were grabbed and dragged outside.

Where Gavin was waiting.

Chapter Twenty

$\mathcal{T}$he prison vehicle and the rest of the convoy were parked inside the center of a huge square compound surrounded by high metal fences. Guard towers spiked up at intervals, and tall floodlights reflected off the razor wire circling the top of the fences. There were several long, low buildings nearby, and a concrete roadway stretched off into the dark. Not a road, Jo decided; a runway. The compound had the look of a small military base.

Gavin gave her a quick look as she stood between two armed men, then he turned his attention on Cage. A pair of men held Cage by the arms, while others surrounded him at a cautious distance of a few feet. A lot of weapons were trained on the vampire.

"Marcus, old buddy," Gavin said. "You look like shit."

Jo watched as Cage summoned up energy and bravado from somewhere to straighten his shoulders and turn a wide smile on Gavin. "I feel like it, too—buddy."

"Bet you wish I'd just kill you and get it over with."

Cage inclined his head in a gracious gesture that was elegant despite his big, burly figure. "If you wouldn't mind."

"I would for old time's sake, if it paid." Gavin shrugged, and jerked a thumb back toward Jo. "At least you got laid while you were on the loose."

Cage's expression went blank, and he pressed his full lips together.

"A gentleman never tells, huh? Never mind, she told me all the details." Cage remained silent, and Gavin motioned to the armed crowd surrounding him. "You know where to put him. And if he gets out again," he added, as they began to drag him away, "you're all dead."

Jo's heart wrenched as she watched Cage disappear. She started to step after him, but the guards caught her by the arms.

A tall, lean man with graying brown hair approached Gavin from one of the buildings. "So you finally brought the creature in."

"Told you I would," Gavin answered. "The Patron will be happy."

"The Patron will be happy when our goals are accomplished."

"You can't accomplish anything without a vampire, and I'm the one who captured him. And remember, I wasn't here when he escaped. It's your research team that let him get away."

"There is no need to assign blame," the other man said. "I merely commented that you returned our subject."

"I didn't hear you congratulating me, Brashear."

Jo struggled with her captors as the men talked. "Sir," one of the men holding her finally called. "What do we do with this one?"

Gavin and Brashear turned to look at her while she futilely fought against being held.

"What's this?" Then Brashear gestured toward a trio of scared-looking women who were being hustled out of one of the vans that had been in the convoy. "And what are they doing here?" Jo recognized the women from the restaurant.

Gavin put a hand on Brashear's narrow shoulder and gestured toward the other prisoners. "Remember how you said that one of the problems you've had with the subject might be caused by not providing him with primary source protein? Since none of us wants to provide it, I brought in some blood donors. Now he can drink it fresh out of the bottle."

"Ah," Brashear said, and nodded. "That might prove to be a good idea."

"Might?" Gavin shook his head, and laughed. "You'll thank me when old Marcus starts fattening up. Starving him didn't get you what you wanted; it just got two of your people killed."

"Not to mention the significant damage to equipment and the compromise of experimental results."

"And he escaped," Gavin added.

"Sir?" the guard questioned once again. "Should we put the woman with the other prisoners?"

"No." Gavin stepped up to her. "She's a present for you, Brashear."

"Really?" the other man asked. "What interest does she hold for my research? What am I supposed to do with her?"

"Cut her up in little pieces, for all I care." Gavin grasped Jo by the chin and jerked her head up, then he stroked two fingers along her throat. "I'm sure you'll want to take samples of the spots where Marcus has been sucking her blood."

"Useful," Brashear agreed.

"What's even more interesting is that he's been fucking her. Fucking and sucking enough for her to be in mental contact with the vampire."

"Really?" Brashear stared intently at her. Jo saw the excitement in his pale eyes and the slight flush of color in his narrow cheeks. And she recognized him as one of the torturers from the white room nightmares.

"Get away from me!" she shouted on a surge of panic. "Get him away from me!"

Gavin laughed.

"Really?" Brashear said again, ignoring her reaction. The word held a terrifying amount of glee. "Get her secured on one of the examination tables immediately."

Gavin stroked her throat again before the guards took her away. "Good-bye, sugar," he said. "It's been fun for me." He was smiling when he added, "This isn't going to be fun for you at all."

*   *   *

Jo hurt all over, but at least they'd given her a shower and dressed her in a clean white nightgown. The scientists were downright paranoid about not getting any dirt in their precious white torture room. Blood, yes; dirt, no.

She wrapped her arms around her drawn-up legs and rested her head on her knees. She felt like Han Solo after Darth Vader had him tortured to get Luke Skywalker's attention. "They didn't even ask me any questions," she murmured wearily.

They had examined her all over with painful, humiliating thoroughness. They'd stuck syringes in her, extracted stuff, injected stuff, attached monitors and probes. They'd even done a dental exam. A lot of what they'd done had hurt; all of it had been frightening and wearying. She was used to pain, and to medical tests and exams; but there had been nothing helpful or healing in the impersonal treatment. She was just a guinea pig to her captors. Neither her protests nor even her occasional screams had drawn any response from them.

When they were finished they'd dragged her here, where she'd slept until a nightmare woke her up. In the nightmare she searched for Cage, but couldn't find him. She woke depressed and disoriented—because he wasn't there.

She was sitting on one of the cots in a large, windowless barracks room. The walls, floor, and ceiling were painted a dull gray, with rows of industrial-style fluorescent lights overhead. A large metal door was the only access. She knew there was an armed guard stationed on the other side of it. Besides the cots, the room held a long table with benches, a toilet and sink, and two of the three women Gavin had taken from the restaurant in Kennedyville—the waitress and the cashier. She wondered where the third woman was.

Jo was glad she wasn't alone. She knew that was selfish, but couldn't help feeling that way right now. She also felt like she ought to apologize for having gotten the women into this.

Worst of all, despite everything, she missed Cage. She worried about him. She knew now that the dreams they'd shared had been memories, or premonitions. It was hard knowing how to define psychic/telepathic stuff, but the two of them were connected—for good or ill. Yet she couldn't feel him now. She felt empty, like something vital had been pulled out of her. Her soul, maybe?

She was terrified of what they must be doing to Cage to have caused this break in their connection. How were they hurting him? What experiments were they running?

He is a vampire, she reminded herself.

Vampires were evil creatures of the night, blood-drinking parasites who preyed on humans. She tried to harden her heart, but the worry kept resurfacing. Just because he was a vampire didn't mean he was a bad person. So far, Marcus Cage had behaved in a far more morally superior fashion than Gavin, his troops, or the gang of scientists. Most of the time.

But—

I miss him.

"I see you're awake," the waitress said. She came over and sat on the cot next to Jo's. As she did, the roar of a jet engine streaked by close over their heads, shaking the building.

"What was that?" the waitress asked, when the noise had faded enough to be heard.

"Gulfstream," Jo answered.

"Are we at an air force base?"

Jo shook her head. "That type of plane's used by corporations or private owners."

The other woman eyed her curiously. "How do you know that?"

"I used to be a pilot. That sounded like a Gulfstream's engines to me."

"A private plane?" The woman sounded desperate when she went on. "But we're at a military base, right? The government's holding us in a quarantine, right?"

"I don't think so," Jo answered.

"But the sheriff came in with some soldiers. They did blood tests. They told Marcia, Karen, and me that we were candidates. For what? And where's Marcia?"

Jo knew exactly why the other women had been taken prisoner, and a hard, hot fist of jealousy curled in her gut, as crazy as that was. The women were scared, and as helpless as she was. There was no reason for her to be angry with them.

"I'm Debbie," the woman told her.

"Jo Elliot," Jo introduced herself.

"I remember you coming in, and all the food you ordered before the sheriff took you away. This is Karen," Debbie said, as the cashier came to sit beside her. "Why did the sheriff take you away?" she asked.

Karen looked at Jo suspiciously. "You infected us with some disease, didn't you? That's why we're locked up here. Is this your fault?"

Jo shook her head. Though if she hadn't called her mother, her mother wouldn't have called the local sheriff's office, and the sheriff then wouldn't have contacted Gavin. Did the local police believe Gavin was a government agent? *Was* this really a secret government project? No, she couldn't believe that.

Cage had warned her that the people chasing him had an unlimited budget, and that cops could be bought. She was fairly certain that bribe money had led directly to where they were right now, and she also knew that her mom was going to have the Kennedyville sheriff's ass. That was the first comforting thought she'd had for a long time.

Just then the door opened at the other end of the room. The third woman was pushed inside, and the door slammed shut behind her. Debbie and Karen rushed to the dazed Marcia as the woman staggered forward. Jo got up and followed.

"What happened to you?" Debbie asked. The waitress took Marcia by the arm and led her to sit on one of the benches by the long table. She sat beside her and put her arm around Marcia's shoulders.

Jo held back, watching them. She guessed that they were longtime friends. She was the outsider, even more than she was used to being.

She'd lost her empathic abilities, and wasn't yet used to dealing with people on a normal basis. All she had to go on was body language, facial expressions, and tones of voice. She'd totally messed up in reading Gavin. She had to go cautiously, observe, guess.

Marcia was the youngest and best-looking of the three women, with a shapely figure and short red hair. That gave Jo a good idea about why Marcia'd been taken first. Debbie was somewhere in her forties, attractive in a rounded, matronly way. Karen was tall, tanned, sharp-featured, and flat-chested; somewhere in her thirties, Jo thought.

"You all right, honey?" Debbie gave Marcia an encouraging squeeze. "Tell us what happened."

Marcia's answer was a moan and to wipe tears off her cheeks.

"What's wrong?" Karen asked. The cashier knelt beside Marcia and took the woman's hands in hers. "You're cold."

"He—" Marcia began. She looked up, and met Jo's gaze. "He has red eyes."

Jo nodded slowly. "Sometimes," she said. She took a step forward. "Is he all right?"

Karen shot to her feet, rounding on Jo. "Who is he?" She turned back to Marcia. "Red eyes?"

"He wouldn't eat me," Marcia told Jo. "He said to tell you that you were on the menu, and nobody else."

"Eat?" Debbie asked. A note of panic entered her voice. "What do you mean—'eat'?"

"He doesn't *eat* people," Jo said. "He just drinks blood." She touched her throat and her wrist. "It's not bad at all, really." She didn't know why she was defending Cage, and she knew she wasn't doing a good job of explaining.

"He's crazy," Marcia said. "They put me in a cell with a crazy man. He crouched in a corner and stared at me for the longest time. Sometimes his eyes glowed. And he had long teeth—like a wolf."

"Like a vampire," Jo said. Debbie and Karen looked at her like she was crazy. "You should get used to the idea of vampires being real," she said. "It will save you a lot of trouble in the long run."

"He was hungry," Marcia said. "He yelled at me about how hungry he was. He's got a deep voice like—"

"A former Marine sergeant."

"—a wild animal."

"Oh, please! Did he hurt you?"

"He wanted to." Marcia gave Jo an angry look. "Because I wasn't you!"

Jo was taken aback. Part of her wanted to think that Cage wanted no one's blood but hers because of an emotional attachment. Then she told herself that the emotion was hatred. He wanted to drain her dry out of revenge.

She put her hand to her throat, and as she did, the door opened once more. All the women came to their feet; the trio huddled together nervously while Jo faced the intrusion alone.

A pair of guards entered. Gavin followed them. The handsome blond man turned a courtly smile on the other women. "Hope you're comfortable, ladies." Then he turned his attention to Jo. "Come along," he said. "Someone important wants to meet you."

Chapter Twenty-one

Everyone in the luxurious meeting room but Gavin looked nervous. Even blank-faced Brashear had a tense air about him. Good. If she had to be handcuffed to a chair, she was glad that she wasn't the only one who was uncomfortable. Gavin leaned against a wall, watching the door with his arms crossed.

They'd marched her across the compound in the midday heat. She had bare feet and was wearing only the short white gown that did nothing to protect her from the sun. Gavin had left the guards outside the three-story building and brought her to this room on the top floor, where Brashear and two of his people were seated at a large conference table. Gavin put her in a deep leather chair and cuffed her wrists to the armrests. No one looked at her, no one spoke; all kept their tense attention on the door. Jo looked around.

The office had a large picture window with a panoramic view of buildings, the guard towers, a hangar, and the sleek Gulfstream jet sitting on the baked concrete runway. There was another plane sitting in front of the hangar, with a pair of techs in coveralls lazily working on it. There were a lot of vehicles parked in the compound, including Hummers, Jeeps, and several three-wheeled all-terrain vehicles. Armed men wearing desert camo patrolled the fenced perimeter.

Beyond the prison was empty desert, with a jagged row of mountains in the distance. The sky was pitiless blue, the earth seared red-brown. It was not a friendly, hospitable view; but she would gladly have run out into the arid, baking desert and taken her chances rather than be locked up with these people. The compound didn't have the spanking-new look of something that had been built specifically for this operation, but the buildings looked very well maintained.

Jo suspected the facility was part of an old, abandoned military base.

"This is a privately funded evil conspiracy, isn't it?" she asked.

Gavin gave a snort of laughter, and one of the seated men looked her way. He had red hair, freckles, and thick glasses. "Oh, yes," he said. Then he looked embarrassed at having spoken and turned his attention back toward the door.

Jo was about to ask who they were waiting for, when the door opened. First a pair of broad-shouldered bodyguard types walked in, then a woman carrying an old-fashioned black leather medical bag. Finally, an old man came tottering in. Everybody at the table stood up when he stepped slowly into the room; even Gavin came to attention. Jo wouldn't have stood, even if she wasn't chained to her seat. She didn't consider that her circumstances warranted showing respect for the authority figures, regardless of age.

And the old guy was *really* old. Montgomery Burns old. He looked like a cricket in a two-thousand-dollar suit. His form was bent and withered, and he used a cane. Only a few silver wisps of hair remained on his head, and there were age spots on top of his wrinkles. His ears were huge. One of the bodyguards helped him take a seat at the head of the table. Nobody else sat while he had a good look around.

His gaze met Jo's for a moment. There was nothing old or diminished in those eyes; they were as sharp as the edge of a blue steel sword. And hungry. He wanted to eat the world.

Now that, she thought, *is a vampire.*

"Gentlemen," he finally said. Despite the frailty of his body, there was still strength in his voice.

Everyone took their seats and turned nervous attention on
the man at the head of the table. The bodyguards and the
woman went to stand by Gavin.

"Hi," Jo called out from the other end of the table. "We
haven't been introduced." She generally wasn't the sort to be a
wise guy, but she'd gone beyond fear. What did she have to
lose by standing up for herself at this point?

She wasn't surprised when she was ignored.

Brashear said, "Good afternoon, Patron."

"Good afternoon, Patron," the others parroted.

The old man gave a slight nod of acknowledgment.

Patron? Jo almost laughed at the medieval images the title
conjured. She half expected Brashear to kneel and kiss the old
guy's ring. Of course, if the old man was providing funding,
security, and a vampire for these mad scientists' experiments,
the researchers were probably willing to kiss anything the old
man wanted.

"Report," the Patron ordered.

Gavin replied. "The subject has been secured. All traces of
the search for the subject have been covered. New security
measures are in place."

The Patron's cold gaze flicked ever so briefly to Gavin.
"You are not going to bother to reassure me that no incident
of this kind will happen again."

"No, Patron." He sounded perfectly confident that he had
his end of the operation under control.

Jo hated to think that he was correct. She wanted to escape,
and even though he was a vampire, she wanted Marc Cage to
escape as well.

"Was the subject in contact with any of its kind?"

"I'm certain he wasn't. He'd rather die than lead us to any
more of his species."

"Pity," the Patron said. "I had hoped the delay caused by
the subject's escape would have some benefits."

"Patron?" Brashear held up his hand, like a schoolboy asking for attention.

The Patron turned a very cold look on Brashear. "You are behind schedule. Your work in finding the secrets of eternity is not coming cheaply. While your subject has all the time in the world, I do not. You are wasting my time. That displeases me."

The words were said with no inflection, yet they chilled the room. Jo flinched, even though she wasn't exactly unhappy to see the mad scientists in trouble with their boss.

Brashear had to clear his throat before he could talk. "Yes, Patron," he acknowledged. "But we believe that there will be major benefits resulting from the escape, despite the amount of time lost working with the subject. We now have new directions in which to take the research. A new research subject." He gave Gavin a look that was half-grateful, half-resentful. Then he looked at Jo. "Mr. Gavin brought us this female, as I mentioned when I contacted you to report that the subject was once more in custody. Test results on her connection with the subject show promise."

The Patron looked at her once more, and Jo felt like a bug under a microscope. "You said the subject fed off her, and that was good for us. How? You told me that prolonged feeding didn't cause physiological changes to a vampire's victims."

"No, Patron," Brashear dared to contradict. "I told you that it was impossible for direct contact with the subject to do you any good."

"He likes girls," Gavin said.

Jo was annoyed with herself for almost smiling. Nothing here was funny; these people were deadly serious.

Brashear got up and came around to stand behind her. He put his hands on her shoulders. Looking down, she noticed that there was a small coiled snake tattoo on the back of his left hand. She found it odd that the scientist had a tat, but a snake certainly suited his cold, reptilian personality.

She tilted her head back to look at him. "Get your hands off me."

Of course he ignored her. He was staring at the Patron. "Here is your immortality."

"That—" the Patron said dismissively, "is a vampire's food source."

"And sexual partner," Brashear added.

The old man's features twisted with disgust. "You know I don't want to hear about how the creatures copulate with humans."

"It's my understanding that the effect is not unpleasant for the victim," Brashear said.

"It rocks your world," Jo said, looking the Patron in the eye.

The Patron went red as a beet. On the other side of the room, Gavin chuckled softly.

"Prolonged sexual contact with a vampire creates psychological and physiological changes with certain human and vampire pairings," Brashear explained.

"That's how I found Cage," Gavin spoke up. "The woman's been with him long enough to have formed a connection. She led me to him."

"Only because you're a lying bastard," Jo said.

"Please allow me to return to my explanation." Brashear squeezed Jo's shoulders hard.

"Explain, then," the Patron said.

Brashear squeezed again, harder. "Stay quiet," he ordered softly. "You are here as an exhibit, not a participant." He turned his attention to the watching Patron. "Tests on the subject show that changes have begun to occur in him. The subject can still satisfy the craving for blood from any mortal source. However, he has become psychologically fixated on this woman. He can drink blood from anyone, but he *craves* her blood. This craving will give us the secret of immortality."

"Does he crave her like a drug? She's an addiction?" the Patron asked. "Will withholding her make him more cooperative?"

"The last thing we want to do is keep the pair separate, because a pair-bonding process has begun. When vampires form pair bonds with mortals, they develop a symbiotic union. This symbiosis results in the mortal partner's life span increasing to equal the vampire's."

Pair bonding? Jo felt overwhelmed. He was talking about her and Cage, wasn't he? And Brashear wanted to use this bonding—her—against Cage.

"You've used me to hurt him already." She shook her head. "Not again."

The Patron looked annoyed. "Why haven't you mentioned this before? I've relied on your expertise about vampires. Withholding information is unacceptable."

"I didn't withhold information. I assumed that this particular knowledge was irrelevant to our research. Vampire and mortal pair bonding cannot be forced. They are an accident of nature. I deal with science, not accidents. Normally."

Brashear squeezed Jo's shoulders again. "I don't believe in luck, either, but this time we got lucky. Or perhaps we created the necessary conditions. The subject was starved and desperate when he escaped. Somehow that led him to a woman with the qualities he needed to form the bond that is unique to each couple. It is this woman's blood that we will need, to discover how ingesting vampire blood leads to the increased life span."

The Patron sat back in his chair, some of the hungry tension going out of him. He looked almost benign when he asked, "Then why aren't you working on a serum right now, instead of displaying this prize captive to try to impress me?"

Brashear's hands moved up from her shoulders to stroke her throat. Jo shuddered at the utter creepiness of his touch. She was already stiff with terror, both wanting and dreading to hear the answer to the Patron's question.

"We can't do anything with her yet," Brashear said.

The Patron frowned, and the room filled with tension once more. "And why is that?"

"Because her body is still free of any contaminants."

"What?" the Patron asked. "What are you talking about? Is the woman going to be a vampire or not?"

"Of course she isn't going to become a vampire. I have told you before that a mortal cannot be changed into a vampire."

"Well, that's good to know," Jo murmured.

"The vampire must share his blood with a bondmate in order to—"

"She hasn't bitten Marcus yet," Gavin summed up. "She hasn't drunk any of his blood."

The Patron's gaze swung to Gavin. "Why not?" he demanded.

Gavin shrugged. "The mood hasn't been right for him to offer her a taste of immortal wine, would be my guess. Old Marc probably needs moonlight, candles, champagne, Sinatra. Maybe even an engagement ring before he lets a girl bite him. He's an old-fashioned kind of guy."

"Well, I'm not giving him a diamond," Jo said flippantly, trying to hide her surprise.

Brashear's hands tightened slightly around her throat. She knew she was too valuable for him to kill, but she didn't fancy being choked until she passed out, either.

"It is likely that the subject was attempting to avoid the very situation we want to create," Brashear said. "We know that he is determined to thwart our experiments, and protect his species' monopoly on longevity at any cost."

"Maybe he doesn't like me," Jo said. "I'm just a food source to him. We haven't got any sort of bond."

"But you will have," Brashear said. "Once you are introduced into the subject's environment, it will only be a matter of time before the sexual, physiological, and psychological attraction will create the necessary trigger to—"

"We don't have time!" the Patron cut him off.

"And you don't know Marcus," Gavin added. "You can treat him like an animal for any regular experiment, but you can't treat him like an animal when it involves the most important thing in his life. You've got to work him into the right frame of mind if you want him to take a mate."

Jo loathed that everyone's attention was firmly on Gavin. She'd been manipulated by Gavin into giving up Cage. She didn't like to think that she was stupid, naïve, or weak-willed. Maybe one or another, but not all of those things at once. She'd been wary of him at first, but Gavin had gotten to her, led her into doing exactly what he wanted. Could he do the same to Marcus Cage? When Cage was weak, drugged, and driven by compulsions that were part of his nature?

She was terrified of the answer.

"Tell us what you would have us do, Mr. Gavin," the Patron said.

Terrified or not, it looked like she was going to find out.

Chapter Twenty-two

Marc paced, alone in the small cell. Alone but for the round black eyes of the monitor cameras in the ceiling that watched his every movement. He hated that they could see him, but that he was blind to his enemies' movements.

He was also blind to their thoughts. They had drugs to ensure that. The effect of the injections didn't last long, and he could feel how they had to keep upping the dosage, but the temporary mental deafness was isolating. It wasn't as if he could ever read minds at any great distance; he'd always had to concentrate hard to read minds. But he could influence thought. That was what they were really afraid of, and they believed it was the only thing he could do. They thought he was a hypnotist, not a telepath, but they were scared enough of that.

Reading thoughts was very hard if someone had a strong will, or was at a distance, especially if you didn't have an emotional connection to the mind you were trying to contact. You had to be able to sneak up on an unsuspecting mind if you wanted to influence a person. No chance that anyone here was unsuspecting.

Of course, there was a more intimate way to share thoughts and emotions. He'd had that kind of communication with Josephine from the moment he sensed her presence in the desert. He'd cherished it, and now he hated it. Just as he hated the drugs that closed his mind, even while welcoming the release from his connection to the woman who'd betrayed him.

How could she do that? He'd let her go, and she'd made him a prisoner.

He was so thirsty for her, he wanted to scream. But he wouldn't do that, not when his enemies could hear. Not when she'd been used against him once already.

If he'd been smart, he would have taken the other woman. He used to be smart. He used to know how to take care of himself. Josephine had made him into a weak fool.

How long had he been pacing? And when would they come for him again? When they came, they came in smoke.

Marc dropped onto the edge of the narrow cot.

He'd been thinking in his own language, and forced himself to translate the concepts into modern English. To say his enemies came in smoke was all very colorful, and even true, but technically, they knocked him out with some anesthetic gas before carting him off for experiments. His people's language was evocative and romantic, but it wasn't scientifically precise.

And he couldn't think it, let alone speak it around these people. He dared not give away even linguistic clues to the origins of his kind, or how they thought. He had to think like mortals, talk like them, be like them.

Normally it wasn't hard. English was his language of choice, America the place he'd been born and raised, and served. The place where he paid taxes, had a home, where his family lived. But his Family was vampire, and he was Prime. Primes protected their own.

Even mates who betrayed them?

He nodded sharply. He couldn't help it. Her blood was in him, sustained him, called to him. Josephine was his. No Tribe sex slave could have it worse than she would, once he got his hands on her again, but she was still his. What did the Tribes call the humans they kept? Cattle? Pets? They never trusted humans, never gave them the chance to take advantage.

Marc looked at the gray walls of his prison and deliberately let himself be aware of the pain that surged through his body. Humans—mortals—had done this to him. With the help of the one mortal he'd totally trusted.

Maybe the Tribes have the right idea.

Even as he had the thought, he became aware of the haze wavering in the air. The cell was being flooded with gas. He surged to his feet, only to fall back onto the cot, his senses reeling.

They were coming for him.

"You awake, City Mouse?"

Her hand touched his cheek softly, tenderly. Desire burned through him.

Marc grabbed Josephine by the wrist and squeezed until the pressure forced a moan of pain from her. "Don't touch me," he ordered. Then he let her go.

The mattress shifted as she got up. With the movement, Marc realized that he was lying on a bed. For a moment, he insanely hoped that he'd only dreamed of being recaptured. But he knew it was all too real when he sat up and opened his eyes.

He was still in a cell, though this one was fitted with a solid door instead of bars. As he got up and turned slowly around, he saw that this was a larger room, with more furnishings. He'd been lying on a double bed covered in fresh linens, instead of a narrow, bare cot. The concrete walls and floor were painted a golden beige instead of antiseptic white. The lighting overhead was recessed and gave off a gentle glow rather than a harsh glare. He spotted a toilet and a shower stall through a doorway, giving at least an illusion of privacy. There was also a kitchen and dining area—a table, chairs, refrigerator, and a microwave on top of a cabinet. It looked more like a studio apartment than a prison.

And there was Josephine. She'd retreated to an empty corner, where she stared at him apprehensively, one hand over the wrist he'd bruised.

She was also naked. They both were. He couldn't help but look at her, and his body couldn't help but respond to what he saw.

It took all his willpower to turn his back on her, trying to combat the lust and thirst that were one and the same. His voice was raw with need when he croaked, "What are we doing here?"

"The luxury suite was Gavin's idea," she answered, followed by a deep sigh. "It's supposed to set a romantic tone."

"You're a naked woman," he said. "That's all the romance I require. It's easier to bite a naked woman," he added.

"Saves you the risk of getting cloth caught in your fangs, I suppose." She sounded calm, but he could feel her fear.

"It's easier to do a lot of things with a naked woman," he added, just to see if it would spike her emotions higher.

It did; and her voice betrayed her nerves when she said, "They want you to bite me."

"Then I won't." It was a hard promise to make, especially when he was furious enough to drain the life out of her.

"They don't think you'll have a choice. Eventually, you'll be too thirsty not to. We both know what happened the night you attacked me."

She was right. The thirst was a living creature of fire inside him. It needed what it needed, despite his fight to control it. He should have taken the other woman. It would have helped bank the fire to a manageable level a while longer.

"If *they* think you're the only woman I'll touch, they're wrong."

"Then you shouldn't have told Marcia that. The red-haired woman you wouldn't touch," she added before he could ask.

"I didn't mean it."

"They don't believe that. Besides, it's not so much that they want you to bite me. They want *me* to bite *you*. They think I'm going to drink your blood. But the last thing in the world I want to do is drink anyone's blood—*especially* yours."

How could he be hurt by this rejection after what she'd already done to him?

He whirled to face her. "Will you stop talking about what *they* want? If it weren't for you, we wouldn't even have to deal with them."

Josephine came out of the corner and was halfway across the cell when she stopped to glare at him. "Me? What do you mean, *me?*"

"What did Gavin promise you? Lots of money?"

"I've got enough money," she answered. "What do I need with more?" She laughed bitterly, and touched one of her many scars. "I've got my health."

The bitter irony only stung him more. "Did he promise you immortality? To heal those scars?" He knew every word was a psychic stab wound, and he was pleased to see her pale and trembling. "You made a mistake. Because, darling, you can't get immortality from him."

"I know that," she said, blinking back tears. She made a sharp gesture. "And he didn't offer."

"Then what did he say he'd give you for turning me in?"

Josephine pressed her lips tightly together, then turned her back on him. He heard her breath catch and a stifled sob. Pain radiated from her like heat haze.

He couldn't keep away from her anymore. He stepped up behind her and put his hands on her bare shoulders before he knew he was going to do it.

She tried to shrug out of his grasp. "Don't touch me!"

"That's what you're here for."

He pulled her tightly against him. His hands moved of their own accord, down her arms and around her to caress her belly, and up her waist to cup her breasts, bringing a gasp from her when the pads of his thumbs pressed against her nipples. He almost forgot his anger with the pleasure of touching her. He breathed in her scent. He wanted her.

"What did Gavin offer you?" he asked again.

She went even stiffer. She tried to calm her emotions, tried to not even think, to hide from him. It was infuriating.

"Tell me." The words were soft, and full of menace.

"You're being a pig."

He turned her around and lifted her chin to make her look at him. "Tell me."

"You." She spat the word out like a curse. "He offered me you."

He dropped his hand and stepped back. "What are you talking about?"

"He said your life was in danger."

"Yeah. From him."

"I didn't know that!"

"You knew I was being hunted. You promised not to turn me in."

"Yes." She ran her hands up and down her bare arms; she looked cold. "But he said you were sick."

Marc grabbed a sheet off the bed and tossed it to her. As she wrapped the material around her, he sighed and rubbed his hands over his face. His head was whirling with confusion. "What did Gavin tell you about me?"

"That you were sick," she repeated.

"And?"

She looked at the floor, the ceiling, and finally back at him. "It made sense at the time."

"What did?"

"That you were an escaped convict who had volunteered for an experiment that went wrong. He said they needed to find you—so they could fix you. He said he wanted to help you."

"And you *believed* him?"

Cage's deep shout filled the room.

Jo took a step closer to confront him. "It made a lot more sense that you merely *thought* you were a vampire, than your actually *being* one. If you had just once said you were a vampire, I might not have believed him."

"*Said?*" Marc shook his head. "Woman, I drank your blood!"

"That could have been a kinky fetish. It's not like you ever showed me your fangs while you dragged me all over the state. Maybe if you'd explained more about this—"

"Every word I told you about this place was the truth."

"But it didn't sound like the truth. It sounded like paranoid delusion. Then Gavin said it was paranoid delusion, too."

"And you believed him?"

She nodded. "Eventually. It took some convincing, but yeah."

"And you led him right to me."

"Yes, and I apologize for that. By the time I figured out that you were right, and he was wrong, it was too late. Besides, then you tried to shoot me."

"I was trying to shoot Gavin. I was so furious, all I saw was him; I didn't see that you were in the way. Now I have to be grateful to Gavin for saving you." He hurried on, not wanting to think about how he had almost accidentally shot her.

He felt some of Jo's annoyance fade. "When did you figure out I was right?" he asked.

"I don't know. I just did."

"You should have figured out Gavin was lying from the beginning. Woman, you're the most sensitive empath I've ever encountered."

"Not anymore. I can't feel anyone but you now. I'm blind and deaf." She pointed a finger at him. "You did that to me."

Marc took an annoyed step forward. "You were hurting," he reminded her. "You had a hole in your shielding a mile wide. I fixed it. I fixed you."

"You turned me off," she accused. "You tuned me to you and no one else. How is that a fix?" She turned away from him.

"I don't take without giving. I gave you shielding again in exchange for your help."

"In exchange for damn near drinking me dry, you mean."

"You could have used a transfusion," he admitted. "But I would have been dead if I hadn't done what I did."

She glared. "Well, your trade didn't work for me." She tapped a finger against her forehead. "I'm not an empath anymore."

"I didn't know."

"Neither did I, until you let me go. And then Gavin had a sheriff pick me up. He interrogated me at the sheriff's office. It was all very official."

"He worked you," Marc said. "He's got a gift for interrogation. I've never known him to need to use force on any of his subjects. He just talks, and smiles, and makes you want to tell him everything." Somewhere in the last few minutes his anger had faded, but it flared up again at realizing that she'd been used. "But you still shouldn't have betrayed me."

She had no time for his petulance. "Get over it."

Marc hesitated for a moment. He ran a hand across the top of his head, where the dark curls were growing back. He made himself look at this tired, defiant, somewhat embarrassed woman.

Yeah, Gavin had done a number on her, and she wasn't happy with herself about it.

They were trapped.

"So what are we going to do now, Girl Scout?"

She gestured toward the kitchen area. "You want a cup of coffee?"

"Better not," he answered. "I'm already a little wired." He followed her toward the kitchenette anyway. He took a seat at the small table and watched as she explored the cabinet and refrigerator. She found some plastic dishes and cutlery, and a jar of instant coffee.

"Starbucks, this is not," she complained. "Water. Where would I find wa—"

"Bathroom," he suggested.

"Right." She came back with a cupful of water and put it in the microwave to warm.

He sniffed when she brought her cup of instant coffee to the table. "I've been away from civilization too long. That actually smells good. How do we rate all this luxury?"

"It's a ploy to get us to fuck like bunnies," she answered.

"Josephine." He shook a finger disapprovingly at her.

"Well, it is." She took a sip of coffee. Then she glanced over her cup at his naked genitalia. "And you want to."

"I always want to." He shifted in the plastic chair. He tried not to think about sex, about the thirst. Just being with her seemed to ease the painful need a little. All the anger he'd burned off in the last few minutes had helped, as well. "Go on."

"For the moment, they've decided to treat us like people instead of lab rats," she told him. "There was a staff meeting where Gavin convinced the Patron that we're more likely to form the kind of pair bond they want if we're left alone. So, no monitors, no cameras spying on us, and some basic amenities like food and a real bed." She sneered as she glanced at the double bed. "Isn't it romantic?"

"If you want romance, I'll take you to Venice."

No monitors? No cameras? He doubted their captors would risk not watching him at all times. But she'd had enough privacy and control taken away from her; it was better for her if she believed they were alone.

She put the empty cup on the table. "I'd like to go to Venice." She gestured around their quarters. "Gavin said you were old-fashioned. A romantic."

"He'd know."

She eyed him suspiciously. "You and Gavin go back a ways, do you?"

"Yeah, we've known each other for years. We used to work together."

"In the Marines?"

"After. Long after." He glanced away, almost embarrassed to explain. "I've done some covert work for the government. Black-ops stuff. I'm the one who recruited Gavin into the agency. We worked together."

"And one day you casually mentioned that you're a vampire to him?"

"No."

"And how could you *work* for the government?"

Marc sat up straight and gave her an offended look. "Are you questioning my honesty?"

"If you really work for the government, sure."

He laughed. "Worked. Past tense. I've been out of the game for a long time."

"But how can vampires—pass as humans?"

He held out his arms, showing off his big, toned body. He had a lot of skin, and it wasn't exactly moonlight pale. "Do I look like a vampire?"

She gave him a long, thorough look, and her lips quirked in

a slightly lascivious smile. Her eyes lit with warm pleasure. It was almost enough to make him blush. It was certainly enough to send lust racing through him.

"The way you look was one of the things that convinced me that you're *not* a vampire. Lestat, you ain't."

"You obviously haven't read the book. He's described as being big and broad. But that's not the point. The point is that real vampires—some real vampires—take medicines that let us live like mortals. We can go out in the daylight, tolerate garlic, and tone the silver allergy down to a rash.

"Gavin's one reason we're stuck in here. Another is that at least one of the mortal scientists who work on developing drugs for the Clans has gone renegade. You have no idea how dangerous that is," he added. "Have you met Brashear?" She nodded. "Did you notice a snake tattoo on his left hand?" Another nod. "That means he was born into the Snake Clan."

The Clans were into symbols and signs and ceremony. The Families considered most of that ancient ritual nonsense, but the Clan marks did help them identify their own.

"He's not a vampire, but he's related to one," Marcus explained.

"Related?"

"We can have children with mortals. Those children are mortal but the Family—or Clan, in his case—still owes them protection and a place in life. Brashear obviously went to work in his Clan's pharmaceutical company, developing the drugs that keep us functioning in the light. And he obviously sold out those he took a vow to protect, to come to work for the Patron. What the Patron's paying him can't be worth it—he has to know that."

"What do you mean?"

Marcus gave Josephine a sober look. "We take oaths very seriously. To break a vow to our kind is a death sentence. Brashear must hate his Clan for some reason, to do what he's doing. Or he's too arrogant to think he'll get caught."

"My impression of him is that he's not going to let anything get in the way of finding the secret of immortality. Maybe he's angry that he was born mortal," she suggested.

Marc thought about it. "Maybe he wanted to be a Prime when he grew up. Sometimes it does happen, but it obviously didn't happen to him."

Josephine surprised him when she said, "Good."

"I don't know how the Patron found Brashear, but Gavin's been a mercenary since he was kicked out of the agency." Marc gave a humorless laugh. "The normal way for a traitor to leave the agency is in a body bag, but Gavin got out before he was caught. I should have caught him," he added bitterly.

"Instead, he caught you."

"Yeah." The word came out as a low, fierce rumble.

"How did he catch you?"

Josephine leaned forward across the small table and the sheet she'd wound around her body shifted, giving him an excellent view of her nicely shaped breasts. He could just make out the tops of her nipples. It was more tantalizing seeing her this way than when she was completely naked. What was half-hidden was always more intriguing, and it would be so easy to grab the sheet and drag her onto the table and peel the material out of his way. He licked his lips as his fangs and his cock throbbed with anticipation.

Not yet. Not until she was ready. Not until she was comfortable.

Right—maybe when hell froze over. He couldn't wait that long. Marc bit down hard on his lust. He would wait as long as he could.

"How did he know you're a vampire?" she asked. "Do you take these vampire drugs? How does anyone know about vampires? Rather, how come no one knows about vampires?"

She was too interested to be afraid—of him, or where they were, and what might happen to them. Marc's head spun with hunger and desire, but he couldn't bear to disturb this moment in which she was free to be herself.

Answering her rapid-fire questions would be an exercise in control, and it was good to have someone to share his secrets with.

And if Brashear's boys were listening? He wouldn't divulge anything that the Snake Clan traitor didn't already know. It wasn't as if he was going to reveal locations of strongholds and citadels, or any other information a mortal child of a vampire would never be privy to.

He ran his hand across his scalp again, then rubbed his jaw. He needed a shave. "Where to start? Yes, I take the daylight drugs. Every Prime has a serum formula that's unique to him. Life's more convenient using the drugs."

"Is it a cure?"

He laughed. "Why would I want to be cured of what I was born to be?"

"Yeah, I can see that. It's an ethnicity."

It soothed him that she seemed to have gotten over being appalled at the idea that there were vampires, and that he was one. As long as he wasn't biting her, that is. And as long as he wasn't offering her his blood.

He needed that completion, though; their captors were right about that. He craved the sharing as much as he needed the tasting.

He dragged his mind back to the conversation. "The drugs don't change us into *Homo sapiens;* it's more that they mimic human traits. I don't know how—I take 'em, I don't make 'em. What I know is that on a normal day I like garlic, and a walk in the sunshine isn't a way to commit suicide."

"You were sunburned out in the desert."

"I was fried. That's because some of the drugs they've used on me have made my normal reactions erratic."

Fortunately, the blood, as well as the physical and psychic presence of a bondmate, helped bring a natural balance to a Prime's world.

There was more to being a vampire than biochemistry and

mutant DNA. There was a psychic component to being a vampire that was as strong as, or stronger than, the physical aspects of what made them different from their mortal cousins.

Even if Brashear had been raised in the heart of the Snake Clan, there were many secrets that he wouldn't be privy to. So much information about what vampires were, what they could do, and what they needed was passed mind to mind to the young from the matriarch Matri and honored Elders. Vampire young took a long time to grow up, and most of what they were taught wasn't learned in a classroom.

Marc made himself get back to her questions. "How did Gavin find out I'm what I am? I was badly injured on a mission. A bomb went off that should have killed me. Gavin got me to a safe house and stayed with me while he waited for me to die. He was shocked when my body repaired itself. I hypnotized him, told him to forget what he'd seen."

"I bet Gavin's not the hypnotizable type. It doesn't work on everybody, you know."

He nodded. "I do now. The best I can figure is that Gavin's a low-level psychic, besides being smart and strong-willed. What I did to him wore off. When he remembered, I think he watched for other clues. We were partners for a long time, and I trusted him, got sloppy.

"Then he sold out an operation for a lot of money and disappeared. I tried tracing him for a while, with no luck. When I got tired of the game, I retired and started my own business."

She looked over his muscular form. "Bouncer?"

He folded his arms across his massive chest. "Executive chef of my own restaurant."

She looked outraged. "You're a chef?"

"I have a cookbook coming out soon. And I'm opening a new place in a Las Vegas hotel. I've been a soldier and a spy, Josephine, and probably will be again. Or maybe I'll become an archaeologist, or film documentaries. I have a long life, and I plan to do everything that interests me during it. Right now, the restaurant business interests me." He smiled at her. "I thought women like domesticated men."

She looked him over again. "You will never be domesticated."

"The saying among my people is *I am Prime*—that means I'm a big bag of testosterone that likes to hunt things. We're supposed to channel all that aggression into sex and community service."

"What kind of community service are we talking about? Running blood banks?"

He grinned. "More like saving the world from nuclear meltdowns, that kind of thing. Well, the Clans mostly do the taking-care-of-humans jobs, but some of us Family boys do the occasional Hoo-Rah thing, as well."

Her brows furrowed. "Huh?"

"Never mind. Getting back to Gavin, I assume he sold his knowledge about me to the Patron. Brashear couldn't have worked on a Prime of the Snake Clan—"

"Why not?"

"Psychological thing," was the explanation he gave. "It's easier for a vampire to hypnotize a relative. Brashear needed to be secure about being in control. To make a long story a little less long—Gavin found me, drugged me, and I ended up here. As to why no one knows about vampires . . . our legends say that thousands of years ago, vampires and humans lived together. Times changed, and we went underground. We actually live among humans, we've just learned how to protect ourselves. But enough conversation," he said, and got to his feet. "I can't take this anymore."

The thirst clawed at him, on every level. If he didn't give in to the hunger while he could still guide it, the consequences would be worse for both of them later.

He held his hand out to Josephine. "Come."

She shot to her feet, and the sheet fell down to her waist. She didn't bother to try to snatch it up to cover herself. She blinked nervously at him, though. Anticipation hummed in her, and so did dread. "What do you want?" she asked.

"I'm taking you to bed."

She stumbled backward, but he caught her before the tangled sheet caused her to fall. He lifted her in his arms, and enjoyed her surprise when her arms came around his neck. It wasn't that she didn't want him—it was just that she didn't know what to make of him. The situation didn't help her mood.

Pretend we aren't prisoners, he whispered in her mind. He carried her to the bed and gently put her down. "I have to do this," he told her as he came down beside her.

A bolt of fear flashed through her. "You have to do what?"

She tried to sit up, but Marc put his hands on her. He kissed her, first her mouth, then each lovely little breast. Then he looked her in the eyes, and said, "I have to thoroughly apologize for acting like a pig." He ran his hands over her breasts. "And you're going to lie back and enjoy the apology."

"Oh." She sighed, and arched into his touch. "Okay."

Chapter Twenty-four

"What are you doing?" Not that she didn't already know. It was just that this had been going on and on and on. He'd been covering her with sharp little nips, each one sending a wave of ecstasy through her. She was quivering like Jell-O, and starting to go crazy.

He looked up from nuzzling the inside of her left thigh. She caught a glimpse of the long, sharp fangs that he'd been stroking against her sensitized skin a moment before. There was a single drop of blood on his lower lip. He slowly licked it off. "This is what I call a tasting menu," he answered, then went back to what he was doing. Slowly.

Jo lay on the bed, her fists full of bunched-up sheets, and shuddered through several more orgasms. She looked up at the ceiling, but what Cage was doing to her sent her far away. He'd lit her on fire, and she loved the burning. When a thought did flit briefly through her head, it was that maybe he should act like a pig more often, because the apology was—

"Don't stop!" she pleaded as he came up onto his knees. Then she saw the huge erection standing up out of the dark curls at his groin and decided that maybe a little apologizing of her own was in order.

"Come here," he said, and held his hands out to her. She reached out and let him pull her up to kneel on the bed as well. She ran her hands over him. Aware of him as never before, she studied him with all her senses. He was hard all over and quivered at her touch.

When she looked at his face, she saw that he was not human.

There was a deep, molten-steel glow in his half-closed eyes, and long fangs pressed against his full lower lip. These changes should have frightened her but were fascinating, instead. More than fascinating—the sight sent renewed shivers of desire through her. That a hint of fear mingled with her primal urge to mate only made the desire stronger.

"May I?" she asked, and brought an index finger up to touch a sharply gleaming tooth. He moaned, and arched away from her. For a moment, she thought he was in pain.

"Oh," she said, realizing what the matter was, and she reached down, cupping her hand around his hard, swollen cock. This time he gasped, and she began to stroke him. "Will this make it better?"

"Woman!" He threw back his head and howled. "Yes!"

She loved the feeling of control, of power. She loved Cage's big, sculpted body, the wild energy and force he was keeping in check, holding back. For her sake.

She moved forward, bringing his penis to the entrance of her vagina. She felt him there and ached to thrust her hips down, to bring him all the way deep inside her.

He held her by the waist, his body as still as he could make it, waiting for her.

She pressed close to him, electric heat going through her nipples as they brushed his chest. "It's all right," she whispered in his ear. "I'm all right. Make love to me."

The next thing she knew, he'd flipped her back onto the bed and was on top of her. He was inside her in that one hard thrust she'd longed for. She lost herself in the pounding rhythm, the earthy scents of sex and sweat, the satiny rasp of skin against skin, the shifting weight and pressure of straining bodies, and the way the barriers of me and you, him and her, disappeared as their minds blended with their bodies. His pleasure built, raw and primal, and became hers. It sent her flying. As the burst of pleasure seared her his fangs pierced her flesh, drawing the bliss out for what seemed like forever.

Eventually she fell from the molten sky. She was sated, her

body boneless and humming at the same time. She couldn't open her eyes, didn't even want to. She couldn't move and didn't want to do that, either. She vaguely felt his arms come around her, holding her tight and safe. It was nice. She sighed, murmured something, and rested her head against his shoulder.

She didn't know how long she slept, but she woke up smiling. It wasn't that having great sex made her forget any of the bad stuff that was happening. She and Marc Cage were prisoners in a desperate situation, but the fear and dread weren't ruling her.

She even remembered what she'd said to Cage before she fell asleep. It was a foolish thing to say under the circumstances. But it was the truth—so what the hell? And if he hadn't heard, or didn't remember, that was all right.

She remembered how terrifying it had been the first few times she'd been this close to Cage. She'd come to what she felt now despite how they'd started, not because of it. To think that Gavin almost convinced her that Cage had brainwashed her into the feelings she had for him. Desperation had brought them together, and now she couldn't imagine a life without him.

Not that she was exactly planning a cozy little future, settled down with her personal bloodsucking fiend—though if she had to give up sex like this, she wasn't sure she'd survive.

What on earth had she done before Cage? Well, she'd masturbated occasionally because she hadn't been involved with anyone for a couple of years.

Good, he thought, overhearing her thought.

You're thinking in your sleep, aren't you? she thought back at him.

His big hand reached out and stroked her breasts, then moved down to coax open her thighs. He found the swelling bud and began playing with it. *Doing this in my sleep, too.*

She wriggled against his hand, and didn't complain as he teased her to a quick orgasm.

Consider me your own personal vibrator from now on.

Jo smiled. *No problem.*

Go back to sleep.

Don't think I can. And if you hypnotize me and make me, I won't let you play with me anymore.

Ha. You'd beg me for it. The pad of his thumb pressed down on her clit, and she sucked in a sharp breath. *Wouldn't you?*

Probably, she conceded. "Rest," she told him aloud, drawing away from him. "I really do have to get up." He opened one eye to look at her, and the worry there was enough to send an ache through her, along with anger at what he'd been through. She stroked his cheek. "I'm not leaving," she told him. *Even if the door was unlocked, I wouldn't be leaving.*

He sighed, closed his eye, and loosened his hold on her so that she could get out of bed. He drew her back into his arms as soon as she came back from the bathroom. His need to touch her was palpable, surrounding her, covering her, coveting her on a mental as well as a physical level. It was possessive, protective, comforting. It was a good feeling. There had been aspects of this from him all along, but they had been covered over by desperation and pain.

He was healing, she realized. The growing connection between them was bringing him back to the person he really was when he wasn't being tortured and starved, and the energy he was giving off was—nice.

You know, for a vampire.

His mental chuckle drifted into her head.

She also knew that he wanted the same kind of complicated possessiveness from her. He was her personal vampire. He needed her to be his personal—what?

Wife, was the answer that came from him. *Bondmate. Soul mate. Symbiote.*

Jo held on tight to his big, warm body, and thought for a while. She felt him withdraw to let her be alone with the things she needed to consider, and knew he would not intrude again until she wanted him to. This was so reassuring that she relaxed to the point of falling asleep.

She ended up dreaming about a wedding where the groom's side were pale, fanged creatures all dressed in black and the bride's side all wore crosses and brandished wooden stakes. Giles from *Buffy the Vampire Slayer* officiated. Far from being afraid, Jo woke up smiling.

This is a hell of a way to meet the man of my dreams.

Am I the man of your dreams?

No, that would be Viggo Mortensen. Or Hugh Jackman. I should have said this is a hell of a way to meet the man I want to be with.

Why not say—the man you love?

She paused. *Because it's a scary thing to say.*

You said it once.

It's a scary thing to say—under the circumstances.

Which circumstance? That I'm the vampire who got you into this mess? Or the mess itself?

I can't blame you for the mess.

I can blame me for getting you into it.

Except that I'm the one who got you recaptured.

I thought we'd worked that out.

We have. She hesitated for a bit, then added, *Except for the your-trying-to-shoot-me part.* She hadn't realized how much it still bothered her until the thought was already shared. *Was it really Gavin you were aiming at? I hate to say that he saved me—but he did.*

This hurt, and Marc cursed Gavin once more. *He made you think he was saving you. Gavin knew who I was aiming at. But, for once, I'm glad that prize manipulator did what he did. I would have hated myself for it if anything had happened to you.*

He felt her sense of betrayal slowly ebbing, and waited for her to make up her mind whether to believe him.

Maybe you shouldn't have shot at anyone, she finally thought.

I was having a bad day.

And they were shooting at you, she agreed. *But—*

I'm sorry.

Aloud, he said, "I don't want anything to come between us." He was looking at the ceiling rather than at her, but his other senses were carefully gauging her reactions.

"I can understand your being a bit ticked off at me," she said. "You thought I'd betrayed you."

"I was crazy—from the sun, the attack."

"You were pissed off."

"Very." *But I still loved you. I didn't try to hurt you.* He rolled onto his side and gently stroked her face. "No matter what I do," he whispered. "Know that I love you."

She buried her head against his chest. "Fine," she whispered against his skin. "Love me. Just don't shoot at anybody when I'm in the way, okay?"

He stroked his hands down her back. "Okay," he promised. "Will you forgive me for endangering you? Forgive me for all the times I've endangered you?" *Trust me. Please. Trust me as you would yourself.* "Can't you feel how much closer we become with every moment we're together?"

She lifted her head. "You're all I can feel." *I trust what I feel.*

But you're wondering if being empathically aware of only me is influencing what you feel about me.

No, I wasn't wondering that. But now that you mention it . . .

I'm sorry I went too far trying to fix you. Let me make it better.

How?

We're telepathically connected right now. I just need to go deeper than this, that's all.

Will it hurt?

You won't feel a thing.

He drew her to him and began to kiss and caress her. Desire began to immediately flash through her.

"I'm—not feeling a thing," she told him between deep, passionate kisses. She liked what she was feeling, but she was confused. "Shouldn't you be—?"

I can make love to you while I'm fixing your head. Please trust me. Surrender your mind and your body—and trust me. Let go, Josephine Elliot.

She couldn't bear breaking off the way he was making her feel. It was as if something inside her soul was opening up, layer by layer. She was blooming.

You complete me, she told him.

I know. As you complete me. You're mine.

Chapter Twenty-five

"How do you feel now?" Marc asked.

"Boneless, bruised, blissful." She stretched out on the wrecked bed linen and wiggled her fingers and toes. It had been many hours since they'd done anything but have sex. "I'm starving. And I could really use a shower."

I meant how does your emotional shielding feel? Is your empathy working right again?

"Oh. That." She was silent for a long time, lying still with her eyes closed. He lay on his side, his head propped up on his hand, and watched her. He'd never get enough of watching her.

He was aware of her senses reaching out, testing. Josephine worked on instinct rather than any training of her psychic gift, but she knew what she was doing.

You feel normal, don't you? he asked.

In balance, she answered. *More like my old self. Only— more.*

We're bonding, Marc told her. *It's nothing to be afraid of.*

Except for that doing-what-the-bad-guys-want-us-to-do part.

What they want doesn't matter. We've been bonding since the night we met.

You're pleased about that. About being with me.

I can't imagine being with anyone else. He walked his fingers over her slender form. *Have to fatten you up a bit, though.*

Because I taste good?

You taste good all over. You're delicious—mind, body, and soul.

I— Thank you, Marcus Cage. How do you feel? she added.

Marc wondered if he looked as smug as he felt. *He* felt wonderful. If they were being monitored, it would not be wise to show his improved condition. Then again, perhaps they didn't fully understand what happened when a bond formed.

They wanted him to take her blood, and he was doing just that. Drinking anyone's blood was sustaining. Blood with sex was physically and mentally satisfying. Forming a bond, sharing body and soul—that was beyond energizing. A bonded Prime was a force of nature, something to be reckoned with.

But their captors didn't understand that it wasn't all enzymes and biochemistry that made a bond. There was something magical at work, as well. Something that couldn't be duplicated in a lab, and it made all the difference in the world.

Brashear would be aware that the more Marc had of Josephine's blood, the more he would want to give his blood to her, and that eventually she was going to crave the gift of life he needed to share with her. Her body was changing with each drop he took from her, though Josephine wasn't consciously aware of it.

No doubt the Snake Clan traitor had a mortal mother or grandmother who shared a bond with a Prime. A fully bonded pair were physically bound to each other, the shared blood providing nourishment for the Prime and extended life for the mortal. That it provided so much more was a private thing between the bonded.

And Gavin was even more ignorant of what it really meant to be a vampire than Brashear was. Granted, Gavin had a lot of self-confidence, a lot of cunning, and a lot of firepower he could call on.

But what was all that against the powers of a fully functioning Prime?

Marc was beginning to believe that he and Josephine had a chance. What they needed was a little more time—time for her mentally to accept what her body would soon want. He wasn't going to force his blood on her; she had to be ready for it.

"You're cautiously happy about something," his empathic lover said.

"Just high on life," he told her.

She grunted and sat up. He let her get out of bed and sat up himself to watch her walk across the room. "Nice butt," he called after her.

She paused and looked over her shoulder, her hands on her hips. She looked for all the world like an R-rated version of the famous Betty Grable pinup photo from World War II.

He responded with a wolf whistle.

She smiled at his response, and continued to sashay, her hips swinging, over to the refrigerator. She found some packaged meals in the freezer and popped two of them in the microwave.

"Those might be drugged," he warned, as the aroma of cooking meat wafted toward him. His stomach rumbled in response.

"Can you recall the last time you had solid food?" She reached into the refrigerator again and brought out pint cartons of milk.

She had a good point. He got up and came to sit at the table.

"You expect to be served, I see," she commented when she noticed where he was.

He shrugged.

"How a naked man can look so nonchalant, I do not know."

"I've spent a lot of time naked. What's for dinner?"

"Drugged meat loaf." She put a loaf of dull white sandwich bread on the table, along with a scattering of ketchup packets. Then she tossed him one of the milk cartons. The microwave timer sounded, and she turned to fetch the trays.

As she reached for the meals, he said, "Maybe the food isn't drugged. They won't want to contaminate your blood."

She turned back to him with an appalled look.

"After you drink mine," he added, bringing the subject out in the open.

Her spine stiffened, and every move she made showed her

furious annoyance, from the way she took the meals out of the microwave to the way she slammed them onto the table and slapped her bare bottom down on the chair.

He peeled the covering back from his entree. As steam rose, he looked through it, and asked, "Did I say something wrong?"

She glared at him. "It's not a joke."

"It's my blood," he answered. "I certainly don't think it's a joke."

She made a face. "But—I can't do that!"

"Why not?" he asked with genuine concern.

"It's all right for you," she said. "You're used to it."

"Drinking blood?"

"Yes. Besides, I don't want to be a vampire."

"You won't be a vampire." He was pretty sure he'd mentioned this before, but maybe he hadn't explained it very well— or at all. Or maybe she hadn't been able to comprehend. Maybe she just hadn't been listening.

Whatever it was that blocked her acceptance, he tried again. "Drinking my blood won't make you a vampire. But the Patron wants—"

"To live forever," she interrupted. "I know that. What I don't understand is why they didn't just grab a female vampire and make her bite him. Wouldn't that solve his immortality fixation?"

Marc really wished she hadn't said that. He did his best to repair the damage, in case anyone was listening. "I'm sure Brashear's thought of that, and knows that it wouldn't work. Vampire females can only bond with vampire males."

That wasn't *exactly* true. Though it had once been forbidden, vampire women now sometimes took mortal lovers. It was true that they didn't bond with them in the same way Primes did with mortal females—the species might have died out long ago if they could—but the sharing of blood did halt the mortal male's aging process for as long as the relationship lasted.

Marc ate a few bites before he went back to the original subject. "We aren't going to get out of here until you do."

Josephine glared at him. "We get out of here in specimen jars if I do. No way am I doing anything to help that old creep."

He shrugged. "They're only going to give us so much time to do the deed on our own." He smiled, with a hint of fang in it. "You know you want to."

"I want more food," she said, and went back to the refrigerator.

Of course she did, and she wasn't hungry because of the blood he'd taken from her. That had been no more than a few drops during many hours of lovemaking. He was back in control of his intake, no longer needing her blood to heal.

"What you're hungry for is me," he told her.

She ignored this. "And I can't believe I just ate meat again without even thinking about it. You've corrupted me, Cage. There's some chocolate pudding. You want some?"

She turned around, holding a pair of sealed plastic cups. "That's not food," he said disdainfully. While he'd eaten greasy-spoon hamburgers and chicken out of necessity, and even enjoyed them, he was not about to eat prepackaged, chemical-laden junk food. "This body is a temple."

"More for me, then," she announced, and brought the pudding back to the table.

"I like what the cold air from the fridge does to your nipples," he informed her.

She ignored him, and they sat in silence while she polished off both containers. Someday he wanted to see that look of intense pleasure on her face when he served her *pot au chocolat*.

"Still hungry?" he asked, when she was done.

She sighed. "Yes."

He held out his arm, the wrist turned toward her.

She made a face. "Euwww." But she didn't look away. She stared avidly at his wrist, the color in her cheeks rising. He didn't think she was aware of licking her lips.

"The lady protests too much."

She bit her lower lip, then finally made herself look him in the eye. "What if I like it? What if I discovered I wanted to drink other people's blood?"

"Then you would be a slut," he answered gravely, "but you're not that kind of girl."

"I'm not going to become a bloodsucking creature of the night?"

Marc couldn't help but laugh. "No. That's my job."

"You're making fun of me."

He nodded. "A little. What we have is nothing to be afraid of, or ashamed of. Just the opposite."

"Gavin is playing you, messing with your head. He knew that if we were put in something like a normal setting, you'd— get all romantic and gentlemanly and want to get married, vampire style."

"Gavin knows me very well." *But not everything about me. Or you. Or what we will be together.*

She waved her arm at their prison. "It'll serve their purpose!"

"No," he said, standing. "It serves ours." He came around the table and took her by the hand. "Come on."

She held back when he urged her forward. "Where? What?"

"You said you wanted a shower," he reminded her, and tilted his head toward the bathroom.

Jo was totally confused by how calm he was, how certain of the rightness of what he wanted of her. She had to admit that she did have a *craving* to share more with him. Logically, she knew it was a dangerous step into the dark. Emotionally, it was a passionate need to move away from being alone, move into a place of light and completion. It was a place where Marcus Cage waited for her, arms open, a place of acceptance, support, protection—for her, for him. Them.

"I really do love you, Cage." She sighed as they entered the bathroom. "I must be out of my mind."

He hauled her close, something that wasn't hard to do in the small space. "Do you love me despite a barbaric courtship? Or because of it?"

Jo rested her hands flat on his chest and looked up into his dark brown eyes. She didn't have to be an empath to sense how vulnerable he was at that moment, how hopeful and afraid.

"I don't know," she answered honestly. "You're you. You were desperate, and scary, but you were—nice. Kind. I understand now that you did what you had to do, trying to protect your people even more than you tried to protect yourself. You did the best you could."

He gave a mental sigh of relief as he drew her into a kiss. A gentle kiss at first, which quickly turned passionate and possessive. And not only on his part. After a few fiery moments Jo realized that she was digging her nails into his shoulders.

Was she trying to draw blood?

The fierceness rising in her frightened her, and she pulled away.

He accepted her reaction, but said, "You can't hurt me, Josephine. Not unless you don't love me."

He turned on the water and drew her into the shower stall. It was a very tight fit. The spray was hard and hot, and steam soon started to rise.

"Nice," she said. She picked up a tube of shower gel from the soap dish and squeezed it all over them. The scent of melon mingled with the steam. "What luxury," she murmured. She leaned back against his chest and closed her eyes as he washed her hair. She'd come to appreciate even the tiniest of luxuries, as well as the way this man mixed gentleness with strength. She knew so much about him, and yet there was so much more to learn. She longed to share all he was. And to share what she was with him. There were so many levels that beckoned, tantalizing, just out of reach . . .

"That feels so good," she said, as he began to massage her shoulders.

"You feel good." *In every way,* he whispered in her head.

She tried to relax, to live in the precious, peaceful moment.

With the peace came clarity. The way he was touching her didn't distract her, but it did heighten her awareness of the—possibilities.

I feel—thirsty for you.

That was the only way to describe the ache inside her. Thirst for a sustenance that would feed her soul.

Then you're ready.

He turned off the shower and, with his arm around her waist, led her back into the other room. Their captors hadn't provided them with towels, so they ended up standing in the middle of the room, dripping water onto the painted cement floor. Jo barely noticed her wet skin growing cold in the air-conditioned room.

He held her out at arm's length. "You won't hurt me." He smiled, and anticipation glowed in his dark eyes. "You can count on that." *And don't be frightened when the guards come in. I'll take care of them.*

Jo blinked in sudden confusion and instant suspicion. She snatched her hands out of his. "What are you talking about? What gu—?"

He snatched her into a kiss before she could finish.

The Patron's mercenaries, he spoke into her mind. *The people holding us prisoner. They'll come for you as soon as you have my blood in you. To keep your blood uncontaminated, they won't use the gas. So they'll come in force when you've finished feeding.*

But—how would they know? Shit, Cage, have they been watching us?

Of course.

I checked for cameras; I'm not completely naïve. I didn't see any.

I haven't found them, either, but they must be there.

He was still kissing her, his tongue working wonders in her mouth. She was furious, and that fury was morphing into physical passion. If there was anybody watching, they were getting quite a show.

If? Why had she let herself pretend otherwise? That Cage

had let her pretend was infuriating. When she thought about what they'd done—

It must have made watching X-rated porn seem tame.

And her actions weren't exactly prim and proper either. She was all over Cage with her mouth and her hands, and straining sinuous muscles, even while she mentally shouted, *You* knew *we were being watched—while we were screwing our brains out! How could you?*

For a hundred reasons. Because I love you. Because you love me. Because I need to make love to you and you alone. Because I needed sex and blood from a bondmate to regain my strength. With my full abilities back, we can escape.

You had sex with me as part of an escape plan?

You have something against escaping?

This last question knocked all the outrage right out of her. Of course she wanted to escape.

When we get out of here, I'm going to kill you.

His laughter filled her mind, and somehow his amusement soothed her ruffled feelings. *One thing at a time*, he thought. *First you have to drink my blood.*

"Fine." She realized that they were tangled up together on the floor like a pair of horny wet pretzels. She found the nearest patch of skin she was certain was his, and bit down.

"Ouch!" He bucked and pushed her off. He knelt beside her. "Not like that," he said, rubbing the tender spot above his navel.

Jo scrambled to her knees to face him. "How, then?" she demanded.

"I do the work."

She watched as razor-sharp fangs slid out over his lips. He lifted his left wrist to his mouth and sank his teeth into his own flesh. Blood welled from two punctures as he held his arm out toward her.

"Like this." He moved closer, and put his other hand around the back of her neck. "Lean forward," he urged. His deep voice was a rumbling, needy whisper. "Drink."

She couldn't take her eyes off the drops of hot, scarlet blood. The sweet scent of it called to her. She was past the point where she could stop herself from wanting it. Needing him.

Heart racing, she bent forward and touched her lips to his wrist. Lightning struck her then, fire from heaven. She was aflame, and so was he. She loved that he was there in the fire with her. They were two souls burning, two bright flames growing together, fusing into one raging inferno.

How long they were together in this private bright place, she had no idea. But nothing so intense could go on forever. Instinct told her that the completion was something to be returned to again and again, but that the world beyond was waiting. They would face the world side by side, stronger for what they experienced within this joining fire.

Though she didn't want it to end, when the fire died down to darkness, she accepted it with an utterly contented sigh.

"Welcome to my world, Mrs. Cage," was the last thing Jo heard before darkness completely took her.

Chapter Twenty-six

Mrs. Cage? Whoa.

It was her first thought upon waking from a brief nap. When Jo opened her eyes, she saw that she was lying on the floor between the bed and the wall. Then she heard the door crash open and people entering, and realized what was happening.

They'd come for her.

Cage had moved her to the one spot that afforded a small amount of shelter. It wasn't much, but it might delay them for a few seconds.

As she sat up, someone fired a shot. Instead of ducking back to the floor, Jo came to her feet, frantically looking around for Cage. All she saw was a blur of motion, and bodies flying as the blur passed by like the angel of death. She had to concentrate to make out the naked human shape of hard muscle and sinew and unnatural power that was the whirlwind.

Cage. She grinned.

A body flew toward her, and she jumped across the bed to avoid the man. He hit the wall with a thud and slid limply down it. Jo landed on the floor and stayed on her hands and knees as she watched Cage go through the guards like a warm knife through butter. Weapons were grabbed and tossed, bouncing with a hard metallic clatter off the walls. There were a few cries of pain.

"Amazing," she said, when he came to a standstill and was the only one standing. She got to her feet and did a quick body count. "There are seven of them. Are they dead?"

Cage turned to look at her, eyes glowing. "Does it matter?"

"Only if they're going to come after us."

"Come on," he said, heading for the door. "We haven't got much time."

Jo ignored him and knelt by one of the men, then quickly unbuttoned his shirt. "Help me," she said, when she had trouble lifting him to get the shirt off.

"What are you doing?"

"I'm not leaving here naked." She glanced at him. "I love your butt, City Mouse, but do you want it hanging out while we run for our lives?"

"Good point." Moving at high speed once more, he found the two downed guards who best approximated their sizes and stripped them.

Jo felt much better once she was dressed in baggy desert camo. One of the guards had been wearing sandals with Velcro closures, and she was able to adjust them to fit her feet. Cage loaded up on weapons and ammo, as well as getting dressed.

"Ready?" he asked, when she fastened the last sandal strap.

She picked up a pistol and stuffed bullet clips in her pockets. "Ready."

"Can you use that thing?"

"Yes."

"Will you?"

She crossed to the open door, paused, and looked cautiously up and down the white corridor. "Let's find out." And stepped out of their cell.

Marc admired Josephine's bravado, but he hurried to take the lead as they moved down the hallway.

"Hold up," he said, before they'd gone very far. "What do you sense?" he asked, when she stopped and gave him a worried look.

She closed her eyes, and he felt her shielding open. She had more control than ever before. While they'd made love and he grew stronger, he had also taught her subconscious how to manage her strong empathic senses. As she sensed the outside world in her own way, he sensed it in his, tasting and scenting the air, and listening with hearing far more sensitive than mortal ears.

"Something's going on," they said together after a few moments.

"There's confusion," she said. "Worry. There's pain." She glanced back toward the cell. "Not just in here."

"Noise at the other end of the compound," he said. "A training exercise that's gone wrong, maybe. Whatever it is, we've got a diversion. Let's take advantage of it."

She nodded, and they hurried down the gleaming white corridor.

"This is too much like the dreams," she said, as they passed several doors.

He squeezed her shoulder. "I know. Only this time we get away." He willed her to believe it. They were armed, their captors were distracted. He was feeling fine.

"No dream," she said. "Not a drill."

They came to an intersection and automatically turned right. Then they paused and looked at each other. The exit they'd raced toward in the dream had been this way.

"It was only a dream." Josephine looked around worriedly.

This was no time to hesitate. "I trust my dreams," Marc answered. He took her hand. "Run," he ordered, the word spoken in a deep, commanding growl.

He ran, and she had no choice but to keep up with him. When a door opened as they approached it, Marc stopped long enough to break the neck of the freckle-faced man who appeared in the doorway.

"I know him," Jo said, staring at the crumpled body. He'd spoken to her at the meeting.

"Did he hurt you?" Cage asked.

She thought back to the medical tests they'd run on her. "Yes."

Marc nudged the body with his foot. "He won't anymore."

They hurried down the hallway again, reached a staircase, and raced down it.

At the bottom, Jo asked, "Was that gunfire?"

"Yes." It had been faint even to Marc's hearing. "Out near the west perimeter."

They went down another white corridor, this one shorter than the last, and at the end was a large, shining metal door.

"What is that stuff?" Jo asked. "Does the guy own a mithril mine?"

"It's pure silver," Marc answered. "I can't touch it." Not without third-degree burns. Even with his body chemistry returned to normal, it still wasn't possible for him to deal with so much of the deadly metal.

"It's not kryptonite," she complained.

He grinned. "Not to you." He stepped back and gestured her forward. "After you."

"Sure." She raised the pistol, shot the lock, and pushed at the door with the flat of her palms. "Heavy," she said as it slowly opened. "Must be worth a fortune. Wonder if it's solid silver or just a sheet of the stuff?"

"You planning on coming back and stealing the door?" he asked. "Wait." Before she could open the door farther, he jumped up and smashed all the lights near the door. When the area was dark he let her finish opening it. "Good. It's night."

"It's beautiful," she said.

Cool air flowed in from the outside, and distant noises came with it. Spotlights lit the compound and scattered buildings. Guards moved in the light, weapons at the ready. Marc and Josephine moved cautiously into the shadows by the wall of the building.

"What now?" she whispered.

Now—? "Steal a Hummer and smash through a fence, maybe? It doesn't have much of a chance, but—"

Josephine took in a sharp breath. "Wait a minute. How many people can fit in a Humvee?" she asked. "Will it take five?"

Marc looked at her in confusion. He didn't like the stubborn set of her jaw. "Five? Five what?"

"People. You, me, and the three women they brought in with us." She pointed to one of the buildings across the compound. "They're keeping them prisoner in there. We have to get them out."

"We? What? No."

"It's my fault they were captured. If I hadn't called my mom— Never mind how it happened, the point is, they're prisoners, too. If we escape, we have to take them with us. We have to help them."

"No, we don't."

Marc knew their chances were already small; if they tried to make this into a group outing, they were doomed.

"They'll kill them. They brought them here to feed you. If we're gone, they're excess baggage, liabilities. Do you really think Gavin will keep them alive?" she demanded.

Marc very much wanted to tell her that the women were not his problem. She was the only one besides himself that he was obligated to take care of. Family took care of Family, and Josephine was now Cage of House Gianna of Family Caeg. The other women were mortals. He had no ties to them; they were— baggage, liabilities.

He looked across the compound, past the bright lights and patrolling guards. He shook his head. "I'd help them if it was feasible. It's not. Once we're free, we'll send back help."

She gave him a skeptical look. "If we get away, you know this base will be deserted before any help can get here."

Without further argument, she bent over and began to run a zigzag course across the compound. Marc had no choice but to follow.

The first bullet hit the ground at his heel, fired from one of the corner sentry towers. The splat it made as it impacted the hard surface told him it was soft metal. A silver bullet. Great.

He wouldn't have heard the second bullet if he hadn't been a vampire. It flew far over his head, fired at the sentry tower from a silenced gun. Marc heard the bullet impact in mortal flesh, the grunt of pain, and smelled the blood. He sensed the presence of another Prime, as well. He kept on running, fast enough to dodge any more bullets, flashed up to catch Josephine around the waist, and dragged her behind the shelter of a parked truck.

Within moments of his hauling his lady to the ground, the second vampire ran up to join them.

"Nice party," the new Prime said. He looked around with a wide grin, then back at Marc. "Are we having fun? Is that yours?" he added with a glance at Josephine.

The Prime had long dark red hair, dark eyes, a wiry build, a silenced rifle, and the overwhelming cheerful arrogance of a cocky young Prime. The cavalry had arrived, and Marc wondered if he was going to have to change its diapers.

"Who are you?" he asked.

The young Prime held up his left arm and showed the tattoo on the inside of his bared wrist. "Colin Foxe, Clan Reynard. When Terry and Annette got your message to us, I volunteered to come take a look."

"Terry and Annette?" Jo asked.

"The werefoxes," Marc guessed. One arm tightly around Josephine's waist, he told her, "I gave them a message to deliver to the Clan they're affiliated with. The message got through."

Colin Foxe smiled charmingly at Josephine. "I'm here to save you." He turned his attention back to Marc. "I actually just came in to scout around and report back to the Clan. But a sentry spotted me, so I figured I might as well do some damage while I'm here."

"Good thinking," Marc concurred. "That made a diversion for us."

"And I saved your life."

No young Prime was going to let that little favor pass. Marc nodded his gracious appreciation while Colin smiled past him at Josephine. Marc showed a bit of fang, just enough warning that he wasn't about to share his mate to show his gratitude for the Clan boy's assistance.

Colin gave a nonchalant shrug. They both knew he wouldn't be Prime if he didn't make at least a token effort to seduce, or in any other way acquire, a pretty sex partner.

"How's the baby?" Josephine asked.

"What baby?" Marc and Colin asked together, drawn out of their silent posturing.

"Terry and Annette's baby."

"I don't know," Colin answered.

"We don't have time for this," Marc said.

"Men," she complained.

"We have to get out of here," Marc said.

So far, none of the other guards in the compound had noticed them. The shooter had fallen from the tower when Colin shot him. Some had been drawn away toward where his body fell.

"We have to get to the women."

"Women?" Colin asked with great interest.

"The other prisoners," Josephine answered him. "Three women."

Oh, no. Marc closed his eyes for a moment. The last thing a chivalrous Clan boy needed to know was that there were other people who needed rescuing, and helpless women at that. Clan Primes lived for that kind of thing.

Colin rubbed a thumb along his jaw. "Going to be tricky getting three other mortals out."

"That's what I've been telling her," Marc said.

"Place is crawling with troops. I hiked in, but we'll need a vehicle to carry that many people. Access in and out is hard, even for SUVs. They can mount up a heavy-duty search operation."

"We know about that," Marc said.

"And they've got a couple of airplanes. So they can do aerial recon and— Planes!" he said, his face lighting up. He looked at Marc. "Can you fly one?"

Joy sparked through Marc like fireworks. He should have remembered about the planes! He jerked a thumb at Josephine. "She's the pilot."

"I spotted a Gulfstream all fueled up and ready to go on the airfield," Colin said. "Can you fly it?"

"Yes," Josephine answered, followed immediately by a panicked, "No!"

"She can fly it," Marc assured the other Prime. He wanted to dance with joy. Instead, he rose to his feet and brought Josephine with him. "We're going home, Girl Scout."

"I—"

"I brought some explosives just in case I got the chance to blow up the lab you told the werefox about." Colin got up. "Where is it?"

Marc hated any delay in getting to the airfield, but he agreed that all the research data they'd amassed about vampires needed to be destroyed. And the scientists with it, with any luck. He pointed toward the lab building.

Colin gave a decisive nod. "You rescue the prisoners," he said. "I'll take out the lab and meet you at the plane." Then he sped off, his running figure a blur to any but vampire eyes.

Marc wanted to howl in frustration. He'd had enough of this prison. He wanted to go home. He wanted his life back. Above all else, he wanted Josephine safe.

Then he looked at her, and she was looking at him with hope, admiration, and utter trust in her eyes.

He sighed. "All right. Fine. Let's go rescue the girls."

Chapter Twenty-seven

"I'm skinny," Jo said. "I think I can get through the window."

"Yeah," he said. "That'll work."

Staying in the dark as much as possible, they'd silently circled around to the back of the building where the women were being held. There were narrow windows high up in the wall. It had been decided that she should go in first and warn the women before Cage came barging in the door. After all, he'd already nearly frightened one of them to death. If the escape was going to go quickly and quietly, they didn't need screaming panic now.

Jo checked the safety on her gun, then stuck it in her waistband and looked around the ground near the wall. "Plenty of rocks. I need one big enough to smash the glass—here we are." She picked up a heavy rock and turned back to Cage.

"Give me a leg up," she requested.

The next thing she knew he grabbed her around the waist, and muttered, "Nobody tosses a dwarf." Then he tossed her.

She was able to grab on to the roof overhang, and plant a knee on the narrow window ledge. This gave her enough purchase to hang on with one hand while she hauled her other arm back and smashed the big rock into the window.

An alarm went off, of course, but Jo continued smashing broken glass until the hole was wide enough for her to slip safely through and ease herself down into the room.

When her feet touched the floor she quickly turned around and saw the three women huddled together by the table on the far side of the room. They stared at her in wide-eyed terror, but they didn't move or make a sound.

Then Jo looked over their heads and saw why. She shouted, "Marc, don't come—!"

But it was too late. The door smashed open, drowning out her warning.

Marc, duck! she thought belatedly.

Marc dropped to the floor in a shoulder roll that took him to the center of the room. Though he dodged a bullet, the slug gouged a shard of concrete from the floor, which grazed Marc's cheek. *First blood to the enemy. How annoying.*

When he rose to his feet, he'd put his big body between Josephine and the man standing behind the trio of terrified hostages.

"Hello, Marcus," Jonas Gavin said from behind his human shields. "I knew this is where you'd come. You've always been softhearted."

Marc gestured toward Josephine. "Don't blame me. This is her idea." He glanced at the bullet that was lodged in the floor at his feet. "Silver."

"I thought it might get your attention."

"Must have terrible accuracy."

"It doesn't need much range close up. I could have shot you if I wanted to. Drop all your weapons."

He couldn't drop all of them—not the fangs, or claws, the speed or the strength, or the psychic talents—but he couldn't use them at the moment, either. One thing about humans, though, was their natural tendency to forget about supernatural abilities if you just behaved normally for a while. Marc did as he'd been told, slowly putting the weapons he'd taken from the guards on the floor, one by one.

Could he dodge a bullet, especially knowing what a fine marksman Gavin was? He put his hands up, showing that they were empty. Gavin kept the gun trained steadily on him.

"You don't want to shoot me, do you, Jonas?"

"I wouldn't mind, but that's not in the cards for right now."

"You're about to point out that I'm more valuable alive." Marc shook his head. "I'm through being a prisoner, Jonas."

Gavin smiled. It was an expression Marc was familiar with. When Gavin had that look, something appalling was about to happen. He grabbed one of the women lined up in front of him by the hair, and pulled her closer. He put the barrel of his gun to her forehead. "I definitely won't miss at this range."

"No!"

Marc put his arm out to catch Josephine when she shouted and rushed forward, and held her tightly around the waist. "No. You're the one he really wants. You're not getting close to him."

"Me? Oh, my blood."

"Come over here," Gavin called to Josephine. "I'll let the women go. I'll even let Marcus go. We don't need him anymore."

Marc held on tight, so Josephine couldn't pull away and surrender herself for the sake of all of them.

She gave a short, cynical chuckle. "Like I'm going to believe anything you promise?"

Gavin looked surprised that his powers of persuasion weren't working. "Then I'll kill all of you."

"Better dead than a lab rat," Josephine answered.

"Good girl," Marc whispered to her. He let her go and put her behind him, retrieving the pistol tucked in her waistband.

Gavin shot at him even as Marc turned and lifted the gun. If the explosion hadn't rocked the building at the same instant, Marc might not have been able to turn out of the bullet's path. As it was, it clipped his cheek and ear, splattering an arc of blood into his eyes. The lance of pain from the touch of silver drove him to his knees, and he dropped the pistol.

Outside the windows and broken door, the night lit with fire. The women screamed. Shattered glass fell like rain.

"Marc!" Josephine shouted above the din.

"Damn!" Gavin shouted.

Marc couldn't see for the blood, but his other senses told him where Gavin was. He followed body heat, scent, the vicious, angry emotions. He knew when the gun was turned on him again. And he moved with the speed of a vampire to reach his enemy before the weapon could harm him again.

There was a satisfying snap of broken bones when he grabbed Gavin's wrist and twisted it. Gavin's scream was the most gratifying sound he'd heard in a long time. Marc held on tight to Gavin with one hand, and wiped the blood from his eyes with the other. Then he held Gavin's head up and made the mortal look him in the eye.

Some vampires enjoy prolonging their enemy's death, he sent the thought into Gavin's mind. For a moment he let himself savor the wild burst of fear that erupted from deep in Gavin's twisted soul. *But you're not worth it.*

With that he broke Gavin's neck and turned back to the business of escaping as Gavin's lifeless body thumped to the concrete floor. For a long moment his gaze met Josephine's across the width of the room. He held his breath, not sure what to expect after she witnessed him killing someone. He knew his empathic mate had felt the death, and he didn't dare try to look into her mind.

She didn't look away from him, or flinch in horror. She was made of sterner stuff than that. She recognized the necessity of what he'd done and acknowledged it with a nod. She didn't even bother glancing at Gavin's body.

"Let's get this show on the road," she said, and paused only long enough to pick up her gun before crossing the room to the other women. "We're here to help," she told them.

One of the women was still screaming. The one Gavin had held the gun on was dazed and glassy-eyed. One of the women pointed at Marc. "He's the vampire!"

"Yeah," Josephine answered. "He's my vampire, and he's here to help you."

"But!" the woman shouted. "But, he's—!"

"A vampire. We all know that. And I," she added, "am the person now holding a gun on you. We don't have time for hysterics or arguments. Just get your asses out that door."

Marc crossed his arms and watched his woman in action, trying not to smile, which might ruin the effect of her performance if anyone looked his way. Not that any of these poor, scared women wanted to deal with a creature of the night. They probably preferred an angry woman with a gun in her hand giving the orders.

"Move!" the angry woman demanded, in a tone that would make a Marine sergeant proud.

The women moved, with Josephine bringing up the rear.

Marc beat them to the doorway and looked around. Across the compound, the lab was burning. The electrical generator must have been taken out, because the only light on the base now came from the conflagration. Just how much explosives had the Clan boy been carrying?

"Looks clear," he said, when the only troops he saw were those trying to fight the fire.

"Which way?" Josephine asked.

"Airstrip. We told Foxe we'd meet him at the plane."

Jo stopped in midstep, frozen with utter terror. "No."

"Yeah. That's what we told him."

She shook her head. "We'll take a Hummer."

Marc's hands landed on her shoulder. "We've been through this, my love. You are our best chance of getting all of us out of here."

The night swirled around her. "No," she whispered. She couldn't. "I can't fly."

"You want to fly," he told her. "You need to fly." His deep voice was dark and honey sweet, seducing her to disaster. It took some doing, but Jo managed to focus her eyes on his face. His earnest expression hurt her, the hope and confidence that filled his emotions burned her. She had to swallow hard before she could get any words out of her fear-constricted throat. "You can't make me do this. Don't make me do this. I can't do this."

He pulled her close. She should have felt safe in the shelter of his arms, but she couldn't.

I can't make you, he thought. *I won't try to make you. But I know you can do it. You were born to fly.*

I'll get you all killed!

No, you won't.

He was so certain. So calm, and patient, and confident in her. It devastated her to know that she'd fail him.

You'll never fail me. And you won't fail yourself.

Marc dropped his arms and stepped away. He stood before her, a burning building at his back, and reminded her, "We haven't escaped yet. The Patron's mercenaries are going to remember about us at any moment. Foxe is risking his life to clear a path to the airstrip for us. Then it's up to you." He gestured toward the three women huddled together, then he held a hand out to Jo. "Time to go."

Up to me. Jo ran a hand through her short hair. *Up to me.* Her heart was trying to pound out of her chest, and she was covered in cold sweat. She hadn't been this frightened when Marc came rushing out of the darkness on that first night.

"Please!" one of the women cried. "You have to help us."

Damn!

Jo swallowed again. "Let's get to the airstrip," she told Marc.

Though she didn't know what was going to happen once they got there.

They found the young Prime standing in the shadow of the hangar entrance. "We have a bit of a crisis," was his greeting.

"You think?" Marc asked.

"It's not just the escape," Foxe answered. "Did you hear the other plane take off?"

"There were explosions, gunfire. I was in a fight. No, I didn't hear a plane."

"The twin engine," Josephine said, coming up beside him. "I thought I heard it."

"Yeah," Foxe agreed. "I managed to keep them away from the jet, but some of the guards managed to hustle an old man onto the other plane and get away."

"Old man?" Marc said. "Goddess—you let the Patron get away!"

"This is worse than I thought?" Foxe asked. "I destroyed the research, and as many of the researchers as I could find. The Snake breed is dead."

Marc frowned at the rude term, but let it go. It was up to the Matri and elders of their own clans to teach children manners. "But the boss got away," he explained to Foxe. "He's the one with the will and the financing."

"Who is he?"

"I have no idea. But we need to find out; he must be stopped."

Foxe put a hand on Marc's shoulder and looked at Marc with burning intensity. "Not we, Prime. Me. I let him get away. Besides, this is more Clan business than it is Family. It's the Clans that are supposed to safeguard the research."

"It is," Marc agreed. "But the Patron threatens all of our kind. Besides, shouldn't it be the Snakes that take the responsibility?"

"I know my Matri. She'd insist I finish what I started tonight, even if I weren't already decided on it. And she'll make sure the Snakes are involved in tracking down this Patron. You don't have to be in it if you don't want. You've been through enough. Besides . . ." He glanced toward Josephine. "I think you have other concerns in the next few months."

Foxe was right. He and Josephine were only at the beginning of their bonding processes. They needed a long, peaceful, intense time together.

Marcus gave the Clan Prime a nod. "Your hunt," he agreed. "But call me in at the kill if that's possible. I want to see this Patron taken down."

"Agreed."

Jo stood apart from the men, not really paying attention to their conversation. There was shouting in the distance and occasional gunfire, though she had no idea what the mercenaries were shooting at. Seeing phantom vampires everywhere, she supposed. And the noise, and the danger that came with it, was growing closer.

She jumped when Marc came up and touched her on the shoulder. "Time to go," he whispered, leaning close to her ear.

"I'm cold," she said, staring at the sleek, small jet sitting nearby on the end of the dark runway.

Dark wouldn't be a problem; it was the kind of airplane that came fully loaded with every kind of instrument money could buy. And it was prepped for takeoff, or the Patron's staff wouldn't have tried to board it. All she had to do was walk into the cockpit, sit down in the pilot's seat, and let her hands and eyes do what they'd been trained so well to do. It meant freedom and safety for them all. Above all else, Marcus Cage deserved freedom and safety. If only she could give it to him.

"I'm cold," she said again.

"I'm here," he said. But he didn't touch her. He didn't make promises, or give reassurances, didn't tell her she was brave and he knew she could do it. He stood at her side, and waited.

"Dammit," she said at last, giving him a hard, angry glare. Then she took a step, then another, approaching the jet with the same trepidation she would a fire-breathing dragon.

The women followed, with the other vampire running ahead to enter the plane first. "Clear," he called from the doorway.

Jo watched Marc shepherd the other women forward. She was tempted to turn and run, but they needed her. Marc needed her.

What if she got them killed?

Gunfire sounded close behind her, and concrete and sparks flew as bullets hit the ground nearby.

That was her answer.

She ran the last few steps onto the jet. Once on board she sprinted through the luxurious cabin, barely aware of the people already strapped into seats, and heard Foxe securing the bulkhead door.

Marc stood by the cockpit entrance. "Anything I can do?"

"Stand by this door and don't let me come out."

"Deal."

She couldn't help but smile at the sound of his deep voice, and she turned that smile on him. "Thanks."

He pointed. "Go."

Shaking like a leaf, she faced the open door, saw the arc of instruments and the runway stretching off into the night beyond the cockpit window. She was about to enter the dragon's mouth, indeed.

"Wait a minute," she said, turning abruptly around.

"Where are we? Where are we going? I can get us in the air, but I need some reference points."

"This used to be Fort Copeland, if that's any help," Foxe called from the back of the plane. "My Clan has a private airport on the Salton Sea. I can get you there, but get us airborne now!"

Jo's roiling nerves settled a little. She knew exactly where Fort Copeland was. This time she didn't hesitate in entering the cockpit. She walked into her world and settled firmly into the pilot's seat. She glanced back once, and Marc blew her a kiss and closed the cabin door.

She ran her gaze and her hands over the familiar controls. Now she was alone. No, she had Marcus Cage with her. Always. "Sort of like the Force," she muttered.

She brought the power up on the engines, loving the fine-tuned hum that turned into a full-throated dragon's roar. She could ride this dragon. Though she was still afraid, a thrill of anticipation sang through her, as well. She'd missed this!

She wanted this. She looked up at the stars overhead. Her heart reached for the sky, and her hands moved, knowing how to take her there.

Marc should have been strapped into a seat, but he waited on his side of the door. His hands were pressed to the cool metal surface, his eyes closed, his concentration completely on the woman he loved. She was in a place where he couldn't help her, but he was there with her. Her fear pulsed through him, then longing took her, and love. The plane began to roll down the runway. He became aware of speed. With the speed came a singing, yearning pleasure.

Then joy burst through her—them—and the plane leapt into the air.

"Yiihaaa! Yes!" Josephine's shout burst out of the cockpit, just as Marc was thrown backward by gravity onto the deck.

He put his head back and laughed with joy, loving her, feeling pretty triumphant himself.

"Yes!" He punched a fist in the air.

They were going to be all right.

Epilogue

Six Weeks Later

"There is nothing more comforting than a long, hot bath. And bubbles makes it even better."

A pair of full champagne flutes in her hands, Jo looked across the vast expanse of rosy marble, crystal, and gold that was their hotel suite's bathroom. Marc grinned at her from the depths of the huge sunken tub. Candles gleamed on the wide marble shelf behind him, lending gold accents to his curly black hair. He was covered up to his broad, bare chest in a rich foam of bubbles. Cinnamon-scented steam rose from the hot water.

"On you, that looks good," she told her husband.

She supposed that technically he was her bondmate. He wasn't going to be her husband until tomorrow afternoon.

"You look like Venus being reluctant about coming out of the sea," she told him.

She crossed the room, loving the feel of the cool tiles on her bare feet and the silky touch of her peacock blue robe against her skin. When she handed him his glass of champagne their fingers touched, and hot pleasure shot through her. Their gazes met.

He said, "You could climb in here with me, and we could *try* to make it a quick one."

It was very tempting, but she took a step back and took a sip from the flute. Marc, who knew a lot about such things, had assured her it was excellent champagne. She liked the taste, but being with him like this made her giddy without any help from the wine.

"You have to come out sometime," she told him. "Come on," she coaxed, letting the silk slide seductively off one shoulder. "My mom's not that scary."

He arched an eyebrow at her, though his gaze was riveted on what she'd revealed of one breast. "Your mother ran a make on me for priors."

Jo shrugged, revealing a bit more skin. "She does that on all my boyfriends."

"I'm not a boyfriend."

"She was a little leery of you at first. You can't blame her, when we showed up with a wild story about thwarting a forced prostitution ring led by that corrupt sheriff in Kennedyville."

"She believed us. And the ladies we rescued corroborated the story."

"After you hypnotized everyone. Which *was* safer for everyone involved and makes a lot more sense than the truth," she admitted.

"The investigation found plenty of evidence about the sheriff's bad deeds."

Apparently there were experts among vampire kind that specialized in operations that kept the vampire world invisible from mortal kind. She didn't blame them for their secrecy, not after what happened with the Patron. She still had nightmares.

And Marcus was there to comfort her every time she woke up with one. And she was there for him.

And now they were getting married tomorrow. And he'd taken her to Venice—sort of. They were staying at the Venetian hotel in Las Vegas, and getting married in the wedding chapel at the hotel. She'd spent a busy few days crisscrossing the country, flying in relatives and friends from both sides. She'd relished every minute spent in the air, even as she'd missed Marc dreadfully when away from him. He'd been putting the finishing touches on the restaurant he was opening in Vegas, getting it ready in time for the wedding reception to be held there tomorrow night.

They had their lives back, they had their careers, they had

the magic of the bond, and they had each other. When he'd captured her that night in the desert, she couldn't have imagined it would lead to this.

"Perfection," she said.

"You are," he agreed.

She turned toward the nearest mirror and marveled at the scars that were fading. She also marveled at the lack of pain. She hadn't realized how much physical and emotional pain had become a part of her life, until he began to heal her. Tomorrow she'd be wearing a strapless wedding gown covered in lace and crystal beads. And to think that a few weeks ago, she'd been reduced to wearing stolen combat fatigues.

"We've had quite a ride, Mr. Cage."

"Indeed we have, Mrs. Cage." As she turned back to him, he added, "Let's not do it again. Now, about my mother-in-law's distrustful attitude—"

"Hey, you didn't have a record—she likes you now."

He sipped champagne and put the glass down on the wide rim of the tub. "You have a strange family."

"In comparison to what? Yours? I like your family," she added. "Even if your great-grandmother's a little scary."

"She has to be. She's the Matri. She needs to be tough to keep the Family in line."

"And I understand why. Your young male relatives are—a lively bunch. If they keep hitting on my sister, somebody's going to get hurt. And it won't be Officer Friendly Phillipa Elliot."

"Josephine *and* Phillipa—your father wanted all boys, didn't he?"

"They're family names. From a grandmother on each side, and my brother is Matthew Elliot III, after Dad and Grandpa. My family has as many traditions as yours."

"Yeah." He smiled fondly. "I like that about them. I like the way your nipple's puckering, too. You want to come here and let me play with it?"

She took a teasing step backward and shook her head. "I told you you had to come to me. And we don't have time to fool around." She pulled the robe back up and tightened the belt. "I'm not going to be late for the rehearsal dinner."

"My family will understand."

"They're all sex fiends."

He stood up in the bathtub, looking more like Mars rampant arising from the foam than Venus. She glanced at his erection. "Correction. You're all sex fiends."

"Famous for it," he answered, and came to her.

It wasn't long before they were making love on the bathroom floor. A quick, happy, wet bout of sex that left them breathless, laughing, and utterly satisfied.

"We better get dressed," he said, after they finished up with a shower that was only slightly quicker than their lovemaking. He took her hand and led her out of the bathroom.

Marc continued on through the living room into the suite's bedroom. Jo came to a halt in front of a low table, staring at the beautifully wrapped box resting next to a huge vase that contained many white roses and one red one.

"What's this?" she called after Marc.

"For you," he called back. "Open it."

Jo touched the roses first and buried her face in the soft blossoms. She nearly became drunk on the sweet scent, and smiled at knowing that roses had thorns. It was all very symbolic, and sweet as well.

Marc came back into the living room, dressed all in black. His powerfully built body was shown off to perfection by the beautifully tailored suit and black silk shirt. She loved the way his curly black hair framed his face.

"Don't stare at me, woman," he said. "Open your present."

She held up the box, wrapped in silver paper and tied with gold ribbon. The bow was as big as a plate. She shook it. "It's so pretty, I hate to."

He folded his arms, and used his Sergeant Cage voice. "Open it."

She grinned and tore into the wrapping. Within moments she put the box on the table, and lifted the white cardboard lid.

When she saw what was inside, she began to laugh. "Good God," she said, taking out one T-shirt after another. *"Adrenalize, Hysteria, X, On through the Night."* She looked at him. "They're all here, aren't they?" He nodded. "Even some I didn't have before."

She laid out the Def Leppard tour shirts in a fan pattern. Being named Jo Elliot, a name almost exactly the same as the British rock band's singer, Joe Elliot, had gotten her a lot of Def Leppard paraphernalia as gifts over the years. She really wasn't that much of a fan of the band, but she'd become sentimentally attached to her shirt collection.

"You found all of them?"

"eBay is my friend," he answered. "You lost your collection saving me. I wanted you to have them back."

"Jo Elliot thanks you." She grabbed him close and kissed him. *And Josephine Cage adores you.*

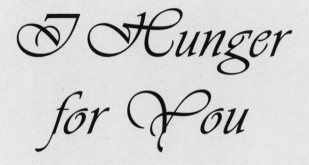

For Scott Ham—
who can be clever and inspiring
even while driving in heavy traffic

Chapter One

"The suspects finally answered the phone. Looks like we have a robbery gone sour. Maybe we can work with their demands."

The negotiator's voice, heard through Colin Foxe's headset, sounded relieved.

"Do you want us to hold?" Colin's team leader questioned.

After a considerable pause, the negotiator said, "Get your team in place, but wait for a go."

There was already an officer down inside; a cop who'd noticed something suspicious while driving by. She'd called it in, then gone inside. Shots had been fired. The situation escalated quickly after that, and now Colin's SWAT team was on the ground and on the move.

He could smell the wounded officer's blood through a bullet hole in the window. He could also sense the faint flutter of her heartbeat. She wasn't dead, but she didn't have much time. He couldn't see inside, since curtains had been pulled across the wide windows at the front of the office building, but he could sense a tangled mixture of physical markers and high emotions.

It was everybody on the team's job to stop this situation, but Colin took it very personally. He'd taken vows to protect and serve humanity that were far stronger and more binding than even his oath as a Los Angeles police officer.

He and his SWAT team were here to see that the hostages and injured cop were saved. It was a great team, well trained, well coordinated, well led; he was proud to be a part of it.

Dressed entirely in black, he moved in line with the rest of the team. Crouching low, they formed in a loose circle that was stealthily closing in on the one-story building. Their target was a small publishing company located in an office park on a quiet side street. There were at least four armed men inside, holding a dozen hostages.

The cloudy night covered the team's movements. They used nightscope goggles to focus on their objective—all but Colin, who'd perched his on the brim of his helmet. He could see in the dark.

Though he was outwardly calm, the excitement of the hunt burned through him. He was *aware,* the extra senses he reined in much of the time now fully focused. He could smell fear, and taste it as well. The threat of violence hung around the office building like a pall of smoke. And one touch of anger scratched across his senses like nails on slate.

He didn't think the fury was coming from one of the perps. It was one of the hostages, and she—yes, that was definitely a strong sense of femaleness—she was royally pissed off. In a hostage situation, it was better to be scared than angry. Scared people were more likely to keep their heads down and do as they were told, increasing their chances of survival. Colin didn't like this; it added risk to the situation. If this woman did something stupid . . .

Telepathy wasn't his strongest sense, and using it might distract him from the team effort. Besides, there were far too many people with heightened senses inside for him to affect one individual. Still, he risked sending one thought toward perps and hostages alike.

Calm down.

I am calm, came the immediate reply.

It took all his training to keep him from surging out of his crouch in surprise. She heard him! And answered! And the brief touch of her mind on his made him red-hot.

Shouts erupted from the building, followed by shots. And screams.

"Go!"

He was up and moving even as the command came.

He was the first one through the door, rushing in just in time to see the flying side kick that knocked away the gun of the man who would have shot him.

"Hey!" Colin shouted at the woman who'd disarmed the shooter.

"Thanks for the distraction." Then she jumped and kicked again, straight up, taking the bad guy under the chin. He dropped like a rock.

Colin grabbed her by the waist as she came back down, and pushed her to the floor.

"Stay put," he ordered, as the rest of his team came boiling in through the door he'd broken down.

Big brown eyes looked up at him, full of shock and fury that sizzled all the way through him. He pointed for her to get under a nearby desk, then turned and took out another gunman. There was already a third man down; no doubt the Karate Kid had gotten him. Which was probably why the shooting had started.

Farther back, in the rooms beyond this reception area, he heard shouts and screaming. Members of the team were heading that way at a run. A medical team was already working on the injured cop; others were cuffing the downed men.

"You could have gotten everybody killed!" Colin yelled at the woman.

"Well, I didn't!" she shouted back.

This was no time for an argument. Colin quickly rejoined his team and got into the well-practiced rhythm of a rescue operation. But even as he helped to secure the rest of the bad guys, part of him was still aware of the impression of soft, warm flesh over hard muscle that he'd gotten in the moment he held her. Her skin held the scent of ginger and her psychic signature was pure heat, as if her blood was laced with chili peppers.

He couldn't let it go. He marched back to the front of the

building as soon as the whole place was secure. By now she
was out from under the desk, and one of the medics was arguing with her. Colin noticed that one side of her face was badly
bruised, and she was cradling her left hand with her right.

Anger shot through him, and a hot, possessive protectiveness. "Who hurt you?" he demanded.

She looked around, and her dark brown eyes locked on his.
"I'm fine."

"That doesn't answer the question."

Her gaze flickered to an unconscious perp on the floor, then
back to Colin. "I took care of it."

Her response only served to redirect his annoyance at her.
He ripped off his helmet and headset to glare at her fully.
"You had no business doing what you—"

"Hey!" She interrupted him. "I saved your ass."

"No, you didn't."

"He was going to shoot you when you came through that
door."

"He wouldn't have." Colin took the woman by the shoulders and was instantly and intimately aware of the warmth of
her skin. "My job is to do the rescuing."

Her anger was incandescent. "You were a little late. Those
men held us hostage for four hours. Where were you?"

"Organizing a *safe* rescue." Everything about her burned
him, but he liked it. She infuriated him, needed to be tamed,
and he liked that, too.

"Did you stop at Starbucks for a few hours on the way?"
She jerked her head to where the medics were working on the
wounded officer. "She could have died. We all could have.
Somebody had to do something."

"So you took it upon yourself to play hero? Bad move, sister."

Her head came up sharply, brown eyes flashing. He could
have kissed her then and there. "I am not your sister."

"And you're no hero, either," Colin shot back.

"Officer," the medic cut in. He put a hand firmly on Colin's arm. "Officer."

The Prime part of Colin almost turned on the medic with bared fangs, as if the man was challenging him for a mate. It shocked him that the instinctive impulse was nearly triggered by a mortal, and it took him a moment to get the vampire part of himself under control. He had to close his eyes, take a deep breath—and let the woman go.

"Ms. Luchese's injured," he heard the medic say. "We need to get her to the ER."

"I told you I'm fine," she said.

This reminded Colin that a few moments ago, his impulse had been to make someone pay for hurting her. He looked at her and said, "Luchese, you always think you know best, and never do what you're told, right?"

She smiled. It was wicked and edgy, and that lit a different kind of fire in him.

"Yeah," she acknowledged.

"Go with the medic," he told her. She would have protested further, but he sent a stern command into her mind. *Go.*

Then his team commander called him, and Colin went back to work.

Several hours later, he met the Luchese woman in the ER waiting room as she came out of a treatment room. There were plenty of cops around, making his presence fairly anonymous in the hubbub, so it didn't look like he was hanging around waiting for her. Yet she spotted him instantly, as if she was as drawn to him as he was to her. He watched her look at him, then look away. He felt her consider walking past him and out the door. Her left arm was in a sling, and a shiny cream covered the bruises on her face. Her shoulders had a tired slump to them, which she consciously straightened when she saw him. Apparently she was ready to do battle all over again.

"You look beautiful," he said, coming up to her.

Her eyes went wide in surprise. She clearly thought he was making fun of her, and asked, "Officer, are you supposed to talk like that?"

"I'm off duty."

"You're not here to—take a statement, or something?"

"Didn't an officer talk to you already?"

"Yeah. He told me everyone got out okay. But why are you—"

"I wanted to check on you." He couldn't help but run a hand up her uninjured arm. He felt her shiver. "How are you feeling?"

"Nothing's broken, just a sprained wrist," she answered. "I don't need the sling, but I promised the nice intern who looked at it that I'd wear it until I'm outside the hospital door." She took a deep breath, and made a wry face. "I'm sorry I yelled at you. You risked your life to save us. Thank you."

He gave a slight shrug, and refrained from telling her that she shouldn't have risked her life when he was there to take care of her kind. Mortal life was precious; it was an honor to protect the helpless—even if Luchese here didn't think she was.

"I was scared," she went on. "That made me—testy."

"What were you doing out in the front office with your captor? Why weren't you tied up in the back with the others?"

"I thought you weren't here to ask questions?"

"Not officially. I'm curious. You were up to something, weren't you?"

"They were making ransom demands," she answered. "They were incompetent idiots with guns. They—"

"Had the wrong building," he filled in. "We know that from questioning them. By the time they figured out they'd screwed up, the officer had called the robbery in. But what were you doing?"

"Trying to split them up, so I could take one down and get his weapon. They were demanding a lot of money, and threatening to kill people if they didn't get it. So I said I was an heiress, and if they'd let me call my family, they'd be rich. I got one of them to take me up front so I could use the receptionist's phone, while one of the others was occupied talking to your negotiator in the back. It worked." She laughed, but the sound was a little shaky. "And I was only there to pick up my friend Courtney for lunch."

He shook a finger under her nose. "Luchese, that was very stupid of you. But brave," he added, as a flash of annoyance went through her. He touched the tip of her nose, then found himself tracing the outline of her lips. Soft, full, warm lips. They sent a wave of hunger through him. He was going to kiss those lips soon. The smoldering look she gave him told him she knew it, too. He was going to taste her. But this was not the place.

He made himself take a step back. "My name's Colin Foxe," he finally introduced himself. "You have a first name, Luchese?"

"Mia," she answered. "Mia Luchese."

Mia. A short, pretty, uncomplicated mortal name. It had nothing in common with the complex, beautiful names of vampire females. Someday he was going to bond with a vampire female, but right now he wanted this human woman.

He reached out and took her uninjured hand. "I'll take you home."

Chapter Two

Six months later

It wasn't true that he came here every night.

Only the nights when he wasn't on duty, or when sex with anyone else was out of the question, or when he was in town. All right, he came here a lot—but that didn't mean he was a stalker.

He certainly wasn't in love; it wasn't an emotional attachment. It was just a physical thing, a visceral thing, a psychic residue messing him up.

In fact, Colin was furious—with himself, and with her—because he hadn't yet been able to let it go.

It was just an ache. He'd go so far as to admit to an obsession. A short-term one.

He got hard just thinking about her, and her scent on the air drove him mad. Occasionally he caught a stray thought or emotion at a distance, and that was worse. Even such accidental intrusion was wrong. The memory of the taste of her kisses, and of her skin—hard muscles beneath ginger-scented, satiny flesh—was torture.

But he knew he'd get over it.

All it needed was time, and detachment, and making love to enough other women to drown the memories of how sweet it was with *her*. He refused to give in to the call to go to her. It had nothing to do with respecting her feelings, and everything to do with mastering his own. Wanting Mia Luchese was an obsession he would master. He was stronger than she was.

So Colin stood here, across the street from her place one more time, looked at her house perched on a hillside above

Coldwater Canyon, and fought the compulsion. He'd beat it. Get over her. Get on with his life.

She was mortal. If nothing else, he'd outlive the object of his desire. She'd get old, and die, and he'd go on—without her.

"Oh, goddess!"

The first month hadn't been so bad. She'd picked up and left town, no doubt researching articles for travel and extreme sports magazines. Even without the writing, Mia could afford to go when and where she pleased. It turned out what she'd told the perps about being an heiress was true. Colin remembered how he'd found out.

The balcony off her bedroom was small, hardly more than a perch with a wrought-iron rail, but it was perfect for looking at the spectacular view. It was a little past midnight, with a cool breeze drying the sweat on their skins, and a full moon high overhead. To him it was as bright as day, and Mia was beautiful by moonlight, her creamy skin bathed in silver.

He'd come to her straight from a very tough operation. Someone had died, and it hadn't been one of the bad guys. He'd needed her, and she'd taken him to her bed. The sex had been frantic, cathartic, wonderful.

Now they were out on the balcony, pressed so closely together, naked skin to naked skin, that he couldn't tell where he stopped and she started. His hands were around her waist; her head was tilted back, resting on his chest while she looked at the moon. He felt her trying to think of something to say or do, to keep his mind from going over and over what had gone wrong.

He welcomed the distraction, and helped her out by asking, "What are you doing living in a house like this?" The Spanish-style house wasn't big but it was very nice, with a pool and a half-acre of gardens surrounded by a high stucco wall.

He knew she was a freelance writer, but she also spent much of her time practicing a lot of dangerous, physically demanding hobbies. She ran, she was into karate and kung fu; she liked target shooting, and competed in traditional archery. She'd told him about the skydiving, the snowboarding; they'd gone rock climbing together. She was female, but not at all soft.

He liked that she shared some of his interests, and that she competed hard even if he never quite let her win. Competent or not, Mia was a mortal woman, and he wouldn't encourage over-confidence even if she was never likely to be in danger again.

She was a major jock, and being a jock on the level Mia practiced took not only time, but money. He'd made sure they didn't have many personal conversations. He listened to what-ever she chose to tell him, but he didn't ask, and he never vol-unteered anything. He'd kept everything in the present tense, because vampires had to guard their privacy, and because he wasn't planning on staying. The less he knew about her out of bed, the better. He shouldn't be prying into her personal life now, but he was suddenly curious.

"I inherited this place," Mia answered. "The house be-longed to my grandmother. It's one of the things she bought when she finally reconciled with her father."

"Reconciled?"

"Long, sad story. I've heard a lot about him, and about his side of the family, but I've never met the old man. He left my great-grandmother when Grandma was a kid. I hear that my great-grandfather's richer than God, and has a few years on Him, as well. Grandma was middle-aged, with kids and a per-fectly good life, when a lawyer brought her a letter and a check from her long-lost dad. Grandma didn't use much of the guilt money he dumped on her for herself, but she invested wisely, and left fortunes to my sister and me."

"So, you have a fairy grandfather—"

"Great-grandfather, and he's more of a—" Mia shrugged, and desire shot through Colin as he felt the movement all along his body.

He moved his hands up from her waist to her lovely, round breasts and—

He remembered the sex now—her sharp gasp of pain and pleasure when he sank teeth into flesh; the way the world turned to fire when he entered her—and it was far more vivid and important than any memory of conversation. It wasn't who she was, but how Mia made him feel that drew him to her like an addiction. He didn't understand what she'd done to him.

It wasn't as if he'd taken much blood from her. He'd done his best to keep the psychic connection between them as tenuous as possible. He'd only wanted her as a bed partner.

He *still* wanted her.

He'd known when she'd returned, knew the instant she was back in L.A. He'd dismissed the knowledge as his imagination, and hadn't given in to the impulse to just drive by her house for another month. But here it was, three months after the end of a three-month affair, and things were getting worse instead of better. He sure as hell hoped she was heartbroken and emotionally devastated, because he didn't want to be alone in this hell.

But she was mortal, a brief candle, a butterfly, a bright burst of fireworks—lovely, warm, and exciting—but ephemeral. How long could something as finite as a mortal creature feel hurt?

She was doubtless over him. In fact, someone as passionate as Mia had probably had at least one lover since they parted.

The very thought of Mia in anyone else's bed set his fangs on edge, and hit him like a hard punch in the gut. But he told himself it was only because Primes were proprietary. He'd unconsciously marked her as his, which was what this returning here night after night was about. It was a sort of instinct.

It's really good practice, he told himself. This pallid obsession was a way of preparing for the extreme emotions inevitable when the opportunity for a true bonding with a female of his own kind came his way.

In the meantime—

Thoughts of the future disappeared abruptly, and Colin's

whole body tensed as Mia's garden gate opened across the street. Pounding need drove through him when he saw her step away from the gate. For a moment she was illuminated under the glow of a streetlight, wearing a red tank top and shorts that showed off her toned body. While she was poised like a pop singer under a bright spotlight, Colin couldn't help but take a step forward, his hands stretched toward her.

She was unaware of him, of course. His kind had a knack for using shadows to their advantage, blending into darkness as if it was their natural coloration. If he tried, he could use his other senses to measure her heartbeat, the temperature of her skin. Her scent was alive on the breeze. When she turned and began to run, he beat down the hunter's instinct to follow.

She's exercising, you fool! She was a normal mortal, doing normal mortal things. He had no business being here, let alone pursuing her. He threw his head back, bumping it against the bark of the palm tree under which he stood. No business being here at all.

So he began to walk—not back to where he'd parked his car, but the way Mia had gone. He was *not* following her— he was just stretching his legs.

Mia didn't normally go running on the streets, especially this late, but something about the night had called out to her. The walls of the house had made her feel claustrophobic, and she needed space. Restlessness clawed at her. Surfing the Net hadn't helped; watching television hadn't held her attention; listening to a book on tape while using the treadmill had bored her. She'd thought about calling her girlfriend Courtney, but her mind was too much on Foxe, and any conversation would only degenerate into another bitching session about "that jerk." Why go over that ground again, when she was trying to forget him? She must have bored her friends to death with the subject by now—she wasn't the suffering-in-silence type.

I'm not suffering, she told herself as she eased her body into the rhythm of running. It was just that sometimes it felt like he was nearby, like she could reach out and touch him, and then—

Then she'd wake up from a dark, erotic dream, and be alone in her bed, and all the sexual energy was still there, simmering—

It was bound to wear off eventually. She'd meet someone else. Life would go on.

Some nights were just worse than others, and this was one of them. Mia figured all she had to do was drive herself to exhaustion; then she could fall asleep without dreaming. So she ran.

Except for the occasional passing car, the street was empty. The sidewalk was clear of pedestrians. There were lights in a few houses, but the neighborhood was mostly dark. Too dark, she thought after a while, and way too quiet.

A sensation of dread began to creep into Mia's consciousness, a feeling that she was being watched, even stalked. That something *wanted* her to be out here. It wasn't anything tangible. She didn't see or hear anything out of the ordinary, though she slowed down and looked around carefully. It was just *there*.

She turned around and headed back home. She trusted her instincts, even if there was no evidence. She knew she was being hunted. She didn't know if making it back to her house would mean making it to safety, but making it home was the only goal she could reach for as she ran through the darkness.

And it was getting darker. It was a cloudless night, but the stars seemed to be fading. Each streetlight she passed seemed dimmer than the last. She couldn't make out any lights in the houses; in fact she couldn't even see the houses anymore. The trees and bushes lining the sidewalk became dark, menacing shadows.

Then the darkness *moved,* resolved into a man-shaped shadow. She thought she caught a glimpse of bright, glowing eyes. The apparition reached for her with pale, clawed hands.

* * *

Colin was running even before he heard her angry shout up ahead. He cursed himself for not noticing the depth of the darkness sooner—that it had solidness, weight, and menace—for not noticing that there was another vampire in the area.

Motion swirled inside the darkness that spread like a scrim across the sidewalk. Emotion swirled as well, and Colin recognized more than just Mia's shock and controlled fear. She was putting up a fight. Like a cat playing with prey, the other vampire projected fierce joy at her puny efforts to kick and punch her way out of trouble. No Clan or Family Prime would take his pleasure like that.

"Tribe." Colin breathed the word as a curse as he sped forward.

It felt as if he had to rip through a curtain covering his mind, but he came through it at a rush to find the pair locked in combat in the small space between a tall hibiscus hedge and a parked SUV. Colin caught a brief impression of Mia twirling and kicking, and the vampire's preternaturally swift feint. The Tribe vampire's light hair was worn in a long braid that hung down his back and swayed as he moved, silver in the moonlight.

Colin grabbed the thick braid and used it to haul the Tribe Prime away from Mia. The Tribe spun around, showing a mocking grin, and fangs bared in challenge. When the other Prime grabbed his braid and tugged, Colin let it go.

"Run!" he called to Mia, and barreled forward to grab the Tribe around the waist and forcibly haul him through a narrow gap in the hedge.

The Tribe fought his way out of Colin's grasp, deeply clawing Colin's arms to do so.

"Scared to fight in front of a girl?" the Tribe asked when they faced each other again.

Colin's own claws and fangs were out by now. He sneered, and gestured the white-haired vampire forward.

The Tribe laughed, and they crouched and circled, taking

on the ritual movements of two Primes fighting over possession of a female. Fangs and claws flashed, bodies moved at
lightning speed. Blows were struck and avoided. The object
was to draw blood.

On the other side of the hedge, Mia shouted, "What's going
on? I'm calling the cops!"

Why hadn't the fool woman run?

"I am the cops!" Colin yelled back.

"What the— Colin, is that you?"

"She doesn't sound happy to see you," the Tribe sneered.

The mockery infuriated Colin, but he didn't let it distract
him. He lunged forward, and this time he got under the other
vampire's guard. Colin's claws raked across the Tribe's smirking face, leaving four thin lines of blood across his cheek.

The Prime howled and leaped away. He disappeared into the
waning night within moments, though cold laughter echoed
back out of the darkness. Tribe Primes weren't known for their
honor, but this one seemed to abide by the rules of mating challenge, accepting defeat at the loss of first blood.

Colin's first impulse was to howl in victory and take possession of his prize—who was on the other side of the bushes.
The emotions emanating from her were anything but simper-
ing delight in having been defended by a champion Prime of
Clan Reynard. He'd made the decision that she would never
know about vampires when they first met, and he fought off
the impulse to change his mind now.

Colin closed his eyes and took a few moments to calm
down. He shook from adrenaline and need, but he balled his
fists and wouldn't move. His body screamed at him that he
was crazy—she was so very close—he should drag her down
on the grass and take her!

"Colin!"

"Go!" he shouted.

Mia stuck her head through the gap in the hedge, framing
her face in hibiscus blossoms. "What are you doing here?"

He'd managed to draw in his fangs and claws just in time. He slapped his mental shields in place, not wanting to give in to what he felt. He didn't want to know what she felt, either, not in the vivid way of his kind.

He stepped forward, relentlessly making her move backward until they were both back on the sidewalk. He could sense the racing of her heart.

He put a hand on her arm. As dangerous as it was to touch her, he kept hold of her and made her walk with him toward her house. "I told you to get out of here, Luchese."

"What are you doing here, Foxe?" she repeated.

"Saving your ass—as usual."

"I was doing fine before you showed up."

"I've heard that before."

"You're the one who could have been—"

"Could have been what?" he demanded when she bit off her words.

She shook her head. "Shouldn't you be chasing the bad guy?" she countered. "Officer."

"I will, after I escort you home. Ma'am."

"That isn't necessary."

"No. But I think I left some CDs at your place," he offered as an excuse. "I stopped by to see if you had them."

"Anything you might have left, I burned, or used as target practice."

"That's fair enough."

Colin glanced at the sky as they walked. Dawn wasn't that far off. Most Tribe Primes made a point of perverse pride in not taking the daylight drugs that allowed Primes like Colin to emulate mortal existence. Mia would be safe from dawn until dusk. And by nightfall, Colin would have tracked down the Tribe scum who had dared to try to touch her. He'd have to inform the local Matri and elders right away that at least one Tribe was playing the old games in Clan territory; then he could get on with his own hunt.

He would not love this woman, but he would protect her.

It was his fault the Tribe Prime had chosen her as a victim. Though Colin hadn't shared his blood with Mia, they had shared an intense physical relationship. Though she wasn't aware of it, Mia was psychic, and they had sometimes touched on that level, as well. The residue of that sharing was what kept Colin coming back over and over, while he waited for the connection to fade.

That residue must also have been sensed by the Tribe Prime. In the old days, when the Clans, Families, and Tribes fought one another, the Tribes counted coup by stealing mortal lovers from Clan or Family enemies. The world was supposedly a safer and more peaceful place for vampires these days, but the Tribes were still vicious, unpredictable bastards.

And it was going to be a pleasure to kill the one who'd attacked Mia.

Mia drew more in on herself with each step, her silence stubborn and angry. She would not glance his way. She suffered his touch, but tried to pretend he wasn't even there. She certainly didn't want him there.

He deliberately didn't talk about the attack. She hadn't mentioned any details about it, and if she'd seen anything as outrageous as fangs or glowing eyes, she'd likely put it down to her imagination or stage makeup. After all, this was Hollywood, where anything was possible. And no sane person believed that vampires really existed.

When they reached her gate, he let her go, though the gesture automatically turned into a caress down the length of her arm. He was too aware of her shiver, and the way her skin heated at his touch. His own breath caught as desire curled through him. They both took a quick step back. His fingers slowly reached to touch her cheek without conscious volition, but at the last moment, she turned her head away.

"Go away," she said, voice tight and barely audible. "Just go away."

It hurt to hear the words, far more than he thought it could. But he could do nothing but obey her. After all, it was what he wanted, as well.

Mia couldn't breathe for a few moments because of the tears that choked her throat.

How dare the gorgeous bastard show up and save her life again?

She fumbled at the latch, and nearly fell through to the other side when it opened. She slammed it behind her as hard as she could. The wrought-iron gate shrieked on its hinges, and bounced back to hit her on the wrist.

She welcomed the sharp pain. It helped clear her head of everything but the memory of his touch, the cocky confidence in the way he moved, the dark red hair that framed his angular face, the heavy arch of eyebrows over the darkest eyes in the world, the way she missed his body covering hers, the sound of his voice, the heat of his kisses.

The way he'd left her for no reason at all.

She swore, and clutched the aching wrist in her other hand. "Have to ice this," she murmured. She went into the house, and made herself think of more important things than Colin Foxe.

Vampires, for example.

Vampires were far more important to someone of her ancestry than obsessing over a callous, uncaring, total jerk like Foxe.

Still, whatever his faults, Colin was a human, and she was glad the vampire hadn't hurt him. No human deserved to be attacked by a vampire.

It *had* been a vampire that attacked her, she had no doubt. The pale-haired monster had been a thing of unearthly beauty, looking rather like Legolas gone bad. It had smiled at her, showing long, bright fangs. It had been overwhelmingly male, and utterly repellent.

My species, right or wrong, she thought, going into the kitchen.

She'd known vampires existed all of her life, but she hadn't known if she'd come into contact with them. Her mother's family had been vampire hunters for hundreds of years, and passed the knowledge down from generation to generation. But nobody in the Garrison family had actually hunted vampires for a long time. Nobody had staked a vampire's heart, or cut off its head, since her grandmother's grandparents, she thought. Mia wasn't even sure how accurate anything her grandmother had told her was. She'd read some old records and family diaries, stuff that made the exploits in *Dracula* seem asinine. But the glory days were gone. Apparently there was some kind of truce in effect with the monsters, and most of the hunter families had gotten out of the business of protecting humankind.

But Mia believed the family legends, and the records. She had made a promise to her grandmother on the old woman's deathbed, a promise to prepare herself in case one day the truce was broken. She'd kept herself strong; learned how to defend herself. She'd done everything she could on a physical level, but nobody had taught her *how* to hunt vampires. She'd been hopelessly outclassed in fighting the monster.

She wished she knew how Colin had driven the creature off. She was also thankful that Colin hadn't noticed the monster's otherness. Maybe you needed vampire hunter genes to see them for the monsters they really were.

There was so much she didn't know.

Like how the vampire had found out that there was a hunter, albeit a very untried one, in Los Angeles. However, he'd done it—found her he had. The truce was broken. She had to fight.

She knew that crosses didn't work, but that garlic did. And silver. She'd inherited a silver necklace from her grandmother. It was a wide, flat chain with an intricate locking clasp, which fitted snugly around her neck. It was heavy, hard to fasten with her sore hand, and Mia had never been one for wearing jewelry—but if she didn't want to get bitten in the neck by a vampire, this necklace would probably help.

Probably.

That was the annoying part, knowing what *might* work rather than exactly what *would* work. By tradition, knowledge of vampire hunting was passed on orally. She had a few documents to draw on only because somebody in the last generation of real hunters in the Garrison family had decided to leave a few obscure, almost coded clues, just in case.

Sitting alone in her kitchen, pressing an ice pack to the wrist she'd bruised, and nursing a broken heart, Mia realized she was woefully unprepared. And it scared her to death.

It was after dawn when she remembered that her grandmother had left her a bank safety deposit box. Maybe there was something hidden in the box that would help her. All she had to do now was remember where she'd put the key, and wait impatiently for the bank to open.

Chapter Three

"Good evening, Lady Serisa." Colin tried not to let his impatience show as he stood at the door of the Matri's Brentwood home. "I need to speak with you."

"And I need to talk to you." The diminutive Matri reached up and tapped him on the forehead with a long, brightly painted fingernail. "Where have you been, boy?"

Being called *boy* didn't suit his Prime's pride. He glared at Serisa, so annoyed that he momentarily forgot the urgency of his mission.

"In case you haven't noticed, we are a telepathic species," she went on tartly. "I may not be *your* Clan Matri, but when I call, you answer."

Colin had been vaguely aware of a nagging voice in the back of his mind, urging him to seek out his own kind, but he hadn't equated it with an actual summons. He hadn't been thinking about vampires lately. He'd been far too occupied with a human woman.

"I have an answering machine," he told Serisa. "And a cell phone and pager on me at all times. You could have called any of my numbers."

"I'm a traditionalist," was her response. "Our secrets are not for sharing in such public ways." She stepped back from the doorway. "Come in."

Colin silently followed the Matri through the house.

The place was large, but in the way of a mansion rather than a Clan Citadel; the tasteful decor showed no evidence that this was the dwelling of a vampire queen. Members of almost all the vampire clans lived in the Los Angeles area, but this was the home territory of the Shagal, led by Matri Serisa and her bondmate, Elder Barak. She was one of the few Matris who chose to live in a crowded human city. His own clan's stronghold was in northern Idaho, which Colin thought was a far more sensible place for the breeding-age females of the Reynards to be hidden away. Though since Serisa was too old to give her clan children, he supposed it didn't matter where she lived.

He really only wanted to give the local Matri his information and leave. He wished he'd called, sent an e-mail, or even used telepathy, when he saw the group gathered in the room where Serisa led him. Apparently he'd interrupted a meeting of the serious, sober, responsible members of the community. Now he was going to have to face all of them.

Boring.

The room was large and windowless, somewhere in the center of the house. There was only one exit, and Serisa lingered in the doorway after she ushered Colin inside. Elder Barak was standing on one side of the room, talking quietly with three other grave elders. They all gave him serious consideration when he stepped into the room.

Colin was relieved to see that Anthony Crowe, from Clan Corvus, was seated in a pale leather chair on the other side of the room. Next to him on a matching couch was Colin's cousin, Alec Reynard, and Alec's bondmate, Domini.

Colin couldn't help but smile at the beautiful, dark-haired female. This drew an automatic frown from Alec, and he put an arm around his bondmate's shoulder.

"Stop it, you two," Domini said, though she leaned into her bondmate's embrace. "Hi, Colin," she added. "You cut your hair."

"You're not supposed to notice details about any Prime but me," Alec said.

Still smiling, Colin sidled closer to this younger group.

"How have you been, kid?" Tony asked. "Haven't seen you around lately."

Colin shrugged. "The team's been busy."

Tony Crowe was retired from the Los Angeles police force. He brightened with interest at Colin's mention of his SWAT team.

"No one is here on a social call," Serisa said, drawing Colin's attention back to her.

"You're usually more fun than this, Aunt Serisa," Tony said. "You could offer the kid a beer."

"I am not pleased with Colin's absence," she answered. "You made a vow," she reminded him. "Remember?"

Her sarcasm stung his pride. "Of course I remember. I can't fulfill a promise if I have nothing to go on."

"How would you know if there was any new information about the Patron if you don't check in with your elders? We haven't had any real contact with you for the last three months."

"That's not true!"

Was it? He'd gone to Arizona to help destroy a lab experimenting on vampires, right after breaking up with Mia. He'd reported on the situation when he got back, then . . .

Colin looked helplessly to Alec. "It hasn't been—"

"Cut the young Prime some slack, Auntie," Alec defended him. "His job fulfills his vow to look after mortals."

"That is not the vow my lady is referring to," Barak spoke up.

"Never mind your work with the police, Colin Foxe," Serisa scolded. "I know what's distracted you. I can feel it whenever I try to touch your thoughts. You've been having sex with a different mortal every night, haven't you?"

"That is what Primes do," Tony pointed out with an unabashed grin.

Mention of mortal women reminded Colin sharply of why he'd come to the Matri. He put aside a sudden rush of dread for Mia and said, "I stopped a Tribe Prime from attacking a human tonight."

Attention focused on him with the intensity of a circle of spotlights, but everyone waited for Serisa to speak.

"Tell me exactly what happened."

At least she hadn't outright dismissed that he'd encountered a Tribe member in her territory. He'd half-expected to be treated like a kid who made up stories.

"This was my fault," Colin began. "That the mortal was targeted." He'd rehearsed what to say on the way over, but they just kept looking at him, which made it harder to explain coherently. He scratched a sudden itch over his left eyebrow. "I made the mistake of having a long-term relationship with this woman."

"Mistake?" Domini questioned.

"What's *your* definition of long-term?" Tony added. "Two nights?"

"Details, Colin." Serisa's command cut across their sarcasm.

"We were together for three months," Colin answered the Corvus Prime. "Which was long enough for a Tribe bastard to target her for one of their sick games. If I hadn't been in the neighborhood when he attacked her, she'd be wearing his brand by now."

Fury ate at Colin when he thought of how Mia would have been used by the Tribe vampire. But being furious was no way to deliver a report. His police training helped him pull away from personal involvement and see the bigger picture.

"Tribe activity is a threat to mortals and our kind. Fortunately, I was in the neighborhood when the woman was attacked, so we're aware that they're in Clan territory. We can only hope this was the first attack. Now that we know at least one of them is in town, we can concentrate on finding him. Of course, it's likely that he's only one of a pack. I can check out missing persons and assault reports for anomalies that could point to Tribe activity."

"There are psychic ways of tracking," Serisa reminded him.

Colin nodded. "But it doesn't hurt to use every method

available to us. The sooner we find him, the safer Mia will be."
Colin was appalled at what he'd said, and quickly corrected
himself. "The safer all the mortals in the area will be."

"Mia's your girlfriend, right?" Domini asked.

"No," Colin snapped. "We broke up."

"Then why were you with her when this Tribe boy showed
up?" Tony asked.

"I told you, it was just a coincidence. I think we need to
focus on the fact that a mortal was attacked by a vampire
tonight."

"And why aren't you protecting this mortal now, by calling
the incident in?" Tony asked.

Tony wasn't on the force now, but he'd been a cop for a
very long time, only leaving after decades of service when he
couldn't stand wearing facial prosthetics and makeup to make
him look older anymore. He might be retired and working as
a private investigator, but he still thought and acted like a cop.

Colin didn't want to admit that Mia didn't want his protection. "I plan on heading back there." He looked at Serisa.
"Some things you don't phone in."

"You were right to come here," Serisa said. "We will look
into the matter." She looked at Alec and Domini. "See that the
woman is safe."

The pair of professional bodyguards said, "Yes, Matri."

"Anthony. Find where the Tribe pack is hiding."

Tony stood. "Yes, Matri."

She turned to her longtime bondmate. "Barak will organize
a plan of attack."

"Wait a minute!" Colin spoke up. "She's my— You can't—
I—"

"You say you are not attached to this woman," Serisa pointed
out. "So the threat to her is not your personal concern."

"But—the Tribe's fight was with me. For her."

"You drove him off, but I don't see the woman at your side.
You have other work."

The look Serisa gave him assured Colin that no argument was going to change her mind about where his duty lay. And it finally occurred to him that she'd wanted to see him because there was finally a breakthrough in the hunt for the Patron.

He was not at all pleased at the thought of leaving Mia's welfare in anyone else's hands, but he was Clan Prime. Duty came first. He straightened his shoulders and kept his temper under control. "What do you want me to do, Matri?"

Laurent of the Manticore had one thing that most Tribe vampires didn't possess: a sense of humor. He didn't know where he'd gotten it, or how, but he knew it was damned inconvenient. As a survival tool, it was totally useless.

"I like to think of it as a rather puckish sense of fun," he said to no one in particular as he stood waiting for Justinian's attention to turn his way. He was standing ankle-deep in plush Persian carpet in a windowless bedroom lit only by a few thick red candles. Justinian was currently occupied behind the velvet curtains of the large bed that was the centerpiece of the room. Though there were a half dozen Primes waiting for the pack leader's attention, the only sound was the panting and groaning coming from the girl the king Prime was currently boning. Laurent found the whole situation faintly embarrassing. He also had a hard time refraining from smirking at the melodramatic setting.

That was one of the problems with the Tribes: they took their brand of evil far too seriously. Their sensibilities were anything but postmodern, or even retro camp. It seemed to Laurent that even people who acted like they still lived in the twelfth century ought to acknowledge that they were actually dwelling in the twenty-first. Instead of belonging to the Society for Creative Anachronisms, his dear Tribe *were* anachronisms.

Well, it worked for them. And they were all he had— though he half regretted being called back into the bosom of Tribe Manticore, after so many years on his own.

"Do you find us boring, Laurent?"

Laurent did a good job of hiding his surprise when Justinian suddenly appeared, standing outside the bed curtains. Though he went stiff with an old, familiar fear, he managed to shrug.

"I haven't been back quite long enough to be bored," he answered Justinian. But he didn't meet the pack leader's eyes when he spoke.

The woman in the bed moaned. Laurent was aware of the hunger that stirred among some of the other Primes, but he kept his own urges under control. And his amusement to himself, when Justinian swept a warning gaze across his followers and the testosterone level dropped like a rock.

His feelings weren't hidden from Justinian. "Our Laurent doesn't play pack games." He took a black satin robe from an obsequious mortal servant and tied it on as the mortal quickly bowed his way back into the shadows.

Belisarius, senior among the pack Primes, said, "Laurent doesn't have the balls to hunger for a woman. Not that we'd challenge you," he added with quick deference to Justinian. The other Primes directed derisive laughter at Laurent.

"Do you have balls?" Justinian asked him.

"I do believe I have," Laurent answered. "Now, ask me about what happened tonight, so we can get on with business."

"I take it you didn't bring back the woman."

"He ordered you to do one small thing—" Belisarius began, but Justinian held up a hand to silence him.

"But there were complications."

It wasn't a question. At least Justinian didn't question his competence.

"There was a Clan Prime guarding the woman," Laurent reported. "I thought you'd want to know. I could have just killed him and brought the Garrison woman to you, but that wouldn't get us an explanation about the Clans' involvement with our rightful prey."

"*My* rightful prey," Justinian corrected.

"You should have brought her here," Belisarius said. "To tell us whatever she knows."

"And have the gallant Clan Primes come running to the rescue?" Laurent looked to Justinian. "You told me this was strictly a matter of justified revenge. Is that true?"

"It's not your place to ask questions," Justinian reminded him.

Laurent remembered how he hated that deceptively mild tone, and how dangerous Justinian was when he used it. "Apologies," he said, and bowed his head.

Justinian let a few tense seconds pass before he spoke. "You were correct not to bring the mortal here. Watch her, Laurent. We'll let her think she's free, while we discover her connection to the Clans."

Chapter Four

Three days later

"Would you like another iced tea?"

Mia looked away from the airplane window at the flight attendant's question. "No, thank you. How soon until we land?"

"About half an hour," the woman answered.

She smiled hopefully, but when Mia didn't request anything else, she moved to the back of the plane. Mia was the only passenger on the small jet flying back to Los Angeles from Colorado, and she wasn't making much work for the staff on her great-grandfather's jet.

The fact that her great-grandfather had a private airplane, and that he'd put it at her disposal, was still pretty shocking. Yes, she'd known he was very rich, but being exposed to the rarefied atmosphere where the super wealthy dwelled made her breathless.

She'd expected the telephone number her grandmother had left her would put her in immediate contact with her great-grandfather, but it hadn't worked out that way. The number belonged to a law firm. She'd used the code phrase that went along with the number, which got a very complicated ball rolling.

Getting to see her elderly relative face to face had taken her through several layers of flunkies; men in more and more expensive offices and suits; men with blanker and blanker faces and blander voices.

Finally, a rough old voice on a speaker phone in the fanciest office of all had ordered the expensive lawyer out.

When she was alone, the old man said, "What do you want?"

It turned out to be very hard to say the words. What if she was making a complete fool of herself? What if it was all myth after all? What if what had attacked her hadn't been—what she thought? What if this wasn't actually Henry Garrison?

But she took a deep breath and said, "I want to know how to hunt vampires."

"Why?" was the gruff reply.

"Somebody has to," was the only answer she could think of.

"For the sake of family tradition? Or is it more personal?"

She thought for a moment before she said, "Both, I guess. I was attacked by a vampire, and I—"

"You've had actual contact with one? Did it take your blood?"

"Yes. No. I—"

"Do you know where it is?"

"Somewhere in Los Angeles."

"That's a lot of territory to cover."

"I know. That's why I need your help. I'm willing to hunt it, but I need to know how."

A soft cackle of laughter issued from the speaker. Then the old man was silent for a while. "All right," he said at last. "I'll show you."

After that she'd been whisked off in a succession of limousines and airplanes, and finally into an SUV that took her up a mountain road to a mansion in the center of a walled compound. Once inside this luxurious fortress, she'd finally come face to face with the last vampire hunter in the family.

Her great-grandfather was not a rush-up-and-give-him-a-big-hug-and-call-him-Grandpa kind of person, but Mia hadn't expected him to be. What she hadn't expected him to be was—kind of creepy. The time she'd spent with him had been instructive, but it hadn't been particularly pleasant. In fact, he spent more time hunched over a laptop working on financial dealings than actually looking at her when they were together. The man was cold, abrupt, and there was a—hunger—in him for vampires.

The fact that he wanted her to bring him a live one freaked her at first.

But his explanation made sense. He reminded her that vampire hunting was almost a dead art. Times had changed, and it would be intelligent to find out what sorts of modern weaponry worked on the monsters.

When he first brought the subject up, Mia was outraged at the idea of experimenting on a living creature. But her great-grandfather pointed out that that was exactly what vampires were—creatures, monsters, parasites.

The Enemy.

She'd signed on to fight a war. There couldn't be any room for mercy when fighting the forces of evil.

That sounds so melodramatic.

Yet it was true. And she had promised to capture a vampire and bring it to her great-grandfather. He'd provided her with drugs that he promised rendered the monsters helpless.

She'd figure out something. And she'd have to do it alone. Even with her new knowledge, Mia still felt unprepared for the challenge.

Oh, no, you don't, Caramia Luchese. I am as tough as nails, and I can do this.

Only it would be so much better if she didn't have to do it by herself. Her great-grandfather had promised her help in transporting the vampire once she'd caught it, but insisted that the capture was her duty alone.

She didn't get it.

Maybe it was some sort of hunter tradition of going mano a mano against the forces of evil. Though if that was the way it was done, it was no wonder the hunter families had died out or gotten out of the business.

Maybe it was a test.

Maybe if she brought her great-grandfather the vampire, he would provide her with more information and resources. Well, she needed his help, so she'd do it his way for now.

She just wished she could tell someone. Unreasonably, stupidly, the one person she wanted to tell was Colin Foxe.

I can't trust him on an emotional level—but damn, the man can kick ass.

Damn, but the man also *had* a fine ass.

Mia ran a hand through her short curls and wondered where that thought had come from. Probably because he'd shown up the other night and—she hated to admit it—saved *her* ass. She'd had a primal reaction to it then that she'd managed to cover with anger, but the effects still lingered. Only pride had kept her from dragging him down on the ground and giving herself to him. She'd felt his excitement after the fight, knew the cockiness he got from the victory. The sex would have been hard, fast, and sweet.

She closed her eyes and tasted the man's kisses, felt his hands on her. The memories alone were enough to stir instant, aching heat.

She had good reasons to hate the man, but he made a hell of a sex toy.

Which was another reason not to bring him into this. She couldn't afford emotional involvement—not lust, not hate. It wouldn't be good for her edge, or his. Besides, how could she get him to believe in vampires? He'd scoff until one was sucking the life out of him.

This thought brought up lovely images of her rescuing him, his gratitude, and her cheerfully rebuffing the gorgeous bastard.

"We'll be landing in a few moments."

The flight attendant's voice brought Mia out of her reverie. This is not a game, she reminded herself as she checked to make sure her seatbelt was fastened.

*   *   *

"What do you mean, you can't guard her if you can't find her?" Colin demanded of his cousin over the cellular phone. "Why can't you find her?" Why had he left Mia's welfare to anyone else?

He stepped out of the small office building of the Van Trier Executive Airport with his phone pressed to his ear, and sudden anger bursting inside him. Even though the sun was setting, he automatically put on sunglasses. His gaze was drawn across the parking lot toward a small jet making a landing on one of the airport's two runways. He put a finger in his left ear to block out the engine noise.

Alec Reynard's voice sounded far too cheerful when he answered. "The best we can figure is that your girlfriend left home voluntarily."

"She's not my girlfriend. And how do you figure that?" Colin shouted over the roar of airport noise.

"Domini and I broke into her house. There was no scent or sign of any vampire having been in the place but you. There was a string of garlic on the back door, so maybe she suspects vampires exist."

"She's Italian," Colin answered, "and she likes to cook. The back door's in the kitchen."

"That's what Domini suggested. You've spent a lot of time over there, have you?"

"You don't believe the girl's in danger, do you?"

"I haven't found any evidence of her being involved with our kind, except for you calling me every hour."

This was only the second time Colin had inquired about Mia, as he hadn't had the time, but he let it go. He didn't know why Alec was needling him and not taking the situation seriously. "Has Tony found—"

"He found and lost the trail of the one you fought, but no evidence of a pack operating in the area yet. Let's hope it was a lone Prime passing through who decided to have a little fun with you."

It would be a relief to think that the Tribe was long out of town. "Tony's still checking, though, right?"

"Of course. And how's your assignment coming along?"

"Slowly," Colin answered. "My team spent most of the last few days on that bank robbery situation that was all over the news. Then we had to do a debrief, and a training sim to see how we could handle it better."

The rest of his team had gone home wrung out and ragged. Colin wasn't tired the way his mortal teammates were, but he was glad for the days off they'd been given. For some reason, he'd found that he was slightly envious of the wives and families the rest of the team had to go home to.

"Now I finally have some time off to work on the Patron info I'm supposed to check out."

"And?" Alec prompted.

"I'm at the airport now. I persuaded a beautiful young woman to look through all the confidential client files, but it's going to take her a while."

"Do you think you've finally run down a lead on this Patron?"

Impatience clawed at Colin. When he'd helped shut down the Patron's immortality research facility in Arizona, he and the others had made their escape on a stolen Gulfstream jet. Tracing the ownership information of the airplane should have quickly led to the identity of the Patron.

Instead it had led to plowing slowly through layers and layers of financial camouflage. The man hid his identity well. After all this time, they still didn't know who the plane belonged to, but some maintenance records had finally been tracked down. That paper trail led to this small, private airport. Now all Colin could do was wait while the mortal female he'd flirted with and hypnotized into helping him looked through confidential files.

He tried to put his mind on how good-looking the office worker was, to stop thinking about Mia, but heard himself say, "Why couldn't the woman stay home so she can be protected?"

"Maybe the woman thinks she can take care of herself," Reynard said.

Colin had forgotten that he was on the phone. "Mortals need taking care of, especially females."

The wave of awareness hit him even before he stopped speaking. If Reynard answered, Colin didn't hear him. All he was aware of was Mia stepping off the plane that had just landed. He was waiting by the gate by the time she reached it. Her gaze was on the ground, a frown of concentration on her face.

"What are you doing here?" he asked.

Her head jerked up, and their gazes met. For a moment there was a light of welcome in her eyes that took Colin's breath away. He almost took her in his arms, but her expression changed to guarded suspicion that warned him to keep his distance.

"What are *you* doing here?" she questioned him.

"Business," was his answer. He moved to let her through the gate and kept pace with her as she walked across the parking lot. "Where have you been?"

"Out of town."

"I know. Why?"

She stopped, and glared at him. "How did you know? Why do you want to know?"

"You were attacked. I wanted to make sure you were safe."

"So you tracked me down here?"

"No. I told you I'm on business."

She took a deep breath, and Colin felt her pull her emotions in and get herself under control. "Thank you for your concern, Officer Foxe."

If she could attempt to be reasonable, so could he. He put his hand on her arm. He was aware of the muscles beneath the warm softness of her skin. That was Mia, steel and velvet. She trembled ever so slightly at his touch, wanting him, and fighting that wanting. He felt the same way. The need was always instant between them.

"Come on, let me drive you home."

She didn't answer, but she did let him lead her toward his car.

But as they passed the small airport office, the office manager stepped out of the doorway. "Officer Foxe!" she called, and hurried up to him.

Standing too close to him, she tilted her head provocatively and said, "I found those records you asked for." She smiled, and the look she gave him was both pleased and hopeful.

Mia stiffened, emotions going cold as ice, and stepped away from Colin. "I have a ride."

Colin moved toward Mia, but the other woman put herself between them. She touched his shoulder. "Come into my office, and I'll show you what I've found."

Damn! Damn! Damn! The woman was beautiful, and he had come on to her. But he hadn't expected Mia to be here!

Now Mia was walking away, and she was likely reminding herself that he'd broken up with her because he'd told her he wasn't interested in being involved with only one woman. Which was the truth, but he still felt as if he'd somehow been caught cheating on her.

Which didn't change the fact that he did need the information the woman had found for him. He'd stop by Mia's place later to check on her.

"Good work," he said, turning a smile on the waiting woman. He put his arm around her slender shoulders, turning her back toward the building. "Let's have a look at what you've found."

Chapter Five

$\mathcal{L}$aurent slept with women. He drank their blood. He took their money. It was a good life. And most important, this low-key lifestyle let him live in choice territory claimed by the Clans without them being any the wiser. He'd been dwelling safely and happily in the warm California nights until his sire showed up with a pack of Primes and all their emotional baggage, and demanded Laurent do his bidding.

He wished he hadn't been lured back into the machinations of Tribe Manticore.

Being an exile had its advantages.

Besides, he only might be my sire. It's not likely he'll say so one way or the other. He uses the truth to keep me in line. If I'm a good little slave, someday he might tell me. Typical tribal behavior.

"But I'm only really in it for the money."

Justinian had said something about their finding out what the Clans knew about Laurent's quarry, but Laurent hadn't heard any news after two nights of hunting. And this was after he'd gone to the trouble of providing the pack with cell phones and teaching them how to use them—after convincing Justinian that this modern method of communicating was safer around Clan boys than using telepathy, since mental activity was more likely to be looked for.

He snorted, and concentrated on the area below his roof perch, where he had a clear view of the entrance of the building across the street. Tonight would be the night.

This was the third night he'd staked out the fitness center

where the Garrison woman worked out. This had seemed a safer place to wait for her than her house, where the Clan Prime might be lurking—waiting for Laurent. She was an exercise fanatic, and bound to show up sometime.

"And there she is," he murmured as he spotted the dark-haired young mortal turn the corner and come striding toward the glass doors of the gym. Energy, purpose, and righteous anger crackled through her aura like flashes of lightning.

It was too bad she was Justinian's prey, because Laurent would quite enjoy a taste of this gifted mortal woman. He shrugged. Maybe after the pack leader was done with her—not that she'd have much spirit left then.

He let himself fantasize while she went into the building. When she left the gym, he could follow her back to her car and take her there. It was a simple, neat plan.

And foiled within a few seconds when the Clan vampire he'd fought for her came walking around the same corner, and followed the woman into the fitness center.

Laurent drew all his mental shielding tightly around himself and kept his swearing silent and on the surface of his mind.

Why couldn't this go easily?

He sighed. After he was sure the Clan vampire had no awareness of him, Laurent took out his cellular telephone.

Maybe, just maybe, he could get someone in the Manticore pack to answer, and give him a little backup.

"Oh, for crying out loud, what are you doing here?" Mia demanded when Colin Foxe walked into the martial arts room.

Bare-chested, he wore a pair of loose-fitting gray sweatpants. There was no one else in this small area but the two of them, so she couldn't just ignore him in the crowd.

He smiled in that infuriatingly charming way of his, and his sultry dark eyes glinted beneath the heavy arch of his brows. "I have a membership."

"But you haven't been here since we broke up."

His smile widened. "You've noticed."

Mia was tempted to keep her claws out and continue snarling at the man, but what good would it do? It would only let him know that she still hurt. It wasn't likely that he was here to explain about the bimbo at the airport, or to apologize for his continuing existence. He certainly wasn't here to beg her to take him back. She knew she should wrap herself in pride and dignity and simply ignore his presence, but curiosity got the better of her.

"You followed me here, didn't you?"

"Yes."

"Because you're feeling protective, Officer Foxe?"

"Yep."

While she rather admired this trait in him, she wished he was feeling protective toward somebody else. "It was a random act of violence that you came upon by accident. Having done the Good Samaritan thing, you can go back to forgetting about me now."

"I take 'serve and protect' seriously."

"Which is about all you take seriously." Damn! There she went being bitter and sarcastic again. "Never mind my whining," she added. "It's late. I'm tired. I want to get in a workout and go home."

She'd wanted to go to bed the minute she got home, but a hunter needed to be disciplined. She hadn't expected Colin to be part of her workout regime.

Colin looked around the empty room and gestured her toward a mat. "Come on. Try to beat me up. You'll feel better."

"I don't want to *try*."

He laughed. "I know." His gaze flicked over her, all hot and arrogant. "You are so sexy when you're pissed off."

It was such a blatant come-on that Mia laughed. After three months of callous abandonment, he thought that she still couldn't resist him.

"You are so—"

"A pig. I know." He spun around and did a backflip onto the sparring mat. He was lithe, lean, wiry as Jet Li.

"I'm impressed," she told him.

Mia crossed to a punching bag set up on a heavy floor stand and proceeded to take out her aggression with some kickboxing moves. She could feel him watching her, which made her clumsy. Which did nothing for her temper. She was *used* to practicing with a group. She'd been doing this for ye—

"You don't look like you've been doing this for years."

She turned in puzzlement at Colin's sarcastic comment. He was closer than she thought, and he lunged toward her. Though she was off balance, Mia reacted to defend herself.

For the next few minutes they punched, blocked, feinted, and kicked their way around the practice room. There was nothing formal about what they did; it was the closest thing to street fighting Mia'd ever experienced.

It was intense, exciting, punctuated by adrenaline and rising lust.

Becoming aware of where this dance was leading, Mia came to a stop. She put up her hands, and Colin backed away. He looked bright and fresh, like he could go on like this all night. She was sweaty and breathing hard.

"You did good," he told her. He bounced on the balls of his feet, grinning. "More?"

It was tempting to continue going at it with Colin, but she knew that come-and-get-me look in his eyes was also an I'm-gonna-have-you promise. And she wanted him, just like she always wanted him, especially at times like this when his hands had been on her, and hers on him. She wanted at the same time to hurt him and to fall on the mat with him and go at it like bunnies.

So for his safety, and her self-respect, Mia said, "No."

He tilted his head to one side, and looked up from under dark, thick eyelashes. "You sure?"

Now he was being cute. She didn't need that. She picked

up a towel and wiped off her face. "I need a shower. And don't take that as an invitation to join me."

"Is sex all you think about?"

She couldn't help but laugh. "That's my line."

He gave a slight shrug. "You know how I like variety. And I've never done it in the girls' locker room."

Mia didn't say anything else, and when she left the work-out room, he didn't follow her, yet she could feel his attention focused tightly on her. She was aware of his straining not to come after her, and she knew he was aware of her fight to keep from going back to him. It was a victory that she made it out to the hall and down the stairs.

She hoped he wouldn't be waiting for her after she took a long, hot shower and then lingered in the locker room for a long talk with a friend. But Colin was waiting by the entrance when she came upstairs, his back to her. He was facing the wide glass doors, talking on his cell phone. There was no way out of the building but past him.

She heard him say, "Thanks, Dom." Then he turned around, smiling at her, the phone already off and tucked away.

She didn't know what to make of this man who had left her suddenly getting so clingy. "I'm fine," she insisted, waving him toward the door. "Go home."

"Right," he said, taking her by the arm. "Let's go home. I'll drive."

"My car's in the lot."

"I know. Mine's parked next to it. I'll drive."

"Oh, for crying out—"

"What were you doing at the airport?" he asked as he ushered her outside.

The fitness center was open twenty-four/seven, and it was late. There was little traffic on the street, and no one on the side-walk but the two of them. This privacy, and the intimacy of his hand on her arm, disturbed Mia greatly. It depressed her, as well. Even his solicitousness was depressing.

It seemed like Colin was always taking her home. To *her* home, never his. She really knew very little about him, except that he loved being the knight in shining Kevlar, and was great in bed. And that he *couldn't be tied down by one woman.*

"If I answer your question, will you answer one for me, for once?"

"I told you I was on business," he anticipated her question. "That woman didn't mean anything to me."

Mia chuckled. "What you do with other women is not my business," she reminded him.

"You were jealous."

"I was annoyed at myself."

"For being jealous."

"What is the matter with you?" she demanded. "I'm trying to be civil, but you keep—coming on to me."

"Sorry," he said, and let go of her. "Is that better?"

She nodded, though she could still feel the possessive warmth of his touch on her skin.

"Now, where have you been? What were you doing at the airport?"

She didn't know why he sounded suspicious. Maybe just because he was a cop.

"I was out of town doing research." It was more or less the truth; let Colin think it was research for a story. "And caught a ride home on a private plane. My turn?"

They turned the corner and walked uphill toward the three-story parking garage at the end of the block. An alley cut between the fitness center building and the garage. The streetlights were spaced farther apart on this side street, and the one nearest the parking lot was out. There was suddenly something very still and spooky about the darkness.

Fighting off primitive uneasiness, Mia said, "I heard about a bank robbery that SWAT was called in on, while I was in the locker room."

Her friend had said, "The news said that a sharpshooter took out two of the robbers. Was that your boyfriend?"

"Were you the shooter?" Mia asked Colin. She felt him tense.

"It was me."

She stopped and turned to face him, putting a hand on his arm. "Are you okay?"

He nodded.

Colin stared at the mortal woman. Just when he thought she was going to rag on him some more about their breakup, she started worrying about him. Every time he convinced himself that his fascination with her was purely sexual, she did something that rattled him.

"I'm fine," he told her, too aware of her touch, too aware of her compassion. "I'm bloodthirsty, remember?" There was no way a mortal woman could understand and accept this literal truth the way a vampire female would.

"Good," she said, growing suddenly tense. She looked around very slowly and carefully, and whispered, "I think bloodthirsty is about to come in handy."

He became aware of the threat a moment before she spoke.

Mia no doubt saw shadows moving toward them, two out of the alley up ahead, and another pair from around the corner behind them.

What he noticed before seeing any shapes was dark mental energy, the malevolent psychic signature of Tribe vampires. They'd dropped their shielding as one, wanting him to know they were there. The intensity of their regard sent a stab of pain through his head.

"Games," he said, and smiled grimly. His blood suddenly sang with the joy of the hunt. "I like games."

"Colin, I think—"

"Don't think. Go on instinct."

She took something out of her gym bag. If it was a gun it wasn't going to do any good, but he didn't tell her so.

"Parking lot," he said. Grabbing her around the waist, he picked her up and ran,

Chapter Six

$\mathcal{M}$ia might have protested being carried like a child, if she wasn't so shocked at Colin's speed and agility. It seemed like it only took him a few steps to reach and dart around the two vampires in the alley. She caught the flash of fangs and glowing eyes as they passed, and brought her hand up enough to squeeze off a blast of aerosol into the vampire's face.

When his only reaction was a sputtered cough and a slight turning of his head, she realized she'd pulled out a canister of pepper spray instead of the garlic mixture she'd reached for. But at least it took the monster's attention away from Colin for a moment.

As Colin sprinted ahead, she could hear the footsteps of the two from the street pounding up to join the ones from the alley.

Somebody yelled, "This is no way to run an ambush. I told you to wait!"

"You don't give orders, exile," an arrogant voice answered.

While the vampires behind them argued, Colin leaped over a ramp barrier and put her down on the other side. All the parking stalls on the ground floor were empty. Her breathing seemed to echo loudly in the vacant space. The garage wasn't well lit, and Colin dragged her farther into shadow behind a thick concrete pillar.

"Don't worry," he told her. "I've called for backup."

She had no idea when he could possibly have done that, but this was hardly the time to argue. "Those—men—" She tried to warn him, but she didn't know how. "Did you see their—"

"Great makeup. It's a cult. Don't worry about it."

He was right, there was no time to worry. "How do we get out of here?"

"Up," he said. He snatched her gym bag from her and dropped it on the ground. "Run," he ordered, and gave her a slight push.

Mia pelted up the curve of the parking ramp. The sooner she got to her car, the sooner she could get to the antivampire weapons stowed in the trunk.

She was aware of the pounding of her feet on the concrete, of the roar of her heart and her own breathing, but she didn't hear Colin behind her. Even a quick look back would slow her down, though, and she needed those weapons!

Besides, Colin was a dangerous man, and he could move silent as a cat.

She didn't look back even when she heard shouts, or the meaty sound of a blow. A few more steps, and she'd reached the second level, where her car was parked.

Damn it! Her keys were in the bag Colin had tossed aside.

She started to turn back, then felt air coldly caress her face as something flew past. The next moment, a vampire was standing in front of her. It was the pale-haired one who'd first come after her.

Mia came to a jarring halt, just in time to keep from running into the monster's widespread arms.

"We meet again," he said.

He was smug, smiling, and even in the semi-darkness she could see the obscenely long fangs protruding over his red lips. He held out a taloned hand.

"Come along, and nobody gets hurt," he told her.

"He's lying!" Colin shouted from below. "Don't let him touch you!"

"Don't listen to him," the vampire said. "You'll beg for my protection after he's dead."

She heard the sounds of fighting. Colin was outnumbered, surrounded. He needed help.

The vampire stepped toward her, and she backpedaled

quickly. Her impulse was to turn and run, but Mia couldn't bear to turn her back on the fanged creature.

"Enough of this," he said, and rushed toward her.

Mia dove sideways and flattened herself on the concrete.

A vehicle swerved into the parking lot below, crashing through the barrier, and then its bright headlights raked up the curving ramp ahead of the roaring engine. Mia watched in astonishment as two figures jumped out the back doors while the huge SUV was still moving. And suddenly Colin wasn't alone in fighting the vampires.

The car kept coming, as big as a tank, straight toward the blond vampire. He jumped just an instant before the SUV would have hit him, landed on the roof with a heavy thud of boots, then leaped again completely into thin air from the second story of the garage.

As he disappeared, the SUV came to a halt next to where Mia cowered against the ramp's inside wall. The driver opened the door and looked calmly down at Mia.

"Hi, I'm Domini. The guy with the beard down there is Tony. The one with the cleft chin is my Alec." The dark-haired woman got out and helped Mia to her feet. "Welcome to—" She put her arm out to stop Mia from running toward the fighting.

"Colin needs help!" Mia protested.

"Help's here," Domini said. "No need for us to interrupt the boys when they're fighting. You know how much they enjoy it."

The woman's cheerfulness and enigmatic words confused Mia further. "Who are you? What are you doing here? And thanks," she added, finally realizing that she'd been rescued from the vampires. Relief flooded her as she realized who the rescuers might be. "Are you hunt—"

Colin ran up to her before she could finish. The next thing she knew, she was wrapped in his tight embrace, and his mouth came down hard and fiercely on hers. All the fear and excitement in her shifted instantly to desire, and she responded just as hungrily. She lost herself to the need.

Until someone coughed loudly.

Domini said, "You guys want to use the back seat? Concrete can be so hard on the back."

"And the knees," one of the men added.

Someone else said, "There are alarms going off. We really ought to leave before the police—"

"The police are here," Colin said, lifting his head from hers.

"But this isn't the kind of rumble you want to report," one of the men said.

Mia was glad that Colin's arms were around her, because her knees were weak. She supposed she ought to be embarrassed by this visceral reaction to danger, but it felt so right to be alive and with Colin. Her body was full of lust, but she fought to focus her attention on the three newcomers. Domini, Tony, and Alec were all tall, dark-haired, attractive, and dressed in black.

"What happened to the—those—" While everyone stared at her, Mia finally remembered what Colin had called their attackers. "Cultists?" She couldn't bring herself to use the word *vampire* until she was sure of who their rescuers were. "Who are you?" she added.

"The cowards ran away when my backup showed." Colin gestured toward the one with the chin. "That's my cousin Alec, and his lady Domini. And that's her cousin—"

"Identifications have already been made," Domini interrupted him.

Tony gave her a charming smile. "You're Mia. I'm delighted. Let's go," he said to Colin.

Colin glared at Tony. "I thought you said there weren't any of them in town."

"I said I hadn't found any yet. Looks like they found you."

"Why?" Alec questioned.

"Has anyone asked the local hunters if they know anything?" Domini questioned. "Aren't they the ones who keep tabs on the bad guys?"

Tony made a sour face. "We don't communicate much with—them."

"Maybe we should. Look, I could—"

"No," Tony cut her off. "I said I'd find out about their being in town. I'll set up a meeting with the hunters—cranks and loons though they are."

The man didn't sound at all happy about it, but Mia was overjoyed to hear mention of local hunters. Chances were that Colin and his friends thought that vampires were some kind of nut cult. Tony clearly thought that those who hunted so-called vampires were also nuts, so this was no time to point out that vampires were real, and that she was a hunter.

Still, if this Tony could help her contact the local hunters . . .

"Come on," Colin said. He led her up the ramp. "Now I really am going to drive you home."

Chapter Seven

The only thing that seemed real in the whole surrealistic incident was Colin's kissing her. Mia's lips were still alive with the memory of it, and her body sparked with need.

But information was more important than need. Her world had changed so radically in the last few days, she didn't know what reality was anymore. Now it looked like even Colin had secrets connected with the dark underworld she'd so recently entered. She needed to know them without giving her own away.

"Colin, I—"

"Don't ask," he said.

Mia's hand was on his arm. He didn't think she was aware of touching him, but the contact sizzled all through him. She'd sat beside him on the drive, stunned and confused, and the hunger for each other buzzed silently between them. Now as he turned onto her street, she was growing curious, restless, wanting answers.

"Those people," she said. "Your relatives. What were they doing—"

"I shouldn't have introduced you."

What was wrong with him? How stupid was he? By all that was holy and sane in his world, he had no business giving information and the names of his kind to an outsider, a mortal.

"I told you I called for backup," he told her. "One of them is a retired cop. The other two—"

Damn! He was doing it again. When had it gotten so easy to spill his guts to this woman who was supposed to be a passing fancy?

"Forget about them," he said. "Your knowing about them isn't important. You won't see them again."

"Why not?" Mia asked. Her attitude stiffened with hurt and anger. "Aren't I good enough to meet your family?"

The question, and the pain she tried to hide, tore Colin in two opposite directions. He couldn't very well say, "No, not really," without hurting her further. He hadn't meant to drag her into his world, a place where she did not belong.

"What were they doing there?" she asked. "What do they—you—have to do with this so-called vampire cult?"

"I can't answer that."

He was going to have to make her forget it all, especially any reference to vampires. But the woman was both stubborn and psychic. It wasn't going to be easy to alter her memories.

"Won't answer, you mean."

"Yeah. Won't," he admitted. "I'm sorry you've gotten involved." He pulled into her driveway and turned off the engine.

He could tell his words weren't reassuring her. In fact, he felt her growing not only annoyed, but more suspicious by the moment.

"Why have you really been following me?" she demanded. "Why are you always around lately? I know you don't want anything to do with me, so there's an ulterior motive, isn't there? Are you using me as bait to draw these—cultists—out?"

"That's a good theory," he admitted. "But the farthest thing from the truth. All I want to do is help you."

Maybe he *had* sort of been stalking her, but he'd thought the only harm was to his own sanity. The results were proving dangerously unhealthy for her, though, as well as for his mental health.

"This is all my fault, Mia. I can't explain, and I know you don't think you have any reason to trust me. And you don't, not on a personal level. But I will get these nuts out of your life, and keep you safe. Then I'll go."

"Maybe I don't—"

Another car pulled in behind his. Was she going to tell him she didn't want him to stay, or that she didn't want him to go? He got out of his car and hurried toward the other vehicle.

Tony Crowe stepped out of Mia's car and tossed her gym bag and keys to Colin. "Thought the lady would like to have these."

Colin caught Mia's stuff and glanced behind him. Mia was standing in the driveway. It was his turn to toss the keys to her as she started toward them. "Go inside."

"I beg your—"

Go inside.

The telepathic order came not only from him but from Tony, as well. Though Tony did add *please* when he intruded into Mia's mind.

Go to bed, Colin said. *Sleep.*

Mia moved with slow reluctance, and kept glancing back toward them as she went toward the front door.

Colin glared at the other Prime when she was safely inside the house. "I don't need your help."

"Yeah. You do," Tony declared bluntly. "Remember Serisa's plan for this mortal? You aren't part of it. Alec, Domini, and I are supposed to protect the woman and find the Tribe pack. Your job is to take out the Patron. What were you doing with her tonight?"

"Protecting her," Colin answered. "Which was more than you were doing. I knew where to find her—"

"Which you should have told one of us."

"I want to protect her."

"Does she belong to you, then? Do you claim her?"

"Of course not!"

"Then do as you're told."

"Serisa of Shagal is not my Matri. She can make suggestions, but she does not rule me. I am Prime."

Tony shook his head. "Don't ask for trouble, kid. This mortal woman dwells in Shagal territory. By right, Serisa of

Shagal has jurisdiction over how all mortals in her territory are protected. Now, if you claim Mia Luchese and bring her into our world—"

"Don't be ridiculous."

"What's ridiculous about it? Mortal women are brought into the Clans all the time. If you want, I—"

Possessive fury warred with outrage, and the world went red around him. Colin lashed out at Tony without thinking.

The other Prime backed away before the blow could touch him and held his hands out in front of him. "Whoa! Calm down. This isn't the time or place for a couple of Primes to get into it."

"Are you challenging me?" Colin demanded. "For *her?*" Jealousy pounded through him, and he didn't care where or when, or with who he got into a fight with over Mia. "First the Tribe, and now you. What's so fascinating about my female, that everybody wants her?"

"I thought you didn't want her."

"I want her until I say otherwise," Colin declared.

"Kid, you are not making a bit of sense."

The worst part was, Colin knew he wasn't. And it was all because of Mia. Not that it was her fault, but . . .

"I am not a kid," he reminded Tony. "I am Prime."

"Yeah, yeah. You've been out of the nest for what, five, six years? Sometimes when Primes get the bonding call early, they go a little nuts."

"Bonding?" Cold fear ran up Colin's spine. "What the hell are you talking about?" he shouted at the older Prime.

"Are you trying to wake up the whole neighborhood?"

The sharp question from Tony brought Colin back to his senses. But before he could deny the accusation of bonding, the door opened and Mia stepped out of the house.

"What's going on?" she asked as she came toward them.

She'd changed into a short silk nightgown. All Colin was aware of for a moment was the outline of her body beneath the clinging fabric, and the length of her shapely legs. Looking at her drove him crazy.

"Hello, there," Tony said.

Colin swore under his breath. Then he said to the other vampire, "I'll deal with her. Get out of here."

Tony looked concerned as he glanced between Colin and the mortal, but he didn't argue. He shrugged, smiled, and disappeared into the night.

That only left Mia to deal with, and Colin wasn't quite sure what to do. His arms came around her automatically when she reached him, and she leaned her warm, curving body into his embrace. His mouth came hungrily down on hers without any conscious volition, and she responded with equal need. He picked her up and carried her into the house, and she was the one who slammed the door with her foot once they were inside.

Chapter Eight

Mia didn't fully understand what was happening when Colin brought her into the living room and they tumbled to the floor together. She'd thought she'd been dreaming about the men arguing in the driveway. It was as if she'd obeyed a hypnotic command to sleep, but hadn't really. It was all very confusing. But apparently she'd been outside in her nightgown, where Colin had been arguing with Tony . . .

And she didn't care, because Colin's touch set her on fire. This was the craziest night of her life. Everything was too intense, too weird.

And being caressed by Colin was too wonderful for her to say, *What the hell do you think you're doing?* Or *Get out of my house!*

She could barely think those things, and he'd know she didn't mean them anyway.

All they needed right now was to be together, thoughts and bodies entwined, melted into one.

It had been like that from the moment they met—as though he could read her mind, and sometimes she could read his. It often became impossible to tell who was touching who, who was satisfying who. They simply disappeared into each other.

In the last three months she'd mourned that intimate connection as much as she'd missed the frantic, fierce, totally consuming way she and Colin made love.

Never mind that he'd left her. Never mind that he would leave her again. She *needed* what he was doing right now. And she wanted him in her bedroom. Pride should keep her from reacting like this.

All she could do was gasp and arch her back when he brought her gown up and over her head. The silk moved against her skin with a sensual slither, drawing sparks of need along her nerves.

He cupped her breasts, teased her hard nipples, then brushed his fingers over her belly and between her thighs. The touch was soft, feathery, and swift, almost all over her at once. Sensation rippled through her, making her frantic.

What good was pride, when she'd never wanted him to leave her bed in the first place?

With a twist and a firm push, Mia put Colin on his back on the hardwood floor. He made a sound between a growl and a laugh, and she echoed it as she pulled off his T-shirt and tugged down his trousers to get at his hot, hard-muscled flesh.

There was nothing gentle in the way she caressed him, or the hungry way her mouth moved over him, nipping as much as kissing his chest and shoulders and throat. God, how she'd missed the taste and scent and texture of him! She wanted to eat him up!

"Draw blood if you want to," he growled as her teeth skimmed his jaw and throat. "'Cause I'm going to."

His hands smoothed up her back and down her sides to cup her ass. Then he flipped her onto her back, and was buried inside her in one hard thrust.

Mia arched up to meet the force of his entry and the swift, plunging strokes that filled her again and again. She loved it this way—fast, frantic, reckless, consuming. She closed her eyes, riding the shattering waves of pleasure.

Then there was a moment of sharp pain, and Mia was lost to the ecstasy.

She was a feast, and he'd been starving too long. Colin buried himself in her soft heat while his fangs pierced the tender flesh of her breast. He suckled there even after he collapsed on top of her, his body spent and sated. Even beyond the sex, the taste of her filled his senses with more intensity than ever. Possessing every part of her was like nothing else in the world.

Damn, he'd missed her! How did she do this to him? Why was Mia so perfect? Her spirit was the perfect challenge. Her body gave him perfect sex. Her blood brought him the perfect high.

Colin was almost grateful to the vampires for attacking her, or he wouldn't be here with her now.

When the memory of the attack intruded on his feeding, he lifted his head, abruptly denying himself the fiery taste he craved. As delicious as Mia's essence was, he had a more important reason for taking her blood than the sheer pleasure of it. Selfish he might be, but there was a higher purpose at work here.

Colin rolled to his side, took a deep breath, and forced his eyes to clear from red-tinged night sight, to focus with more human vision on the woman lying beside him. She drifted somewhere between sleep and waking, her body satisfied and utterly relaxed. It wasn't possible to keep from touching her, so he brushed his fingers across her cheeks and through her dark hair. He relished the way the short curls twined around his fingers, but it also reminded him that he couldn't afford having a human woman clinging to him.

Right now she needed his protection. Though he supposed a proper Prime would not have used protecting a woman he'd left as an excuse to have sex with her.

"Tough," he murmured, unable to call up much guilt for what he'd just done.

Should he make a promise to a matri that it wouldn't happen again? He wasn't that strong, or unselfish. And why shouldn't the humans sometimes pay just a little for the protection Primes gave them? Especially when the payment gave the human as much pleasure as it did the Prime.

Colin smiled, in no doubt about what Mia had gotten from the exchange. He'd been exquisitely aware of all her responses, reveled in all the orgasms he'd given her.

He bent down and kissed her throat. Lust coursed through him, but he was caught in an even deeper wave of pure affection.

He got to his feet with her in his arms, naked and blissed out, and carried her upstairs to the bedroom, where he could conduct the delicate mental work of convincing her mind that almost everything that had happened tonight hadn't been at all what it seemed.

He had even less guilt about brainwashing Mia than he had about the sex.

Mia woke with a faint taste of copper in her mouth; an odd but not unpleasant sensation. There was also a ringing in her ears, and it took her a muzzy moment to realize that the sound was her telephone.

Totally exhausted and wanting nothing more than to be left alone, Mia forced herself to get out of bed and pick up the handset on the other side of the room.

"So, is it true you hooked up with that jerk cop again? Morgan said he saw you and Foxe leaving the health center together last night. You weren't just working out together, were you?"

Mia winced at Courtney's angry voice. She'd spent a lot of time complaining to her best friend about Colin.

"There was a bit more to it than exercising," she admitted.

"Why?"

Mia almost felt guilty when she answered. "It just happened. We were mugged, or maybe it was carjackers—"

"What? Are you all right?"

She ached all over, but not from being in a fight. "I'm fine." Her memory was a little fuzzy on the exact details of what had happened in the garage. "We were attacked by three or four guys. And this is embarrassing, but I totally reacted like a girl—let Colin defend my honor, or whatever—"

"You? The kick-ass martial arts queen?"

"It's true. I don't know why. It's almost as embarrassing as letting him bring me home and—"

"You slept with him? Out of gratitude?"

Mia squirmed. "Why are you abusing me this early in the day?"

"Somebody needs to abuse you. You have no control where that jerk is involved. I cannot believe that you let him stay the night."

Mia sighed. "He didn't stay."

"Well, isn't that typical? What does that tell you about him? Couldn't he stay the night and be comforting in case you were upset?"

Mia didn't disagree with her friend's harsh criticism. "At least he *was* here. He has many faults, but the desire was mutual—this adrenaline thing kicked in. It's not as if we thought about it; there's this almost perverted, animalistic—"

"Oh, yeah?" Courtney sounded almost amused. "What'd you do?"

Mia looked at her body, thinking she'd see a few bruises from the wild sex, but her flesh was unmarked, even though aching muscles told a different story. "I vaguely remember a lot of scratching and biting, but maybe I did all that. And I'm not telling you any more."

"Listen, hon, even if the sex was great, you can't let him break your heart again. You told me to tell you that if you ever saw him again."

"I know." Hell, the man wasn't here, and it hurt that he wasn't here. Last week she'd halfway thought that she might someday get over him. Now this *hunger* she had for Colin Foxe was back in full force. She was such a fool. "Maybe I shouldn't have had sex with him, but—"

She couldn't explain her reactions to Colin, not when the gut lust he caused sometimes overrode her higher brain function. Last night had been completely out of control, for both of them, she was certain. She didn't think they'd made it to the bedroom, even if she'd woken up in her bed. Alone. It was disturbing not to know how she'd gotten from there to here, or when Colin had left.

"He didn't say good-bye."

"That's typical."

"Yeah," she agreed, though she'd been talking to herself rather than to Courtney.

But she was more disturbed by the holes in her memory, and by the nagging worry that something wasn't right, than she was by her friend's comments. Dream images flashed through her mind, mixed in with what she could remember from last night. Which wasn't as much as she should.

She rubbed a hand across her face. She just didn't feel right. "I'm really not awake, Courtney. Let's meet for lunch and talk about it later, okay?"

She hung up before Courtney could answer, and went to take a shower.

Hot water helped, but she could still feel Colin's touch on her body. The hot water also helped clear her foggy mind. Memories and actions fell into place as she scrubbed herself vigorously with almond-scented bath gel.

She remembered the flight back from Colorado. It took her a while longer to remember why she'd been to Colorado in the first place. In fact, for a few minutes she firmly believed the notion that vampires were real was a ridiculous dream.

For a few minutes she was frightened that she was crazy.

When she closed her eyes and let the water pound against her face and throat, memories of the attack last night came back to her. Except, one set of memories kept overlaying another.

In one image—the one that insisted it was the real memory—she watched Colin fight off a group of carjackers in a dark garage.

The other images were far more chaotic and crowded, and buried beneath the more logical attack. There were monsters in these memories. Not only monsters, but more people. She and Colin hadn't been alone. She still hadn't been much use—that shameful memory was real—but other good guys had ridden to the rescue in a big black SUV.

For a moment she could almost make out the license plate number of a Lincoln Navigator, but the image faded and wouldn't come back.

"Damn." She struck a fist against the wet tiles of the shower wall. "Remember!"

The vampire attack was the truth, wasn't it?

Yep. Reality was the scary, weird stuff.

Why had her subconscious tried to fool her into thinking otherwise?

She supposed that the trauma of facing real vampires was just more than she'd been prepared for, even if she'd thought she was ready.

Or maybe vampires kept their existence secret by telepathically projecting false memories at people. Her great-grandfather had mentioned that the monsters had hypnotic powers. The vampires projecting false images at her and Colin as they fled made as much sense as the changed memories being trauma-induced. More, if she wanted to believe she wasn't going just plain crazy.

But the brainwashing hadn't lasted long. She was glad that the real memories surfaced so quickly, even though she was left standing in the shower shaking from them. Well, she wasn't exactly glad—but concentrating on vampires would keep her mind off Colin. She left the shower, and dressed.

She was in the kitchen with a mug of green tea cupped in her hands before she thought of the rescue squad again. She squinted, trying to recall exactly what they'd done and said, but those memories remained blurred.

They'd shown up . . . maybe they'd already been chasing the vampires. They had to be official vampire hunters, and she needed to hook up with them.

One of them was named Tony, she recalled. He drove my car home.

That's right. Colin brought her home in his car, and the other man followed. The men had argued about something in the driveway, but she couldn't remember what.

And it didn't matter, because she'd just thought of a way to find Tony. After all, she did have a backup team of sorts she'd been told she could call on.

Mia put down her tea and picked up the kitchen phone. She called her great-grandfather's high-powered attorney. "Can you help me find out a man's identity from his fingerprints?" she asked.

Mia smiled when she was told that it was possible. Her addiction to all the CSI crime dramas on television had paid off.

Chapter Nine

"You made her forget *everything* about last night?"

Colin did not take kindly to Alec Reynard's tone. "That's not what I said," he replied.

He sat back in the small booth and took a sip of beer. They were in a bar in downtown Los Angeles that catered to customers of a supernatural nature, so there was no need to moderate their voices. It was the middle of the afternoon, the place was nearly empty, and the two vampires had met for an information exchange.

Colin would have preferred to be watching over Mia, but it was judged that she was safe in the daylight. They also kept telling him it wasn't his job, and Alec had demanded a briefing on Colin's activities after Tony left.

Alec looked concerned at Colin's answer. "What exactly *did* you do?"

"I just rearranged her memories."

The older vampire shook his head. "I'm not sure that's a good idea."

Colin didn't want his cousin's advice, but part of Prime training was to at least listen to the so-called wisdom of one's elders, especially Primes of one's own clan. He and Alec were both Reynard Clan, though from different lines and houses. Besides, Alec was buying the beer.

Colin took another sip from his cold bottle of Corona and grudgingly asked, "Why not?"

"I tried messing with Domini's mind and memories when

we first met. I thought it would be best if she forgot any weird stuff she encountered." He shook his head. "It didn't take."

"This will take, and I was very careful."

Though maybe he had been in a bit of a hurry. Touching Mia's mind was as arousing as touching her body. He hadn't gone deeply into her subconscious, just far enough in to overlay and rearrange memories. Then he'd gotten out of her head and house before giving in to the temptation to rouse the sleeping woman and have sex with her again.

"Besides, Mia's not like Domini," Colin pointed out. "Domini was born to be one of us. Mia is merely human."

"Merely?" Sarcasm was thick in Alec's voice.

"Don't start with me." Colin cut off the lecture he knew was coming. "I took my vows. I take of mortals' bodies and blood, but they are not my kind. I care for Mia, but she's—"

"Not your kind? You racist pig."

"You can be as pissed off as you want, but I made my choice the first time I attended a Convocation of the Clans. I don't remember what serious stuff the Matri and elders met about, but I do remember the partying, and what it was like to be surrounded by all those beautiful, mysterious, sensual Clan women. Bonding with a mortal woman is fine for other Primes, but it is not for me," Colin told his cousin.

"You're saying that you think bonding with a mortal woman is second best?" Alec sounded dangerously annoyed.

Colin ignored Alec's politically correct attitude. "I'm saying that I want *our* life, to live within *our* culture, to bond with a Clan female, to be the father of her house."

Alec was thoughtful for a moment, then shrugged off his annoyance. "Okay. I agree that's not a bad life to aspire to."

"It's what all of us really want and need, no matter how much time we spend among mortal kind. It's nature's joke on us that there are more Primes than there are females, so not all Primes can have a vampire mate. In the old days, we Primes could at least fight each other to the death over mating rights to our women. It cut the male population, and it was good for the gene pool."

Alec laughed. "I'm glad the Matri Council outlawed that practice centuries ago. Though I certainly don't mind a nice first-blood fight over a woman—or I didn't, until I found my bondmate."

"That kind of combat's one hell of an aphrodisiac." Colin finished his beer. "I thought Flare was quite impressed when I blooded Kiril at the Convocation last year."

"Did she sleep with you?"

"No."

"Then my sister wasn't impressed. Don't tell me you want to bond with Flare. She's restless and bad-tempered and mean."

"You only think that because she's your sister. She's hot. Very, very hot. Our women are pure fire, compared to fragile mortal women."

Except for Mia.

Colin pushed the thought of her out of his head, though his body grew taut with memories. He made himself think about vampire women.

"I don't know which one I want yet. Maybe Flare, maybe Maja, or Chaviva—there's a dozen or so to choose from. I've got years before I need to make up my mind, before the bonding urge strikes between me and a Clan woman. In the meantime—" Colin smiled lecherously and held his arms wide, taking in the whole city. "So many mortal women, so very much time."

Oddly enough, the only mortal image that came to mind was Mia, and he didn't feel as enthusiastic about many future decades of casual mating as he should.

He changed the subject. "I checked out the lead at the Van Trier airport yesterday, before all hell broke loose with the Mia incident."

Alec leaned eagerly forward across the table. "Did you find out anything? Are we any closer to this Patron? I'd like to know a name instead of having to use this pretentious Patron crap."

Colin grinned. "Yeah. We Primes are the only ones allowed pretentious titles."

"We've earned that right over thousands of years of tradition. This Patron is just some creep trying to live off of us. And he's willing to kill to do it, both our kind *and* mortals. I hate that it's taking so long to track him down."

"You don't have to remind me," Colin said. "I was there, at his Arizona lab facility. I'm the one who let him get away," he added, angry at himself.

"Did you find anything useful at the airport?"

"I got an address for a law firm that leased hangar space for a Gulfstream for a client. The lease was for two years, but the plane hasn't flown in or out of Van Trier for a while. Since we have the Patron's Gulfstream hidden away in Arizona, *it* also hasn't been flown out of Van Trier."

"Sounds like it could be the same one."

"I need to check out this law firm. Or maybe it would be better for someone else to follow this lead. I'm not a detective; my job's to hunt the Patron when we discover who he is. And Mia—"

Colin's head came up sharply, words lost as all his senses focused on Mia. She was—somewhere.

Somewhere she wasn't supposed to be. Doing something she shouldn't be doing. With someone else. With a male.

Colin growled deep in his throat and left the bar, totally intent on finding Mia.

As she sat on a bench on a shaded sidewalk in Santa Monica and gazed at the one-story, hacienda-style apartment complex across the street, Mia wasn't sure what to do next.

Oh, she knew what she had to do; it was finding the right approach that was giving her trouble. Marching up to the door and ringing the bell, rather than calling first, had seemed like a good idea until she got here. But now she wondered if the direct approach was the correct one.

She now knew that Tony's full name was Anthony Crowe.

He was a retired homicide detective with LAPD, with a brilliant service record and lots of commendations. He owned the renovated 1930s building, where he had resided for twenty years.

Though the man she remembered didn't look old enough to be retired. She hadn't noticed any gray in his black hair or beard. Of course it had been dark, and her memories still wove in and out of two very different scenarios, unless she concentrated hard enough to get a headache.

Maybe he'd been seriously injured in the line of duty and forced to retire early. There was always a nagging worry in the back of her mind that something awful would happen to Colin, though he naturally thought he was indestructible. She guessed that Colin knew Tony from the police connection.

Mia reminded herself sternly that she hadn't tracked down Tony Crowe to discuss Colin Foxe—

Foxe. Foxe and—Crowe.

What an interesting coincidence that both men had animal names. And hadn't her great-grandfather said that vampires ran in packs and used animal names? Though the only group he'd mentioned specifically called themselves the Snakes.

How charming.

Crowe and Foxe were relatively common names, though, and crows and foxes were fairly harmless creatures. Her revved-up nerves were creating connections out of simple coincidences.

She'd been sitting on this bench for a good half hour, stalling like this. She didn't know why approaching Crowe was harder for her than finding her grandfather.

Except, maybe, for the insidious voice in her head that kept telling her there were things she shouldn't know, shadows she could not explore, secrets meant to be kept.

That voice sounded a lot like Colin's, and it was beginning to piss her off.

The voice only grew stronger as she forced herself to rise and cross the street. A low stucco wall with a decorative iron gate separated a gardened courtyard from the sidewalk. The gate

wasn't locked, so Mia went inside. A small tiled fountain bubbled in the center of the courtyard. Mia paused as a pair of startled doves took flight off the rim of the fountain, then marched
up to a dark, carved wooden door and rang the doorbell.

A male voice said, "Yes?" through an intercom a few moments later.

"Mr. Crowe?"

"Yes," he answered cautiously after a pause.

"My name is Caramia Luchese. You don't know me, but we
met last night. You know where, and why," she added.

The door opened, and a man who was distinctly not a senior cit-
izen, but *was* Tony from last night, stood in the doorway. "Miss
Luchese," he said. "I get the distinct feeling that you have no concept of leaving well enough alone." There was an amused twinkle in
his eyes, but that didn't stop him from looking extremely dangerous.

"How can I leave well enough alone when it concerns me?"
she answered.

"Does Colin know you're here?"

"Colin has nothing to do with this," she answered, confused
and annoyed.

"Really?" he questioned, coolly amused. He smiled, and
looked her up and down in a way that made her flushed and
flustered. "How did you find me? And is it me you want? And
would you like to come inside to explain it all?"

His voice was a rich purr, and Mia felt like Little Red Riding Hood invited into the Big Bad Wolf's den.

She gestured toward a table and chairs set on a brick patio
beneath a pair of palm trees, suddenly feeling that discussing
vampires out in the open might be best.

"Why don't we talk over there?"

"Sweetheart, we shouldn't be talking at all."

She didn't like the endearment from a stranger, but let it go.
She also didn't like it when he took her arm and led her over to
the shaded patio, then waited until she was seated before he
said, "Would you like some lemonade? Cookies?"

"There's a certain smug amusement to your gallantry, Mr. Crowe," she answered, keeping her tone calm. "I don't understand that."

"Oh, it's a Prime thing." He glanced toward the street, then at his watch. Then he sat in the other chair after moving it closer to hers, though this put him directly in the bright sunlight. "We have a few minutes to get to know each other. Tell me everything you know."

She looked at him suspiciously. She wasn't sure how she expected this confrontation to go, but the man's confident amusement was unsettling. "Everything I know about what?"

"Vampires, of course. And not just the monsters that have been pursuing you. Do you know why they're after you?"

"No, I don't know—wait a minute."

She'd come to get information from him, and he was attempting to control the information, to learn from her rather than tell her anything.

"What do you know about vampire hunters?" she asked, keeping stubbornly to her own agenda. "How do I get in touch with them? Are you one?"

"Vampire or hunter?"

She smiled. "Sorry, I phrased that poorly."

"Not necessarily."

"Is Colin a hunter?"

"He's definitely a predator." He gave her an assessing look. "More than he knows, I think."

Mia hated her unconscious rush to bring Colin into every conversation, especially after months of trying to do a memory dump of the man. But he'd come back into her life at the same time the vampires showed up, and she couldn't believe it was a coincidence.

"When we were attacked last night, Colin wanted me to believe that the monsters are a human cult. But he was just trying to protect me, wasn't he?"

She wasn't sure if she was going to be pleased or furious if she found out that Colin Foxe was the very thing she was looking for.

"I think he very much wants to protect your life," Crowe answered. "And that he's trying to protect himself, as well."

"How is he involved in this? How are you?"

"I'm always fine, darlin'."

First *sweetheart,* now *darlin'.* She could tell he was trying to rile her, and tried hard not to show her annoyance.

"You know what I meant."

"How am I involved with vampires, you mean, rather than the state of my health?" He leaned closer and chuckled. The sound was low and sexy. "I'm involved in every way possible."

"Get away from her, Corvus."

Mia sprang to her feet at the threatening sound of Colin's voice. Tony rose as well, laughing, and turned to face Colin. Mia had to move a few steps sideways to see past Tony Crowe's broad shoulders. Colin's face was a mask of fury. Every whip-cord lean muscle was taut, as though he was just barely holding himself back from attacking the other man.

"What are you doing here?" she asked Colin.

"What are *you* doing here?" he demanded, but he directed most of his anger at Tony. "What do you think you're doing?"

"I was waiting to see how quickly you'd show up, Reynard."

"Did you think I'd let you do whatever you please with my—"

"Your what?"

"My—" Colin pointed. "Her."

"Is she is, or is she ain't?"

Crowe smiled, and he seemed to have very sharp teeth all of a sudden. Colin took a step closer.

Though she saw two men facing off in the hot afternoon sunlight, Mia had a strong impression of watching a pair of leashed fighting beasts getting ready to go at each other with fangs and claws and hard male muscle. A shiver of fear went through her, like an ice cube being run down her spine. She wanted to run, and she didn't like the sensation. Before being chased by the vampires last night, she'd never backed down from any challenge. She couldn't be a coward again. Besides, it seemed this confrontation was somehow over her.

She cleared her throat. "Excuse me, but—"

"Stay out of this," both men said at once.

"Screw you," was her automatic defiance at this high-handedness. "I'm not being fought over like a piece of meat."

She always got reckless when her temper flared, but she didn't turn her back on the men as she edged away from the patio. They seemed momentarily stunned by her words, and while they stared, she moved toward the courtyard gate. She was almost ready to break into a sprint when a hand landed on her shoulder, bringing her to an abrupt stop.

"Don't run," a voice warned her.

When she turned around, she saw Alec from the garage rescue party. The woman called Domini came up to join him a moment later. Then Colin and Crowe were there, as well. Mia had the impression of being surrounded by a pride of hungry lions.

"Back off, boys," Domini said.

Surprisingly, the men all took a step back. Yet that didn't make Mia feel any less trapped.

"What's up?" Domini asked.

Tony answered, "I think our young Prime has gotten the girl in trouble." He looked at Alec. "Can't you *smell* what's going on between them?"

"What are you talking about?" Mia and Colin demanded at the same time.

Tony chuckled and shook his head. "They haven't got a clue."

"To what?" Domini asked.

"Just look at them, hon," Alec told her. "With all your senses."

"Oh," she said after a moment.

"Do you know what I think?" Tony asked. "I think we take them to the Matri. Right now."

Chapter Ten

The room was decorated in a luxurious, *Arabian Nights* harem way, with a big bed, a thick Persian carpet, a sitting area with a pair of comfortable chairs and a full bookcase, and a marble fantasy bathroom. But there were no windows, and she'd been locked in.

She'd been kidnapped, firmly but politely taken away by the people who'd come to the rescue the night before. Her only consolation was that Colin had been abducted as well. They'd been put in different cars and brought to a secluded mansion hours before. She hadn't seen him since they'd stepped inside the house.

A group of men had taken him away; several older women had joined Domini and escorted Mia to her nicely appointed prison. Domini looked concerned, but everyone else's expressions had been neutral or downright hostile. Mia got the impression that they found her presence thoroughly inconvenient.

She'd been left alone for a while, then Domini came in and introduced her to a Dr. Casmerek. He'd wanted blood and urine samples. Of course she'd refused, in a very physical way. She'd tried to get past Domini to get to the door, and almost made it. But Domini was unnaturally fast and strong, and the combination of aikido and Krav Maga fighting techniques she used took Mia by surprise. The woman's unconventional style didn't make her give up, though.

The doctor stayed out of the way until the fight was over. A few things got broken; Mia hoped they were priceless antiques.

Mia ended up grudgingly giving him the fluid samples, but she was pleased that at least she'd put up a fight, at least *tried* to control the situation.

Domini smiled at her and said, "You did good," before she followed the doctor out, leaving Mia alone in the locked room once more.

What sort of medical tests was this Dr. Casmerek running on her?

Mia paced while she fretted. Every now and then she paused to listen at the door, or to pick up a piece of broken porcelain or glass. After a while she had a nice little collection piled on a table. None of them were large enough or sharp enough to make a decent weapon, but at least thinking about it helped.

She didn't know exactly where Colin was, but she had the feeling he was close by—she almost believed she could find him if she could get out of the room. The weirdest thing was, she thought she could feel him wanting to be with her. She'd had sensations like this about him before, but never as strongly as now.

And what good would finding him do her? Though it would be kind of fun to be the one who came to the rescue this time.

And then he could explain to her what was going on. He knew these people, though he hadn't seemed very lucid when he showed up at Tony Crowe's. And he'd been just as confused and outraged as she was by the others' actions.

Was Dr. Casmerek running tests on him, too?

And what did Colin's mood swings and their being kidnapped have to do with vampires?

After a while she picked a book at random from the case and settled on one of the deep, comfortable chairs. It was a big, heavy book, with fine leather binding. She was contemplating how she might be able to use it to smash someone if she waited by the door when the door opened silently across the room.

Mia swore under her breath at the lost opportunity and rose to her feet as Domini came in, followed by Alec.

"Sorry to have kept you waiting so long," Alec said.

As kidnappers went, these people were certainly polite.

"The matris will see you now," Alec said.

"The what?" Mia asked. "Where's Colin? Is he all right?"

The man and woman exchanged an infuriatingly knowing glance.

"He might not be when the matris get through with him," Alec answered. "They wish to see you, as well," he went on.

His tone implied that there was no questioning the wishes of this Matris person or persons. All Mia cared about was getting out of this room and finally finding out what was going on. And, all right, she wanted Colin. His presence wasn't always necessarily reassuring, but it was—important—to her.

"Fine," she said. "Lead on."

Mia walked toward the door, but Domini put a hand on her arm before she could leave.

"One thing," she said. "The medical tests came back. The good news is that you're not pregnant. At least, I assume you take it as good news."

Mia flushed deeply, appalled and embarrassed. She shook off the woman's touch. "I didn't ask to take any tests," she reminded Domini. And what was the bad news? she wondered. Were they testing her for some sort of disease? She was too proud, and scared, to ask.

"I don't mean to seem rude," Domini said. "And of course you don't think this is any of our business, but believe me, it really is for your own good."

"And Colin's," Alec added. "Shall we?" He gestured toward the door.

All Colin could do was pace like a trapped animal back and forth across the thickly carpeted bedroom, which got boring very quickly. He'd been furious when they'd brought him to the Citadel, and his mood hadn't gotten any better in the long hours since.

No windows. The door was guarded. Other people were allowed in and out, but Colin Foxe was trapped in another clan's stronghold.

He was angry at this intrusion into his privacy. He was impatient at the interruption of the hunt for the Patron. He was annoyed that Mia had been brought to the Shagal house, and even more angry that he was not allowed to see her. He was infuriated at the long hours he'd been made to wait, all but a prisoner in a guest room, without any explanation.

Even the usually forthright Dr. Casmerek had refused to tell him anything, other than to say that the blood he wanted from Colin was for tests.

What sort of tests? None of this made any sense. What by the devils of darkness had his involvement with Mia gotten him into?

And worst of all, when lovely Cassiopeia, Matri Serisa's only daughter and heir, had come into the bedroom and offered to spend the night in his bed, he hadn't even been interested. She was a beautiful, sensual, exciting vampire woman who no Prime in his right mind would turn down. Yet Colin had barely been able to keep his rejection polite enough not to cause offense.

"What is the matter with me?" he asked, turning to face Anthony Crowe as the door opened and the other Prime came into the room.

"We're scheduled to discuss exactly what's wrong with you," Tony answered.

"I turned down Cassie Shagal," Colin went on. "Can you believe that?"

He was totally stunned at his uncharacteristic behavior. He wasn't going to ask himself why. What he needed was to get out of here, get away from all this Clan crap, and get his head together on his own.

"Can I go now?" he demanded.

"Not yet."

"There are rules against this kind of treatment!"

"Yep. But there are extenuating circumstances that have to be worked out involving you and Miss Mia."

"Have you sent Mia home? Did Matri Serisa make her forget about us?"

That would be the best thing for her, even if Colin did resent anyone else touching Mia's mind but him. If he let himself think that perhaps some Prime had probed the mortal woman's thoughts, he knew a jealous red rage would overtake him. He did not want to be jealous of Mia. He wouldn't let himself be.

He took a deep breath, and made himself say, "I'm sorry I acted like I did at your place. There was no reason for it. Was there?" he added, as jealousy shot through him once more.

Tony shook his head and looked at him steadily for a moment before he said, "A few things have to be settled before you two can leave. Come on."

Colin suddenly caught his breath on a scent, a sense.

"Mia."

Colin pushed out of the room ahead of Tony. Though he hadn't been able to feel her presence for hours, he was now keenly aware that she was close by. But there were two other Primes waiting in the hall, and Tony at his back.

He was ready to start a brawl with all three to get to Mia, but she appeared around a corner and ran toward him a moment later. He had her in his arms before he noticed Alec and Domini following her. Tony grabbed him and pulled him back before he could kiss Mia, then Domini stepped between them.

"Hey!" Mia complained.

"Hands off!" Colin shouted. He was surprised when Tony let him go. The problem was now getting around Domini, since there was no way he would use force on a woman.

"No way," Domini said before he could think up a plea or a cajoling word. "Serisa—"

"Actually, there is a slight change of plans," Tony broke in. "Serisa and the other ladies want these two to have a little talk before they get on with other matters."

Colin spun to face Tony. "Talk? I don't want to talk to the woman."

"What?" Mia asked indignantly behind him.

He turned back to her. "I want to get you safely back home," he explained.

He could tell she was scared, and covering it up with her usual bravado. The others couldn't see it, or didn't care, but he knew that Mia was upset.

"She might be home," Domini said.

Colin hadn't a clue what Alec's bondmate meant.

"Who's Serisa? And what does she want us to talk about?" Mia shot a look at Domini. "What do you mean, I might be home?"

It occurred to Colin that Mia was following the enigmatic thread of conversation better than he was. She was no fool. Out of her depth, of course, but sharp.

"Don't worry, you will get explanations," Tony told Mia. He concentrated on Colin. "But first Serisa wants you to explain everything about us to her. *Everything*," he added firmly. "Truth first," he added, with one of his annoying grins, "then consequences."

"The truth?" Colin was appalled. "She can't handle the truth!"

"Aaron Sorkin, *A Few Good Men*," Domini muttered. When everyone stared at her, she smiled at Alec, then focused her attention on Colin. "I handled the truth, didn't I?"

"But you're one of us," Colin objected.

"I wasn't then."

"Yes, but—"

"Will you people stop arguing, and tell me what's going on?" Mia demanded.

Colin hated that every gaze was on them. Even worse, Mia's needs called to him all tangled up with his own.

"Fine," he finally agreed. "She's going to have to forget it all, but I'll tell her."

"Everything," Tony admonished. "Including what you've done to her."

"*What* have you done to me?" Mia asked.

Colin was far too aware of the crowd. "Not here."

Tony pointed toward the bedroom. Colin grabbed Mia's hand and hustled her inside. This time he was glad when the door shut behind them.

Once they were alone, he turned to her and gave her the blunt truth.

"I'm a vampire."

Chapter Eleven

"No, you're not."

Her response certainly wasn't unexpected, but Colin couldn't help but be indignant. "What do you mean, No, you're not? I ought to know what I am: a vampire Prime of Clan Reynard."

She shook off his hand and backed away to look him up and down. "That's not possible."

Colin did his best to see the situation through her eyes, and tried to sound soothing. "I realize that you're confused."

"Oh, yes, I'm confused. But don't try to tell me that you're a vampire."

"It's not only me," he told her. "Everyone in the house is a vampire. Except Domini, and maybe a couple of the Primes' mortal bondmates, but they're special cases." He sighed, and held up a hand. "Never mind, I'm going too fast. Let's concentrate on you and me, and get this over with."

"Yes," she said. "Let's."

There was a gleam of anger in her eyes and in her spirit that stabbed at him. Maybe he was choosing his words wrongly, not being tactful enough. It was hard to tell with women. They were hard to talk to, but he'd been told to be honest.

"You've seen vampires," he reminded her. "I tried to make you forget that we exist."

There was a long moment where the sense of anger and betrayal sizzled around her, but she got it under control. "It didn't work. Not for long, anyway."

He was surprised by her mental resilience, and rather proud of her, despite the inconvenience. "That's the trouble with trying to manipulate psychics," he explained. "You can never be certain it's going to work. You seem to be getting stronger. What did you do, go to Tony when the false memories wore off? And why Tony? How'd you find him?"

A stubborn mask came over her features, and her mind. "Aren't you the one who's supposed to be doing the talking?"

"There's plenty of things you need to answer for."

"You first."

Her tone cut like a knife.

More than that, it excited him. Every fiery look from her, every word, stimulated him more. Though the passion that seethed inside her was from anger, Colin knew instinctively how to channel and change it to the kind of passion that brought pleasure, and completion.

"Mia. We can do better things than fight." His voice was full of sultry promise. He took a step toward his beautiful human, reaching for her. She gasped when his fingers touched the side of her throat and slid across her shoulders, and the familiar, delicious crackle of desire passed between them.

Then she danced away to the far side of the room. She held her hands up before her when he would have followed. "I don't make love to vampires."

He smiled and glanced toward the king-sized bed in the center of the room. Just because they were stuck in here didn't mean they couldn't have some fun. He nodded toward it, all cocky and sure of himself. Mia always came to him in the end, no matter how much they fought.

"Then maybe I won't confess to being one."

"Good. Because—"

"But that would be a lie. And I'm told that's not allowed."

He sat down on the end of the bed and patted the spot next to him for her to join him. "You've been making love to a vampire for months, Mia. Come and make love to one again."

Mia slowly turned her back on Colin, though she could still feel his gaze on her. For hours all she'd wanted was to be with him, but now she couldn't bear to look at him. But that didn't keep the memories from rising up to haunt her through all the layers of confusion.

She didn't take strangers home; she wasn't that kind of woman—but here they were in her bedroom, with no more conversation than the words they'd exchanged in the hospital. Somehow he knew the way to her home, into the most private place where she lived. She welcomed him into this sanctuary, and gave herself up to the desire that had been waiting for him to kindle.

He didn't touch her like a stranger, but as the lover who knew and fulfilled her every desire. When she touched him, she knew every hard-muscled inch of him. The scent and heat and taste of him was a homecoming rather than a revelation.

They were meant to fit together, and they did, falling onto the bed, ripping off each other's clothes, moving together, mouths and hands finding all the right places with frantic, fulfilling urgency. There was no gentleness in this coupling; they both rode the wildness, loved it. There were moments of pain that only intensified the pleasure. They clawed at each other as he thrust into her. Clawed and scratched and—

Bit.

Mia touched her right breast, as the memory of the first time it happened washed over her with erotic intensity that almost sent her to her knees.

"You *bit* me."

"Upon occasion."

How could he sound so damned smug?

She whirled around and glared at Colin. His biting *her* wasn't the only thing she remembered about their wild love-making, but she wasn't ready to face the rest of it.

"You bit me!"

"I tasted you," he corrected. "That's what we call it. We never take more than a few drops of blood at a time, but it heightens our partner's pleasure, and ours. You remember the pleasure, but not what we do."

How could he say that, when she was remembering it right now? She also remembered the taste of copper in her mouth. "You are so obtuse, Colin Foxe."

"But I'm sexy."

Sex *had* been the basis of their relationship. But sex with a vampire? Her stomach twisted at the thought.

"Biting me doesn't make you a vampire," she said. "And vampires aren't sexy. Except maybe Angel and Spike, but they're fictional. Real vampires are monsters. I've been attacked by them."

"Tribe vampires are monsters. I'm Clan."

Tribe. Clan. Family. She'd heard the terms. Her great-grandfather had told her that vampires divided themselves into three distinct types. He'd also told her that the distinctions made no difference. Vampires of any type were inimical parasites, meant to be killed by humans. That Colin knew about the different kinds of vampires frightened her.

"Is this some kind of test? I'm trying to find vampire hunters, but when I think I find the hunters, I'm told they're vampires. That doesn't make sense."

Colin stood up slowly, and he looked very annoyed. "What do you want with hunters?"

"Vampires have been attacking me," she reminded him.

This calmed him a little. "How do you know about the hunters?"

She wasn't ready to answer this. "I've seen you in the sunlight. Vampires can't bear the light."

She remembered being with him on the beach on the hottest day of the year. She remembered making love at midday in her garden, laughing about getting their butts burned if they weren't careful. They'd rubbed coconut-scented sunblock all over each other. She remembered the way his skin felt, slick with the cream and warmed by the sun.

And she remembered talking to Tony Crowe in his courtyard, how he'd turned his face up to the clear California sky.

And how Colin and he had faced off in the middle of the bright Los Angeles afternoon.

"How can you all be vampires when you run around in the daylight?"

"We take drugs. Lots of drugs. This is the twenty-first century, woman. Do you think we haven't changed with the times?"

That was one of the things her great-grandfather wanted to know. That's why he wanted a live vampire to study. Maybe she should take Colin to her great-grandfather.

And if she could think like that, it must mean that she was beginning to believe he really was a vampire. Which would mean . . .

That she'd been sleeping with the enemy.

A wave of self-loathing overtook her, strong enough to drive her to her knees. Colin was beside her almost before she hit the floor. Then his hands were on her.

"Monster!" she shouted. "Get your hands off me, you disgusting parasite!"

He backed off, and there was hurt in his voice when he said, "Hey!"

She looked up at him, realized she was on her knees in front of a vampire, and got to her feet. She wasn't going to show weakness in front of him—in front of *it*. Looking at him, even knowing what he was—what he proudly proclaimed to be—she still had trouble seeing past the man she'd cared for to the beast he truly was.

It made it worse that she couldn't look at him without wanting him. She'd have to put the yearning down to some sort of telepathic glamor he exerted on her, which made her want him. Because if wanting him was something that came from inside her, then she was a weak, perverted fool.

Mia was looking at him as if she'd never seen him before, and Colin accepted that. What ground on his temper was that she radiated intense hatred and anger—not only at him, but at herself. What was that about?

Maybe she wanted him to apologize for what he was, which was not going to happen. "I'm proud of being a vampire. We're faster, stronger, longer-lived, and have better sight, hearing, and vision than humans. We're psychic as hell."

She sneered. "You're better than humans, is that it?"

"The Clans are protectors of humans, Mia. We look after your kind."

"My *kind*. What arrogance." She crossed her arms. "And what's the bill for being so tenderly looked after by your superior species? Do you do it for free?"

"Yes, of course. Well—"

"Do you look after us like shepherds with their flocks?"

"Yeah," he answered. "Like that."

"Sheep end up being slaughtered, Foxe. They're protected until the shepherd decides they make a tasty stew."

"Oh, come on!"

"How many people have you slaughtered?"

"I'm a *cop*."

"Cops kill people, and get away with it. What a great cover for a vampire. Didn't you just shoot a couple of bank robbers in the line of duty?" She laughed bitterly. "And to think I was worried about how you reacted to killing those men. How many innocent people's blood have you taken while wearing the uniform?"

For now he'd accept that in her ignorance she could ridicule what it meant to be a Clan Prime. But there was no way he let her get away with accusing him of being a bad cop!

Colin took a furious step toward her, only to spin toward the door when it opened.

"Time's up," Tony Crowe announced.

Chapter Twelve

"Not now!" Colin shouted at Crowe.

Mia was relieved to have Colin's attention diverted from her. The wild look in his eyes when he came toward her had scared her. She'd never been frightened by him before, and she cursed herself for rousing the temper of a monster when she didn't yet know how to defend herself against him.

Damn it! Why hadn't her great-grandfather been more helpful? Why hadn't she found the human vampire hunters before running into this nest of monsters?

She was such a fool for mistaking Colin, Tony, and all the rest for hunters just because they'd fought off the other vampires. Had she stumbled into the middle of some territorial dispute?

"I'm just the messenger," Tony answered Colin. "Did you tell her about us?"

"I've been trying to. She just called me a bad cop. A Prime has to defend his honor."

Tony gave her a disapproving look. "We're very proud that he qualified for SWAT at his tender age."

"He's thirty-two," Mia said. At least that's what he'd told her—as if anything Colin Foxe said about himself was true.

"They let you out of the crèche awfully young, didn't they?" Tony said to Colin.

"I'm old enough to kick your ass, old-timer."

"I might let you try, pup." Tony came farther into the room, and looked Mia up and down in a way that made her blush.

"But you know what you'd be giving up if I won. I'm a hundred and three," he added to Mia. "Think of all the experience I have to offer you."

"Hey!" Colin put himself between Mia and the other vampire.

"Enough," a woman's voice said from behind them. "Anthony, be good." A small, dignified woman swept into the room, commanding everyone's attention with her regal manner. She bent a stern look on Mia that made her feel about five years old before she addressed Tony again. "Unless you mean to rescue this young woman from an untenable situation."

"Should the need arise, Lady Serisa, it will be a privilege."

"Good. Come along. We've been waiting to settle this long enough."

Serisa left, and they all followed without a word. Colin reached for her hand as they walked down a wide hallway, but Mia sharply snatched it away.

Don't touch me!

Fine.

Mia realized that neither of them had spoken aloud. Telepathy? It made sense that a vampire was a telepath, but how could she send thoughts to him, as well? Come to think of it, she remembered hearing his voice in her head even before they met, telling her to calm down. How had he gotten into her head like that? How did she get into his?

She had to put her speculations on hold when they entered a large room full of people. Full of vampires—just because they looked like people didn't mean they were. They were all attractive and well dressed, though mostly in black. They were all staring at her.

A tall, barrel-chested man came forward. He had gray at his temples and deep lines around his eyes. When he spoke, his voice was deep and mellow. "I am Barak, elder of Clan Shagal. Welcome to our Citadel." He glanced toward the woman. "Serisa is my lady. She is Matri here."

Then he smiled at Mia, and the expression in his gaze was so kindly and concerned that it left her wishing that Barak was her great-grandfather. She couldn't help but smile back.

He took her hand and made sure she was seated comfortably in a deep black leather chair on one side of the room. Then he moved to stand in front of Colin.

"Sit," Barak ordered him brusquely.

"I'll stand," Colin answered. He looked around the crowded room. "This looks like a trial. What am I being accused of?"

The atmosphere in the room grew even tenser as Barak and Colin stared at each other for a few moments. When Barak nodded and Colin came striding past him to stand next to her, people relaxed. There were even approving looks and a few smiles when he put his hand on her shoulder. Mostly, Mia was aware of the comfort that came from contact with Colin in the midst of all these strangers.

She looked up at him. "You confuse the hell out of me, Foxe."

He looked down at her. "The feeling's mutual, Luchese."

"Which brings us to the heart of the matter," Serisa said. The small woman stepped to the center of the room. "We are not dealing with accusations, but with concerns. Some facts must be verified, acknowledged, and addressed." She turned to Tony Crowe. "Thank you for bringing the situation to our attention. Perhaps you should explain what you saw that alerted you."

"Alerted him to what?" Colin questioned.

"What are we being accused of?" Mia demanded.

"Kids," Tony said, and shook his head. "This is for your own good, so shut up and let's get this over with." He addressed Serisa. "One of my impressions about the girl is that we have an amateur vampire hunter on our hands."

"Amateur!" Mia piped up indignantly. Even if it was true, this Crowe person didn't have to announce it to the world. "I came to you for help," she told him.

He smiled. "But you didn't recognize me for what I am, did you? You had no idea what Colin is, after months as his lover.

He didn't tell you anything, did he? And whenever you figured anything out, he tried to make you forget, right?"

Mia couldn't help but nod, and shoot Colin an angry look.

Tony addressed Serisa once more. "The boy has her so messed up, she isn't really sure of what's going on."

"Boy!" Colin shouted. "Messed up? I've never done anything to her. Except make her forget things she isn't supposed to know. For her good, and ours," he added.

"You haven't forced your blood on her?" Barak asked.

"Of course not!"

"If she didn't have your blood in her, would the Tribe pack have decided to hunt her? If you weren't linked, would they have come after her?" Serisa questioned.

"That isn't why they're hunting me," Mia said, but everyone's attention was on Colin.

"I've tasted Mia, yes. I freely admit that I've taken her blood. But I have never, *never* shared my blood with her. I wouldn't do that with a mortal woman."

"I don't think he *thinks* he has," Tony said to Serisa.

"Yet you are certain of the mingling."

"I am."

"Why are you listening to him? I'm right here! I know what I did with Mia."

"I don't think you do," Tony replied. "I met the young lady when Alec, Domini, and I answered a call for help from Colin against a Tribe attack. My impression from the first moment was that they were bonded. I quickly came to understand that neither of them were aware of it."

"Bonded?" Colin's hand squeezed her shoulder. He was utterly stunned, and unaware that he was hurting her.

She shrugged off his touch and rose to her feet. While there was a tension in the air, she wasn't feeling physically threatened. But she did fear she was in danger of being talked to death.

"Does the term *beating around the bush* have meaning for

you people?" she demanded. "You've kidnapped us, and now you're interrogating us. Why? What business is it of yours, what Colin and I did together?" Had she known he was a vampire, she certainly wouldn't have slept with him, but she wasn't going to try to claim that the sex hadn't been consensual. "Maybe he messed with my memories, maybe he bit me, but that's nobody's business but ours."

And why were they so concerned about one of their own drinking someone's blood? That was what vampires did, wasn't it?

"Besides, we broke up," she went on. "It doesn't matter anymore."

"You can't break up," Serisa said. "You're bonded."

"We aren't," Colin insisted. "It's not possible. She's human."

He sounded desperate, appalled, and this hurt Mia as though he'd slapped her. She spun to face him. "Is there something wrong with being human?"

Ignoring her, Colin stepped up to confront Serisa. "This is impossible. You can't put this on me." His expression was stricken.

Serisa's answer was cold. "I do."

Domini stepped forward. "I'm sorry no one's bothered to explain bonding to you," she said to Mia. "They forget that a mortal isn't going to automatically know what they're talking about when they speak of bonding and bondmates. Basically, you and Colin are married. You are physically, spiritually, and psychically connected."

"Don't be ridiculous," Mia snapped.

"And it's permanent," Domini added.

Part of her recognized the truth of what the other woman said, but the rest of her rejected it with almost hysterical fervor.

"I cannot be"—she couldn't bring herself to use the words *bonded* or *married*—"attached to a vampire."

"We have the blood tests to prove it," Dr. Casmerek spoke up. "You can't argue with science."

"Yes, I can," Mia said.

"I am *not* bonded with this mortal," Colin asserted. "I did not give her my blood." He glared at the doctor. "I don't care what your tests show. You're lying."

"What reason would I have to lie, Prime?"

"Can you bear to be away from her?" Tony asked. "Don't you miss him when he's gone?"

"It's more than love," Domini said. "It's a wonderful craving."

"What's so wonderful about it?" Colin demanded.

"Bonding is the most wonderful thing that can happen to a Prime," Barak said.

Colin sneered. "With a human?"

"Watch it," Alec warned. Several other males echoed this sentiment.

Mia was tempted to join the argument and defend her rights, but part of her also wanted to defend Colin. After all, whatever was going on was between them, and not this loud, outraged crowd. She forcefully reminded herself that these were *vampires*, not concerned family members. Vampire in-laws? Good Lord, what an awful thought!

If only there was some way she could sneak out unnoticed while the others argued. She began to sidle slowly away from the arguing group gathered around them.

"Wouldn't I know if I was bonded?" Colin demanded.

"Not necessarily. You wouldn't be as aware of the signs as a more mature Prime. The tests show positive, but I'm not sure how it was triggered," the vampire doctor said. "You're rather young for the biological imperative to have kicked in."

"Much too young," Barak said. "What were you thinking of?"

"It's not the sort of thing you think about," Tony said.

"I—" Colin started.

"A traumatic event could have triggered the need," Serisa cut him off. "If their minds met while she was in danger, he would have responded instinctively. His desire to protect his mate could have kicked in and accelerated the bonding process. How did you meet your bonded?"

"Hostage situation," Colin answered. "I rescued her."

Mia swung back toward him. "Hey!" She curbed her outrage to acknowledge, "He and his whole team rescued us."

Tony Crowe's arms suddenly came around her from behind. "But will he rescue you now?"

The words were a seductive whisper in her ear. He pulled her closer, making her aware of hard male muscle and inescapable strength. She didn't let her shock stop her from thrusting a heel toward his shin and her head back toward his jaw.

But Colin was there before either blow connected. She caught a glimpse of bared fangs and burning eyes; Colin's handsome features were transformed into those of a bloodthirsty animal.

The next thing she knew, she was on her hands and knees on the carpet, and her mind was full of Colin's psychic voice shouting, *She's mine!*

Her soul greeted this declaration with the harrowing knowledge that she *was* his. She belonged to Colin Foxe, a vampire who fought another monster for possession of her.

Gentle hands reached for her and helped her to stand. Domini looked into her eyes and asked, "You okay?"

Mia shook her head. "It's all my fault."

Domini glanced over her shoulder. "It's already over."

She turned Mia to face the center of the room. Colin was being held between Barak and Alec; he still looked ready to kill.

Tony Crowe stood a few feet away, looking smugly satisfied, even though a bloody cut scored his cheek. "Always a groomsman," he said with a mock sigh. "Never a groom. Are you bonded or not, Colin?" he asked.

"Mia is mine!" Colin looked around, the fire in his gaze challenging every male in the room. "She's *mine*."

"I think we were all aware of that," a new voice said. A beautiful, slender woman walked out of the shadows on the far side of the room. She put a hand on Colin's cheek, and he seemed to calm down instantly.

"Matri," he said, and leaned his head into her caressing touch.

A bolt of jealousy shot unexpectedly through Mia, but Domini put a hand on her arm when she would have stepped forward.

"It's okay," Domini whispered. "She's Anjelica, the head of his clan. His great-aunt, I think."

"She doesn't look like anybody's great-aunt," Mia whispered back.

"You flatter me, Prime's Chosen," Anjelica said, turning to Mia. The older woman smiled and held a hand out toward her. "We've had enough of wrangling and explanations. You've been through enough. I came here to celebrate the happy occasion of a bonding ceremony. I think we'll have the ceremony this evening." She shot a stern look at Colin. "Don't you agree, Reynard Prime?"

Colin didn't even look at Mia. He bowed his head and looked up at Anjelica from under his heavy dark brows. Mia saw that his gaze was defiant, and felt his seething anger—anger he directed at her.

But his voice was totally neutral when he spoke to the other woman. "Tonight, Matri. As you desire."

Chapter Thirteen

"Look what we caught."

"Caught him sneaking outside the house."

"He didn't put up much of a fight."

Laurent kept silent and didn't offer any resistance as the trio of Manticore Primes manhandled him into the room and shoved him to his knees before the pack leader.

"So you've come back," Justinian said, stepping up and slapping Laurent's already bloody face.

"We thought he'd run for good," one of the Primes who'd caught him said.

Justinian sent a look around the room that reined all his pack into silence. Even though the lesser Primes backed off, Laurent was all too aware of the malevolent attention focused on him. They were hungry for any excuse to vent aggression, and right now he appeared easy prey to them.

Laurent focused his attention on the truly dangerous one in the room. He made himself look at Justinian, and smile. And rise slowly to his feet.

Justinian let him do these things without striking him again. "Well?" he demanded. "Why did you desert the pack two nights ago? Why have you come back? Why were you skulking around my lair?" He sent a hard look to his beta Prime. "Did he betray us to the Clans? Have they hunted us to this lair?"

"No, Justinian," Belisarius answered promptly. "We made a careful search of the area. There are guards on watch." He gestured toward Laurent. "He is the only—"

"Do you want me to answer your questions or not?" Laurent interrupted, annoyed at having lost Justinian's attention. The night wasn't getting any younger.

And why were Tribe Manticore too damned old-fashioned to use the drugs that gave the Clans and Families the advantage of living twenty-four/seven, instead of creeping around in the dark like a bunch of movie vampires? Oh yeah, the Clan wouldn't let them.

He pushed that frustrating question out of the way, and went on. "I didn't desert the fight in the garage, I escaped a Clan attack—just like your boys did. The point of the exercise is to keep the Clans off our asses. When your loyal minions ran back here—where the Clan might have been able to follow—I went looking for information. That was why you brought me in on this operation, right? To find the woman without the Clans getting wind of a tribe in their territory?"

"Not that you've managed to keep our presence secret," Belisarius accused.

"The Clans have no right to dictate where and what we hunt," Justinian proclaimed angrily. Then he shrugged, acknowledging the reality of the situation. "Yet they do. I didn't come to Los Angeles to start a war, but to get what is mine back."

"Hold that thought," Laurent said. "Because I think that's a strategy that might come in handy."

Justinian gave him a fiercely stern look. "Go on."

"I wasn't skulking around," Laurent went on. "I returned only after I had something useful to offer you, and I was scouting out the property to make sure neither Clan nor human hunter had found the lair when your boys jumped me."

"Hunters!" Justinian shouted. He spat on his fancy carpet. Then he swore in a harsh and ancient language. "How I loathe those murdering, thieving mortal pests. At least fighting vampire-to-vampire has some honor in it, some challenge. But being forced to fight mortals—" His lips drew back in a vicious, fanged snarl.

"It's a dirty job, but somebody has to do it," Laurent muttered under his breath.

"What?"

"Nothing. Can I go on now?"

"You may." Justinian regally granted his permission.

"I keep a low profile in this town," Laurent said, "but I'm the most well-informed vampire in Los Angeles. I've spent the last couple of nights finding out what the Clan wants with the woman, and with us, now that they know I'm not the only Manticore in town."

"How dare you call yourself Manticore?" Belisarius demanded.

His comment was followed by angry snarls from others in the pack, but Justinian held up a silencing hand.

"And what did you find out, might-be Manticore?"

"Wannabe," someone muttered.

Laurent reined in his Prime reaction to start a brawl. He was already restraining the urge to taunt them that it had taken three of them to subdue him when he'd actually been *trying* to get inside.

"What I found out is that the Garrison woman had been the plaything of a Reynard Prime, but he'd moved on before we found her. His interest was in her hot little body and a psychic edge she brought to the sex."

"Sounds like you're going to enjoy more than just torturing her," Belisarius said to Justinian.

The pack leader nodded before looking back at Laurent. "You're saying this Clan maggot had no idea who she is?" Justinian demanded suspiciously.

Laurent nodded. "For him she was a bed toy he met during some heroic rescue, I hear. I don't think they talked much."

"Why talk to a woman? And a mortal at that," Belisarius spoke up.

The other lesser Primes laughed. Laurent and Justinian ignored this byplay.

"Then why was the Clan male there when I sent you for the woman?"

"A blood call, is my guess. I think he drank a little too deep, and the craving hadn't worn off yet. He was trying *not* to return to her, in typically noble Clan fashion. So he was hanging around moping, and got in my way instead." Laurent snorted in disgust. "He assumed I wanted her for myself because he'd had her first, which was better than guessing the truth. But now all the Clan allies have closed ranks to protect the woman. They've taken her to the Shagal citadel."

Justinian hissed, and looked around at his small Manticore pack. "How am I to get my prey out of such a guarded place?" He glared at Laurent. "How are *you*?"

"I have more news, before I get to that."

"More? Worse, you mean."

"Another complication, at least. It seems that the Clans are on one of their noble quests to root evil out of the world. They're looking for some mortal bad guy who calls himself the Patron. Sounds sort of like a Tribe title, doesn't it?"

"The Patron, eh?" Justinian chuckled. "Do they know about Garrison?"

"Not yet. We have the advantage there, and I think we're going to have to use it. You see, the Clans are planning on turning the information about our being in town over to the vampire hunters."

Justinian drew himself up in outrage. "They'd deal with humans against their own kind?"

Yeah, well, boss, the times they are a-changin'. "My sources tell me that old Tony Crowe had an appointment to talk to the hunter leader yesterday, but events at the Shagal place prevented him from keeping it," Laurent said.

"What events?"

"I haven't a clue, but every Clan member in town is gathered there. And some flew in from Idaho. I'm guessing your prey is involved. No doubt Tony plans to reschedule the meeting. That'll leave the woman with the Clans, and the hunters on our tails. We need to act fast."

"What would you have us do?" Belisarius demanded. "Raid the Citadel? Battle the humans? Run?"

Running would have been Laurent's first choice, except for the promised payday. He kept his attention on Justinian. "I do have a suggestion."

It involved using brains rather than fangs, so there was no guarantee this lot would go along. But the only one who had to was the pack leader. The others would obey without question. Such blind obedience had never made much sense to Laurent. Right now, he wondered why he was tempted to reclaim any place in the Tribe. Maybe when this was over, and he was rich, he'd reevaluate his social ambitions.

Justinian considered him in silence, and tension grew in the room. The other Primes were not at all happy that the pack leader had brought Laurent into their midst. They itched for any excuse to fall on him and tear him to pieces. If Justinian repudiated him now, there was going to be a lot of bloodshed here tonight—though Laurent was the only one who wasn't certain most of the blood was going to be his. He felt mental probes from the others, telepathic taunts and threats, and ignored them. It was the silent, unmoving Justinian he concentrated on.

After a long time, just when Laurent could feel the boys getting ready to pounce, Justinian finally spoke.

"All right: what do you suggest I do?"

"As you desire." Mia paced back and forth in the bedroom, muttering furiously as she walked. "What did he mean, *as you desire*? Who the hell is that woman? What does she mean by bonding ceremony? Who is she to give orders? Since when does Colin Foxe take orders from anybody?"

"He takes orders from his matri," Domini answered.

Mia spun around on the deep plush carpet to face the vampire woman. Domini was seated on one of the chairs near the book-case, her legs drawn up, looking calm and ever so slightly amused. She'd accompanied Mia back to the bedroom—appar-ently to wait with her while some sort of wedding ceremony was being cobbled together.

"I've been through this," Domini had said when they'd come in. "I can help."

Mia had ignored the offer in favor of angry pacing. She'd been so intent on fuming that she'd forgotten Domini's pres-ence until now.

"And only *his* matri, at that," Domini went on. "Colin's a stubborn one. That's one of the reasons Serisa sent for Anjel-ica. She knew he's in too crazy a state right now to answer to anyone but the head of his clan. When a matri gives an order, Primes obey. They're matriarchal, and the only thing that keeps those big, bad boys in line is a strict code of honor and respect for women." She grinned conspiratorially at Mia. "And we women must only use our powers for good."

Mia digested what Domini told her, and ventured, "So An-jelica rules the—Primes—of Colin's clan."

Domini nodded. "That would be Clan Reynard. Serisa is head of Clan Shagal. Clans contain houses, and each house is headed by a daughter, aunt, sister, or female cousin of the matri. So a Prime, say my Alec, would introduce himself as Alexander Reynard, House Anjelica, Clan Reynard. It's complicated, like any culture. It has a certain old-fashioned charm, but somebody really ought to write a manual for new vampire inductees."

"Joss Whedon, maybe," Mia suggested.

Domini laughed, then grew serious. "Advice: no pop cul-ture vampire jokes around the older generations. They rarely get it, and if they do get it, they think it's disrespectful."

Mia filed this tidbit away. At least someone was finally telling her something about vampires, even if it was a vam-pire. "Okay. How do I tell the older generations from the younger, when they're all immortal?"

"Hardly immortal, just long-lived, and that's a good question. You just *know* after a while. It's not polite to ask a vampire's age, but speech patterns and personal style give clues. When I first met my grandmother, she was wearing a lace bustier instead of a leather one, and that's how I could tell the difference, even though she looked about twenty-five."

"I don't plan to be around long enough to tell."

Domini's expression was sympathetic, but slightly impatient. "Get over it, Mia," she advised. "Bonding is always meant to be. Nobody asks for it. You belong in Colin's world now."

"You mean I belong *to* Colin." Fury bubbled in Mia. "Maybe you don't see anything wrong with a mortal being some sort of blood slave to a vampire, but the mortal isn't happy about it."

"Blood slave?" Domini asked. "That's a Tribe term. How do you know about the Tribes?"

"My family are vampire hunters," Mia blurted out, and lifted her head proudly. "The Garrisons." If they could have their clans and houses and whatnot, she had an ancient ancestry, as well. "I'm from an old line of vampire hunters."

"Really? Me, too."

"I thought you were a vampire."

"My grandmother's a vampire, but my . . . Wait a minute, does Colin know about your affiliation? You haven't killed any—"

"No. No one in my family's hunted in generations. I only vaguely knew that vampires existed, before the blond one attacked me."

Domini twined a strand of long, dark hair around her finger and looked thoughtful for a moment. "This should be between you and Colin, and you'd better tell him soon."

"Why? Will the shock be too much for him? He's already ashamed enough to be involved with a mortal."

Domini shook her head. "It's hard on both of you that the matris decided to make your situation so public, but they were worried that he'd broken some very strict laws about bonding. They felt it was necessary to confront him like that, since he's young, stubborn, and more headstrong than most Primes."

"Oh, that's a joy to hear."

"If they'd thought for a moment that he'd forced you—"

"He didn't."

"See, you care for him. Or you wouldn't be so quick to defend him."

"He doesn't want *me*. And I don't want him . . . to be a vampire." Mia sighed dramatically. "But I suppose it's too late, on all counts."

"That's the spirit," Domini said with false cheer. Growing serious, she added, "Remember that he belongs to *you*, too. Don't let him get away with any shit."

Mia couldn't help but smile. "You sound like my friend Courtney. Oh, my God! Courtney!"

Domini jumped up from the chair. "What's wrong?"

"Courtney's going to kill me!"

Domini's hands landed on her shoulders. "Where? How?"

Mia realized that the woman was taking her literally. "Sorry. I— Courtney's my best friend. We've known each other forever, and we promised to be each other's maid of honor. And I don't want to marry Colin, I mean, not like— But since I have to, well, I just can't get married without Courtney being there! I mean, I don't want to have a wedding ceremony without having any say in the arrangements. Which sounds totally hysterical," she added.

"Yeah."

Mia felt unaccustomed tears well up. Not only was it impossible to contact her best friend, but it certainly wouldn't be right to bring Courtney into a lair of vampires. And it hurt terribly to be cut off from her friend. From her family. She had no friends here, no one she could really believe and trust. Not even Colin, who so clearly didn't want a human mate.

"So much for my special day," she murmured, and turned away from the other woman.

She took a deep breath. Domini was right: she needed to get over it, get on with it, and figure out what to do with what she had to work with. Maybe she could come up with some way of escaping during this blood bond ceremony, or at the reception.

Mia began to laugh as she wondered what sort of wedding reception vampires held. Domini looked at her, but there was a knock on the door before she could say anything.

The door opened, and Alec stepped inside. "We have a new wrinkle in the situation. The ceremony might be a little later than we planned." He gave Mia an uncomfortable glance.

"What did Colin do?" she asked.

"He just smashed Tony over the head and fled the Citadel. It looks like we're going to have a search party instead of a bachelor party."

Chapter Fourteen

$\mathcal{M}$ia was aware that someone spoke to her, that someone touched her shoulder, but it didn't matter. There was a landscape painting on one wall of the bedroom. It looked like maybe it was a view of the Italian countryside, a warm, sunny place far, far from here. Mia stared at it and wished herself away.

"Anywhere but here," she murmured

He didn't want anything to do with her. He'd abandoned her. Left her in a den of vampires. Even if he was a vampire too, at least he was her—

"Mia. Mia, focus."

The voice belonged to Alec. The tone was one that expected to be obeyed. Mia ignored him.

"Mia, where is he?" Domini asked gently.

This got her attention, and Mia finally turned back to the couple. "Gone," she said, looking at Alec. "You said he was gone."

"But where is he?" Alec asked. "It would help if you told us."

"What's he talking about?" Mia asked Domini.

"You're bonded to him," Alec said impatiently.

Domini put a hand on his shoulder. "She really doesn't comprehend what it means yet. You are psychically linked to Colin," Domini told her. "*You're* psychic."

"No, I'm not." She remembered sharing thoughts with Colin. She knew that kind of communication came from both of them and wasn't just because he was a vampire. "Unless— Is being able to share thoughts with one person psychic?"

"It's a beginning," Domini said. "Your talent must be latent.

Mortals tend to put up natural barriers to their own gifts, but one day your full potential will just explode. It'll develop as your relationship with Colin grows."

"But right now we need to find Colin," Alec insisted.

"What relationship? Hell, if the man wants to go, let him. Leave him alone. And I don't want to be here, either," she reminded the vampire couple.

"You can't be left alone. The matris have declared—"

"I don't answer to yo' mama!"

Alec's mouth hung open in shock for a moment.

Domini put a hand over her mouth, but her eyes sparkled with laughter. "Twenty-first century, my darlin' bondmate," she said when she had her amusement under control. "Young people these days, and all that."

Alec shook his head. "Mia, we of the Clans are a civilization with ancient laws and strict codes of conduct. Colin has agreed to the bonding ceremony. For him to go back on his word given to his Clan Matri is punishable by death. Twenty-first century or not, Colin's life is forfeit if he breaks his word."

Mia gasped, and this time she couldn't stop the tears, or from shaking as sobs wracked her.

"What's the matter?" she heard Alec ask. "Ow! What?"

"You just told a woman that a man would rather die than marry her," Domini said.

"I didn't say that! Besides, he can't *not want* to marry her. There must be something else going on."

"Tony's convinced that unconsciously bonding has made Colin unstable."

"Tony is currently unconscious. And when he wakes up, everyone in the Citadel is going to know that Colin's gone. Then Serisa and Mother are going to hit the roof, and the shi—"

"You mean you haven't told anyone else yet?" Domini asked.

"He managed to get out without anyone but me noticing. That's why I need your help, Mia. You, Domini, and I can leave the Citadel to find him."

"Shopping," Domini suggested. "They'll understand Mia wanting a dress for tonight."

"Once away from the Citadel, Mia can lead us to Colin, then we can bring them back here."

"Or we could leave them alone to work through their problems," Domini suggested.

"It can't happen that way," Alec answered.

Mia registered Alec's sounding all adamant and stern, and Domini's pragmatism, and she almost laughed. As insane as this situation was, the couple sounded so normal in the way they dealt with each other. Then it registered with her that Alec thought Colin was behaving this way because he was sick. Guilt and concern overrode the tearing pain of abandonment.

"Did I make him sick?" she asked, turning back to them. *Or is he just a jerk?*

Either way, he was still a vampire. Why did she keep forgetting the intrinsic evil of these people? Probably because she had Colin's blood flowing through her veins.

Abomination. The ugly word swam up from the few things she'd learned from her grandmother. It was the term vampire hunters used for those who consorted with the enemy.

She pulled herself together. She wanted to get away and they were offering her a way out. Once she was away from the Citadel with only these two guarding her, she'd be able to find a way to escape.

"I'll help you find Colin," she told them. "Let's hurry."

Colin stood in the shadow of the low stucco building and waited while the woman crossed the small parking lot. He didn't know where she lived, but he knew where she worked, so this was where he'd come to find her. It wouldn't have been prudent to barge in and grab her, so he stood outside and telepathically called until she came outside.

If he'd had his cellular phone with him this would have

been easier, but his fellow clansmen had deprived him of his modern possessions.

The young woman he wanted was slender, long-legged and blond, young and attractive, and wearing a short blue print dress that showed off all her best assets. She wasn't his favorite person in the world, even though he appreciated looking at her. In fact, he considered her an inconvenience, but it wasn't as if he'd made an effort to get to know her. Right now she was important to him.

He waited until she was at her car before he made his move. He was standing behind her before she could open the car door. When he touched her shoulder, she jumped and turned, and her eyes went wide in surprise.

"What the hell are *you* doing here?"

He smiled, cocking his head to one side. "I came for you."

She frowned at him and started to protest.

But Colin looked into her eyes and slipped past her weak mental barriers with ease. *I can explain everything. And you're going to love this.*

"What the *hell* does he think he's doing?"

The sudden jab of possessive anger that went through Mia caused as much physical pain as mental pain. Enough to make her screw her eyes shut—which only gave her a disturbingly vivid image of the couple standing next to a red car. She knew the car, and the woman.

"What's he doing with her?"

Mia's head hurt so much she was barely aware of Domini sitting beside her in the backseat.

"Colin?" Domini asked.

Alec stopped the car so quickly she was thrown forward against the seatbelt. The jolt broke her concentration, but not so much that she wasn't *aware* of the connection linking her to—

"That cheating son of a—"

"Colin," Alec said.

Mia looked at Domini. "I've felt when he was with other women before, and told myself it was imagination. But I just *saw* him."

Domini nodded encouragingly. "The more blood you share, the closer you become."

They were surrounded by heavy traffic on the busy street. Many car horns sounded, and Alec responded by driving slowly on. "Where is he?" he asked Mia. "Which way do I go?"

Mia put her head back against the seat's plush headrest and closed her eyes once more. The air conditioner hummed, and cool air slid over her skin. Domini's hand was warm on her arm. All these sensations were easy to block out. When she let herself concentrate on it, she became exquisitely *aware* of where Colin was.

She'd been fighting the hunger to be with Colin for months. In fact, the struggle not to find him had become a habit, one that had driven her nearly crazy.

It was time for her to give up the fight. The vampires wanted to find Colin. And she *needed* to.

And when she did, all her instincts urged her to whomp his ass for daring to be with another woman.

"Left," she told Alec. "Left at the next street."

"Sweet," Colin said.

He was speaking of the maneuver the black SUV's driver had used to force him to pull the red sports car over to the curb and block it from pulling out again. He might have been concerned if he hadn't recognized the vehicle, or been aware that Mia was one of the passengers.

As it was, he acceded to the situation and said to the woman beside him, "This is fun."

While she wasn't completely in his thrall, he exerted enough influence over her to keep her calm. He got out of the car, and the woman followed him. Mia jumped out of the back of the SUV and rushed toward him. He recognized the look in her eyes, having felt the same way when she was with Tony.

"What the hell do you think you're doing with my best friend?"

"Hi, Mia," Courtney said, coming up beside him.

Mia lunged.

Colin caught Mia in his arms before she could do any damage to anyone.

"Sweetheart, I know exactly how you feel," he told her.

Then he kissed her, and the usual fire threatened to explode between them. Damn, he loved kissing her!

She resisted for a moment, which only made him more urgent. Then Mia ground her body against his, and Colin forgot everything but the urge to lay her down on the hood of the car. Her nails pressed hard against his shoulders told him she wouldn't mind.

"You're holding up traffic, Officer."

Colin heard Alec's comment as though from a great distance, but awareness of the other Prime helped him to reluctantly break the kiss. For a moment he saw only red, and all he could breathe was Mia's scent. They were standing in the street with cars flashing past inches away. He moved onto the sidewalk, where the others joined them.

Then Mia moved away from him, and he was able to get himself fully under control.

She looked from him to her friend. "Courtney, what are you doing with Colin?"

There was still an edge of jealousy in her voice, and Colin couldn't help but smile at this proof that she wanted him. "I felt your need to be with your friend so strongly, I had to do something."

"That was a bit impulsive," Alec said.

Colin concentrated on Mia. "So I was bringing her to you to be a bridesmaid. I wanted to do something nice for you."

"Aw . . . ," Domini said.

He ignored the sarcasm. Mia was all that mattered. She was looking at him not just with confusion, but with a certain amount of cautious hope. She touched his cheek, and the connection was as electric as ever.

"You kidnapped Courtney? For me?" She sounded unwillingly pleased.

Courtney laughed. "He asked nicely." She gave Colin a wry look. "Which I didn't expect from him, but I have to admit, I'm beginning to understand what you see in him."

"Did you hypnotize her?" Mia asked him.

"I used charm," he answered.

"So of course I said I'd come with him," Courtney went on. "Especially after he told me how the two of you had been in intensive couple's counseling for the last week. I was wondering why you weren't answering my calls. I was worried, girl, and I think this quickie wedding idea is a little on the impulsive side, but if that's what you want, you know I'm here for you, like I always am." Courtney took a deep breath, and added, "Do you even have a dress yet?"

"That's exactly where we were heading when we ran into you," Domini said. Colin was relieved when she stepped in to take charge. "Why don't you two head back to Serisa's," she told him and Alec, "while the three of us head over to Rodeo Drive. Don't worry," she added to Alec's dubious look. "I'll be sure to have them back in time for the party."

Chapter Fifteen

"When I was born," Serisa said, "the world was still lit by candles, by fires, and gaslights and oil lamps. And we have always walked by moonlight and starlight, which are the reflections of distant fire. We saw the world by fire, and fire has always burned in us. In this age we live by both sun and candlelight, but the quest to find our bondmates has not changed. Two here have fulfilled that quest. We of the Clans come together to witness the binding of Two Who Burn as One."

Serisa stood on the edge of a wide terrace, her back to a garden fragrant with roses and jasmine. The terrace was lit by hundreds of white candles, and filled with arrangements of red and white flowers in crystal vases. Overhead the moon shone as a silver crescent, and stars were visible despite the lights of the city. Anjelica and Barak stood to the Shagal Matri's right and left, and a small table was in front of them.

All the other vampires were gathered on the terrace, as well. They applauded her words and spoke their approval.

"When two fires join to blend into a greater flame, that is when we know our greatest joy."

There were more murmurs of agreement.

Mia stood on the other side of the terrace in her orchid gown and looked around in shocked wonder at the proceedings. She carried a bouquet of orchids as well, and one was tucked into her short brown curls. She felt beautiful, even though butterflies fluttered in her stomach.

She was as nervous as any bride, she supposed.

While a part of her tried to remind her that she was caught up in a monster movie nightmare, she couldn't listen to that part of herself right now. She was touched, genuinely touched and pleased at the beauty and goodwill that surrounded her. They had done this for her. Best of all, Colin had—

"Ready to rock?" Courtney whispered.

—brought her friend to be with her. She'd been promised that Courtney would be taken safely home afterward, with only pleasant memories of the event. *And no bite marks,* Tony had said. *I promise.*

Mia smiled at Courtney, then at Domini, who was also standing with her.

"You look beautiful," Domini told her.

"Thank you."

It was Lady Anjelica who had found Mia's dress. Anjelica and Serisa showed up at the exclusive dress shop only moments after Domini had ushered her and Courtney inside—a subtle reminder that Mia was a prisoner. There'd been no chance to escape, but the shopping had been glorious. The dress finally chosen was long and slinky; the bias cut gave the dress an elegant but sexy 1930s look. It made Mia feel rather like Jean Harlow.

Maybe she wasn't draped in virginal bridal white, but this was hardly a traditional marriage. "I guess *until death do you part* takes on new meaning when your're dealing with vampires," Mia whispered.

Domini nodded.

"What?" Courtney asked.

On the other side of the terrace, Serisa raised her hands and said, "Let the Bonded be brought together."

"You know, you didn't have to hit me," Tony said.

He was standing to Colin's left while they waited in the garden. Colin didn't glance his way; his attention was focused on the brightness on the terrace above.

"Yeah, but it was fun," he answered.

"You should thank Tony, instead of taking your resentment out on him," Alec said from his other side.

Though he would have preferred to have his own friends or his brother standing witness with him, Colin was grateful enough that his cousin and the Corvus Prime were with him. But he didn't want to hear their advice on women, even if this was the traditional time to offer it.

"Of course, if your friends were standing here," Tony picked up Colin's thoughts, "they'd be ragging you about settling for a mortal."

"And then you'd have to beat the crap out of them," Alec added.

Would I? Colin wondered. He would, because his bond-mate's honor was his honor, and a Prime's honor was everything. "I'm more old-fashioned than I thought."

"Good thing, too," Alec answered. "It means you'll do right by that girl, whether you want to or not."

"I'll take care of her."

"Like a person, not a pet," Tony insisted.

As Serisa said, "Let the Bonded be brought together," Colin took a sharp breath, all the dread of this moment suddenly forgotten. Mia was up there.

He moved across the garden and up the marble stairs with swift urgency. He vaguely recalled that Alec had told him this part of the ceremony symbolized climbing from dark into light as he reached the candlelit terrace. But symbolism didn't matter, as long as Mia was up there waiting for him.

"You are so beautiful," Colin said as he and Mia met.

She was more beautiful than he remembered, even though he'd seen her only a few hours ago. Why hadn't he really noticed how beautiful she was before?

He reached for her. She swiftly gave her bouquet to Courtney and took his hands. He wanted to say more, but neither thoughts nor words would come, only emotions. He was so good at erecting psychic barriers, at compartmentalizing his feelings, but suddenly he had no barriers at all.

What good were barriers when they kept him apart from Mia?

She looked into his eyes, which were aglow with hope. She smiled. It was shy, tentative, but it set him on fire.

Colin drew Mia into his arms. Their bodies came together, and their lips touched. For that instant everything became clear, and he became whole. They became whole.

As if from a great distance he heard Lady Serisa say, "The Blessing of Fire is granted to Reynard Prime Colin and his lady Caramia."

Caramia. Mia. *His* Mia. What a beautiful name, Caramia. As lovely as any vampire name.

Caramia, he whispered into her mind. *Caramia mine.*

Colin, she answered.

The next thing Mia knew, they were facing Barak and the matris across the width of the silk-draped table. Courtney and Domini were standing on her other side; Alec and Tony flanked Colin. A gold cup was placed at the center of the table. It looked heavy and ancient, and was decorated with Egyptian symbols and filled with red liquid.

For the first time Mia felt a moment of panic. Was she going to have to drink *blood*? In public?

Barak leaned forward and whispered, "It's all right. It's a sort of cinnamon drink; cold and hot, sweet and fiery, all at once."

"Kind of like magic Moutain Dew," Colin added.

Mia stifled a giggle as Serisa gave them a stern look. The Matri was obviously not going to allow any levity to mar this grave and solemn occasion.

Serisa reached out. "Give me your left hand," she directed Colin. "Your right," she told Mia. She entwined her fingers with theirs over the cup.

Mia and Colin were already holding hands, and energy

poured through her and from her, making her part of a psychic circle. When Serisa spoke again, it was directly into her and Colin's minds.

Your yearning souls sought and found each other all uncaring of your conscious wills. Your minds must bend to the will of your joined souls. You fight the inevitable to your cost. To wound each other is to wound yourselves. Bend or break, but the bond will remain. Live in joy at what you have found, for the true and complete soul bonding is rare among vampire and mortal kind. Those who seek it do not always find it. You have not sought it, yet the treasure is yours. Guard it, nurture it. Guard and nurture each other.

"I will," Mia said, though she hadn't meant to speak.

After a hesitation, Colin also said, "I will."

Then Serisa placed their hands on either side of the gold cup. "Witness," she said to the others.

Alec, Tony, Courtney, and Domini all gravely responded, "I witness."

The metal beneath Mia's fingers suddenly began to grow warm. Then the liquid within the cup began to glow. She almost didn't believe what she was seeing, but she was completely fascinated.

Are we doing that? she asked Colin as the light continued to grow.

Yeah. He was as awed as she was.

The light and warmth spread into her, through her, through Colin, and back to her. This was magic, true magic, true completion.

When the moment was right, and they somehow *knew* it was right, they gently lifted the cup. Colin held it to Mia's lips for the first sip. She held a few drops on her tongue while she held the cup to Colin's lips, then Alec took the cup from them. She closed her eyes and let this magical potion take her.

It tasted exactly as Barak had described, and more. It tasted like the essence of love.

"Your souls merge, your blood entwines, forever claiming what you are to each other." Anjelica spoke for the first time. "Colin Foxe, Prime of House Athena of Clan Reynard, your Matri recognizes the undeniable truth of your Bonding. Caramia Luchese, mortal daughter of Catherine, your Clan welcomes a new daughter into our keeping. Kiss now, and let the Binding be sealed."

Colin took her in his arms, and when their lips met, she forgot everyone and everything but Colin, and that he tasted of love.

"Great party," Colin said to her, after one more Prime finished giving good wishes and advice and moved away.

Mia was well aware that her "bondmate" was getting tired of all the attention, but they'd been told it was their duty to stand here by the terrace steps and speak to the guests. Mia was still too full of excitement at finally learning about vampires to be bored. For example, she found it interesting that instead of a reception line, the vampires solemnly came up one by one for private conversations.

"Great party, indeed," she replied, gazing around at groups of people who were laughing and flirting with each other.

Couples kept disappearing down the garden stairs and into the house. There was a joyous air of sexual tension in the atmosphere. It was pretty obvious that people got laid a lot at vampire parties. These were highly sensual, sexual beings, and quite comfortable with it.

"Maybe we should dance or something," she suggested to Colin, relishing the idea of moving slowly with her body pressed against his. "The bride and groom can do that, right? It's a way for us to be left alone for a while."

A group of guests were playing classical music on one side of the terrace; the vampire musicians were very talented. She supposed that they had plenty of time to develop their skill.

"They're playing a waltz," Colin said. "Do you know how to waltz?"

"No."

"Me, either. And we don't use terms like *bride* and *groom,*" he explained. "Not for a bonding ceremony. We're mates, bondmates, bonded, but it's hard to translate into mortal terms. It's not gender-specific like husband and wife. It goes deeper than that."

She caught his sense of profound surprise that they shared this special vampire thing, and she nodded. "Me, too."

"We can't fight it," he said, responding to her understanding of him.

But did that mean that he wanted to fight it? Did she? Should they? Not right now; she was having too good a time. "Are you having a good time?"

He kissed her cheek. "Like I said, it's a great party."

Mia took another sip from a crystal flute and sighed. "This is the best champagne I've ever had."

"I'll get you another glass," Colin offered.

She put her hand on his sleeve when he turned toward the buffet table. "You know I never let myself have more than one glass of wine at a party."

He was still for a moment, then turned back to her with a puzzled look. "I do?" She nodded. He frowned. "I guess we don't know each other very well yet."

She settled her arm more snugly around his waist, leaning against him. Desire buzzed through her as it always did when he was near, and there was no frantic edge to it, no darker undercurrents. She was enjoying him, enjoying being with him, loving the anticipation of making love to him.

"This feels good," she said.

"You smell good," he answered.

"It's the perfume. Turns out Serisa uses the same brand my grandmother did. When she spritzed it on me, all these childhood memories came flooding back. It was kind of like having her with me—though I doubt she would have approved of you."

He laughed. "What sane granny would?"

"What about your family?" she asked. "I know that Alec's a cousin, and that Anjelica's a great-aunt, right?"

"Right."

"What about the rest of your family? Will they approve of me? Do you wish they were here?"

"We'll have another ceremony for your family," he said. "A mortal-style wedding."

He had evaded her question. "Will your mom and granny and brothers and sisters come?"

"I don't have a sister, but my mother and brother will welcome you into the Clan. Both my grandmothers are dead," he added. "And don't say you're sorry, because Grandmother Genevieve was nearly six hundred years old when she passed away. Even for a vampire, that's ancient."

Mia's mind boggled at this information. And it reminded her that her great-grandfather—who was ancient by mortal standards—had talked a lot about how wrong it was for something as monstrous as vampires to hold the secret to eternal life. It seemed that they weren't exactly immortal, but . . .

"Six hundred. Whoa. That's impressive."

"So was she. I'm told she was a tough old matri, but the old lady I remember was sweet, and loved to spoil kids."

Mia wondered just how vampires spoiled their children—and about vampire children, and about having vampire children.

"What about your other grandmother?" she asked, grasping for a focus before her mind completely boggled.

Anger and pain clouded Colin's expression. Mia didn't think he was going to answer, but after a moment he said, "I never knew Grandmother Antonia, my father's mother. She was captured by one of the tribes long before I was born. Those are the bad-guy vampires out of mortal legend," he told her. "They're as much our enemies as they are yours. They take our women when they can, as they did my grandmother. Like they tried to take you." His hold on her became suddenly tighter, more possessive and protective.

The tense moment was interrupted by the approach of another Prime. Mia hadn't yet seen a vampire who wasn't spectacularly handsome or beautiful, but this blond male also had an aura of sorrow and weariness about him that was almost palpable.

His smile was still charming, though, and there was a hint of goodwill in his hazel eyes when he looked at her. "I wish you joy, lady of Reynard. And you," he added, looking to Colin, "I wish you all the time in the world to enjoy what you have. Cherish each day." Then he kissed Mia's hand and walked away.

Colin looked after him with the sort of awe Mia had never expected to see from her cocky SWAT cop. "I didn't think he'd be here," he murmured.

"Who is he?"

"David Berus, Clan Serpentes. The Viper himself."

"And that translates to a language I understand as . . . ?"

"Bravest of the Brave, the most primal of the Primes. And the only one who's ever survived losing a bondmate. It drove him crazy for about fifty years. I hear that's why he volunteered to be the guinea pig when they first developed the daylight drugs. He didn't have anything to lose, so he let the scientists experiment on him. He was the first to walk in daylight—though I don't suppose seeing the sun made up for what he lost."

Music still floated across the terrace, the tune melancholy. It added to Mia's sense of sadness over what Colin told her about the other Prime's loss. "How did he lose her?" she asked. "I thought bonding was forever." To lose forever would be awful.

"A band of Purists murdered her," Colin answered. "The evil fanatics cut off her head. David was on the other side of the world when it happened, probably saving mortal lives. The mortal hunters don't care what kind of vampires they kill, as long as they kill vampires."

The hatred he projected frightened Mia. How was she supposed to explain that she had set out to be a vampire hunter herself?

Domini had advised her to tell Colin about her family soon, and it sounded like good advice. But it probably wasn't the best subject to bring up to a vampire husband on one's wedding night. That it felt so very right to be married to this vampire was confusing enough.

"You know," she said, with a shaky smile, "I think I will let you get me that second glass of champagne."

Chapter Sixteen

"Can you read my mind?"

Mia really meant, Can you reach deep into my thoughts and rip out anything you want to know about me? But this didn't seem like the time or place to ask such a blunt, frightening question.

Colin thought this was an odd question for Mia to ask, when they were finally alone. They'd just endured a ceremony that he found downright medieval and silly. Everybody at the party had escorted them into Serisa's most luxurious guest room, where they'd been put into bed together. A shivaree? Or maybe the shivaree thing was the old bride-kidnapping custom. His memory of folklore was dim at the moment.

He guessed maybe Mia didn't want to talk about how strange the last few minutes had been, but it still seemed like an odd question. He studied her as she sat propped up against a pile of pale satin pillows, with a sheet drawn up to her bare shoulders and a pensive look on her lovely face.

"We've been sharing thoughts for months," he reminded her. "Mostly communicating without even knowing it."

"And you've been messing with my memories."

"For your own goo—" He stopped when she shook a finger at him, and made him laugh. Okay, it was time to stop being defensive. "I only touched the surface of your mind," he promised her. "I never consciously went deeper than that."

"But you could?"

Okay, a little paranoia on her part was understandable, but they had better things to do with the rest of the night than talk.

He began tugging slowly on the sheet covering her as he answered. "The kind of mind reading I think you're talking about is really very hard to do, at least if you don't want to leave your subject brain-damaged. I've heard that Tribe vampires mentally rape their victims—but we do *not* want to talk about that."

She shook her head. "Definitely not."

Mia was safe here, and was going to stay safely in the Shagal citadel until the Tribe vampires who'd hunted her were dealt with. Or maybe he'd take her to his own clan's stronghold in Idaho. But that would mean introducing her to the likes of Flare and Maja, the Clan daughters he'd been courting. Although he cared deeply for Mia, he wasn't ready to acknowledge that a Clan match was forever out of his reach.

Bend or break, Serisa had said. But he had to do this in his own time and way. He had no choice but to make the effort. And—

"Colin?"

He blinked, and looked at Mia. Without noticing it he'd pulled the sheet down around her waist, baring her lovely round breasts. The warm tint of her tanned skin contrasted beautifully against the pale satin. He pulled the sheet all the way off, taking in her sensually rounded hips and the firm curves of her legs.

She reached out and touched his cheek, and the contact sent blazing heat through him.

"Colin, are you with me?"

"Oh, yeah," he said, and bent his head to take a nipple in his mouth. He suckled, and teased it with his tongue and teeth when it grew stiff, loving the taste and texture. Mia's breasts were wonderful.

Her response was as quick as his need. She caressed his back and shoulders while he moved down her body, breathing in her warm female scent, tasting her skin with quick licks and kisses.

He was aroused by the sharp awareness of blood rushing

beneath warm flesh. His fangs were extending quickly, and his cock was already hard. Flesh and blood both called to him, the need to possess both growing in him. He sensed and savored the way her body changed as she became more and more aroused.

Mia tried not to let herself go, not to lose herself instantly this time. But Colin's gentlest caress was explosive, making it almost impossible not to fall into sensory overload. She couldn't stay lucid for long when he touched her.

She was aware of the soft mattress beneath them, and of the smooth satin sheet and pillows at her back; the brush of cool air was a stark contrast to the heat of their naked skin. But most of her world was taken up by the feel of sinewy hard muscles beneath her hands, and the glory of Colin's clever mouth working wonders, moving from her breast to her stomach, and farther down. Every few moments the edge of a fang brushed across her skin. Anticipation of the sharp combination of pain and ecstasy set her senses reeling.

This searing expectation was familiar, but this was the first time she was actually fully aware of what was happening.

"And I like it."

Colin lifted his head. "What?"

She ran her fingers through his hair. "Don't ever stop."

Colin laughed, and she felt the sound against her skin. The same way she felt his pleasure at giving her pleasure. She closed her eyes and rode sensation while his head came between her spread thighs. His highly skilled tongue darted and licked across her slick, swollen flesh. She squirmed and moaned as lightning seared deep inside, where it coiled and grew, tighter and larger, and finally burst through her.

Colin cried out at her orgasm. His body arched away from hers, then he grabbed her by the waist and pulled her to him across the smooth satin sheet, and his cock entered her in one smooth, hard thrust. This set off another orgasm, and her reaction drove him crazy—which drove her wild.

As the feedback loop rolled through them, their bodies came together in hard, frantic thrusts, thrashing limbs, and breathless, frenzied kisses on salty hot skin.

Mia was blinded by the roaring rush of orgasm after orgasm, but it still wasn't enough. The craving grew even as he came inside her and his release flashed nova-hot through her. The taste of Colin's skin was delicious, but what was beneath the surface still called to her. There was no way to resist, and her teeth pressed into Colin's shoulder.

Her mouth filled with sweet copper fire, though there was only a drop or two on her tongue. Vampire blood was so sweet.

Colin pulled away with a hard, surprised jerk, and he was up off the bed an instant later. Mia watched him in a languorous fog, too heavy-limbed and brain-fogged with utter satisfaction to react to anything.

Colin, on the other hand, was full of furious energy. He grasped his shoulder and shouted, "You bit me!"

His glare could have ignited a wildfire, but Mia only smiled a little. "Uh-huh."

"You. Bit. Me." He spoke slowly and clearly, each word an accusation.

Mia languidly reach up and stroked the spot on her left breast where he had bitten her while they'd been making love. It was nice to remember him doing it, and how wonderful it had felt at the time. Though she wasn't quite sure when he had taken the quick nip that sent her into ecstasy. There'd been a lot of ecstasy in the last few minutes—hours?

She smiled as she continued to pet the healing mark. "That was nice."

Colin gazed at her breast and he felt himself growing hard again, just looking at Mia's naked body. His fangs ached to bury themselves in the exact spot she was so provocatively stroking. She was looking at him with a dazed, adoring, satiated expression that normally would have made him preen. Normally, he'd jump back into bed and start making love to her again.

But there was something very disturbing going on here, and he had to concentrate, hard as that was. As hard as *he* was.

"You *bit* me," he said for the third time.

"Yeah." Her eyes glittered with invitation, and she lifted a hand toward him. "Come here, and I'll do it again."

He curbed his natural impulses with some effort, and concentrated on justifiable anger. He had to turn his back on her. "You had no right to bite me."

"Why not? You bite me all the time."

He whirled back to her. "I'm a vampire! I'm supposed to bite you!"

"Is there something wrong with biting back?"

"Yes! You can't taste my blood without—"

"Your permission?" Irritation crept into her voice. "Why should I have to ask you for a bite, when you never asked me if it's okay?" She sensually stroked her breasts. "Which it is."

Her nipples were standing up, perky and demanding his attention. His body was growing tight with desire, but this had to be settled. "Because—"

"It works both ways, Colin."

"How long have you been biting me?"

She gave a slow, one-shoulder shrug. "I don't know. It just happens sometimes, when we get really wild. I don't usually remember doing it. Don't you remember getting bitten?"

"No."

"I didn't remember you biting me, either. So I guess that's fair."

"It's not fair. It's crazy. I deliberately made you forget when I tasted you."

"Well, maybe I made you forget."

"That's not possible!"

She gave another shrug, followed by a conciliatory smile. "Are we going to argue on our wedding night?"

"We are not married!" he shouted furiously, as a sense of betrayal took him. "We're bonded! We're stuck with each other forever!"

"Stuck?" Her voice sounded as sharp as broken glass.

"And it's your fault!"

Her hurt beat at him through his fury, through the ache of lust. For a moment, he hated himself for hurting her. He didn't mean it, not the way she thought he did. It was just—

Just that it wasn't supposed to happen this way!

He'd had his life planned out, knew all the right moves, the way a Prime's life was supposed to progress. It had all been going so fine until the night Mia Luchese kickboxed her way into his life.

Though that wasn't fair, and he knew it. He had pursued her, been determined to have her, the moment they met. But she was the one who caught him—and right now he hated the feeling. A few hours ago he'd made a vow to himself to accept his fate, to make the best of the situation.

Right now, all he wanted to do was walk out.

But she was hurting too, and she was his bondmate.

"Damn!" he snarled, and turned back to her.

Only for a knock to sound on the door before anything could be said or settled.

Chapter Seventeen

"Don't you dare open that door!" Mia demanded as Colin crossed the room. She was in no mood to be interrupted; no way was she going to let him get away with blaming her for all this. "Come back here and fight like a vampire!"

Colin snatched up her abandoned clothing as he passed the foot of the bed and tossed it to her. "Get dressed."

"Fuck you!"

"Don't tempt me."

His voice was cold, but the anger and implied threat radiating from him frightened Mia.

Colin didn't know who dared to interrupt them, but he was set to tear the intruder apart. He paused only long enough to make sure his bondmate's modesty was protected.

But when he reached the door, Colin leaned his forehead against it for a moment. Despite the wild urges racing through him, a small, sane voice was trying to remind him that it was a Prime's duty to think before reacting. He was intensely aware of the smooth grain of the wood and the faded scent of the varnish. His sharp senses also detected both a male and a female waiting in the hallway. This gave his animal side some reassurance that the Prime on the other side of the door wasn't here to steal his mate.

The knock came again.

When he opened the door he found Barak and Serisa waiting in the hall. Barak was standing protectively in front of his bondmate, as though anticipating an attack.

Colin kept his hands at his sides, and his voice almost polite. "Yes?"

Serisa peered from behind her mate's wide shoulder and gave Colin's naked body a quick glance as she said, "We would not have interrupted you unnecessarily."

Colin accepted her once-over as his due. Bonded or not, young or old, a vampire had to be dead not to *look*. "Yes," he said again, his voice just barely calm enough not to give insult to the Matri.

"Your presence is required," Barak said. "Immediately."

Colin ran a hand across his face. His nerves were already frayed, but he knew they wouldn't have disturbed him if it wasn't important. SWAT call or Prime duty, he was used to having his private life disturbed.

Still, he couldn't help but say, "Why now?"

"We are sorry," Barak said. "But we have a situation with Tribe Manticore that concerns you and your lady."

"And requires your presence," Serisa added. "Both of you."

Mention of Tribe vampires redirected Colin's anger. He'd heard of the Manticores; real old-fashioned bad boys considered trash even by the low standards of the other tribes.

"I'm not letting my woman near a Manticore."

"It is required," Serisa said. "By the terms of the Understanding."

Colin frowned at the Matri. "Understanding? What are you talking about?" Suspicion gnawed at him. "Is this Understanding like a treaty? Do we have a treaty with the Tribes?" His voice rose in outrage at each question. "How come I've never heard of this?"

Barak put up a calming hand. "We have arrangements for parlays with the Tribes—a holdover from ancient times when the mortal hunters targeted all vampires. We do not stand with them, ever, but exchanges of information are sometimes necessary. The Manticore pack leader claims rights under the old ways."

"An *Understanding*," Colin scoffed.

"They approached our sentries just before dawn," Serisa told him. "They offered their vulnerability to sunlight as a show of good faith. They risked their lives for the chance to speak with us." She sighed. "I had no choice but to allow them a daylight sanctuary, and parlay."

Colin thought she should have let these Manticores stand out in the sunlight and fry.

"For the parlay, Justinian of the Manticores says he requires your and Mia's presence," Serisa said.

"Please get dressed and come with us now," Barak said.

Colin was torn by several conflicting impulses. He was compelled to obey, because he'd been trained to obey the Matri and elders. He also wanted to tell them he wasn't letting Mia anywhere near the vampires that had attacked her, and slam the door in their faces.

He glanced over his shoulder to where Mia knelt in the center of the wide bed, wrapped in the cream-colored satin sheet. Her expression was one of curiosity, but her emotions still radiated anger and hurt. He felt them like a burning coal in his head, and in his soul.

He couldn't stand her pain.

"Your indulgence, Matri, Elder, but we can't join you right now." Colin took a step back, and began to slowly close the door on the surprised couple. "Tell the bottom-feeders we'll be there—when we're there," he finished as the door firmly shut.

He put everything going on outside this room out of his mind as he crossed the thick carpet to stand at the foot of the bed.

Mia watched his approach warily. "What do you want?"

"Let's talk," he said, holding up his hands before him. He took a deep breath, determined to stay calm. "Just talk. Okay?"

"Talk?"

She looked at him so suspiciously that he almost laughed. At least he felt her temper cooling down a little. That was his Mia: she flared white-hot at light speed, but she calmed down quickly enough. Her hurt wasn't going away, though.

He sat down on the end of the bed. "Come here."

When she didn't move, he grabbed her by the ankle and pulled her to sit beside him. He put his arm around her shoulder, partly to be comforting, partly to keep her from getting up and stalking away. She was stiff in his embrace for a moment, but soon relaxed against him. They couldn't help but want to touch each other. He waited in silence for her curiosity to build.

"What do you want to talk about?" she finally asked.

She looked up at him with those big brown eyes, and he wanted to do several things other than talk. Which would have been fine if she was just another mortal girl he desired.

"We don't have much time. Did you hear about the Tribe visitors?"

She scowled. "I heard. But—"

"When did you first bite me?" he interrupted. "Do you bite all your lovers?"

"All my lovers?" She laughed. "You're the only lover I've ever had."

"What?" His arm tightened around her. After a moment of shock, his memories rolled back to the first time they'd made love. All he remembered was passion—hot, hard, frantic, unbelievably mind-melting sex. He remembered the effects, but the details were vague. "Uh . . ." Colin swallowed hard. "Are you sure?"

He expected her to be offended, but she chuckled. "A woman generally remembers these things. You are the only lover I've ever had."

"But—it—you—we—"

"Fucked like bunnies. Or vampires, I guess."

"But you seemed so—involved. Shouldn't a virgin be more . . . virginal?"

She laughed again, obviously relishing his almost embarrassed confusion. "This isn't the Middle Ages. I read a lot of books with sex scenes, and saw a few R-rated movies before you came along—and I think instinct plays a part in knowing what to do."

"So—" He thought about it for a moment, then ventured, "When I bit you for the first time . . . you responded by . . . you followed my lead?"

She gave this some consideration. "Yeah. I guess that makes sense."

"So I'm your first, huh?" He pulled her even closer, her bare skin warm and soft against his side. "How about that." Too bad they didn't have a few more minutes.

"Oh, *please,*" she complained. "Don't sound so smug, you slut."

"Guilty," he told her.

"And I knew every time you cheated on me. Did you know that?"

Colin started to say that he hadn't technically cheated on Mia, since he had officially ended their relationship. But since they'd unknowingly fallen into the bonding process during the months they'd been lovers, and he suddenly felt the pain he left in her like deep, aching scars on his own soul, he understood her anger.

"It must have confused you," he said. "Knowing I was with other women, but not knowing how you knew."

"Did you know I was aware of you?"

"I tried not to think about you at all." She tried to draw away, but he wouldn't let her. "I know that's harsh, but it's true. I tried to forget you."

"Because I'm not a vampire."

"You were pretty upset to find out that I'm a vampire. You wouldn't have wanted me if you'd known the truth from the beginning."

"You can say that again," she muttered.

The comment hurt his pride, but Colin kept his hard-won calm. They didn't have the time to work out all their problems right now. "We have years—"

"That you'll be stuck with me," she interrupted.

"But I can't imagine being stuck with anyone else," he said. "Even when I was with other women, all I could see was you."

Mia gave him a furious look. "Oh, that really makes me feel good."

"Do you want me to say something sickeningly romantic?" She frowned, but shook her head. "I could say I wish all those nights in other women's beds hadn't happened. All I can say is that they *shouldn't* have happened, knowing what I know now. If I'd thought for a moment that we were bonding, I would have—"

What would he have done? Returned to Mia and begged her to take him back, instead of lingering near her and hating the need to be with her? If he'd suspected the start of a bond, he might have run off to his Clan citadel, seeking telepathic help, or to Dr. Casmerek's vampire clinic for some kind of scientific answer. But could they have helped? Would it have been right?

"My culture teaches that bonds are meant to be. Apparently the longer a Prime lives unbonded, the more he craves the bond and searches for his one true love. I'm still confused about what happened between us."

Mia was thoughtful for a moment. "If I hadn't bitten you and made you forget it, you probably wouldn't be in this mess."

"Don't apologize."

"I'm not. I'm just acknowledging my accountability. When I first figured it out, I was upset about it, but then I figured I had as much right to bite you as you did to bite me. It brought us mutual pleasure."

He couldn't deny the incredible pleasure, and the need for more of the same. So Colin tried his best to be as accepting of the situation as Mia was trying to be—he knew she was still pretty rattled, even though she was trying to be objective. He rubbed his shoulder, aware of a sweet, phantom ache. The girl had sharp teeth for a mortal.

"And we did it a lot—tasted each other—even if I don't remember the times you bit me. I wonder why I don't remember?"

"We're stuck with each other," Mia said. "Till death do us part, I guess."

The vision of empty, lost, bondless David Berus flashed through Colin's mind. He shuddered at the thought of ending up like that. "Till death do us part," he told his bondmate. "And that will be a long long time."

"But you're immortal, and I'm—"

"Been watching *Buffy* reruns?"

"Right. Not immortal, just long-lived. Domini tried to explain that." He hadn't noticed that she'd put her head on his shoulder until she lifted it. "Domini also said something about my mysterious psychic talent being stimulated around you." She laughed. "You stimulate every other part of me. Could it be that when you made me forget, I bounced it back at you?"

He rubbed his chin. "I—suppose."

He wasn't sure if anything was settled, but fury wasn't buzzing between them anymore. That would have to do for now.

He stood and drew Mia to her feet. "We have plenty of time to explore our psychic connection later. Right now, we'd better get to the Matri's meeting before they send a commando team in for us."

Chapter Eighteen

"Nice," Laurent murmured, standing arrogantly in the center of the luxurious room. He looked around with the air of one who owned the place. "Very nice."

If there was one good thing to be said about the Clans, it was that they lived well. Not ostentatiously, mind you. Oh, no, the cultured, civilized, extremely old-money self-proclaimed good guys of the supernatural world had class, style, élan.

Laurent wanted to get him some of that. Or at least enough cold, hard cash to fake it. Being nouveau riche was fine with him.

In the meantime, he noted the tasteful paintings and sculptures, the numerous leather couches and chairs grouped around low tables, the subdued glow of the lighting, the rich color and texture of the carpet.

He was not unaware of the danger of the situation. Truce or not, he, Justinian, and Belisarius were standing in the den of their mother-loving enemies, with every Clan Prime in the territory ranged in a circle around the walls of the windowless room. No one had invited them to have a seat, of course. He supposed being offered a drink was out of the question.

And what exactly did Clan folk drink, anyway? It was a certain bet that their women didn't allow them to keep blood pets around the house. No way one of those poor, whipped bastards could just reach out and grab himself a hot one without Mama saying, "You put that mortal girl down right now!"

Laurent couldn't help but smile at the image, earning him a furious look from Belisarius.

"Relax," he whispered to the beta Prime. "So they have us outnumbered. We have—no, wait, we *don't* have right on our side. You may continue being terrified."

"I don't take commands from you."

Laurent managed to successfully hide his amusement this time, wondering if Belisarius realized just how stupid his automatic response sounded.

Justinian turned a fierce look on him. *This is taking too long, exile.*

Patience, my lord. We must be patient.

And wait on a woman's whim as to whether she will talk to me, and when?

Justinian's frustration at having to deal with the Clan women was understandable. It didn't help that they'd been kept waiting far longer than Elder Barak had promised. Laurent hoped the pack lord didn't blow their best chance out of impatience and outraged pride. Laurent gave a wary, assessing look at the Clan Primes ranged around the room. Though they weren't aware of it, Laurent recognized many of them. Every Prime in the city, except for the little Reynard shit who'd started this, was giving them cold, hard looks. The Manticores would never get out of here if there was a fight.

Maybe even worse than the uneven numbers was the fact that the Clan vampires were memorizing their faces and psychic signatures. Hiding in this territory was no longer going to be possible.

"This had better work," he murmured, and drew dirty looks from the vampires he'd talked into coming here.

Before Justinian or Belisarius could say anything, a group of people entered the room. The Clan boys all straightened, practically coming to attention at the sight of several of their regal, proud women. The smallest of the lovely females seemed to be in charge. She was not young, but age only added a lovely patina to her beauty. She walked hand in hand with a barrel-chested male with dark skin for a vampire, and grizzled gray hair.

"Serisa and Barak of Shagal, aka Clan Jackal," Laurent said to Justinian.

He'd given the Manticores a briefing on the local players, but now he matched faces to the names. The Tribes were always amused and contemptuous of the humble scavenger names the Clans went by. Laurent figured the Clans saw their monikers as some kind of self-deprecating joke these grand chevaliers played on mortals and the rest of the supernatural world.

Not that this was the time to be analyzing names; his job was to get what they wanted and get out of here alive. A lot was going to depend on keeping Justinian and Belisarius from doing anything fatally stupid. They had both tensed at the sight of the female.

Be polite, he advised Justinian. *Be diplomatic. Or let me do the talking.*

Laurent knew his last comment was a big mistake even before Justinian gave him a poisonous look, for it was an implied challenge to the senior vampire's dominance.

Laurent bowed his head and took a quick step back.

Serisa spoke before Justinian reacted further. "Don't sneer at me if you want to get anything accomplished. I don't like dealing with you, either, but at least I don't resent you simply for your gender."

Justinian drew himself up haughtily. The Primes along the walls tensed. Then Justinian smiled, and swept Serisa an elegant bow.

"Forgive my rudeness. It's a bad habit I'll try not to indulge in in your presence. Our cultures are different, Lady, but my intent is to abide by the rules of your house, though I am not certain of all of those rules. Cut me some slack, please?" He spread his hands before him in a conciliatory gesture.

His last words held a certain charm, at least enough to make Serisa smile. Laurent noted that the smile didn't reach the shrewd old Matri's eyes. The Primes relaxed, but not much.

"A little slack," she agreed. "So we can get this over with as quickly as possible."

Justinian inclined his head with graciousness that took Laurent by surprise. "When you hear what I have to say, you will be glad you allowed this parlay, Matri."

"And why is that?" she asked.

Before he could answer, two more people entered the room, and everyone's attention turned toward the couple.

Well, well, well, isn't that sweet, Laurent thought. *They're holding hands.* He was willing to bet that they wouldn't be after the Clan brat found out the awful truth about his girlfriend.

No, not girlfriend, he realized as they came closer and the psychic energy that swirled between the pair permeated his own shielded senses. *Oh, shit! They're bonded!*

Bonding wasn't something the Tribes allowed, but Laurent had been around enough Clan and Family types to recognize the signs. He put a hand gently on Justinian's sleeve and telepathically pointed out this new wrinkle in the proceedings, while the lovebirds went to stand with the Matri's group.

Everyone was staring at her. She'd gotten stared at a lot the last couple of days and she was very uncomfortable with the looks she was getting from the trio in the center of the room—which included the blond vampire.

"You do know that's the one who attacked me, right?" she whispered to Colin.

He squeezed her fingers. "Oh, yeah," was his grim answer.

He aimed a murderous glare at the Tribe vampires, but didn't say anything as he led her to stand near Serisa and Barak. Domini was there, and Anjelica, along with a couple more Clan women and several older males. Mia felt young and way out of her depth in this crowd, and would have been happy to slip to the back behind everyone and not be noticed.

But apparently she and Colin were the center of attention.

She wondered if they were ever going to be able to get away to start leading their lives and working out their relationship.

Serisa clapped her hands. "We are gathered in truce with our enemies," the Matri intoned.

Did the vampire leader have a ceremonial statement memorized for every occasion?

All the vampires, including the Tribe ones, clapped once. The combined effect was like a somber clap of thunder. Mia exchanged a glance with Domini, who claimed to be nominally human. Domini had her arms crossed, and she gave the faintest of shrugs when Mia caught her eye. Mia was almost reassured, knowing she wasn't the only one out of this particular ceremonial loop.

"Speak, Justinian of Manticore," Serisa said.

The one called Justinian took a step forward. Like all the other Primes she'd seen, Mia found him handsome, with a commanding presence. But unlike the Clan males she'd encountered, there didn't seem to be any sense of humor leavening the haughtiness of his bearing. He looked the way a vampire ought to: arrogant, cruel, and really, really pale.

"The Clans and Tribes disagree on almost every point," he began.

Justinian's voice was deep and compelling, and made her think of a high-powered trial lawyer. For some reason that image made Mia very uncomfortable—as if maybe she was the one on trial.

"Over the centuries, this has led us to misunderstand each other. But when it comes to the hunters, when it comes to survival of our kind, we are forced to cooperate." He produced a slick, sincere-seeming smile. "I have come to tell you that you are unknowingly harboring a female from one of the mortal bloodlines that have murdered our people for centuries."

"Would that be me?" Domini spoke up, taking a step forward and shielding Mia in the process. "If it is, you can leave now, because that thing with the Purist was settled long ago."

Justinian turned a look on Domini that could have melted titanium.

"Silence, female!" he snapped. Then he looked her up and down and sneered. "Mortal female, at that."

"So much for the civilized veneer," Domini murmured.

"Bi—" Justinian managed to stop himself before uttering the rest of the word.

The tension in the room escalated, and Alec moved forward. Tony Crowe put a hand on Alec's shoulder to stop him. The blond vampire did the same with Justinian.

Justinian shoved away his hand, but the blond turned to Serisa. "There's a story that needs to be told," he said hurriedly. "One that goes back several mortal generations. Allow us to tell you the root of our grievance and claim. We came here in good faith." He gave Domini a mildly reproachful look. "Bait a Prime of any of our kind, and he responds."

Domini frowned. "Okay. I did that." She pointedly did not address Justinian. "My apologies, Matri."

The friction among the Primes eased down a notch.

"Tell your story," Serisa directed.

The blond waited for a nod of permission from Justinian before he said, "For several centuries, a mortal family named Garrison pursued Tribe Manticore. These murderers made it their mission to hunt us to extinction."

His words made Mia uncomfortable, and she could almost see their point of view.

"But the Manticore accepted the terms of the Great Truce of 1903," he went on. "We tried to pursue the peaceful coexistence promised by the truce. The Manticore disappeared into the night, to take blood as we need, but to live without killing. And the Garrisons retired from hunting. They still had the blood of our dead on their hands, but we vowed not to seek revenge. We lived by the truce." He looked around and asked, "Has anyone ever heard of a Manticore killing a mortal?"

After a short silence, Barak said, "Not for over a hundred years."

"When the truce freed us from the necessity of always being on the run, the Manticore finally had the time to amass a great deal of wealth. We used this wealth to protect our young, to try to fit into the modern world. We might have become one of those tribes that blended into the neutral ways of the Families."

Mia interpreted this statement as some sort of playing on the Clan vampires' sympathies, and it seemed to be working, at least a little.

"Whatever might have happened," he went on, "we will never know. Because our future was destroyed by a man named Henry Garrison."

Oops, Mia thought, as shock rattled her.

Colin had put his arm around her shoulders; now it tightened in reaction to her psychic outburst.

"What?" he asked.

The blond went on, "Garrison was from the generation of the hunter family born after the truce was signed. He had no personal vendetta to pursue vampires, no reason to hunt us. But he came after us anyway. Not because of what we are, but because of what we had. This Garrison stole everything from us and made himself a wealthy man."

"A very wealthy man," Justinian added. "And Tribe Manticore has dedicated nearly a century to hunting him. It is our right to take back what is ours, but Garrison hides himself very well. It has taken us decades to find even a member of his family. And what do we encounter, when we finally have the key to his whereabouts within our reach? We find that the Clans have offered protection to this vampire murderer's great-granddaughter." He pointed at Mia. "To her."

Everyone turned to look at Mia.

"And by the way," the blond said, "these days, Garrison likes to be known as the Patron."

Chapter Nineteen

Colin's arm was no longer around her shoulder. In fact, he had stepped away and was the one looking at her with the most intent scrutiny.

Though the gazes turned on her were neutral and questioning, the psychic temperature in the room was decidedly cooler. And the air of danger was palpable just under the surface.

Mia went cold, and tried not to shake—but Good God, she was a mortal among vampires! And the blond had done a fine job of working the room.

She turned her glare on the Manticore vampires. "These are the ones who have been trying to kill me," she reminded the Clan members.

"We have been trying to—"

The blond hesitated, and Mia was willing to bet he was trying to come up with words that were more diplomatic than *capture, torture, interrogate.*

He settled on, "We have questions for the hunter. It was natural for us to approach her with a certain amount of caution."

"He jumped out of the bushes and grabbed me," Mia said. "If Colin hadn't rescued me, I don't know what would have happened." She glanced at Domini, then over at Alec and Tony. "And remember the attack in the parking garage?"

"We came here to claim our right to deal with the Garrison woman," Justinian said.

"She is now a member of Clan Reynard," Anjelica spoke up. "You cannot have her."

Mia flashed her Matri-in-law a shocked look. "What? Would you just turn me over to them otherwise?"

"We came to claim her," the blond said. "But we had no knowledge that the mortal had managed to connive to bond herself to a Prime. Of course, now our negotiations over the Garrison woman have become more complicated."

This guy was good. He was making it sound like she'd wormed her way into Colin's clan on purpose.

"My name isn't Garrison," she pointed out. "Henry Garrison *is* my great-grandfather, but—"

What was she supposed to say? That she'd only met the old boy a few days ago, that she didn't like him—and that he'd sent her out hunting vampires?

"I know very little about the man," she finished.

"He's richer than God, and about as old," Colin said. He took her by the arm. "That's what you told me about him once. Don't you remember?"

"Yeah—vaguely."

"You didn't tell me he's the Patron." His voice was soft, deadly, and very, very scary. So was the cold look in his eyes.

Being scared always made Mia angry. She jerked her arm away from Colin's grasp. "I didn't know."

Colin looked calm, but she was all too aware of the seething fury beneath the surface. "If you will excuse us, Matris, I need to talk to my bondmate in private."

"Yes. We need a few minutes to work this out." Though *this* was so complicated, Mia had no idea how to begin.

"I protest," Justinian said. "This hunter-spawned female has her psychic claws in your young Prime. That makes him vulnerable to any poisonous lies she plants in his mind. It is the Manticores' right to question her. Let me—"

"You have ten minutes." Serisa cut him off. She made a shooing gesture. "Go out on the terrace and talk."

*   *   *

"When were you planning on telling me?"

Colin sounded far too calm, when she'd been waiting for an explosion. He'd been standing with his back to her for a couple of minutes, looking out at the landscaped hillside stretching down from the house. The marble terrace was empty; every sign of last night's celebration was gone.

Mia squinted in the bright light that poured down on them. She was aware of a growing headache, and wished for a pair of sunglasses.

She also wanted to go home.

She wanted her house, her profession, her life. She wanted to call her mom. She *definitely* didn't want anything to do with her great-grandfather.

"He ran out on my family," she reminded Colin. "Remember that I told you how he abandoned them? I didn't know anything about—no, that's not quite true. I knew about the Garrisons being hunters, but not about how he—"

"When were you going to tell me that you are a vampire hunter?" He turned slowly to face her. When she didn't immediately deny the charge, he lifted one heavily arched brow. "Well," he said, and put his hands behind his back. "Isn't this interesting?"

Mia would have preferred him to shout.

"Domini said I should tell you right away, but there hasn't exactly been time."

Surprised hurt spread from him like a shock wave. "Domini knew about this, but you didn't tell *me?*"

"There wasn't time!" Mia repeated. "The subject came up just before the ceremony." She crossed her arms and took a defiant stance in front of him. "And I don't know why I have to defend myself just because my ancestors and yours didn't get along. We're not the Hatfields and the McCoys, you know."

"Who?"

Okay, maybe Colin didn't know anything about American history. Or maybe it was mortal history he was weak on.

Mia tried another tack. "I'm not the enemy. I don't want to hurt anyone in the Clans."

Her own sincerity surprised her. It hadn't been so long ago that she'd lumped all vampires into the evil-monsters-that-must-be-destroyed category. What had changed her mind? Was it because they'd given her a beautiful dress and made her and Colin marry each other? Because they threw a great party? Maybe it was because the Clan vampires had defended her from the Tribe ones?

"Your people don't seem to have any kind of evil agenda toward humans. I haven't witnessed anything but your helping people." She looked at him with admiration. "You're a SWAT officer."

"Didn't you accuse me of using that to cover up killing people?"

She winced. "I was angry when I said that. Scared and totally confused at finding out you were a vampire."

"How could you be confused when you already knew about vampires?"

"I didn't know *you* were one! All I knew was what little my grandmother told me, which she learned from her grandfather and only half believed herself. A lot of information can get lost or garbled in that amount of time."

He looked thoughtful for a moment. "I guess mortals have a different view of time. What's within living memory for one of us can be ancient history for you."

She nodded. "Exactly. I knew I had a legacy, and a feeling I should do something about it, but—"

"Is that why you're such a jock? So you could kick vampire butt?"

She was embarrassed, since her training didn't stand up well against the reality of his kind. "I like being physical. But yeah," she admitted, "I've worked my butt off preparing for a scenario I never really thought would happen. And I certainly never intended to become a bad-ass vampire hunter until that blond guy jumped me."

"Tony said you were looking for the hunters." Colin slapped a hand to his forehead. "I am such an idiot. He kept saying you were a wannabe hunter. Why didn't I pay attention? Because I can't think around you." As if in proof, he grabbed her by the shoulders and drew her into a hard, fierce kiss.

She opened her mouth beneath his and responded just as fiercely. Heat raced through her, mutating the high drama of their argument into passion—deep physical and emotional need. She ran her hands down his back and thighs, reveling in the feel of warm skin and wiry muscles.

The kiss ended as abruptly as it began, leaving her dizzy with desire and totally frustrated. "Hey!"

He gave a harsh, breathless laugh and shook his head. "I can't think. All I want to do is that. And more."

"Me, too." She was crazy about Colin.

Or maybe just plain crazy. Here they were in the middle of yet another argument, faced with a threat from those Manticore jerks, yet lust still sizzled and threatened to burn away all brain cells used for logical thought.

"We'd better not," she agreed. "Besides, you're still pissed at me."

"Yeah," he agreed.

"I still don't completely know why."

"Because of the Patron." Colin put his hands on her shoulders. "Don't you realize who this man is?"

"The man who deserted my grandmother's family," she responded. "This does not endear him to me. And apparently he got rich by stealing, but since that claim comes from vampires who attacked me, I'm not necessarily willing to believe that." But she couldn't deny that Henry Garrison and the Patron were the same man; she had heard one of his staff address him as Patron.

"Running out on your family and stealing from the Manticores are things he did in the past," Colin answered. "They're nothing compared to what the Patron is up to right now. He's a very, very dangerous man. Dangerous and sick, and ruthless."

Mia was stung, even if she didn't have much respect for Henry Garrison. "Dangerous and sick and ruthless is exactly what I thought about *your* relatives a couple of days ago. How can you say such things when you don't even know the man?"

"Oh, I know him," he answered. "I've taken a vow to destroy him."

"You what?" Mia jerked away and stared at her bondmate in horror. "I can't let you kill one of my relatives!"

"He's willing to kill mine."

"Yeah, but you're vampires—and he doesn't know any better. He's a traditionalist!"

"He's insane," Colin went on before she could protest further. "He doesn't care about saving the world from vampires. He wants to live forever. He thinks vampires are immortal, the way all hunters used to, and that he can steal the secret of immortality from us. And he has the money and mindset to pursue research into immortality. He uses mercenaries, and funds rogue scientists, kidnaps vampires and mortals, and has his scientists run hideous experiments on them."

She didn't believe she was hearing this. "That's the plot of a B movie. No one could get away with doing stuff like that."

"With enough money, you can get away with anything. The Clans have been funding private scientific research for a long time. In fact, your great-grandfather hired away several of our scientists for his research. I've been at the abandoned military base where the Patron's scientists ran their nasty experiments. I helped blow the place up. I helped rescue his prisoners. I was *there,* Mia. I know exactly how dangerous your relative is. He has to be stopped."

"But—"

He grabbed her shoulders again. For a moment she thought he was going to shake her, but he drew her close and stared intently into her eyes. "You're going to help me."

It was not a plea, nor was it a threat, but it was a cold, hard statement that would brook no argument.

She didn't try to argue, but she did say, "You could say please."

"Please."

Mia took a deep breath, and closed her eyes for a moment. She missed her preconceptions about vampires. It was so much easier to believe the crumbs she'd gleaned from family history, and what little her great-grandfather had told her. Right now, she felt like she was trying to pick her way through a minefield of conflicting realities. Everyone she'd met, every situation, gave her a different view of what it meant to be a vampire. But she had to make some hard choices.

To complicate things much more, now she was linked physically, emotionally, and psychically to a vampire, and to his clan.

Or at least that was what they wanted her to believe.

"My head hurts," she said. "It really does."

"I know." Colin's fingers moved to her temples and began a gentle massage. "Me, too."

"I want to go home."

"Me, too."

"And I'm sick of hearing about this Patron."

"*You're* sick of it? Sweetheart, he's been dominating my life for months. When I wasn't thinking about you, I was working on finding him. The closest I'd come to a lead was the night I ran into you at the airport, and—" His hands were suddenly back on her shoulders. "The airport—the same one the Patron's plane used. The same one you used."

Mia's heart slammed hard in her chest, and her stomach flip-flopped. She felt exposed, as if she was about to be accused of a horrible crime. Worse, she felt inexplicably guilty even before being accused.

"You're working with him!" Colin declared. "He found out I was the one hunting him, and he sent you to trap me!"

"Oh, for crying out loud!" she responded without thinking. "Why is it always about *you*?"

He laughed harshly. "I suppose it was a coincidence that we met when you were a hostage?"

"Yeah." Of course it was. It had to be. "Don't try to make me paranoid that my great-grandfather set up the worst day of my life so that I'd start dating a vampire! Then *you* followed *me* to the hospital, remember? And I didn't contact you after you broke up with me, did I?"

Her questions made him thoughtful. He looked away, then back at her. "Meeting me was the worst day of your life?"

He sounded dead serious, but there was a faint spark of teasing in his eyes. Maybe it was her "always about you" comment that had cut through his rising paranoia.

"Meeting you was—interesting. Being taken hostage that day was frightening." She looked around her. "Though I guess it was good practice for being kidnapped by vampires."

"We were both kidnapped by vampires," he reminded her. "What were you doing at that airport?" he went on, relentlessly back on the hunt. "And just how did you find Tony? Why? You *are* working for the Patron," he decided.

"Working with him," Mia answered. "Or at least, I thought I was." Colin gaped at her in surprise, which didn't help her already frayed temper. "You look like you thought I was going to lie to you and say, Oh, no, I haven't had anything to do with the Patron. Come to think of it, I haven't. The man I went to for help, after I was attacked *by vampires,* is the only living relative I have who has ever had contact with vampires. I went to him for help," she reiterated.

"You could have—"

"Come to you?" Mia shook her head. "How could I? I was trying to *protect* you—from vampires."

When Colin started to laugh, Mia couldn't help but join him. Well, at the time she hadn't known how absurd that was.

They were still laughing when Barak appeared on the terrace and said, "Time's up."

Chapter Twenty

"Tell them," Colin said to Mia when they were once more standing before the Matris and the elders.

The Manticores stood at their back, but Colin had put himself between them and his bondmate. He realized with dread that no one in the room was going to like Mia's explanations, but the Manticores were the only ones that posed any real danger to her. The problem was, she couldn't really understand that yet.

Mia turned a confused look on him. "Tell them what?"

"Everything you know about the Patron," he clarified. "Everything you've done with him, or for him."

"Oh. Okay."

He'd thought she was going to protest. When she didn't he put a hand on her shoulder. It was meant to be reassuring—at least he tried to mean it that way. His head was still whirling from everything that had happened between them, the information overload of the last few hours. He was confused and furious—at Mia, because of Mia, for Mia.

But he was there for Mia. Whether she wanted him or not.

Mia took a deep breath, and focused on Serisa. "Henry Garrison is my great-grandfather. Until they attacked me"—she jerked a thumb over her shoulder—"I never had any contact with him. After the first attack, I knew I needed help fighting vampires. I didn't know how to contact the local vampire hunters. In fact, it didn't even occur to me at that time that I should try going that route. So I contacted Garrison."

"How?" Justinian demanded.

"With difficulty," she answered, without bothering to look at the Manticore Prime.

"And after you contacted him?" Serisa asked. "What then?"

"Then he asked me to bring him a vampire. For experimentation."

She said it without any hesitation, without any show of fear. Colin wasn't the only one in the room who gasped.

"You're working for the Patron?" Domini asked. "You're helping him with his sick research?"

"I didn't know it was sick at the time, did I?" Mia asked in turn. "He told me he wanted to learn more about vampires, that he wanted one to study. He didn't say anything to me about research into immortality."

"What about our money?" the blond Manticore asked. "Did he mention anything about where he keeps large sums of stolen cash?"

"There are more important things than money," Serisa declared.

The blond gave a derisive snort of laughter.

"What about our claim?" the leader of the Manticores spoke up. "The Garrison woman can lead us to what is ours, what was stolen by a mortal. Is it not our right to question her, under the agreements established to protect our kind from vampire hunters?"

"The Patron poses a threat to all our kind," Barak said. "You have the right to assist in the hunt for him."

"What if the female won't help you?" Justinian persisted. "If you deem finding Garrison important for all vampires, but the woman won't cooperate, what then? We have a claim on her information; you must allow us what is ours by right."

Colin spun around to bare his fangs at the Manticore Primes. "Do you know how much I will enjoy killing all of you, if you try to touch what is *mine*?"

"Well, excuse *me* for having a free will and the ability to make my own decisions."

Colin whirled back around to find Mia standing with her arms crossed and a look of complete disgust on her face.

She turned slowly, aiming her annoyance at everyone in the room, and didn't speak until she was looking at him again. "Perhaps it would be nice if someone would kindly *ask* me to help," she suggested.

"Good point," Domini spoke up.

Silence loomed with a tense crackle, like the still air before the explosion of a thunderstorm.

Finally, Anjelica asked, "Will you help us, Caramia?"

Mia sighed, and her shoulders slumped, but she put her hand out to stop him when Colin moved to come toward her. The weariness and worry that emanated from her disturbed him, no matter how infuriating she was. She faced the women of the Clans.

"Let me think about it," she answered them. "Just give me some space to think."

"No!" Justinian protested.

Serisa studied Mia for a few moments; her expression was both worried and calculating. Finally she said, "Very well."

"Wait, wait, wait, just like the Matri wants."

Colin glanced at the newcomer and reluctantly answered. "If you don't like it, leave."

"My master has chosen to remain. I live to serve, and all that. How about you? Do you always do what you're told?"

Colin had been sitting alone on a bench at the back of the garden when the blond Manticore Prime came strolling down the path. He'd been out here for a couple of hours, long enough to watch the sky go through a fine pastel sunset and to watch stars and moon come out. He hadn't exactly been enjoying the solitude, but this was one of the last people he wanted interrupting his thoughts.

"Do you always hang out where you're not wanted?" Colin answered. He'd been told the pest was named Laurent. "It's after sunset. Why don't you people leave?"

"Justinian won't go until he has what he wants." Laurent took an uninvited seat on the bench. "Think of me as his interpreter of the modern world. You wouldn't like Justinian without me around."

"I don't like Justinian anyway."

"Ah, but he's on his best behavior at the moment. He's much worse than you imagine—which makes us quite proud of him. But since you boys don't seem to have a handle on decadence, perversion, and guile, you need my help pointing it out to you. He needs me to keep reminding him how upright, upstanding, and honest you folks really are. Frankly, I don't know how you good guys manage to have any fun."

"Nobility has its boring side," Colin conceded. "But the dragon slaying"—he bared his teeth in a smile—"a manticore's a type of dragon, isn't it?—and rescuing the fair maiden has its rewards."

Laurent stretched his long legs out in front of him. "If I read the signs aright, there's no more maiden-rescuing in your future. Not that your woman isn't lively enough in bed, I suppose, but to be stuck with only one . . ."

"I could happily kill you, you know."

"It'd give you something to do. This place is nice, but dull."

"You've got that right."

Maybe he was tired and wired, or maybe he missed the mocking camaraderie of his SWAT unit, but Colin almost found the Tribe vampire's attitude amusing. He didn't forget the guy was everything mortal legends thought vampires were, though, or that he was at the Citadel because of an agenda that could threaten Mia.

"But while our attempting to kill each other would be diverting, that would be breaking the truce, as I am speaking in friendship," Laurent went on.

"And how is that?"

"I was only offering my condolences on your bonded state, one Prime to another—as we of the Tribes don't believe that monogamy is the natural condition for a Prime. Do you know how we avoid the bonding state?"

"No."

"Do you care?"

"Does it involve violence toward women?" Colin asked, quietly and dangerously serious. His fists were clenched to fight the urge to strike.

Laurent studied him carefully for a moment. "Maybe I shouldn't have brought up the subject."

"I guess not." He forced himself to relax a little.

"She's a dangerous woman, you know."

Colin smiled. "I know."

Laurent shook his head. "Can you control her?"

"That's none of your business."

"Do you think you can trust her?" These words were spoken with far more seriousness than anything else the Manticore had said. "She's Garrison's," Laurent went on. "Your blood is in her, but so is the Patron's DNA." He stood and moved away. "Can a bond overcome birth? Where does her loyalty really lie?"

With those words, Laurent faded into the night. Tribe members were the masters of vanishing into shadows. For all their bad habits, they had a certain dark style.

And he left Colin with dark thoughts. He tried to let Laurent's words roll off him, to remember that the Manticore was working his own agenda. Of course, that didn't make everything Laurent said a lie. And there was the matter of trust.

One thing that bothered Colin was how worried Mia had been about having her deeper thoughts read. Fear of violation? Or was she hiding some plan of the Patron's? He didn't know, and he hated thinking about it.

It had been a rough couple of days, and it just got rougher and rougher.

Colin tiredly stretched out on the bench and stared up at the night sky for a while. He drifted off for a while, but restless need wouldn't let him sleep.

After a while he stood up, stretched, and headed back toward the house. "That's it. Time's up. She's had enough time to think."

A sense of panic drove Mia to sit up and look around frantically. She heard someone move. "Colin?"

"No," Domini answered from what seemed a long way away.

Mia blinked and rubbed her eyes. It had been dark, and she'd been dreaming and— "Was I asleep?"

"Yes."

Domini sounded very calm, reassuring. Mia looked toward her. Domini was on the couch on the other side of the bedroom where Mia had been kept before the bonding ceremony. It took Mia a few more moments to piece together the memory of being shown in here and left alone.

She rubbed her eyes again. "I was supposed to be thinking, but I think I just crawled into bed and passed out."

"You needed the rest," Domini answered. "They don't need to sleep as much as we do, so they'll run us ragged without realizing it."

"How long was I out?"

"Maybe three hours. Not long, but maybe long enough to help you think straight." Domini gestured toward a covered tray on a low table near her. "There's tea and food. Would you prefer coffee?"

Mia got out of bed and crossed the room. Taking a seat in one of the chairs, she eyed Domini. "Did they send you to talk to me because you're a mortal who's bonded to a vampire? Are you going to convince me that I can trust you because we have so much in common?"

Domini reached over and flipped the tray covering. The scent of Earl Grey tea perfumed the air, and Mia's stomach began to rumble at the sight of a plate of sandwiches, and another one piled with fancy cookies.

"We do have a lot in common," Domini said, not seeming concerned at Mia's suspicious attitude. "Though I'm not *exactly* mortal." She looked Mia in the eye and added with quiet intensity, "And it is all about trust."

Mia poured herself a cup of tea, spooned in sugar, then snatched up half a sandwich. It was ham and cheese, and she ate it in three bites. Then she gulped down the wonderfully warm, sweet tea. She tried the cookies next.

She sighed when she was done, and the plates were mostly empty. "What do you mean, not exactly?" she asked, looking the other woman over curiously. "Are you turning into a vampire?" A jolt of alarm ripped through her. "Will I?"

Domini gave her a stern look. "Even the most amateur hunters know better than that."

Mia let out a relieved sigh. "Okay, I forgot that one for a moment. But if you're not—"

"I will eventually become a vampire," Domini said. "It's rare, but it sometimes happens. But the only reason I can change is because my grandmother is a vampire. My grandfather is mortal. And—here's where what you and I have in common comes in—he's from a family of hunters. Actually, he's from a family of Purists." When Mia looked at her blankly, she said, "You don't know about the Purists?"

"I know very little about hunters," Mia said.

"You were trying to find them, Tony said. But you didn't know where to find them?"

Mia nodded.

"That tells me that your great-grandfather has no interest in legally hunting rogue vampires. Tony is our local liaison with the hunters. Since we found out the Patron's name, Tony has been trying to find out if the hunters know anything about Garrison. Though they have the family name in their database, no one has heard of him. If he's so rich and wants to hunt vampires, why send an untrained female out alone, when there are official resources he could contribute to?" She clasped her hands over a raised knee, and tilted her head to one side. "My guess is that the old man set you up as bait. But you need to make up your own mind about him."

Mia poured herself more tea and gave Domini a skeptical look. "Then what are you here to influence me about?"

Domini smiled. "About your place in vampire society."

"You mean about where my loyalties should lie?"

"About trust. You have to make up your mind who deserves your trust."

Mia put the fine china cup down so hard it rattled the other dishes. "Hey! I don't know you."

"You know me better than you do your great-grandfather. At least you've spent more time with me."

Mia had to nod her agreement to this.

"I know that Earl Grey is your favorite tea—and that when Colin offers you the choice, you're going to take the ruby instead of the diamond."

"What?"

"Sorry." Domini tapped her forehead. "Having a psychic episode. I get flashes of future events. Junk stuff, usually. But that brings me back to how hunters and vampires are really a lot alike, and how this knowledge will help you make a more informed decision about helping find the Patron."

"How are hunters and vampires alike?"

"There's a lot of psychic talent in both groups, and they intermarry a lot more than either will admit." She held up a hand and leaned forward earnestly while Mia digested this information. "But the decision about the Patron is still yours."

Mia remembered how adamant Colin had been about her helping him on his Patron-smashing quest. "You think so?"

"Oh, the boys will huff and puff and try to guilt you into living up to their noble ideals, and Colin will be the worst. But they won't *make* you do what they want. They are the good guys."

"The Manticores aren't good guys."

"No," Domini agreed. "The Manticores, and the other Tribes like them, are one of the reasons that some mortal vampire hunters still exist. The Tribes are the reason that the Purists still hunt all vampires, and that even the more reasonable hunters will never completely trust the Clans or the Families. As long as the Purists exist, vampires can never completely trust mortals. People like Garrison, people who use anybody for their own selfish reasons, just make it harder for everybody to trust anybody." Domini uncurled herself from the couch and stood. "But the point is still, who do you trust? Who's your family? And what are you going to do about it? That'll be Colin," she added, just before a knock sounded on the door.

Mia watched Domini open the door and glide out as Colin entered and announced, "We have to talk."

Chapter Twenty-one

"Oh, for crying out loud! Hasn't there been enough talking? There's a couple of ham sandwiches left," Mia added as her bondmate crossed the room.

He was wearing jeans and a tight black T-shirt that emphasized his leanly muscled body, and she couldn't help but appreciate how good he looked. They'd only been separated for a few hours, but seeing him sent a surge of longing through her. More than a strong physical reaction, a sense of security blossomed up from some deep part of her now that he was with her.

The front part of her brain could argue that this was a false sense of well-being, but it didn't argue hard at the moment. Besides, it had never been the front part of her brain that was attracted to Colin. She'd gone on instinct with him from the first.

Which was probably not good in the long run. Or was instinct what mattered? Where did trust come from? The gut, or the logic center of the brain?

It's lust, she reminded herself. It rhymes with trust, but it's not the same thing.

And just where does the heart come into it?

"How's the thinking coming along?" he asked.

"I think I'm thinking too much about anatomy," she answered. "Or maybe it's philosophy. Either way, it doesn't make any sense."

"Anatomy, huh?" He picked up a sandwich and settled on the wide arm of her chair. "What did Domini want?" he asked around a bite of food, and put a hand on her shoulder. The contact between them was as electric as ever, even if he had been touching her like this an awful lot lately. There was something proprietary about this touch, this one spot of contact that linked him to her.

She leaned sideways, letting her shoulder and head touch his side. His hand moved from her shoulder to the back of her neck, and his thumb began to work at muscles she hadn't realized were tense.

"Domini was being a cheerleader for your side," she answered.

"My *side*?"

She sighed, partly in exasperation, partly because what he was doing felt good. "Oh, don't get all huffy."

"Have you picked a side yet?"

"I've been adopted into Clan Reynard, haven't I?"

"Bonded."

"It's the same thing."

It amazed her that neither of them were speaking these words in anger. There was tension between them, all right, but her body was growing tight with desire.

"Have you thought about the Patron?"

"Some. Mostly I took a nap."

"That wasn't very productive."

"I dreamed about you."

"As you should. Was I naked?"

She gave a snort of laughter, and as she did, Colin somehow managed to slide down from his perch to squeeze himself beside her in the plush armchair. It was a tight fit, one that made her pleasantly aware of every bit of Colin's hard, toned body.

"We need to talk," he said, and kissed the back of her neck. Then his lips brushed the side of her throat, and up to her ear.

The breath caught in her throat, but Mia managed to say, "Keep doing that, and we won't be able to talk."

Wanna bet?

She laughed. Not out loud, but inside her head, sharing her amusement with him on the psychic level. Desire bubbled up from the laughter, and burst like sparks that heated from the soul out to the skin.

It's been hours, he thought. *I missed you.*

She felt the truth in the thought.

Who would have thought the truth could be so sexy? It sent desire rippling through her in a way that was strong, deep, and devastating. There was a new level calling to her here. A challenge to go beyond everything she'd experienced before.

Mia liked challenges.

I like you thoughtful, Colin.

Colin. The name had taste and texture, color and depth, in her mind. Sweet, spicy taste, scarlet silk and sharp iron entwined in texture, shifting color of fire.

Caramia.

He thought her name, and she became aware of his response to her—the velvet touch of yellow roses, the taste of cinnamon candy, warm coffee with cream and lots of sugar, the rush of wind during free fall.

All the great guitar solos ever played burned through them: Eric and Carlos and Jimi and Lenny and—

After a while, Mia managed to pull back into herself enough to think, *This is so, so—*

Psychedelic?

Yeah. Don't you have any Coldplay in there?

Me, I like Metallica.

She found her voice. "Does this sort of thing happen often?"

"I don't know—I'm new here." His voice sounded raw with desire, with emotions he'd never known before.

Mia knew how he felt. Not only because she felt new herself, but because they were bound together. They were in this together.

She opened her eyes, to find herself gazing into Colin's. And she realized that her eyes hadn't been closed; they'd just been lost in each other.

"Nice," she said.

He pulled her into his lap, and his hand came up under her shirt to stroke her breasts. "Nicer," he said.

His fingertips barely touched her, barely moved, spreading a slow fire from the outside in.

He held her still, not letting her move. And he kept on caressing and kissing her with the slowest and gentlest of touches. He stripped her of her clothes, but without any hurry, thoroughly stimulating every new bare spot, taking delight in learning her responses. He took such delight in her body, it was as if he was discovering her sensuality for the first time.

It made her feel like this was their first time, as well.

But Colin's subtlety kept her a millisecond away from the desperately desired cataclysm, driving her crazy.

Before long, she was begging him for more.

"More?"

He loved being in control of her pleasure—and it was fine with her.

"*More.*" She let out a long, desperate moan. *Everything. Anything.* "*Colin!*"

His triumphant laugh bubbled through her like champagne. He picked her up and swung her around with a speed more than human, so fast that the room swirled into blurred colors. She threw her head back against his shoulder and let the roller-coaster ride take her even further away from herself, further into her need for him.

She was dizzy in every possible way when he finally dropped her on the bed.

"This is like skydiving without a chute!" She held her arms up toward him.

He undressed so quickly, she was only aware of a blur and of clothes being tossed all over the room.

Colin was laughing when he dropped on top of her. His mouth covered hers even as she gasped. His tongue swirled and teased, drawing her even further toward rapture. But the kiss didn't last nearly long enough.

Using more of his natural strength and speed, he flipped them over, switching their positions. Now he was on his back, and she was poised over him. His hands held her waist, and her legs were on either side of him, her knees pressed against his narrow hips.

Mia could feel the tip of his cock straining upward, barely grazing the wet and swollen entrance of her sex, sending jolts of heat deep inside her. She instinctively tried to move her hips downward, to join his body with hers. All she wanted in the world was him in her, to be filled. It was a hunger like nothing she'd ever known before.

But he wouldn't let her move.

She arched her back, felt his cock twitch in response.

"Colin!" she complained. "You're going crazy, too!"

He gave a dark and sexy laugh. "Yep."

"Why are you doing this?"

Because I can.

He was loving the control, and holding on to it with all his might. And he was loving her responses to that control. She'd never been more aware of her body, of the cravings that only Colin could excite and satisfy. Her breasts were heavy, her nipples aching. Her nerve endings were on fire, and coiling heat burned inside her. There was no blood craving involved right now, but the lust was all-consuming.

"Colin!" she pleaded. "Enough!"

He was covered in a sheen of sweat, muscles tautly straining, his dark eyes glittering, and he was shaking from holding back. "You want me?"

"Yes!"

His smile was dangerous. His voice was low, and commanding. "Make it slow."

His hands came away from her hips, and moved to cup her breasts. The shock wave that went through her when his thumbs grazed her nipples would have set off an orgasm, but Colin's voice in her head murmured, *Easy.*

Mia lowered her body onto his cock, taking him into her with the slowness he commanded. A climax wracked through her with every little movement, but somehow she found the willpower to take him the way he wanted, though she was screaming inside for pounding speed.

She kept on stroking him, setting a slow, slow, sliding rhythm for a long, long time. She brushed her breasts across his chest, joined her mouth to his on every downstroke. She twined her tongue with his with hot, fleeting kisses. Their breathing grew more and more ragged, the connection between them more electric.

His hands roamed over her, stroked her clitoris, bringing her to another climax. When she moaned, the groan that came from deep in his throat matched her sound.

She couldn't stop her response to that heartfelt groan, and her hips ground down hard against his. He bucked as she plunged.

His orgasm took her with the same explosive intensity as it did him.

The next thing Mia knew, she was lying stretched out on top of Colin, and he was holding her as she shook like a leaf.

"It's okay," he murmured, lips close to her ear. "It's—that was—"

"*Wow,*" she finished for him. For some reason there were tears stinging her eyes. Tears of joy, of exhaustion, of release, tears for all sorts of reasons. She couldn't ever remember crying over great sex before. She wiped her face against Colin's shoulder, surprised that she wasn't uncomfortable showing this vulnerability. But if the man could get inside her head, and she into his—

Mia fell asleep before this thought was complete.

She was called out of very pleasant warm darkness when Colin shifted and said, "We're going to be in trouble for keeping the Matris waiting."

For a moment, still foggy with sated lust and bone-melted exhaustion, Mia didn't have a clue what he was talking about.

She didn't even remember where they were, other than a very comfortable bed.

Then the whole mess came back to her, and she sighed and sat up. Colin was propped up on a pile of pillows, one arm thrown over his head, and he didn't look at all guilty for keeping the tribunal waiting. She couldn't help but trace a finger around the unrepentant smile quirking his lips.

"Didn't you say you wanted to talk to me when you came rushing in here?"

His eyes narrowed in thought. "Oh, yeah . . . the Patron. How are you going to help me save the world from him?"

She noted that he wasn't asking if she'd help. "Can I ask you a question?"

"And waste more time before we have to face the honorable old ladies?" He propped his other hand behind his head, and grinned. "Sure."

Anjelica and Serisa sure didn't look like old ladies to her, but Mia let that go. "Why do you want to save the world?" she asked seriously. "You really believe in the hero mystique, don't you? Why do vampires protect humans?"

"Mortals," he corrected. He looked at her breasts and smiled happily for a moment before pulling his gaze back up to her face. "Vampires are humans, too—superior humans, sexier and more virile humans. Mortals need protection from themselves, and from—"

"Morally superior, horny vampire snobs."

"No, no." He shook his head. "We snobs take vows to protect and serve."

"But why? How long has this been going on? What do you get out of it?"

He gave her a hard look. "Will the answers help you make up your mind about the Patron?"

She supposed she couldn't put it off much longer. She swallowed, and steeled her resolve. "Yes."

"For one thing, taking care of mortals is fun. It beats Primes fighting each other for dominance and territory. The matris and elders figured out a long, long time ago that we need outlets for aggression. I learned in vampire school—"

"You have vampire school?"

"You don't think I went to Harvard, do you?"

"I don't think you could get into Harvard."

"I went to UCLA." He caressed her cheek. "I learned in vampire school that the Clans' protection of mortals started being codified back in ancient Egypt—something about a bunch of vampires being saved from some disaster by priests of Osiris, and taking a vow before the god of death to protect the priests and their families."

"Nice legend."

"I don't think it's a legend—there's written records of this pact someplace. It's the basis for the code we live by. Some of us." He held out his left arm to show her the fox head tattooed on the inside of his wrist. She'd noticed it before. "Those of us who serve mortals take the vow and wear the mark of our Clan."

"So nobody makes you do it."

He nodded. "And there have always been perks to the job."

"Damsels in distress taste delicious."

"They certainly do. And I guess there were Primes who protected ancient cities and were treated as gods for it. It's a pretty good life—you kick the occasional bad guy's ass, and get to live in a palace and have all the women you want in return."

"Too bad that times changed."

"And as times changed, the Families got into leading mostly normal lives, but the Clan Primes went into a tragically misunderstood gothic hero period." He looked pained. "I am so glad I wasn't around for that. I suspect they wore poet shirts and black capes when they appeared out of the night to save the damsels."

Mia grinned. "Not your style."

"And then politics came into the picture, complicating the choices between good and bad. My own family worked on both sides of the French Revolution. Some saved the aristocrats from the evil peasants; some saved the downtrodden peasants from the decadent aristocrats. There was a lot of damsel tasting on both sides."

Mia laughed. "Vampire family feuds can't be pretty."

He shook a finger at her. "We're Clan."

"You know what I meant."

"Yes. But the distinction between Clan, Family, and Tribe is important."

"Why?"

He looked surprised, and opened his mouth a couple of times before he answered. "The Tribes are bad guys. Always have been, always will be."

"Didn't the blond guy say something about Tribes having blended into the Families?"

"Yeah, but I wasn't listening too hard."

She remembered that he'd been busy trying not to show how pissed at her he was on finding out she was involved with hunters and the Patron. She didn't want him pissed at her now. She would much rather have conversations than arguments with Colin.

"What about Clan Primes in the modern era?" she asked.

Colin was aware of Mia's mental barriers going up, though he hoped she wasn't consciously aware of doing it. He suspected part of her sudden distancing herself was because of the damsel in distress comments. They likely reminded her of his reluctance to be permanently involved with a mortal woman. It was a fact, and there was no use arguing about it anymore.

"You know about modern Primes," he told her.

She moved across the wide bed and stood up, putting mental distance from him as she moved away. "We better talk to your people now."

She sounded reluctant and unhappy. Her nervousness sang against his senses. She didn't trust that the Primes were right about the Patron, did she? Her lack of trust reminded him of what Laurent had said about trusting the kin of the Patron.

Right now, all he wanted was to fulfill his vow to destroy the threat the old man posed, then get on with his life. A Prime fulfilled his vows, no matter the consequences and complications to his own life.

But how could he make a mortal woman understand that no matter how much they talked about the history of the Primes?

"Yeah," he answered Mia, getting out of the opposite side of the bed. "It's about time we had that talk."

Chapter Twenty-two

"This is taking too long," Justinian complained.

He got up and began to pace around the dining room where the Manticores had been invited by their Clan hosts, after hours of being kept in the meeting room. Laurent's senses told him it was past dawn, though the room was windowless.

Another day living in the lap of luxury—if the Clan mamas don't decide to kill us or toss us out to fry.

"We are being treated as guests," he carefully advised the impatient pack leader. "We must have patience."

"Patience is for the weak Clans. Do they always talk and never act?"

Laurent shrugged.

Belisarius glared across the table at Laurent, then got up and went to stand against a wall. From there he kept his attention on Justinian, playing the loyal subordinate vigilant on his master's behalf.

Laurent stayed in his seat and continued to sip his dinner. The warmed wine mixture was beyond excellent. In fact, it was the best blood he'd ever had outside its natural container. There were subtle flavors in the mixture that he couldn't identify. Possibly the brew was laced with some of the drugs the Clans favored.

Drugs that helped them dwell in the daylight? He doubted they'd offer what they considered a gift to Tribe vampires. Especially knowing that the Manticores would pitch a fit, feeling that their bodies were polluted. Well, Justinian would, and

Belisarius would follow his lead. More likely, the drugs Laurent tasted were those that helped the Clans keep their blood cravings to a minimum.

Laurent could understand why they might want to feed those drugs to dangerous, uncivilized Tribe members. In his opinion it was akin to chemical castration, but one dose wasn't going to permanently fix him, so there was no use getting mad about it. Not when it tasted so good. He looked at the goblet after he finished the last sip and placed it on the table.

Could he get a second glassful? Would it be bad for him?

He wondered how long the Clan members could go between natural feedings using the stuff, and why they wanted to. He could understand the advantages of dwelling in daylight, even if other Tribe members couldn't, but voluntarily turning yourself into a eunuch? He shuddered. Did they do it for the sake of living more openly among mortals? Because they really believed that creatures of the darkness could be *good*? Hell, it wasn't as if a vampire had to kill mortals to take their blood—though draining the life out of helpless victims was an appealing prospect.

Laurent smiled.

"Too long!" Justinian shouted.

Laurent looked up to see that the door had opened, and Justinian had yelled at Matri Serisa as she walked in.

"I agree," she said serenely, and took a seat at the head of the table.

Several people followed her into the room, among them the Garrison woman and her Prime keeper. Laurent hoped the fact that the pair weren't touching or looking at each other was good for the Manticore cause. The group took seats around the table, leaving the chair to Serisa's right for Justinian. The Garrison woman sat on the Matri's left.

Justinian glared at everyone for a few moments, then stalked over and took his seat. "Well?" he demanded.

Serisa looked to her left.

"I'm willing to help." The mortal woman looked at Serisa when she spoke.

"Willing?" Justinian growled. He brought the flat of his hand down on the shining wood of the table. "The female should not be allowed to speak, let alone set conditions."

Mia looked at Justinian, temper flaring in her eyes. "You're a rude jerk, but I'll help you get your money back."

Justinian smiled, showing fangs. "And will you *help* with our revenge as well?"

"Oh, cut out the melodrama," Foxe said.

Laurent schooled his features and emotions, not wanting to show that he completely agreed with the Clan Prime.

"Of course I'm not helping you get revenge," Mia said. She looked around at everyone at the table. "If my great-grand-father is doing bad things, I'll help you stop him."

"Bad things?" Colin Foxe echoed. "Hon—"

Serisa gestured him to silence. "How will you help us and Tribe Manticore?" she asked Mia. "Will you tell us where to find him?"

"I'll take you to him," Mia answered. She looked at Foxe. "I'll get you in to talk to him, search his compound, whatever you need to stop his operation. But you can't kill him," she added. "I won't let you kill my great-grandfather."

"That is unacceptable," Justinian said.

Laurent thought that Justinian spoke just before Foxe would have said the same thing.

"He's an old man," Mia said. "He's in his nineties. Maybe that's not old to your kind, but among ours that makes him ancient. He isn't going to live that much longer."

"Which is why he's trying to find the secret to immortal-ity," Foxe pointed out.

"But there isn't one. So, you shut down his experiments, destroy the research records. You make him forget vampires exist. Do whatever you have to do, short of killing him. You have to promise that," she insisted, concentrating her plea on Colin Foxe.

While Justinian seethed and Belisarius fought the urge to attack the Garrison woman from behind, Laurent decided it was time to get back to the important point. "We don't care about the Patron's medical experiments. We want our money back."

Mia flashed him a smile. "And that's the solution right there. Take away my great-grandfather's wealth, and he can't fund any mad scientist stuff."

"And how can you give us his wealth?" Justinian demanded. "Do you know where he keeps a vault full of gold?"

"No, but I know where he keeps his laptop," the woman answered tartly. "If you can't find out how to break into his financial records with that, you really are a bunch of pathetic medieval losers, aren't you?"

After a moment of shocked silence, Justinian mastered his outrage and sneered at her. "And we are supposed to trust *you* to bring us this laptop?"

"Yes."

Justinian laughed. "Such calculating openness, such false naïveté. We do not forget the female's treacherous blood." He looked earnestly at Serisa. "Do you? Do you really think she will betray her blood?"

"She will bring the laptop to us," Serisa answered, ignoring Justinian's skepticism. "We will share whatever information we find about the Patron's finances with you."

Justinian banged his hand on the table again.

"This is where you're going to have to compromise, Matri," Laurent said before Justinian broke into a rage that could turn violently ugly. "From our point of view, you have just told us that you will take charge of the wealth that was stolen from us. You say *share information,* but what we hear is *take what is ours.*"

"Don't the Clans have enough wealth already?" Justinian

demanded. "Are you so contemptuous of the Tribes that you would stoop to stealing from us?"

Serisa's head snapped up proudly. "Of course not!"

Justinian gave a satisfied nod. "Then you cannot object to my sending one of my Primes to retrieve this laptop for us."

Finally, Serisa nodded.

Justinian looked at Laurent. "You."

Belisarius stepped forward. "But he—"

"Laurent goes," Justinian snapped. "Understood?"

Awestruck by the possibilities, Laurent was unaffected by the glares being turned on him not just by Belisarius, but by Fox and the woman, as well. He was also fully aware that Justinian's question had been aimed at him, and of its dangerous implications.

"Understood," he answered. He smiled at Foxe. "So, partner, when do we assault the Patron's fortress?"

"No assault!" Mia waved her hands. "No violence. Nobody gets hurt."

"He's surrounded by security, isn't he?" Foxe asked.

"All rich people have bodyguards. They're just doing their jobs to protect him."

"We do not want innocent casualties," Serisa said.

"The Patron uses well-armed, trained mercenaries," Foxe said. "I've fought them; I know what they can do."

"That was a different time and place." Barak spoke for the first time. "You destroyed his private army. We do not know if he has had time to rebuild his organization. Mia could be correct about the people currently guarding the Patron. We will approach this operation with an initial nonlethal action plan."

"Aw," Laurent complained, and got an agreeing look from Foxe.

"*Initially* nonlethal?" Mia protested.

"We cannot go in unprepared," Barak told her.

"You can't do anything without me," she pointed out, and crossed her arms. "And I have a plan."

Chapter Twenty-three

Everybody's going to be really pissed at me if this doesn't work, Mia thought as the car approached the rendezvous point at the Van Trier airport.

She and Colin were seated on opposite sides of the spacious back seat, not touching. They hadn't spoken for a while, either, not even by telepathic contact. Ever since the op started, Colin had been focused on nothing else.

To set everything in motion she'd made a phone call, and they'd been picked up by a car sent by her great-grandfather's lawyer. So far, so good, but those who'd argued against doing it her way weren't going to like it if anything went wrong.

Colin had been one of the ones who argued about her coming along, no matter how necessary her presence was. She didn't know whether he was trying to protect her, or if it was because once the action got started, Primes were macho males who ran the show. She had a nagging fear that he didn't quite trust the Patron's great-granddaughter. And she almost didn't blame him if that were the case.

Even more important, if her plan didn't work, people and vampires both could end up dead. She wanted no deaths on her conscience.

Well, maybe the smart-mouthed blond Manticore guy.

No, not even him.

"What a rough, tough slayer I made," she whispered, and got a quelling look from Colin in response.

She quelled the impulse to stick out her tongue, since Colin's gaze flicked briefly toward the driver. The driver ultimately worked for the Patron. The less gratuitous chatter, the better, if this makeshift undercover operation was to work.

Colin was half tempted to reach over, pat Mia's hand, and reassure her that she would do just fine. She might not be up to slaying vampires, but she could hold her own in a fight against mortal opponents.

He was spoiling for a fight, but he had to hope that it didn't come to one. One of the reasons he hadn't wanted Mia along was that if she got into trouble, his first impulse would be to protect his bondmate. That impulse could cloud his judgment in the middle of a dangerous situation. And maybe another reason he didn't want her in a fight was because he wasn't sure which way her instincts would impel her to jump.

But he admitted that her presence was necessary. She was the key. But having her with him was dangerous in many ways. Not only did he worry about her safety, he had trouble keeping his hands off her. This was not a situation where a Prime's natural lust for his bondmate was welcome. Not touching her was a misery, but it was the only choice for now.

"Remember to stay in character," he'd told her before they left the house. "Keep your hands to yourself and your mind on business."

His tone and attitude had angered her. "Do I look like a lust-crazed idiot to you?"

"Yes," he'd answered, not adding that he was even more crazed than she was. It was better to have her pissed at him and in character, even if having her angry brought its own dangers.

Now, as the car pulled to a stop next to another dark sedan, he chafed at not being in charge of the situation, but tried to tell himself that this was no different than an op led by his mortal SWAT commander. Except that he had total faith in his commander's abilities.

"Let's go," he said.

Mia steeled her resolve at Colin's words, trying to emulate

his calm. She got out of the car and approached the man standing at the rear of the other car, recognizing him as one of the lawyers she'd dealt with before.

"Where is the object?" he asked when she reached him. Then he looked suspiciously at Colin. "Who is this?"

Mia was pleased with the man's reaction; he obviously didn't recognize Colin for a vampire. She'd been worried that there was some secret way his nature could be detected, and now she was a bit more confident this would work.

"He's here to help," she told the lawyer. She gestured toward the trunk of the car she and Colin had come in. "We brought what my great-grandfather requested."

"You'll want to verify the merchandise," Colin said. He made it sound like a drug deal.

He walked to the back of the car, and she and the lawyer followed. The lawyer looked nervous.

Mia was now glad that she'd had to agree to this addition to her original idea. "Pop the trunk," she ordered their driver.

It was after dark, and there were no other cars in the parking lot. There were lights illuminating a runway where a small jet was prepped for takeoff. The muted roar of its engines added a keening background noise to this tense meeting.

The lawyer looked at the handcuffed male lying curled up in the trunk. The prisoner was wearing a hooded sweatshirt and sunglasses, and his ankles were bound as well as his hands. "This is the experimental subject the Patron requested?"

"Yep, he's a vampire, all right," Mia answered. She reached into the trunk and lifted Laurent's upper lip. He didn't oblige her by showing even a hint of fang. "He's drugged to the gills with the stuff I was told to use," she added. "So you don't have to be afraid he's going to bite you."

"The subject has the required blood anomalies the lab is looking for," Colin contributed. "Let's get him loaded, shall we?"

The lawyer looked around as if he was afraid they were going to be overheard. And even though Colin's expression hadn't changed, she knew he wasn't happy with her saying the V word. He certainly hadn't been happy when he'd found out that she'd been furnished with vampire catching equipment, even though they hadn't used it. The blond in the trunk had flinched a little at the mention of drugs; maybe he was afraid of needles.

The lawyer gently lowered the trunk lid. "Thank you for your assistance," he told Mia. "I will take charge of the subject from this point."

"Just what does that mean?" Mia frowned. "My great-grandfather instructed me to bring him the subject."

"I know nothing of those instructions. Your presence is no longer required."

"Oh, no. That's not how this plays out." This lackey was *not* going to snarl up their plan.

"He's not going anywhere without us," Colin seconded. "We're taking him to the Patron."

"That is not possible," the lawyer answered adamantly.

Mia felt her temper rise. "It's imperative," she snapped.

"You will be well compensated for your services," the lawyer said.

"I don't *need* compensation. I am Henry Garrison's great-granddaughter; this is a family matter. I did this for him, and for a good cause. It's not finished until I know the subject is in his possession. Understood?" If this *idiot* didn't—

"My instructions are explicit. I am to take charge of the subject at the rendezvous point and convey it to the research facility. No mention was made of you"—he glanced at Colin—"or anyone else accompanying me."

Mia's temper flared white-hot.

Get out of my way! she shouted as she glared at the lawyer. *Just do as you're told and get out of my way!*

Colin took a swift step back, his vision flaring bright white and fading quickly to black, the inside of his head ringing with Mia's telepathic shout. He heard a gasp escape Laurent from inside the trunk.

When Colin's vision returned, he saw the lawyer on his knees in front of Mia with his hands clutching his temples, his features a mask of pain. Mia was still glaring at the man, practically incandescent with fury, and he wouldn't have been surprised if flames suddenly shot out of the tips of her fingers. He'd always known her temper could flash, but he'd never known it could burn.

He rushed to his bondmate's side and snagged her around the waist, turning her to face him. "Calm down. Focus it," he commanded when she didn't take her gaze off the mortal.

Colin's touch steadied Mia, made everything solid again. He brought the ground back under her feet, put the sky back over her head. His voice brought her back from a dangerous edge. The world had gone away for a moment, leaving only her will. She'd held it like lightning in her hands, and she'd used it like a weapon.

She blinked now, and night air laced with jet fuel and desert dust rushed into her lungs. She coughed, shook her head, and told the man on the ground, "Get out of here."

He sprinted to his car and was gone within seconds, tires screeching as he fled the airport.

Mia collapsed against Colin. "That was me," she said, bewildered. "I did that." Feeling like a lost child, she looked at him for help. "What did I do?"

He held her and explained, "Telepathy. Very strong telepathy."

She rested her forehead on his shoulder and breathed in his scent, starting to feel dizzy. When she looked at Colin again, his face was slightly out of focus. "Domini said I had a psychic gift. That sometime it would just explode."

He nodded. "That was quite an explosion." He touched her cheek with the back of his hand. "It's your gift, and your curse."

She smiled, but it took an effort. She felt exhausted. "Like Spider-Man?"

"With great power comes great responsibility," Laurent's muffled voice came from the trunk.

Mia looked toward the car. "We'd better—"

"Not yet." Colin held her tighter. "Wait for it."

"For wha—"

The pain hit like a star going nova inside her head, driving her down into merciful darkness. She thought she heard Colin say, "That's what," just as the darkness closed over her.

Chapter Twenty-four

"Is she still out?" Laurent asked.

Colin glanced across the seating area of the plane's luxurious cabin. The other Prime was buckled into a plush chair opposite the couch where he was seated with Mia. She was lying with her knees drawn up and her head resting in his lap. The pilots were behind the closed cockpit door, and there was no one else on board.

He'd been gazing at her worriedly for a long time, running his fingers through her dark curls. Until Laurent spoke, he'd only been aware of the silky texture of her hair and the muted roar of the jet engines as they flew northeast.

And worry. He was very much aware of aching, desperate worry.

"Is she going to be all right?" Laurent asked.

Fear knotted in Colin's gut, and a hint of primal jealousy began to creep into his emotions. "Why would you care?"

Laurent raised his cuffed hands dismissively. "Oh, please. You have nothing to worry about from me on her account."

"You came after her," Colin reminded Laurent.

"That was just business. She's too dangerous for my taste, my friend." He tilted his head to one side, studying Colin. "You do know that she's dangerous, right?"

Colin looked back at Mia with pride. "We like them dangerous."

"Dangerous females are liabilities. Dangerous mortal women are even more dangerous. Mortal women with psychic gifts— that's the world turned inside out, upside down, and really,

really sick, my friend. You *are* going to ditch her once we're inside the old man's place, right? Or at least put a collar and leash on her, if you plan on keeping her."

"I'm keeping her," Colin growled.

"I know you've been forced into that, and I know you don't like it. You can't trust her, and she's taking us into a lion's den. You better keep an eye on her, and you better keep her under control. If you're going to be her keeper, take a lesson from how we Tribe Primes handle our mortal women."

It would have been tempting to get up and hit the Manticore Prime, but no Clan Prime would strike a helpless prisoner. Laurent probably knew that, and so felt he could say whatever he wanted with impunity. And he seemed genuinely disturbed by Mia's gifts, which amused Colin. But Colin also found the Manticore's attitude very disturbing.

"And how is it you treat your mortal women?"

Laurent heard the danger in Colin's tone, and backed down a bit. He shrugged. "They make nice pets, I'm told. I wouldn't want to keep one, myself. A night and a bite with as many pretty ones as I can score, that's how I relate to the mortal herd."

Laurent's words made Colin squirm. It was like looking into a mirror and seeing a warped reflection. He was no different than a Tribe bastard, when it came down to what was really important. A strong shudder ran through him, and he tasted bile.

Laurent laughed softly. "I see that you know exactly how I feel."

"I knew I should have put a gag on you," Colin said.

The Manticore frowned and rattled the cuffs. They both knew that he could pull them apart any time he wanted, but Laurent was willing to stay in his role as vampire prisoner for the sake of his tribe's agenda.

Perhaps he had some honor, after all. No—even though some of the tribes had been forced into less vicious behavior in the last century, the Manticore were not among that group.

Laurent's actions were motivated by greed, and probably fear of his pack leader.

"Justinian trusts you to do the job, does he?" he asked.

Laurent laughed softly. "Justinian would never be fool enough to trust anyone completely." He nodded toward Mia. "Unlike some people I know. When she turns on you, remember that I told you so."

This conversation was going nowhere. Besides, Mia was beginning to stir to consciousness, and the plane was beginning its descent.

"Hello," he said when Mia lifted her head. She groaned, and he helped her sit up very slowly. Her skin was still a little cool to the touch, and there were dark circles under her eyes. "How do you feel?"

Mia put her hands over her face and mumbled, "Head. Hurts."

If it would just fall off and roll gently away, she'd be perfectly happy. Who wanted a head, when it felt like this?

Colin put a comforting arm around her shoulders. "Do you feel kind of blank? Like the inside of your mind is stuffed up? Mental congestion?"

"Yeah."

"Good."

She managed to turn her head just far enough to give Colin a scathing look. "Good?"

"That means you didn't suffer any permanent brain damage, and you'll be better soon."

Ahh, soon—good. Then, "*Brain* damage?"

She heard nearby laughter, and decided that it came from Laurent. Then she realized they were on the plane. They must be on the way to Colorado, though her memories stopped back at the airport parking lot.

Colin patted her arm reassuringly. "You just overloaded a few psychic circuits with your tantrum. With a little rest and a lot of training, you'll be fine."

"You've done the same thing," she concluded.

"When I was a kid, yeah."

Mia didn't like the implication that he considered her psychic gifts somewhere in the juvenile range. Then again, she had a raging headache, so she couldn't objectively conclude if he was being insulting, or if she was just cranky from the pain.

"Is the plane landing?" she asked.

"Yeah. Looks like you woke up just in time."

Just in time? She scrubbed her hands across her face. Just in time for—

Oh, yeah, she had a role to play.

Mia sat up straight and disengaged herself from Colin's embrace. She noticed that Colin didn't try to stop her. In fact, when she glanced at him, he'd put on the distant persona once more. She did her best to look cool, calm, and competent, even with a raging headache and worries about whether this was the right thing to do. And whether she and Colin would ever—

"Heads up," Laurent announced from across the aisle. "We're going wheels down."

"What are you doing here?" Henry Garrison asked Mia. He then pointed a bony finger at Colin. "Who is he? How did you get in here?"

The old boy wasn't happy. But then, Colin doubted that Garrison was ever happy about anything, maybe just less annoyed from time to time. There was a sour anger in him that permeated everything around him. While the room was large and well lit, Colin had the sense of being trapped in a small, dark space with a hungry rat.

He didn't know whether to feel sorry for Mia, that this was her eldest living relative, or worried about the flawed genetics of his future offspring.

He had only seen Garrison at a distance the night he'd helped destroy the research facility, but Colin recognized the thin old mortal, though not the pair of unmoving bodyguards who stood watch behind him. They hadn't been among the mercenaries who'd hustled the Patron onto the airplane he'd escaped on.

There was a wide desk between the old man and where Colin and Mia stood. The only thing on the desk was an open laptop computer. Its matte silver case stood out in stark contrast to the ornate wooden desk, gilt-framed floral prints on the walls, Oriental carpet, and dark velvet wing chairs that made up the room's furnishings.

Somehow, Colin didn't think the Patron was the sort for Victorian decor. This suggested that Garrison had moved in hastily, taking over the remote old mansion sight unseen, and hadn't had the time to make many changes. So hopefully the security system wasn't up to modern standards yet, either. Every little weakness would help in shutting the Patron's operation down permanently this time.

Colin had taken careful note of every step of their movement into the heart of Garrison's compound. Security was tight, but there were obvious weaknesses. The small airport where they'd landed was several miles away from the site, which lessened the Patron's chance of easy escape. This place wasn't as isolated as the facility in Arizona had been, either. There was a perimeter fence and guards at the entrance, but this was no fortified camp. And there was only this one building, though it was huge. When they'd come in, Laurent had been taken down a staircase off the main hall. Colin guessed that the Manticore Prime was now locked in a basement room.

He and Mia had been brought up a sweeping staircase with an ornately carved balustrade to this room at the end of a long hall. A heavy door had been shut behind them, and they'd come face to face with the querulous Henry Garrison.

"Well?" Garrison demanded when he wasn't answered immediately.

Colin and Mia were standing side by side, like kids called into an angry principal's office, but they weren't touching. And Mia didn't look at him when she took a step forward.

"You asked me to bring you a specimen."

Garrison waved her words away impatiently. "I changed that plan. Weren't you informed?"

"I changed it back."

Colin almost smiled. His Mia was not one to be intimidated; he looked forward to watching the old man try to put her in her place.

Instead, the old mortal smiled. It was a thin, grudging, brief movement of his lips, but a spark of real humor lit his cold eyes for a moment. "Apparently you inherited some of my strong will," he told his great-granddaughter.

"I don't know if it comes from you or not," was her answer. "We don't know each other, but we do have a common cause." She gestured at Colin. "We have Mr. Faveau's organization in common, as well."

The name Faveau had been chosen at Tony Crowe's suggestion, Tony being the mortal vampire hunter expert. The Faveau were a family that still hunted, had always hunted, and the name would be known to someone who had grown up in the hunter society of the last century.

"Faveau?" Garrison spared Colin a long, searching look. "You don't look like a Faveau."

"You haven't seen a Faveau in three generations," Colin answered coolly. "We don't all marry our hunter cousins these days. Times have changed, Mr. Garrison. It's time that hunting methods change, as well."

Garrison looked back at Mia. "Why have you brought him here?"

"I wasn't as prepared to capture a vampire on my own as you and I assumed. I needed help." She took a deep breath before she admitted, "I would have gotten killed if the hunters hadn't rescued me. I owe—"

Garrison cut her off. "What you owe them is hardly my concern."

"They want to help," Mia told him, "and they have skills to offer."

"Ms. Luchese told us about your research project," Colin said. "We propose an alliance. We have information to exchange; we've been studying samples of the vampire daylight drugs we've managed to obtain from their clinic in Los Angeles."

That got Garrison's attention. He steepled his fingers, trying not to show any excitement, but Colin could tell that the old mortal's hands were shaking a little.

"Oh, really," Garrison murmured. "You have samples, data?"

"Yes. But we don't have the resources and facilities that Ms. Luchese tells us you do. We have similar goals, Mr. Garrison. We should work together. We even brought you a captured subject as a goodwill gift."

The old man sat back in his high-backed leather chair, and thought for a while. "This could prove productive," he said at last. "The data I'd been gathering for years was recently destroyed. I've disliked the idea of starting over."

"Then let us combine our research," Colin proposed. "The results could put an end to the parasites that prey on humanity, forever."

Mia gave him a brief glance that said he'd gone a bit over the top with this last statement, and Colin agreed with her. But Garrison didn't take any note of the melodramatics.

"I'll think about it," he said. "I'll definitely think about it. We'll talk again. It's late now." He looked at Mia and said, "Go to bed, child."

Colin wondered if the old man meant for his gruff tone to sound grandfatherly.

"Show these two to guest rooms," the Patron ordered one of his guards. "You did well, Caramia," he said as the guard led them toward the door.

Much to Colin's surprise, Mia flashed the old man a shy, delighted smile before stepping out into the hall.

"Thanks, Grandpa," she said.

Chapter Twenty-five

Thanks, Grandpa, Colin repeated over and over with growing alarm as he paced from one side of the third-story bedroom to the other. *Thanks, Grandpa?*

He so disliked being away from Mia. Disliked? Hell, he was growing close to frantic. Bondmate crap, he told himself, tempting him to be unprofessional. He had to stay on the program, follow the procedure they'd set up. So far they hadn't encountered any contingencies they hadn't planned for.

Except—*Thanks, Grandpa.*

What had she meant by that? Was her Garrison blood kicking in to lead her to the dark side?

It didn't help that he couldn't feel her thoughts at the moment. He was aware of where she was, by the blood connection between them. He knew her scent on the air, and the sweet surge of her heartbeat from every other mortal's in the building. But he didn't feel the essence of *her,* and he missed it.

He knew she'd be fine in a little while, that the numbness would wear off. But in the meantime, the separation made him realize just how much a part of him she'd become.

And it wasn't even the horniness that bothered him the most. Oh, he hungered for the touch and taste and responses of her body, as he always did. But he missed *her.* Her voice, her laughter, the conversations they'd been having, in between fights.

And it seemed like the arguments were growing farther apart, the conversations closer. He missed talking to Mia. There was so much about her he didn't yet know, despite the psychic and physical bond between them.

For example, what did she mean by *Thanks, Grandpa*?

The words grated on his senses, set off warning bells of paranoia. Suspicion.

He should have gagged Laurent.

And what about Laurent? Colin looked at his watch. Had the Manticore broken out of his cell yet? Even though he was only a Tribe Prime, Laurent was still Prime. He could take care of himself.

But Mia was only mortal. And as tough and resourceful as she was, it was his duty as Prime, and his right as her bondmate, to be her protector.

Bondmate.

For the first time, Colin smiled. He knew it was a sloppy, sentimental smile, and was glad he was alone as the unfamiliar romantic feeling came over him. This was no time for him to show vulnerability; he had a job to do.

Speaking of which, this had gone on long enough to give Laurent time to escape and to destroy any new research material down in the labs. Colin's job was to make Garrison forget about vampires; Mia's was to retrieve the laptop to give to the Manticores. Then they were going to leave. It was a simple, nonviolent, gentle, peace-loving—stupid!—plan. Colin didn't believe for a minute that it would go down so easily, and he was sure Laurent didn't, either. But Matri Serisa had approved it.

Unfortunately, she was not a war matri like his own clan's legendary Lady Anjelica, who had directed engagements against mortal Purist hunters and Tribe renegades. There was even a rumor that Anjelica had fought Nazis in the French resistance, though Clan females weren't supposed to put their precious selves in harm's way.

He bet Anjelica would have authorized the use of deadly force if necessary. But Serisa was the one who approved the op. Fortunately, Serisa's bondmate Barak was a war leader, and more practical. He understood the need for having a Plan B.

Right now they were still on track with Plan A, but being separated for any length of time was not part of the plan.

Colin paced some more, and after about five minutes, he decided that he'd had enough. He was going to find Mia.

He listened at the door for a moment, and detected the heartbeat and breathing of a guard posted in the hallway. No need to go through the mortal if he didn't have to.

He crossed to the room's large window. He was three stories up at the rear of the mansion, which was perched at the edge of a cliff. Not only did this provide a spectacular view, it afforded a natural security measure. There'd be a lot more than three stories to fall if you tried to get out the window. Which he intended to. The walls were brick, which an experienced rock climber like himself could scale. Especially an experienced rock climber who came equipped with long, strong claws.

Mia was one floor below and to his right, on the same side of the house. It was late on a cloudy night, but Colin also had excellent night vision. He smiled. This was going to be fun.

Thanks, Grandpa. What on earth had she meant by that?

Mia sat on the heavily carved Victorian bed and looked at the white lace canopy that arched above her head. The room was all pink and white and girly. She was getting really sick of being tucked away in luxurious cells, to be brought out when other people were ready to make pronouncements and decisions.

She was also thoroughly confused by her own behavior. Her hands were clenched tightly together, her stomach was full of acid-winged butterflies, and the headache that had plagued her since she mind-zapped the lawyer was still throbbing against her temples. Frankly, she was a wreck. She needed action, and she wanted Colin. Though she thought he was pissed at her, from the look he'd given her at her *Thanks, Grandpa.*

Colin probably thought she was on the Patron's side. Maybe she was a better actress than she thought, and she'd been really deeply into the moment. Or maybe there was some residual sympathy for the old man's cause lurking somewhere inside her.

Maybe the old man was the one telling the truth, and all the others were the ones lying to her.

She smiled at this thought, and relaxed a little. *Oh, yeah, every vampire I've met has been part of a vast conspiracy to convince me that my opinion of them is the most important thing in the world.* Mia shook her head. *And to think I pointed out to Colin that everything isn't always about him.*

Maybe they were bonded because they were a lot alike. She hoped they were alike in the good ways as well as the egotistical bad ones. Or maybe it was just the sex—she ached for him at the thought.

At the same instant, something tapped on glass behind her. Mia jumped to her feet and whirled toward the room's window. She almost screamed when she saw an upside-down face grinning at her wildly through the lace curtain.

She rushed to the window, pulled back the curtain, and lifted the window. There was no ledge. Colin's hands were braced on either side of the window frame, and the rest of his body was held up like a gymnast's at the top of a vault. The thought of the drop he was hanging above terrified her.

"For crying out loud," she whispered fiercely to the vampire clinging head over heels to the outside wall. "You look like a scene from a Dracula movie."

His maniacal expression turned to surprise. "I do?" He laughed softly. "I hadn't thought about that."

She glanced toward the door, where there was a guard posted, as he swung himself into the room. As soon as his feet hit the floor, Mia grabbed him in a tight embrace, her heart hammering in her chest. "You could have been killed!"

"No way. That was easier than rock climbing."

He sounded way too smug, and far too pleased at her getting all huggy on him. Now, wasn't that just like Colin? Which was just the way she liked him, God help her.

She loosened her hold to tug his head down to hers. His hair was silk against her hands, and the touch of his skin overwhelmed her. She kissed him, all her tension fueling her hunger. He cupped her rear and pulled her against him, and their hips ground together in quick mutual arousal.

Colin just wanted to get Mia on the bed, get her under him, get inside her, and feel his cock tightly surrounded by all the soft, yielding heat tha—

"Whoa, whoa, whoa," he said. He let her go as if he'd been burned. He *was* burning up, on the edge of losing his mind to his desire for her.

"Whoa what?" Mia asked, staring at him with a stricken look in her eyes. Her desire was a perfume surrounding her, calling to him.

Colin took another step back, shaking his head, trying to get his arousal under control. "Not now," he whispered, motioning toward the door.

Mia closed her eyes. She was trembling. He watched her helplessly while she got herself under control. And he kept his hands behind his back, because just looking at her was almost too tempting.

When Mia opened her eyes, there was anger in them.

He desperately wanted to calm her, comfort her—find out what was pissing her off.

He said, "Laurent's escape is overdue. We have to do something."

"Are you sure he's still locked up?"

Colin nodded, but before he could say anything, the door opened.

Four of the guards entered, all carrying guns. Garrison came in after them with an aide at his side. The old man leaned on a cane. Colin was aware that there were other armed men out in the hall.

He could take them out if he had to, but—

"Grandpa!" Mia shouted, and rushed forward.

Weapons were raised, but she ignored them, though she stopped short of touching the Patron.

"I'm so glad you're here!" She pointed at Colin. "He wants me to help him steal your data. The hunters don't really trust you, and I didn't ask for their help catching the vampire. When they surrounded your people at the airport, I couldn't think of a way out of bringing him here. And then he showed up in here and told me he wasn't going to wait for you to make a decision—"

Garrison cut her off. "You are a very talkative young woman."

"I guess that doesn't run in the family," Colin said, which focused Garrison's attention on him. Colin glared at Mia. "How did you manage to call for help? And why? Is blood so much more important than the cause?"

She whirled to face him. "You have no right to force the issue. I won't let you sabotage my grandfather's work."

"Blood is what it is all about, Faveau," Garrison spoke up. "Finding out what's in their blood that makes them what they are. It's a pity you chose not to wait for my decision. I sent for you to tell you that I would work with your people."

"You can't trust them," Mia put in.

"So it seems."

"But you still need their data."

"You won't get any help from us now," Colin said.

"Which is why you won't get out of here alive," Garrison calmly responded. "If we have no mutual need—"

"But there *is* someone that needs him." Mia smiled slowly, and her expression was diabolical enough to make Colin nervous. "The vampire. Why don't you put the vampire hunter in with the vampire for a while? If the creature's hungry . . . I suspect Mr. Faveau would rather share his data than become snack food for the thing he hunts."

"Bitch," Colin said to her, then told Garrison, "You can't torture what you want out of me."

The old man shrugged one frail shoulder. "But there's no harm in trying. Dump him in with the creature," he told his guards.

As he was led out the doorway, Colin heard Garrison say, "Caramia, child, you are an asset to the family after all. Come and join me for a drink."

Chapter Twenty-six

The pain was so bad, Laurent could barely stand it. The blinding bright lights far overhead burned his eyes, even though they were closed. The temperature was cranked up to the point that it nearly scalded his skin, and they'd stripped him down to his underwear so there was a lot of skin to burn. But the restraints were the worst, fastening his arms behind his back. The searing agony around his wrists was so great that he'd gnaw his hands off to get free of the pain, if he could only get to them.

Lying on the floor, curled up in a ball and concentrating hard on trying not to scream, he almost didn't hear the door open. Someone was shoved inside, and the door closed again before he could gather the strength to lift his head, let alone make a lunge for freedom.

When he did manage to lift his head and pry his eyes open, it took several tortured moments for his gaze to travel up a long, lean body dressed in black and finally reach the face of the newcomer.

"Oh, it's you," he managed to croak out.

Colin Foxe squatted beside him. Squinting in the hideous light, he looked Laurent over. "What happened to you?"

"I don't do drugs," Laurent rasped out.

He wasn't sure if he was more furious at the Clan vampire who was merely inconvenienced by the things that were killing him, or at the Tribe alphas who forbade the use of the elixirs that would keep away this pain. Mostly, he just wanted the pain to go away. He wanted it to go away so badly that he couldn't stop the moan that escaped him. But this one sound of weakness was the closest he'd come to begging.

Foxe reached out and turned Laurent onto his stomach. "Damn. They put silver on you."

"I—noticed."

Laurent could have broken the steel handcuffs he'd worn when he entered the cell. But before he had the chance, someone had picked up an ampule from a selection on a cart and stuck a needle into his neck. When he woke up he was alone, stripped, and silver bound his wrists. Silver was a soft metal, and even a mortal female could twist off the cuffs that hooked his arms together. But the burning agony of silver against his skin paralyzed him and made the task impossible.

Colin saw that Laurent's skin was badly burned. The daylight drugs only offered him partial protection from silver burns, so he pulled off his shirt and wrapped it around his hands before touching the manacles. Even with the protection of layers of cotton, Colin's skin grew uncomfortably warm before he was able to pull the soft metal apart. It took a few more moments to pry Laurent's wrists out of the cuffs. Once they dropped to the floor, Colin stood and kicked them aside.

Colin didn't offer to help Laurent up, but turned his back to give the other Prime privacy to get himself together. A couple of minutes passed before he heard Laurent take a deep breath and slowly rise to his feet.

Colin turned back and said, "We wondered why you were late."

"The bastards were tricky." He gave Colin a very annoyed once-over. "Now we're locked up together. What happened? Did the girl turn you in, too?"

"Yes."

Despite the lines of pain that still marred his face, Laurent managed to look smug. "Didn't I warn you not to trust her?"

Colin picked up his shirt and put it on before saying, "You

warned me." He gave the other Prime a warning look. "And if she wasn't so softhearted, I wouldn't be here to save your ass."

"Save my—she betrayed you, dude!"

"No, she betrayed the guy I'm pretending to be. When I told her that you might be in trouble, she managed to get the old man to toss a vampire hunter in with a vampire. Not bad for a spur-of-the-moment Plan B. The woman has promise, and I can't wait to tell her so." He smiled fondly, as though this was a revelation to him.

All Laurent wanted was to get out of here. "Fine," he told the besotted fool. "All praise to your lady, and other flowery Clan crap." He gestured toward the locked door. "What's next?"

"Back to Plan A. Only now we bust out and destroy all the data we can find."

Right, he'd been supposed to destroy computer disks and stuff like that. Who cared? What mattered was the payday—not that the noble, and rich, Clan boy was concerned with that.

"Lead on," he said.

Colin crossed to the door and dug his claws into the lock plate. While the Clan Prime pried out the lock, Laurent went to the table, picked up one of the filled syringes, and moved close to Colin.

"How's it coming?"

After a moment Colin said, "Done."

Laurent didn't know what was in the syringe, but he had no qualms about sticking it into Colin's shoulder and pressing the plunger. Being a prisoner had taken up too much of the night, and he needed a head start to the premises. Justinian had ordered him to bring back Garrison's wealth, and he wasn't ready to defy the pack leader's wishes yet.

"Sorry," he told Colin as the other vampire fell heavily onto the floor. "But I've got to put my own Plan B in motion."

*   *   *

Mia hoped Colin wasn't mad at her. After all, she'd done the right thing, and he had gone along with it. She wished she could feel him; then she wouldn't be so confused and worried.

The headache was finally gone, so maybe she'd have the full use of her abilities back soon. Being deprived of these brand-new senses made her more aware of them, made her *want* them. They completed her, enhancing her connection to Colin.

She hated that she didn't know where he was right now. She'd thrown him into trouble, and she'd just have to trust him to get out. And it came down to who you trusted, didn't it? Just like Domini said. Colin was easy to get pissed off at, but impossible not to trust when push came to shove. Did he realize she knew that, though?

She followed her great-grandfather down the corridor to a small elevator with an ornate brass gate. A pair of his guards followed them closely.

Mia tried hard to keep her mind on the moment, but thoughts of Colin kept rolling around in her head.

Did he know she wasn't angry with him for pulling away from her just before the bad guys showed up? She knew he'd felt her emotion, but she hadn't had time to explain that she was annoyed with herself.

She had no business tempting him—them—in the middle of a dangerous situation. She'd gotten thrown into all this action without any training, and now she had to deal with this bonding thing and—

She took a deep breath as they stepped into the narrow elevator cage. Mia squeezed in first, and the old man followed, standing with his back to her. She still didn't want anything to happen to the old man, but she was more convinced than ever that he was dangerous and had to be neutralized.

There wasn't any room for the bodyguards, so they hurried down the stairs so they'd be waiting on the first floor when the elevator finished its slow descent.

"How did he get into your room?"

The old man's voice had a cricket rasp to it, and he was leaning heavily on his cane. But there was no doubting the strength of his will or the sharpness of his mind.

"How did you know he was in my room?" she answered. When he didn't reply immediately, she let the subject go, and guessed, "You don't have long to live, do you?"

"No mortal does." He sighed and turned his head to look at her. "I have very little time, and the vampires cheated me out of much of it a few months ago. Now I must rush to rebuild what was lost. Perhaps I could have used your help sooner."

Mia could barely keep her revulsion in check. It sickened her to realize how much this man had destroyed and abandoned in his quest for eternal life. Had he actually lived the life he'd been given? Did he know what he'd given up, or care at all?

"You're just evil, aren't you, Grandpa?"

The elevator stopped as she asked her question, and the door slid smoothly open to reveal three people waiting for them. The guards were lying at the bottom of the stairs, and the scent of blood filled the air.

Mia's emotions spiked with terror as she recognized the tall male who stepped forward, smiling coldly. He held a hand out. "Come with me," Justinian said. "I'll teach you about evil."

I'm getting good at this, Laurent thought as he ripped another door off its hinges.

The action not only got him into the locked rooms on the third floor, but also alleviated his growing frustration.

There had been a guard at either end of the hall when Laurent came dashing up the stairs, but he'd moved on them with speed no mortal could match. Disarming and disabling them had helped him work through his annoyance at his treatment.

Once the guards were out of the way, he began his hunt. Recovering the Manticore's stolen fortune was all he'd signed on for.

He didn't give a damn about the traditional revenge aspect of the scenario; he didn't care about this mad Patron's evil experiments.

If the old guy could find the secret of immortality for mortals, it might threaten vampire existence, but vampires had been threatened throughout history. Laurent didn't see any reason why they wouldn't survive the menace from the Patron—as long as he wasn't the one being personally experimented on.

Besides, if the Patron managed to find his magic live-forever potion, think how much Garrison's company's stock would be worth. Laurent rather liked the idea of the Manticores taking control of Garrison's holdings. It would satisfy their right to reimbursement, and solve Justinian's need for revenge. Everybody would profit. Maybe he could talk Justinian into it.

But first, he had to find Garrison's computer. The mortal woman was right that the laptop likely held all the financial information they needed.

The room he stepped into this time had the look of an office. He might finally be getting somewhere.

First he ripped apart the desk and found nothing. That was fun, but then he got himself under control and began a more methodical search of the room. It didn't take him long to find the safe tucked behind a large portrait of a very ugly woman. The gleaming steel door of the safe was set flush against the wall. Brute strength wasn't going to do any good here, but what was the use of having extremely fine hearing if one couldn't use it to listen for the correct combination while carefully spinning the tumblers? He pressed his head against the cool steel and got to work.

Patience, he told himself. Patience.

To his delighted surprise, it didn't take long at all to open the door. He was even more delighted to find a small leather computer case resting inside the safe.

"All right!" he congratulated himself, and reached for the case.

His elation died the moment he had the computer in his grasp.

They were here, earlier than he'd expected or wanted. He'd been concentrating too hard to notice their arrival, but he was acutely aware of the pack's presence now. Most were concentrated in one area of the house, but there were others scattered around the grounds. So Justinian had brought the whole pack with him. That hadn't been the plan.

It sent a chill up his spine; even though he was with them, he wasn't one of them. Laurent held Justinian's triumph in his hands, and that should count for something. But his fellow Tribe Primes were so unpredictable, especially in large groups, where they egged each other on.

He turned slowly away from the safe. It was easy enough to follow the Manticore's mental signature down the flights of stairs to the first floor.

The first thing Laurent noticed when he found the pack was that there were over a dozen Primes scattered around the ballroom. The place was so big, even a dozen vampires didn't take up much of the space. There was a crystal chandelier blazing overhead, but it didn't throw that much light into the room. A huge, empty fireplace and several groupings of heavy old furniture made up the rest of the room. No windows, Laurent noted; that was always a plus in a building designed for mortal inhabitants.

"And speaking of mortal inhabitants," he murmured, spotting the pair surrounded by Primes in one of the seating areas.

Justinian and Belisarius were standing in front of them, and another pair of Primes were poised behind the couch. One had his hands on the old man's bony shoulders. The other had a hand twisted in the female's short curls.

"Oh, hell." Laurent rushed forward, but was stopped by a stern look from Justinian. Laurent held up the leather case in his hand. "I have what we came for. Let's get out of here."

"I'm not done here." Justinian looked back at the prisoners. "The Garrisons have to pay."

"What are you going to do? Mind-rape them for information? You don't need to do that. We have what rightfully belongs to the Manticores. We can leave."

"What use is a black bag?" Belisarius sneered. "All his money couldn't fit in that."

"It's not the bag that's important, but the data in the computer inside it. You do know what a computer is, right?" Laurent knew that sarcasm was dangerous, but he just couldn't help himself.

"Garrison's data will be password-protected," Belisarius said to Justinian. "I can rip those passwords from his mind if you wish."

Okay, so Belisarius wasn't completely ignorant, just stupid and brutal. And the old man probably deserved what he got.

Probably? Laurent shook his head in disgust at this softness. There must've been wimp juice in the drink he'd had at the Clan house.

"Do what you want with the old man—" he began.

"I will," Justinian purred.

"But remember that the Garrison female also belongs to the Reynard Prime. Hurt her, and you risk a war with the Clans."

"He's afraid of the Clans," Belisarius sneered.

"We've been through this before," Laurent said with a sigh. He gave up and stepped back. He knew from the glittering edge to Justinian's emotions, the look of greedy anticipation on Belisarius's face, and the general eagerness for blood sport pulsing in the psychic atmosphere that the time of reasonableness had passed.

"You guys just can't hold it together, can you?"

Of course, Laurent was ignored.

Justinian concentrated on Garrison. "Will you trade the passwords for the female's life? Remember that she is your only chance at immortality, old man. So will you trade your empire for something more important?"

Garrison looked steadily at Justinian, and replied calmly, "Of course not."

The female didn't look surprised.

Justinian looked delighted. "We'll see." He told Belisarius, "Make her scream."

Chapter Twenty-seven

Colin was lost in thick, clinging fog that enwrapped him so he couldn't see or taste or feel where his body ended and the fog began. He was alone. Completely alone. And something was terribly, terribly wrong. The fog allowed him fear, and pain that boiled up from his soul. There was so much pain—in his heart, in his head, permeating his body, blocking out any chance of joy or completion or—love.

He was lost, and he'd never love again. Or be loved.

I wish you all the time in the world to enjoy what you have. Cherish each day.

David Berus's voice rang in his head. Then the Serpentes Prime's hand was on his shoulder. They stood together—

And looked down on a grave.

"No," Colin said. He closed his eyes and turned away. "No!"

Mia was gone. Dead. Lost.

"Isn't that what you wanted?" Laurent asked. "She wasn't worthy of you."

Colin whirled to the Tribe Prime, ready to kill. But Laurent wasn't there. "Liar!" he shouted to the phantom. Yet he knew that the one who lied was himself, about who he wanted and needed. He was an arrogant fool, unworthy of her.

David Berus wasn't to be seen, either.

Colin was alone in the fog, fog that was swiftly turning to fire. Colin didn't care. He burned from the inside out now, aching hunger gnawing at him.

"This is how it feels," Berus said from out of the fire, "to lose what you love."

Colin had a memory of childishly admiring Berus for having survived the loss of his bondmate. Now that admiration turned to compassion.

And to hopelessness.

"I can't live like this," he called to Berus.

"It isn't living."

This was hell. Having Mia ripped from him was hell. Being without her was hell. She was—everything.

"She can't be dead."

"Why not?" Laurent sneered.

"Because."

"Not an answer, Clan boy."

It wasn't any of the Tribe bastard's business. So Colin held the all-important words inside, speaking only to his empty soul.

Because I never had the chance to tell her how much I love her, Colin thought.

Pain ripped through the left side of Colin's chest, and a shout of pure fury stabbed into his mind. His eyes flashed open in shock, and he was momentarily blinded by the light of the bright, bright room.

"Touch me there again, and I'll rip your heart out!"

Colin sat up so fast that he cracked the back of his head on the wall he'd been slumped against. Mia's fury and fear ripped through the fiery fog and brought him fully awake.

Mia!

Colin!

She was alive! He was out of hell!

Colin! Help!

She needed him—and it was her fierce energy that brought him back to life.

"Mia!" he shouted, and jumped to his feet.

At least he tried, but for a moment all he could do was flail helplessly on the cell floor. What the hell was the matter with—

Laurent. A jab of pain. Then he was dizzy and down. He'd

been drugged by the Manticore. He'd been lying here halluci-nating while his woman needed him.

Move, he told himself. *Carefully. Steadily.* He took slow, deep breaths. Got his legs under him. He stood, and waited until he was certain he could keep standing.

While he did all this, he fought to keep from shaking with fury and shared pain as Mia's torture played out in his mind.

A few seconds was all it took to be sure he could function, but those seconds brought him a lifetime of anxiety before he flew out the door.

She wasn't screaming enough to suit Belisarius, and Laurent wished she would—then maybe Belisarius wouldn't hurt her so much.

Belisarius was having way too good a time. His actions ex-cited the others, who shared laughter and encouragement, and made bets about how long the mortal would last.

Justinian stood back with his arms crossed, watching his beta Prime torture a helpless woman like a proud papa watch-ing his boy at a track meet.

Laurent stayed still and silent in the shadows, and wished it would stop.

The old man didn't seem to be paying attention at all.

When Belisarius lifted a hand with claws fully extended, Laurent looked away. So he was the only one who saw the streak coming through the open doorway.

Foxe was awake and coming to the rescue—of course. Surely he was aware that there was a pack of excited, blood-thirsty Primes surrounding the object of his noble desires?

And Laurent was the only Prime in the room aware of the approaching threat. Not only did Foxe move fast, his psychic shielding was incredibly strong. That made his approach dou-bly silent and dangerous.

Laurent supposed it was his duty to shout out a warning to

his Manticore brethren—but they ought to have been on guard in the first place, he decided. So he stepped even farther into the shadows, and waited to see what would happen.

Strength of numbers or purity of heart? He certainly didn't care to place a bet.

One moment, Mia was only aware of the sharp claws arcing down toward her face. The next thing she saw was a black streak rocketing toward her. Then Colin put himself between her and her tormentor.

Colin's attack forced the other vampire to drop his tight hold on her upper arm. Mia stumbled back and fell to her knees. Though she was bruised and scared, the elation of having her bondmate defend her overrode everything else.

She wanted to help Colin, but the fighters were moving so quickly she could barely see more than flashing fangs, raking claws, and fiercely straining muscles.

She looked around and saw the other vampires moving in, circling the fight, waiting to see how Colin's battle with their comrade played out before they joined the attack. Her heart sank at the realization that her man didn't have a chance. Even if he defeated the one he was fighting, the others would be all over him.

Mia scrubbed a hand across her face. *Think!* She'd gotten Colin into this deadly situation—how was she going to help get him out of it? Her thoughts raced. Silver, garlic, hawthorn, sunlight, high-caliber bullets, mortar rounds, C4, napalm, nuclear radiation, Stinger missiles— *Think, woman! What's at hand?* There must be an arsenal of weapons against vampires in this place. All she had to do was get through the line of vampires and find something she could use.

Colin threw Belisarius onto a low table, and the old furniture was crushed beneath the impact. Wood splintered, and the two Primes scrambled for sharply pointed shards to use as stakes.

"Dust him, Colin!" Mia shouted encouragement.

The fighters lunged closer and she had to scramble backward onto the couch to get out of Colin's way. She kicked at

Belisarius in passing. Her foot connected with his jaw, and Belisarius turned his head.

Colin drove his wood splinter into the side of the other Prime's neck. Blood spurted, and Belisarius howled. Then Colin's fangs sank deep into the other side of Belisarius's throat, and his claws ripped deep into the Manticore's chest.

Mia felt the instant Belisarius died, like a psychic candle suddenly being snuffed out. She had a moment of elation at Colin's survival, but it turned to terror even as Colin sprang to his feet to face the circle of Tribe Primes, Belisarius's blood on his face and hands. Despite Colin's snarling triumph and defiance of the pack, they were still deeply, deeply in trouble.

Mia rose to her feet. She was aware that her great-grandfather slumped sideways when she moved, but she didn't have time for concern for the old man right now. She stood side by side with her bondmate as the pack slowly circled them, eyes glowing, fangs bared.

"Take them apart," Justinian ordered. "Do it slowly."

This was definitely a scene out of her worst nightmare. Only in her nightmares the man she loved wasn't with her. Maybe she was going to die, but at least she wasn't alone.

"What have we got to fight vampires with?" she whispered out of the corner of her mouth.

Colin wiped the blood off his mouth, and his hands on his shirt as he looked beyond the encroaching pack. Then he flexed his fingers and gave her a bright, reassuring smile.

"Personally, I think other vampires are good to fight vampires with," he said.

Then Barak, Tony, Alec, David Barus, and others whose names she didn't know came out of the shadows, encircling the Tribe vampires.

"Back to the original Plan B," Colin said. Then he put himself between her and immediate danger as the fighting started all over again.

*   *   *

Mia took her gaze away from the body on the couch when Tony Crowe came up to her. "Is it over?"

Colin was outside, searching for those who were trying to get away.

"It's all over except for the cover-up," Tony answered.

The fight hadn't gone on for very long, but it had spread all through the house and the estate grounds. Mia hadn't taken part; she'd been giving CPR to her great-grandfather. And that had been done out of hopeless duty, because—

"He's gone," Tony said. "No light of soul left at all."

"I know." She also knew that the old man hadn't had a soul for a long time. "I don't know if one of the vampires killed him, or if it was just his time." She rubbed the back of her neck. "I did what I could."

"I'm sure you did."

She supposed he was thinking that Garrison's death left the vampires one less loose end to tie up. She couldn't blame him for feeling that way, but was glad he was too polite to say so.

He took her by the shoulder and turned her away from the couch. "We'll take care of everything. And thank you," he added. "Your plan worked."

Mia gave him a sardonic look. "Which part of my plan involved you and the bad guys showing up?"

"Ah. Those elements were factored in later. We knew we couldn't trust the Manticores to abide by the rules, so we—"

"Didn't follow the rules, either," she contributed. "Not that I mind."

"They followed Laurent, we followed you. Our only surprise was that Justinian's people got here first." He gave an eloquent shrug. "It all worked out. There were mortal casualties," he told her. "I'm sorry, but the Manticores killed two of the guards."

In movies and television shows, no one worried about the spear carriers. She'd hoped to keep very real humans from getting hurt. "It would have been much worse if you hadn't shown up. Did you kill Manticores?"

"A couple of them got away, but most of them surrendered," he answered. "That's almost too bad, because now we have to lock 'em up and reeducate them, and that takes years."

Suddenly a thrill ran through her and Mia turned away, all her senses focusing on the most important thing in the world. Colin had entered the room, and she didn't care about anything else.

He came to her, took her hands, and smiled, but he spoke to Tony first. "It looks like Laurent and Justinian got away."

"We'll keep looking." Tony stepped away.

Colin took her in his arms, and Mia collapsed gratefully into his sheltering embrace. They did nothing but hold each other for a long time.

"Hell of a night," he finally said. Then he held her out at arm's length. "Are you all right? What can I do to help?"

Mia was incredibly touched by his gentleness and concern. She couldn't answer for a moment, overwhelmed just by looking at him. He was strong, brave—handsome. She'd known all these things, but now she recognized and absorbed how much everything he was, was a part of her.

"As you are a part of me," he told her. "Come on."

He put his arm around her waist, and they went out into the morning light. The breeze was scented with pine, and morning sunlight sparked off snow-covered peaks. Mia took a deep breath. Then Colin kissed her and took her breath away.

"I was so afraid of losing you," he said when they finally came up for air. "Afraid of losing you before we really found each other. I've been a fool and a jerk and a complete—"

"I know." She put her fingers over his lips. "Don't make a speech about it, okay?"

He kissed her palm and she thought she was going to melt. "You deserve a speech."

His earnestness sent joy flooding through her. "Yeah, but it wouldn't match the groveling abasement I've lovingly imagined."

"That's harsh." His eyes sparkled teasingly. "Do I get down on my knees, in your fantasy?"

"Yeah, but not in the apology fantasy." His low, wicked chuckle sent a thrill through Mia. "Just apologize and tell me you love me, and we'll be okay." She held him close.

"I'm sorry."

He ran his hands down her back and looked thoughtfully out at the mountains. For a moment she grew cold with dread. Maybe he wasn't able to say the words.

"I've never told you that I love you, have I, Caramia?" He laughed softly. "Of course, your name says it all. *Cara mia* means 'my love,' doesn't it?"

"Yes."

He rubbed his cheek against hers, and whispered in her ear, "I'm never going to call you anything else. I love you, Caramia."

"And I love you."

"Really?" he asked eagerly. "Since when?"

"You first."

"Probably when you yelled at me for being late to the hostage rescue. I thought it was lust, but the connection went so much deeper. You?" he urged.

"When you showed up at the hospital to see if I was all right."

"I just wanted to get into your pants."

"Yeah, but it was still sweet. And you get extra points for saving me from Belisarius. I *really* love you for that." She fluttered her eyelashes at him, but she meant it when she said, "I knew you'd come for me, my hero."

"Damn right. You know I'll always be there for you, right?"

"Damn right." She gave Colin her complete and utter trust.

"I was so scared of losing you. The bondmate in danger thing really helped me put things in perspective. You tired, Caramia?"

"Exhausted. And tired of the whole situation. Let's go home."

"To your place," he said. "You've got more room. You're going to have to adjust to being married to a cop. That won't be easy, Caramia."

"It has to be easier than adjusting to being bonded to a vampire."

"I guess."

"And you have to adjust to being married to a vampire hunter."

"What!" He held her out at arm's length again. "No way."

"Yes," she answered. "There are bad guys out there that need policing. It's part of my heritage, and I'm going for it. But properly, officially, with your help and training."

He clearly didn't like it, but he didn't argue. Mia figured there'd be plenty of time to argue when they got home. Arguing was one of the things they did very well together. They had a long lifetime to do lots of things well together.

He put his arm around her shoulders once more and led her toward the driveway, where they approached a lovely, low-slung red sports car. She didn't know who it belonged to, or if there were keys in it. But she did know that Colin Foxe had every intention of driving away with her in it.

"You know what I'm going to do when we get back to Los Angeles?" he asked as he held the passenger door open for her. "After making love to you for a couple of days?"

"What?"

"Take you to Harry Winston's and buy you a proper wedding ring. Something with lots of diamonds."

"Or rubies," she answered, succumbing to a sudden impulse. "I think I'll let you buy me rubies."

She glanced for the last time at the mansion perched on the mountainside as Colin slid into the driver's seat.

"Let's go home." She smiled at him, and at being with him forever, as they drove away.